The
Pemberley Chronicles

*A Companion Volume to Jane Austen's
Pride and Prejudice*

DEVISED AND COMPILED BY
Rebecca Ann Collins

SOURCEBOOKS LANDMARK™
AN IMPRINT OF SOURCEBOOKS, INC.®
NAPERVILLE, ILLINOIS

By the Same Author

The Women of Pemberley
Netherfield Park Revisited
The Ladies of Longbourn
Mr Darcy's Daughter
My Cousin Caroline
Postscript from Pemberley
Recollections of Rosings
A Woman of Influence
The Legacy of Pemberley

Published by Sourcebooks Landmark, an imprint of Sourcebooks, Inc.
P.O. Box 4410, Naperville, Illinois 60567-4410
(630) 961-3900
FAX: (630) 961-2168
www.sourcebooks.com

Originally printed and bound in Australia by The Pink Panther. First published 1997.
Reprinted 1998. Revised and reprinted May 1998. Reprinted 1999 and 2002. Revised
and reprinted 2003. Reprinted 2004 and 2006 by SNAP Printing, Sydney, Australia.

Library of Congress Cataloging-in-Publication Data

Collins, Rebecca Ann.
  The Pemberley Chronicles : A Companion Volume to Jane Austen's Pride and Prejudice /
Devised and Compiled by Rebecca Ann Collins
     p. cm.
  ISBN-13: 978-1-4022-1153-9
  ISBN-10: 1-4022-1153-8
  1. Bennet, Elizabeth (Fictitious character)—Fiction. 2. Darcy, Fitzwilliam (Fictitious
character)—Fiction. 3. England—Social life and customs—19th century—Fiction. I.
Austen, Jane, 1775–1817. Pride and Prejudice. II. Title.

PR9619.4.C65P46 2008
823'.92--dc22

                                    2007049507

Printed and bound in the United States of America
VP 10 9 8 7 6 5 4

To the beloved Jane Austen

An Introduction . . .

A LIFELONG FAN OF JANE Austen, Rebecca Ann Collins first read *Pride and Prejudice* at the age of twelve and fell in love with its characters. Since then, she has gathered a wealth of information about its author and her work, seeking to inform herself about the life and times of the "Pemberley families."

Two things set in train the current stage of her splendid obsession: the BBC's magnificent production—which brought Jane Austen's brilliant, witty story and characters so dramatically alive in a stunning visual context—and the appearance in bookshops of a rash of sequels. Some of these turned the lives of the characters into a soap opera in which Elizabeth and Darcy, for whom one had developed an abiding love and regard, appeared suddenly to behave like figures out of *Dynasty!* It was in this context that Miss Collins began work on the chronicles, placing her favourite characters in their original environment: nineteenth century England.

She at no time presumes to imitate the literary style of the original author, nor does she distort the essential core of main players, who are so well drawn in the novel, with tortuous twists of character or bizarre behaviour that seem gratuitous and hard to believe. Rebecca Collins is concerned to observe them in the context of an era of profound economic, political, and social change, perhaps the most dynamic period of English history, certainly the most interesting.

She observes them as they make their way through the changing landscape, with only an occasional push from the chronicler—a change of direction or emphasis rather than of character. All the main characters essentially remain recognisably Jane Austen's, except that they age, mature, mellow, and sometimes depart the scene.

Children are born and others—both old and young—die, as they did in all the families that Miss Austen herself knew, personally. Consequences flow from tragedy and triumph alike. It was ever thus. As the Pemberley families face the changes that confronted all the people of England, Ms Collins, not content to hang the bland "happily ever after" tag upon them, observes the impact upon their lives. How Elizabeth, to whom Pemberley represented elegance and stability as well as love, copes with personal tragedy is as important as the influence of the commercial entrepreneurship of Mr Gardiner on the landed gentry facing rural recession.

Coincidentally, the author's assumption of the pen name and identity of Rebecca Collins is a useful device, allowing her the freedom of an internal narrator, working from personal, anecdotal, and documentary sources within the Pemberley group, without appearing to take undue liberties with their privacy.

The story lines are clearly drawn and the characters observed with affection and humour, as one would expect from a member of their circle. All those interested in the story of *Pride and Prejudice,* its historical and social setting, will enjoy this companion volume.

If you watched spellbound as millions did as it unfolded on your television screen and, seeing the two couples drive away as the closing credits and that magic music rolled, you wondered where life would have taken them, then Emily Gardiner's prologue, which opens the chronicles, will start you on that journey.

It is for these readers, and not for the J.A. Specialists or the literary establishment, that Rebecca Ann Collins has compiled *The Pemberley Chronicles.* It is to them, as much as to the beloved Miss Austen herself, that the book is dedicated.

November 1997.

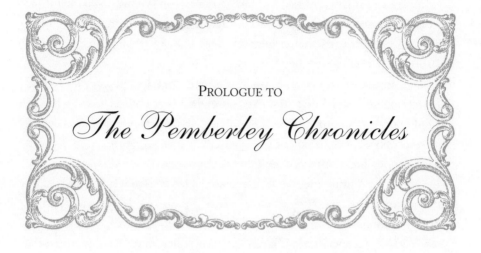

PROLOGUE TO

The Pemberley Chronicles

THE WEDDINGS ARE OVER. There are rose petals everywhere. Jane and Elizabeth Bennet have been married to Mr Bingley and Mr Darcy on a shining Autumn day, and everyone is smiling with the joy of sharing in their happiness. "They looked more beautiful than princesses," said the little maids, Caroline and Emily Gardiner, who with Kitty Bennet and Georgiana Darcy had assisted the brides.

"Could anyone have looked happier than Lizzie?" asked her aunt. "Not unless you looked across at Jane, who seemed as if she was all lit up like a candle," said Colonel Fitzwilliam. Both bridegrooms looked extremely well. Mr Bingley was the favourite, of course, being universally charming. But even those who had reservations about Mr Darcy, thinking him proud and reserved when he first came to Netherfield, could not deny how well he looked: tall and very handsome, his countenance suffused with delight as he and Elizabeth stepped out into the sunlight.

Sir William Lucas said over and over that we were losing the brightest jewels in the county and Mr Darcy was a real dark horse, because no one had guessed he was in love with Lizzie, whereas everyone knew, he said, from the very first evening they met, that Mr Bingley had lost his heart to Jane. Sir William even claimed credit for the match, having been the first to call on

Mr Bingley and invite him and his party to Meryton. He was boasting of his success to Mr and Mrs Gardiner, who knew a good deal more of these matters, being particular friends of both Mr Darcy and Elizabeth, but they just smiled and let him chatter on.

Later, on the way home they would comment that, had he known it was at the reception at Lucas Lodge that Mr Darcy had first noticed Lizzie's beauty and found himself wanting to know her better, Sir William might have become quite impossibly conceited about his role in their marriage, too.

Jane and Charles Bingley are gone to London, where Charles wants to show off his beautiful wife, while Lizzie and Darcy have left for Oxford en route to the estates on the borders of Cheshire and Wales that are part of Darcy's family inheritance. Mrs Gardiner, who helped Lizzie and Jane pack for their journeys, says Lizzie is longing to see Wales, never having visited the area before. They are all to meet in London some six weeks hence to dine with the Gardiners.

The servants gathered up the debris on the lawn, and the guests began to leave. Some of them seemed more reluctant to go than others. Mr Bennet looked as if he would like them to be gone, but Mrs Bennet would not stop talking, endlessly, to Mrs Long, Aunt Philips, Lady Lucas, and anyone else who would listen, detailing her joy at having her two most beautiful daughters so well married and settled. She was full of news too about Jane and Charles and their journey to London and bemoaned the fact that she knew so little of Elizabeth and Darcy's plans, except the couple were to be at Pemberley for Christmas. She was still too much in awe of Mr Darcy to ask him outright.

As we were to learn later, while the Bingleys headed for London, Darcy hoped the time and the environment of the lovely border country would give Lizzie and himself a chance to be alone together as they never could, amidst the bustle of friends and families at Longbourn.

They broke journey and spent their first few days at a very pleasing hostelry outside the university town of Oxford. At Oxford, Darcy, a Cambridge man himself, took his wife to meet an old friend, a clergyman, who had spent some time at the Kympton living in Derbyshire prior to returning to continue his theological studies at Oxford. Dr Francis Grantley was two years Darcy's senior, learned and witty with it, not at all sombre and pompous as some clergymen one could name! "Poor Charlotte," Elizabeth sighed for her friend as she recalled with a shudder the silliness of Mr Collins. Dr Grantley was quite another matter, said Elizabeth in her letter to Mrs Gardiner, written before the couple left Oxford:

> *I am sure, my dear Aunt, that you would like him very much indeed. He is Mr Darcy's dearest friend and they have known one another for many years, since Dr Grantley was assistant to the curate at Kympton, the picturesque little parish we visited in Derbyshire last Summer. We spent all day with him, visiting some of the wonderful libraries and College Chapels, including his own college, St John's, which has a renowned Chapel choir and delightful gardens. Mr Darcy has invited Dr Grantley to return to the living at Kympton, which is now vacant, during his sabbatical and I for one would welcome it; we could do with another gentleman of education and taste at Pemberley!*

Elizabeth was interrupted at this point by her husband, who came in to dress for dinner, having given instructions for their journey to Bristol on the following day. In a touching gesture, he had brought her a rose, picked fresh from the garden, taking her by surprise, as he would do often in the future. Recounting the incident to her aunt, Elizabeth confessed she was more pleasured by these unexpected and spontaneous expressions of affection, than by the ritualised courtliness affected by many men in smart society.

She let him read her letter while she completed her preparations. It was the first time she had let anyone other than Jane see any of her letters, and she was conscious of what it signified between them. That he was pleased with what he read, she knew from his smile as he handed it back to her and the warmth with which he embraced her before they left the room to go to dinner. There would be an openness between them that would enhance the intimacy of their marriage, and she was excited by its rich promise for their future together.

Later that night, Elizabeth rose quietly from bed as her husband slept, and finished her letter to Mrs Gardiner:

> *You will be happy to learn, dear Aunt, that my dear husband approves of my excellent judgement—not only with regard to my appreciation of Dr Grantley but more especially in my love and esteem for himself—as expressed earlier in*

my letter; both feelings, he assures me, are returned in full measure. I need not say again how very happy we are, but I almost fear that were I not to say it, you may not know how completely certain I am of the correctness of my decision to marry Mr Darcy. I know my dear father had his doubts, but you, I am sure, did not share them. Indeed, in your letter to me after Lydia's dreadful faux pas, relating the part Mr Darcy played in resolving the problems caused by Wickham and Lydia's stupidity, you were most generous in your praise of him, and had I not already realised that I loved him, I would certainly have been persuaded to look again at this paragon! I am so glad, however that I needed no such persuasion; having come to understand how deeply I cared for him, it was good to have your confirmation of his virtues. Since then, every occasion that we have been together, whether alone or in company, has only served to confirm my good opinion of him. Dear Aunt, he is a most generous and honourable gentleman and as I have discovered since our marriage, a truly loving husband.

Thank you again, my dearest Aunt and Uncle, for your part in bringing us together; for persuading me to visit Pemberley on that beautiful morning. We have spoken often of those Summer days in Derbyshire, and Mr Darcy agrees with me they will forever be part of our most precious memories. He sends you his love and best regards.

A sudden sound outside the window, and Darcy stirred in his sleep. Elizabeth, fearful of disturbing him, hurried to conclude her letter:

Mr Darcy tells me that Dr Grantley has agreed to spend his next sabbatical at Pemberley, where he will have access to the library for his work. He is, I am told, a theologian of some repute. Even better, he will be with us at Christmas, when you will be able to meet him, a pleasure I can promise you, with confidence. Georgiana will also be there, more pleasant company to look forward to.

We leave tomorrow for Bristol but are to stay at Clifton, so should you have time to write, we shall be at the Royal at Richmond Terrace for ten days.

It is late, and I should close this before I go to bed, so it will be in your hands as early as possible. Do give our love to the children and say we look forward to seeing them. (Caroline and Emily were the sweetest of little maids and though our bridesmaids Georgiana and Kitty were very handsome, the little ones got most of the compliments!)

   I'll say goodnight with love,
   your affectionate niece, Lizzie.

The following morning, after breakfast, they left for Bristol. Elizabeth looked forward to the journey, which took them through Gloucestershire, with which she was not familiar. Darcy, on the other hand, had travelled these roads often en route to Cheltenham, Gloucester, and the family properties in Wales. He was, therefore, well informed and able to prepare Lizzie for the scenes and vistas to look out for as well as provide some of the information about the places they could visit along the way.

The countryside was new and interesting to her; there were many places to study and admire. Darcy was a particularly good teacher, and Elizabeth was eager to learn. It was, for her, a most satisfying and salutary experience. She was both disarmed and charmed by her husband's patience in answering all of her questions and pleased to discover how much she could enjoy depending upon him.

Reaching their destination late in the afternoon, Elizabeth was tired with travelling all day, and Darcy, whose solicitude for his bride knew no bounds, insisted that she should go directly to their rooms, while he had their luggage carried upstairs. Within the next half-hour, not only did she find herself ensconced in a spacious and comfortable suite of rooms overlooking the river, well down from the bustle of Bristol, but a pleasant young woman had presented herself, offering her services as a lady's maid. When Darcy appeared, some time later, he was accompanied by a manservant who brought in a collation of cold meats, cheese, bread, and fruit for the travellers, as well as wine and a great pot of tea to comfort the weary.

To complete her happiness, Darcy had in his hand a letter from Jane, which had awaited their arrival at Richmond Terrace. Elizabeth cried out and hugged him with an excess of enthusiasm that quite astonished and delighted her husband, who was singularly unaccustomed to such overt displays of affection. For Lizzie, no amount of appreciation was too much for the care and pleasure with which he had surrounded her.

As she later wrote to her sister Jane:

There was not one more thing I could have wished for, except perhaps to share my pleasure with you, dearest Jane, which I am doing now.

After they had eaten, Darcy went out for a walk around The Mall, urging his wife to take some more refreshment and rest awhile. Elizabeth was not at all averse to complying with his instructions. Comfortably tucked into a chaise lounge with a fire to warm the room, which was pleasantly invaded by an Autumn breeze, she opened up Jane's letter. It was, just as Elizabeth had expected, full of her happiness and her husband's kindness and love. Jane could barely get the words out to convey to her sister all the new experiences she was enjoying. Marriage, combined with the excitement of London, with its balls and parties and crowded shops, a rush of new places and people—she must have been left breathless by it all. It was almost with relief that Lizzie read that they were to spend a week away at Maidenhead, at the invitation of one of Bingley's friends.

Oh Lizzie, I have to confess we are both looking forward to it mainly for the peace and quiet. We have spent so little time alone for we are forever surrounded by kind friends, who will insist on our dining or going out to balls with them. They are all full of compliments and mostly very charming, but I tire of all this and long to curl up on the sofa and dream as we used to . . .

Elizabeth laughed out loud, since this was exactly what she was doing. She knew just what Jane meant as she read on:

Dearest Lizzie, do you recall our conversation on the night before our wedding?

Elizabeth remembered it well. Despite the conviction that they had both made the right decision in accepting two of the most eligible, fine, handsome, young men they were ever likely to meet, there had been a moment of trepidation as the two sisters had embraced before parting that night. That they loved their chosen partners they knew only too well, for they had carried the secret in their hearts over many months. Nor were they in any doubt that they were deeply loved by two men, who had made them the envy of ladies for miles around.

Still, there was anxiety perhaps from the lack of an example of a happy marriage at home, for though they rarely spoke of it, Jane and Elizabeth knew that their parents' lack of mutual respect and understanding and their obvious incompatibility had made for a very poor sort of marriage. Both sisters had been determined never to fall into such a trap, however well baited it may be. Elizabeth remembered her aunt's sage advice, when she had thought—nay feared—that Lizzie might be falling in love with Wickham. A cold shiver passed through her at the thought of her escape.

Jane's happiness and her confidence in the love she had found with Charles Bingley spilled across the pages of her letter:

> My dear Sister, I want so much to set your heart at rest on my behalf. I have been so blessed that I have no doubts at all and indeed I wonder at my ever having had them. Mr Bingley has made me so happy. Lizzie, I am the happiest person in the world!

Once more, Elizabeth laughed, this time softly and indulgently, as her mind slid gently on to the subject of her own marriage and the happiness she and Mr Darcy were finding each day they spent together. The letter fell to the floor, as she gazed out at the distant horizon across the river, letting her thoughts follow. It was in this pleasant reverie that Darcy found her when he returned from his walk.

On reading Jane's letter, he understood her mood and was happy to match it for the rest of the evening. As on previous occasions, when they had been alone together, neither needed to say very much to express feelings deeply held: sensations that Darcy had struggled for months to overcome and Elizabeth had not known she could feel. Yet, now, as they discovered their need for each other, they flowed easily and naturally. As always, there was a mixture of passion and playfulness between them; of laughter and love, which would ensure that theirs would be an ardour free of the cloying effects of excess. Elizabeth's excellent sense of humour and Darcy's quiet dignity would always lighten and balance their marriage.

Elizabeth decided to postpone her reply to Jane for a day or two. She wanted time to absorb and enjoy the experiences she was sharing with her husband. She did not feel capable of putting her present emotions on paper; she could barely express them to the man she loved so much and then only with some degree of shyness and much loving encouragement. She longed to share her joy with her beloved sister but wanted more time to hold it close to her own heart first.

~❦~

Clifton and its salubrious environs afforded Elizabeth and Darcy many hours of entertainment. Having visited many more castles—old and new, some in the strange pseudo-Gothic style—than either of them had hoped to see in their lives, they decided they would see no more but would enjoy a leisurely drive through the West Country. They stopped at Kingsweston to admire the exquisite prospect stretching across three counties, broke journey at Cheltenham, and then proceeded to cross the border into what was for Elizabeth new, uncharted territory amongst the mountains and valleys of Wales.

The wildness of the Welsh landscape, at times almost over-powering, added a new dimension to their enjoyment. Travelling slowly, without the pressure of timetables, Darcy and Elizabeth found time and solitude conducive to their mood. That Darcy ardently and sincerely loved her, Elizabeth was left in no doubt. For her part, she was learning to enjoy being so deeply loved and found new excitement in falling more in love with a man she admired and esteemed. That this man was now her husband—a circumstance unthinkable a mere six months ago—made her smile.

More and more she longed for the days when they would be at Pemberley together, the environment in which she was sure they would find the greatest happiness, where their dearest wishes could be fulfilled. As they travelled, they had talked of their future plans, and Darcy made it very clear to Elizabeth that she would be Mistress of Pemberley in her own right and should feel quite comfortable with her role. He invited her to talk with Mrs Reynolds and suggest what changes she felt were needed. "You must feel free to suggest whatever you decide is appropriate, Lizzie, because Pemberley is your home now, and I shall depend on you to tell me what needs to be done to improve it."

It was of no use to protest that there appeared to be very little that needed improving in such a gracious dwelling. Darcy would reply with a degree of reasonableness that there was always something that needed improvement.

Darcy was finding that he was enjoying more and more the lightness and humour that Lizzie constantly brought into their life together. Almost in spite of himself, he enjoyed her teasing ways and often found himself responding in like manner. As he later confessed to Bingley, Lizzie was clever enough to balance playfulness and gravity with ease, never overdoing one or the other, and her keen sensibility told exactly how far she could go, never embarrassing her husband in any way. While this was new to Darcy, it had also brought an element of fun and liveliness into his life, which had been too serious for too long. Since his father's death, he had carried all the responsibilities of his family, and it had left very little time for the lighter side of life. He was almost thirty years of age and determined that the next decade of his life was going to be a good deal more interesting than the last. With Elizabeth at his side, he was sure this would be easily achieved.

Before leaving for London, Lizzie wrote to Jane with news of all the fascinating places they had visited and yet could not hide her longing to see her sister:

> *I would have written before, dear Jane, but for the reluctance I felt to put pen to paper, knowing we were still weeks away from seeing you. Now we are but five days from being in London, I can write and know that there will be but a day or two at most from the moment this letter is in your hands to the time we shall see you again. Can it be five weeks since we left Longbourn? You and Mr Bingley to speed to the excitement of London, while Mr. Darcy and I have wandered through several counties—at a most leisurely pace. And yet, from your letter and my own feelings there appears to be no difference in the degree of our happiness. Pray, dearest Jane, that it will be ever thus.*

Elizabeth explained that Mr Darcy had business in London, which involved both Bingley and their Uncle Gardiner. He had suggested that the ladies might take in the theatre and the London shops and perhaps, a soirée at one of London's salons.

> *I cannot tell you how highly Mr Darcy rates the advice he seeks from our Uncle Gardiner. This, dear sister, is especially pleasing to me, because I already knew that he liked both our Uncle and Aunt exceedingly well, ever since our chance meeting at Pemberley, last Summer. However, to know that he would seek them out for advice, denotes a new level of regard, not at all a part of his desire to please me.*

His appreciation of Mr Gardiner's experience and judgement and Mrs Gardiner's good taste and subtle gentility had endeared Darcy to her quite early in their courtship. This new evidence of his respect only strengthened her esteem and love for him.

The letter she had received from Mrs Gardiner had remained unanswered until they were two days from London, since plans had already been agreed between them to dine with the Gardiners. Writing a short note, which Darcy arranged to send by express with some papers for her uncle, Lizzie entreated her aunt to forgive her for not writing more fully, but promised that there would be many hours to spend together, while their husbands attended to business, when the three of them would scarcely catch breath for all the news they would have to impart to each other:

I promise you, my dearest Aunt, that Jane and I will be at your command—it will be almost like it was before last Summer. Oh, how much has happened since then! Mr Darcy and I look forward most eagerly to being with you very soon. He sends his love to all of you.

Your loving niece, Lizzie.

THE PEMBERLEY CHRONICLES

Part One

CHAPTER ONE

Reunions

SINCE HER MARRIAGE TO Mr Darcy some seven weeks ago, Elizabeth had wanted for nothing to complete her happiness, unless it was a chance to see her sister Jane again. Which is why her excitement increased markedly as they drove into London and around mid-morning found themselves approaching Mr Bingley's house in Grosvenor Street. Her husband could not conceal his amusement, as she cried out, "There they are!" like a little girl on her first visit to the city. As the carriage pulled up, she could barely wait to be helped out, before she flung herself into the welcoming arms of her sister.

Charles Bingley, who had been waiting beside Jane, smiled broadly as he exchanged greetings with Darcy, now his brother-in-law. They waited for the sisters to break from their warm and tearful embrace, the men's expressions of indulgent affection mixed with a degree of helplessness. It was Mr Bingley who intervened as the servants unloaded the travellers' trunks onto the footpath. Putting a solicitous arm around his wife and her sister, he said, "Shall we go indoors and let the luggage be taken upstairs?" He led them indoors, while Darcy followed, carrying Elizabeth's silk shawl, which had slipped off her shoulders as the sisters embraced.

They passed from the open hall into the comfort of a warm, pleasant room, where a fire crackled in the grate and a sideboard with an ample array of food and drink welcomed the travellers. While the gentlemen helped themselves to sherry and warmed themselves in front of the fire, Jane and Lizzie escaped upstairs, ostensibly so that Lizzie could divest herself of her travelling clothes and boots.

There was nothing the sisters wanted more than the privacy of a bedroom, where they hugged and kissed again as the words tumbled out, with neither able to wait for the other to finish a sentence. There was mutual acknowledgement that they had missed each other, they were both blissfully happy, they had the best husbands in the world, and they wished everyone could be as blessed as they were. The only matter upon which they could not agree was the question of which of them was the happier.

There was so much to tell, but it had to wait awhile; Jane promised they would have the afternoon to themselves as Bingley had planned to take Darcy out to his club to meet mutual friends.

Coming downstairs, they found Georgiana Darcy and Mrs Annesley come to call; they were staying in town at Mr Darcy's elegant townhouse in Portman Square and had been invited over by Jane to meet the returning couple. Georgiana, whose love for her brother was matched only by her devotion to her sister-in-law, whom she regarded as the sister she had always longed for, greeted Elizabeth with warmth and affection. Jane, looking on, wished she too could feel the same confidence of gaining the affection and approval of her in-laws, Caroline Bingley and Mrs Hurst. She felt not a little sadness as she saw the obvious satisfaction that Darcy felt as Lizzie and Georgiana embraced and talked together for all the world like loving sisters.

But, being Jane, she soon shook herself free of any trace of melancholy, as her husband came to her side and whispered, "I've arranged to take Georgiana and Mrs Annesley back to Portman Square, after which Darcy and I will go on to Brooks for an hour or two—that should give you and Lizzie plenty of time together. How would you like that, my love?" Jane replied that she would like it very much indeed and added her heartfelt thanks to her husband, whose sensitivity was a source of constant pleasure. As she said later to Lizzie, "I can hardly believe that he is so good and kind a man and yet preferred me above all others, knowing he could quite easily have had any of a dozen young ladies of greater substance and standing than myself." To which, Lizzie's reply was a reproachful reminder to her sister not to let her natural modesty trap her into undervaluing herself.

"For there is no one I know with a nature as good or a disposition as sweet as yours. Believe me, Jane, Mr Bingley is well aware of it and is considered, by his friends, to be a singularly fortunate man."

Earlier, they had partaken of a light luncheon of fresh rolls, sliced ham, cheese, and fruit, with tea, hot chocolate, or wine, as desired, before Georgiana and her companion left with the two gentlemen, who promised to be back in time for dinner. As the servants cleared away the remains of the repast, the two sisters returned upstairs to the comfort of Jane's boudoir to spend the rest of the afternoon in the kind of happy exchange of news and views that only two loving friends—both newly wed and blissfully happy—could hope to enjoy. Unhappily, the news from Longbourn was not good. Mrs Bennet, whose health was never the best, had not been well, having suffered from exhaustion after giving away two of her daughters at once. Their father, in his last letter to Jane, had asked that Lizzie be permitted to complete her travels undisturbed by this news.

"You know how it is, poor Mama will insist on having everyone over for Christmas; but this year, Lizzie, your kind invitation to us and Uncle and Aunt Gardiner to spend Christmas at Pemberley has relieved Mama of the strain. Because she cannot undertake the journey to Derbyshire, Papa has decided that he will remain with her at Longbourn, while Mary and Kitty will travel North with Aunt Gardiner," Jane explained. At this piece of bad news, Lizzie cried out, for she had been hoping so much to have her father at Pemberley, because she wanted him to see how happy she really was, especially in view of the doubts he had expressed at the time of Mr Darcy's proposal of marriage.

Jane offered some comfort, "Lizzie, Mr Bingley and I have talked about this. We knew how disappointed you would be if Papa could not be with you, so we have a plan. How would it be if Mr Bingley and I returned home at the New Year and had Mama to stay at Netherfield, so Papa could come to you for a few weeks?"

"Has he agreed to this?" asked her sister, somewhat surprised.

"Not yet, but we think he will, if Mr Darcy will ask him, tomorrow," said Jane. "Tomorrow?" Lizzie was astonished and more so when Jane replied, "He is to be at Aunt Gardiner's where, you will remember, we are all asked to dine tomorrow."

Elizabeth's pleasure at the news that she would see her father sooner than expected was much enhanced by the realisation that her sister Jane had gained in marriage a totally new confidence. If there was one criticism that could have been made against Jane, for all her sweetness of nature and strength of character, it was a diffidence—a reluctance to make judgements. To Elizabeth, it seemed as if this tiny flaw, if one could call it that, had disappeared since her marriage to Mr Bingley. However, she said nothing, not wanting to embarrass her sister. Besides there was so much to talk of their new lives, their husbands, their travels and so much love and happiness, that they quite forgot the time, until a maid ran upstairs to tell them the gentlemen were back.

Lizzie wished to bathe before dressing for dinner, and the luxury of a hot bath scented with lavender oils, prepared for her by Jane's maid, reminded her that this was London and not the inns of Gloucestershire or Wales, which, despite their charm, had been less than modern in their toilet facilities.

When they joined the gentlemen downstairs, they found there, to their surprise, Colonel Fitzwilliam, who had not been heard from since their weddings, when he had carried out his duties as Darcy's groomsman with aplomb.

Having greeted both sisters with affection and expressed satisfaction at finding them looking so well, he let Bingley explain his presence. "We found him at the club, where he has been staying all week," said Bingley, which led Jane to protest that he should have come to them.

"You could have stayed here, we have many empty rooms."

"I did not wish to intrude," Fitzwilliam said apologetically, "and I had no idea when Darcy and Elizabeth were expected."

"Well, you are here now, and you must stay," said Bingley firmly, as if that was the end of the matter, "until your ship is to sail." Amid cries of astonishment from the ladies of "What ship?" and "Where is he sailing to?" Fitzwilliam explained that he'd been at a loose end after the end of the war with France, and when he was offered a berth on a ship going to the new colonies of Ceylon and India, he had accepted. "That's the other side of the world!" said Jane, but Fitzwilliam assured her it was opening up fast and many people were going out there.

"I wanted a change of scene," he added by way of explanation.

It was an explanation Jane did not fully accept. Later that night, she reminded her sister that it was Charlotte's opinion that Fitzwilliam had been very partial to her, when they had been at Rosings last year, before Mr Darcy entered the picture. Elizabeth laughed and brushed it aside as a rumour, mainly a product of young Maria Lucas' romantic imagination. Fitzwilliam had left promising to return the following day to go with them to the Gardiners, to whom also he wished to say his farewells.

As they went to bed that night, Darcy and Elizabeth both agreed on the remarkable change in Jane since her marriage. It was a change Darcy welcomed for her sake and that of his friend, Bingley. "She will make him a stronger and better wife, and that will make him a stronger and better man," he said, adding more gently, "it was an aspect of your beautiful sister I used to worry about, my love, because I knew how important it was for Bingley." Ever ready to tease her husband, Elizabeth asked if he'd had any doubts about her own strength, to which Darcy replied firmly, "None at all, because, my dearest, you never left me in any doubt right from the start. Indeed, it was what I first admired in you, apart from your beautiful eyes, of course."

So pleased was his wife with this response that she stopped teasing and relaxed into the gentleness that she knew he loved. Darcy had never doubted his own feelings; Lizzie wanted him to have no doubt at all of hers. On such openheartedness was their marriage founded that concealment or archness was unthinkable.

The following day, plans were made to visit the shops on the other side of town, since the ladies wished to see the shoemakers and milliners. While break-fast was being cleared away, a carriage drew up, and, to the huge delight of their nieces, Mr and Mrs Gardiner were announced. The visitors, though unexpected, were warmly welcomed, especially by Mr Darcy. Elizabeth noted with great sat-isfaction the obvious pleasure with which he greeted them, and the sincerity of his welcome left no doubt in her mind of his regard and affection for them.

Mr Darcy's instant response of open friendliness and respect for her aunt and uncle, when they first met at Pemberley last Summer, had been the turn-ing point in her own appreciation of his character. Their relationship had grown slowly and with increasing confidence upon this foundation. It had grown in strength, and each time they had met with the Gardiners, whose esti-mation of Darcy was of the highest order, Elizabeth found her opinion endorsed by them. That Darcy, whose family had, by his own admission to her, encouraged an inordinate level of pride in class and status, could have devel-oped such a strong relationship with Mr and Mrs Gardiner, was remarkable in itself. That his behaviour to them was not merely correct in every particular of courtesy and etiquette, but was genuine in the friendship and affection he showed them at every turn, was proof enough for her that her husband was a man of estimable qualities. That she could be so much in love with a man she had almost loathed a year ago was well nigh miraculous!

Elizabeth knew she could have married him in spite of his low opinion of the stupidity of her sister Lydia or the silliness of her mother, but never could she have formed an alliance with anyone who did not share her love and regard for her favourite aunt and uncle. Their mutual respect was now something she took completely for granted. It was an essential part of their love for each other.

It was agreed that the ladies would drive to the shops in Mr Gardiner's carriage, while the gentlemen would stay behind to discuss matters of business. Soon, capes, shawls, and bonnets were fetched, and they set out determined that they would not be seduced into buying French fashions, which seemed to be in vogue! In the carriage together, Lizzie and Jane were keen to discover what business it was that their husbands were discussing. Mrs Gardiner was able to enlighten them, just a little. "I do not know the detail of it, my dears, but I believe your husbands have been clever enough to realise the great opportunities for trade with the new colonies and have expressed a wish to invest in your uncle's business. I think a partnership has been suggested."

"A partnership!" Both sisters were intrigued. They were well aware of the Bingleys' links with trade—it was the source of their fortune—but Darcy?

Elizabeth felt sure he would tell her all about it, when there was more to tell. Having satisfied some of their curiosity, Mrs Gardiner protested she was far more interested to hear how her favourite nieces were enjoying being married. The girls had no difficulty convincing their aunt of their current state of bliss; she could see for herself. "And what about Christmas?" she asked, to which Lizzie replied, "That's been settled—you are all to come to Pemberley at Christmas."

And so they went out to the shops in excellent humour and spent an hour or more in the pleasantest way. Lizzie bought some new boots—her own were worn with travelling, she declared, and Mrs Gardiner insisted on buying her nieces two pairs of French gloves in the most modish colours of the season. Mrs Gardiner was delighted to find Jane and Lizzie so happy. She was young enough to understand the intoxicating effects of love and marriage on two lovely young women, recently wedded to two of the most eligible young men one could hope to meet.

When they returned to Grosvenor Street, they parted almost at once, since the Gardiners had to hurry back to await Mr Bennet, who was arriving by coach around midday. Driving back to Gracechurch Street, Mr Gardiner was as anxious as his wife had been to hear the news about his nieces. "And how are Mrs Darcy and Mrs Bingley, my dear? Such grand names!" he said in jest, almost mimicking his sister, Mrs Bennet.

Mrs Gardiner was delighted to tell him of their happiness, "I am so pleased, Edward, I could not be more so if they were my own daughters. Indeed, I should be well pleased if Caroline and Emily were half as fortunate as Jane and Lizzie."

It was a verdict she was to repeat to her brother-in-law, Mr Bennet, over lunch, appreciating his keenness to hear news of his daughters. Her husband added, "And having spent quite some time with Mr Darcy recently, what with one thing and another, I can safely endorse those sentiments, Brother. There would not be two young men more deserving of your wonderful daughters than Mr Darcy and his excellent friend, Mr Bingley."

Mr Bennet waited impatiently for the evening, when he would see his beloved Jane and Lizzie again. His memories of their wedding day were a blur of activity, smiles, and the unending chattering of his wife. He had missed his daughters terribly and longed to know they were happy. When the party from Grosvenor Street arrived, Mr Bennet noted that Jane and Lizzie looked extremely well.

The young Misses Gardiner—Caroline and Emily, given special permission to dine late with their cousins—admired the exquisite jewels, gifts from their husbands, and fine gowns they wore and begged Lizzie to tell them all about the wonderful places she had visited.

After dinner, there came the usual request for music. Lizzie obliged with a song and invited Caroline and Emily to join her in a pretty ballad, which they had all learned last Summer. It was a great success, and an encore was immediately demanded. Fitzwilliam, who had a fine tenor voice, was pressed into service next; he delighted everyone by singing a pretty little duet with young Miss Caroline Gardiner, whose sweet, clear voice harmonised perfectly with his. Mr and Mrs Gardiner looked so proud that Jane, sitting with her aunt, thought she would surely weep with joy, but she merely gripped her niece's hand very tightly and applauded enthusiastically when it was over. Colonel Fitzwilliam bowed deeply and kissed Miss Gardiner's little hand in a very gallant gesture, at which Bingley jumped to his feet and applauded again.

Mr Bennet did not need to ask if his daughters were happy. He could see, from the glow on Jane's face and the sparkle in Lizzie's eyes, that they had no regrets about the men they had chosen to wed. Watching his sons-in-law as they stood engaged in animated discussion, he turned to Lizzie, who had just brought him his coffee, "I have to say, Lizzie, that Mr Darcy appears to be much more cheerful and relaxed. Marriage has done him a deal of good, and it must be all your own good work, eh?" "Whatever do you mean, Papa?" asked Lizzie, pretending to be quite unable to understand his drift.

"Why, Lizzie, I have never seen Mr Darcy smile so much and look so pleased. I do believe I even heard him tell a joke—or perhaps that was Bingley?"

"Well, I did assure you he was perfectly amiable, did I not?"

"You did, my dear . . ." he began, but at that moment, Mr Darcy approached, and Lizzie went to him, leaving her father smiling, quite certain his daughter's happiness was not in question. Was it Chance or Destiny, or was Mrs Bennet right after all? Poor Mr Bennet would never know the answer. Later, when the guests were gone, and he sat with his brother-in-law before a dying fire in the drawing room, he returned to the topic.

"They are fortunate to have married two such fine young men—but then, Jane and Lizzie deserve the best," he observed. Mr Gardiner was quick to agree, adding that while Mr Bingley was a most charming and amiable young fellow, it was Lizzie's Mr Darcy, whose nobility of character, generosity, and devotion to his wife had endeared him to them, who was their favourite.

"Mrs Gardiner and I are agreed that, had your Lizzie been our daughter, there is no other man above Mr Darcy to whom we would have preferred to entrust her happiness." This was high praise, indeed, and Mr Bennet was content. He could return to Longbourn and face Mrs Bennet's unending chatter about all the servants, carriages, and fine clothes they would have, knowing that both his daughters were cherished and happy.

The following day, as Mr Bennet waited for his coach, Darcy called very early in the morning. He'd come to invite his father-in-law to spend a few weeks with them at Pemberley, in January, since sadly he was unable to join the family at Christmas, due to Mrs Bennet's state of health. "If you would advise me, Sir, of dates and times, I shall send my carriage to meet the coach at Lambton," said Darcy, adding that they were all looking forward to his first visit to Pemberley. His graciousness, generosity, and good humour completely won over Mr Bennet, in whose estimation Mr Darcy had been rising very rapidly. He accepted the invitation gladly adding that he was looking forward very much to using the excellent library of which he had heard so much. Darcy looked very pleased, and they parted, each man having increased his respect for the other, both looking forward to their next meeting.

Darcy returned to Grosvenor Street and found Lizzie in their bedroom, looking out on the deserted street below. She had risen late and assumed he had gone out riding with Bingley. When he told her of his visit to her father, she turned to him in tears, "My dear husband, I told him you were a good and amiable man, but I did not say you were perfect!" at which he coloured deeply and fumbled for words, saying it was of no consequence . . . simply a part of his love for her. Elizabeth was in a teasing mood, "You should have let me see, rather earlier in our acquaintance, how kind and generous you really are; it might have saved us both a great deal of heartache," she complained.

Darcy, touched by the warmth of her love so sweetly expressed, was serious as he held her close. "How could I, Lizzie? How could I lay claim to qualities and values I barely recognised, until you, my dearest, made me acknowledge my own inadequacy." She tried to hush him then, unwilling to rake up the memories of her reproof and his agonising over it, but Darcy was determined to acknowledge it. "No, my dear Lizzie, it is all your doing. If I have done some good things, if I have been less selfish and arrogant, it is because of you, because I loved you and sought your love in return." His voice was very low with the unaccustomed weight of emotion, and Lizzie, knowing the strength of his feelings, let him speak, responding only with a loving kiss.

Later, Georgiana came over and stayed to lunch. They made plans; Georgiana and her companion would travel to Pemberley on Tuesday, with instructions for Mrs Reynolds to prepare for the arrival of Mr and Mrs Darcy with the Bingleys, a week later. They would be staying on in town only until Fitzwilliam sailed. Mrs Reynolds was also to arrange for the accommodation of the other guests at Christmas; Lizzie noted that the list did not include the Hursts or Caroline Bingley. Jane had already reassured her that the Bingley sisters and boring Mr Hurst were invited to Rosings, by Lady Catherine de Bourgh! "Ah well," Lizzie remarked, "They're sure to get on exceedingly well. No doubt much time will be spent expressing their indignation at my daring to defy Her Ladyship's orders and marry her nephew!" The other guests were the Gardiners and their children, Kitty and Mary Bennet, and Dr Grantley, who would be arriving on Christmas Eve. Darcy explained that his sister always had her own party on Christmas Eve for the children of the Pemberley Estate. Jane thought it was a wonderful idea to have a party for the children of the estate, and Georgiana said that it had been her brother's idea, when she, as a little girl, had been unhappy that the children of their tenants and servants had no party of their own at Christmas.

"He started it, and it was such a success, we've had it every year." Lizzie thought how well it fitted with Mrs Reynolds' picture of a caring Master, whose tenants and servants rewarded him with singular loyalty.

Looking across at Darcy, she felt proud to be his wife, proud of the innate decency and goodness that was now so clear to her. She felt ashamed of the prejudice that had been allowed to cloud her judgement, when they had met, but just as quickly she put aside her guilt, blaming Wickham for poisoning her mind with lies. She looked again at her husband; this time their eyes met, and they smiled.

The Bingleys intended to stay on at Netherfield Park only until Spring, when the lease ran out. Charles had already sought Darcy's advice on purchasing a suitable estate, not far from Pemberley, unless as he said, "You want Jane and Lizzie to be forever pining for each other." Darcy agreed that this would not do at all and promised to make inquiries about suitable properties in the area. The prospect made Jane and Lizzie very happy indeed. Elizabeth realised that Mr. Bingley seemed to thrive on the bright lights and social whirl of London and her sister Jane, to whom this was an exciting new world, appeared to match his enthusiasm. Darcy, on the other hand, loathed the social obligations and artificial rituals of the London Season, and Elizabeth had no taste for them either. They couldn't wait to get away to Pemberley, but there were contracts to be signed and Fitzwilliam to be farewelled, so they remained in London, moving into Darcy's townhouse at Portman Square.

They spent many hours in Galleries and Museums, attended a soirée and a chamber concert, and when they dined at home alone, indulged in that favourite pastime of loving couples—congratulating themselves on their excellent judgement in marrying each other!

The following Sunday, their last in London, with the Bingleys visiting friends in Windsor, Darcy and Lizzie took advantage of some rare Winter sunshine and drove down to Richmond. This beautiful spot on the Thames, which had become quite fashionable with the London set, afforded them the privacy they craved.

They talked of Jane and Bingley—for they had both noticed how Jane seemed much less diffident about showing her feelings. Recalling Jane's concealment of her affection for Mr Bingley and the inordinate length of time taken by Charles to declare his love for her, Elizabeth rejoiced that they appeared so much in love, with so very little concern as to who knew it. Darcy said he thought they had both matured a good deal in the last year. Elizabeth agreed but wondered aloud whether everyone was as cautious in such situations; but, even as she spoke, before she could finish her sentence, she saw her husband's wry smile, stopped, and started to laugh. "Oh dear!" she said, as Darcy smiled and shook his head, "Neither of us were particularly cautious, I'm afraid."

They recalled that first occasion at Hunsford, when Darcy had declared himself in the strangest way, rushing headlong, throwing caution and sensibility to the winds, and Elizabeth had responded with a degree of sharpness of which she had never dreamed herself capable. She begged him not to remind her of the hurt and harm she had done, with her reproaches, but Darcy disagreed, claiming that her frankness and honesty had been just what he had needed to jolt him out of his smugness and complacency. "It forced me to look at myself to confront the fact that I had no right to claim the status of a gentleman unless I behaved like one to all those I met and mingled with. No, Lizzie, had you not spoken and taught me the lesson I had to learn, we might never have found out that we cared for each other." Lizzie's cheeks burned as he went on, "Look at us now, could we ever have been this happy if we had not been honest with one another?"

"You are probably right in that, dearest, but are we in danger of becoming a tiny bit smug and complacent ourselves?" She was teasing him, but he replied seriously, "Never Lizzie, whilst ever you set such high standards for us both." Lizzie smiled. "I must agree we are very happy and comfortable together. I had feared we might be too reserved with each other, but it has not been so," she said.

"That is because you, my love, with your open, honest manner, would defy anyone to be reserved," he said, smiling as he added, "it was the quality I found most engaging and hardest to resist."

This time, Elizabeth could not help but tease him. With her eyes sparkling, she quipped, "Especially when you were so determined to do just that!" Darcy would not permit her to continue, not even in jest, protesting that he had proved his love and would do so again, if necessary. At this point, Lizzie decided she would tease him no more; there was never any doubt at all of his love for her. "Could we go home?" she asked, softly, and sensing her changed mood, Darcy rose immediately and helped her into the carriage.

There was something very special between them. Theirs was no "unequal marriage" of the sort her father had warned against: a marriage in which one partner found it hard to respect the other, the kind of union that, they acknowledged without ever saying a word, existed between her parents. This type of marriage Lizzie had dreaded all her life. She and Jane had frequently vowed to remain unwed, rather than submit to that ultimate indignity. With Darcy, Elizabeth already knew she had a marriage after her own heart; she could unreservedly say that the love they shared was stronger for the esteem they had for each other.

They drove back into town, wrapped in a warm, affectionate silence, and went directly to Darcy's townhouse in Portman Square. "We're home," he said, helping Lizzie out. They embraced as she alighted into his arms and went upstairs, leaving their coats and scarves in the hall.

That evening, they dined with Fitzwilliam and the Bingleys. He was sailing on the morrow for Ceylon and India, where he was to work with the East India Company for at least three years. He confessed to being suddenly sad to leave, knowing it would be a long time before he would see England and all his friends again. He had dined the previous evening with the Gardiners, and all these farewells were taking their toll upon his spirits.

Elizabeth had sensed the sadness that seemed to overlay his earlier enthusiasm and said so to her sister. Jane was convinced that it had more to do with losing Lizzie than leaving England. Their husbands, on the other hand, much more interested in the business opportunities than in Fitzwilliam's state of mind, did not remark upon it at all.

Two days later, they were on the road themselves, deciding to make the journey North before the weather worsened. When it was decided to break journey in Oxford, Elizabeth was delighted. It would give Jane a chance to meet Dr Grantley. Jane, who had heard so much about him from her sister, was in complete agreement with her after they met and dined with him that night. His distinguished appearance, cultured conversation, and remarkable reputation quite overawed her, until his unassuming manner and friendliness drew her out.

When they retired after a most pleasant and stimulating evening, Jane expressed her surprise that he was unmarried. Lizzie laughed and warned her against matchmaking—which had been the bane of their lives at home. Jane protested that she had no intention of doing so but added, "Lizzie, he is such a charming and educated gentleman, that I find it impossible to believe, that had he wished to marry, he could not have found a suitable partner. Surely, he does not intend to remain a bachelor?" Lizzie laughed and begged her to remember that Dr Grantley was but a few years older than Mr Darcy, so there was hope for him yet!

And so, on to Pemberley . . .

CHAPTER TWO

... To make a celebration

THE DRIVE TO PEMBERLEY took them through wooded country stripped partially bare by the Winter winds. Though Elizabeth had been to the house both before and after her engagement to Darcy, she was, on this occasion, assailed by a tumult of emotions, which kept her unusually silent. Beside her, her husband was also quiet and thoughtful, but this was not particularly unusual for Darcy. It was left to Charles Bingley to keep up a commentary for the benefit of his wife, pointing out every item of interest, every lovely aspect, quite unashamedly showing off his familiarity with his friend's fine estate. There was no snow on the ground; in fact, the sky was clear and blue. But the clouds gathering up ahead suggested that there might be snow on the way.

Elizabeth's mind kept harking back to the first time she had come here driving from Lambton with her aunt and uncle, hoping merely to get a visitor's view of Pemberley, never suspecting that they would meet the owner himself, returning unexpectedly early. She recalled her confusion and embarrassment on seeing him standing there not twenty yards from her, his face suffused in a deep blush. She smiled to herself as she remembered their encounter and all that had flowed from it.

Had it really been only last Summer? She sighed and turned slowly from contemplating the cold wintry woods to look at her husband. She was rewarded with a warm smile that confirmed her suspicions that he was remembering too. Unwilling to break the spell of the moment, she said nothing, knowing there was no need for words. The magic moment was gone, however, as Bingley asked, "Not much longer now, is it, Darcy?" to which he replied, "No, just half a mile down the road, and we shall be into the park." Lapsing into a reverie again, Lizzie recalled how it had looked last Summer as they descended into the valley and drove towards Pemberley House. The handsome, stone building had made her catch her breath as her aunt and uncle admired its elegant lines and noble proportions, set as it was in a beautifully landscaped park, against a background of wooded hills.

When they had been here again in Autumn, after her engagement to Mr Darcy, she'd had more time to appreciate the myriad of colours in the woods above the house as well as the streams and valleys below it. Darcy had taken special pleasure in showing her his favourite views, and they had walked along the stream till it reached its confluence with the river, which meandered along a lovely winding valley as far as the eye could see. When she had pointed out that it was an ideal spot for a picnic, Darcy had immediately promised they would have one there next Summer, to commemorate her first visit to Pemberley. She had teased him gently then, asking if he really wanted to perpetuate the memory of that day, which had been so embarrassing to both of them. To which Darcy had replied, "But of course, dearest, for after the initial astonishment, I think we got on very well indeed. For my part, it was the day that saw the resurrection of my hopes. I shall never forget the happiness I felt after I had seen you here at Pemberley." This time, Elizabeth, who had never seen it in Winter, almost gasped at the first view of the house, its graceful architecture thrown into relief by the starkness of the Winter landscape and the dark foliage of the pine and fir trees in the grounds around it.

Jane, who by now had changed her seat so she could see the way ahead more clearly, was asking questions about the estate, and Darcy, with the courtesy of a gracious host, was answering her enquiries.

Listening to them, Elizabeth wondered again at her blindness in believing Wickham's wicked lies that had Mr Darcy as a haughty, short-tempered man with little or no patience for those he presumed to be beneath him. Every circumstance had proved her wrong, as she experienced not only the love and affection he lavished upon her but much more the generosity and genuine graciousness of his behaviour towards all members of her family. As a husband, brother, and friend, Mr Darcy had passed every test. Involuntarily, Lizzie smiled, and Bingley caught her eye as she did. Bingley, whose admiration for his friend knew no bounds, smiled broadly and said in his own amiable way, "I told Jane, Darcy would be the man to tell her about Pemberley; he's so besotted with the place."

"I can understand why," said Lizzie, as the carriage crossed the bridge and drove to the great front door.

They alighted and went up the steps into the hall, to be received by Mrs Reynolds, the housekeeper, who had not seen them since the wedding. Her delight at having her Master back was so apparent it was quite moving, especially to Elizabeth, whom she greeted with warmth and deference, asking if they had had a comfortable journey and showing them into the saloon, where a lively fire was burning and a table was laid for afternoon tea. There, waiting for them was Georgiana, whose greeting was as affectionate and warm as their parting had been, just a week ago. She was obviously delighted to have her brother home again, and of course, now her affection extended to Elizabeth.

Jane was overwhelmed with the scale and grace of the rooms and the elegance of the furniture and accessories. "Oh Lizzie," she whispered, "It's beautiful." Elizabeth's eyes sparkled, but she forbore to tease her sister, as she had done on that night many months ago when she attributed the first stirrings of her love for Darcy to her appreciation of his beautiful estate.

After tea, they were shown upstairs to their rooms—to rest awhile before dinner, which was always at seven in the Winter unless they had company, other than family. Mrs Reynolds, concerned for their comfort, provided Elizabeth and Jane with a lady's maid, her niece, Jenny, a pleasant young woman with a strong family resemblance to her aunt. Mrs Reynolds hoped she would be satisfactory, and Lizzie, who had shared a maid with her mother and four sisters, assured her that Jenny would do very nicely. Before leaving them, Mrs Reynolds took the opportunity to explain that she had, in consultation with Miss Darcy, decided that it was not appropriate to present the household staff to the new Mistress of Pemberley as soon as she had arrived after a very long journey. However, the staff would be ready to receive them in the hall before dinner. Lizzie thanked her for her kind consideration and added she was looking forward to meeting them. She understood the formal protocol, and as Darcy explained later, it was a significant day for the staff, too. There had not been a Mistress of Pemberley for many years, since the death of his mother. "Will you be there too?" she asked, a little anxiously, and sensing her nervousness, he smiled and answered, "Of course, my dear," and she was instantly at ease again.

When they went down to dinner, Lizzie was glad she had worn her new green silk gown and the jewels her husband had given her; the servants, all of them, were so smartly turned out. With Mr Darcy at her side, she acknowledged them all, and she accepted their good wishes and the welcoming words spoken by Mrs Reynolds. A little girl—the daughter of one of the men—approached with a bunch of Winter roses, and everyone was charmed, when Lizzie, quite spontaneously, bent to thank her with a kiss. Looking on, Darcy knew that these men and women had been enchanted, just as he had been—not just by the beauty, but also by the unaffected charm of their new Mistress. He had known most of them all his life and could sense their pleasure and approval.

Dinner was a simple but excellent meal, with soup, fish and poultry, roasted vegetables, and a dessert which was declared to be Darcy's favourite, as well as the best wines from the cellar. Elizabeth could barely suppress a smile at the spoiling of the Master that seemed to be the order of the day.

After dinner, it was time to talk of plans for Christmas, with Georgiana pointing out gently that there were but ten days to Christmas Eve and her important party for the children of the Pemberley Estate. Lizzie and Jane promised to help, and it was decided that on the following day, the three of them would sit down after breakfast and draw up some plans. Darcy and Bingley were going to be riding into Lambton, so they would have the morning to themselves.

Later, Georgiana and Lizzie were persuaded to oblige them with music, and again memories of last Summer came flooding back as Elizabeth played and sang with her sister-in-law, who was now much more at ease than before. Looking across at Darcy, she saw again the expression that she had first seen in this very room. At that time, it had led her to wonder at his feelings for her; she knew now that it was a confirmation of them. The last time they were in this room and she was at the instrument with Georgiana, they may have both preferred to conceal their feelings from each other and the rest of the company; now, they were in love, and it mattered not who knew it. Mrs Reynold's smile as she brought in the candles and bade them all goodnight suggested that she knew it, too. Lizzie recalled their conversation when they had visited Pemberley last Summer as strangers—Mrs Reynolds was not sure there could be a woman good enough for her Master, who, she had assured them, had been the "sweetest tempered, most generous hearted boy in the world." Even allowing for some partiality born of loyalty, it had been agreed that this was high praise indeed. Lizzie could now assert that to the best of her own intimate knowledge, that boy had grown into the most generous and kindhearted of men and the best of husbands. She acknowledged herself the most fortunate of women, that he had chosen her to be his wife. Based on her reception and the kindness, concern, and respect extended to her, Lizzie had reason to believe that Mrs Reynolds approved of his choice.

As they went to bed that night, she told Darcy of that conversation and was assured that he had not always been the perfect little boy Mrs Reynolds recalled. He confessed that he may well have been selfish and stubborn in his behaviour as a young man. "And I need not tell you, my love, that Pride sometimes got in the way too."

"Oh, hush," said Lizzie, not wanting to spoil this lovely evening with memories of recriminations, but Darcy persisted, wanting her to understand the extent of her own influence upon him and the depth of the change he had wrought upon himself for her.

"Since you wish to credit me with this happy transformation, I will certainly accept it, my dearest," she said, "but believe me, I have often reproached myself for the harshness of my judgement, the cruelty of my words, and the hurt I must have caused you. So, shall we say we have both accepted our faults and pledge never to hurt one another again? Are we agreed?" Darcy nodded, took both her hands in his, and drew her close; he had no words to express the happiness of this moment, and neither had she, but, no matter, for none were needed.

The following morning, Mr and Mrs Darcy rose late, dressed, and went downstairs to find that most of the others had done the same, except Bingley, who had always been an early bird. Lizzie recalled how very early in the day he used to call on them at Longbourn, much to the confusion of Mrs Bennet. She reminded Jane of the day he had proposed to her, having arrived before any of them were dressed, and the total chaos it had made of their mother's plans; the sisters laughed together at the memory, commenting as they did on the delightful consequences of that day upon all their lives. "Of course, Lizzie, I had no idea then that you and Mr Darcy were in love and so close to becoming engaged,"

Jane teased, prompting both Darcy and Lizzie to protest that they barely knew it themselves at the time, and it was to the amazing intervention of Lady Catherine de Bourgh that they owed the good understanding that followed and actually led to their engagement.

Jane laughed a delightful happy laugh as she took both their hands and drew them to her side, "I well remember the visit of Lady Catherine to Longbourn, and I swear I would never have believed at the time that any of us would owe our happiness to her!" Elizabeth looked quickly at Darcy's face, but he was laughing with them and proceeded to declare that Lady Catherine was bound to suffer even more discomfiture very soon, when she discovered, shortly after Christmas, that her nephew James, brother of Colonel Fitzwilliam, was engaged to Miss Rosamund Camden, the daughter of one of Darcy's neighbours.

Lizzie and Jane knew nothing of this; Darcy proceeded to explain that the couple had met a year ago when the Fitzwilliams had stayed at Pemberley. "Rosamund is several years older than Georgiana," Darcy explained, "and a very personable young lady. Naturally, James spent most of the time with her. They have much in common—both coming from similar farming families—and I was not surprised to hear from Fitzwilliam that he was sorry to be missing his brother's wedding, which he believed would take place at Easter."

"And why are you so certain of the effect this will have upon Lady Catherine?" asked Elizabeth, unaware of the ineligibility of Miss Camden as a bride for Darcy's cousin.

Darcy smiled, "Because as you well know, my dearest, my aunt likes to manage people's lives, and she had hoped that James would look favourably in the direction of a certain lady, whom you both know well," he said, and of course, they demanded to know who it was. "It's Miss Bingley," he said quietly. Jane and Lizzie were amazed. "Miss Bingley? Caroline?" they cried, unable to believe their ears.

Darcy chuckled. "Indeed. Her fortune is twice that of Rosamund Camden's. She and her sister have been presented at Court and own a valuable house in London, and that would carry more weight with my aunt than almost anything. In addition, Miss Bingley is very deferential to Lady Catherine and Miss de Bourgh, and that is much appreciated. Indeed, I believe they are at Rosings this Christmas." Jane testified that this was indeed true. "Well, Lady

Catherine will be hoping that Fitzwilliam will soon be joining them, unaware that he is already with the Camdens at Rushmore Farm, near Lambton, which is where Bingley and I are going later today," said Darcy, obviously enjoying himself in the telling of it.

"That is indeed as droll a tale as ever I've heard," said Jane, and Lizzie had to agree that her husband had certainly surprised them.

Bingley, who had been out riding very early, returned as they were finishing breakfast, which ended the conversation, since none of them wished to offend him in any way. He sat down to breakfast, assuring Darcy he would not be late for their ride into Lambton, adding, "I am very keen to see the horses; Fitzwilliam recommended a particularly promising pony." Lizzie and Jane exchanged glances, but clearly, Darcy had not said a word to his friend of his aunt's plans for Caroline Bingley!

After breakfast, the gentlemen set off for Lambton and Rushmore Farm. Lizzie and Jane were immediately drawn by Georgiana into the morning room, where the warmth generated by a crackling fire augmented the rather watery sunshine that struggled through the clouds.

Unaccustomed to the vagaries of the Northern weather, Jane shivered, and Georgiana, concerned, asked for a shawl to be brought for her. Lizzie, alerted by her husband, had dressed in warmer clothes and seemed comfortable enough but was solicitous of her sister, who did not have a particularly strong constitution.

Plans for the children's party were soon on the table. Mrs Reynolds needed to know details of their requirements, so she could instruct the cook, the maids, and the butler. Lizzie was feeling a little tired, when after a couple of hours, they had not got very far with ideas for the entertainment.

Georgiana wondered if there was something new they could do as everyone was tired of Punch and Judy, and not all the children could be trusted with fireworks. "Do they sing?" asked Elizabeth, suddenly. Both Jane and Georgiana said, "Sing?" looking quite confused.

"Yes," said Elizabeth, "after all, it is Christmas, and they could sing Christmas carols." "Oh Lizzie," cried Georgiana, "what a wonderful idea!"

"It's a lovely idea, Lizzie, but how would they learn them?" asked Jane.

"We shall have to get them together and train them," said Lizzie.

"Do you mean like a choir?"

"Exactly, a children's choir—the Pemberley Children's Choir," said Lizzie. Both Jane and Georgiana were delighted, and immediately, there was a sense of excitement. Mrs Reynolds, who came in to ask if they would like some tea, was requested to provide the names of staff with children who could be taught to sing Christmas carols. A little confused and uncertain at first, she soon got into the spirit of things and provided a dozen or so names. By the time the gentlemen returned, much had been accomplished. Neither could quite believe that a choir of Pemberley children could be trained to sing carols in less than ten days, but they were willing to help the ladies try. From then on, the music room and an adjoining sitting room became a hive of activity, with preparations for the Pemberley Children's Choir taking precedence over all else. Darcy was particularly pleased to see how well Georgiana worked together with Jane and Elizabeth.

The staff whose children were to be trained to sing were so delighted they couldn't do enough to help—many staying on after their work was done to help with costumes and decorations. A stage had to be built at one end of the large room that was always used for the party; Bingley supervised the carpenters, while Mr Darcy organised the transport for the children. They seemed to enjoy singing, but few of them, except for a very young lad with a high sweet voice, had ever been in a choir. Elizabeth played, and Georgiana sang along with them, while Jane plied them with tea and ginger bread, courtesy of the cook. It was hard work, and every so often, Elizabeth wondered what had possessed her to suggest a choir! Then, they would behave and sing like angels, and she knew it was all worthwhile. It was amidst all this activity that a message came from the inn at Lambton that the Gardiners had arrived, with Mary and Kitty, and would be driving up to Pemberley on the following day. The news, which Darcy whispered to Elizabeth in the midst of a rehearsal, immediately lifted her spirits, for there were going to be several more helpers and a few excellent to passable voices among them. That would make a considerable difference to their little choir.

~

When Elizabeth and Jane came down to breakfast the following morning, the clouds that had threatened sleet or snow all of the previous day had been blown away overnight by great gusts of wind. The gardeners were out early, clearing away the debris, piles of fallen leaves and shattered branches, which lay all over the park. A very pale sun struggled above the horizon.

Darcy and Bingley returned from their early ride, and Mrs Reynolds was quick to produce fresh pots of tea and hot food for the gentlemen, who were coming in from the cold. Jane and Lizzie had already commented with some amusement at the way in which the men of the household were thoroughly spoilt by the staff. Having grown up in a house full of women, where their father spent a good deal of time trying to keep out of the way of the womenfolk, they found the situation at Pemberley quite diverting. Jane thought it was probably the result of Mrs Reynolds taking on the care of the children when their mother died. Lizzie suggested it was more a mutual admiration society, because the servants felt that lavishing attention on their wonderful Master and his sister was their appointed role, while the Master and his sister would wonder how they would ever get on without the help of their staff. "Oh Lizzie," Jane protested, "I do believe you are too harsh; besides, I cannot see any harm in it."

"Nor can I, but you must admit, it is the relationship of mutual dependence that holds them together so well. I cannot see a similar situation at Longbourn, could you?" Jane confessed that it did not seem likely and added that while the servants at Bingley's house in Grosvenor Street were most efficient and attentive, they did not appear to have the same familial attitude that existed at Pemberley. It must have something to do with being in the country, she thought.

Elizabeth did not entirely agree but kept her counsel, not wishing to offend or hurt her beloved Jane by pointing out that, grand though Mr Bingley's house was, it was not Pemberley, where generations of servants had served the Darcy family. While the servants at Grosvenor Street had been hired for their excellence, those at Pemberley had been mostly born into service, and loyalty was their strongest suit. There was certainly no suggestion that Darcy and Georgiana had any reservations about the staff, and they appeared content to leave most of the management of the household to Mrs Reynolds. Mr Darcy had urged Elizabeth to instruct the housekeeper about arrangements for the Christmas guests. Mrs Reynolds herself had, on the day after they'd arrived home, apologised for troubling her but asked if Elizabeth had any special instructions for the meals. Content to leave things in her capable hands for the moment, Elizabeth had thanked Mrs Reynolds but pointed out that since she had plans already in hand, Elizabeth would not want to make changes. However, perhaps in the New Year, after she had got accustomed to the way things were done, she might wish to make some suggestions. The happy smile on the housekeeper's face convinced her that she had said absolutely the right thing.

It was midmorning, when the sound of horse's hooves and carriage wheels on the gravelled drive attracted Jane and Lizzie to the windows of the upstairs sitting room. No sooner did they see the Gardiners, than they ran downstairs to greet them. The servants were helping the travellers out and unloading their trunks, when Lizzie and Jane embraced their aunt and uncle, the young Gardiners, and their younger sisters, Mary and Kitty, whom they had not seen since their wedding in October. Kitty was especially tearful, having missed her two elder sisters terribly, while Mary had so many books and manuscripts with her, she appeared to have come prepared for long periods of study and practise on the piano.

Darcy was already out greeting Mr and Mrs Gardiner and welcoming them back to Pemberley. Elizabeth did not doubt that they would all have recalled the last occasion when they had stood there together. How much had changed since then; she caught her aunt's eye, and they smiled.

It was left to Mrs Reynolds to persuade everyone to come indoors and enjoy the warmth of a fire and tea in the morning room. Georgiana, who had been practising in the music room, came out to join them, and the halls of Pemberley, which had been so quiet a mere half hour ago, were filled with many voices, including those of the four young Gardiners.

Caroline Gardiner, who was meeting Georgiana for the first time after the weddings of Jane and Lizzie, was delighted to be asked to help with the choir. After tea, Mrs Gardiner went upstairs with her nieces to take a look at their rooms, unpack her presents, and enjoy a long conversation with her favourite young women. This time, she had good news for them. Their mother was feeling much better, and was planning to go North to Newcastle to Lydia and Wickham, who were expecting their first child in Spring. Jane and Elizabeth gave silent thanks that they were not at Longbourn to share in their mother's enthusiastic and expensive preparations for the birth of her first grandchild.

More news, this time from the Lucas household: it appeared that Charlotte's sister, Maria Lucas, was being courted by the new doctor at Meryton. "Maria Lucas!" cried Jane, "but she is younger than Kitty."

"Only by a few months," said Lizzie, "but nevertheless, this is a surprise. How did it come about?"

"Apparently, Lady Lucas was unwell and sent for Mr Jones the apothecary, who happened to be away visiting his daughter. In his stead came a young man recently arrived in Meryton, a Dr John Faulkner, a physician, who has set up his practice in the town." Mrs Gardiner explained, and seeing that her nieces were agog for more, she went on, "Of course, young Maria Lucas was on hand to assist her mother and to offer Dr Faulkner tea afterwards."

"Is that all?" Lizzie sounded disappointed, but her aunt had more to tell.

"Your mother tells me that he has visited Lady Lucas four times in the last fortnight, and Hill has heard from the Lucases' cook that he spends most of his visit, having tea and walking in the conservatory with young Miss Maria."

"No doubt Mama is very vexed," quipped Lizzie "that Kitty has not been preferred by the new doctor."

"But Kitty is not likely to be planning to catch herself a suitor, however much mama might wish it," said Jane. Mrs Gardiner agreed, saying Kitty had seemed quite unfussed by her friend Maria's achievement, except to say "Dr Faulkner was much less boring than Mr. Collins!" "So it seems Kitty approves of Maria's choice," said Jane, to which Lizzie added that it was hardly Maria's choice; more likely Dr Faulkner had done the choosing.

Their aunt decided she had to stop her nieces from having young Miss Lucas married off to the Doctor in the next few minutes. "Now, let us not run on so fast, my dears, there is not even talk of an engagement as yet—much less a wedding," she warned, and Lizzie laughed.

"Yes, and we know one cannot count on these romances always turning out as one might expect. But I do not want you to think that I don't wish young Maria well. She is a very pleasant girl, and I do hope she is happy." Jane and Mrs Gardiner agreed, and the conversation was closed abruptly as they were interrupted by Emily and Caroline who came to say luncheon was on the table.

Later, the children came to rehearse their concert of carols, and what a delight it was for the visitors. When they had run through the chosen carols—mostly of old English vintage—and been heartily applauded by their audience of family and servants, Elizabeth and Georgiana invited the four Gardiner children to join them.

Ranging from ten year old Caroline and Emily, who was seven, to Richard and Robert, who were six and four, they could all sing and made a spectacular contribution to the volume and quality of the choir. Mary was happy to assist with the accompaniment and so released Elizabeth to sit with her guests, while Kitty was totally engrossed with making appropriate Christmas hats for the children. Mrs Gardiner suggested the older children hold little candles, a European custom she had found appealing, while on a visit to France.

Later, after hot chocolate and cake had been duly consumed, Georgiana persuaded Caroline to try a solo carol, and they chose the gentle *Virgin's Lullaby*, which almost had the listeners in tears. The excellent work done by the ladies received much praise, while Mr Darcy had never looked happier.

❧

Christmas Eve dawned cold and bright.

After breakfast, everyone who wanted to got rugged up and went into the woods to collect boughs of fir, pine cones, and holly for decorating the rooms and the stage. The younger members of the family enjoyed this part of the preparations most and spent all afternoon making garlands to hang across the windows.

Shortly before lunch, a carriage arrived, bringing Dr Grantley, who apologised for being late but assured everyone he was willing and ready to help, "I'll do anything," he offered, and Lizzie, seeing poor Jane and Georgiana working very hard in the music room, sent him along to help them. With everyone pressed into service, the house hummed. Bingley and Darcy wandered in and out of the rooms, amazed at the activity. Darcy swore he could not recall an occasion when there was so much going on at Pemberley.

By late afternoon, everything was in readiness. The children had all been fetched and costumed like little choristers. The fires burned brightly and burnished all the dark oak and copper as well as the glowing red berried garlands around the walls and over the windows.

By six o'clock, the room had filled with guests and neighbours, and when the children walked in carrying their candles, there were gasps of surprise. Their glowing faces and sparkling eyes told of their excitement.

Jane, Elizabeth, and Georgiana shepherded them into place, and then, Dr Grantley read the story of Christmas from the Bible. It was the perfect touch, suggested by Georgiana and gladly carried out by Dr Grantley. When the singers began, a little nervously at first, but stronger and sweeter by the minute, the tears in the eyes and the smiles on the faces of the audience told the story. The parents of the children of the estate ranged from yeoman farmers to grooms, maids, and gardeners. Never before had they seen their children afforded such an opportunity as this to participate in the festivities at Pemberley. When it was known, mainly through Jenny and Mrs Reynolds, that it was all Mrs Darcy's doing, her popularity among them soared. When they broke for an intermission, to allow the little voices some rest, Elizabeth came over to Darcy who was sitting with the Gardiners. She had wanted reassurance that it was proceeding well; what she got was adulation from everyone around her. Elizabeth glowed, and Mr Darcy could barely contain his joy. If Mrs Gardiner needed any proof of the success of this match, for which she and her husband felt partly responsible, she had it there in front of her as Darcy reached across and took Elizabeth's hand and said, "I cannot honestly remember a happier Christmas Eve, since I was a boy."

When they went upstairs, Elizabeth embraced her aunt. "If it had not been for you, I may never have come to Pemberley last Summer, never have met him again in such happy circumstances, and never found the happiness we have today," she said. Mrs Gardiner had never doubted that Jane and Bingley would have a felicitous union, for they were both so similar, so attuned to each other, that it was not difficult to imagine them making a harmonious marriage. With Lizzie and Darcy, it was more complex: they were both strong characters, with high standards and high expectations; she had, despite her love for both of them, worried that their very strength could lead, even unwittingly, to tension and unhappiness. Seeing them in London some weeks ago, she had been very impressed with the promise of maturity in their relationship. Seeing them at Pemberley together confirmed her hopes. Here indeed was the happiest couple she had ever had the pleasure of knowing. She could only pray that their future would be as blessed as the present.

Later, Darcy and Mr Gardiner joined them. Sensing the unspoken query in Lizzie's eyes, Darcy explained that Jane and Mr Bingley had sat down with Georgiana and Dr Grantley to a game of whist. "Whist!" exclaimed both ladies together, unable to believe that anyone had sufficient energy left at the end of this day for a game of whist.

"Indeed," said Darcy, "a somewhat merrier version of it than usual."

"I was just saying to Mr Darcy how well Lizzie and Miss Darcy have done in putting together the entertainment this evening. No one would believe that most of the children had never sung in a choir before," said Mr Gardiner.

Darcy agreed enthusiastically and, putting an arm around his wife, said, "I am very proud of them, especially Lizzie, whose idea it was. I have never enjoyed a better Christmas Eve, and what's more, my dear, Dr Grantley is so impressed, he has asked that they sing when he takes Evensong in the chapel, tomorrow."

Lizzie and Mrs Gardiner were delighted. "Now that is an honour, indeed. Knowing the reputation of the choir of St John's, I must say it is very kind of Dr Grantley," said Lizzie, adding that the four young Gardiners had made a vital contribution to the success of the evening. The Gardiners gently disengaged themselves on the pretext of getting their lively children to bed. Darcy and Elizabeth smiled and did not try to keep them from going. Much as they loved the Gardiners, it was the first time in almost twenty-four hours that they had found themselves alone together, and the pleasure was as sweet as it was unexpected.

A light snowfall overnight created a picture book Christmas scene as the family and guests went to church in the village below the Pemberley Estate, where Dr Grantley joined the resident curate, Mr Jenkins, in conducting the service. The little church was full with the young "choristers" sitting together at the front. The singing was sweet and strong. Elizabeth was delighted to hear the voices of the children in natural harmony. Exchanging glances with Mrs Gardiner and her husband, she vowed to carry on the Pemberley Children's Choir, "We'll make a tradition that Pemberley will be proud of," she thought, as she listened.

Later, the young curate congratulated her, "I've never had such fine singing here before, Mrs Darcy. I believe we have you to thank."

Elizabeth blushed. "Oh no, Mr Jenkins, many people including Miss Darcy and my sister Mrs Bingley helped. And ultimately, it was the children themselves; they were so keen to learn to sing."

"Well, it looks to me we could have the beginnings of a proper choir at Pemberley," said Mr Jenkins, who was Welsh and heir to a fine tradition of choral singing.

"I think we should build on this excellent foundation," Elizabeth agreed, and her husband added, "I think you have started something here, my dear." They invited Mr Jenkins to join them at Pemberley for Evensong that night and stay to supper, an invitation that was readily accepted by the young clergyman.

Christmas dinner was a splendid feast. Mrs Reynolds excelled herself, and the cook had produced delectable dishes of game and poultry prepared in the traditional style, as well as a range of side and corner dishes to tempt the palate on a cold afternoon. Punch and mulled wine were served before, and hock and claret accompanied the courses, until finally Christmas pudding and a festive centrepiece of fresh fruit and syllabub, with small bowls of nuts and preserved ginger, were placed on the uncovered table.

Elizabeth was so pleased, she thanked Mrs Reynolds and asked to be taken to the kitchen so she could thank the staff and especially the cook for the splendid meal. No previous Mistress had done such a thing. The staff was surprised and gratified at the gesture and thanked Mrs Darcy for her appreciation. It was clear that she had made an excellent debut at Pemberley.

The festive mood seemed to affect everyone—as the diners rose and proceeded to the music room to sing and play, while the children played Hunt the Slipper and Hide and Seek—their voices ringing through the halls and corridors of the house. The often awesome atmosphere of the stately building was lightened with an infusion of fun overlaying generations of formality and tradition.

Darcy, too, appeared to have shed the shyness that masqueraded as a serious and taciturn disposition and revealed a whole new aspect of his nature. His hospitality and concern for his guests were impeccable and moreover, were warm and sincere. Jane, tiring a little of entertaining the children, came over to where Elizabeth sat, a little apart from the company. "You seem tired, Lizzie," she said, as she sat down beside her.

Lizzie nodded but added, "Yes, but, oh so happy, Jane . . . I cannot believe that a year ago we were all so sad and despondent." Jane smiled as only the truly contented woman can and said, "I know exactly how you feel, Lizzie. Mr Bingley and I have noticed how much Mr Darcy has changed—he is so much more sociable; he does not seem to stand apart as he used to before. We are quite sure it is all due to you, Lizzie. He is happier and therefore more at ease with everyone. Bingley is very pleased." Elizabeth smiled and wondered at the perceptive comments of her sister; she knew in her heart that Jane was right but was reluctant to accept all the credit for herself. She hastened to say that Darcy had always been amiable and had no improper pride; his shyness and uncertainty of acceptance had led to a reputation for hauteur, which was, for the most part, undeserved. Jane put an arm around her, "I have no need to be convinced of this, dear Lizzie, Mr Bingley has always told me that his friend was the best of men, and I know you would not have accepted him if it were not so."

Afterwards, Georgiana came to sit with her; as they watched Darcy move among the guests, she said, "Lizzie, I cannot tell you what a lovely Christmas this has been," and spoke with such warmth and sincerity that Elizabeth had to believe this was more than a polite expression of thanks. "I have no memory of enjoying myself so much, and I am sure that my brother feels the same. You only have to look at him to see how happy he is. Lizzie, it is all due to you, and I am so very grateful." Elizabeth coloured with pleasure and some embarrassment; she had not expected all these compliments, and much as she enjoyed the appreciation, it troubled her a little to accept so much praise. Darcy, seeing them together, came across and put his arms around them both and hugged them in full view of everyone. It left no one in any doubt that the Master of Pemberley was having his happiest Christmas in many years.

To complete a wonderful day, after everyone had exchanged gifts, they filled the little chapel at Pemberley for Evensong. This time, the choristers were joined by the family and visitors, Mary, Kitty, and the Gardiner children together with the resounding Welsh tenor of Mr Jenkins making the place ring with the loveliest sounds ever heard in this great house. Darcy, standing beside his wife, felt for the first time that he was making his own mark as the Master of Pemberley; with Elizabeth beside him, he was confident this was only the beginning of a new era. Elizabeth sensed his happiness and gently pushed her hand into his to share a moment of tenderness. Bingley and Jane looked across at them, and, catching her sister's eye, Elizabeth smiled, her felicity there for all to see.

❧

On the morning of Boxing Day, the traditional Christmas boxes were handed out to the servants and farm workers of the Pemberley Estate. Darcy's generosity was now clear, with the very substantial rewards he gave to people who had provided services to the family through the year. Through the day, they were visited by the tenants and their children. Later, Mr Darcy and Georgiana invited Elizabeth to accompany them as they drove out to the far side of the estate to visit two families, who had not been able to attend the Christmas festivities at the house.

In the case of the Lawsons, the father was an invalid—having hurt his back in a farm accident, and the mother had worked for years to bring up their children—one of whom was apprenticed to the Pemberley stables. Georgiana explained to Elizabeth that her brother had always insisted on coming himself to visit them. It being Boxing Day, they brought the usual Christmas box, as well as a hamper of festive fare packed by Mrs Reynolds. Seeing the pleasure this brought to the Lawson family, especially the hardworking wife, reminded Lizzie of the words of Mrs Reynolds praising Darcy's generosity and his concern for his tenants.

Georgiana showed she was learning valuable lessons from her brother. Her caring and gentle nature was touched by the misfortune of the Lawsons. She spoke sympathetically, without any hint of patronage, to inquire into the needs of the family and, like her brother, seemed ready to provide some practical help. Learning that one of the children was ill with a bad cough, she promised to send a vehicle that afternoon, so the child could be conveyed to the apothecary at Lambton.

That she had made the promise without even consulting her brother suggested to Elizabeth that brother and sister were agreed upon these responsibilities and she didn't need to seek his approval. It was an indication of the remarkable level of personal responsibility accepted by Mr Darcy for the people on his estate. It was reinforced by their next visit to a very old man, Tom Hobbs, a former horse trainer who had lost a leg in an accident and had lived with the pain and disability for many years.

As Georgiana helped put away the rest of the fare, she talked with his daughter. Elizabeth overheard the girl say, "He cannot stop talking about you and Mr Darcy, Ma'am. He knows how kind you have been to us. It is so good of you to come out in this weather." Elizabeth recalled again the words of Mrs Reynolds, last Summer. "He is the best landlord and the best Master . . . there is not one of his tenants or servants but what will give him a good name," she had said.

At the time, they had made allowance for a degree of partiality on her part, because of her long association with the family, but time and again Elizabeth had seen evidence that served to enhance the veracity of the housekeeper's words. The very genuine concern and kindness in his actions and manner towards the people who lived and worked on the Pemberley Estate were plain for all to see. He made no speeches about it, but the strong sense of responsibility he demonstrated convinced her that her husband was indeed "an excellent man," as well as being "the best landlord and Master, ever."

Later, she shared her experiences and feelings with her aunt and sister, as they relaxed in her private sitting room enjoying shortbread and tea. Mrs Gardiner also recalled the words of Mrs Reynolds and added that she had never found it difficult to accept the housekeeper's praise of Mr Darcy, because it had been more than confirmed by his amazing generosity and single-minded pursuit of Lydia and Wickham. "I realize, Lizzie, that it was all done for love of you, but even so, his general demeanour and his behaviour to your uncle and myself were always so pleasing, so much more genuine than some other gentlemen we have known, that I could not possibly believe him to be other than the best of men," said Mrs Gardiner, making her niece very happy indeed.

That evening, as the younger members of the party dressed up in masks and costumes for the customary pantomime, the sisters watched their husbands help to set the stage for the performance. Georgiana and Dr Grantley were busy organising the music, and Mrs Gardiner with the help of the maids was putting the finishing touches to the costumes. Jane and Lizzie, who had the task of judging the best performance, sat apart in the alcove at the back of the room. They did not need to say very much; there was such a close understanding between them, they could enjoy the felicity of their situation, without saying a word. Of the success of Elizabeth's first Christmas at Pemberley, they had no doubt at all.

CHAPTER THREE

A seal upon thine heart

THE WEATHER CLOSED IN after Boxing Day and made travelling much more difficult. It was generally acknowledged that staying indoors was the best option, and several activities were organised to keep everyone entertained. Mary was quite content to spend hours in the library or the music room, oblivious of the weather outside or the people inside the house. The Gardiner children were generally well able to entertain themselves with a range of games, and Kitty was still sufficiently youthful to join in.

Dr Grantley, who was working on a paper on early English church music, was grateful for the assistance that Georgiana could give him, and the two of them spent a great deal of time in the library and the music room, going through the extensive collection, which was the work of many generations of the Darcy family.

Elizabeth spent some time with them and came away fascinated by the extent and variety of the resources available to them at Pemberley. She talked to Darcy about providing a scholarship, perhaps in memory of his mother, for students of music, who may wish to use the library. She was convinced that the treasures of the Pemberley collection could be shared with others who had no opportunity to appreciate them in this way. "It is such an excellent collection, much too valuable to be hidden away," she declared, adding that Dr Grantley had said that there were students of his at Oxford who could benefit from a visit to the library. Darcy promised to consider it and talk to Dr Grantley.

He was, in fact, quite delighted that his wife, like his mother, had realised the richness and value of the Pemberley heritage. He experienced a twinge of guilt that he had ever doubted Elizabeth's suitability to be the Mistress of Pemberley. He thrust the thought out with the absolute certainty he now felt about her ability to fill the role with distinction and be an adornment to their family.

~❦~

The following day, a party from Rushmore Farm came to call, in the middle of what could almost be called a blizzard, so blustery and cold was the weather. Though not the best day for entertaining, it did give Elizabeth and Jane an opportunity to meet James Fitzwilliam and Rosamund Camden, who had become engaged at Christmas. Recalling Darcy's droll tale of Lady Catherine's vain hope of marrying James off to Caroline Bingley, Jane and Lizzie could not help but wonder at her lack of judgement—for the gentleman was so unlikely to suit Miss Bingley as to make the whole idea ludicrous.

James Fitzwilliam was a solid farmer if ever there was one. He was plain speaking and fairly ordinary in appearance, unthinkable then that a sophisticated and fashionable woman like Miss Bingley would be an appropriate partner for him, in spite of his lineage. Rosamund Camden, on the other hand, seemed a sensible young woman, with sufficient personal style to fill her role, whenever her husband succeeded to his title and estate. Mr and Mrs Gardiner agreed that the couple appeared well-suited and they had no doubt at all that James Fitzwilliam would not have been making a good marriage had he followed the wishes of his Aunt Catherine, instead of his own heart. Before the Camdens left, an invitation was issued to all at Pemberley to dine at Rushmore Farm the following day.

After days of poor weather, when they had stayed mostly indoors, everyone and especially the children looked forward to the visit to Rushmore Farm, where Bingley promised them they could see the famous horses of the Rushmore Stud. Unfortunately, these plans were disrupted on the following day, when Jane became unwell and quite unable to leave her bed. Mrs Gardiner was determined to stay behind with her. Elizabeth was also reluctant to leave her sister but was persuaded by both Jane and Mrs Gardiner that she ought to accompany her husband.

The evening dragged on for both Elizabeth and Bingley, whose anxiety about Jane could not be concealed. Elizabeth apologised to her hosts for her pre-occupation and was persuaded only with difficulty to accompany Caroline and Georgiana on the pianoforte, when they agreed to sing after dinner.

Darcy, realising the extent of her anxiety, had proposed an early departure and they made their excuses to the Camdens. On the short journey home, he tried to reassure her. He knew Jane was not very strong and prone to colds and chills: they recalled her unhappy illness two years ago, during a visit to Netherfield.

On their return to Pemberley, Bingley alighted from the carriage and ran up the stairs to the room where Jane was resting, while Lizzie went in search of her aunt. She found her in the sitting room taking tea and talking with Mrs Reynolds, whose countenance did not suggest that there had been any bad news. Both women smiled as Lizzie rushed in, taking off her cape as she entered. Even before she could speak, Mrs Gardiner stood up and came to her. "Sit down, Lizzie," said her aunt, seeing her anxious expression, "Jane is going to be quite all right."

"What did the doctor say?" she asked and seeing her aunt smile, "Do tell me please, what is it?"

Mrs Gardiner spoke gently. "He said what I expected him to say, Lizzie, but I had no right to tell you until the doctor had seen her: your sister Jane is going to have a baby."

Elizabeth cried out, tears filling her eyes; she leapt up and ran out of the room, ran back in again, hugged her aunt and Mrs Reynolds, and then ran upstairs to her sister's room. She found Jane sitting up in bed with her husband beside her, both of them looking very happy indeed. The sisters embraced, and there were more tears.

Bingley decided to leave them alone for awhile and went down stairs to give Darcy the good news. They could barely speak for the emotion that welled up in them. "Oh darling Jane, what a wonderful Christmas present!"

"Lizzie, I cannot believe how fortunate I am; I am sorry to have caused all of you so much concern," said Jane.

"Oh hush, I was concerned that you might have caught a chill in all this bad weather, but my aunt says she expected the doctor's verdict. I have to say, Jane dearest, I cannot wait to be an aunt." Lizzie's voice bubbled over with joy, as her sister reached out and held her hand tight. "We have already decided that Mr Darcy and you are to be godparents," she said, and Elizabeth was ecstatic.

Darcy was so pleased for Jane and Bingley that Elizabeth felt the tiniest tinge of regret that she had not been able to give him the news herself. Later that night, preparing for bed, she ventured to tease him about being godfather to the Bingley's child. But he had anticipated her and refused to be teased, saying only that he knew how much it meant to Jane and Bingley and what good parents they would make. "Bingley," he said, "is very fond of children and will make an excellent father."

"As I know you would," said Elizabeth, determined to find out how he really felt. This time, he did as she plainly wished him to, as he took her in his arms and said, "Of course, my dear, when we have our own children, I have no doubt that we shall make excellent parents," adding with a smile, "I know you will insist upon it."

On the following Sunday, the weather had cleared sufficiently to enable the Gardiners and Bingleys to leave Pemberley for London and thence to Netherfield Park and Longbourn. Bingley, in particular, had been very reluctant to have his wife put at risk in any way by rough weather and bad roads. Elizabeth had been very touched by the extraordinary care he showed towards her sister.

Parting from both Jane and Mrs Gardiner at once was heart wrenching, and for Lizzie, it was also a realisation that she was now on her own at Pemberley. Without her aunt and sisters, she felt suddenly alone, despite the loving support of her husband and the admiration and affection of her sister-in-law. This prompted her to invite Kitty to stay on while Mary returned home.

"You could stay on until after Father arrives and return to Longbourn in the Spring with him," she suggested and was a little surprised at the cheerful alacrity with which Kitty accepted, asking only that her mother pack a couple of her favourite dresses and a bonnet, to be sent over with her father's things when he came to Pemberley. Elizabeth was pleased. She and Jane had only recently discussed the change in Kitty since being separated from Lydia. "Yes, and I do believe if she were to return to Longbourn, our mother will very likely take her North to Newcastle, when she travels there in March," said Jane, adding, "and all the good work we've done will be undone."

"Indeed it will, and I am sure it will not be in Kitty's interest to fall in with the type of person with whom Wickham and Lydia are likely to keep company," observed Lizzie, thinking, as she spoke, that it would never do for their family to have to contend with another catastrophe of the kind visited upon them by Lydia and Wickham.

She could imagine the outrage of Lady Catherine de Bourgh and the sneering comments of Caroline Bingley, which would surely sour her own marriage, should such a circumstance arise again. Darcy's forbearance and generosity of spirit were likely to be sorely tested, and neither he nor Bingley would feel comfortable trying to explain away another faux pas by one of their sisters.

For Kitty's sake, too, it was far better that she complete her development in the society of people far superior to those her errant sister could provide in Newcastle. Strangely, it seemed Kitty had come to the same conclusion, because she appeared to spend much of her time with Georgiana, actually practising the piano, helping with her music and the Children's Choir.

Elizabeth wept as she parted from Jane; they had grown even closer together since being married, and the knowledge that Jane would probably not return for the wedding of Rosamund Camden and James Fitzwilliam, later that year, saddened her sister considerably.

Darcy noticed her distress and moved to console both sisters with a promise that they would surely be visiting Netherfield very soon. After many affectionate hugs and kisses and faithful promises to write almost at once, if not sooner, they were gone, leaving a tearful little party on the steps, for even the servants had grown so fond of the lovely Mrs Bingley. With her sweet nature and gentle ways, she was their favourite.

Close behind them, the Gardiners' carriage, with Mr and Mrs Gardiner, Mary, and the little Gardiners hanging out of the windows, rolled forward, and there were more hugs and tears. When the two carriages had disappeared from sight, Elizabeth turned and found her husband close beside her, took his arm, and went indoors, not even trying to hide her tears.

CHAPTER FOUR

Letters

I N THE MONTHS THAT followed, many letters flowed between Pemberley, London, Netherfield Park, and Longbourn. Elizabeth had not spent more than a few days before she longed to put pen to paper. In her private sitting room, overlooking the park, she pondered on all that surrounded her at Pemberley. It was not just the years of tradition and family history or the exquisite treasures of Darcy's forebears, nor was it the presence of an army of servants and tenant families, who regarded her husband with so much deference and respect, that now flowed through to her. It was much more than that. It was a sense of stability, an environment of elegance and harmony that prevailed throughout, almost defying the ravages of conflict, to create a pervading atmosphere of tranquillity. It was this same stability she had begun to appreciate in her husband, with his unswerving consistency of behaviour, based upon a high sense of personal honour and responsibility. Combined with the constancy and tenderness of their mutual love and esteem, it was an ideal Elizabeth may only have dared to dream of.

There was no doubt, however, that she was missing her beloved sister. Writing to Jane, she struggled to put her thoughts into words:

> *I have tried, these many hours, to think how I might best convey to you, my*
> *dearest Jane, the sense of loss I feel at your departure from Pemberley. Each*

night since you and my dear Aunt and Uncle left us, we have sat but a short time at the table after dinner, yet no sooner have we risen and gone upstairs to our sitting room, than we speak longingly of the days just gone and the evenings filled with laughter. Oh Jane, both of us miss you so. Darcy has promised that we will visit you soon, probably when father returns to Longbourn. There is no need for me to tell you how much I look forward to seeing you, again.

Meanwhile, I cannot let you believe that we are all gloom and despondency, for that would be unfair to the efforts of Mr Darcy to engage my interest in a dozen different schemes. Tomorrow, we hope the weather will be as good as it is today, which only means cold and dry, instead of cold and wet, for we are invited to a reception for the Duke of Wellington at the estate of the Earl of Lichfield in Staffordshire. The Duke is being feted for his splendid achievements at Waterloo and elsewhere, now that the war is over. The family at Pemberley has had a long association with the Ansons, whose family are the Earls of Lichfield. Mrs Reynolds has told me that Darcy's father, who was much loved and respected, was a close friend of the late Earl.

Afterwards, Darcy has promised we shall visit Lichfield, where my dear favourite Doctor Johnson was born, to attend a choral recital at the great Cathedral there. It is a pleasure I should only have dreamed of, dear Jane, and one I shall enjoy all the more knowing that Darcy will share it with me. He has an excellent understanding of music and will often help Georgiana or myself in reading and interpreting some of the new European compositions. This is especially good for me, since my knowledge of music is mostly self taught, as you know, and not particularly extensive. Georgiana and Dr Grantley are to accompany us; although they are not asked to the reception, they will visit the castle and High House at Stafford, while Mr Darcy and I attend the function for the great man. As you know, Dr Grantley has a great interest in Church music, and Georgiana has been helping him with the material in the Pemberley collection, and he is very appreciative of her interest in his work.

Will you forgive me, my dear sister, if I mention this with some little trepidation, but I fear Georgiana is in danger of falling in love with Dr Grantley. I have not spoken a word of my suspicions to anyone but you, so I beg you keep this to yourself alone. Do not ask me if it is requited, dear

Jane, for Dr Grantley is of an age and a level of maturity, being a year older than Darcy, that enables a man to keep his feelings to himself. Georgiana is of such a tender age, being younger than Kitty, that he may not wish to encourage her in any way. If my husband knows anything of it, he has not indicated it to me, but I am sure he will have noticed that they are together for many hours each day. Let us leave it until we meet; there may be more substance to the matter by then, or perchance there may be no more of it, since Dr Grantley returns to his College at Oxford in the Spring. I must close now but will write again when we are returned from Staffordshire. Do give our love to Bingley, and, dear Jane, I beg you please look after yourself. You are always in my thoughts.

Yours very affectionately, Lizzie.

On returning from Staffordshire, Elizabeth found two letters waiting for her. The first, from her father, had been expected for some time, since Mr Bennet had accepted Darcy's invitation to visit Pemberley in the New Year. Elizabeth was overjoyed to read that he was finally coming, having ensured that Mrs Bennet was safely off to Newcastle. He asked Elizabeth to tell her husband that the coach would arrive at Lambton on Saturday afternoon, remembering that Darcy had offered to send the carriage for him.

While I regret that I have delayed my visit to Pemberley, I think, my dear, you will agree that it was done in a good cause, for by waiting until your mother was ready to leave for Newcastle, taking her maid Sarah with her, I have spared your sister Jane the responsibility of entertaining both your mother and Mary for several weeks. I would have felt guilty had I done so and would not have enjoyed my stay with you quite as much as I intend to. As it happens, Mary is gone to Netherfield Park; Hill and John will watch over Longbourn, while I avail myself of the delights of Derbyshire in general and Pemberley in particular. Please tell your husband I am looking forward very much to burying myself in his remarkable library, of which I have such excellent reports.

Elizabeth hurried over to find her husband and give him the news. She found him in the sitting room, reading a letter from Mr Gardiner, thanking them for their hospitality over Christmas and urging them to consider a visit to London, preferably before they went on to Netherfield in Spring. When she handed him her father's letter, Elizabeth was delighted to see the genuine pleasure with which he read it and turning to her, said, "There you are, my dear, I knew you would soon be smiling again. I know how much you've been missing your father—why you're looking better already." Elizabeth knew he was sincere, despite the teasing tone of his voice.

"I shall ask Hobbs to arrange for the carriage to meet him, unless you and Kitty would like to go, too." Elizabeth considered this but decided she would prefer to wait for her father at Pemberley, with Darcy beside her. She said so, and from his approving smile, she knew it was the right thing to do.

Tea was served and as the others helped themselves, Elizabeth took hers upstairs hoping to read the second letter she had received, in the privacy of her sitting room. She had recognised the hand; it was Charlotte's and posted at Hunsford. Even before she opened it, Elizabeth felt a sense of gleeful anticipation; Charlotte would surely have news from Rosings where Lady Catherine must have held court during the festive season, with the Bingley sisters and Mr Collins showing appropriate respect.

On opening it, Elizabeth read it quickly through and then re-read it as she was wont to do when she wished to savour the pleasure of a letter from a favourite source. The first few paragraphs contained sundry pieces of information relating to household matters and then there was news from the domain of Lady Catherine de Bourgh.

Charlotte wrote:

Dear Eliza,

You probably will not be surprised to hear that your marriage to Mr Darcy has not found favour with his aunt. She seemed to think you had done it out of spite or some determination to flout her Ladyship's wishes. It was a judgement with which Mrs Hurst and Miss Caroline Bingley seemed ready to agree with alacrity, though it must be said that Mr Hurst did not wish to become involved. He was of the opinion that Mr Darcy "had had his eye on Miss Eliza Bennet since the day of the Netherfield Ball," and this rather threw them all into confusion. You will be pleased, I am sure, to hear that Mr Collins and I remained staunchly aloof from any vilification of your selves and when the opportunity arose, I remarked to Miss Bingley that I was quite certain both her brother Mr Bingley and his friend Mr Darcy were considered extremely fortunate to have married two of the most handsome ladies in the county.

"Oh Charlotte, I can wager anything, she did not like that," said Lizzie, chuckling to herself, visualising the scene at Rosings and enjoying the discomfiture of Miss Bingley as Charlotte described it.

More than for herself, Elizabeth found it hard to be charitable to the Bingley sisters on account of their treatment of Jane last Summer. It remained a mystery to her that their brother could be such an amiable and sincere gentleman while growing up in the company of sisters whose meanness of understanding and total selfishness of character were hard to conceal. She could not restrain her laughter when she read of Lady Catherine's response to the failure of her nephew James Fitzwilliam to present himself at Rosings for Christmas.

Her Ladyship appeared most put out when a message arrived on Christmas Eve, from her nephew James, elder brother of Colonel Fitzwilliam, saying he was unavoidably delayed up North and could not get back to Kent for Christmas. Mr Collins did try to discover why Lady Catherine was so particular that he should be here, but no one seemed to know.

Elizabeth, recalling Darcy's tale of Lady Catherine's plans for her nephew, laughed out loud. When Darcy came in search of her, Elizabeth had reached the last page of Charlotte's letter:

My main reason for writing, dear Eliza, is to tell you that I am going to be at Lucas Lodge from the beginning of March until my baby is born in May and probably for a month afterwards. My dear parents have asked me to stay, and Mr Collins agrees with me that Dr Jones would engender more confidence, having attended almost all members of our family, than the physician recommended by Lady Catherine. Again, I doubt that I have pleased her Ladyship with my decision, but I am convinced I must do as I see fit.

Elizabeth gave a cry of joy, as if she was cheering Charlotte on in her defi-
ance, and Darcy looked on in astonishment, until she acquainted him with the
reason for her satisfaction. She passed the letter to him, having read the last
paragraph, in which her friend expressed a wish that Lizzie should not fail to
visit her when she came to Longbourn. Elizabeth had not been unaware of Mrs
Collins' condition, having heard of it at the time of her own wedding in
October, but her happiness was intensified by Charlotte's news that she would
be at Lucas Lodge—probably without her odious husband, so that a visit would
bring real pleasure. "It will be almost like old times," she said, and Mr Darcy,
who had always felt some regard for the pleasant, sensible, and long-suffering
Charlotte, agreed. They laughed together at the news from Rosings, especially
the remark from Mr Hurst about Darcy and Elizabeth and Charlotte's description of Lady Catherine's aggravation at the non-appearance of her nephew.

"She cannot have learned of his engagement to Rosamund," said Darcy,
adding that he was glad not to be at Rosings to hear her reaction.

Finding him in this very light-hearted mood, Elizabeth pressed her request
for an early visit to her sister at Netherfield, with the possibility of seeing
Charlotte at the same time. It wasn't difficult to extract a promise that when her
father returned home in four weeks' time, they would all go, probably via London.
In addition, he had other, more advanced plans. "I know how much it means to
you, dearest, and I have already made arrangements for our stay in London, probably for four days. I have only been waiting on Mr Bennet's arrival to discover
whether he would like to join us or stay here with Dr Grantley and Kitty.

"Once we know his preference, you can make whatever arrangements you wish
with Mrs Gardiner for your entertainment during the day, when Mr Gardiner and
I will be busy with matters of business. Your uncle has also obtained tickets for the
Opera, and we must confirm our arrangements as soon as possible," he said.

Elizabeth was delighted. She threw her arms around Darcy and thanked
him with an enthusiasm that both surprised and delighted him. As soon as matters were decided, she intended to write to Jane and Charlotte and give them
the good news. As for Mrs Gardiner, she was owed a letter, and Elizabeth
decided it was going to be written without delay.

Outside, the weather was still wintry, but in her heart, it was already Spring.
This feeling of lightness flowed through into her letter:

My dearest Aunt,

It gives me so much joy to write with good news, and so much of it. First, my father arrives on Saturday for four weeks, having ensured that my mother has safely left for Newcastle to be with Lydia. He apologises for his tardiness in coming to us but is certain that it was in a good cause, since it preserves dear Jane and Bingley from having Mama to stay for two weeks before her journey North. I have no doubt at all that Jane and Bingley are profoundly grateful, although they are both much too polite to say so.

My second is that Charlotte Lucas has written to say she is going to Lucas Lodge for the next three months until her baby is born. The greatest good news, dear Aunt, is Mr Collins needs must stay behind at Hunsford, since the spiritual needs of his parishioners and the wishes, nay commands, of his patron Lady Catherine must come first. Which means, when Father returns to Longbourn next month, we are to go, too. I shall be able to see Charlotte without her husband's constant attentions and interruptions. What bliss! Can you imagine?

We are also to stay a week with Jane and Bingley, at Netherfield Park, to which I am looking forward very much. With Mama away, Mary is with Jane at Netherfield until Papa and Kitty return.

Speaking of Kitty, she has started to practise her piano again and is getting quite good at it. She is happy to help us out with the Children's Choir, which has become a fixture of late. Last Sunday, the Rector— Reverend Huw Jenkins—who is Welsh and with an excellent voice himself, thanked Kitty especially for the hard work she had put in with the choir. She looked very pleased with the special attention she received. We are all agreed that the change in Kitty is very good news indeed.

Even better news, Mr Darcy has arranged for us to come to London for four or five days. The date is not as yet set, but he will send an express to our Uncle Gardiner as soon as it is settled.

I do look forward to London in March, so close to Easter too. I believe we are to go to the Opera with you, and I shall have to order a new gown for the occasion. Not having been to the Opera in London, any advice from you on an appropriate style will be much appreciated. I think I should also purchase a new bonnet, for daytime, if we are to go driving in Hyde Park together. Would you advise me if your milliner has something suitable? I must stop for now as Mrs Reynolds wishes me to look at the rooms they have prepared for Father. I shall write more tonight.

Mrs Reynolds escorted Elizabeth to what they used to call "the quiet wing" of the house, since it was situated away from the main living rooms and the nurseries. The Library, accommodated in a fine room from whose windows one could look out on almost every aspect of the grounds except the woods behind the house, was elegant and inspiring, with its remarkable collection housed in a series of magnificent cabinets. Reading tables and comfortable chairs all placed to take advantage of the natural light pouring in at the windows gave the room a most welcoming atmosphere, unlike some cold and musty rooms which passed for libraries in many houses she had visited. Elizabeth was sure her father would enjoy this place. Mrs Reynolds wished to point out a special reading desk and chair that Mr Darcy had had moved into an alcove beside one of the windows overlooking the park. "The Master said it would suit Mr Bennet, Ma'am," Mrs Reynolds explained, and when Lizzie asked where it came from, she was astonished to hear her say, "From Mr Darcy's father's study." Elizabeth's pleasure showed plainly on her face as Mrs Reynolds led her down the corridor and across the main landing to a suite of rooms comprising a bedroom of medium size with its own dressing room attached and beyond a little sitting room, complete again with its own writing desk and book case. "The Master asked that these rooms be prepared for Mr Bennet, Ma'am, but he insisted I was to ask you if you approved and if there was anything more you wanted done."

There were tears in her eyes as Lizzie looked around the rooms, and so overwhelmed was she by the generosity and kindness of her husband, she failed to hide them from Mrs Reynolds. The housekeeper spoke gently and with understanding, "It is very like the Master, Ma'am, as you would know, he is kindness itself and nothing is too good or too much trouble for a friend. He said Mr Bennet was a learned and well-read gentleman, with a partiality for a quiet atmosphere, Ma'am. So this was the right room for him, being so close to the Library too."

Elizabeth agreed, "He is right, my father's favourite room is the library."

Mrs Reynolds smiled. "Mr Darcy said as much, Ma'am. He is a good judge of people."

Recalling her father's impression of Darcy, an impression largely fostered by her own uninformed and prejudiced views, Elizabeth's tears fell, coursing down her cheeks, and only the sound of footsteps, unmistakably those of Mr Darcy, saved her from further embarrassment.

Mrs Reynolds moved into the corridor as Darcy entered the room and seeing Elizabeth, said, "There you are, my dear, I've been looking everywhere for you."

"I've just been showing Mrs Darcy the rooms we have made ready for Mr Bennet, sir," Mrs Reynolds said by way of explanation, and as Darcy turned to thank her, she slipped away, leaving them together.

He asked at once, "What do you think, Lizzie? Do you approve?" He seemed eager to have her approval, as he had been when they first met in the grounds of Pemberley last summer. Then seeing her tears, he was immediately concerned, "Dearest, are you not pleased? Is anything amiss?"

"Oh no no, not at all, it's so kind of you to go to all this trouble," she said, and as he took her hands, she wept and had to be comforted.

"You like it then?" He was keen to please her.

"Yes indeed, it's perfect. My father will love the library and this beautiful room."

"That was my intention, and I hoped you would agree. I felt your father made his library a haven from the ups and downs of domestic life and I thought he would like a similar atmosphere here. Should he care for company, he needs only to walk downstairs, and he would be just outside the main living room." By this time, Elizabeth had recovered her composure and smiled at his eagerness to convince her.

"Dearest, he will love it, it's exactly the way he likes it. My father, as you know, is not the most sociable of people; he enjoys good books and his own company. I must thank you most sincerely for your concern for his comfort."

That night, Elizabeth finished her letter to Mrs Gardiner. She wrote of the arrangements Mr Darcy had made for her father's visit:

Unlike my uncle, with whom Darcy struck up an easy friendship from their very first meeting, as you will remember, my father has been a difficult person for him to get acquainted with, and it was not made easier by the terrible business of Lydia and Wickham.

Darcy, who is a very loving brother, takes his responsibilities as a guardian very seriously, and being extremely careful of his young sister

could not understand the easygoing attitude of my parents to Lydia's
behaviour. Now, however, he is so transformed, so anxious to make up for
any hurt he may have caused, that he is kind and generous to a fault. I
must be the most fortunate creature in the world, dear Aunt, do you know
of any other?

On Saturday morning, Mr Bennet arrived at Pemberley, the carriage having called for him after breakfast at the inn at Lambton. Elizabeth waited for
him with Darcy and Kitty at her side. She was conscious of the fact that it was
the first time her father was visiting Pemberley and indeed the first time since
their wedding that Mr Darcy and she were to welcome him together.

In spite of the wintry cold, Pemberley looked splendid against the sky, and
Lizzie hoped her father, whose good taste in art and writing had influenced her
own appreciation, would notice the elegance of line and proportion that characterised the handsome house. She was not disappointed. No sooner had he
alighted and embraced his daughters—Lizzie twice and Kitty with special mention on how well she looked—than he turned to Darcy, who greeted him most
warmly and welcomed him to Pemberley. Mr Bennet responded with genuine
enthusiasm. "This is indeed a fine place you have here, Mr Darcy; there are not
too many places I have seen which manage to avoid looking bleak and cold in
Winter; Pemberley certainly does that. The park with those stands of evergreen
trees looks much less bleak than some of the bare grounds I saw on my way here."
Darcy was clearly pleased and, as he ushered him indoors, explained that the park
and grounds at Pemberley had been lovingly designed by his late mother.

Elizabeth and Kitty following close behind, exchanged glances and smiled.
They recalled that their father it was who had taken an interest in the layout of
the grounds at Longbourn, while Mrs Bennet had shown no interest in it at all.
Once inside, Mr Bennet turned again to his favourite daughter, "Lizzie, you
look so well, I must compliment your husband. Mr Darcy, congratulations, I am
sure I have never seen Lizzie look so radiant. Marriage obviously suits both you
and Jane, I saw her and Bingley before I left Longbourn, and they're looking
extremely well."

Embarrassed, Lizzie, who knew her father was teasing her, turned to her
husband and urged him to pay no attention, but Darcy, catching Mr Bennet's

mood, was determined to join in the game. "Why thank you, Sir, I'm sure I agree with you; I have not seen Lizzie look more beautiful than she does now. However, I cannot take all the credit; she has been happier than ever since we had your letter advising us of your visit." Elizabeth blushed, mainly with the pleasure of hearing the ease with which her husband and father appeared to exchange these pleasantries, without a hint of awkwardness. And yet, there was regard and respect in Darcy's tone, which truly pleased her.

As she wrote later, to Jane:

I cannot say too much about the warmth and sincerity of Mr Darcy's welcome to our father. In his conversations and general demeanour, he has in every respect been so pleasing, often deferring to my father, where I may not have done. We have had so many conversations, Jane. Did you know that Father was seriously concerned about the lack of schooling for children of many tenant farmers? At dinner, we were joined by Dr Grantley and Georgiana, and Papa expressed his outrage that while Britain was "well nigh bursting with national pride" after the war with Napoleon, the nation had only haphazard and inadequate schools for its children, except for the sons of the rich and privileged, of course. Surprisingly, both Dr Grantley and Mr Darcy agreed with Papa, and indeed Darcy went so far as to say that his father had once wanted to start a school for the children of Pemberley's tenants but had been opposed by the then-curate of the parish of Kympton, who had probably seen it as a threat to the authority of the church, which provided only a Sunday School.

I have put that information aside in a corner of my mind, Jane, and I intend to ask Darcy if we may not try again, since we have at present, no incumbent at Kympton. It would be good to have a school for the children of the estate.

Dear Jane, when I think how much we learned to appreciate the value of reading, it does sadden me to think so many young children are without any teaching at all. Dr Grantley pointed out that scholars at Oxford are mostly the sons of the rich and not all appreciate the value of learning. So many of our great men are self-taught, and it seems a shame that only a few of our girls are ever taught at all. Oh Jane dearest, I seem to have run on so, forgive me, but it has been such an exciting day. Papa is rather tired from travelling and has retired to his rooms, but hopes to be awake bright and early tomorrow, when Darcy has promised to drive him around the park and show him more of the countryside. I shall continue this letter tomorrow, when I hope to be more certain of our plans for London.

Goodnight, dear Jane.

Mr Bennet's stay at Pemberley brought both him and his daughters more pleasure than any of them had anticipated. For Elizabeth and Kitty, it was an opportunity to see their father in a new light. Away from the dominating, intrusive presence of their mother, their father expressed a range of opinions on subjects dear to his heart; subjects to which he had never cared to speak out. Because he knew they were of no interest to his wife, he had unfairly assumed that his daughters would have no interest in them either.

Yet now at Pemberley in the company of Darcy and Dr Grantley, he was much more expansive and talked of many matters that had concerned him, matters that were in the news, like the increasing moves towards enclosing the farmlands and taking over the commons or the rapid and unconscionable increases in rents.

He found in his son-in-law and Dr Grantley men of like mind, well-educated, well-read, and more amenable to enlightened ideas. Elizabeth listened with increasing astonishment to the flowering of her father's reformist zeal and wondered at the frustration he must have experienced these twenty-odd years, with so little opportunity to express his opinions in congenial company.

"You will have seen it in this county too, Mr Darcy," he said after dinner one night, "I certainly see it all over Hertfordshire, every landowner with a little property and a modest house has decided to re-build or expand or improve, call it what you will, acquiring a field here, enclosing a meadow there or worse still, adding bits of classical architecture to perfectly good English houses." Both Darcy and Dr Grantley agreed immediately; to Elizabeth, it was like a breath of fresh air to hear their views.

Dr Grantley complained that people in London were being taken in by the new tribe of decorators and designers who were re-modelling everything in the Classical image, whether or not it was appropriate. Darcy said he had been approached twice by disciples of Humphry Repton, who had offered to force the stream that ran through the park into a series of cascades, ponds, and fountains, ornamented with classical statuary! Elizabeth cried out on hearing this, only to be reassured by her husband that it was the very last thing he would permit at Pemberley. Mr Bennet congratulated him on his good sense and judgement. "Because," he said, "Pemberley is the kind of handsome, solid house that needs no such embellishment. The naturally flowing stream enhances the house and the park because of its very simplicity; it does not need fountains and peacocks." Everyone laughed at the idea of peacocks in the park at Pemberley until Dr Grantley pointed out that Lord Derby had just added a new wing with a dining room that overlooked an enclosed garden that housed exotic birds imported from India! Mention of India reminded Elizabeth of the exotic tastes of Warren Hastings as exemplified by the interior design of his famous residence Daylesford, which they had visited on their travels. Darcy observed that it was far too ornate and exotic for his taste.

Their evenings passed in musical entertainment and excellent conversation, of a level Elizabeth had rarely enjoyed at Longbourn. She had the satisfaction of knowing that her father had shown, as her Uncle Gardiner had done before, that he was the equal of any gentleman. Recalling her encounter with Lady Catherine, Lizzie permitted herself a little smug smile. It was a special pleasure for her to see how easily Darcy and Dr Grantley engaged him in conversation and the degree of respect they accorded his views. Frequently, the Rector, Mr Jenkins, would call and stay to dinner, adding his views to the conversation or his excellent voice to the singing, with Kitty to accompany them on the pianoforte. Elizabeth noticed that Mr Jenkins was there more often of late and believed him to be rather lonely and glad of the company.

Mr Bennet was so enjoying himself, that he had no desire at all to go up to London; he expressed a preference for accompanying Dr Grantley, Georgiana, and Kitty on a drive to the Peak District. He had heard a great deal about the area from Lizzie and the Gardiners, when they toured there last summer, he said. Elizabeth was surprised that Kitty preferred to stay but was later not quite so surprised, when it was revealed that young Mr Jenkins, the Rector, had been invited to join their party.

Completing her letter to Jane, briefly, for there were preparations to be made, Elizabeth mentioned the interest that Kitty was showing in the work of the little church at Pemberley. She added that the Rector was perhaps as great a source of interest as the rest of the Rectory. "He is a very well-mannered and thoughtful young man, and Mr Darcy likes him," she said, but she urged Jane to keep her counsel on this, "until we meet and can speak privately." To Charlotte, Elizabeth was particularly cordial, since she felt she owed her oldest friend some special consideration. Their friendship had been shaken, when Charlotte chose to marry Mr Collins, and Elizabeth felt the need to make amends.

She wrote:

> *I am looking forward very much to seeing you, dear Charlotte. God willing, we shall meet in May, before your baby is born, and have the time to talk as we used to in days gone by. God bless you,*
>   *Your friend, Lizzie.*

CHAPTER FIVE

Relations and friends

I N THE SPRING OF 1816, London was a thriving, exciting metropolis and a
political, mercantile, social, and cultural centre. Many people came there to
do business, to make political or social contacts, or simply to see and be
seen in the right places, with the right people.

For Darcy and Elizabeth, their visit to the big city meant much more than
this. While Darcy did have business to negotiate and Elizabeth intended to do
some shopping in the fashionable emporiums recommended by her aunt, their
main interest was the opportunity to enjoy the company of the Gardiners, with
whom they shared a most satisfying relationship. Whether talking of matters
pertaining to business or attending some entertainment in one of the numerous
venues around London, both Darcy and Elizabeth were completely at ease with
Mr and Mrs Gardiner. On matters concerning themselves or their families, they
were able to speak frankly and openly, because there was between them a strong
sense of trust as well as an affectionate concern for one another.

Darcy and Mr Gardiner needed to discuss a proposal to extend their business, based on reports from Fitzwilliam on the opportunities involving the trade
in Tea and Spices from the Eastern colonies of India and Ceylon.

While Darcy had little experience in the business of trade, he was wise
enough to see the direction in which British commerce was moving, and being

no longer hobbled by snobbery, he found working with the practical and amiable Mr Gardiner rewarding and engrossing. He was content to leave the actual organisation and administration of the business in the hands of Mr Gardiner but took a lively interest in its progress. Darcy was also aware of the other consequences of the great expansion of industry and commerce that was taking place in England. It had been troubling him, and Elizabeth knew he felt strongly about it.

After dinner one night, he mentioned the subject of the new industries that were spreading across the country. "Are you aware," he asked quietly, "that there are factories being opened up in places such as Sheffield and Birmingham, which employ young children? I've had a letter from Fitzwilliam, who speaks with some horror of child labour in the Colonies; I wonder if he knows that it is happening here, in the very heart of England." Elizabeth and Mrs Gardiner exchanged glances. It was obvious from his countenance and the tone of his voice that Darcy was speaking very seriously. Mr Gardiner responded cautiously, wondering how extensive the practice was.

But Darcy persevered. "I understand it is very popular with the cotton spinners and weavers," he said, adding with some sarcasm, "The children are thought to be small enough to crawl under the machines and clean them," and hearing Elizabeth gasp, he looked at her and added, more gently, "I have this on the best authority, my dear. I know it seems unbelievable, but it's true. What is more, I'm told that all over the Midlands and in parts of the West Riding and Cheshire, the landscape is being blackened with pits and smoke while the trout streams are being choked with wool scour and dye wash." He sounded angry, and Mr Gardiner, realising that Darcy was always passionate about the land, agreed that it was a worrying trend. Elizabeth and Mrs Gardiner had remained silent at first, but they added their voices in support of Darcy, only to find that their guest, a banker, was adamant that this was the way of the future.

"It's progress," he declared, "and there is a price to be paid for it."

"If that is true, I want no part of it," said Darcy in a voice so determined that everyone at the table was left in no doubt of the strength and sincerity of his words. "I have no desire to see the fields and rivers of England sullied and the ordinary working people and their children enslaved by the owners of pits and workshops, just so they can make a great deal of money."

Mrs Gardiner was quite surprised, pleasantly so, on hearing Darcy speak out. Being from the same part of England, she shared his apprehension about the despoiling of the land and was glad to hear it spoken of so passionately. She whispered to her niece, "Lizzie, this is a side of Mr Darcy we have not seen before." Elizabeth assured her aunt that she had become aware of Darcy's concern since their marriage and knew it to be a matter of considerable importance to him.

Elizabeth's pride in her husband grew as she heard his words. She had never heard him speak of these matters with such a degree of passion before, but she knew he had concerns, because from time to time he had been troubled by information he had received.

Recently, there had been incidents reported of rural labourers' being thrown out of work as their masters enclosed the small farms and the commons and introduced "labour saving" machines. Their families, deprived of food and shelter on the farm and rendered homeless, wandered the streets, begging from passers-by.

Worse still, laws had been recently passed to make the casual taking of game punishable by transportation or, in some cases, death. Poachers, as they now were trying to grab a hare, fish, or pheasant to feed a hungry family, might well find themselves arrested, charged, and sentenced to be transported to Botany Bay. Their wives and children either went with them or starved.

Elizabeth knew that Darcy had protested strongly about this abuse of the poor at a meeting with some of the new landowners in the neighbourhood. She'd heard of this from Rosamund Camden whose father had agreed with Darcy and supported his stand. Many others did not. They were caught up in a rush to produce more with less and enrich themselves at the expense of the landless poor who had worked hard for them for generations.

The banker, Mr Fletcher, appeared to be unmoved. "Does that mean you will not enclose the commons on your property, Mr Darcy?" he asked.

"I most certainly will not," replied Darcy, reddening as he spoke, "The commons and some of the woodlands have been set aside for the use of everyone. It would be a gross injustice to enclose them and deny the village people use of the land."

Young Caroline Gardiner, who had been called in by her mother to help with the tea and provide some after-dinner entertainment at the pianoforte, heard part of the conversation and when an opportunity arose asked her mother why Mr Darcy was so angry. On being told, she expressed total sympathy with his point of view and, as Mrs Gardiner later told Elizabeth, solemnly promised that she would never marry anyone who had enclosed their fields and turned out their farm workers. "She was completely at one with Mr Darcy," said Mrs Gardiner as Elizabeth took a cup of tea with her before retiring, "Caroline thinks that you and Mr Darcy are the most wonderful couple in the world, Lizzie, and tonight, she was so impressed by his eloquence and anger that I can wager she will soon want to join the Reformists or even Mr Cobbett's Radicals!" Elizabeth laughed and when she went upstairs, related the tale to Darcy, who would not agree that it was precocious of young Caroline, saying only that the child had intelligence beyond her tender years and it was indeed a pleasure to find that a little girl not yet thirteen could be so moved by injustice.

Later that night, Elizabeth confided in her husband the sense of loyalty and pride she had felt as he spoke at dinner. She added that she wished she had known more about the circumstances of the textile trade; she would have had an opinion to offer when Jane had written to her about the new and lucrative business that her in-laws, the Hursts, were investing in. "I know all about it; I believe his sisters and Mr Hurst have actually persuaded Bingley to buy shares. Well, I intend to enlighten him about the pernicious nature of the enterprise, and if I can, I shall persuade him to sell out," said Darcy.

"Sell out?" Elizabeth could not believe her ears, "Do you think he will?" Darcy's face and voice had the kind of determination that Elizabeth had learned to recognise as implacable.

"I certainly intend to try my best, my love; I hope to convince him that his valuable patrimony will be far better used to purchase a very attractive property in Leicester, some twenty miles from Pemberley," he said, with a sly smile. The news sent Elizabeth into transports of delight as he went on, "Since he is soon to be a father, it is surely time he acquired a family home. He has frequently asked me to look out for a suitable place. Your sister is naturally keen to be close to us, so I have done his bidding, and I am fairly confident that if you and Jane were to add your considerable powers of persuasion to mine, we shall soon convince Bingley of the wisdom of moving his money from the hideous squalor of the textile industry to the still green and pleasant vales of Leicestershire."

Elizabeth, who had not heard Darcy speak with such passion and eloquence on the subject before, was quite amazed at his scheme. She couldn't help admiring his determination and dedication, but even more was she delighted at the thought of the Bingleys moving to Leicestershire, not twenty miles from Pemberley. "Will you not tell me where this Paradise lies?" she asked, and Darcy told her it was one of the properties being sold by Lord Thompson, who was getting too old to leave his own considerable estate in Hampshire and travel around the country. Two of the smaller properties—one in Leicestershire and another in Staffordshire—were to be sold, although this was not publicly known. Darcy was familiar with both properties and was certain the one in Leicester would suit the Bingleys well. "We could look it over on our way to Longbourn and Netherfield, next month—would you like that?" he suggested.

"I can think of nothing I would like better," answered his wife, and so it was settled.

When it was time to leave, their farewells were drawn out and sad as they left the Gardiners. Darcy and Mr Gardiner had successfully negotiated their business, while Elizabeth and Mrs Gardiner had spent many hours together, undisturbed and alone but for young Caroline and Emily, so they could talk to their hearts' content. Elizabeth's affection for her aunt was exceeded only by her love of her sister, and both aunt and niece were looking forward to being with Jane in August, when her baby was due. The Gardiners were to stay at Longbourn. "Your father insisted," said Mrs Gardiner, smiling, "He made me promise I would be there to keep your Mama calm." Elizabeth laughed. She knew exactly what her father had meant but added hopefully that, just maybe, having been with Lydia when she was brought to bed would help her mother remain calm.

She was grateful that her aunt had not pressed her about her own prospects of having a child. They had talked about it once, when Lizzie, feeling a little low in spirit, had admitted to having some anxiety about it, and Mrs Gardiner had hastened to reassure her; after all they were not as yet married a year, she'd said.

Returning to Pemberley, they found the party happily engaged in a variety of pursuits. Dr Grantley, who was shortly returning to Oxford, having completed his research in the Library, was working with Kitty, Georgiana, and Mr Jenkins the Rector, on a new program for the Children's Choir. Choosing the right music—not too ambitious, but with more variety than their first program—was an important matter, Kitty declared. Rosamund and James had visited and asked if the choir would sing at their wedding in the Autumn.

Georgiana and Kitty felt this was a huge honour and could hardly speak lucidly as their words tumbled out to express their delight at the invitation. There was so much to be done, Georgiana asked if Kitty may be allowed to stay on at Pemberley to help. Their friendship had come on apace, much to Elizabeth's delight. Mr Jenkins declared solemnly that they could not possibly manage without Kitty, and even Dr Grantley appeared to agree that she was so "good with the children" that she was invaluable to the project. Darcy and Elizabeth could not, in the face of such unanimity, see any objection, and it was left to Mr Bennet to give the final answer.

When he was applied to for permission, Mr Bennet seemed quite bemused. "Of course, Kitty may stay. Lizzie my dear, I cannot believe she is the same silly young person to whom I had to speak so severely, so often at home," he said, with a twinkle in his eye, "your own influence and the excellent example of your young sister-in-law have completely altered her shallow, foolish ways. No, Lizzie, Kitty is transformed—let her stay, the longer the better—if you and Mr Darcy can bear it." Of the last condition, there was no question, so it was settled. Kitty would stay on. The smiles on all their faces attested to the popularity of the decision.

That Sunday, after Evensong, Mr Jenkins stayed to dinner. He and Kitty seemed to have a great deal to discuss, not all of it appeared to do with the choir either. On retiring to their room that night, Elizabeth could not resist asking Darcy if he had noticed their growing closeness, and he immediately smiled and said, "Of course I have, dearest, I would have had to be blind not to notice. I think we can safely say that Mr Jenkins is deeply smitten and Kitty is not entirely unaffected either." Even though she knew he was teasing her, Elizabeth was surprised at the accuracy of his observations. She wondered how he could have failed to notice a similar situation between his sister and his friend, Dr Grantley. Indeed, he'd said nothing at all on the matter, and Lizzie did not feel she wanted to interfere.

On the subject of Kitty, however, he was even more generous in his praise than her father had been, frankly admitting that he had been too harsh in his original criticism of her, for she was then too young and her character too immature to be so judged. Elizabeth was pleasantly surprised to hear him say, "Kitty is developing into a very pleasing young person; Georgiana is very fond of her, and I am sure with a little guidance and a mature influence in her life, she will surprise us all." So astonished was Elizabeth at this statement that she failed to seize the moment and ask if he thought Mr Jenkins would be a sufficiently mature influence, for by then he had turned and put his arms around her as if to indicate that they had talked enough of others and he was of a mind to concentrate on themselves.

~✥~

Two days later, Dr Grantley left to return to Oxford, having said his goodbyes and thanked everyone individually, wishing them well and promising to return.

In vain did Lizzie look for any sign that he and Georgiana had reached an understanding; she found none. Having spent so much time together, perhaps, she thought, they had come to the realisation that they were not suited. After all, he was older than Darcy, and Georgiana had an almost fatherly regard for her brother. Neither was there any sign of sorrow at their parting, as one might have expected; no trace of a special friendship except when she smiled so sweetly for him as he turned and waved before entering the carriage that was to take him to meet the coach at Lambton. Elizabeth found it difficult to hide her disappointment. Darcy had not said a word; nor had Georgiana.

Writing to her Aunt Gardiner, Elizabeth expressed her bewilderment:

It is difficult to believe that after all these weeks, during which they have spent so much time together, there has not been some understanding reached between them. At first, I had thought her too young to appreciate his worth, but the more I saw them together, the more interests they seemed to share, and the more they appeared to suit one another. I am indeed disappointed, my dear Aunt, that Darcy has not spoken of it at all, and yet I am reluctant to mention it myself.

Perhaps, I should really mind my own business and stop worrying, but as you know, Georgiana has had one unfortunate disappointment when she was but fifteen, and I would have been very happy to see her settled with someone worthy of her, as Dr Grantley undoubtedly is. However, there is nothing for it, now he is gone back to Oxford, and we are not likely to see him for several months.

For myself, I shall concentrate on the journey to Netherfield and Longbourn and hope all goes well with dear Jane and Charlotte too. I had forgotten that Lydia will be having her baby very soon; we must pray for a safe birth in her case as well. Concerning Kitty, I hope to have some news soon. We are due to leave for Longbourn with my father, and it is reasonable to suppose that Mr Jenkins may want to declare himself prior to Papa's departure.

Two weeks later, on the afternoon before they were to leave for Longbourn with Mr Bennet, Kitty approached Elizabeth in her sitting room. She was remarkably calm for Kitty, though a little flushed, and her hands were held tightly together. Elizabeth knew at once that some moment of truth was about to be revealed. She guessed that Mr Jenkins may have proposed. She was right. He had indeed, that morning, as they walked back from church, and Kitty had accepted him. Elizabeth was pleased for Kitty but astonished at the insouciance with which she had gone through it. She held out her hands, but Kitty, instead of grasping them, wrung her own and said, "But Lizzie, do you think Papa will consent? He has been so angry with me ever since Lydia and Wickham . . ." Her voice trailed away, and Elizabeth put her arms around her.

"Kitty, of course he will, if Mr Jenkins asks him, and you are both quite sure it is what you really want. Why should he not?"

"Oh. I don't know, I've told Huw—Mr Jenkins everything, even Lydia's foolish behaviour, and he said it did not matter, he loves me, Lizzie!" Elizabeth felt genuine concern for her young sister, realising how little time their parents had spent with their children, preparing them for the vicissitudes of life and love! Their mother, apart from her obsession with marrying them off to eligible, preferably rich, men, had done little to advise them of the pitfalls along the road to matrimony. Their father, concentrating solely on keeping them fairly well-provided for in a material sense, had shown little interest in his daughters.

Jane and Elizabeth had been fortunate enough to develop an intimate and rewarding relationship with their aunt, Mrs Gardiner, but the others had no one of equal sensibility or maturity to turn to and were largely left to their own devices. Realising that it was necessary to reassure Kitty quickly, Elizabeth spoke soothingly and vaguely of their father's being no longer angry but quite well-disposed towards her. Kitty then asked if it was all right for Mr Jenkins to approach Mr Bennet, while he was at Pemberley. Unsure of the etiquette, they had been reluctant to do anything that might offend anyone at all. Elizabeth was certain Mr Darcy would not mind, but wanted to be sure. She urged Kitty not to worry, dried her tears, and left to find her husband.

Meanwhile, Darcy, who was beginning to wonder why his wife was so late dressing for dinner, was surprised to see her but not at all surprised by her news. In fact, he informed Elizabeth that Mr Jenkins had already confided in him and been assured of his blessing and support, should he and Kitty succeed in obtaining Mr Bennet's consent. "What did you say?" she asked, pleasantly surprised at this new turn of events.

"I had to be certain that they were quite firm in their decision; I was assured they were, and I agreed that if they could wait until after Christmas to be married, I would have the Rectory renovated for them and would increase the Rector's stipend, by an agreed amount each year, so he could more comfortably support his wife." Elizabeth's delight was indescribable, and she could not wait to tell Kitty the news. Kitty was astonished, "Mr Darcy said that?" and when Elizabeth nodded, "Oh Lizzie, he is a wonderful man; Mr Jenkins thinks so. I've always been a little afraid of him, but oh dear, I do think the same now."

With Lizzie's having reassured Kitty that it was quite proper for Mr Jenkins to approach her father after dinner when he retired to the library, the sisters embraced and went downstairs. Kitty went directly to her brother-in-law and thanked him. He smiled and wished her every happiness. Darcy was painfully aware that he had misjudged Kitty, whose fault had been her youth. A lack of direction from her parents and the wrong example from her sister Lydia had placed her temporarily in jeopardy. Observing her over the last few months, it had become clear to him that Kitty, removed from the influence of Lydia, was a totally different young woman—gentler, quieter, and more thoughtful. He was pleased to acknowledge this to himself and his wife, as he had done the night before.

Shortly afterwards, Mr Jenkins approached Elizabeth and apologised for not having sought her approval first. Elizabeth assured him that she did not feel in the least offended, since Kitty was eighteen and well able to make up her own mind. However, she added that she was pleased with her sister's decision and wished them happiness. Mr Jenkins was clearly pleased with this reply. He then spent the rest of the evening deep in conversation with Kitty.

After dinner, Mr Bennet retired to the library, forewarned by Elizabeth to expect Mr Jenkins. "If it's about Kitty, my dear, I have to say I'm delighted. He seems a thoroughly respectable and sensible young man; so long as he knows that Kitty has no fortune of her own." Elizabeth remarked that she didn't think he had any illusions on that score and enlightened her father about Mr Darcy's part in the matter. He was thoughtful for a moment, then breaking into a smile said, "Good God, Lizzie, what will your mother say when she finds out I've given Kitty away, while she was in Newcastle?"

Mr Jenkins went into the library and came out very soon after with a message for Kitty; her father wanted to see them both. Kitty was still apprehensive, but Mr Bennet, seeing her tears, told her she was a good girl and deserved a good husband. He added he was confident that Mr Jenkins would look after her better than her father had done these eighteen years. Before Kitty could protest, he waved them away. "Remember, my dear, that your sisters Jane and Lizzie are your dearest friends and your best examples. If you must thank anyone for your present happiness, you should thank them."

~❦~

Mr Bennet, Mr Darcy, and Elizabeth left for Longbourn the following morning. They had left a day earlier than expected, so they might look at the property in Leicestershire and call in at the Gardiners,' in London.

There were a few tears, but no real sorrow at this farewell. Kitty and Georgiana seemed already like sisters—being of an age when young women are fond of confiding in each other—they looked forward to spending plenty of time together. Elizabeth had already informed Mrs Reynolds of Kitty's engagement to Mr Jenkins. She was not surprised to learn that the staff at Pemberley had anticipated it for some time. Mrs Reynolds promised to take good care of both young ladies. Mrs Annesley, who had been away visiting friends, had returned, so they left the girls in excellent hands.

The stability and certainty of Pemberley and all it stood for had given Elizabeth the kind of confidence she appreciated; just as marriage to Darcy had given her the emotional fulfilment she had yearned for all her life. When, as a young woman, she had contemplated matrimony, she had often doubted if her dream of a passionate relationship could be realised. It had made her wary, even distrustful of suitors. Yet, in the warmth and generosity of Darcy's love, Elizabeth had found complete contentment.

Writing later to her Aunt Gardiner, Elizabeth recalled the moment as a point in her life with Darcy, when every feeling came together:

It is not that I ever doubted the correctness of my decision, but that I had gone through so many turbulent emotions in my relationship with him in the course of one year, that I was unable at first to sort out my true feelings. But, today, as we drove away from Pemberley, I knew the strength and goodness of my husband and the love we shared was at the very centre of all those feelings and it would travel with us, no matter where we went, or what fate befell us. I know you will understand, dear Aunt, because you have enjoyed the blessing of a good marriage. I pray that what I feel now is the foundation of a similar state for Darcy and myself.

The letter was posted in London, surprising her aunt when it arrived a day after they had been at Gracechurch Street themselves, but on reading it, Mrs Gardiner understood exactly why it had been written.

CHAPTER SIX

Family matters

ELIZABETH WAS EXCITED BY the prospect of seeing the property in Leicestershire, if only because it was close enough to Pemberley to make for regular visiting. Both Mr Darcy and Mr Bingley were well aware of the close and affectionate bond that existed between their wives. That the current distance between them distressed both Jane and her sister was well-appreciated. Jane's husband had promised at an early date to seek a resolution to this situation, by moving from Netherfield Park, when the lease expired, to a house he intended to purchase for their family home. That he had requested Darcy's help in finding a suitable place was an indication of the value he placed on his friend's taste and judgement as well as his determination to acquire the best property his money could buy.

Elizabeth was unfamiliar with Leicestershire and depended upon Darcy to draw her attention to places of interest. A county rich in historic places— Roman antiquities, Norman churches, ruins of medieval castles and abbeys, and the site of the battle of Bosworth Field—all lay within a short distance of each other. Farmers working the fields might well turn up artefacts from any of these periods of history. Leicestershire was closer to the hub of English history than either Hertfordshire—where Elizabeth had lived most of her life, or Derbyshire—where she expected she would spend the rest of it. Mr Bennet asked about Oakham Castle, which was a site he remembered visiting many years ago, and Elizabeth was surprised at the amount of information Darcy was able to provide about this example of 12th century Norman architecture.

As they crossed the river and the ancient Roman Road that ran North into Nottinghamshire, the rocky outcrops or "scarps" jutted out from the softer pastures that supported good herds of cattle and sheep. The landscape was very different from anything Elizabeth had known, being at once harsher and more interesting than the gentle fields and woodlands of the South, but in her opinion, less majestic than the celebrated beauty of the Peak, Matlock, and Dovedale, which she had enjoyed on her tour of Derbyshire last Summer.

Passing through the village of Ashfordby, the road to Melton-Mowbray branched away to the North, and they gradually climbed out on to a long ridge which afforded an excellent view of the entire valley to the Southeast as well as the rising scarps and sandstone caps to the North.

Situated on gently rising land, surrounded by attractive woods and an ample park of some two hundred acres, which included a farm and an orchard, was Ashford House. Though it had none of the breathtaking impact of Pemberley, Elizabeth was immediately attracted to the house and its environs. A large place, initially of Jacobean design, complete with arched windows and steeply pitched roofs—Ashford House, bathed as it was in Summer sunlight, with a fine collection of trees throwing dappled shadows on the lawn, was the very picture of an English country house. The slopes behind it were well-wooded, and the rising steeple of an old Norman church emerged in the middle distance, against a clear blue sky. Elizabeth was charmed.

Darcy dampened her enthusiasm somewhat by suggesting that while it might look very good on the outside, where nature had played its part well, the previous tenants may not have been as kind to the interior. But, in this he was only proved to have been cautious, as usual, because the manservant who admitted them informed them that the master had instructed that everything was to be in readiness for Mr Darcy's visit, and so it was; the interior was impeccable.

From the warm and welcoming hall to the gracious library, sitting and drawing rooms, and excellent dining room overlooking a rose garden, the house spoke of care and comfort. Everything she saw, the handsome fireplaces, fine hangings and furniture, and several elegant bedrooms, convinced Elizabeth of the rightness of Darcy's judgement. She could see Jane here. She turned to Darcy and smiled when he asked, "What do you think, my dear, would it suit?"

She replied, without hesitation, "Perfectly well, I shall have no trouble recommending this place to Jane; it's beautiful."

Darcy permitted himself a satisfied smile, as Mr Bennet joined in to praise his judgement. "There can be no doubt, if as you say, Bingley wishes to purchase a place, this property would be an excellent choice," he said.

They spent an hour or so looking out of windows, admiring the aspect—North towards the wooded ridge, or sloping away to the meadows, and a fast tumbling stream to the East. A useful little dairy and a hothouse for nurturing fruit and green vegetables in the cold seasons both added to the desirability of the property. Finally, Lizzie had to be dragged away from the spacious kitchen and pantry that looked out on a perfect kitchen garden, so they could make good time on their journey to London.

As they journeyed, Elizabeth's enthusiasm continued unabated, until teasing her Darcy said, "I shall soon begin to worry that you like Ashford House better than Pemberley, Elizabeth," which brought such a strong denial, he had to retract his words immediately.

In London, they went directly to Darcy's town house in Portman Square and, having rested and partaken of tea, went later in the evening to Gracechurch Street, to dine with the Gardiners.

Elizabeth and Mrs Gardiner had barely sufficient time to eat, so busy were they giving and receiving the news. First, there was Kitty's engagement to Mr Jenkins, whom the Gardiners had met, but of whom, except for his remarkable voice, they recalled little. Mrs Gardiner wanted to know more, and Elizabeth amused everyone with the statement that they would not know Kitty when they met her, so changed was she from the naïve, rather silly young person she had been before. "I do not wish to be thought complacent, Aunt, but if we succeed in keeping Kitty to ourselves and by that I mean away from Newcastle, where the greatest peril lies, I am convinced we shall have gained a remarkably pleasing young sister, with much promise for the future," said Elizabeth, looking across to her husband for support.

Mrs Gardiner looked at him and smiled. "Is this right, Mr Darcy? Or is Lizzie teasing me with this tale of Kitty's miraculous transformation?" she asked. Darcy, not usually keen to venture opinions on his in-laws, was, on this occasion, completely supportive of his wife.

"No indeed, Mrs Gardiner, Lizzie is quite right. We have been very proud of the way Kitty has worked with my sister Georgiana to improve her perform-ance on the piano, and of course, everyone has admired the generous work she has done with the Children's Choir," he said, and both Mr Bennet and Elizabeth smiled with pleasure at his words.

For Elizabeth, who was painfully aware of the low opinion Mr Darcy had held of the impropriety and foolish behaviour of her younger sisters, this was a special moment, and she loved him all the more for saying it to her family, in her presence. As for Mr Jenkins, Darcy assured them that Dr Grantley, who had known him at St John's in Oxford, had vouched for him when he first applied for the living at Pemberley, and since then, Darcy had found no reason to doubt that he was anything but a fine and sincere young man and very devoted to Kitty.

Mr Bennet, at this point, volunteered that he was of the same opinion. "I shall be eternally grateful to Elizabeth and Mr Darcy for affording Kitty an opportunity to extend and improve her circle of friends and her mind at the same time; a consequence that has not always been apparent in Kitty's case," he said.

"And when do they plan to marry?" asked Mrs Gardiner, unable to resist the inevitable question.

"Probably after Christmas," said Lizzie, explaining that Mr Darcy had plans to renovate the Rectory, drawing more praise for her husband from the Gardiners, who already had the highest opinion of him. Then there was the excitement of Ashford House, which Elizabeth was absolutely certain would suit Bingley and Jane to perfection. She was so excited that Mr Gardiner teased her about liking it better than Pemberley and for the second time in a day, Elizabeth was compelled to deny this, amidst a great deal of teasing.

This time, it was her father who came to her rescue, "The reason for Lizzie's excitement is quite plain to me," he said. "She knows her sister will depend totally upon her opinion and with Bingley so confident that Mr Darcy is the best judge of such things, they cannot go wrong. I will wager London to a brick that Lizzie will have her sister ensconced at Ashford House, not twenty miles from Pemberley, before Christmas."

It was scarcely four months since the sisters had been together at Pemberley, yet Elizabeth and Jane were both tearful and ecstatic at their reunion. At Darcy's suggestion, they had driven directly to Netherfield Park, having left London very early that morning, arriving around midday.

The warmth of summer had more impact in Hertfordshire, and together with a naturally healthy glow, it had given Jane a lustre that Elizabeth noticed immediately. "Dear Jane, you look beautiful!" she cried, contrasting her own still pale complexion with her sister's radiant health. Jane blushed at the compliment, but everyone agreed that she looked remarkably well. Elizabeth felt tears sting her eyes. Jane's beauty was of a very special kind. The serenity her marriage had given her greatly enhanced it.

There was so much to talk about that the sisters had to go away upstairs. They repaired to the same spacious bedroom that they had shared some years ago, when having been caught in the rain as a consequence of one of her mother's foolish plans, Jane had been very ill and had to stay at Netherfield, with Lizzie arriving to nurse her through her fever. The room brought back so many memories, that they were both overwhelmed by the thought of all that had happened since they were last there together. When they could finally speak rationally, Jane asked, "Tell me, Lizzie, what news have you of Kitty? I cannot believe she is already engaged to Mr Jenkins."

Elizabeth told her what had happened, and she was at first scarcely able to believe it, but then as she heard it all, including Mr Darcy's kindness and generosity to the young couple, she wept with happiness and embraced Elizabeth. "Oh Lizzie, how happy I am that you were spared the agony of a marriage with Wickham and waited for Mr Darcy. How grateful I am that we are both blessed with good and generous husbands. Poor Charlotte is at Lucas Lodge; she is soon to have her baby, and yet I feel for her, because it seems she would rather be away from Mr Collins. I could not bear to be separated from Bingley at this time, and I cannot help thinking that it must be so hard to be alone."

"Not if one has a fool for a husband," said Elizabeth, sharply, still angry that her dear friend Charlotte had, by marrying the stupid Mr Collins, so compromised her chances of a dignified and happy marriage. "We must call on Charlotte tomorrow. I shall send a message when Father returns to

Longbourn, that we will visit later in the day." The time sped by as they talked and made their plans, while downstairs lunch was served, and Bingley, who had been hearing of the solid advantages as well as the delights of Ashford House from both Darcy and his father-in-law, came upstairs himself to persuade the ladies to join them.

~

The following day, Mary—who had been at Netherfield since Christmas—and her father left for Longbourn soon after breakfast. Mr Bennet had enjoyed his sojourn up North but nevertheless looked forward to his own fireside and library, even more so because his wife was still at the side of her daughter Lydia in Newcastle. The prospect of perfect silence and peace at Longbourn attracted him greatly.

Elizabeth sent a note to Charlotte, which John was to deliver immediately and then the ladies would drive over for afternoon tea. Charlotte had not seen her dear friend Elizabeth in nine months. She was overjoyed at the prospect of seeing her and Jane that afternoon. No sooner had they alighted from the carriage than she was out to greet them, admiring them both and wanting to know how Elizabeth was. They embraced and greeted each other warmly. "Dear Eliza, you look remarkably well, and what a fine gown this is—doesn't she look quite the lady of fashion, Maria?" Charlotte began, and young Maria Lucas, who had last seen Lizzie at her wedding, seemed completely in awe of her now. Her eyes widened as she nodded and agreed with her elder sister. But she was much more interested to hear about Kitty, disappointed that her friend was not with them. The news that Kitty was about to be engaged and was likely to be married at Christmas astonished them both.

"Kitty engaged!" said Maria. "She vowed she would never wed, after Lydia . . . ," her voice trailed away, in some embarrassment at having brought up the forbidden topic of Lydia's escapade with Wickham. But Elizabeth was no longer troubled by it, and while Jane reddened a little, she laughed and brushed it aside, saying, "Well, it seems she has changed her mind; having been away from the foolish influence of Lydia for nigh on a year, Kitty, believe me, is a changed and mature young person. I assure you Maria, she is quite transformed and we are all very proud of her." Charlotte was herself amazed at Elizabeth's news, but unlike her younger sister, Charlotte's own quiet wisdom enabled her to understand how the excellent marriages of Elizabeth and Jane and the social opportunities afforded them had advantaged Kitty, too.

When they had finally satisfied all of Maria's curiosity about Kitty and Mr Jenkins, Elizabeth and Jane were ushered by Charlotte into the parlour, and there they were served a splendid tea. Lady Lucas had not been very well, said Charlotte, apologising for her mother's absence, and Sir William was expected later; he'd been out shooting on a neighbouring manor.

Meanwhile, Charlotte asked to be told all the news. "Eliza, we heard from Lady Catherine, shortly before I left Hunsford, that you and Mr Darcy had not only displeased her by your own union, but were now responsible for thwarting her plans for her other nephew—James Fitzwilliam—Darcy's cousin. Is this true?" Even Charlotte could not keep a straight face, and she lost control altogether when told of the abortive plans of Lady Catherine to contrive a match between her nephew James and Caroline Bingley.

"Miss Bingley?" Charlotte could not believe her ears, "Oh Eliza, we met her and her sister Mrs Hurst. I do beg your pardon Jane, but I gather you are not entirely without criticism of your sister-in-law," and as Jane nodded and smiled to indicate she had no inhibitions on that score, Charlotte continued, "As I was saying, she was at Rosings last Christmas, and, oh dear, she was impossible to please. There was always something amiss, though she did not dare say so to Lady Catherine. But Eliza, I cannot honestly say that I see her as the Lady of the Manor." Both sisters agreed that they could not imagine it either, pointing out that they had met James Fitzwilliam and his bride to be—Rosamund Camden—and did not believe that a better marriage might have been made by Lady Catherine.

"Should the opportunity arise, Charlotte, you may wish to set her Ladyship's mind at rest. Mr Darcy and I had nothing whatever to do with the match; the couple were already engaged before we met them at Christmas," said Elizabeth, with a twinkle in her eye. "It may not change her opinion of me, but she may at least understand that yet another of her nephews is sufficiently adult to make his own marriage arrangements, without interference from her."

From the tone of her comment, Charlotte gathered that there had been some earlier attempt by Lady Catherine to intervene where she had no right to do so and was determined to hear the tale. Elizabeth, who was an excellent mimic, regaled them with such a vivid description of the visit of Lady Catherine to Longbourn and her strenuous efforts to intimidate Elizabeth into promising never to accept Mr Darcy, that she had all of them in gales of laughter.

Charlotte, whose admiration for her friend increased as she listened, confessed she had not laughed so much in months, "I wonder how I shall keep a straight face when I am next at Rosings," she said, as Lizzie went on to explain that far from achieving her goal of preventing her nephew's engagement to her, his aunt had actually advanced it. In this and other agreeable conversations the afternoon passed, and as the sisters were preparing to leave, Sir William Lucas arrived. His delight at seeing them there enhanced the pleasure he had of having spent a very good day with his friends, bringing home a good bag of game. Upon discovering how long Elizabeth and Darcy were to be at Netherfield, Sir William announced his intention to have a dinner party in their honour at Lucas Lodge and extracted a promise that they would all be there.

On the way home, Jane, who had been rather quiet all afternoon, spoke softly, "Do you see what I mean about Charlotte, Lizzie?" Elizabeth nodded gravely and reached for her sister's hand, "You were right, dearest Jane. Charlotte's happiness is solely in looking forward to the birth of her child. She did not once mention Mr Collins, odious man! Oh Jane, I feel guilty that you and I can be so happy, so blessed in our dear husbands, and Charlotte, who has no less a right to the same happiness and good fortune, needs must put up with such a poor substitute for a happy marriage."

"It is clear that she is happy to be back at Lucas Lodge."

"No doubt she is relieved to get away from the strictures of Lady Catherine de Bourgh," said Elizabeth, remembering Charlotte's long suffering forbearance at Rosings, when Lady Catherine probed and queried their every action, while the obsequious Mr Collins only encouraged her rude intervention. Jane agreed, "I cannot believe that it would have been very comfortable for Charlotte, to be under such scrutiny, when she was first married and went to live at Hunsford."

"And to prepare to face Lady Catherine whenever she deigns to honour them with a visit? I cannot imagine anything worse!" said Elizabeth with spirit and sincerity, "She is such a rude, meddling old woman. Oh Jane, it must have been intolerable!"

Jane's countenance revealed her distaste at the prospect. "I must say that when Mr Bingley and I were married and went to London, I was pleased to find that we had the house at Grosvenor Street all to ourselves, except for the servants, of course." Elizabeth concurred, recalling that she and Mr Darcy had greatly appreciated the time they had spent together after their wedding, travelling through several counties and staying where they chose, free of the scrutiny of friends or family.

There was still plenty of light in the sky as the carriage turned into the drive at Netherfield Park. As they reached the house, they could see Bingley and Darcy on the lawn. "I wonder what has happened," said Jane, realising that it was unusual for the gentlemen to be out at that hour.

As they alighted, Mr Bingley came up to Jane and, taking her arm, led her indoors. Mr Darcy did likewise, whispering as they went that there had been an express communication come for Jane from Newcastle. Lizzie hurried into the main parlour, where Jane was seated and Bingley had just opened up the express letter. That it was news of their sister, whose confinement was imminent, she was sure. As Jane took the letter from Bingley, Lizzie sank down beside her. It was in Wickham's hand and announced the birth of their son— Henry George. The brief message said both the child and Lydia were well and a letter would follow. There followed a request that Mr Bennet and Elizabeth be informed of the news and concluded with the usual felicitations. It was signed George Wickham.

Jane's tears expressed her relief that Lydia and the child were both safe and well. She seemed delighted that her parents were blessed with a grandson and hastened to send a servant with the message for her father. Elizabeth, on the other hand, could not feel the same unalloyed pleasure, remembering all that had gone before with Wickham and Lydia and her own unthinking acceptance of Wickham until his duplicity was exposed. The hurt it had caused to Darcy, whose character had been so unfairly impugned, she would never forget nor forgive. It seared her soul to think that her first nephew, her father's first grandchild would be Wickham's son. Conscious of all that Darcy had been through because of the stupidity of her sister and the dishonourable behaviour of Wickham, she was unable to rejoice simply, as Jane had done.

Sensing her unease, Darcy tried to reassure her that he had long ceased to care about Wickham and she must not let what had happened in the past upset her again and again, each time he touched their lives.

"We are far too happy to be distressed by those memories, my dearest Lizzie. There is no reason why Jane and you should not be happy on this occasion." Grateful for his generous spirit and the assurance of his affection, she brightened up considerably and went in search of Jane.

She found her upstairs, composing a letter to Lydia, congratulating her and urging her to take good care of herself and her baby. It was as simple and sincere as Jane's responses usually were. As her sister appeared, she stopped, "Do you wish to write something too, Lizzie?" she asked. But Elizabeth could not.

"No, Jane, it is best you write for us all. Send her our love and good wishes, and let us hope she will be less foolish in future—now she is a mother."

Jane was shocked by the harshness of her sister's voice. "Oh no, Lizzie, you must not say that. I'm sure Lydia will settle down."

Elizabeth shook her head. "Do not depend upon it, dearest Jane; do not forget that Lydia is not yet eighteen and still as vain and silly as ever. Unless by some miracle, her feckless husband is transformed into a mature and responsible person, I cannot see our sister settling into sensible motherhood."

Seeing the shocked and troubled look on Jane's face, she relented, "Oh dear Jane, don't look so upset. I may be wrong; I hope I am; I hope they turn into exemplary parents with perfect children."

"Oh Lizzie, please do be serious, do you really think Lydia is unchanged?" asked Jane, almost pleading for some hope.

"I do not know Jane, how could I? I have not seen her in more than a year. She may have redeemed herself. But, I am not very confident." Looking a little less certain, Jane folded and sealed her letter, and they took it downstairs to send off to the post before joining the gentlemen for dinner.

Despite the best intentions of Sir William, the dinner party at Lucas Lodge did not eventuate. At first, it was postponed because of Lady Lucas' continuing ill health, but in the following week, Charlotte herself was brought to bed without warning.

Elizabeth and Jane were visiting her one warm afternoon, and while they were having tea, Charlotte was taken ill with severe pains. Fortunately, Dr Faulkner had called to see Lady Lucas and stayed on to have tea and continue his courtship of Maria, with whom he was walking in the garden at the time. Elizabeth ran into the garden and called out to them. Dr Faulkner proved to be most capable, calmly organising everything, giving clear instructions, and swiftly moving to make Charlotte as comfortable as possible.

At his request, Elizabeth sent a servant for Mr Jones and arranged for her sister to be driven home. "I think I shall stay and see if Charlotte needs me. You could send the carriage for me later," she explained to Jane, who went reluctantly, realising that it was for the best. Not knowing quite what she could do for Charlotte but wanting very much to be with her friend at this time, Elizabeth went to her and sat with her while her maid and the housekeeper bustled around with their preparations for the doctor. Mr Jones arrived within the hour, by which time Charlotte appeared calmer, but shortly afterwards the midwife was called in, and Lizzie had to leave the room. She spent a couple of difficult hours unable to do anything to help except perhaps pray and once sat down to scribble a note to her aunt but could get no further than the first two lines. She went outside to a Gazebo, where she sometimes used to read with Charlotte and found young Maria there, curled up, very frightened, and quite unable to cope.

After what seemed like an eternity, Dr Faulkner came in search of them, and seeing his face with relief written all over it, Elizabeth knew it had to be good news. "It's a little girl, and . . ." He got no further, for Maria had hurled herself into his arms and Elizabeth, knowing it was useless to try to get anything more coherent out of him, ran indoors, where she found Charlotte, a little pale but otherwise well. Elizabeth went to her at once and took her hand.

Charlotte smiled and thanked Elizabeth for staying with her. Her daughter lay in a crib beside her. "Eliza, meet your namesake—Catherine Elizabeth Collins" she whispered, and in spite of herself, Elizabeth was crying for joy. "I was going to ask you, but she became impatient, rather like you do, and I did not have the opportunity."

Elizabeth reassured her, "I am delighted you have given her my name, Charlotte." Charlotte apologised, "I am sorry about the Catherine; I'm afraid it could not have been otherwise—Mr Collins insisted, if it was a girl, it had to be Catherine, but she'll always be 'Little Eliza' to me."

"And to me," whispered Lizzie, as she said goodnight and left.

Elizabeth and Darcy were glad to be leaving for Pemberley, since news had arrived that Mr Collins was on his way from Kent, travelling by coach and having sent express messages to practically everybody in the county to announce the birth of his daughter. Having seen the curious letter her father had received earlier in the week, in which Mr Collins had presumed to warn Mr Bennet of the imminent birth of a male heir and its effect upon the entail of Longbourn, Elizabeth had no desire whatsoever to meet him.

"Stupid, odious man!" she said to Jane, as they spent their last evening together at Netherfield, "Fancy writing such a letter to Papa; he has lost none of his pompous self-importance! Poor Charlotte, how does she cope?" They visited Charlotte later and having left congratulatory messages for her husband and a gift for little Eliza, said their farewells.

Jane and Elizabeth parted reluctantly, but Bingley travelled with them, for he had been almost convinced by Darcy to sell his shares in the heinous textile industry and invest the money with the rest of his inheritance in Ashford House. He wished, however, to see the property himself before making the final decision.

Jane was quite content to depend upon the judgement of her husband and brother-in-law, knowing already in her heart that Elizabeth's recommendation alone had sufficed to convince her of the complete suitability of the property. As her father had said on another occasion, so certain was Jane of her sister's taste and good opinion, that she needed only the additional attraction of the place's being a mere twenty miles from Pemberley to declare herself completely satisfied.

As the sisters parted this time, they smiled, promising each other that they would soon meet again. Jane's child was due in August, and God willing, she would be safely delivered of the baby. "Just think, Lizzie," Jane whispered as they embraced, "we may be at Ashford House by Christmas."

"I shall pray that you will. Dearest Jane, take care," said Elizabeth, knowing that she and Darcy would do everything in their power to make it happen. If Bingley purchased Ashford House, they would certainly be there by Christmas.

CHAPTER SEVEN

New beginnings

RETURNING TO PEMBERLEY, ELIZABETH and Mr Darcy found Kitty and Mr Jenkins engaged. Kitty wore a ring on which it appeared Mr Jenkins must have expended most of his worldly goods. Happily, it turned out that the ring had been his mother's and Mr Jenkins was in no danger of being pauperised by the purchase. Elizabeth was very relieved. They were so obviously pleased with themselves, that she did not have the heart to say anything to disappoint them. They admired the ring, wished them happiness, and broke out a celebratory bottle of champagne. Later, however, Elizabeth expressed some reservations, that the couple had not waited to visit Longbourn and have Mrs Bennet meet her future son-in-law, before becoming formally engaged. "I am convinced," she told her husband as they dressed for dinner, "that Mama will blame me; she will feel that I have deliberately neglected to inform her of Kitty's engagement."

"That should not concern you, Lizzie," said Darcy. "No more than it concerns me that Lady Catherine believes I am in some way responsible for subverting her plans for Fitzwilliam and Miss Bingley." Elizabeth laughed at the memory but was uneasy. She had no desire to upset her mother or cause trouble between Mrs Bennet and Kitty.

"I think," she said tentatively, "I shall write directly to my father and have him send Mama a letter. It may not save me from her censure, but it will spare Kitty and Mr Jenkins an inordinate amount of aggravation." Darcy agreed.

Elizabeth's letter to her father relating their safe return to Pemberley and the news of Kitty's engagement contained just one piece of advice:

> *Mr Darcy and I both feel it is best that Mama be told of Kitty's good news as soon as possible. We are also agreed that it would be best coming from you, Papa, perhaps with a promise that Mr Jenkins will be invited to Longbourn to meet Mama, on her return from Newcastle.*

That night, Lizzie asked her husband's opinion of her letter and received praise, "Very diplomatic indeed, my dear. I can see no cause for offence at all." said Darcy. When, a week later, her father's reply was received, they were both amused by his response:

> *As for the matter of Kitty's engagement, it has all been done, my dear Lizzie, exactly as you and Mr Darcy have suggested. Have no fear, while you are indeed in loco parentis while Kitty is at Pemberley, remember that I gave them permission to become engaged. I have said as much to your mother, adding copious praise of Mr Jenkins. I am certain that when your mother reads it and realises that she is about to be relieved of another of her lovely daughters, she will be so overcome with joy, that no other concerns will signify at all.*
>
> *However, your suggestion that Mr Jenkins be invited to visit Longbourn when Mrs Bennet returns is an excellent one. I intend to despatch such an invitation forthwith. I trust my dear that Mr Darcy and you can survive without his ministrations for a week or so in the Autumn. Mary and I are bearing up well. Mrs Hill and John do their best for us, but we miss you all, Lizzie, especially you and Jane. God bless you both, and I look forward to your next visit . . .*

Lizzie felt deeply for her father; it was clear that his life had changed so totally in the last eighteen months; she was sure he was experiencing great loneliness, which in the midst of her present happiness, saddened her greatly. Darcy sensed her sadness, and though he said little at the time, he had made up his mind to invite Mr Bennet back to Pemberley at the earliest opportunity. Despite their lack of communication earlier in their acquaintance, he had, during the last few weeks when there had been time to get to know him better, come to understand and respect his father-in-law. Mr Bennet's alert, well-informed mind and his great zest for reading, combined with the quick, sarcastic sense of humour that played upon everything and everyone, made him a most stimulating guest. Darcy, whose own view of the world always had a sardonic edge, now softened somewhat by his wife's sensibilities, had appreciated Mr Bennet's observation and wit.

There were, however, other matters of more immediate concern, which demanded Darcy's attention. Recently, his steward had been asking questions about the new developments in farming. With some of the landholders in the area enclosing commons and fencing out their old tenants and farmhands, many people were anxious and insecure. Georgiana had spoken to her brother of the fears of her maid—whose parents and grand parents had lived and worked on the estate for generations. Even Mrs Reynolds, whose husband had been his father's manservant, was concerned. Her son, who was a gamekeeper, had hoped to take up the tenancy of a vacant farm, with a cottage and pigpen. His wife, a local girl from the little village of Trantford below Matlock, had already seen her parents ousted from their small holding, when the new absentee landlords sent the bailiffs in to enclose their fields and prepare them for pasture.

Darcy wished to reassure them that they should not have any fears of such developments on the Pemberley Estate. Talking to his chief steward and the men who worked to run the estate, Darcy gave an assurance. "There will be no compulsory enclosures at Pemberley. We have plenty of land here, some of which is lying fallow and not fully used. Should we wish to increase our flocks or extend our cultivation, we can do so without enclosing the commons, woodlands, and meadows. And every family on the estate will have access to the river." Turning to his Steward, he said, "I want to get that message to all our people; they will not lose their cottages or their farms. Miss Darcy, Mrs Darcy, and I are the only persons concerned. The estate is not encumbered in any way, and no one else can influence the way Pemberley is managed. What we do and who lives on our estate, under what conditions, is our business entirely. I can assure all of you that we have no intention of undertaking any enterprise that will cost any of you your homes or your livelihood. Everyone is free to continue working and living here, unless they wish to leave, voluntarily."

If the Steward and his men were at all surprised by the vehemence of the Master's words, they certainly did not show it. The Steward's confidence and loyalty were demonstrated by the way in which he appeared almost to take Mr Darcy's words for granted, as if he had never doubted his intentions. Four generations of his forebears had served Darcy's family, and they had always trusted each other. The other men, mostly tenant farmers, did look relieved and expressed their appreciation to Darcy as they filed out. It was heartening to have good news to take home to their families. On the following day, they would gather their labourers and farmhands together and tell them too.

As Darcy walked back to the house, the sun was setting, casting lovely, long, indigo shadows across the park. Elizabeth and Georgiana came out to meet him. "We thought we might have tea out here," said Elizabeth, "it's such a beautiful afternoon."

"What a good idea," he said, drawing both of them to his side.

"You look tired," Elizabeth observed, and his sister agreed he looked weary. Darcy explained, "I've been speaking to the men. They've been worried by all the talk of enclosures in the neighbourhood. There are moves afoot to enforce the law and deprive tenants of their rights to use the woods and commons. I hope I have set their minds at rest."

As they reached the lawn where the table was laid for tea under a graceful, spreading elm, Mrs Reynolds came towards them. She had just been speaking with her son, who had told her of Mr Darcy's assurances to the men. There was gratitude in her eyes, as she grasped his hands and thanked him. Unembarrassed, touched, and pleased to have achieved what he had set out to do, at least in her case, Darcy repeated his reassurance that no one would be thrown out of their cottage or farm on the estate.

"You did not need me to tell you, Mrs Reynolds, you should have known I would never countenance such a thing."

"I did indeed, Mr Darcy, but my son was most anxious," she explained and thanking him once more, left to fetch the tea tray.

It was an index of her affection that she would often personally carry out a service for the Master, which would usually be the task of a maid or footman. With Georgiana and Darcy and now, increasingly, with Elizabeth, she did not stand on ceremony. Darcy spoke passionately. "It is unforgivable that men and women who have worked the land and served us for generations should be so bewildered and fearful, because of laws made to accommodate the greed of others," he said, "Laws are meant to make the lives of citizens better, not worse."

As he explained the gist of his message to the tenants and farm workers of Pemberley, both women listened eagerly, conscious of their perceptions of him in his role as the Master of Pemberley. To Elizabeth, here was more proof of the astonishing generosity of her husband, a character trait she had not expected to find in him when she had first made his acquaintance, but one for which she and her family had every reason to be grateful. To Georgiana, it was her brother being himself; she had never known him to be otherwise.

When they had finished their tea, Georgiana asked to be excused. She was expected at the church for choir practice. Kitty had gone ahead. "It's a special programme for Rosamund's wedding," she explained.

"When can we come and listen?" asked Elizabeth.

"Oh! Not just yet," she said as she disappeared indoors, leaving Darcy and Elizabeth alone, in the luminous twilight. They sat in silence awhile, enjoying the quiet evening. A flock of starlings flew over the house, wheeled around, and flew out towards the woods, with the rays of the dying sun gilding their wings. Reluctantly, they agreed that it was time to be going indoors.

The following week, Mr Darcy received from Sir Edmond Camden an invitation to attend a meeting of landlords in the neighbourhood. Since it was summer, he had decided to ride over to Rushmore Farm with his Steward and a groom. Aware of the controversy surrounding some of the enclosures that had followed the passage of the Enclosure Laws by the Parliament, Darcy had been prepared for an argument with some of his neighbours but not for the level of anger he encountered. Like Sir Edmond, Darcy was unwilling to enclose common and woodland for agriculture, to the detriment of tenants and farmworkers, who had lived and worked on his family estates for generations.

Since childhood, their families had impressed upon them the sense of responsibility that must accompany the ownership of land. The relationship, though paternalistic, was one of mutual obligation and in many cases engendered respect for each other. It was something that had been conspicuously absent in France. No one who had seen the forces unleashed in the terrible conflict of the French Revolution could ever forget.

For Darcy, who had been at College while the revolution erupted and tore France apart, the bloodstained hands had seemed to belong to men on both sides. Though it was not in his nature to be fired by revolutionary causes, he could not help seeing that the exploitation of peasants and labourers had led directly to the overthrow of the French regime and the Terror that followed. At that time, when life had been cheap in France, it had been easy to feel morally and socially secure as an Englishman. But, the onset of the agrarian revolution in England had brought deprivation to a large number of small holders and peasants and the enrichment of a privileged group of rich landlords who had a stranglehold on the Parliament.

Those like Dr Grantley and William Camden, Rosamund's young brother, had shared his concern, but neither had been placed as Darcy had been on the death of his father, in a position to do something about it. Many others, sons of English landlords across the country, seemed not to notice the evil consequences of the enforced, arbitrary processes of enclosure upon the people they displaced. They spoke glibly of "improvements" or "the price of progress," unconcerned that for the farm labourer these "improvements" had taken away their open fields, their commons, woods, pastures, and in many cases their cottages, which had been passed down from one generation to the next.

The "dandies" and "swells," as they came to be called, spent hardly any time getting their shoes, much less their hands, dirty with English soil. Most of them left the management of their properties to bailiffs and stewards, at whose mercy were the now-landless rural poor, while they spent their time in the assemblies of London and the country mansions of their peers. For two or three years, Darcy had ignored the way landlords around the country had used their political power to strip the peasants of basic rights, while they enriched themselves. His family had never needed to exploit their tenants and instead had encouraged and received a high level of personal loyalty. Now, some ten years after the first Enclosure Bills, there was pressure being applied to those among the landed gentry who did not conform.

At the meeting hosted by the Camdens, there was a new group of landowners—lately rich and prosperous—bemoaning the sudden reversal of their fortunes, after the war. The demobilisation of the armies and the crashing grain prices caused by markets flooded with wheat from the very fields they had enclosed and made more productive were causing a rural depression such as England had not seen in living memory.

The new rich, who had little knowledge of the ebb and flow of fortunes in farming, were impatient of the slump in corn prices and the declining value of farms, which they had purchased, hoping to make a fortune. They demanded to know why some landlords were not using the new Enclosure Laws, which Parliament had passed to enable them to maximise their profits and minimise their losses.

Several rather trashily dressed young men asked questions of Sir Edmond Camden, implying that he and some other older landlords were dragging their feet and not supporting the efforts of the newcomers to make the best of their land holdings. One of them, a haughty looking, overdressed man carrying a heavy riding crop, called out across the room. "Darcy, I believe your people are preparing for the harvest." Mr Darcy, to whom he had not been introduced, looked across at him but said nothing. "Well, are they?" he persisted, "And do you intend to let them proceed to feast and get drunk and dance at your expense as well?" Darcy muttered something about that being his own business. William Camden, standing beside him, ventured an answer, "Harvest Home has been a tradition here for centuries. It is about as important as Christmas," he said.

"Not on my land it isn't," said the original speaker, raising his voice so all may hear him, "and if you let 'em carry it on, you're a damned fool!" Darcy bridled, visibly angry, but said nothing. Another man, standing next to William, added, "Look, it only encourages them to drink, and then the others will be demanding it too. I certainly have no intention of throwing away my good money on feasting and drunken revelry."

Still another of the men addressed Sir Edmond, "What about your rents, Sir Edmond? Do you intend to raise them next season?" Sir Edmond said curtly, "I do not."

"What about you, Darcy?" Darcy took a deep breath—he was offended and angry at having to engage in a discussion with them but was determined to make a point.

"I have no intention of increasing the rents of the tenants and farmworkers. In difficult times, when crops have failed or prices have fallen, my family, like Sir Edmond's, has provided some relief for our tenants and labourers.

"Most of them have lived on the estate for generations; their fathers and grandfathers have worked the land; they are making a reasonable living and working very hard for it. I can see no reason to burden them with an impost they cannot afford. I have no wish to see them deprive themselves or, worse, their children of food or clothing, just so I can collect more rent."

There was a sullen silence in the room as Darcy, warming to his theme, continued, "As for enclosing the commons, I would not even consider it. There is no land for sale on the Pemberley Estate. We have plenty of arable land lying fallow, should we wish to expand cultivation; we have no good reason to enclose the commons."

"Does that mean you will not support us?" the first man demanded. William had by now informed Darcy that this man was Barlow, a stockbroker from London, who had bought up several small holdings in the neighbourhood.

"You have no need of my support, sir," Darcy replied. "You are free to use the law and do as you please on your land. On my own estate, I shall do what I think is in the best interests of my family and the people who work for us."

"But do you not see that those of you who are working outside the Enclosures Act are making it damned difficult for us who need to use it to make a profit on the lands we have recently purchased?"

Mr Darcy shrugged his shoulders. "I'm sorry, but that is not my problem. As I see it, we have a system, which allows each landholder to use or not use the processes of the Enclosures Act. In the case of the Pemberley Estate, we have no need to use its provisions, nor do I need to increase the rents of my tenants."

He turned to William and indicated that he had had enough of this and wanted to leave. William Camden, the only one of Sir Edmond's sons to show any interest in the family farm and stud, had watched Mr Darcy's determined stand against the "Johnny-come-lately" Londoners with admiration. But he was also well aware of the anger of these men. They had been to see his father a few days ago, before it was decided to call the meeting. They were confident in the rightness of their cause, certain that only through widespread enclosure and extensive mechanised farming would England feed her increasing population and the landowners prosper. Sir Edmond had tried to calm things down, pointing out that Mr Darcy was acting within his rights and should be free to manage his estate as he thought fit. James Fitzwilliam, who was not well-known to the newcomers from town, spoke up, too. He reminded the gathering that unlike new landholders with recently purchased acreage, families like his had farmed the land for centuries and they had responsibilities towards their tenants and workmen.

This brought a hoarse laugh from the "town toffs" as William called them, which seriously irritated Darcy, who spoke from the doorway, "You might not acknowledge it, but there is a thread of mutual obligation that runs through the fabric of our society, which we have to thank for the security we enjoy today. While French peasants joined the poor in Paris to forge the revolution, English farmers were not seduced by slogans, because the system we have here assured them of freedom and security of tenure. If you destroy those threads and rend the fabric of English society, you do so at your own peril."

As Darcy walked out, his Steward and groom, who had waited outside the meeting hall, fell in beside him. There had been some audible voices agreeing with him but many discordant ones, grumbling, disputing his right to speak out. William, feeling somewhat uneasy at their overt hostility, followed Darcy out to the stables. They stopped awhile to talk with Sir Edmond and his steward, who were both apprehensive that Darcy was riding back to Pemberley in the gathering darkness. "Would you not prefer to leave your horses here and take my carriage?" Sir Edmond offered. "My groom can bring them over tomorrow." Darcy was not very concerned.

"They are hardly likely to attack us, surely. It would be foolish, after they've been clearly seen here."

"You could not count on them being anything other than hotheads, sir," said Sir Edmond's steward. "If you insist on riding out to Pemberley tonight, I'd be of a mind to accompany you with a few of my men."

Sir Edmond quickly endorsed the idea, and Darcy was reluctant to argue. Moreover, he was anxious to get back to Pemberley, since it was already later than he had expected to be. Darcy and his two men mounted their horses and rode on ahead, while William Camden, James Fitzwilliam, Camden's steward, and some half a dozen men followed at a discreet distance.

There was a half moon rising, still rather low in the sky, but the late Summer night was only half-dark. Instead of riding through Lambton as they had come, Darcy suggested they take a shorter route across the woods, along a familiar bridle path that crossed the boundary of the two estates. They rode on untroubled by anything untoward, until they had almost reached the point where the path descended steeply towards the stream. As arranged, Darcy's steward whistled to indicate to those following that they were almost home; once across the stream they would be within the park and quite safe from any trespassers. There was a rustling and sounds of horses, which they took to be the party from Rushmore turning back. Then, a shrill, quite different whistle pierced the night, and without warning they were in the midst of a crowd of some six or seven men, some on foot and others on horseback, all with their faces hidden under hats or scarves. The steward's horse reared up in fright and its cry must have reached the others, who wheeled around and rode back as fast as they could, arriving just in time to find Darcy confronting a stocky man with a heavy stick upraised, while his Steward and the groom were grappling with two others on the ground.

Obviously outnumbered, they were very relieved to have the party from Rushmore arrive in time to subdue and arrest the vicious ruffians, no doubt in the pay of some disgruntled dandy who blamed Darcy and his ilk for the fall in his profits. Darcy's Steward, Thomas, and the rest of the men from Rushmore Farm decided that they would take the miscreants back and hold them until the morrow, when they would be brought before the magistrate. William Camden and his groom accompanied Darcy the rest of the way to Pemberley House, ignoring his protestations that he was quite safe.

Elizabeth, anxious as darkness began to fall, was at an upstairs window watching out for her husband, when the small group broke out of the grove and crossed the bridge. Recognising Darcy as he rode towards the house, she ran downstairs and was at the front door before he had alighted from his horse. Seeing William Camden with him and noting that Thomas and the groom were missing from the party, Elizabeth sensed something was wrong. However, she knew better than to make a fuss, waiting until he was upstairs and had flung off his coat and boots before she asked the reason for his somewhat ruffled state and the missing men. Not wanting to alarm her unduly, Darcy made light of the matter, not telling her too many details, attributing his own rather dishevelled condition to the rough ride through the woods on a windy night. Elizabeth was not fooled. She was determined to discover what had taken place to cause her husband to return in some disarray, minus two of his servants and accompanied by William Camden and his groom. She knew Darcy would not lie to her if she asked him directly, but seeing he was tired, she did not pursue the matter, intending to find out some facts first. Meanwhile, after holding her very close for a moment, as if he was afraid for her safety rather than his own, he went away to bathe and dress for dinner. Georgiana was at dinner, and not wishing to alarm her, they said no more. That night, Darcy, clearly exhausted, was not averse to retiring early and soon fell fast asleep. Elizabeth on the other hand, unable to sleep, wrote to Rosamund Camden, begging her to ask her brother William for more information. She suggested they meet at the church on Sunday.

On receiving Elizabeth's letter, Rosamund approached her young brother immediately. Since no one had told him otherwise, William had no reservations about telling his sister exactly what had happened that night. The urgency of Elizabeth's note and the anxiety it expressed told Rosamund that this was a matter that could not be delayed until Sunday. On the pretext of consulting Elizabeth about some detail of her wedding clothes, Rosamund came the following afternoon to Pemberley, while Darcy was out.

Her account of the incident so terrified Elizabeth that she wept and was quite unable to think rationally for a while. Rosamund assured her that Sir Edmond, who was also the magistrate, had come down very hard on the villains, who had been captured and produced before him. He had asked his daughter to set Mrs Darcy's mind at rest; he would be taking further steps to ensure that those responsible for the abortive attack would be incarcerated and the men behind it would pay dearly, too. Rosamund did not know whether the identity of the men behind the attack was known but assured Elizabeth they would be found.

It was some time before Elizabeth could collect her thoughts, so anxious was she about her husband's safety. She thanked Rosamund again and again, for her prompt attention to her request and decided to write first to her Aunt Gardiner and seek advice.

When Darcy returned later that evening, Elizabeth tried very hard to conceal the fact that she knew any more than she did when he had left her that morning. She talked with false brightness about the approaching wedding and asked if Darcy was looking forward to being best man for his cousin. Darcy soon began to suspect that all was not as it seemed, and when they retired for the night, he chose the moment to probe the matter, only to find that he had opened the veritable floodgates of emotion, anxiety, fear, and bewilderment.

Never in her relatively sheltered existence had Lizzie experienced anything like the threat of violence against any member of her family or circle of friends.

Moving from the peaceful but modest environs of Longbourn to gracious, elegant Pemberley, it was the very last thing she had expected to confront. Though she had heard talk of unruly behaviour of newcomers to the district, they were so far removed from her, so unlikely to cross her path, that it was a matter to which she had given no thought at all.

To discover that, despite the elegance and comfort of their life at Pemberley and the very high regard in which the family of Mr Darcy was held all over the county, there were emerging new and hitherto unexpected forces that impinged upon their lives was unsettling. It had shaken her more than she cared to admit, and she could not conceal it from her husband.

Astonished by the strength of her feelings and the extent of her distress, Darcy, who had hitherto treated her concerns rather lightly, relented. He realised that his best efforts to spare her anxiety had only exacerbated the situation. He apologised for not having taken her fears seriously. Quietly and clearly, he told her what had occurred and explained his subsequent actions.

As she realised that both Mr Darcy and Sir Edmond had the ability to take action against the men involved and to protect themselves in the future, she was better able to accept it as a rash attempt by stupid, foolhardy men to intimidate their neighbours. "There is nothing they can do, dearest, nothing" he said, reassuring her, hoping his firm words would convince her that her fears were groundless. "We know who they are, and we have their measure. Should they make one more mistake, they will face transportation, no less. I cannot believe that any of them will fancy a stretch at His Majesty's pleasure, upon a wretched prison hulk or worse in New South Wales."

Despite the gentleness of his tone, a result of his concern for her, the determination in his voice gave her some comfort, and for the first time, she smiled. "Is it not likely that they will try again?" she asked, but he was very certain.

"If they do, they will not succeed, my dearest; they have shown themselves to be hot-headed and stupid. Should they try again, we will be ready for them." Elizabeth seemed reassured and agreed to set her fears aside, but not before she had extracted from him a solemn promise that he would take no risks and go nowhere alone. Impractical as this seemed, Darcy was happy to give her his word. He had every intention of taking good care and was unlikely to walk into a trap again.

The incident had convinced him of the rightness of his own convictions. That the rural English heritage he loved was, despite its strong foundations, fragile enough to be shattered by the actions of men with no lasting links with the land, whose only motivation was greed.

The mutual dependence and shared responsibility, which was the basis of the community in which he had grown up and in which he hoped to raise his own family, provided the security that was the hallmark of rural England.

Recent developments had started to rip that security away, and the desperation of the dispossessed poor was being mirrored by the desperation of those who had grabbed their land but found it brought them small profit. That it had manifested itself in an attack upon him had come as a shock. But the intrusion of violence, however abortive, into the groves of his beloved Pemberley hurt more than the attack upon himself.

❦

Mrs Gardiner was about to go out when Elizabeth's letter arrived. It was of such a size—being thick and closely written—that she decided to postpone her expedition to the shops. Her niece, always an interesting correspondent, could not be kept waiting. She gave Mrs Gardiner a most colourful account of the attack on Darcy, not hiding her concern or her anger but reassuring her aunt that Darcy and Sir Edmond had the matter in hand:

> *It is still difficult for me to write of the fear and alarm I felt on realising that Darcy had been attacked, here, within the park at Pemberley. Had it not been for the resourcefulness of Sir Edmond's men and the courage of Darcy's groom, who was hurt grappling with two of the villains but hung on to them nevertheless, I dread to think what might have happened. Darcy assures me that the guilty men have been severely dealt with and their masters, whom the ruffians betrayed easily no sooner were they apprehended, have been confronted and warned to stay out of trouble. We are particularly fortunate that Rosamund's father is the magistrate for this part of the county; Darcy and Rosamund both tell me he is feared up and down the land.*

Mrs Gardiner was deeply shocked by the revelations in Lizzie's letter. Recently, the Gardiners had begun to tire of the constant hustle and bustle of their part of London, which was growing heedlessly into a commercial quarter, where all manner of people gathered to ply their trade. With four children—

two of them girls, they had wondered about the wisdom of continuing in their house in Cheapside. Elizabeth's letter convinced her that it was time to make some decisions about moving out of London.

Elizabeth continued:

My dearest Aunt, how I longed for you or Jane to be here—or at least not quite so distant from me, that I might seek some comfort.

I have been afraid and yet I must not let the staff see my anxiety, nor let it trouble Darcy. He has said and done every possible thing to comfort me and allay my fears, but never having expected such a terrible thing to befall us in such a beautiful spot as this, I am still not able to restore my earlier calmness of mind. As I write, I look out over the park and my eyes track the stream to the point where the bridge lies across it and the path disappears into the woods. Seeing it now in the bright sunlight, it is hard to believe that just out of sight, in the shadow of those same trees, the attackers lurked in darkness. What might have befallen my dear husband had he been alone or had with him only Thomas, who is almost as old as Papa, I shudder to think.

Please do not be unduly alarmed, dearest Aunt, but it does seem to me that suddenly we are confronted with very different circumstances to those in which we grew up. I need very much to see you and talk with you before long, even if it is only to reassure myself that we are not in danger of losing that happy life we once enjoyed . . .

There was no doubt that Elizabeth had been badly shaken by the incident, and Mrs Gardiner had almost decided that she would take her daughters and go to Pemberley for a few days, when another letter, this time by Express Post, was delivered. Tearing it open, fearing it contained bad news, she stood in the hall reading it, with some degree of apprehension.

Moments later, with a joyful cry, Mrs Gardiner ran into her husband's room with the news that their niece Jane had been safely delivered, almost a month earlier than expected, of a son.

The letter, from Mr Bingley, begged Mrs Gardiner to come as soon as she could. Not only did Jane long to have her and Elizabeth at her side, but he was apprehensive that Mrs Bennet might arrive posthaste from Newcastle and take up residence at Netherfield, unless Jane had another companion already present.

While not wanting to appear disrespectful towards his mother-in-law, Bingley's lack of enthusiasm for such a visitation was quite plain. Jane, he said, had expressed a preference for the company of her aunt. Mrs Gardiner did not waste a moment. Instructions were given and arrangements made, notes despatched, and, finally, packing—that inevitable chore—was done, and less than twenty-four hours later, they were on their way.

Meanwhile, a similar letter, this one carried by a servant from Netherfield Park, had reached Elizabeth and Mr Darcy. In her excitement to be gone to her sister's side, all thoughts of footpads and ruffians were banished from her mind as she flew around the house, making preparations for the journey.

Seeing her thus—bright eyes shining, a smile constantly playing on her lips, humming a tune as she tripped briskly or ran to complete some task, Darcy was more than happy that, unexpectedly, the son of Bingley and Jane had arrived to restore Lizzie's happiness and with it his own.

A further reason for their joy lay in the invitation the letter contained to be godparents to young Jonathan Charles. For Darcy and Elizabeth, whose affection for Jane and Bingley was a very special part of their lives; it was an honour requested and promised many months ago. Elizabeth knew how much this child meant to her sister; she knew he would bring fulfilment to an already felicitous marriage. She longed to be there to share Jane's happiness.

It was with real joy in their hearts that they set off for Netherfield.

CHAPTER EIGHT
Of heirs and graces

N O CHILD, BORN BEFORE or since young Jonathan Charles Bingley, had or was ever likely to have such a clamour of congratulations and good-will surround its birth. That was the considered opinion of his grand-father, Mr Bennet, whose joy at the birth of Jane's son had left him with a look of perpetual felicity that was not at all in keeping with his usual sardonic view of life. Unlike his wife who had been in a state of high excitement about the birth of Lydia's son some months ago, Mr Bennet had succeeded in avoiding the event by virtue of its having taken place in Newcastle.

When news arrived that Jane had been prematurely brought to bed, however, he had felt it was his bounden duty to proceed to Netherfield House and keep his son-in-law company through the anxious hours until Jonathan was born. Thereafter, he was available to dispense refreshment and good news to any and everyone who called to inquire after the well-being of mother and child.

Whether it was the universally acknowledged beauty and sweet nature of his mother, the unfailingly amiable disposition of his father, or the recognition that there must be an heir to inherit the growing fortune of the Bingleys was not clear. Whatever the reason, there was no doubt that Netherfield Park was the nearest thing to a place of pilgrimage for the next week.

The birth of Master Bingley was an event of some circumstance in the neighbourhood. As the news became more widely known, friends, acquaintances, tenants, and nosey neighbours arrived, many bearing flowers, fruit, and other small tokens, some hoping for a little peep at Mrs Bingley and the baby and feeling very disappointed that Jane and her son were not as yet ready to receive visitors. The servants were run off their feet, and Mr and Mrs Gardiner were kept busy receiving the callers, since Charles Bingley hardly left his wife's side for long.

Mr Bingley had been profoundly grateful for the arrival of Mrs Gardiner, who immediately proceeded to take charge of the household, while her husband, in his thoroughly practical way, assisted with matters such as placing the usual notices in the appropriate journals and meeting the coach at Meryton— the coach on which Mrs Bennet was arriving from Newcastle. Only her brother would be able to convince Mrs Bennet that she was not required to rush immediately to Jane's side but should go home to Longbourn, where she could rest and change before visiting her daughter and grandson in the evening. Despite her loud protestations that she must surely go forthwith to "poor Jane," Mr Gardiner would have none of it. "Do not distress yourself, Sister, Jane is quite recovered, and little Jonathan seems very well indeed; his lungs are certainly in excellent order," said Mr Gardiner, persuading her that there was no immediate need to rush to Netherfield. "After your long journey from Newcastle, it would be best that you take some refreshment and rest awhile, before you call on them. Mrs Gardiner has been at Netherfield these last two days and is doing all that needs be done. You can rest assured Jane is well looked after."

"And where is Lizzie? Has she arrived?" Mrs Bennet asked.

"Mr and Mrs Darcy are expected at any time," her brother replied.

"Mr and Mrs Darcy! Oooh! Doesn't it sound grand?" Mrs Bennet swelled almost visibly with pride as she said it. "Do you know, Brother, when I mentioned their names in Newcastle among the regimental ladies—especially those who were Lydia's friends, they were just green with envy at the immense good fortune of our two girls. Lizzie and Jane have done so well." Her brother agreed and added that the news about Kitty was good also.

"Indeed it is, you could have knocked me down with a feather when Mr Bennet's letter arrived telling me Kitty was engaged! 'Kitty engaged,' I said, 'now isn't she the sly one!' Who would have thought? And brother, what an excellent match—the young man is Rector at Pemberley!"

Glad to have got her off the subject of going directly to Jane's bedside, Mr Gardiner instructed the driver to take the road to Longbourn, knowing how grateful the members of the family at Netherfield would be. Even better, he was to escort her there and return to Netherfield in the carriage, thereby ensuring that she had no independent means of transport, until Mr Bennet sent his carriage over to fetch her in the afternoon.

Mrs Gardiner was at the window of Jane's bedroom, looking out over the park and into the lane beyond, when she saw her husband's carriage turning into the drive. Close behind was another vehicle, which turned out to be carrying Darcy and Elizabeth, who had broken journey overnight, in London. Mrs Gardiner went quickly downstairs and out to greet them. Mr Gardiner had alighted and met them at the entrance. As the servants moved to unload their trunks, Elizabeth embraced her aunt and uncle and wanted to go to Jane at once. "Is she well?" she asked and on being reassured immediately added, "And Jonathan?"

"He is very tiny, but he's healthy, and he is a beautiful boy, Lizzie," replied her aunt, trying hard to keep up with Elizabeth as she ran up the stairs. As they reached the landing, Mr Bingley appeared at the top of the stairs, his face wreathed in smiles.

"My dear Lizzie, Jane has been longing to see you," he cried as he greeted her warmly and led her to Jane's room.

Jane's delight at seeing her sister at last was matched only by Elizabeth's own. She was paler and looked a little tired, but there was a glow, almost a luminous quality, about her face and a sweetness of expression that made Lizzie catch her breath. Her beauty, which had always been exceptional, had acquired a new fragility, like very fine china, which made her seem even more precious to a loving sister.

Leaving the sisters to embrace and exchange news, Bingley went to fetch Mr Darcy, while Mrs Gardiner fetched Jonathan from the nursery. Elizabeth was captivated by him, small, rosy, and fine-featured like his mother, with a little tuft of honey gold hair. Jonathan was still asleep, when Jane took him in her arms; Bingley stood beside her, ever the proud father.

Looking up at her husband, Lizzie saw the softening of his features as he smiled when little Jonathan opened his eyes. She bent and took the child from her sister's arms; as she did so, Jane, Bingley, and Mrs Gardiner exchanged glances at the very pretty grouping they made. There was no doubt in any of their minds that both Darcy and Elizabeth must long for their own child.

Later that day, when they were alone, Jane asked her sister the inevitable question. "Lizzie, you will not be angry at me for asking, will you?" she said, a little uncertainly.

"Of course not, dearest Jane, you know you can ask me anything. What's more, in this case, if you promise to keep a secret, I might just have a happy answer for you," Elizabeth replied. Jane was immediately excited and demanded to be told.

Elizabeth's face was suffused with colour as she explained that she was hopeful but unsure and needed to see the doctor before she could tell her husband the news. "I shall have to talk to my aunt first," she said, and Mrs Gardiner coming in with some tea for Elizabeth, overheard her remark and demanded to know what it was she was to be told, and why could it not be told now.

On hearing Elizabeth's news, she gave such a girlish whoop of delight that Lizzie had to hush her and beg that the knowledge be limited to the three of them until they had been to Meryton and seen the doctor. Jane was not at all sure she could keep it a secret from Bingley but promised solemnly to try her very best.

She did, however, make a very helpful suggestion that might obviate the need for Lizzie and her aunt to travel to Meryton, in what looked like worsening weather, to consult Dr Faulkner.

Jane explained that her own doctor was due to visit in a day or two and suggested that Elizabeth should consult him instead, thereby avoiding any possibility of the news that she had been to see a doctor in Meryton, getting out and about in the neighbourhood, with all the attendant rumour and gossip.

It was an idea that appealed to Elizabeth very much indeed. "How long can you stay with us, Lizzie?" Jane asked, to which her sister replied that while Darcy had business in London next week, she had no need to hurry back to Derbyshire for at least a couple of weeks.

"We must be back at Pemberley in October, for Rosamund's wedding, of course," she said. Jane explained that Jonathan's christening would be in three weeks' time, and Lizzie was sure they could both stay until then. "Should Darcy need to go back, he will certainly return for the christening," she said. Mrs Gardiner interposed that Mr Gardiner had told her he and Mr Darcy had business in London, which meant they would have the house to themselves for a few days. The words were hardly out of her mouth when there was a commotion and an eruption of noisy laughter downstairs, followed by the unmistakable voices of Mrs Bennet and her sister Mrs Phillips on the stairs. Soon afterwards, a maid appeared with the two ladies, who sailed into the room. Elizabeth tried to withdraw but not before her mother and her aunt had both remarked on how well she was looking and when was there going to be a new addition to the Darcy family? Elizabeth did not deign to answer, and since her sister was the real centre of attention, she succeeded in escaping further scrutiny.

Meanwhile, Mrs Bennet turned to Jane, "Jane, oh my dearest daughter, how fortunate you are that I was able to get away. Lydia could not have spared me two weeks ago; she has only just engaged a very suitable nurse, a Scottish woman, who comes highly recommended, to look after Henry. I must say, he is such a big boy already and so like his father." Elizabeth winced and was relieved when the nurse brought in little Jonathan for his grandmother's inspection. "Oh my dear, he is very small!" she cried, and Mrs Phillips agreed. Elizabeth, unable to bear it any longer, went quietly out of the room, feeling guilty at leaving her sister but knowing that Jane had always been able to cope better with their mother's ramblings.

At dinner, it was much the same. Mrs Bennet's tales of life "up North" with the "regimental ladies" as she insisted on calling them, took up most of the time, when she and Mrs Phillips were not giving Mr Bingley advice on bringing up Jonathan, advice Elizabeth was sure flowed over him, leaving no recollection whatsoever. Mercifully, her father, realising that neither his daughter nor his sons-in-law could be expected to put up with both Mrs Bennet and Mrs Phillips for an entire evening, declared that everyone must be very tired after all the travelling they had done, called for his carriage, and left for Longbourn, taking with him his wife and her sister. He could see the gratitude in Elizabeth's eyes as they said goodbye, even as Mrs Bennet was heard promising to return as soon as possible.

While her husband and brother-in-law were far too polite to show it, a huge sense of relief swept over Elizabeth. She hoped, nay she knew, her father would ensure that her mother would not be back for a day or two, at least. There would be dozens of household matters that would require her attention, and no doubt she would be wanting to call on Lady Lucas, Mrs Long, and all her other friends in the neighbourhood with her news and gossip from Newcastle. Feeling guilty at what she felt was her disloyalty but yet unable to do anything to change how she responded to her mother, Elizabeth decided to make the best of her time with Jane. She wanted to spend time with her sister. Jane and Lizzie had always been close, but the last two years had drawn them even closer, as their lives had been so totally changed, yet linked together through their husbands. With Mrs Gardiner taking charge of the household, the two sisters had their hearts' greatest wish, being left to their own devices—free to talk for hours together, except when Jane was called away to Jonathan. They had never been happier either: Jane, with every dream fulfilled, Elizabeth wanting only to fulfil her hope of a child to match her sister's happiness. Lizzie longed to tell her husband but determined to wait to be certain, not wanting the heartbreak of disappointment to touch him, too.

As they prepared to retire for the night, Lizzie asked Darcy when he was going to London with Mr Gardiner and how long they would be away. Darcy revealed their intention of leaving on the Monday and said they would probably be away all week, because they planned to visit a property in Derbyshire as well. When she expressed surprise, he explained that it concerned the Gardiners' desire to move out of London. A property had recently come to Darcy's attention, and he had recommended that Mr Gardiner take a look at it. Elizabeth's surprise turned to astonishment as he continued, "You see, dearest, following our little confrontation with the gentlemen from London, Sir Edmond was approached by an agent for two of them—absentee landlords both. They are losing money, and their land is losing its value. They want to sell out before the prices fall even further. Sir Edmond cannot make an offer, he's the magistrate who cautioned them—it would not be right, but he mentioned it to me, and since your uncle had often spoken of buying in Derbyshire, I thought immediately of him."

"My aunt will be delighted. She has always wanted to return to Derbyshire. You know how well she loves it," said Elizabeth.

"Indeed, I do," said her husband, "and that is the real value of this property. It is a manor house and farm, not five miles from Lambton, with its own trout stream, orchard, and dairy. Parts of the property have been recently enclosed and hedged for cultivation of corn, but the meadows and woodlands are still free and should probably be allowed to remain so. Now, if your uncle likes it, he may well be able to negotiate a very good price." Elizabeth was unable to control her delight.

"That means we shall be neighbours!" she cried.

"That thought had also crossed my mind, Lizzie," he said, clearly pleased as she threw her arms around his neck and hugged him, responding tenderly to the warmth of her affection.

Even sweeter news came on the following day, when Bingley announced that Ashford House in Leicestershire was ready and as soon as Jane was fit to travel, they would be moving in. Since the lease at Netherfield ran for two more months, "They would have ample time," he said, and added, "This time, it will be our pleasure to have you all over at Christmas." For Elizabeth, there was very little more she could ask for, except confirmation of her own special news. This came the following day, when Jane's doctor visited Netherfield Park and having pronounced Jane and Jonathan to be in excellent health, proceeded to see Elizabeth. He confirmed her hopes of a child, probably due next spring. Elizabeth, Mrs Gardiner, and Jane embraced each other and wept as the joy swept over them.

Mr Darcy and Mr Gardiner had been over to Meryton. On his return, Darcy looked for Elizabeth and not finding her downstairs, went in search of her. Finding her alone in their room, he was anxious and puzzled. She had obviously wept, but she was smiling. "What is it dearest?" he asked, with some trepidation. When she told him, she had the pleasure of seeing his usually serious face light up, as he picked her up in his arms.

"Elizabeth, my darling, are you sure?" She nodded and told him that she had seen Jane's doctor that very day, "He says it will be in Spring—probably in May." They kissed, embraced, and laughed, sharing a moment of very private joy, admitting to each other how much they had longed for this news.

Then, becoming serious again, they decided that apart from the Gardiners, Jane, and Bingley, they would tell no one else. "Dearest, I should like us to keep the pleasure of this blessed news to ourselves for a little while," he said, and Lizzie agreed. She also wished to savour the joy of knowing and keeping her secret, before the whole family and the neighbourhood demanded their share.

"We shall tell them after Jonathan's christening, when we are about to leave for Pemberley," he suggested. "That way, we shall not have you set about with everyone in the neighbourhood giving you advice."

"How well you know me already," she said, softly, "that was my wish exactly." It was for both of them the greatest moment of happiness they had known so far. Darcy confessed he had not expected such joy, but Elizabeth, not letting him grow too sombre, reminded him that they had decided, a year or more ago, that they were to be the happiest couple in the world. Catching her mood, Darcy responded warmly. "Of course," he said, smiling, "and you must never let me forget it."

❦

If one had wished to paint a sky of a brilliant blue and tinge the autumn leaves of the oaks in shades of russet and gold, one might have done worse than paint the day when young Jonathan Charles Bingley was baptised. Proud grandparents, parents, and godparents vied with friends and neighbours to get a glimpse of the little boy who seemed to bring a smile to the face of everyone who set eyes upon him. Jane and Bingley were overwhelmed with good wishes. No one in the neighbourhood could remember so much interest in the birth of a child before, but then, as Elizabeth said to her husband, "Jane is a very special person."

It was indeed a memorable event and a beautiful early Autumn day for it. Not even the presence of Bingley's sisters, Mrs Hurst and Caroline, who had travelled from Bath for the christening, could spoil Elizabeth's joy. Looking particularly well herself, with her own secret shared only with those dearest to her heart, Elizabeth graced the baptism of her nephew with a confidence that no amount of insincerity and artifice on the part of the Bingley sisters could shake.

Of artifice there was certainly a good deal, for both women seemed determined to make themselves, rather than Jane or Jonathan, the centre of attention. Dressing in the very latest of modish clothes and wearing hats trimmed with spectacular plumes, they might have been attending the Coronation at the Abbey, rather than a simple family christening at a country church. Jane, wearing her favourite shade of blue and a completely natural Madonna-like smile, put them all to shame. Bingley, together with most of the congregation, had eyes for none other.

So wrote Elizabeth to her friend Charlotte Collins. Charlotte was unable to travel to Hertfordshire; she was close to being delivered of her second child. She had written, however, begging to be excused and promising to call on Jane when she came to Lucas Lodge at Christmas. Elizabeth had to inform her that her sister and brother-in-law would be gone before Christmas to their new place in Leicestershire.

> *Jane has asked me, dear Charlotte, to say how much she appreciates your pretty gift and kind wishes. She hopes sincerely that you and Mr Collins will find time to visit them and stay a few days at Ashford House, prefer- ably in April or May, when it will be very pretty with the Spring. Dear Charlotte, if I may add my own good wishes and ask you to consider com- ing to Pemberley as well, since we are but twenty miles from Ashford Park, it will be a pleasure to have you.*

Elizabeth's affection for her friend remained undiminished, despite the stu- pidity of Mr Collins and her initial anger at Charlotte for accepting him. She was even more pleased to discover that Darcy had a very good opinion of the character and good sense of Mrs Collins, though he could not abide the pompous verbosity of her husband.

There was also the extra affection she merited for having invited Elizabeth to stay at Hunsford two years ago, thereby providing for her an opportunity to visit Rosings and meet Mr Darcy and Colonel Fitzwilliam in a social setting far removed from the tribulations of Longbourn or Meryton, which had so afflicted Mr Darcy.

She had, on occasion, teased her husband and obtained from him a confes- sion that he had been trying hard to put her out of his mind, when he met her again, quite unexpectedly, at Rosings. "And do tell me, were you on the verge of success?" she would ask, determined to obtain full value for her question. Darcy looked shamefaced as he admitted that he had not been succeeding at all.

"It was not for lack of trying, my dearest Lizzie, but as you know, I was totally out of my depth. Finding you staying with Mrs Collins, so close at hand, made it a hopeless proposition."

"So, it is to Charlotte we owe at least some part of our present happiness?" she asked, and Darcy gladly admitted that this was indeed the case. Elizabeth also took her friend into her confidence about the child she was expecting in May, hoping Charlotte would find it an added reason for visiting Pemberley next Spring.

Elizabeth's parents were told after dinner, on the last evening of their stay at Netherfield Park. The uproar at Longbourn, with her father's quiet pleasure being totally eclipsed by the jubilation of her mother, who would no doubt feel compelled to advise the entire neighbourhood of her daughter's condition, convinced Elizabeth that she had done the right thing by concealing the news until the last possible moment.

The wedding of Rosamund Camden and James Fitzwilliam should have been a big social event. Preparations were afoot for a celebration of some considerable significance.

As it happened, the sudden death of the bride's mother, a month from the appointed wedding day, caused a complete change of plan. The family decided that despite their grief at the loss of their mother, it would be better to proceed with Rosamund's wedding. Sir Edmond, devoted as he was to his wife of some twenty-five years, could not countenance the disappointment his daughter would suffer, if she were compelled to postpone her wedding.

A few days after the funeral, Rosamund and her father came to Pemberley to explain that there would not be the lavish wedding they had planned but only a family breakfast after the ceremony at the church, to which close friends and relations would be asked.

Elizabeth had not known Lady Camden at all well, but her friendship with Rosamund was warm and sincere. Her grief affected Elizabeth deeply, and feeling rather helpless, she offered to assist in any way she could.

Writing later to Jane, she explained:

Poor Rosamund, it is the worst possible thing, to be so bereft just before her wedding. Dear Jane, it is difficult for me to know how deeply she feels the loss of her mother, since I have never been as close to Mama as Rosamund was to Lady Camden. Being the only daughter must also have made the bond stronger, and apart from myself and Georgiana, she has really no one to whom she might turn for consolation.

Elizabeth gave Jane an account of all that had taken place. She could not resist including more praise for the generosity of her husband and his concern for the Camdens:

It is not only his family and mine that benefit from his generous nature; it is anyone in his circle who needs his help. I had not known how often he has extended his hand to help those who live on his estate, until Mrs. Reynolds enlightened me, when I made casual mention of it while we were visiting Rushmore Farm. Dear Jane, because he speaks rarely of it, his work in helping people in need is not widely known. It is not just our sister Lydia and Wickham, however undeserving, who have recently been beneficiaries of his goodness.

In a similar letter to her Aunt Gardiner, Elizabeth noted that she was sure she was not telling her anything she did not already know, recalling that only a year or two ago, Mr and Mrs Gardiner had recognised the nobility of Darcy's character, long before she did.

She wrote:

Of course, I may plead that in my case, I had not been privy to the words and deeds that you and my uncle were able to hear and see. I cannot, however, excuse my own prejudice, which had for so long blinded me to the qualities that you were able to recognise in him, because you were sufficiently clear sighted and had not permitted your judgement to be clouded by rumour and malice.

After the wedding, Elizabeth wrote again to her sister, expressing some degree of surprise:

We had all had some fears for Rosamund, knowing she was sure to recall her mother at almost every moment. But truly, Jane, we need not have worried. Rosamund was calm and very composed that morning. Mr Darcy believes that James and Rosamund are well-matched and will be happily married. I am inclined to agree, though I do not have his advantage of knowing both parties since childhood.

Jane, I know you will be very glad to hear that our dear Kitty did very well with the little Children's Choir, which performed so beautifully, everyone remarked upon the sweetness of their singing. There was, especially, a little Welsh hymn taught to the children by Mr Jenkins, that was quite perfect. We are all very proud of Kitty, Georgiana, and the children, of course.

Now that the wedding is over, Kitty and Mr Jenkins are to visit Longbourn, so he can be introduced to Mama. They leave tomorrow with Georgiana for London, where they will stay with Uncle and Aunt Gardiner (Kitty means to purchase some of her trousseau in London, and our aunt has kindly consented to advise her, for Kitty knows nothing of London) and then proceed with my aunt as companion to Longbourn. No doubt, Mama will make a great deal of the matter of meeting Mr Jenkins. I look forward to receiving from you, my dear sister, a complete account of the visit. While they are all away, Darcy plans that we should visit a family property in Wales. I saw one of them when we were travelling last year after our wedding, but I had not the time nor, I confess, the calmness of mind, to fully appreciate the beauty of the countryside. This time I shall do better, though I wish I could sketch and paint as Georgiana does. You will have to be satisfied with my descriptions.

Do give our love to your husband and darling Jonathan. We look forward to seeing you all at Christmas.

Your loving sister,

Lizzie.

CHAPTER NINE

New vistas

A DAY OR TWO BEFORE Darcy and Elizabeth set off on their journey to South Wales, a letter arrived for Darcy from Bingley's brother-in-law Mr Hurst. Writing from London, he advised that they—that is, Mr and Mrs Hurst and Miss Caroline Bingley—were joining a large party from Bath, where they now lived for most of the year, to travel to Paris. "Paris?" cried Elizabeth as Darcy read the letter aloud, "Why Paris?"

"Patience, my dear Lizzie, the answer to your question follows," said her husband and proceeded to read the letter. It said that Paris, after the defeat of Napoleon Bonaparte, was fast becoming a fashionable, cosmopolitan city, worthy of a visit by a party from England. Mr Hurst assured Mr Darcy that he had been told by many gentlemen of quality, who had recently crossed the Channel, that there were already a number of prominent members of the English and Irish aristocracy who had set up fine establishments in Paris and entertained French and visiting English persons at soirées and coffee parties. He named a couple of ladies of very high renown indeed and suggested that his wife had obtained assurances that they would be invited to their famous cultural gatherings. As Darcy read on, Elizabeth became more puzzled by the writer's motive in penning the letter until at the penultimate paragraph, Darcy suddenly stopped and exclaimed, "Good God! He invites us to join them! Lizzie, Mr and

Mrs Hurst would be delighted if you and I would join their party. It seems they had hoped Bingley and Jane would go, but the arrival of Jonathan has rather dashed their hopes." Elizabeth could not believe her ears, and when he added, "What do you say, Lizzie, shall it be the salons of Paris or the valleys of Wales?" she laughed out loud.

"I cannot imagine why they would choose to invite us; what motive could they possibly have?"

"I dare not speculate upon that, Lizzie, but Hurst has obviously decided to ensure he has some company; he cannot know too many of the party from Bath. He has realised that he would be on his own, while his wife and Caroline attended all those soirées and parties, and has decided to persuade us to join them." Elizabeth could not believe that it was a prospect her husband would appreciate.

"How fortunate that we are already engaged to go to Wales," she said, quietly. Darcy smiled rather mischievously and said, "My feelings exactly, my dear, I shall write at once and decline on the grounds that we are about to leave for Wales, which has, I might add, a remarkable number of County families, some excellent houses, and some of the most beautiful landscapes in the country. I cannot vouch for salons and soirées, but I can wager we shall not miss them. Do you not agree, my dear?"

Elizabeth laughed and agreed that indeed they would not.

When she wrote of this quite amazing occurrence to her Aunt Gardiner, Elizabeth did not fail to mention the obvious scorn that Darcy had shown for the Parisian expedition of the Hursts and Caroline Bingley, nor the delight she herself had taken in it:

Imagine if you would, dear Aunt, Mrs Hurst and Caroline, dressed in the height of fashion, complete with plumed chapeaux, attending the salons and soirees of Lady X or Dame Y. Maybe I am unduly suspicious, but I cannot help feeling that the invitation came at the behest of the Bingley women, who must have hoped to show me up as a country girl with none of the sophistication and panache one expects of the aspiring Parisienne! I need not tell you how delighted I was when Darcy wrote to decline (not that there was any danger of our ever accepting) on account of a previous arrangement to visit Wales. I quote from his letter, "I have long wanted to show Elizabeth the very particular beauty of South Wales, including the magnificent Brecon Beacons area, which lies to the East of the property my family acquired some fifty years ago. We are both looking forward to it very much indeed."

By the time Mrs Gardiner received her letter, Darcy and Elizabeth had already left Pemberley, travelling through Birmingham, Worcester, and Cheltenham, where they broke journey, before crossing into Wales.

This was now a journey of many shared pleasures, since Elizabeth was inclined to hold Darcy to his promise in his letter to Mr Hurst, to show her all the particular beauties of South Wales. They stayed at little towns and villages until they finally reached the manor house a few miles uphill from Llandovery, an old Celtic market town, which traced its history back to a Roman fort and its reputation as a commercial centre to a licence to trade granted by Richard the Third. The property that Mr Darcy's family had acquired lay in the fertile upper Towy valley, reaching from the softly undulating pasturelands to the rocky foothills of the Cambrian mountains. An abundance of trout in the rivers and streams as well as plenty of game catered for the tastes of the gentlemen, but for Elizabeth there was no greater pleasure than walking. Although under serious orders not to overtire herself, she would spend many happy hours with her maid, an avid walker herself, exploring the woods and meadows, while Darcy attended to matters of business with his Steward.

In Wales, too, the pressure to enclose land was growing, but on Darcy's property, which ran cattle, produced food, and provided many men and women with good farm jobs, there was none. There was, however, another problem that was spreading rapidly through the countryside of the English Midlands and South Wales. The presence of coal in huge quantities had always meant that some areas of the country were destined to be industrialised. The demand for coal, essential to the iron and steel industry, meant increasing numbers of men, women, and children moving to the squalid little towns that clustered around the mines. Smoke, grime, and the ubiquitous slag heaps dominated the once-pretty landscapes of many parts of England and Wales, as well as the lives of the hapless people who laboured and lived there.

Elizabeth had remarked upon the freshness of the air in the Towy valley, but her husband had looked rather sombre and responded that there was no knowing how long it would last. Finding him somewhat melancholy one evening, Elizabeth asked if she may share his thoughts. Immediately contrite at having shut her out, he was keen to explain, "I'm sorry, dearest, it is not that I do not wish to share my concerns with you; it is more a matter of my inability to understand them myself. We have spent several days here, enjoying the magnificence of the Welsh landscape, and yet all the time the threat of an expanding coal industry hangs over it. There seems to be an irresistible power in the hands of those who own these mines. They control the government and are able to roll over the objections of any local landholders." Elizabeth was shocked at his sense of helplessness.

"But surely, there are no plans for mines here?"

"Not just now, but I am told the Lord—— has been making inquiries; should he succeed in securing mining rights on the slopes above the river, there would be very little we could do. The slag heaps would cover the hillsides, and the streams would be choked with run-off from the mines." He sounded so unhappy that Elizabeth said nothing for a few minutes; then, wanting to console him, she sighed and said,

"At least, they cannot touch Pemberley." He smiled and took her hand, "Yes, they can never get their hands on Pemberley, but Lizzie, this is more than just a question of Pemberley and my family; it is a matter of England's heritage; this landscape is all we have. To despoil it is to destroy our children's inheritance. I am determined to see that this valley is not destroyed, if I can possibly help it."

Elizabeth wrote to Jane and again to her aunt—quiet, serious letters from the heart:

There is so much beauty here and yet, so much ugliness, lying in wait to tear it all apart for profit. Every day, we see places of spectacular beauty, but because they are within reach of coal miners, they seem doomed to become part of the great black mass that is spreading across the land. Darcy is very depressed at the way the countryside is being despoiled and vows he will do something about it.

On the last night they spent at Llandeilo, they dined with the family of Sir Tristram Williams, who had been a friend of Darcy's father and whose mother was related to his aunt, Lady Catherine. They talked of the unhappy state of England's rural people. Darcy had heard a number of alarming reports of action by desperate labourers and miners who were being thrown out of work by greedy mine and factory owners, cutting their losses in the face of a deepening recession. Sir Tristram's son, a lad not yet eighteen home on vacation from College, railed against the "do-nothing government" and determined that he would join the Reform Party and enter Parliament, since that was the only way to stop their mendacity.

He surprised them even more with his support for his older sister, Jessica, who declared that women should have the vote, because, "We would then elect some of the right people to the Parliament at Westminster, not just landlords and mill-owners, whose only interest is in increasing their own wealth. England needs some Reformers," she said.

"I shall be one of them, and I shall teach the slavers and spoilers a lesson," declared her brother, fiercely.

David's parents indulged him and smiled at his fiery sentiments, but Darcy said later that he wished he had been as keenly aware as David, with as much determination to right the wrongs that he could see around him. "Unfortunately, when I was young David's age, I was too satisfied with my own life to even think about the problems of others. I see now that the selfish lives we led, ill prepared us to recognise our real enemies." Elizabeth protested, "Darcy, I will not have you say that. You are not selfish; indeed you are quite the least selfish man I know."

"That, my dearest, is because I have, thanks in no small measure to you, learned my lesson. A little late, perhaps, but it is well-learned," he replied. "I promise you, Lizzie, I will do everything I can to teach our children their duty, not just to their family and friends but to all those who share this land with us." Elizabeth was able by now to recognise determination in his voice. She knew he meant every word.

Leaving Wales, they stopped at an inn, where, to their horror, they learned of a dreadful accident which had cost several travellers their lives, when a coach had overturned, throwing its passengers into a gorge. Despite the best efforts of engineers and road builders all over England, many roads were still quite hazardous. Elizabeth was depressed by the bad news and longed to be back at Pemberley—her safe haven of stability in an increasingly changeable world.

It was late evening when they reached the surrounding woodlands, and Elizabeth looked out as if she was making the approach for the first time, realising now how much she had come to regard it as her home. She loved the glow of the setting sun on the reddening Autumn foliage and never failed to be impressed by the first glimpse of the stone work of the house, as it came into view on the far side of the valley. She felt a deep sense of peace and well-being, which seemed to seep in from her surroundings and fill her heart and mind. As if he had read her thoughts, Darcy took her hand to help her out, smiled, and said simply, "Here we are, Lizzie; is it not good to be home?"

"Oh, indeed, it is," she replied, with a heartfelt sigh of relief.

There were several letters waiting for them at Pemberley. Elizabeth, having greeted Mrs Reynolds and instructed her maid Jenny on the disposition of her luggage, hurried to her room to read hers. By the time Darcy came upstairs, she had scanned them once very quickly and was about to settle down to read them over again.

The first letter she opened brought good news from her Aunt Gardiner. She wrote of Kitty and Mr Jenkins, whom they both had come to like very well, for his gentle humour and perfect manners:

> *Were he not a clergyman, dearest Lizzie, one would have felt constrained to suggest that he had missed his calling. He is all that Kitty needs to counter balance her immaturity, and yet he seems to enjoy and value her youthful enthusiasm greatly. He could not be stopped from describing in minutest detail all the effort Kitty and Georgiana had put into the training of the Children's Choir; their performance at the wedding of Miss Camden was no less than perfection, we are told. It certainly augurs well for their union that he is so pleased with her and she is so eager to please him.*

There was more about their shopping expeditions and Kitty's choice of a particular shade of green for a winter gown that Mr Jenkins liked and much more. This brought a smile to Elizabeth's lips.

Jane's letter, which had been written over several days, was more in the nature of jottings in a diary than a letter. She had had very little time to write about anything in detail, except for a visit from her in-laws, the Hursts and Miss

Bingley, recording in somewhat incredulous words the fact that they were going to Paris!

Just think, Lizzie, they are with a large party from Bath—retired generals and admirals mostly, who wish to see Paris after the end of Bonaparte! Can you imagine Caroline Bingley and her sister among them? They spoke of invitations to salons and soirées, but with only Mr Hurst to escort them, I cannot believe they will enjoy it very much. Indeed, Mr Bingley tells me Caroline has some French, mainly to read and sing, but not to parlais and Mrs Hurst has none at all. Lizzie, without a sound understanding of French, I confess I am confused as to how they will get on.

Jane was clearly puzzled. Elizabeth laughed and read it all out to Darcy, who responded with a comment that it was to be hoped that there would always be a couch available at the soirées, large enough to accommodate Mr Hurst, when he fell asleep during the recitals.

Jane also had news of Kitty:

Kitty is expected with Aunt Gardiner tomorrow and we are to dine at Longbourn on Thursday. I shall write again to give you an account of the occasion, but from what our father has said, I imagine it will be one of Mama's favourite days. The Lucases and the Longs are invited, and no doubt Aunt Phillips will attend. I am very glad Aunt Gardiner is to be with us.

Jane apologised for the shortness of her letter and the scrappiness of its execution; little Jonathan had been unwell with a cold and needed her all the time, she explained. She concluded with love to both of them and wishes they were with her also. Jane's eternally generous and kind nature would not let her say it, but her sister could sense the frustration she felt at having to shield Kitty and Mr Jenkins from the excesses of her mother, without Elizabeth beside her for support.

Most interesting of all Elizabeth's letters was one from Georgiana Darcy. She had spent a week with the Continis—an Italian family with whom they had become friends some years ago, in London. A talented and artistic couple, they had immediately liked Georgiana, and with her brother's permission, she had accompanied them to the Opera and recitals of Chamber Music by an Italian maestro.

Georgiana wrote enthusiastically of galleries visited and a particularly beautiful performance of "The Magic Flute" which she had attended with the Continis, only to find Dr Grantley in the audience:

Signora Contini invited him to join us in their box, and afterwards he came to supper at Portman Square, and it was quite remarkable how much he knew of Mozart and the Opera. Dr Grantley is in London to attend a Synod of the Church, which he has explained to me is the Parliament of the Church of England. They have long discussions and make important decisions about the Church, he says. He is therefore very busy all day, but Signor and Signora Contini have invited him to dine with us again at the end of the week on the day before we are due to return to Pemberley. For that evening, Signora Contini has engaged a String Quartet, and she suggests that I might join them in a performance of a Piano quintet, the music only recently received from Paris. It is very beautiful, and while I do not know if I shall succeed, I intend to practice every day to master it. Dr Grantley is very sure that I shall, but then he is always very kind.

There was no mistaking the affectionate tone of her letter, and Elizabeth wondered if it was not time to talk to her young sister-in-law about Dr Grantley.

Meanwhile, Darcy's silence on the subject puzzled her. She passed the letter to him and watched as he read it. A slight smile was all he permitted himself as he handed it back to her. "Georgiana seems to be enjoying herself in London," she remarked, hoping to draw him out.

"She always does," he said. "The Continis are very fond of her; they lost a young daughter some years ago and treat Georgiana as if she were their own. Signora Contini is a singer of some renown, and her husband is a very keen patron of the arts. It means my sister is well-placed to see and hear some remarkable performances when she is with them."

This did not satisfy Lizzie at all. She was not looking for a dissertation on the Continis and the Arts rather for some insight into Darcy's thinking on the subject of Dr Grantley and Georgiana. She tried again, using a different opening,

"What a coincidence that they should meet Dr Grantley at the Opera." This time Darcy put down his own letter, smiled, and shook his head.

"You must do better than that, my dear; I know you wish to talk about them, but until there is something to speak of, I have nothing to say." He was smiling, but his expression gave nothing away.

"Oh you are vexing," she cried and then, deciding that she was going to play the same game, "Ah well, I suppose I shall have to wait to hear it from Georgiana, when she returns." Elizabeth was certain that Darcy had noticed the growing friendship between his sister and his dearest friend. She was impatient to discover his thoughts, but she had too much respect for him to pry—knowing he would tell her when he was ready. But her patience was wearing thin.

Elizabeth awoke the next morning before the sun had climbed above the wooded hills behind the house. Darcy had risen and was out riding, as he did most mornings before breakfast. Looking out over the park, she was sure she could see him with his groom in the distance, but so deep were the shadows in that part of the park, that she could not be certain. Her husband's dressing room afforded a clearer view of the path leading from the woods. Elizabeth went through the unlocked door to the window, beside which stood his desk. His manservant had obviously been and laid out his clothes; beside them, fallen to the floor, was a letter, two pages of fine white paper, closely written in perfect copperplate. Before she realised what she was doing, Elizabeth had picked it up and unfolded it to reveal the writer's name. When she saw who it was, she stood still as if rooted to the spot. The letter was from Dr Grantley; it was dated from London—just three days ago. Elizabeth recalled immediately that it had been written some twenty-four hours after Georgiana's letter to her. Why had Darcy not revealed its contents to her? Elizabeth was very confused, and against every one of her normal instincts except that of curiosity alone, against her better judgement, she read quickly, her cheeks burning, fearful lest a servant should come in and find her.

What she read only confirmed her own observations. Dr Grantley was deeply in love with Georgiana but had not approached her until he was sure of his own feelings and her brother's judgment. Having met her again in London, he was convinced of his own inability to go on seeing her without revealing his feelings and attempting to discover if they were welcome and perhaps returned. Yet, he wanted Darcy's permission to do so. "Oh why do you all need his permission?"

Lizzie almost cried out loud—recalling Bingley and Jane, "Why do you not follow your heart?" Reading on, she found the reason. Dr Grantley was aware of the cruel episode involving Wickham, which had so nearly wrecked Georgiana's life. Darcy had confided in him at the time, and he did not wish to do anything that would cause either Georgiana or Darcy any pain or hurt. Elizabeth soon understood why Darcy had said nothing to her. Dr Grantley begged him to treat the entire matter in confidence, until it was resolved.

> *I ask it only because, whatever happens, I cannot break with you and your family. Darcy, you are such precious friends, that I should be desolated to lose you—should your sister not accept me. If that should happen, or you should feel that I am too old for her or have some other objection to my suit, it would be a terrible loss, but so much worse if it meant that I could not continue our friendship, because my affections and my disappointment were too widely known and spoken of. I have no right to ask this of you, Darcy, but because we have been as brothers for many years, I hope it will not be too difficult for you to agree.*

Elizabeth hurriedly folded up the letter and left it as she had found it. The rest, what she could recall of it, simply spoke of his love for Georgiana and asked Darcy's permission to propose marriage to her. There was a further paragraph containing a proposal for a trust to be set up, so the considerable income from her inheritance should be saved for her future use, but Elizabeth wanted to know nothing more. She ran back to her room and washed her burning cheeks with cool water. Jenny came in with her tea and informed her that Mr Darcy had sent a servant to Lambton, with an urgent packet for the mail, to go immediately to London.

Elizabeth tried to appear unconcerned, "It was probably a business matter for Mr Gardiner," she said, knowing full well it was Darcy's response to Dr Grantley.

She did not know how she would get through the day; Georgiana was due home the following evening. Poor Elizabeth, she had never meant to deceive him, yet there was no reasonable way to tell her husband what she had done and avoid his censure. How could she compromise the trust they shared? What possible excuse could she offer and be forgiven? Feeling wretched and unhappy, she feigned a headache and retired to her room, drawing the blinds and urging her maid to make her excuses. She had no appetite for breakfast. She was sure Mrs Reynolds and Darcy would put the appropriate construction upon it, recalling she was weary from the long journey home. Before she went to bed, she bathed her face again and prayed that Darcy would be late returning from his ride around the grounds.

Some hours later, she awoke to find him sitting beside her, worried that she had been taken ill and anxious to know if he should send for the doctor. Elizabeth immediately sat up and feeling a little unsteady, was glad of his arm to help her out of bed. Having reassured himself that she was not in need of a doctor, he sent for Jenny. On coming downstairs later, Elizabeth found her husband waiting for her in the morning room. She suggested in a bright but not very convincing voice that she should ask for some tea, and though Darcy did not demur, it was quite clear that he was preoccupied.

After tea, he took her arm and led her out into the gentle Autumn sunlight on the terrace and closed the doors leading from the house. There, to her amazement, he apologised to her. He told her he was sorry he had been rather short with her the day before; he had not intended to hurt her feelings or refuse to answer her questions; he had been protecting the confidences of another. Today, he had taken action that enabled him to be more forthcoming.

Elizabeth was by now even more confused. With the dubious advantage of having read Dr Grantley's letter, she had no idea how it was now possible for him to talk about it to her, without breaking a confidence. Worse still, she could not reveal her own knowledge without totally losing his trust. While all these wretched thoughts whirled through her mind, Darcy took out two heavily folded letters—one she recognised as Dr Grantley's, and the other was in his own hand and on his personal notepaper. He passed them to her in the order in which they were to be read. Sitting down, Elizabeth read again, slowly and carefully this time, the letter she had raced through that morning. Then, without saying a word, she reached out for the other and read it through. It was obviously a copy of the letter he had sent to London; in it, Darcy not merely gave his friend his blessing but came as close as he possibly could to giving him hope of success. Darcy reassured Dr Grantley of his good opinion, his love, and his best wishes for the fulfilment of his friend's dearest wish.

He added:

Based upon every indication I have had and keeping in mind that young ladies cannot always be expected to tell their older brothers everything, I feel I am able, Francis, to assure you that Georgiana has the very highest regard for you. Her most recent letter to Elizabeth, after your meeting in London, contains a degree of affection and esteem she has never before expressed for anyone. I am convinced she loves you, though whether she knows how well or how deeply, I cannot speculate. That, I am sure, you will discover soon enough. Elizabeth and I will look forward to seeing both of you on Sunday at Pemberley, with, I hope and trust, some good tidings. Since writing this, I will have shown Elizabeth your letter and my reply. I have not spoken of it to her or any one else until now, but I know you above all others will understand the need for me to tell my wife, for there are no secrets between us. I know she shares my good opinion of you and will wish you success. God bless you both until we meet,
  Yours etc,
  Fitzwilliam Darcy.

When Elizabeth had finished reading, she handed Darcy both letters. He had expected her to be full of questions, but she turned very quietly and embraced him, letting him hold her as tears filled her eyes. Conveniently, Darcy attributed her emotional response to the state of her health as well as her affection and love for Georgiana. "You do approve then?" he asked, a little uncertainty in his voice.

"Of course I do," she cried, smiling for the very first time that morning. "I have been so anxious for her, seeing her falling in love with him, not knowing how he felt nor how you would respond, unable to say a word to protect her from disappointment if things had not turned out right. Yet I knew that he would surely speak to you first, and when you said nothing to me, I was afraid it would all come to nothing. My anxiety was for dear Georgiana, I was not prying or wanting to gossip." Darcy hushed her at once, "Of course not; I never thought for a moment that you were. Yet, as you could see from his letter, Francis had begged me not to speak of his love to anyone, lest it all came to nothing in the end. He had the same concerns. But as you can also see, as soon as I was able, I wrote to him and told him that you had to know—I could not keep it from you, my dearest Elizabeth. You do understand, do you not?" She smiled, accepting everything; glad that her small sum of guilt could now be repaid tenfold with love and trust.

On the following day, preparations were afoot for the return of Georgiana. Her favourite rooms were opened up and aired, and all was in readiness. When the carriage turned into the drive, Elizabeth, watching from an upstairs window, smiled and turned to her husband, "It is settled for certain, they are both here." Darcy agreed that it was unlikely that they would have undertaken the journey from London together, had Dr Grantley been refused. When they alighted and he helped her out, the expression of sweet contentment on her face told the story. Mrs Annesley was no sooner out of the carriage than she whispered in Mrs Reynold's ear, "They are engaged," which caused such a joyous reaction as to bring tears to her eyes. She was seeing her little girl grown up, and it was too much for the usually dignified Mrs Reynolds.

Georgiana embraced her brother and thanked him before turning to Elizabeth and hugging her close. "I shall tell you everything, Lizzie," she promised. For the moment, there was enough happiness around to warm all their hearts.

After dinner, while Georgiana and Dr Grantley repaired to the music room, Darcy explained to Elizabeth what arrangements were proposed to be put in place for Georgiana. Dr Grantley had been ignorant of the extent of her private fortune until very recently. This had given him pause, not wishing to be thought some kind of fortune hunter—but having consulted his lawyers, he had suggested to Darcy that a trust be set up to protect her inheritance and preserve its income, for the sole use of herself and any children they may have. Having a good income of his own, he believed Georgiana's interests would be best served by retaining her current guardians—Mr Darcy and Colonel Fitzwilliam—as trustees.

Darcy, though not for a moment would he have questioned the motives of his dearest friend, was delighted, because it would clearly mark him as a man apart from the fortune hunters, against whom he had always been vigilant on his sister's behalf. "Have you no reservations about the difference in their ages?" asked his wife. It was a matter she had been anxious to discuss, but Darcy showed no such concern, saying only that he felt Georgiana needed the strength and security of a man she could trust and depend upon, knowing his declared love was a mature and genuine emotion.

"It is in her interest, and knowing Francis Grantley as well as I do, I can safely say that there is no man to whom I would entrust her with greater certainty of her happiness," he said with such conviction that Elizabeth knew there was no room for doubt.

Writing to her aunt, Elizabeth broke the news with great pleasure:

After the unhappy experience with Wickham, it is not surprising that the family would be wary of suitors, especially young and impecunious ones! Dr Grantley, a scholar of repute with a good income in his own right, was apparently quite unaware of the size of Georgiana's fortune. He was drawn to her because of their shared interests, her elegance, good taste, and gentle nature. I might add, and I am sure you would agree, dear Aunt, that she has also freshness and a youthful loveliness, assets one would find difficult to ignore. When he did become aware of her inheritance, he was determined to find a way to divest himself of it. It is typical of Dr Grantley that he should want to avoid any taint of the fortune hunter. I believe they have also decided upon a longer engagement than usual, wishing to wait until after Georgiana's eighteenth birthday—next Spring. Meanwhile, we look forward to entertaining Dr Grantley very often at Pemberley. Darcy is absolutely delighted, of course, to entrust his beloved sister to one of his best and most trusted friends. He has only tonight written a letter to Colonel Fitzwilliam in Ceylon, giving him the good news.

Let me take your mind back, dear Aunt, to the time when we were led to believe by Miss Bingley that her brother was very partial to Miss Darcy. Judging from Mr Darcy's remarks, which carried not a single hint of ambiguity on the suitability of Dr Grantley, would you not agree that Miss Bingley's remarks were more in the nature of wishful thinking? She hoped, no doubt, to promote her own cause as much as her brother's. How totally are the tables turned. Mrs Reynolds is almost speechless with joy. She thoroughly approves of Francis Grantley, and while I am sure she cannot believe that any mortal person is good enough for her dear Miss Georgiana, Dr Grantley must come close. With this high degree of agreement and general satisfaction, you can imagine that we, at Pemberley, are at present enjoying a singularly pleasant and happy atmosphere. It wants only the addition of yourselves to make perfection.

On the day following, as if there was an insufficiency of good news, a letter arrived from Mr Gardiner confirming that he had closed the deal with the agents for the purchase of the property at Lambton. Having taken Mrs Gardiner and all the children to see it and being assured that everyone loved it, for one reason or the other, he wrote:

> *I must be forever in your debt, Mr Darcy, for having drawn my attention to this property. My family, especially Mrs Gardiner, is delighted with the place, and the added pleasure of being but five miles from Pemberley has sent young Caroline into transports of delight. She is, as you know, Elizabeth's particular favourite and looks forward to seeing more of her in the future. In the New Year, when both our boys will be enrolled at school in Oxford, we hope to move to Oakleigh Manor.*
>
> *Meanwhile, we—that is yourself, Mr Bingley, and I—should meet to discuss arrangements for our London offices, since I expect to sell the house on Gracechurch Street. We should have no great difficulty finding suitable offices to rent nearer our warehouses. Many businessmen and stock traders have sold out or gone bankrupt. Commercial property is fast losing value; we should be able to take advantage of the market, since we have not suffered similar devastation.*

Mr Gardiner, whose long experience in trade and commerce had stood them all in good stead with the onset of the recession that was tightening its grip over England, explained the need for planning. His well-honed skills, combined with Darcy's natural caution and Bingley's willingness to take sound advice even if it meant quelling his own enthusiasm, had successfully steered them away from speculative ventures and debt—the twin destroyers of men and institutions of the day. Husbanding their joint resources and holding them available for future investment had proved an excellent policy. Now he was advising them to plan ahead, look beyond the present misfortunes to an England that would certainly recover, and be ready to take advantage of the upward swing.

> *Make no mistake, Mr Darcy, this recession will surely end, and when the market is at the very bottom of the trough, people and nations will start to buy again, and if we are prepared with sound plans and sensible strategies,*

we shall do well. There is nothing worse than letting the gloom of the current situation blind us to the potential of tomorrow.

He sent his regards and looked forward to a meeting at an early date. Darcy, who had had little or no experience in the world of Commerce, was more than grateful to have the benefit of Mr Gardiner's wise counsel at a time when no one in business or government had predicted the chaos that was developing around them.

The landed gentry were the least able to understand the new forces that the Industrial Revolution had unleashed. Darcy knew that many of his acquaintances and friends had no notion what was happening to the country. Familiar with the traditional cycles of a rural economy, with its droughts, floods, crop failures, and fluctuating prices, they depended upon a process of natural rotation to restore and sustain them. If one crop failed, another succeeded. Prices swung up and down.

They were unprepared for the creeping recessions of industrial society, with the devastation of mill closures and starving poor begging on the streets, simply because ordinary people were too poor to buy food and clothing, and nations, deep in debt, could no longer import British goods for their people.

Aware that his family had been, for the most part, protected from the impact of the recession that was rolling across the nation, Darcy had realised how exceptionally fortuitous had been his introduction to the Gardiners, through his marriage to Elizabeth. Mr Gardiner had proved a mentor and friend as well as a shrewd business partner.

After dinner that night, he acknowledged to his wife his debt, explaining in greater detail than he had ever done before the worth of her uncle's contribution to their own well-being and financial security. "Had I been less well advised, had I not been made aware of the need to protect and hedge the value of our own properties, quite apart from the additional value of the investment in Mr Gardiner's business, which he runs with such remarkable success, there is no certainty that I would not have suffered losses, too."

Elizabeth was quick to point out that it was unthinkable Darcy would have been as rash or naïve as several of the prominent gentlemen whose fortunes had disappeared before their eyes. "Certainly, I agree that my natural caution and reserve may have saved me from the excesses that have destroyed them, but it may equally have prevented me from deriving the benefits of sensible enterprise." Elizabeth agreed and in her heart rejoiced that Darcy had chosen in this way to indicate very clearly that, far from being materially damaging to him and Mr Bingley, their marriages had proved to be beneficial, through their very association with their Uncle Gardiner.

Writing later to Jane, she related the burden of her discussion with her husband, and added:

> *How fortunate we are, my dearest Sister, to have in our close circle such a couple as Aunt and Uncle Gardiner, who in every way are examples of what is worthy and honourable. Add to this my husband's acknowledgement of the skill and wisdom of our uncle's management of his business enterprise as well as his gratitude for the advice that he and Mr Bingley have had from Mr Gardiner, and we can be satisfied that Lady Catherine's fears regarding the damage done by an alliance with us were quite laughable.*
>
> *You will recall, dear Jane, how depressed we were, after Lydia's stupid elopement. How wretched were my predictions for our future prospects of marriage. Will you forgive me for having contributed to your distress at the time? Quite obviously, I was wrong. There was no question of our association's ever damaging them, quite the contrary. While neither you, dear Sister, nor I, need such assurances from our dear husbands now, it is nevertheless comforting to know that it is true. To have this knowledge, while having also their love and esteem, is surely to have happiness of a very high order.*

For Elizabeth, her uncle's letter and the conversation with Darcy that followed it, had crowned a week of increasing joy. With Jane and Bingley moving to Leicestershire—a mere twenty miles from Pemberley and now her favourite aunt and uncle coming to live at Lambton, her cup was full.

As she picked up her pen to finish her letter to Jane, she wondered at the good fortune that had blessed them both and, indeed, most members of their family. For the present, at least, there was nothing more she could ask for, to add to the sum total of her happiness, except the safe delivery of her child, due in the Spring.

CHAPTER TEN

By fortune truly blest

WELL BEFORE CHRISTMAS, THE smooth running household of Mr and Mrs Bingley at Netherfield had been organised, packed, and moved to Ashford Park in the county of Leicestershire. Jane and Jonathan had temporarily moved to Longbourn, where Mrs Bennet had her heart's desire, with an afternoon tea to which every neighbour, friend, and acquaintance was invited to meet her beautiful daughter, Mrs Bingley, and her grandson. No grandmother could have been prouder or more voluble in her praise of him. "The heir to the Bingley fortune," which in times of increasing trade and commerce, had grown quite remarkably, was how his grandmother saw him.

Jane's presence with her son considerably brightened her father's life. Ever since his two favourite daughters had married and moved away, Mr Bennet had suffered a deep sense of loss. Knowing both Jane and Elizabeth were happy was certainly a great comfort to him, but he missed them terribly. The birth of Jonathan and Jane's return to Longbourn for however short a time were special pleasures, and he was determined to enjoy them.

Jane's happy contentment was obvious to everyone, and her father had the grace to acknowledge to himself, at least, that God or good fortune or both had intervened to bless her life, despite the unpropitious circumstances of her home and family. Her mother's foolishness, her youngest sister Lydia's stupidity, and his own neglect could well have ruined any chance of happiness for Jane as it could for Elizabeth. It had been a salutary lesson for all of them, a lesson learned late, but well. That he had acquired two excellent young men as sons-in-law and, with Kitty's engagement, was about to have another worthy addition to the family, all accomplished with a minimum of effort on his part, did contribute to some degree of smugness, it has to be said.

Jane's own sweet reasonableness, which caused her to dismiss as irrelevant confessions of negligence or inadequacy on her father's part, only served to enhance his present feelings of self-satisfaction. "Dear Papa, you have no guilt to carry on my behalf. There was nothing done or left undone, by you, that would have changed my life significantly. Mr Bingley has assured me of this, and I believe him. If there was a time when he was uncertain about me, it was due to a misunderstanding of the strength of my own feelings, and for that, I can blame no one but myself. However, once he was reassured of my feelings, through the fortunate intervention of our dear Lizzie and Mr Darcy, he determined to return to Netherfield and ask me himself, and you know the rest," she said, ensuring by her generosity of heart, that her father would not blame himself for any of her sorrow, however short-lived.

When everything at Ashford Park was in its place, and Netherfield had been closed, Mr Bingley came to take his wife and son home. There were tears, advice, and blessings to spare, and finally, with the promise of a reunion at Christmas, they were permitted to leave. Jane had so much confidence in the taste and judgement of her sister and brother-in-law that she had not insisted on seeing the property at Ashford before it was purchased. She had, however, accompanied Mr Bingley, their steward, butler, and housekeeper on a tour of the place, before the move was undertaken.

So completely delighted was she with the house, its furnishings and accessories, the gardens, the park that surrounded it, even the woods, walks, and streams that all seemed to be in exactly the places she had imagined they would be, that she pronounced it a perfect choice. On hearing of this, Elizabeth declared that she wished there were twenty more Janes in the world and they were all as amenable and easy to please. Congratulating her husband on selecting the property and then persuading Bingley that it was the right thing to do to sell his shares in the squalid textile industry in order to purchase Ashford

Park, Elizabeth noted that Mr Darcy must now be feeling very satisfied with his success. "Certainly," he replied, "Especially in view of the recession that is now overtaking the textile industry. It was a wise decision. I am indeed happy to have been able to advise Bingley to do what was both right and financially sensible."

"And to have made both his wife and yours happy with the result; surely, a doubly successful enterprise, would you not say?" Darcy looked up at Elizabeth quickly, suspecting she was teasing him again, but in truth, she was not. For her part, Elizabeth continued to be astonished at the lengths to which he would go to assist his friends. She had witnessed it time and again. It was almost as if he accepted that he had a responsibility to help those of his friends and relations whose well-being mattered to him. That this altruism extended to her own family—even its miscreant and undeserving members—she already knew, and Elizabeth loved him dearly for it.

Lydia and Wickham, now expecting their second child, had not shown much gratitude for Darcy's efforts on their behalf, but Elizabeth and Jane, learning of the extent of his involvement from Mrs Gardiner, never failed to appreciate his remarkable generosity of spirit. Seeing his quizzical glance, she rose and went to him. "I was being absolutely sincere, my dearest, you must know how happy I am that Jane and Bingley are to move to Ashford Park," she said, "If the truth were told, I am sure they would have continued at Netherfield for another year, had it not been for your persuasion. Jane is very easygoing and would not have nagged Mr Bingley about it . . ."

Darcy interrupted her in midsentence, "I cannot see Jane ever nagging anyone, my dear, and as for her amiable husband, he has been talking of buying a property ever since his father died but has been happy to enjoy the ease of renting for all of this time. To be fair, he did ask me, very soon after Jane and he were engaged, to look for a suitable place, which is all I have done. It was simply fortuitous that Ashford Park was available." Elizabeth laughed and teased him about being so modest about his part in the enterprise but proceeded to assure him that she had learned from her sister that Bingley was immensely grateful for his assistance and advice.

As for Jane, she could not imagine any place better situated or so well-appointed, and she gave all the credit to Darcy and Elizabeth. "So you see, dearest," said Elizabeth, "We have been credited with a triumph of taste and good judgement." Darcy smiled and said it was something he always enjoyed doing—

giving good advice and having it so readily accepted. "Have you any particular advice for me?" asked Elizabeth, in a mood to divert him from serious matters. "Indeed I do, my dear," he replied, taking her arm, "I suggest you accompany me upstairs—to look at a particular suite of rooms."

Elizabeth had already approached Mrs Reynolds about preparing a nursery. She had suggested accommodation closer to their apartments, and Mrs Reynolds was sympathetic, though a little surprised. The previous Mistresses of Pemberley had always preferred to sleep undisturbed by their babies. It was the way the "gentry" raised their children. "If you would tell me what you would like, Mrs Darcy, I will have it done in time for Spring," she had said, helpfully suggesting an early start to the work.

Elizabeth had wished to consult her husband first, before giving any orders, and she wondered at his already knowing of her request. His words anticipated her question. "Mrs Reynolds mentioned your discussion about a new nursery to Georgiana. She used to have rooms across the landing from our mother's, but she has long since moved into her own apartments on the other side of the house. Georgiana thought you might like to have the rooms redecorated as a nursery. They are very light and spacious, with a pretty view."

Elizabeth's delight was not in any way diminished by the fact that it was so unexpected. That Georgiana should be as generous as her brother did not surprise, but that Mrs Reynolds should have thought to initiate and Darcy to develop the idea added to the comfortable feeling of being drawn into the warm circle of Pemberley, where everyone seemed concerned about each other. It was a habit of caring that she was beginning to recognise as characteristic of the people here, due in no small measure, she decided, to the nature and practice of the Master. It was this atmosphere—rather than the prospect of fine jewels, splendid carriages, and an army of servants, in which her mother had revelled upon her engagement to Darcy—that Elizabeth appreciated most. The rooms proved to be exactly as Darcy had described them. With plenty of light and air, and an attractive view of the Rose Garden, which would be exquisite in the Spring, they were easily accessible from the main apartments and had accommodation for a nurse as well. Seeing she was happy with them, Darcy urged Elizabeth to proceed to give her instructions, so the work could begin. "As I have said before, dearest, it is your home, and I would like you to feel free to have done any work you wish."

"Are you sure you have that much confidence in me?" she asked.

"Lizzie, I know you are unlikely to have the woods felled, the stream diverted, or the gallery turned into a bowling alley, so I urge you to tell Mrs Reynolds what you want done. She will have the tradesmen do the rest."

Elizabeth was supremely happy. There was so much joy in her life that from time to time, she felt undeserving—as if it was too much to accept as her share of happiness. But that did not prevent her enjoying every moment. As she settled into her marriage with Darcy and learned to give and receive the mature love that was the core of it, she grew also in maturity herself and like Jane, found contentment easier to enjoy. The strength and emotional stability that Darcy provided, without the boredom that often accompanied those virtues, the warmth of Georgiana's friendship, together with the concern and care that Mrs Reynolds and her staff wrapped around her, made for a most pleasing and happy state.

She wrote to her friend Charlotte, who had just been delivered of another daughter—Rebecca Ann:

> *I am indeed happy, dear Charlotte. The added pleasure of having my dearest sister Jane less than two hours' drive from Pemberley, with the promise that in Spring, my uncle and Aunt Gardiner will move to Lambton a mere five miles away, shortly before my own baby is expected, is almost too much for one fortunate heart. I should have liked to have come to visit, dear Charlotte, but as you were when our dear Jane was delivered of Jonathan, so I am afraid am I quite unable to travel further than a few miles. I hope to go to Ashford Park at Christmas, but only for a day or two as I am warned that overtiring myself will not do. But, my dear friend, I hope and pray for your good health and that of both your little girls and trust we shall see you here soon. Jane tells me you have agreed to come to her in May; God willing, we shall see you at Pemberley, too.*
>
> *God bless you,*
> *Eliza.*

The good fortune that followed Elizabeth touched others in her family circle, too, that year. At Christmas, which was celebrated at Ashford Park in the kind of lavish style that Mr Bingley was accustomed to, Dr Grantley and Georgiana announced their engagement. The beautiful ring on her finger was admired for its design and envied for its value, by every other young woman present. For Elizabeth and Darcy, however, it was the near-certainty of Georgiana's happiness with Dr Grantley that mattered most. Her gentleness was so perfectly complemented by his strength, and the pride he clearly felt in gaining her affection matched well her youthful devotion to him.

Jane, who was seeing them together for the first time since their engagement, declared it to be "truly a match made in heaven." "There is so much of genuine goodness in both of them, Lizzie, so open and honest in disposition are they, that there can be no other conclusion," she declared, and for once, Elizabeth agreed completely. Even Jane could not exaggerate their virtues.

Two days later, letters from Longbourn confirmed that Maria Lucas was to wed Dr. Faulkner at Easter and Kitty was to be her bridesmaid. Dr Faulkner had a thriving practice at Meryton but no house in the district, so the couple would live at Lucas Lodge—for the foreseeable future. Kitty and Mr Jenkins would be married in June and planned to travel to Bristol to visit his family home, before returning to the Rectory at Pemberley. Kitty had wanted to wait until after Elizabeth's child was born, so her sister could attend her wedding. Meanwhile, tradesmen worked to improve the Rectory, as Darcy had promised, and to redecorate and furnish the new nursery at Pemberley.

In spite of the unhappy state of the nation, the families on the Pemberley Estate and its neighbouring properties had survived the worst of the recession, thanks largely to responsible management by their owners and the hard work of their tenants. A determined effort had been made to assist the poor and dispossessed. No one starved in the environs of Pemberley or Ashford Park that Christmas; no unfortunate being was left homeless in the cold through the greed of landlords. This was no mean feat considering the widespread poverty and suffering that afflicted vast areas of rural England throughout the year.

The churches and parish councils at Lambton, Pemberley, and Kympton had all played their part, seeking out people in trouble and helping families cope. Darcy and Elizabeth together with Dr Grantley and Georgiana used Boxing Day to distribute much food and clothing to the families in and around the Pemberley Estate. The choir of children sang as lustily and sweetly as ever at their party on Christmas Eve, where food was so plentiful that many of their families took away as much again as they had eaten. At Pemberley, the festivities were quiet and unostentatious, with the gladness and good cheer deriving mainly from the warmth of friendship and Christian kindness.

In the New Year, the Gardiners moved to Lambton, sooner than antici-pated. Winter had brought home to all Londoners, save those who lived in ivory towers and palaces, the extent of suffering and anger in the community. Mr and Mrs Gardiner had been feeling increasingly uneasy, living comfortably though by no means luxuriously, in the midst of such deprivation. The large itinerant population that wandered the streets made life less safe and hastened their decision to move.

Once settled at Oakleigh Manor, where they acquired a whole new set of social responsibilities, they were, especially Mrs Gardiner and her daughters, regular visitors at Pemberley. Caroline, at fourteen, an accomplished, charming, and intelligent young lady, was devoted to Elizabeth and adored following her around Pemberley, while Emily, who was just nine, was a great reader and scrib-bler, and could only be persuaded to leave the library at meal times. The two families, already bound by ties of respect and affection, would grow even closer together. Elizabeth and Jane depended upon their aunt as they might upon a beloved elder sister for companionship and advice. Darcy, Bingley, and Mr Gardiner not only had a thriving business partnership; their friendship had developed from a coalescence of interests as well as a strong foundation of mutual affection and regard.

At Easter, Jane attended Maria Lucas' wedding and returned with the only piece of sad news they had heard in a year or more. Lady Lucas was sinking slowly from a long, unremitting illness and Maria's wedding had in fact been brought forward for her mother's sake. A nurse now lived permanently at Lucas Lodge, and Maria and her doctor husband would reside there for as long as her mother needed his care. As Kitty wrote:

She is not expected to survive the Summer, Lizzie. Maria and Nurse Williams are her constant companions. Dr Faulkner is very kind and attends Lady Lucas on every occasion—to ease her pain. Truly, Lizzie, he is such a good doctor, we cannot imagine what they would do without him.

Jane confirmed Kitty's news. She also said that Charlotte had promised to come to Ashford Park and Pemberley, but unfortunately, Mr Collins could not be long away from her Ladyship at Rosings and would have to return to Kent after a week with the Bingleys—no doubt to report to his patron on the state and style of the Bingleys' establishment. Charlotte, however, would stay on and bring her two little girls as well to Pemberley. This singular piece of good news was almost sufficient to help Elizabeth overcome the sadness of Kitty's letter, but, unwilling to outrage her sister's sensibilities, she said nothing, except that she was looking forward to seeing Charlotte and her daughters, prompting Jane to draw a comparison with themselves in childhood, when Charlotte, Jane, and Lizzie had been the happiest threesome in Meryton.

Later, Elizabeth wrote to Charlotte extending an invitation to her to stay at Pemberley for as long as she could tear herself away from Hunsford and Rosings Park. Elizabeth smiled as she sealed her letter. What pleasure to look forward to Spring, her friend Charlotte, her baby, and no Mr Collins! Dear God, she thought, it will be almost heaven.

~❦~

In the midst of the first Summer storm of 1817, when Doctor Stephens was away in Derby on a Saturday afternoon, umpiring a game of cricket, with only her Aunt Gardiner and Mrs Reynolds to assist with her arrival, Elizabeth's daughter was born.

Darcy, who had to be called from a meeting with Mr Gardiner in Lambton, was for the first time anyone could remember, quite incapable of doing anything more than pace the floor and demand news of his wife every five minutes. Fortunately, Dr Grantley, who was visiting Georgiana and Mr Gardiner, kept him company. They urged him in vain to be patient and kept him from riding out in the rain to fetch the errant doctor.

Darcy was quite furious with the doctor. "How could he have gone to Derby for a cricket match on such a day as this?" he asked, "And what sort of cricket would they play in this weather?" It was of no use to point out that no one had expected to see Elizabeth brought to bed till at least the end of May and it had been a fine morning for the cricket.

Mrs Gardiner, who had had four children of her own, Mrs Reynolds, similarly qualified, and young Jenny managed very well indeed. Little Cassandra Jane was born late that afternoon and was declared by all to be the loveliest baby they had ever seen. She was presented to her delighted parents by Mrs Gardiner, just as Dr Stephens arrived, breathless and apologetic, too late to do more than declare that the ladies had done very well indeed and both mother and daughter were in excellent health.

Darcy, who had been threatening dire consequences for the doctor's neglect of his duty, was so delighted with his wife and daughter, he was all smiles and thanked Dr Stephens, as though he had been present all the time. With the luxury of an estate free of entail, Darcy was untroubled by questions of a male heir. While he was confident that some years later they would have a son, who would carry on the family traditions at Pemberley, it was, he said, not a matter of great consequence.

The cause of his happiness was the safe delivery of a beautiful little girl—and his only concern, her health and the comfort of his wife. Elizabeth, who had secretly hoped for a son, had no time for disappointment. Her time was taken up with the demands of a lively daughter, whose resemblance to her handsome father and lovely mother was being discovered by every visitor who called to see her.

It was a long time since there had been a child born at Pemberley, and every tenant and neighbour wanted a glimpse. In the time-honoured tradition, they all felt they had to see some family resemblance in Cassandra that no other visitor had detected. One saw her father's noble brow; another, the lovely dark eyes and the glowing complexion of her mother. Mrs Reynolds even thought there was a hint of Mr Darcy's late mother in her eyes.

Elizabeth, who had been forewarned by her husband to expect all this attention, took it in her stride. She was sensible enough to know that Cassandra Jane belonged to Pemberley as much as to her proud parents. To her happy godparents Jane and Charles Bingley, Cassandra Jane was going to be "a beautiful little friend for Jonathan." To her mother and father, she was the centre of their universe.

CHAPTER ELEVEN

Angry voices and honourable gentlemen

A BRIEF NOTE FROM MR Darcy had informed Lady Catherine de Bourgh of his sister's engagement to Dr Francis Grantley of St John's College, Oxford. Soon afterwards, Georgiana Darcy had written to her aunt—advising of her own engagement and promising to visit Rosings, in the near future. She had consulted both her brother and sister-in-law before writing and had been forewarned to expect a volley of probing and personal questions. When there was no response to either communication, Georgiana was anxious that she had, unwittingly, offended her aunt but was equally uncertain of what she should do next.

The birth of Cassandra Jane had brought with it the particular pleasure of being an aunt herself, which thrust all thoughts of Lady Catherine into the background, until one day in June, when she was sitting with Elizabeth and Cassandra in the nursery. It was a time both young women enjoyed since it gave them an opportunity to talk, as sisters do, of many matters, significant or sentimental as the case may be. They were discussing the possibility of Cassy's growing up with an interest in music and painting. Elizabeth felt sure that being surrounded by so much beautiful art and music at Pemberley, there was no question Cassandra would acquire a taste for it but added, if she did not, then her Aunt Georgiana would have to take her in hand.

They were interrupted when Jenny came in with a letter for Georgiana, from Lady Catherine. It acknowledged hers and the information it had contained concerning her engagement. With no further comment, the writer peremptorily summoned Georgiana and Dr Grantley to Rosings in July, suggesting that the third week of the month would be the most convenient. Almost as an afterthought, she sent her compliments to Mr and Mrs Darcy and hoped they and their daughter were well.

The tone and timing of the letter amused Elizabeth, who declared, "There you are, Georgiana, you need not have worried about displeasing Lady Catherine at all. She has probably investigated Dr Grantley's family background and prospects and finding them quite satisfactory, she now wants to meet him; so you are commanded to present yourselves at Rosings!"

Georgiana laughed and asked, "How can you be certain that she approves?" On this point at least, Elizabeth could reassure her, "Of course she approves, if she did not, she would probably have driven over in her chaise and four to tell you so and demand that you end it at once!" Elizabeth's eyes were sparkling as she spoke, and Georgiana refused to take her seriously. But her brother, who had come in as Elizabeth was speaking and had heard her words, laughed as he assured his sister that it was indeed true.

"Lizzie is absolutely right; believe me, Georgiana, if Lady Catherine had disapproved of Francis Grantley, we would have heard about it."

"Then you think Dr Grantley and I should arrange to go to Rosings?"

"Certainly, and you had better make certain that he has all the information at his command, for Lady Catherine will want to know everything about him," said Darcy, then seeing the alarm this was causing his sister, he relented and confessed he was only teasing.

Elizabeth intervened to point out that the dates suggested by Lady Catherine would probably suit Georgiana and Francis Grantley well, since they would all have travelled to Hertfordshire for Kitty's wedding the previous week.

Darcy did, however, have another, pleasanter surprise for both of them. He had only just received in the mail a letter from Colonel Fitzwilliam. He wrote that he was returning to England in the Autumn, "in time for Christmas at Pemberley and Georgiana's wedding in the New Year." Both Elizabeth and Georgiana were delighted with the news but also a little puzzled. While she could understand his eagerness to attend Georgiana's wedding, Elizabeth could not help feeling that there was more to his decision to return earlier than planned.

As Darcy read out more of the letter, it became clearer; Fitzwilliam had received much news of the present unrest in the country and the Parliament. He had always been more interested in politics than his cousin, and having met with some members of the Reform Group, he was anxious to be involved. He wrote:

> *There seems to be a great deal of talking about reform and very little action. I cannot help thinking that the time is right to demand more representative government in Britain than we now enjoy. So many nations of Europe are achieving a level of democracy greater than ours, and the American Colonies have declared themselves for Independence and Democracy; it shames me to have to admit that our Parliament is filled with members of the landowning aristocracy elected from rotten boroughs to govern us.*

Elizabeth and Georgiana sat in stunned silence. "So you see," said Darcy, "Fitzwilliam is returning to join the Reform Movement."

"I would never have guessed he was so keen," said Elizabeth, still incredulous.

"He has always had strong views on the subject," said Darcy, "He could not abide the old high Tories who dominate Parliament. I have known that. What I did not know was that he had become sufficiently passionate to involve himself directly in the movement. Well, we shall see what he says and does, when he arrives," he said, putting away the letter. Darcy then informed Elizabeth that he intended to invite Fitzwilliam to stay at Pemberley on his return, if she had no objection. Elizabeth made no objection at all; she had always enjoyed his company.

"Does he say what he intends to do, apart from joining the Reform Movement?" she asked. Darcy nodded, "He writes that he wants to settle in this neighbourhood, he hopes to purchase a property, as he says 'Within riding distance of Pemberley'—which must mean he is seriously interested."

"Could he be planning to marry?" Elizabeth asked. Darcy shook his head, "If he is, he is keeping it a secret. He makes no mention of it, nor do I see any other indication of such an intention in his letter. No, my love, I believe the answer lies in the head rather than the heart; he wants to settle in this part of the country, so he can ultimately stand for Parliament here."

"Do you really believe that?" asked his wife, astonished at this information.

"Certainly, he has always been interested in politics, since his days at Cambridge; but being an officer in the army precluded him from taking an active role." Elizabeth could hardly believe that the gentle, well-mannered Colonel was an ambitious politician, but quite clearly Darcy knew more about his cousin than she could have gathered from her pleasant but short acquaintance with him. She still believed there was a lady in the picture, somewhere, but Darcy laughed and warned her against matchmaking, before he left them to go away and write to Fitzwilliam—inviting him to stay at Pemberley until he found a suitable property of his own.

Charlotte Collins and her two little daughters—Catherine and Rebecca, having spent two weeks with Jane at Ashford Park—came to Pemberley. Darcy who had always acknowledged Mrs Collins with respect, as a sensible and intelligent woman, made them very welcome, and Elizabeth was truly delighted to spend some time with her friend again, especially as it was to be free of the encumbrance of Mr Collins. Charlotte brought good news from Jane for her sister: she was expecting her second child. Elizabeth wanted to tell her husband at once, but they found he had already walked down to the stables with the groom and the news would have to wait till later.

Meanwhile, with their three little girls in the care of their nurses, Charlotte and Elizabeth prepared to spend a few days of leisure together. Their friendship went back many years and had been a source of fun as well as comfort, when she and Jane had longed to escape the shallow prattling of their mother. Charlotte's mother, Lady Lucas, was a kind, well-meaning woman and had always welcomed the two elder Bennet girls as her daughter's particular friends. Apart from the temporary coolness that had existed between them following Charlotte's engagement to Mr Collins, an event that had bewildered and angered Elizabeth to the point where she had been rather insensitive to Charlotte's feelings, they had continued to remain affectionate friends.

Charlotte's complete freedom from envy regarding the excellent marriages of Jane and Elizabeth, her sensitivity to the feelings of the Bennet family—in the matter of the entail on Longbourn—and her genuine concern for their happiness and well-being, set her apart as a true and valued friend. They spent most of that day talking of their families, especially their younger sisters—Maria and Kitty, who had also been firm friends since childhood.

While Elizabeth knew little of Dr Faulkner, she had heard nothing but good about him from every source and was sure Maria would be very happy. Charlotte agreed, adding that his devoted care of her mother, who was very sick, went far beyond the call of mere duty. On the subject of Kitty, they were both agreed that her removal from the influence of her giddy younger sister, Lydia, had wrought a total transformation of her character and outlook upon life.

"I had not met Kitty in almost a year, when I called in at Longbourn with Maria before the wedding, and I do not mind telling you, dear Eliza, I was not prepared for the remarkable change in her. She is still young and somewhat excitable, to be sure, but there is no harm in that. What is so pleasing is the change in her temper and values."

Elizabeth agreed, "Mr Jenkins has certainly made a change in Kitty," she began, but Charlotte interrupted gently, "While I accept that Mr Jenkins' influence must be taken into account, I think it is you and Jane who must take most credit. Both of you have shown her, by example, how a young woman conducts herself in the best circles of society and may enjoy the good things of life in genteel moderation, without falling into excess and impropriety." Elizabeth coloured at these compliments from her friend but was happy to accept them all the same.

The following day, the Gardiners came to dinner, and later in the week Rosamund Fitzwilliam called and insisted that they all come over to Rushmore Farm, which was most interesting for Charlotte, who had never before visited a horse stud. The Gardiners would not take no for an answer either, wanting Charlotte to see for herself how well they had settled into life in Derbyshire, after some twenty years in London. It was on returning from Oakleigh, on a balmy afternoon, that they found sad news waiting for them.

An express had come from Sir William Lucas. Lady Lucas had passed away early that morning, and Charlotte was summoned to Lucas Lodge. As the tears welled up in Charlotte's eyes and Elizabeth embraced her dear friend, Darcy went immediately to find Mrs Reynolds and organise their journey to Hertfordshire. He determined that Charlotte and her children could not travel post, unaccompanied. They would have one of his carriages, with a trusted man from Pemberley to escort them. He assumed a message had already gone to Mr Collins in Kent and no doubt he would arrive for the funeral. Everything was done to enable them to leave in time to reach Coventry before dark.

Charlotte was overwhelmed by Darcy's concern and generosity. As she prepared to leave, barely an hour later, he assured her they were in good hands. He said the driver had instructions to do exactly as she asked but suggested they break journey at a hostelry he recommended for its safety and comfort. Charlotte, he said, need not worry at all about arrangements, his servant would attend to all of that. Having again expressed his condolences and asked for them to be conveyed to Sir William and Maria, he reassured her, "Have no fear, Mrs Collins, you will be delivered safe and sound to Lucas Lodge," and added, "Bingley and I will call on you and your father in a day or two." Charlotte thanked him from the bottom of her heart, whispering in Lizzie's ear as they said farewell, "My dear Eliza, you have a most thoughtful and generous husband. Look after him."

Elizabeth had already asked her to forgive her own inability to travel to the funeral, but Charlotte, in her usual calm way, waved away her apologies, "I know you cannot travel at this time, Eliza, but at least, I know that your thoughts will be with us. My mother always thought very highly of you and Jane; she hoped you would marry good men. Having seen both Mr Bingley and Mr Darcy as I have these last few weeks, I know her wishes for you have been more than fulfilled."

Suddenly, Elizabeth felt sad, wondering at the way their lives had changed, since they had been girls together. Charlotte was her oldest friend. Not even the tragicomic circumstances of her marriage to Mr Collins could destroy their bonds of friendship.

When they had gone, she turned to her husband and was surprised by the expression of deep concern upon his countenance. It was at these moments, she understood fully how fortunate she was. That she could ever have thought him cruel, callous, and indifferent to the feelings of others was incomprehensible to her now. She was ashamed to acknowledge that he had been as harshly misjudged by herself, as by others whose ignorance might be their excuse. She'd had none to blame but her prejudice. The gentleness in his treatment of Charlotte in her sorrow, his compassion combined with the swift practical assistance he sought to provide, had filled Elizabeth with pride and love. She was no longer surprised, just very proud of him. Putting an arm around her, he took her upstairs. "You must rest, dearest; there is nothing more to be done. I shall send a message to Ashford suggesting to Bingley that he and I attend the funeral. We may have to leave tomorrow." Elizabeth agreed; she was suddenly very tired and longed for a bath and bed. Her mind kept returning to Charlotte, her nurse, and two little girls, on the road to Hertfordshire and her mother's funeral.

The following day, Elizabeth decided that she would take Cassandra and Jenny and travel to Ashford Park with Darcy, where she would stay with Jane until their husbands returned from the funeral of Lady Lucas. Jane and Elizabeth had much to talk about. They were rarely apart for a week, but one sister would feel she could not possibly spend another day without seeing the other. Sometimes they visited one another; at others, they met at Oakleigh, where their beloved aunt and uncle were always overjoyed to see them.

On this occasion, the sadness of Charlotte's loss was softened by Jane's news of another child. "It does mean we shall not be having our usual party at Christmas, Lizzie, but Aunt Gardiner has claimed the right to have us all at Oakleigh, because it will be Caroline's birthday on Boxing Day!" said Jane.

"So it will. She has grown up these last two years—why Emily still seems a baby, but young Caroline is quite the young lady," said Elizabeth. "Can you not remember the days when she would climb into your lap and refuse to leave until you had read her a story?" Jane did remember, very well.

"She is certainly grown up and so beautiful too, Lizzie. I do believe it was one of the reasons for our aunt and uncle deciding to leave London for the country."

Elizabeth was puzzled. "How do you mean?"

"Aunt Gardiner was over here with the girls while Charlotte was with us last week. We were talking of the tall tales coming out of London these days. Lizzie, there are all sorts of stories of wild parties and loose living men and women—all encouraged by the lack of discipline at the Court. Well, it seems there was a lot of truth in some of the tales, and Lizzie, Aunt Gardiner was especially concerned about the girls."

Elizabeth was speechless for a while then, recovering her composure, asked, "You cannot mean that they were in any danger?"

"Not in any physical danger, but by example. You know how it was with Kitty and Lydia and all those Officers and silly women in Meryton?" Elizabeth nodded; she certainly remembered them! "Well, it is, according to my aunt, twice as bad in London. The Prince Regent and his swell friends are forever being accused of indulging in gambling, feasting, and drunken brawls and other equally wild practices, which set a very poor example for the ordinary folk. And, Lizzie, my aunt says there is now in fashion a new continental dance they call the waltz, in which the ladies are clasped close to their partners and whirled around the room. She believes all this is more than too much for her young Caroline and Emily to endure."

Elizabeth smiled; she had heard of the Viennese waltz and was not entirely convinced that it would bring about the end of British civilisation. Jane was much less sanguine, "I cannot help thinking, Lizzie, that ever since the old King was declared mad and locked away, things at the Court have got much worse. On our last visit to London, we were quite embarrassed by the large numbers of rather raffish young men who attend the assemblies and parties. They have neither taste nor distinction and seem only to drink, jest, and brawl around town." Jane warmed to her subject as her sister listened, "Mr Bingley's friends are equally concerned. The Middletons have retired to Hampshire, the Hursts have moved to Bath permanently, and Caroline Bingley has gone with them. Now, I cannot believe they would have left London unless they felt compelled by some unpleasant circumstance, Lizzie."

"What does Bingley think?" asked Elizabeth, beginning to be concerned by her sister's narration.

"Bingley thinks the problems are caused by the lack of any leadership from the Prince Regent or the Tory government," said Jane, "He says it is time they did more than arrest people and send the poor to prison." Elizabeth was surprised at the extent of her sister's information. It was the first time Jane, who usually listened and said very little during similar discussions, had appeared involved and genuinely concerned. She wondered briefly what had happened to bring this about and then recalled that while she had been busy having Cassandra, Jane had been spending a great deal of time with the Gardiners, whose contacts in London were numerous and varied. It was no wonder, then, that she had all the town gossip down pat. Her anxiety was very real; she seemed like one who had floated down a pleasant stream in a frail little boat thinking herself safe in a familiar environment, until quite without warning, she becomes aware of dangerous rapids ahead. It was so unlike Jane that

Elizabeth determined to talk to her Aunt Gardiner about it, to satisfy herself that she was not being unduly alarmed by rumours.

Later, however, when she had spoken with her aunt and uncle, who came over from Oakleigh Manor to dinner, Elizabeth herself began to be convinced of the reasons for their uneasiness and Jane's fears. She learned that young women and girls—some not twelve years old—were being attracted into the city by promises of everything from humble jobs in domestic service to excitement, romance, and ultimate fame and fortune among the ranks of the Regency bucks in the Prince Regent's entourage. "Believe me, Lizzie, foolish young women are coming to London, hoping to be picked up to become some toff's mistress!" said her aunt.

"I cannot believe it, Aunt. How has this come about?" she was somewhat sceptical. Her aunt was severe in her condemnation.

"You need only look at the dissolute and self-indulgent life of the Prince Regent and his courtiers to understand what is happening. Where there is no example for young people to follow, you will get chaos, and that is what we are seeing in London today." Mr Gardiner was no less indignant, "Is it not a shocking thing, my dear Lizzie, that the nation that fought and twice defeated Bonaparte, seems to have lost direction and principle? The Regent and his courtiers are only interested in their own pleasure; they waste more money in a day than would feed a family for a month. Our government seems bewildered, unable to provide any solutions to our problems, and the men in business seek only greater and greater profit. Greed, dear Lizzie, is a terrible God!" A thought occurred to Elizabeth, and she asked her uncle if he had been in touch with Colonel Fitzwilliam and made him aware of what was happening.

"Certainly, why Colonel Fitzwilliam, when he returns, will be a full partner in our business enterprise. I've kept him well-informed" said Mr Gardiner.

"And do you know when he expects to be back in England?"

"Indeed I do. He wrote last week to say he would be here for Christmas, for Caroline's birthday, and of course, for Miss Darcy's wedding in the New Year. The colonel agrees with me as does Mr Bingley, Britain needs some new leaders and new laws to reform our system."

Elizabeth nodded sagely and smiled. A vital piece of the puzzle had just fallen into place. Her uncle must have been the Colonel's chief source of information. Mr Bennet had often said that his brother-in-law was a "good Whig" because being in trade, he could not possibly be a Tory! But not even her father had suggested that Mr Gardiner might be a Reformist, yet it now transpired that he was probably encouraging Fitzwilliam to join the Reform Group and stand for Parliament.

For a young woman who had spent most of her life totally disinclined to pay any attention to matters political, Elizabeth found herself getting very interested indeed. She felt she would be looking forward to the return of Colonel Fitzwilliam with much greater interest than she was a week or two ago. She couldn't wait to tell her husband about it.

Mr Darcy and Bingley returned from Lady Lucas' funeral with letters of thanks from Sir William, Charlotte, and the rest of the family and a special invitation to Jane and Elizabeth to stay at Lucas Lodge, when they came to Hertfordshire for Kitty's wedding in July. Jane wondered whether her parents would be offended if they did not stay at Longbourn but changed her mind immediately on hearing that the Wickhams were expected to stay there.

Returning the following day to Pemberley, Elizabeth could barely wait to get upstairs, before she began to relate the events of the previous day and the information she had gained from Mr Gardiner, especially his news about Fitzwilliam's political leanings. She had expected Darcy to be very surprised, but to her great disappointment, he appeared to be very well-informed himself. "You forget, my darling Lizzie, Mr Gardiner is as much a partner of mine as he is of Bingley's and yes, Fitzwilliam's too. He has kept us all informed. He has extensive contacts in the city and in business circles; he also lived in the heart of London's commercial district for twenty years—he knows it better than any of us. Do you recall the week Mr Gardiner and I spent on business in London and at Oakleigh, while you remained at Netherfield with Jane?" Elizabeth nodded, recalling that Darcy had returned almost certain that her uncle would purchase Oakleigh Manor. "Well, it was then he first told me why he was so keen to leave London. It was not just your aunt's desire to return to the county she grew up in. They were both growing increasingly uncomfortable with the environment in the city—the poverty, the large numbers of people who were coming into the city aimlessly, the lack of discipline at Court and among the hordes of camp followers of the Prince Regent. Believe me, Elizabeth, he was seriously concerned for the safety of his family and the poor example it set for the children."

"And have you spoken of it since?" she asked.

"Yes, we have spoken of it often. He knows that I have never enjoyed spending much time in London. All that frantic merrymaking and drinking is not to my taste. It hasn't affected me because I don't live there, but I agree with him, it's destroying the heart of London society. I must admit, I had no idea that he was so committed to the Reformists. That is new, but I suppose it is the next step. Fitzwilliam is obviously keen, and if your uncle supports him, they may succeed in getting him elected. We have not discussed Fitzwilliam's intentions, but I do know that Mr Gardiner knows of several others—especially men in trade and commerce, who appear to be interested in working for reform. So, my dearest Lizzie, we may well have an 'Honourable Gentleman' in the family soon."

He had lightened the mood with his remark, but it was quite obvious that Darcy was taking Mr Gardiner's views quite seriously. He had a good deal of respect for both of them and valued their judgement. Elizabeth knew that Darcy's own tastes had never run to the foppishness and snobbery that seemed to obsess the fashionable classes in the city. He had abjured the competitive class conflict that was now a national pastime among the rich and, as he said, "buried himself in Derbyshire" for most of the year, travelling up to London for business or special occasions and then staying only for short periods at Portman Square. After their marriage, it had been much the same. While she enjoyed the occasional excursion to the capital, there was little to attract and keep her there, especially now that the Gardiners had moved to the country. Of one thing Elizabeth was certain: Fitzwilliam's return was going to be the start of a very interesting period for all of them.

Kitty Bennet was married at Longbourn to the Reverend Huw Jenkins on a fine day in July, with a gentle breeze rendering the warm sun more temperate and dappled shadows softening the harsh mid-Summer's light. While she had neither Jane's elegance and classical beauty nor Elizabeth's striking dark colouring and lively charm, Kitty made a very pretty bride. She had a youthful, delicate air and made a charming picture, with her two bridesmaids—Caroline and Emily Gardiner, who were well-practised at following their cousins up the aisle. There were many in church that day who remembered them from the wedding of Jane and Elizabeth, a few years ago, and some of them remarked on how grown up and beautiful young Miss Caroline Gardiner looked on this occasion.

Sitting next to her sister, Jane whispered, "Oh Lizzie, isn't Caroline beautiful?" While Emily still had a childlike quality, her sister at fourteen was very much a young lady. Tall for her age, slim, and very graceful, Caroline was more remarked upon than the bride. Her parents were very proud indeed, not just of their daughter's beauty, but of the poise and decorum that marked her behaviour at all times.

Particularly striking was the contrast with the still silly and immature Lydia Wickham, who in spite of being a mother of two little boys, was unable to resist the temptation to flaunt herself and flirt with every man in sight, while her husband wandered around seemingly indifferent to the behaviour of his wife. It seemed that Wickham was quite bored with his wife and did not care who knew it. He appeared a good deal more at ease with other men's wives, those who put up with his ingratiating smiles and compliments, at least.

By the end of the wedding breakfast, Elizabeth was getting very tired of hearing her mother proclaim the virtues of "Lydia's boys." Lydia loved it, and Wickham merely basked in the attention as if he was the object of it all. It seemed three years of marriage had added nothing worthwhile to either of their characters. Jane and Elizabeth, who had the protection of their husbands, were relieved that he did not try to join them at the table or afterwards, when they were seeing the wedded pair off on their journey to Bristol.

Mrs Gardiner, however, had noticed that he appeared to pay special attention to young Caroline and was quick to approach them and, in her daughter's presence, pointedly asked after his wife and sons. Unabashed, Wickham immediately turned on his charm for Mrs Gardiner's benefit—launching into a paean of praise for Lydia and the boys, who he assured her were the delight of their lives. Having seen their behaviour at Longbourn over the last twenty-four hours, where they were alternately indifferent or indulgent towards their children, Mrs Gardiner found his hypocrisy breathtaking but said nothing.

Later, when they were back at Lucas Lodge, she confided in her nieces. "I cannot believe that neither of them have any shame at all," she said.

"My dear Aunt, you should not be surprised; they are both quite brazen and appear to imagine that everyone in the family and in this neighbourhood has totally forgotten his appalling behaviour when the regiment was at Meryton and the circumstances of their marriage," remarked Elizabeth, annoyed that Darcy had had to put up with the vexation of watching Wickham simper and court approval, all the while knowing the true nature of the man. Jane, on the other hand, was more dismissive.

"I agree. I should have been ashamed to have attended the wedding after all that has gone before. But I think Mr Wickham is no longer a danger to anyone we know; I have made it my business to inform any of our acquaintances, who may ask about them, of the unpardonable way in which they deceived everyone and the irresponsibility of both Lydia and Wickham. I cannot believe that any-one, who has behaved as they have, will not have forfeited the regard of all respectable people."

Elizabeth was astonished at the strength of her usually gentle sister's remarks but was equally delighted that Jane felt as she did. Jane and she had been saved from the damage that Wickham and Lydia had wrought only by the generosity of her future husband and his determination to spare her the pain of sharing in her stupid sister's shame. His love, which she had at that stage rejected—in a moment of blind prejudice and ignorance—had stood between all of them and the opprobrium that society stood ready to heap upon them. Recalling it alone sent a cold shiver down her spine. She was delighted to see Darcy approaching with Mr Gardiner; her welcoming smile brought a warm response from him as he took her outstretched hand. "Are we ready to leave?" Mr Gardiner asked, and the ladies scattered to say their farewells and gather their belongings.

"Very soon," said Elizabeth, "But not before we find Charlotte and thank her. Maria, there you are, have you seen Charlotte?" They found her and taking her aside thanked her warmly and sincerely for her kind hospitality and invited her to visit them again.

Mr Bennet, too, had to be consoled, now there was only Mary left to keep him company. Darcy made sure he was invited to visit Pemberley whenever he wanted a change of scene.

Mercifully, Mrs Bennet had gone ahead with Lydia and Wickham, and Elizabeth felt no real need to follow them to Longbourn, choosing to send her farewells through her father and Mary. With the Wickhams' staying on a few more days, she was sure her mother would scarcely notice. When Lydia was at home, Mrs Bennet appeared to crave nothing more than opportunities to indulge and cosset her daughter and her children. The Wickhams clearly pleased her mother more than they did poor Mr Bennet, who had nothing in common with either of them. Elizabeth did not leave without extracting from him a promise to visit Pemberley again after Christmas. It was a promise he found easy to give. "Your husband has already asked me, my dear," he said cheerfully, "and as I told you on a previous occasion, I cannot refuse him anything. So yes, Lizzie, you shall have me back at Pemberley in the Spring."

Now her sister's wedding was over, Jane, who was tiring a little, wanted to get away too, and Bingley obliged at once. They were all breaking journey overnight in London at the Bingleys' house in Grosvenor Street.

The Gardiners, most of them, were already in their carriage, and the younger ones were bidding everyone a lively farewell. Caroline stood waiting for her mother, who was finding it hard to leave an old friend. Elizabeth noticed again how elegant and grown up her young cousin looked. Weddings were good occasions to see people in a new light, she thought. She noticed, however, that her father looked a little weary and said so. Darcy, waiting a little impatiently for the carriages in front to move on, agreed, adding that while it had been a good day for Kitty, and she was surely a fortunate and happy young woman, for some members of her family, it must also have been a rather trying day.

His understated comment exactly matched her own feelings. Quite clearly, her father had found little pleasure in the occasion. Elizabeth smiled and reached for Darcy's hand. There was no need for words. They had said their goodbyes; setting off for London and then Pemberley, Elizabeth and Darcy felt only the pleasure of going home.

CHAPTER TWELVE

England's green and pleasant land

AUTUMN WAS LATE THAT year in Derbyshire. The mild evening tempted Elizabeth to ask that tea be served on the West lawn, where they could sit in the golden light of the setting sun, look up at the great, wooded hills behind Pemberley, and enjoy their glorious colours. She had not yet become accustomed to the scale and magnificence of the grounds and woods around this great estate, much less to being Mistress of it all.

On this evening, Elizabeth had company. Darcy and Mr Gardiner had gone to Liverpool on business, arranging the changeover of their trading interests from London to the West coast ports. The gentlemen were expected home in time for dinner. With her two boys away at College, Mrs Gardiner and her daughters were spending a few days at Pemberley. They had spent the morning tramping around the park with Caroline, who never tired of walking in the woods and the early afternoon in the library with Emily, who could not tear herself away from the books.

Having changed for dinner, they had agreed that the evening was too mild and beautiful to warrant staying indoors. Caroline and Emily, sitting on a rug between their mother and Elizabeth, were taking it in turns to read aloud from a new book of poems. Elizabeth had bought it in London on her last visit and made a gift of it to the girls. Emily already knew some of the poems by heart and had just finished one of her favourites—a slight piece by Wordsworth about daffodils "fluttering and dancing in the breeze" in his beloved Lake District. She spoke it well and, when she had finished, asked if they could visit the Lakes. Elizabeth and Mrs Gardiner exchanged glances and smiled as they remembered the last time they had planned to travel to the Lakes, the initial disappointment they had felt, and of course, the consequences that had flowed from their choosing to visit Derbyshire instead. When the girls detected that there was a secret their mother and cousin shared, they demanded to be told and would not be satisfied until some abbreviated version had been provided. The rest of the tale would have to wait until later, their mother said, adding that they may need to get Mr Darcy's permission to fill in the details. This puzzled the girls greatly, but it was quite clear they were not going to get any more information out of either Elizabeth or their mother, whereupon they gave up and returned to the poetry.

It was then Caroline's turn to read, and she chose Wordsworth too, but quite a different piece. Caroline had spent most of her life in London, and she had loved the city, especially the river, along whose banks the family had often walked on a Sunday morning after church, sometimes to Richmond Hill, where the view of the river was so pretty that many smart Londoners had built houses there, overlooking the Thames. The sonnet composed on Westminster Bridge appealed to her, and her gentle, modulated voice lifted as she read the lines,

> *"Never did sun more beautifully steep.*
> *In his first splendour, valley, rock or hill*
> *Dear God, the very houses seem asleep.*
> *And all that mighty heart is lying still."*

As she finished, her little audience applauded. She looked up at Elizabeth, "It is so beautiful, Cousin Lizzie. This is such a good collection of poems. Do you not agree, Mama?" Before her mother could reply, footsteps were heard approaching on the path from the house, and an unfamiliar voice said, "I certainly agree and that was very well-read, Miss Caroline." Everyone turned around, and Elizabeth jumped up to find Fitzwilliam standing in front of her.

"Colonel Fitzwilliam! What are you doing here?"

He was smiling, quite unabashed, greeted her with much affection, and apologised for surprising them. "Mrs Darcy, Elizabeth, forgive me, I know I am not expected until the end of the month, but I had a rare chance of a berth on a boat that was leaving early. Ever since I received Darcy's letter, I've been anxious to return to England, as soon as possible."

Turning to Mrs Gardiner, he spoke warmly, "And this is indeed an unexpected pleasure meeting you here, Mrs Gardiner, Miss Caroline, and little Emily, too. I have to confess, Miss Caroline, I heard your reading of Wordsworth's sonnet and waited till you had finished before I spoke. It was excellent, rendered with so much feeling." Caroline was obviously pleased. He asked after Mr Darcy and Mr Gardiner and on being told that they were expected to dinner, declared that he could not have chosen a better moment to arrive at Pemberley. No sooner had he sat down and accepted a cup of tea, than he turned once more to the book of poems. "I have purchased a copy myself," he said, "It is all the rage in London."

"And do you have a favourite poem?" asked Emily. He smiled as he answered, "Indeed I do, you will find it at page nine," and as the girls turned the pages eagerly, "It's called Jerusalem."

"Jerusalem?" Elizabeth was not familiar with the poem. "What is its subject?"

"England, the English countryside, and the despoiling of it," said Fitzwilliam. "The poet, William Blake, is troubled by what he sees happening around us." He had committed the poem to memory and spoke the lines quietly, but with feeling,

"And did those feet in Ancient time
Walk upon England's mountains green
And was the Holy Lamb of God
In England's pleasant pastures seen
And did the Countenance Divine
Shine forth upon our clouded hills
And was Jerusalem builded here
Among these dark Satanic mills?"

Elizabeth and Mrs. Gardiner listened in silence as Caroline, having found the poem in the book, read the second stanza with him,

"Bring me my bow of burning Gold
Bring me my arrows of desire
Bring me my spear, O clouds unfold
Bring me my Chariot of Fire
I shall not cease from mental fight
Nor shall my sword sleep in my hand
Till we have built Jerusalem
In England's green and pleasant land."

As they finished and looked at one another, Mrs Gardiner and Elizabeth applauded, while Emily, her eyes wide, sat completely entranced.

Caroline coloured and suddenly broke the spell by asking if Mr Blake had written many other poems. But she never got an answer, because Mr Darcy had arrived at that very moment and, hearing their voices, came around the house at great speed, almost running into his cousin, who had stood up on hearing him approach. "Fitzwilliam! When did you arrive? Have you been long in England?" Darcy asked, simultaneously astonished and delighted to see him. As they greeted each other warmly, Fitzwilliam explained and apologised all over again, assuring Darcy that he had taken rooms at the inn at Lambton—in case there were other guests at Pemberley.

"What nonsense!" said Darcy, "there is plenty of room here; you know that, Fitzwilliam. We can send a man to fetch your things, if you will write a note to the landlord." Elizabeth agreed with her husband.

"There is no question; you must stay at Pemberley. It will be a waste of time for you to return to Lambton tonight. Mr Gardiner will be joining us for dinner; surely, you will want to stay and meet him." Fitzwilliam was easily persuaded and went immediately with Darcy to arrange for his things to be brought over from the inn, while Elizabeth sent for Mrs Reynolds to make arrangements about his rooms.

Mr Gardiner arrived in time for dinner, having stopped to settle some bills and attend to domestic matters at the farm. His pleasure at finding Fitzwilliam at Pemberley, a full month earlier than he had expected to see him in England, was overwhelming. The Colonel, with whom he had corresponded over the past three years on matters of business and pleasure, regarded Mr Gardiner with great respect as an astute and honourable businessman, as well as a trusted friend. He had been very impressed by the entire family when he had met them during the preparations for the wedding of Darcy and Elizabeth. Mrs Gardiner he found, as Darcy had predicted he would, to be a woman of great decorum and excellent taste, while all her children and especially the girls were exemplary in their behaviour and exceedingly well-taught.

Their being resident in London had meant that before and after the wedding, Fitzwilliam had met them often, finding their company more congenial than that of his fellow officers in the London clubs. Not having sufficient money with which to play the gaming tables and not being inclined to follow the Casanovas in their quest of compliant ladies, he was frequently on his own and was often asked to dine at the Gardiners. As a bachelor, with no home of his own to go to, he had enjoyed immensely and was grateful for their generous hospitality. He had become a regular visitor, especially on Sundays; he had looked forward to it and had begun to believe that they did, too. Leaving for India had been a considerable wrench, for which letters did not entirely compensate. He had missed them all very much.

Meeting them again, without warning, at Pemberley, brought back all those memories. Both men had a great deal to discuss, and Darcy, knowing that he would have plenty of time to talk with his cousin, while he was staying at Pemberley, left them together, pointing out in a slightly sardonic remark to Elizabeth that it certainly wasn't only ladies who could be accused of talking endlessly when they met. Elizabeth laughed and said she had always found Fitzwilliam had a good deal to say for himself, so she was not at all surprised. This brought an immediate riposte, about her preference for strong, silent men, of course!

Unaware that he had caused any comment, Fitzwilliam was deep in conversation about several matters dear to his heart. While in India, he had become aware of the unease that Mr Gardiner and some of his fellow businessmen were feeling over the direction in which the nation appeared to be heading. Most frustrating of all had been the inability of the middle class to get an effective voice in Parliament and have the government take their concerns seriously. Now, he knew more about the disillusionment that had set in across all of English society. "It seems that those who support the Tories are unhappy because they are not repressive enough, while the Reformists and the Whigs are critical of the lack of freedom and the inadequacy of our Parliamentary system to represent all of society—not just the rich landlords," he observed, and no one disagreed with him.

Mrs Gardiner and Elizabeth took the girls upstairs to bed. They were tired after a long day and the excitement of Fitzwilliam's unexpected arrival. Both aunt and niece were clearly pleased by his return; he had been a favourite of theirs, with his gentlemanly manners and friendly disposition. As they tucked Emily into bed, Mrs Gardiner remarked, "Colonel Fitzwilliam has certainly brought some excitement back with him, Lizzie," and Elizabeth agreed, adding, "But I must confess I had never believed him to be particularly political."

"What's political?" asked Emily, and before either of them could speak, the answer came from her sister, in the bed across the room,

"You are very ignorant, Emmy, it means to be interested in the way the Parliament runs the country. Is that not right, Cousin Lizzie?"

"It certainly is," said Elizabeth, eyebrows raised and very impressed. As they left the room, her aunt said, "It's Edward and his friends, of course. They're forever talking about the Parliament and demanding reforms. Caroline seems to absorb it all. I know it seems precocious, but your uncle believes that the girls need to know as much as the lads."

"And he is quite right, Aunt. Ignorance is the surest way to disaster. Our family knows that only too well," Elizabeth declared as they joined the gentlemen downstairs.

They had already moved to the drawing room, but the conversation continued unabated, over coffee. During the short time he had spent in London, Fitzwilliam had heard of the chaotic situation in the city and at Court. He had met up with two friends who were involved with the Hampden Clubs and the Union Societies, promoted by aging Radical Major Cartwright and sympathetic Whigs like Burdett and Brougham. Fitzwilliam declared that he was of a mind to join the movement, "However, I must talk it over with you, Darcy and Mr Gardiner," he said.

Mr Gardiner counselled caution, pointing out that the government was being very vindictive towards its opponents and it might be sensible to study the political landscape well, before lending his support to one of the movements. Fitzwilliam was grateful for the advice but assured them that he was absolutely committed to working for reform. "I will not continue to hang my head in shame each time I hear of an American Declaration of Independence or a Bill of Rights in some European nation, while we still struggle under a system that denies the majority of us the vote." There was no doubting his sincerity, and Elizabeth was truly happy to hear Darcy agree with his principles, while he advised his cousin to consider his decision carefully. "But Darcy, if we do not demand reform, no one will; I am determined." Mr Gardiner asked carefully, "Would you stand for Parliament, Colonel Fitzwilliam?"

"If need be, yes, I will. If that is the only way to get reform, I will stand for Parliament," he said with so much conviction and firmness that it left no one in any doubt of his determination. Darcy looked across at Elizabeth, and as their eyes met, they smiled. They recalled a conversation a few weeks ago, when Darcy, having received Fitzwilliam's letter, was sure he intended on his return to join the Reformists and stand for Parliament. Elizabeth had not been so certain.

Later that night, as she brushed her hair and prepared for bed, Elizabeth acknowledged to her husband that he had been right, after all. He was gracious in victory, allowing that he had some prior knowledge from conversations with her uncle. However, he did admit that he had not anticipated the energy and eagerness for action that his cousin had shown. And there were many more things that he wanted to accomplish. Darcy revealed to Elizabeth that they had talked of half a dozen matters at least. "To begin with, he is no longer the disadvantaged younger son, dependent upon his father for an allowance. His position with the East India Company brought him into contact with a whole new group of businessmen—planters, traders, merchants, and he was able, with some good advice from your uncle and others, to make several excellent investments in both India and Ceylon—in commodities like tea, cotton, and spices, which are in great demand here and all over Europe. I believe he even has a half share in a gem mine in the hill country of Ceylon—producing sapphires and rubies," said Darcy, and seeing his wife's eyes light up, he added, "all worth a king's ransom, no doubt."

"And is my uncle going into this business too?" she asked.

"No, he is interested in the established trade; that is what he knows best," Darcy replied. "Fitzwilliam is to become a partner in the trading company along with Bingley and myself. The rest of his investments are his own." Elizabeth sighed; she could hardly believe the transformation in Fitzwilliam, from a very unassuming, if pleasing young man to the enthusiastic, energetic, no less pleasing, but very different person who had appeared at Pemberley that evening. She confessed to being rather confused. Darcy understood the reason for her bewilderment. In three years, the comfortable, easygoing Fitzwilliam had changed, and Elizabeth, who had liked his former persona, was anxious lest she should lose touch with the new one, by failing to keep up with him.

"Do not be anxious, Lizzie; he is by far a stronger, better character now, more self-reliant and confident of his views, but his essential nature and disposition remain unchanged. There has always been a basic goodness of heart, a sense of justice in Fitzwilliam. Unfortunately, without the means to follow his inclinations, he was unable to do anything about it. I have heard him complain about the injustices of one system or the other, but he had to be discreet as long as he depended upon the munificence of his relatives, or was employed by the Crown. Remember, my dear, that his father and our mutual aunt—Lady Catherine, who are his principal benefactors—are such arch conservatives that the slightest hint of radicalism on his part could have meant a severe reprimand or even a reduction of his allowance," he explained. Elizabeth recalled a conversation with Fitzwilliam during a walk in the woods at Rosings, some years ago, in which, among other matters, he had confessed to her the privations suffered by younger sons of titled families. He had especially bemoaned the loss of independence. "And do you mean that he is now better able to follow his heart in matters of marriage as well as politics?" she asked. Darcy answered without any hesitation, "Undoubtedly. I cannot believe there would be any constraint upon him on that score, except in matters of character and disposition."

"And Lady Catherine would not pursue him as vigorously as she might have, had he been dependent upon her good opinion and generosity?"

Darcy knew she was teasing and followed suit, "There is no knowing how assiduously Lady Catherine may prosecute her cause in the case of Fitzwilliam; he is a particular favourite of hers."

"As you were," she interposed, smiling.

"Indeed, so there is no means by which one can predict her actions; but one thing can be said with absolute certainty: Fitzwilliam's fortune is now considerably more than anything they can take away from him. And, unlike theirs," he went on, "his assets have an ever-increasing value, based as they are upon trade and commerce, the fastest growing enterprise on earth. That being so, he is free to make whatever choices and decisions he wishes. One can only hope and pray that they will be the right ones, for him."

"And surely, my dear, you intend to see that they are?" she asked, a teasing little note creeping into her voice. Darcy put his arms around her and, as if to signal the end of the conversation, snuffed out the candle on her dressing table before saying, "Dearest Elizabeth, have I not learned my lesson? Never again will I interfere in the personal affairs of a friend. I still suffer when I recall how much pain I caused two people we both love dearly, by my intolerable arrogance." Elizabeth hushed him; she would hear no more. She well knew how much he regretted causing the hurt and sorrow that had flowed from his well-meaning but insensitive intervention in the lives of Bingley and Jane. But that was a long time ago, and as things had turned out, he had been completely forgiven.

❧

A day or two later, after Fitzwilliam had moved his things and settled in at Pemberley, he was consulting Darcy about the purchase of a property. He had put aside a reasonable sum of money, including the proceeds of the sale of some assets left to him by his mother, to buy himself a home. "Darcy, I am not looking to purchase some grand mansion or manor. A good, solid house with a decent sized farm and some acres of woodland is all I crave," he said, as they sat in front of the fire.

Elizabeth was reading but could hear the conversation. "I have no interest in being a landlord, I have neither the time nor the inclination to manage a large estate, nor do I intend to maintain a large establishment with dozens of servants. If there are tenant farmers, we shall have to work out an arrangement whereby they will, for the most part, manage their own businesses. I would, of course, require some labour on the farm, for which I shall pay a fair price, but apart from that, it's going to be the simple life for me." Darcy, though he was a little surprised, did not discourage him. His advice was practical and carefully considered, "Well, with the collapsing prices of farm land, you should have little difficulty. Where are you intending to settle? Are you still determined to be a neighbour of ours?" he asked. Fitzwilliam laughed, "I would very much like it, if I could remain within riding distance of yourselves and Mr and Mrs Gardiner, not just because I love Pemberley, but because we intend to do business together."

Elizabeth put her book away. "And do you intend to be an active partner in the Company?" she asked.

Fitzwilliam laughed. "As active as my partners want me to be," he said. "I have interests in the Colonies, and Mr Gardiner is anxious to establish some contacts with enterprises there. These are matters for discussion." Darcy nodded and agreed but did not pursue the matter. He was still amazed at his cousin's enthusiasm.

When Elizabeth revealed that they were considering giving a dinner party to welcome him home, Fitzwilliam was equally keen. "Will you have dancing afterwards?" he asked, his eyes sparkling, to which Darcy, who was not the keenest of dancers, replied, "If you wish to dance, Fitzwilliam, and you can persuade the ladies to join you, we shall certainly have dancing."

Everyone in the neighbourhood who knew Colonel Fitzwilliam and some who did not came to dinner at Pemberley the following Saturday: Charles and Jane Bingley, all the Gardiners, the entire Camden clan, Rosamund and her husband, Kitty and Mr Jenkins, who had recently returned from Wales, as well as some young people from the village. Georgiana and Mrs Annesley were returning from London, and Dr Grantley was expected from Oxford. It was a large party, and both Elizabeth and Mrs Reynolds were keen to ensure it was a success.

The dinner was a triumph, with a carefully selected menu and delectable dishes to suit every taste. Afterwards, there was the usual clamour for entertainment and particularly—music. Fitzwilliam had always been keen on music. Elizabeth recalled his enthusiastic support of her efforts at Rosings, all those years ago. She obliged with a song or two, and so did Kitty, accompanying her husband, whose fine Welsh voice was much admired. Georgiana, now a far more confident performer than she had been when Elizabeth first saw her play, made light work of a difficult composition, and Caroline, whose voice had been enhanced with training, sang a beautiful English lyric and had everyone applauding.

While she was being vastly praised for the sweetness of her voice and the excellence of her phrasing, Caroline was collecting the sheets of music into her folio, when Colonel Fitzwilliam joined them and invited her to sing with him the duet they had sung some three years ago, before his departure for the colonies. The music was found, and though Elizabeth could not recall it very well, she was persuaded to accompany them. The song was so delightfully rendered it held everyone in the room spellbound, with even the footmen reluctant to bring in the coffee, lest they break the spell. When it was over, there was such a burst of applause that young Caroline blushed as Fitzwilliam most gallantly kissed her hand.

Caroline, now a very ladylike young person, curtseyed to return the compliment and bowed deeply, before retreating to the back of the room, where she clung a little uncertainly to her cousin Jane's hand. Only then did she realise that she was trembling. Jane squeezed her hand and held it, "That was beautiful, Caroline, simply beautiful," she whispered, and Mr Bingley leaned across his wife to endorse her words of praise.

Mrs Gardiner and Elizabeth exchanged glances, but neither said a word. Elizabeth wanted to know how Fitzwilliam had recalled the words after three and a half years. "However did you recall it so well?" she asked, after congratulating him on the performance. To her surprise, he told how he had not been able to forget the melody for months after he had left England and in a moment of great nostalgia had written to Mr Gardiner requesting that he purchase a copy and send it to him in Ceylon, where he was stationed at the time. There being none available, Caroline had made him a copy in her own hand, which was despatched by the next mail.

"It brought me so much pleasure, just seeing the words and being able to sing them so far from England. Since then, it has become my favourite party piece," he declared.

"And could you always find a willing partner to sing it with you?" Elizabeth asked, a little wickedly.

"Oh yes," he said, "but never one who matched the original for perfect harmony and sweetness of tone. As you can see by her performance tonight, Miss Gardiner has a most enchanting voice."

Elizabeth agreed. "Indeed, she has," she said, as they joined the other guests. And enchanted you certainly seem to be, she thought to herself. She was rather glad young Caroline had not heard this last, extravagant compliment, for Elizabeth had heard more than his words, in the gentle inflections of his voice, and a tiny grain of anxiety began to insinuate itself into a corner of her mind. However, it was such a happy occasion that she determined to push it out of her thoughts.

The following morning, Darcy and Elizabeth had come down to a late breakfast, to find that Fitzwilliam had risen early and ridden over to Lambton with Bingley. Jane, who was enjoying a solitary cup of tea, since most of the other guests had left either the previous night or very early in the morning, knew only that Fitzwilliam, on hearing that Bingley was taking his usual morning ride, had persuaded him to ride to Lambton. "I cannot be certain, Lizzie, but I did hear some mention of a farm near Matlock," she said. Elizabeth raised her eyebrows and said nothing more. Darcy seemed to know something but was disinclined to discuss it.

When it was close to midday and they had not returned, Jane, whose anxiety was probably because her baby was due in a month, seemed to become concerned about her husband. Darcy left the room and was about to go out, when they heard the horses. Soon afterwards, Fitzwilliam burst into the morning room, with an obviously exhausted Bingley bringing up the rear. "Where have you been? Jane has been most anxious," said Elizabeth, betraying her irritation a little. Fitzwilliam, immediately contrite, went over and apologised profusely to Jane. He had never intended to keep her husband away so long, he said, but there was this farm, in the dales below Matlock, beside the Derwent. Mr Gardiner had told him about it last night, and he absolutely had to see it. Since it was such a fine morning, he had decided to go at once.

"Bingley, I am sorry, it was thoughtless of me, but it was just the most perfect place. Darcy, you must see it and tell me what you think."

"Would it make any difference if I disagreed with you?" Darcy asked, not hiding his amusement.

"Darcy, of course it would." Fitzwilliam was indignant. "You know I value your opinion above all things. I may not always change my mind on account of it, but I certainly take it seriously."

"Bingley, what is this farm like?" asked Darcy, more inclined to trust his brother-in-law's opinion in the face of his cousin's enthusiasm.

Bingley shrugged. "It is certainly a very pretty farm, exceedingly pretty with an excellent view of the heights and meadows sweeping all the way to the river. The house is small but seems comfortable, and the garden's pretty," and that was about all he was going to say, since Mrs Reynolds had sent in fresh food and tea and Bingley was very hungry.

When they had finished, Jane and Bingley decided they would leave almost at once, in order to be home before dark. Their carriage was sent for, and after fond farewells, they drove away. Darcy, still uneasy about the speed with which

Fitzwilliam was throwing himself into everything, tried to caution him. He chose reassurance rather than a warning. "You know you can stay here for as long as you need to, Fitzwilliam. You do not have to rush into anything."

His cousin was grateful but insisted that he had no time to waste.

"Of course, I know that, Darcy, and it's very good of you and Elizabeth, but I must settle somewhere, the sooner the better. I feel I want a place of my own before I can start my work, and this place is very promising, you'll see."

"What does Mr Gardiner think?"

"He says it is very good value; there are no real disadvantages. It is half a mile from Matlock—you could walk to the village and close enough to Chatsworth to make it interesting. I like it well enough already, but Mr Gardiner says I should think carefully and make up my own mind."

"He's right, of course," said Darcy and then, on a sudden impulse, "Fitzwilliam, you can tell me to mind my own business if you wish, but I have to ask you. Is there any particular reason for making such haste? You are not secretly engaged to someone . . . ?" He was not even permitted to complete his sentence.

"Engaged? Of course not! Darcy, whatever made you think that? No, there is no other reason except I am thirty-three years old and feel I've spent half my life doing very little. I did not have the means, even if I had the inclination. Now, I have both, and there is so much to be done, Darcy, I want to start forthwith." There was no mistaking his sincerity, as he went on, "I see how happy you are with Elizabeth and Bingley with Jane; even little Georgiana seems to have more purpose to her life than I have. I just want to get mine in order, and to do that, I must have a place of my own. I've never had one."

Darcy apologised for having pried into his cousin's personal life, but Fitzwilliam was most magnanimous. "I know you meant well, and believe me, if there had been a lady, Elizabeth and you would have been the first to know." Having settled the matter of a lady, he returned to the question of the farm, and Darcy decided that they would go on the morrow, if only to set his own mind at rest. He felt responsible even though Fitzwilliam was older than himself. He had always come to him for advice, and Darcy could not refuse him now.

And so to Matlock they went, this time, in the carriage because Elizabeth expressed a desire to go, too. They drove first to the Gardiners' and discovered that Mrs Gardiner and the girls were coming as well. They went in two carriages since the Gardiners had decided to drive into Matlock, afterwards. Elizabeth joked that they were a party large enough for a picnic and had she known in advance, she would have packed a picnic basket, seeing it was such a fine day.

Although the village of Matlock lay not far from the northern boundaries of Pemberley, Elizabeth had not been there since her marriage to Darcy. She had happy memories of the Peak district, so beloved of her Aunt Gardiner, from their holiday in Derbyshire three summers past, and recalled with vivid pleasure all of her feelings—of confusion, happiness, and delight, which she had experienced at her unexpected meeting with Mr Darcy at Pemberley. She had confessed, much later, to her aunt that the journey back to the inn had been a mere blur, during which the strange behaviour of her own heart had dominated her thoughts and prevented any appreciation of the dramatic untamed landscape of the Peaks. Mrs Gardiner had teased her then with the assurance that once she was settled at Pemberley, why the Peaks would be no further to visit than the environs of the Pemberley Estate.

Elizabeth smiled to herself at the coincidence in their lives that at this moment had brought them all together in this place. Unlike the rather severe beauty of the Peak, whose stony summit seemed to glower down upon the deep valleys and wooded gorges below, the dales were sunny, welcoming, and friendly places. They had visited Dove Dale, too, and Elizabeth recalled the delight of standing on the path that ran beside the river Dove and looking up at the heights, thickly wooded, green, gold, and ashen, on the lower slopes rising to the sheer, hard edges of steep hills, shimmering in the sunlight.

The road curled its way through the dales, and then a mile shy of Matlock, it branched out towards the ridge of hills that rises to the summit of High Tor. Gently dipping into a wide curving valley, suddenly, the road petered out in a patchwork of green meadows and brown stubble falling away towards the river in the distance. At the high end of the valley, where the woods trailed down from the hills towards the most appealing natural hollow, filled with wild daisies and rampant mint, was the house. It stood four square, its welcoming, well-proportioned frontage facing the neat front lawn.

They climbed out of the carriages and stood there looking at the scene, until the excited voice of Emily broke in, "Oh look Mama, there's a dog," as a retriever came racing out of the bushes at the far end of the valley. A man followed the dog out and, seeing the visitors, came towards them. Colonel Fitzwilliam, Darcy, and

Mr Gardiner went to meet him. He appeared to be the caretaker; they wanted to ask some questions and apply to see inside the house. Meanwhile, Elizabeth, Mrs Gardiner, Emily, and Caroline walked up the gravelled path and up a shallow flight of steps to the porch, which protected the entrance to the house.

The gentlemen had disappeared behind the house to look at the important features—stables, outhouses, and barns—while the ladies, obviously pleased with what they saw, were eager to see inside. Mr Gardiner walked with the man towards the outer edge of the meadow which sloped rather steeply towards the river, whose gentle curve seemed to cradle the small valley, before it flowed more swiftly down to the gorge beyond. Across a low stone bridge lay the home farm's fields, worked at present by two families, who had served the previous owner until his death in the war. It turned out that the property had been sold once during the war; the owner's widow had left the area and returned to her native Scotland, when the rush was on to purchase every farm in sight. With the collapse of prices in the rural recession, it was for sale again. Mr Gardiner discovered that the two tenant families had no desire to leave; they had nowhere to go to and, if the new owner let them stay on, would provide labour for the home farm. By the time he joined the others, Mr Gardiner had decided that this was a property well worth considering.

When he had walked through the house, with its solid construction, well-proportioned rooms downstairs, and five pleasant bedrooms and a sitting room upstairs, as well as a large, typical farmhouse kitchen and scullery, he was convinced that Fitzwilliam should make the owner an offer.

The ladies were similarly delighted. Mrs Gardiner thought the best part of the house was the dining room with its view of the lower slopes of the hills. Elizabeth liked the well-proportioned drawing room, but for Caroline there was no place better than the large room upstairs that ran the width of the house and afforded, from all its windows, splendid views across the river, to the woods and the ridge of hills beyond. "I think this would make a wonderful music room," she said, and Fitzwilliam, hearing her, declared without hesitation that it was exactly as he thought it should be.

"A music room, indeed, it will be perfect for just such a purpose," he said. Elizabeth managed to avoid Darcy's eyes, but Mrs Gardiner caught her looking very thoughtful and said, "I'll give you a penny for them, Lizzie." Elizabeth doubted if her aunt had any idea what Elizabeth was thinking. She simply smiled and said nothing, for the moment.

On the journey home, Fitzwilliam was eager to have Darcy's opinion of the property. He had said little, except to agree that its location was quite spectacular. Pressed for an opinion, he was candid. "You are exceedingly fortunate, Fitzwilliam. If you are quite satisfied and can negotiate a fair price, I suggest you close the sale as quickly as possible." His cousin was delighted.

"Darcy, do you mean that?"

"I certainly do. It's an excellent little property, since that is the size and type of place you are looking for, I think it would suit you exceedingly well," he said. Fitzwilliam beamed. He already knew Mr Gardiner's opinion; to have Darcy's approval as well was all he needed.

"I shall contact the owner's agent tomorrow," he declared, and there was no mistaking his delight. He turned to Elizabeth, smiling, "You liked it, too, Elizabeth?" he asked.

"Oh yes, I think it is a charming place," she replied, "You will need some new rugs and drapes, I think, and the scullery could do with a good scrub down." Fitzwilliam assured her that he would have everything inside renewed in time, and new curtains would present no problem at all. Could he count on her advice, he asked, hopefully, to which Elizabeth replied that, of course, they would do everything to help.

When they arrived at the Gardiners' place, it was past midday, and Mrs Gardiner insisted that they have some light refreshment before proceeding to Pemberley. The invitation was gratefully accepted. They had only just sat down to luncheon when a rider arrived with a letter for Mrs Gardiner. It was from Mr Bingley, announcing the safe arrival of their daughter—Emma Jane, born in the early hours of that morning. She had not been expected for at least two weeks! "Early again, a typical Bingley," said Elizabeth. It was a gentle joke in the family that Mr Bingley was always early for everything. It dated from the days when he used call to see Jane at Longbourn, often arriving before breakfast. Arrangements were soon made for a visit to Jane on the following day.

The year ended on a celebratory note, despite the background of unrest in the cities, where bank foreclosures ruined businessmen and farmers alike. There had been attacks of arson and skirmishes in the streets, and an increasing wave of petty crime had resulted in much alarming talk, with frightened householders fearing attacks in their homes and travellers wary of being on the road after dark.

It was not the familiar friendly face of England. The cruel boom followed by bust characteristic of the industrial era had unnerved the populace.

In spite of this, at the election that year, the Tory government was returned, with some losses in London alone. The Reformists and Radicals decided that the lily-livered Whigs had failed and they intended to go all out to press, not just for the defeat of the Tories, but for Parliamentary reform as well.

Buoyed by his success at negotiating, with the help of Mr Gardiner, an excellent deal on his property, Fitzwilliam decided to try to further his political career by applying to stand for Parliament at the next election. Unfortunately, his youth and enthusiasm were not enough to counter the influence of more longstanding members of the Reform Group. Turned down, he returned disappointed but determined to try again. Calling on the Gardiners to break the bad news, he found them deep in their preparations for Christmas and stayed to help. Both boys were home for Christmas, and together with Caroline and Emily, they helped cheer him up.

When it came to Christmas, the Gardiners were traditionalists. It was their turn to host the festive family gathering, and they took it very seriously. Mrs Gardiner and her cook prepared large quantities of traditional fare, and the children spent many hours hanging decorations and choosing gifts for each other and their parents.

Fitzwilliam, who had never experienced this type of Christmas at home, found the warmth and friendliness of their household irresistible. As his own place was unlikely to be ready before the New Year, he was still staying at Pemberley but, in fact, was spending more and more time at Oakleigh, on matters of business as well as pleasure. Elizabeth, who came over on occasion to lend a helping hand, was not surprised to find Fitzwilliam there, as he had often spent the day with them. It was of no use to offer him a seat in her carriage; he always preferred to stay on and ride home later.

On Christmas Eve, Caroline and Emily were expected at Pemberley to help with the children's Christmas party. Fitzwilliam set off shortly after noon to fetch them. When they arrived at Pemberley, closer to five than four o'clock, there was only Caroline. Emily had become ill, having eaten too many nuts and sweets, they said. Georgiana, who had been waiting very patiently, was so grateful to have her help with the children, she rushed Caroline indoors and waved Fitzwilliam into the drawing room.

Elizabeth, however, had been watching from her favourite window and could not fail to notice the glow of pleasure that seemed to wrap them and the easy familiarity with which young Caroline gave her companion her hand, so he could help her out and then appeared to be in no great hurry to withdraw it, after she had alighted from the carriage.

Fitzwilliam had the look of a young man who had somehow lost control of his feelings. He smiled unnecessarily and for too long, he appeared to feel no need of food or drink, he was unfailingly polite to everyone while appearing not to hear a word anyone said, and he kept looking around the room until he found the one face he wanted to see. To Lizzie, the symptoms were unmistakeable.

Halfway through the evening, Elizabeth happened to be standing beside Dr Grantley and Georgiana, when Caroline appeared with one of the little children, who had become unwell. The speed with which Fitzwilliam rushed to her side to help and the concern he showed for her, because she had carried the child, who was not at all heavy, brought a smile to their lips, and Dr Grantley whispered something to Georgiana, which Elizabeth could not hear, but which she was quite sure was a reference to the couple they were observing.

Later that evening, Mr Gardiner arrived to take his daughter home, and Elizabeth was relieved, not because they had been guilty of unseemly or censurable behaviour, but because she feared for them. She loved Caroline as if she was her own sister, and while she was confident of her virtue and Fitzwilliam's integrity, she could not help worrying about the consequences of their romantic involvement. She recalled Jane's sorrow, her own unhappiness, both of which were short-lived and had ended happily, but if Caroline were hurt at such a tender age, how would she cope? She resolved to talk to Darcy about it, but the occasion did not immediately arise.

～≈～

Christmas Day was busy and crowded with dozens of things to do, which thrust the matter of Fitzwilliam and Caroline into the background. Not so on Boxing day, which was also Caroline's birthday. The Gardiners were having a grand dinner and dance in her honour. Fitzwilliam had asked at least three times at exactly what time they would be leaving for Oakleigh. When they arrived, Caroline was still upstairs. Family members were already gathered in the hall, and other guests were still arriving. The large drawing room had been prepared for dancing, with a small chamber group providing the music, with two other rooms arranged for the dinner. At seven, precisely, the music makers played a modest fanfare, and young Caroline came downstairs on the arm of her very proud father. To say she looked beautiful seemed inadequate to describe her on that night. In a dress of cornflower blue, with soft lavender ribbons and a corsage of violets, her hair in a modish Grecian style, she carried herself with so much grace that she brought tears to her mother's eyes. There was applause which she acknowledged with a curtsey and a smile, and then, the music started.

It was at this point that Elizabeth held her breath. Was Caroline going to let everyone into her secret, by dancing the first dance with Fitzwilliam? If she did, it would be an indiscretion, however minor, that they may both later regret, Elizabeth thought. To her enormous relief, it was her cousin James—a young man of impeccable credentials, the son of Mrs Gardiner's brother John—who took Caroline's hand and led her in to the dance. Later, she danced with her brother Richard, with Bingley and Darcy and her Uncle John, while the Colonel waited patiently for his turn. It had been an agonising wait for him, during which they both did everything right. He danced with Elizabeth and Jane, with Georgiana and Emily, but it seemed there was only one person in the room he was waiting for. Whenever he was not engaged in the dancing, his eyes would follow Caroline, as she moved down the line, turned, and returned to the figures of the dance. Occasionally, their eyes would meet, and sometimes, they smiled.

Finally, Fitzwilliam claimed his reward for an hour or more of patience and discretion, and thereafter, she danced only with him for the rest of the evening or at least until dinner was served and the musicians took their rest. Elizabeth and Jane were together, waiting for their husbands to join them for dinner. Jane spoke first, "Lizzie, Caroline and Colonel Fitzwilliam make a very handsome couple, do they not?" Elizabeth laughed.

"They certainly do, Jane, and only a blind man could fail to see that they are in love." Jane smiled. Neither were prepared to say anything more, at the time.

END OF PART ONE

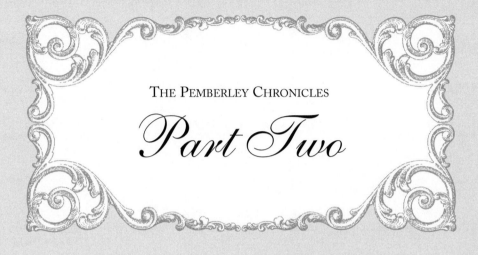

THE PEMBERLEY CHRONICLES

Part Two

CHAPTER THIRTEEN

A marriage of true minds

T HE MORNING OF GEORGIANA Darcy's wedding day dawned crisp and fresh, as though Nature herself knew this was a very special day at Pemberley. And indeed, it was. There had not been a young woman married from this great house in two generations, and this was a very special young woman. Nowhere was there a single voice that wished her anything but the greatest happiness.

Elizabeth awoke early, unable to sleep with excitement and anticipation. During the five years that she had known her young sister-in-law, she had grown to love her dearly. There was, truly, no one, apart from her own beloved sister Jane, for whom she had felt such warmth and affection. Her husband was well aware of and greatly appreciated Elizabeth's efforts to cultivate the relationship, which he felt had been wholly beneficial to his sister, transforming her from a shy, rather diffident young girl with very little self-confidence, into a charming and talented young woman.

Elizabeth was disinclined to take all the credit her husband wished to accord her for Georgiana's development, sharing it gladly with Dr Grantley, whose maturity, intelligence, and excellent judgement she greatly admired. But, no one who had known the awkward fifteen-year-old Miss Darcy and watched her emerge slowly into the sunlight like a butterfly from a chrysalis, could doubt the value of Elizabeth's influence upon her.

Mrs Reynolds, the housekeeper, was one whose doting eye could see no fault in either her Master or his sister. Yet, she had acknowledged Elizabeth's part. As they made the final preparations for the wedding, Elizabeth had said, "It is going to be an important day for all of us, Mrs Reynolds, not just for Miss Georgiana." Mrs Reynolds agreed that they had all waited many years for such an occasion at Pemberley, adding in her quiet way, "It is indeed a very special day, Ma'am, and if I may say so, we all know how much is owed to you and your sister—Mrs Bingley."

Elizabeth had been pleasantly surprised by her lavish praise of both herself and Jane, for their kindness to Miss Darcy. "You see, Ma'am," she explained, "With her dear mother gone, there was no one to set her an example. The Master was very loving and did all he could for her, but it is not the same, is it, Ma'am?" Elizabeth agreed that it was not, saying, however, that she was sure Miss Georgiana must have had governesses, companions, and friends. "Oh yes, Ma'am, but not those who could be as you have been, like a sister to her. I have watched how she has grown, in herself as a young person, since you and the Master were wed. She is a real lady now. Oh I know she used to sing and play and amuse us all, but she was ever so shy and quiet in company. And if you don't mind my saying so, Ma'am, and some might say it is not my place to say it, but I did not think that Miss Caroline Bingley was a good influence upon our Miss Georgiana at all."

Elizabeth had bitten back her enthusiastic agreement with this judgement, but her smile had betrayed her. She felt she was in good company. Darcy himself had remarked upon the shallowness and lack of substance in the conversation of the two Bingley women, happily contrasting it with the interesting contributions made to any company by Miss Caroline Gardiner, who was so much younger, yet much better informed and well-read. Both Jane and Elizabeth had formed the impression that he had, for the most part, put up with the Bingley sisters because of his friendship and regard for their brother, for whom he clearly had great affection.

Darcy had no doubt at all that his sister had benefited immensely from the new acquaintances she had made since his marriage to Elizabeth but most particularly from the affectionate relationship that had grown up between Georgiana and her sister-in-law.

On returning from his customary morning ride, Darcy came in to the bed-room and found Elizabeth looking out at the park and the woods in their soft Spring colours. As he joined her at the window, she turned to him and said, "Isn't it a perfect day? I am so happy for them. They deserve the best possible start to their marriage." Darcy agreed.

"They certainly do, but even if the heavens had opened up and the rain had poured down, I doubt if it would have spoilt their day. I have never seen Georgiana so happy, and Elizabeth, my dearest, she, we, all of us owe much of that to you." She was about to hush him and put her hand up to do so, but he would not be silenced. He took her hand in his and held it as he spoke, "No, my love, it cannot be denied, no one who has known Georgiana can fail to see how she has been transformed over these last four years. She has told me herself how much she values the close and affectionate relationship you share. Her trust in you and your judgement, her admiration for your honesty, even the light-hearted fun you have together, these are all important to her. They have changed her life, quite remarkably." Elizabeth protested, "You make me very proud indeed, when you credit me with all this, but do you not agree, my love, that Dr Grantley has been the greatest influence upon Georgiana—his maturity and width of vision must have materially changed so much of her thinking."

"Of course it has; I do not deny that. Francis is my dearest friend, I know him to be the best of men; I do not doubt that he has broadened her horizons and developed her mind, but Georgiana needed, indeed craved, the company and affection of a sister, and you, my dear Elizabeth, gave her that in full measure."

Elizabeth recalled the day almost five years ago at the inn at Lambton, when Darcy had brought his shy, young sister to meet her for the first time. Even as she sang the praises of her perfect brother, Georgiana had confessed that she would have loved to have had a sister. At that time, Elizabeth had had very little hope of becoming that sister by marriage. Her relationship with Mr Darcy had just begun to thaw, after their chance meeting at Pemberley. Shortly afterwards, the disastrous events of Lydia's elopement had almost shattered any hope she may have had. As she contemplated the changes in her own life, changes that had affected others—including Jane, Kitty, Mr and Mrs Gardiner, and now her cousin Caroline, Lizzie smiled and, suddenly, shrugged away her concerns, recognising how much the love they shared meant to both of them and the people they held most dear. Turning into his arms, she embraced him with a degree of warmth that made him smile and suggest that perhaps it was a perfect day for all of them, not just for the bridal couple.

The wedding guests filled the church, and included for the first time in years the bride's aunt Lady Catherine de Bourgh and her daughter Anne, while all around overflowing into the Rectory gardens were people from the estate—tenants, labourers with their wives and children, who cheered as the bridal carriage approached and the bride alighted, supported by her brother. Waiting for her was her tall, distinguished groom. They were married by Kitty's husband, with a homily preached by a close friend and colleague of Dr Grantley, quoting Shakespeare's sonnet—"Let me not to the marriage of true minds admit impediments—."

The choir of Pemberley children sang the wedding hymns like angels, filling the church with sweet sounds. Later, the guests returned to Pemberley for a splendid reception. Every eye was turned upon the bride, whose elegant figure was perfectly gowned in satin and French lace. While Dr Grantley had been a visitor to Pemberley for many years as a friend of Mr Darcy, not many people knew him well. Now they were all eager to meet the man who had not just won Miss Darcy's heart but was widely admired and praised by everyone who knew him. Not even Lady Catherine could find fault with Georgiana's choice. She had accepted the invitation sent in the names of Mr and Mrs Darcy, without comment. Clearly pleased by the deferential treatment accorded her at the church, as the most highly connected personage present, as well as the aunt of the bride, she was remarkably condescending in her manner towards Elizabeth and Jane, when she met them with their husbands.

While there was no hint of real appreciation, she seemed to have accepted, with as much grace as she could muster, that the marriage between Darcy and Elizabeth had not polluted the hallowed portals of Pemberley, as she had feared. Her affection for Georgiana was genuine, and the very real bond that existed between her niece and Elizabeth, a bond of which Georgiana had spoken with great warmth during her visit to Rosings with Dr Grantley, had served to soften her aunt's attitude, just enough to preserve them from her usually sharp tongue.

Before they left for the Lakes, which Georgiana had always longed to visit, Dr and Mrs Grantley came to thank Darcy and Elizabeth. There were tears as the sisters embraced, and Georgiana whispered, "Oh Lizzie, I can never thank you enough. Were it not for you, this happiness could never have been mine."

Elizabeth refused to believe this. "Georgiana, you cannot mean that."

"Indeed I do, and thank you for being such a wonderful sister to me," she insisted, before turning to her brother and enfolding him in a great hug that threatened to ruin her beautiful corsage. Darcy's face betrayed his deeply felt emotions as his young sister left her family home. Elizabeth understood how he must feel and held his hand in hers as they said farewell to the couple and saw them to their carriage. In a flurry of rose petals and cheers from the guests, they were gone.

Mr Bennet had observed, in his usual sardonic manner, that Lady Catherine must have wanted very much to see how well or ill the new Mistress of Pemberley conducted herself and the wedding had provided a good occasion to make a judgement. If that was the case, there would have been little if anything to upset Her Ladyship's sensibilities; it was generally acknowledged that the arrangements were excellent. The army of servants and helpers, who had been trained for days to serve and cater to every whim of the guests, did exactly as they were asked, with not so much as a broken glass or a spilt sorbet to spoil the occasion. Lady Catherine almost acknowledged it herself when, on her declaring she was ready to leave, Darcy and Elizabeth escorted her to her barouche. "You have done well, Fitzwilliam," she said. "Your dear mother would have approved. The arrangements were well done. My compliments to you too, Mrs Darcy—no doubt you have played a part in all this."

Elizabeth accepted this comment with a bow, and a gracious, "Thank you, your Ladyship."

When she added, "And I am happy to see that Pemberley still looks as good as ever," Darcy thanked her, but after she had departed, they had to laugh at his aunt's words, which appeared to suggest that she had feared Pemberley may have fallen into disrepair in her absence!

❧

Following an almost idyllic Spring of 1819, the rest of the year turned, suddenly, sour. The short-lived recovery from the agricultural recession gave way to a mood of sullen depression in the country; especially in the textile manufacturing districts of the Midlands. The collapse of the textile industry, with the loss of hundreds of jobs, resulted in a fearful development, with a spate of machine breaking and arson attacks.

The improvement in foreign trade over the last two years had masked the gradual destruction of the smaller textile mills. Those who had lost their farming rights and migrated to the towns to seek work in the new industries found they were out on the streets, again, this time in alien surroundings far from home and any help, save the grudging charity of the poor house. Many were desperate and turned to petty crime or worse.

Colonel Fitzwilliam was visiting Pemberley, when Mr Gardiner arrived with news of a particularly bad attack, which had led to the arrest and charging of several men for machine breaking. The penalty, if they were found guilty, was death by hanging or slow death by transportation to Van Dieman's Land. Fitzwilliam was furious, "What do they propose to do?" he demanded, "hang or transport half the population of the Midlands?" Darcy agreed that the options appeared limited. If there were more attacks upon property, it was likely to provoke even more repression.

"With no leadership at all from the government, the poor and disillusioned can only turn to the Radicals," he said. Fitzwilliam countered that the so-called Radicals were not revolutionaries demanding the heads of the rich, as in France, but conservative men like Major Cartwright—founder of the Hampden Clubs which demanded reform of Parliament, and respected Whigs like Sir Francis Burdett and Lord Brougham.

"These are not men who want to turn the nation on its head, Darcy," he persisted, "they merely ask for a better deal for the poor and representation for the men who create the wealth of this country—the traders, the merchants, the professionals, and the middle class."

Darcy was not optimistic, nor was Mr Gardiner.

"I cannot believe that this government will agree to any reforms; they are committed to maintaining the power of the landlords whose representatives support them in Parliament. They are very impatient with anyone who goes against the tide," he said, gloomily. Fitzwilliam jumped up, irate and impatient, expressing his determination to join Cobbett's pamphleteers and petitioners, who were agitating for reform.

"If that is the only way we can get our voices heard, I fear I shall have no alternative," he declared, his voice rising with anger and frustration.

Mr Gardiner's two daughters had been spending the day at Pemberley. Elizabeth suspected that the arrival of Fitzwilliam, unannounced, may have had more to do with their presence than a desire to ask after his cousin's health.

After the meal, both girls had gone upstairs with Elizabeth, while Darcy and his cousin remained in the sitting room. Hearing their father's voice, they prepared to go downstairs, but, while standing at the top of the stairs, they heard Mr Gardiner's words and Fitzwilliam's angry outburst, whereupon Caroline ran back into Elizabeth's sitting room.

Elizabeth followed Caroline, found her sobbing, and immediately went to comfort her, without knowing the cause of her distress. "Caroline, what is it?" she asked. Caroline refused at first to say anything but was gradually persuaded to tell Elizabeth of her fears that Fitzwilliam would join one of the Radical groups and put himself in harm's way.

"He could be arrested or killed, Cousin Lizzie; these are dangerous times, Papa says so." Elizabeth could hardly believe her ears,

"Caroline, what are you saying? Why would Colonel Fitzwilliam want to do that?"

"He is determined to do something about the poor people who are being thrown out of work and onto the streets. He says it is unfair that we should enjoy the benefits of their suffering, and, Lizzie, I agree with him, I really do, but I am afraid, because he could be in terrible danger." Elizabeth was silent for a moment, and suddenly into that silence Caroline blew her little nose and said, "I am very afraid, but I cannot say anything."

"Why?" asked Elizabeth, scarcely recovering from the surprise.

"Because . . . because I love him, Lizzie; he doesn't know I love him, and it would not be seemly for us to talk about such matters. Oh Lizzie, I don't know what to do," she was sobbing again. Elizabeth was reluctant to say too much but decided that the best way would be honesty.

"Have you never spoken of your feelings, either of you?" she asked.

"Of course not!" Caroline seemed shocked at the question.

"And have you told anyone else, before today?"

Caroline shook her head, still sobbing, "No, nobody, there was no one to tell." Elizabeth held her close, trying to reassure her that it was very unlikely Colonel Fitzwilliam would place himself in that kind of danger, but to console her, she promised to ask Mr Darcy to speak to him.

"You know how well he respects Mr Darcy; he will listen to his advice; I am sure of it."

Caroline was ecstatic. She threw her arms around Elizabeth. "Would you?

Oh Lizzie, I knew you would help me. Please, please could you also ask Mama if she would permit him to . . ." Elizabeth stopped her in midsentence. "Caroline, my dear, one thing at a time, please. Your Mama and Papa cannot possibly permit anyone, however good or suitable, to call on you, when you are just fifteen," she remonstrated.

"Mama was married at sixteen," Caroline retorted.

"She certainly was, but I still think it may be a little early for you to make such an important decision. Listen, my dear, once I know some more, after Mr Darcy has spoken with Fitzwilliam, I promise I will talk to your mother, but you must be patient."

It was almost half an hour later, having washed her tear-stained face and tidied her hair, that Caroline was ready to go downstairs. Her father waited to take them home. Emily, meanwhile, had retired to her beloved library, and Elizabeth went to fetch her. When they returned, Darcy and Mr Gardiner were in the hall, while Caroline and Fitzwilliam were deep in conversation beside the fireplace in the sitting room. To Elizabeth's surprise, they were both smiling and obviously happy. It was as if nothing untoward had happened at all.

Elizabeth determined that she would speak to Darcy that night. When she first told him of the scene with young Caroline, Darcy was surprised. He admitted he had noticed some degree of partiality towards Caroline on the part of Fitzwilliam but had not taken it too seriously. As for Caroline, she was, he said, a talented and lively young person with such an endearing nature, as to cause no one to read more into their friendship than was understandable and acceptable. She was, after all, he pointed out, just a child, and Fitzwilliam was twice her age.

"Darcy, that is exactly what I said to her, but her response was such that I was left in no doubt that there is, at least in the early stages, a much closer bond between them," Elizabeth said. "Could you not speak to Fitzwilliam?" and seeing the look of anxiety that crossed his countenance, she added, "He is your cousin and I know he respects and values your advice."

Darcy was reluctant to interfere. He reminded her of the exceedingly unhappy consequences of his last intervention in the affairs of another young couple and his absolute determination to avoid a similar disaster. Elizabeth understood his reservations, but for the sake of young Caroline, for the sake of their friendship with the Gardiners, some one had to find out what Fitzwilliam's intentions were. "We cannot now pretend that we are unaware of the situation, even if we have turned a blind eye before today. I know I shall blame myself if she is hurt and my Aunt Gardiner will never forgive me," said Elizabeth, and she looked so unhappy that he relented.

However, he did try to allay her fears, "Elizabeth, I know you are afraid that we may be making the same mistake that resulted in your sister Lydia's unfortunate entanglement with Wickham, but, dearest, remember there are very great differences. Caroline is nothing like Lydia; she is intelligent and sensible; even if she thinks she is in love, she will not do anything stupid. I am sure of it. On the other hand, I would wager my entire estate on Fitzwilliam's honour and integrity. He is no Wickham, my dear, and we are all well aware of his sound financial position, so I think we need have no fears on that score." Elizabeth agreed but was still fearful that a combination of youthful innocence with high emotional sensibility could well undermine even the most virtuous of characters and begged her husband's help. Understanding her anxiety, he agreed.

That night, Elizabeth, unable to sleep, rose and wrote to her sister:

My dearest Jane,

A circumstance has arisen which I must discuss with you as soon as possible. It is a matter of extreme delicacy and concerns some of those dearest to both our hearts, so I cannot speak openly about it in company— even among the family. This being so, I shall arrange to travel to Ashford Park on Wednesday and hope we shall have some time to ourselves. Meanwhile, I must beg you to remain silent on this matter. Please do not disclose, even to Bingley, the true reason for my visit. I shall say that I wish to consult you about something concerning Cassy. I do not wish to alarm you, so let me assure you that it is not a matter which materially affects either you or Bingley directly; rather it is a delicate "family matter" which, if unresolved, may cause unhappiness to those whom we all love dearly. There now, I have confused you completely, have I not? Dearest Jane, have patience, I shall be with you on Wednesday and all will be revealed.

Your loving sister,
Lizzie.

On the Wednesday, as arranged, Elizabeth went to Ashford Park to spend the day with her sister. Mr Darcy intended to see Fitzwilliam, who was at his house supervising refurbishments. Darcy felt it would afford him an opportunity to raise the subject that had so concerned Elizabeth.

Elizabeth, meanwhile arrived at Ashford House to find Jane all of a flutter, eager to discover the cause of her sister's concern. While they partook of morning tea, Elizabeth gave her sister a detailed account of her own observations of the situation between Caroline and Colonel Fitzwilliam and the distressing incident of two days ago. "But Lizzie, she is just a child," said Jane, disbelief written all over her lovely face. Elizabeth laughed and threw up her hands.

"How many more times will I hear that! Oh Jane, I do not mean to upset you, but that is what all of us think; in truth, however, Caroline has grown up before our eyes, and we have not noticed it. I believe that Colonel Fitzwilliam, arriving as he did last Autumn, seeing Caroline after three and a half years, saw the blossoming of a young woman, while we had all been seeing only the child." Jane's eyes widened, "You are quite right, Lizzie; unlike most other people, he has treated her quite differently; he kissed her hand and paid her compliments, like she was a young lady, which she is. Our Mama was engaged at fifteen." Elizabeth agreed but did not wish to be distracted from her cause.

"That may be so, dearest Jane, but our present concerns are rather different. As far as we know, neither our aunt nor our uncle is aware of the situation. They are probably doing as we did, thinking of her as a mere child. Furthermore, we have no notion of Fitzwilliam's feelings in the matter. Does he realise that Caroline's emotions are so deeply engaged? I think not. If he did, would he welcome it?"

"Do you not have any indication of his feelings, Lizzie? I confess I have not paid as much attention to these matters, since having Emma. She takes up most of my time, when she is not asleep. But Lizzie, what about you and Mr Darcy? Have you not observed them more closely? Was there no hint of his feelings?" Jane asked. Elizabeth took some time with her answer, explaining her own inclination to treat some of her observations lightly and adding to that Darcy's reluctance to interfere in his cousin's life.

"We must assume, since our aunt has said nothing to us on the matter, that he has not approached them—and that would explain why he has said nothing directly to Caroline."

Jane looked troubled, and when she spoke, her voice was gentle with sympathy born of her own experience only a few years ago.

"Oh Lizzie, if only Caroline could be spared this sorrow and at such a tender age too." Her kindness and concern were a reflection of her own gentle nature.

The sisters spoke no more about Caroline's unhappy situation, because Mr Bingley returned with young Jonathan, who immediately demanded the attention of both his mother and his aunt, so precluding any further discussion of the subject.

After luncheon, Jane had to go to Emma, and Bingley insisted on showing his sister-in-law-the beautiful display of Spring flowers in Ashford Park. Since moving from Netherfield, he had become far more interested in the grounds and was proud of his success.

As evening approached, Elizabeth grew anxious. Darcy was to join them for dinner. She hoped and prayed that his approaches to Fitzwilliam had not been misunderstood or rebuffed. That would be disastrous. When he did arrive, Elizabeth was surprised by his light-hearted manner. Indeed, Jane pointed out that he seemed perfectly cheerful. "Could it be that all is well, Lizzie?" she asked, hopefully. Elizabeth was impatient to discover the results of his efforts, but Darcy was never one to be hurried, and on this occasion, he was helped by the fact that it was not a matter they could speak of while the servants were about serving dinner. It was, therefore, only after they had withdrawn to the drawing room and Jane had sent the servants away, that he was able to enlighten them.

First, he spoke quietly with Elizabeth, taking the opportunity of Bingley's absence from the room. He told her his meeting with Fitzwilliam had been a good one and there was some news, which he thought they should all hear. Darcy felt it was not fair to expect Jane to keep it from her husband. He had Fitzwilliam's permission to tell them. Jane and Elizabeth could hardly wait to hear what he had to say. Bingley, unaware that that there was anything to be concerned about, returned to the room remarking cheerfully that this was very nice indeed, very much like old times at Netherfield Park.

Darcy waited until his brother-in-law had sat down with his coffee and port, but before he could speak, Bingley asked if anyone was going to sing or play tonight. He wondered if Lizzie could be persuaded. Jane, unable to bear the suspense any longer, touched his arm and said gently but very firmly, "Dearest,

Mr Darcy has something important to tell us," and when her husband looked a little surprised, she added, "it concerns Colonel Fitzwilliam."

"Fitzwilliam? Why, what is the matter? Is he unwell, Darcy?" Bingley asked, genuinely concerned.

Darcy confirmed that Fitzwilliam was very well. "He is at this moment at his farm, having his house refurbished. That is where I have spent most of today, and what I have to tell you concerns a matter dear to his heart." Now, even Bingley was interested. Darcy went on, "It also concerns someone for whom we all have great affection—Miss Caroline Gardiner." Bingley was quite taken aback. Darcy revealed that he had visited his cousin and, having apologised for interfering in his personal affairs, had questioned him about his feelings and intentions towards Miss Gardiner. Even as he spoke, Darcy could see the astonishment on the faces of Jane and Bingley. Elizabeth, at least, had been prepared for some of what followed.

After the initial surprise of Darcy's approach, Fitzwilliam had conceded that Elizabeth, as Caroline's cousin and confidante, was entitled to ask what his intentions were towards her. He appreciated that her age and innocence made her vulnerable, though he had immediately asserted that she was in no danger from him. Darcy found it difficult to express Fitzwilliam's concern, except to say that he had not sought such an assurance from him; he was confident of his cousin's honourable conduct.

Fitzwilliam had confided that since last Christmas, he had found himself falling in love with Miss Gardiner. Afraid at first to even admit it to himself, he had feared he would offend her parents, for he recognised that they regarded her as a child—as did everyone else. Jane and Elizabeth exchanged knowing glances as Darcy told of Fitzwilliam's unhappy and largely unsuccessful efforts to suppress his feelings. To make matters considerably worse, he began to suspect that Caroline reciprocated his undeclared feelings; it was apparent on every occasion, every time they met, each time they sang or danced together; all their conversations seemed to make it increasingly obvious, though neither spoke openly of their feelings.

Soon it was clear that it would not be possible to keep it from Mr and Mrs Gardiner. While he feared their disapproval, he had felt a strong sense of duty to be open with them. Fitzwilliam then determined to lay his cards on the table, whatever the consequences. While Caroline was at Pemberley after Georgiana's wedding, he visited the Gardiners and opened his heart to them. Darcy went on, "He says he promised he would do or say nothing without their permission, assuring them that in all things concerning their daughter he would be guided by them. He asked for no marriage settlement, promising rather to settle a part of his own fortune upon her, as soon as they were engaged. He promised also not to press for a marriage date until after her sixteenth birthday. He told me, as he had told them, that he had never loved any other woman as deeply and with such pure affection and begged to be allowed to speak to her, if only to declare his feelings."

By this time, Jane had become quite tearful and held tight to her husband's hand. Elizabeth asked, "What did they say?"

Darcy looked solemn. "They were understandably cautious, because she is so young, and wanted some time to think about it. Meanwhile he has promised not to speak of it to Caroline."

"Oh poor Caroline," said Jane, her voice almost breaking, "and poor, poor Colonel Fitzwilliam, how terrible he must feel." Darcy added that it seemed to him his cousin was relieved that he had been able to confide in him. He had lived with his secret for too long.

Elizabeth broke the silence. "Were my aunt and uncle surprised at his approach?"

Darcy shook his head. "Not entirely. I gather they had had some intimation of the situation. We are not always as successful at hiding our feelings as we may think, Lizzie. I believe, from what Fitzwilliam tells me, that in spite of their reservations, which are entirely on account of their daughter's very tender age, they have assured him of their regard and affection for him. They appreciate very much the discretion he has shown in his behaviour and the honesty and openness of his approach to them. He is convinced that they would make no objection were it not for her extreme youth. They worry about letting her become engaged so young." Jane, despite her tender feelings, was reasonableness itself.

"Surely, there can be no other objection. I cannot see how my aunt and uncle would object to the match, especially as they truly love each other." Darcy replied that he could certainly vouch for Fitzwilliam.

"I have known him all my life; he is undoubtedly very much in love. Every aspect of his behaviour in this matter confirms it." Bingley intervened to say how much he respected and liked Fitzwilliam.

"An absolutely honourable fellow, a perfect gentleman," he said. Darcy smiled, modestly acknowledging the praise heaped upon his cousin, pointing out that there had always been a very good relationship between Fitzwilliam and the entire Gardiner family, with whom he had corresponded regularly for three years while he was away in the East. He was now, in addition, a valued partner in Mr Gardiner's company. Should they be permitted to marry, Darcy said, he felt they would have an excellent foundation for a successful and happy marriage. Elizabeth spoke again. "How soon does Fitzwilliam expect to receive an answer?"

"He is to call on Mr and Mrs Gardiner on Sunday. Lizzie, I have taken the liberty of saying that we will be delighted to invite Misses Caroline and Emily over to Pemberley. We shall have to send a note to Mrs Gardiner tomorrow."

Elizabeth assured him she could find an excuse for an invitation, quite easily, and then asked, almost in jest, "And what of this nonsense about Fitzwilliam joining the Radicals?"

"He did say he had volunteered to assist with the petitions. As you know, he feels very strongly about the lack of leadership from the Parliament, and the petitions are demanding reform. Fitzwilliam has agreed to help with mustering support. I cannot see any danger in that." Darcy laughed and added, "As for being involved in anything more perilous, you can set Caroline's heart at rest on that score; he has no intention of putting his life in any danger. He has much pleasanter plans in mind for the future."

On the long drive back to Pemberley, through the woods that were now dark and silent, Darcy was quite clearly tired, and Elizabeth decided not to return to the subject. He was, for the most part, thoughtful, saying little. She was surprised, when he took her hand and asked in a low voice, so as not to be overheard by the coachman, "Elizabeth, are you pleased with me?"

"Pleased with you, do you mean generally?" she teased, and then, seeing his disappointed expression, she relented and assured him of her complete approval. "I cannot believe that it would have been easy to ask Fitzwilliam all those questions without offending him, yet you've done so well. Of course I am pleased with you, my love. I cannot tell you how glad I am to know that my aunt and uncle are aware of and able to deal with the situation."

"And to deal with it so well, as Fitzwilliam tells it," said Darcy. "For my part, I was concerned to know that my cousin was doing the right thing. I have only the greatest respect and affection for your aunt and uncle and their children. Caroline is especially dear to you, and I was unwilling to leave the situation as it was, without satisfying myself that all was well."

"And do you think all will be well, in the end?" she asked, anxiously. He nodded, "I certainly hope and pray it will," he said, putting an arm around her and drawing her close. And to that prayer, Elizabeth could only say "Amen."

Emily and Caroline arrived early on Sunday, looking forward to being back at Pemberley. Emily promptly retired to the gallery. When she grew tired of reading, she liked nothing more than to go out into the long gallery and gaze at the paintings, especially the fabulous Italian collection that was housed in a special place where the light would show the paintings to advantage.

For Caroline, the treasures of Pemberley lay, not in the furniture and accessories, but in the people. She loved hearing the stories of the men and women who had lived there from anyone who had time to tell them. Mrs Reynolds enjoyed telling her stories of three generations of the Darcy family she had known. Fitzwilliam had been amused by her interest, but Darcy encouraged it, happy that some member of the younger generation was interested in the past. He told her all about the eccentric Darcy ancestors, those about whom Mrs Reynolds did not know much or was tactfully silent.

After a very pleasant day, during which both girls had enjoyed being spoilt, they had dressed for dinner and were about to go downstairs, when Elizabeth's maid Jenny hurried upstairs to say that Colonel Fitzwilliam had arrived and was waiting in the sitting room. Darcy went down to him, while Elizabeth had to prepare Caroline for the encounter. She had already reassured her about his intention to help with Mr Cobbett's petition, but now she had to reveal that he had been to see her parents.

Caroline was aghast. She could not have known that there had already been an approach made and so trembled at the thought that their disapproval may mean the end of her dream. "Oh Lizzie, what do you think he has said? Would Mama have been very angry?" she asked, fearful of what may lie in store.

Elizabeth reassured her, "You need have no fears of your Mama; she is the kindest, wisest person I know. Now, come along with me, we must not seem to be dawdling for no good reason."

They went downstairs, and as they reached the door of the sitting room, Darcy appeared and said, "Elizabeth, Caroline, there you are. Fitzwilliam is waiting for you." He said no more, but Elizabeth thought he looked pleased and took that to be a good sign. Caroline almost ran away but, taking her cousin's hand to give her confidence, composed herself quite creditably, before entering the room.

Fitzwilliam was standing at the window, looking out over the West lawn. He turned and smiled, and Elizabeth knew then there would be no heartbreak for young Caroline. Having greeted both of them, he begged her pardon and asked to have a word to Elizabeth. After they had spoken, he returned to Caroline, who was sitting by the fire, and held out both hands to her. Elizabeth left the room, indicating she would be close at hand, if they needed her. She had no desire to intrude upon the moment of joy she knew would follow.

When she returned with Darcy later, they were still holding hands, sitting together on the couch by the window. They appeared to say very little, but there was no doubting their happiness. Caroline embraced Mr Darcy, kissed Elizabeth, and ran upstairs. When she was finally ready to return, she became rather shy but soon overcame it. Each time she seemed to demonstrate more maturity and common sense. The decorum that they displayed in their behaviour in company spoke volumes for the sensitivity and good sense of both.

Fitzwilliam stayed to dinner and, when he was leaving, said rather grandly, "I have an invitation for Mr and Mrs Darcy from Mr and Mrs Gardiner, to dine at Oakleigh on Wednesday. I shall call tomorrow morning after breakfast, to take Caroline and Emily home to Oakleigh; I know Caroline is longing to see her parents." Caroline, transformed by happiness, smiled and glowed, but said nothing. Only when she put her arms about Elizabeth and hugged her close, did she speak, "I shall never ever forget your kindness, dearest Lizzie, and Mr Darcy's," she whispered, as they parted for the night.

Elizabeth and Darcy could only look on indulgently. Having known the pain and frustration of separation in love themselves, they wished their cousins every happiness. They agreed, however, that they could wish them only as much joy as they had together, refusing to be dislodged from their position as the happiest couple in the world, by anyone.

CHAPTER FOURTEEN

To build Jerusalem

OMENTOUS AND FAR-REACHING changes were sweeping across England throughout 1819 and 1820, spilling inevitably into the lives of the people whose stories are recorded in these chronicles. Pemberley and its neighbouring estates lay at the very heart of the English counties where most of the changes were taking place. It was impossible for any family living there not to be affected by what was happening around them.

Throughout 1819, the shocking consequences of the depressed state of the nation's rural economy were seen everywhere, with bankruptcies and evictions on all sides. Proud, hard-working men and women were being turned out from places where they had lived and worked for generations, onto the streets—their livelihoods destroyed, their homes and workshops seized by the bailiffs. Cold charity, offered in small servings, bred such resentment and bitterness as few had experienced before.

When, with their leaders demanding redress and reform, they massed, marched, and paraded, the government brought down repressive legislation, and the magistrates sent in the yeomanry. The worst incident took place in August of 1819—when some sixty thousand unarmed workers, massing in St. Peter's Field at Manchester, were attacked by sabre-wielding troops on horseback, leaving eleven dead, hundreds wounded, and millions shocked by the savagery of the day's events. In an ironic comment on the "Heroes of Waterloo," this dreadful incident came to be called the "Peterloo Massacre."

Colonel Fitzwilliam and two of his associates had travelled to Manchester but, fortuitously, were not at St. Peter's Field. Caroline, now happily engaged to him, preparing for a wedding within the year, had begged for a promise that he would not go, and having given it, Fitzwilliam nobly resisted the temptation to attend, despite his overwhelming curiosity. His friends, however, obtained plenty of information from those who had been either participants or observers on the day. When the truth about the attack by the yeomanry began to come out from eyewitnesses returning to their villages, some of the newspapers, controlled as they were by the very men who had been responsible for the policies that had caused the violence, suppressed or ignored it. Not so, the *Matlock Review,* which was jointly owned by Sir Edmond Camden and his nephew Anthony Tate. The son of Sir Edmond's sister, Anthony had inherited his share of the paper from his father. Since he was still a student at Cambridge, he left the running of the business to his mother and uncle. Sir Edmond's sister, Therese, was, by force of her personal circumstances, a much more independent and liberal minded woman than many others of her time. She had married young, had two sons, and was widowed early in the war against Napoleon. Compelled to take on the responsibility for managing the family farm as well as raising her children, Mrs Tate had relied a great deal on the advice of her elder brother. Like him, she deplored the abandonment of the old tenant farmers and their exploitation by the new mill owners. She steadfastly refused to enclose the commons that lay adjacent to her farm, permitting her tenants to graze their sheep and fish or trap game in the woods, as they had done for generations. She used her influence with the editor of the *Review* to speak up for justice for the dispossessed, a stand that was not popular with several new landlords, though it had the support of men like Mr Darcy, Colonel Fitzwilliam, and Mr Gardiner.

Using the information provided by Fitzwilliam and his friends as well as the eyewitness accounts of several farm labourers, mechanics, peasants, and unemployed mill workers, the *Review* gave the story plenty of publicity. Bloodcurdling tales were told—much to the chagrin of the magistrates who had ordered the attack, of panicking yeomen in their bright, "toy soldier" uniforms, slashing at unarmed people with their newly sharpened sabres. For days afterwards, crowds gathered in market places, homes, paddocks, and common lands—wherever they felt safe from further attack, to talk about the "Peterloo massacre."

For the government, it was a disaster. The reverberations would go on for years. "No decent English heart could not but be ashamed that Englishmen had spilt the blood of other ordinary, hard-working English men and women, whose only crime was to demand a fair hearing and Parliamentary reform!" wrote the editor of the *Review*. There were calls from the local magistracy and conservative Tories for even harsher measures, but the majority of English people were horrified at the use of such force against unarmed peasants and workers and said so at meetings up and down the country. Fitzwilliam, attending a meeting of "concerned citizens," predicted that the "Martyrs of St. Peter's Field" had not died in vain and their deaths would change the Reform Movement forever.

Indeed, it appeared to have made Radicals out of several hitherto uncommitted middle class groups, who had heard the reasonable words of men like Bamford and Charles Greville. They warned that if England were not to go the bloody way of France, the rich and powerful had to heed the growing resentment of the poor and propertyless, who felt excluded from the heritage of their nation. Reform and change, they said, were not simply necessary; they were essential for England's survival. Fitzwilliam, whose political ambitions were taking shape, campaigned wholeheartedly for the cause.

Change, albeit of a somewhat milder nature, was happening within the Pemberley families, too. Mr and Mrs Darcy were now the proud and loving parents of a son—William Charles, born a few weeks before Christmas, lightening the mood of a rather depressing year. For Darcy and Elizabeth, it was the fulfilment of a wish they had not admitted to publicly. While there was not the pressure of an entail on Pemberley to require a male heir, there was the desire for a son to inherit his father's role in the community. Elizabeth, who had always missed having a brother, had longed for a son. William was rather a small baby, but he was a gentle child and gave little trouble as an infant. Elizabeth, whose daughter Cassandra was a truly beautiful little girl, declared that if William grew up to fulfil his early promise, she would be perfectly content with her children.

Her friend, Charlotte Collins, had been delivered of a third daughter, Amelia Jane, much to the disappointment of her husband, who was seeking to make more secure his inheritance through entail of Longbourn, on the death of his cousin—Mr Bennet. That Mr Bennet appeared to enjoy excellent health at present did not seem to affect in any way the ambitions of Mr Collins.

Mrs Bennet, however, was inclined to gloat and would publicly declare that the Collins' lack of male children was a form of divine punishment. Anyone in Meryton who would listen was regaled with the news that "poor Mrs Collins" had had another daughter, while all of her married daughters, except Kitty, who had, as yet, no children, had produced sons. The irony of her own state—of having five daughters and no sons, seemed to escape her completely. Moreover, Mrs Bennet, recently returned from Lydia's third confinement in Newcastle, brought unhappy reports of friction and worry over Wickham's wandering eye. She had little to do but entertain her friends and spread the gossip, with no thought for the sensibilities of her elder daughters or their husbands.

Jane, visiting Elizabeth for William's christening, brought the unhappy news to Pemberley. She and Bingley had been godparents to Charlotte's little daughter, who Jane declared to be "the loveliest little girl I have ever seen." Visiting Longbourn on the return journey, she had received a full account from her mother of the news from Newcastle, and it had alarmed her. Waiting discreetly for a time when their husbands were out riding and the servants and nurses were out of earshot, Jane expressed her unease about their wayward sister and her unreliable husband.

"Lizzie, if even half of what Mama tells is true, it is not a good situation at all." She said, proceeding to detail some of Mrs Bennet's reports. "It would seem that neither Wickham nor Lydia take their marriage vows seriously," she said and appeared more than a little shocked when Elizabeth declared, in what Jane took to be a rather cavalier fashion, "Well, that should come as no surprise. I cannot believe that anyone honestly credited either of them with serious intentions. Their marriage was brought about by the intervention of Mr Darcy and Mr Gardiner, who had to patch up the disastrous mess into which they had got themselves." Jane protested; her kind heart would not let her dismiss them so easily.

"How can you say that, Lizzie? Surely all of us hoped for some improvement, some change in their behaviour?" Elizabeth was unmoved.

"My dearest Sister, your goodness, your unfailing charity, will not let you see what is so plain to all of us—Wickham and Lydia are unlikely to want to change. She is still silly and vain and continues to flirt outrageously; he, it must be said, is at least less blatant about his desires; if what you have heard is true, he seems to be rather more discreet, though no less culpable in his behaviour, than our sister."

"Is there nothing we can do?" asked Jane. Elizabeth looked uncertain.

"I suppose, I could stop sending Lydia the small sums of money I have sent her for the children, as some form of censure, but I doubt if that will have any effect upon her behaviour. She will probably apply to you for help, instead." Jane looked surprised and embarrassed.

"Lizzie, has she been appealing to you for money?" she asked. When Elizabeth nodded and said, "For years," Jane shook her head in despair.

"Oh Lizzie, I fear you are quite right. We are never going to change Lydia; she has been receiving regular payments from me and Mama ever since Henry was born!"

The realisation of the irresponsibility and manipulative nature of their sister and her husband devastated Jane and angered Elizabeth. But both agreed that there was very little to be done, except hope and pray that they would not act so brazenly as to bring shame upon their families again. "I'm grateful that Darcy says little or nothing about them. He knows Wickham only too well, and, as for Lydia, there is nothing one can say that will improve our opinion of her. We are all aware that their relationship owes little to love and even less to logic. They were brought together forcibly—for my uncle is sure that Wickham had no intention of ever marrying her, because their desires had got the better of what little virtue and good sense they might have had. To put it plainly, Wickham was bribed into marrying Lydia." Seeing her sister's unhappy expression, Elizabeth took her hand, "I know you think I am being harsh, but, Jane dearest, when I stop to think how close they came to wrecking all our lives, to destroying not just our chances of happiness, but the lives of those we hold most dear, like Papa, I cannot find it in my heart to feel much sympathy for them in their present predicament. They were given the best possible chance that could have been salvaged from the wreckage of their relationship, after that stupid, wicked elopement. Now, if they wish to throw it all away, they can do so without any tears from me." A reminder of how close they had all come to losing everything, including any chance of a good marriage, dragged Jane back to reality.

"You are right, Lizzie; I realise that they are responsible for their own actions. We are not to blame for their troubles," she sighed, sadly.

The return of their husbands interrupted any further discussion of the painful subject. Other members of the family were expected to join them, and both sisters were looking forward to the arrival of the Gardiners and Colonel Fitzwilliam, who had been away in London for the past week.

The Gardiners, after some initial concern, had taken Fitzwilliam to their hearts. His devotion to their daughter had won him a special place in their affections, and both Mr and Mrs Gardiner would go to great lengths to help him with arrangements for his new home and forthcoming wedding. On this occasion, they had been shopping for items of Caroline's trousseau, but Mr Gardiner, whose long familiarity with London's commercial district was a great advantage, was able to advise his future son-in-law on a number of matters concerning his new establishment and obtaining the services he would require.

When they arrived at Pemberley, they were full of information about the scandalous goings on in London, more particularly at the Court, since the death of the mad King George III. Fitzwilliam was scathing in his criticism of the Court and the Parliament—for the charade that was in progress over the succession and the vilification of the Queen, by a King who openly and unashamedly paraded his mistresses. "And in the Parliament, those elected to govern us remain consumed by these ridiculous matters, while all over England good, decent people are sinking deeper into the mire of depression," he declared and added, "There are those in London who swear that we will soon have another revolution to sweep all this corruption away." Everyone else expressed the hope that it would not come to that.

"Several members of the Whig Party have declared themselves in favour of reform, and it is surely possible to hope that this could be brought about without violence," said Mrs Gardiner. Mr Gardiner expressed the hope that trade would save the day as it had some years ago, when all seemed lost.

"If only the government would bring its mind to bear on trade—there is so much to be done. The Dutch, the French, and even the Belgians are working hard at developing trade with the colonies, while our government fiddles with the marriage problems of the King!"

Darcy agreed wholeheartedly. He could see no solution to the current troubles, he said, unless the prosperity of the entire nation was uplifted. "There is little to be gained by the rich and the powerful withdrawing into their fortresses, while the poor and dispossessed beg in the streets, watching their children starve," he said, with the kind of firmness and certainty that made it difficult for anyone to disagree with him. Not that anyone seemed to want to do so, Elizabeth noted. "In times past," he went on, "those who owned and enjoyed the rich harvests of this country contributed to the alleviation of suffering of the poor and the sick. My father would have been ashamed to have homeless men and their families begging on street corners for the charity of strangers, or being forced into the poor house because they had no land to farm and no paid work on his land."

Fitzwilliam chimed in on a topic that was as dear to his heart as to Darcy's—the destruction of the rural English community. "What has happened to us, to England? Why do we, who have always helped our people, suddenly turn them away?"

"Well, as a matter of fact, Fitzwilliam, we have not," said Darcy. "At Pemberley, we have turned out nobody who wishes to stay on the estate and work here. Those who have left have gone because they wanted to, and there have been very few of them; some have found work in the towns, but others have returned, unhappy with their new masters."

Elizabeth, who had listened quietly, ventured the information that her maid Jenny's brother had gone to the mills at Manchester, on the promise of good wages and advancement. However, less than a year later, he was back—working as an undergardener happy to be back at Pemberley. Darcy supported her view, adding that there were several instances where the mill owners had provided jobs that demanded long hours of work in appalling conditions for very low wages.

He continued, "Indeed, I have plans, about which I intend to talk to Sir Edmond and others, to involve ourselves more deeply in the life of the community. I think we ought to make a greater contribution towards the welfare of the people who live on our estates, providing help with schools and medical care." On hearing Darcy's words, Kitty's husband, Dr Jenkins, asked if Mr Darcy would help with a school for young children on the estate to be run by the parish church. Kitty was keen to get it started, and there were other parishioners willing to assist her, he said. Not only did Mr Darcy show an interest in the idea, he promised to meet Dr Jenkins to discuss it further. It was, he said, the sort of thing that could help people in these hard times.

"If we could provide a school for young children, it would help their parents cope with some of the problems they face," he said.

"And at least, the children would be safe at school, while their parents worked," added Elizabeth, who was delighted that Darcy had supported the plan. It was an idea that attracted her, and she decided to pursue it herself.

These discussions usually petered out when the meal was served, but on this occasion, Elizabeth noticed that it seemed to continue all through dinner and was picked up again when they withdrew for coffee. It was only very much later she came to understand that the seeds of an exciting plan had been sown on that day. Her husband's vision of fostering a new community spirit, healing the fractured land, was yet to become clear to her.

Later that evening, Mrs Gardiner, Elizabeth, and Jane sat together in Elizabeth's private sitting room, where hot chocolate in front of the fire was an inviting prospect at the end of the day. Jenny set the tray down on the table and bade them goodnight. The gentlemen were still downstairs talking business and politics, while the children had been taken to bed. Young Emily came in to say goodnight, before she went to bed too, and her sister Caroline followed minutes later, lingering to let her cousins admire her exquisite ruby and diamond ring. When she had left them, Elizabeth remarked on how very well she looked, adding that they certainly seemed a very happy couple.

What pleased Jane most was the decorum they showed in their general behaviour in company. "There is no doubt that they are in love, and they obviously enjoy being together, but they cause no embarrassment to others," she said, and Elizabeth and Mrs Gardiner both smiled, remembering Jane's own extraordinary behaviour, when she and Bingley first met. Her extraordinarily high standards of decorum, coupled with her natural reserve and Bingley's modesty, which had led Darcy to believe that Jane had no deep attachment to his friend, had almost destroyed their romance. Happily, Jane knew nothing of that unfortunate episode. Bingley had clearly never betrayed his friend's part in it, and, for that, Elizabeth was very grateful. It would surely have hurt her sister very much.

Mrs Gardiner agreed with Jane, "I must say, Lizzie, Colonel Fitzwilliam is the perfect gentleman. I admit I had my concerns, not because of the difference in their ages, because after all I have been happily married to your uncle—a man fifteen years my senior and have appreciated his maturity and knowledge, greatly. Rather, it was because I feared that being so very young, Caroline may not have known her own mind. One rarely does at fourteen."

"And you have no such reservations now, Aunt?" asked Jane with a smile, for she and Lizzie had noted how Fitzwilliam treated Mrs Gardiner with great affection and respect. "No, none," her aunt replied. "Of course, Mr Darcy has always spoken well of him, and your uncle, who has done business with him for many years, will not hear a word against him. There is no question of his honour, and I have to confess that I have had not a moment's concern on that score, since his engagement to Caroline."

Jane interposed, "Of course, he is Mr Darcy's cousin, that must surely be a recommendation," but Elizabeth laughed merrily, reminding them that Lady Catherine de Bourgh was Mr Darcy's aunt, adding mischievously, "And, what of Miss Bingley, whose relationship to our dear Bingley beggars belief? No, Jane, relationship offers no certainty of character likeness between the parties. Why, think only of our own sister Lydia and the whole idea is destroyed."

At the mention of Lydia, Mrs Gardiner closed her eyes, as if she could not bear to contemplate the picture of her errant niece. "My dears, I had hoped not to speak of Lydia and her husband. Such foolish behaviour is rare indeed. It seems beyond anyone's ability to convince those two of the need to maintain any standards at all. It grieves me to say it, my dear Lizzie and Jane, but hardly a month goes by without a hurriedly scribbled note arriving with a request for some form of help with bills, payment of arrears of salary to nurses or tradesmen, and with no promise of any repayment at all."

Her nieces were shocked. They had not imagined that Lydia, who was already applying to her mother and sisters, was also appealing to their aunt for money. It was a most humiliating circumstance. Elizabeth had kept it from her husband all these years, sending small sums of money out of her own income, whenever a request was made. "You should not continue to help her, dear Aunt. She has used all of us, and while there may be some justifiable claim upon her family, there is none upon you and you must not let her use you so," Elizabeth said firmly, her face flushed with embarrassment. Jane was silent; her feelings of shame would not let her speak.

Mrs Gardiner thought rather differently, "Your uncle knows it all, my dears, you must not be upset. He says someone has to help her, or she will run up huge bills and borrow money from strangers, at high rates of interest, and compound the problem. It is better this way, even if it does spoil her further."

Jane and Elizabeth rose and embraced their aunt. To her wisdom and kindness as much as to their uncle's generosity, they owed a great deal. Hearing the voices of their husbands who were coming upstairs, they moved out onto the landing to meet them. They had spent such a pleasant evening together, none had noticed the lateness of the hour.

*

Elizabeth wrote to her father, inviting him to Pemberley in the Summer of 1820. She had heard from Jane that their mother was going with her sister Mrs Philips to Ramsgate, both sisters having decided that they deserved a holiday from their respective families!

On mentioning this to Mr Darcy, I have been urged by him to write immediately to invite you, Papa, "to take the opportunity to escape the domestic scene and visit Pemberley, where the pleasures of fishing, shooting, and plenty of reading" await you. I should add to this the company of at least two of your daughters—for Kitty is but ten minutes' walk across the park or fifteen by road, two sons-in-law, and your grandchildren, of course! Pemberley is at its prettiest from late Summer to early Autumn. Could you ask for more? We are engaged in planning for a new school that Kitty and Dr Jenkins want to set up for the younger children on the estate. Mr Darcy is providing the building and the furniture, converting and restoring a hall which stands in the grounds of the Rectory, and the teachers will at first be volunteers from the community. You will not be surprised to hear that I shall not be teaching drawing or painting—how wretched were my early efforts at home—but have agreed to assist with singing and reading. Mr Darcy believes that it will help in building a community spirit to counter the destructive effects of the enclosures that have created so much misery for the poor people in these parts. On the other side of the district, Colonel Fitzwilliam and the Gardiners are attempting something similar—at Kympton, with the assistance of the parish council. More when you arrive, dear Papa, we do so look forward to your visits. Mr Darcy asks that you send a message giving the time of arrival of your coach at Lambton, and the carriage will be there to meet you.

Cassandra sends her love. She looks forward to more of the stories you read to her when you were here last year. I think we can be confident that she will make some calls on your precious time.

Mr Bennet's response was short and to the point:

My dear Lizzie,

Your letter has convinced me that it is quite useless to spend even another day at Longbourn. Mary has already gone to Jane. I shall be on the coach on Wednesday. Do tell your husband that his offer of a carriage to meet me at Lambton is, as usual, happily and gratefully accepted. I look forward with great satisfaction to reading with Cassy; indeed I have acquired a new book with just such a purpose in mind.

Throughout that Summer and into Autumn, the families remained in the country, unless there was an absolute necessity to travel to London. The pleasant Autumn weather and the relative peace of the countryside provided ample reason to stay at home, while recent reports from the city offered every argument to avoid it.

Colonel Fitzwilliam, who had gone to London to lobby members of his Reform Group, wrote to the Gardiners:

. . . You are right to avoid London, for it has become a veritable mad-house—with the populace and the Parliament involved in an unseemly battle, as to who was the more disreputable, the King—as yet uncrowned or his unwanted and unloved Queen.

Darcy, Elizabeth, and Mr Bennet were dining with the Gardiners that evening. Fitzwilliam was to join them later. Caroline read, with appropriate dramatic emphasis, parts of his letter, which had arrived a day or two ago:

The streets are filled daily with a rabble, who support one side or the other—marching, shouting, waving banners, molesting innocent passers-by, and generally causing mayhem. Many feel we are close to revolution—but I cannot believe that we are to become involved in such an exercise on the back of such a dreary cause as this . . .

Mr Gardiner pointed out that Fitzwilliam was in London to lobby the Reformists for support with the plans they had for providing schooling and health care for the poor. "There is hope that the Whigs will support a new bill to let municipalities play a part in running some of these services. It will depend on the support they can get from the Reform Group, of course."

Mr Bennet, who had been very impressed with the work that Kitty and her husband were doing at the Rectory at Pemberley, was interested to hear how the plans at Kympton were proceeding. "Caroline is very much involved," said her father, very proud indeed of the role his daughter was playing, "She and Emily are to start a singing class for the young children and Mrs Tate, who manages the *Review,* will help Mrs Gardiner with the reading and writing classes." Mr Bennet, who had often expressed outrage that English children were left to grow up illiterate, unless their parents had sufficient money to have them privately taught their own language and literature, indicated that he was suitably impressed, though he remained outraged at the government's lack of interest.

Caroline continued, from Fitzwilliam's letter:

> *I cannot get a sane word out of anyone in the Parliament on the subject of reform either. The Romantics of the last decade—Sir Walter Scott, Coleridge, Southey, and would you believe, my dearest Caroline—your favourite Wordsworth—have all turned into ardent Tories and are demanding more repression and harsher penalties for the poor if they dare to question their masters. Wordsworth has even called for a police force to curb the people and laws to control the press.*

There was at this point a yelp as if she had been bitten, and Caroline cried out, "I shall never again read another novel by Scott or a poem by William Wordsworth." Everyone laughed; surely that was one promise she could not keep, they said, but Caroline was quite determined. "How could they want more repression of the people, and why would a poet like Wordsworth call for control of the press? It would be a betrayal of everything he believed in." Impressed by her passion, Elizabeth ventured an opinion, "Dear Caroline, many a youthful romantic has turned into a boring conservative with age. Wordsworth is no different to many others."

"Well I shall not," said Caroline, in a spirited voice, "And if a poet cannot speak for the people, what chance have the rest of us?" Then turning to Mr Darcy, she asked, "Mr Darcy, do you intend to turn into a boring old conservative, too?" Her mother gasped, but Darcy laughed and proceeded to answer her quite seriously, "Caroline, I am conservative, by nature, I prefer to preserve the best features of our society, and I value our traditions, but that does not mean I support injustice and repression. I am uncomfortable with this government, which supports the demands of the privileged and represses the poor. I do not accept that age or birth has anything to do with it; it is a question of having a sense of responsibility for your fellow men. I have always believed, as my father and grandfather did, that those of us who are fortunate in life must play our part in helping those who are not. I don't mean just doing charitable deeds and giving to the poor—all of us do that. I mean taking responsibility to contribute materially to the improvement of their lives, because it also improves the community in which we all live."

"Do you mean by that, Mr Darcy, building schools, libraries, and hospitals?" asked Mrs Gardiner, whose interest in the subject had increased with her own involvement in the Kympton Parish School. Darcy nodded his agreement, "Indeed I do, Mrs Gardiner, but not just building them; helping to keep them going, supporting the people who do the work, because healthy, educated people are going to be happier to live and work with than sick, ignorant folk, and that must benefit all of us as a community." Caroline gave a little cheer.

"Does Colonel Fitzwilliam know your mind on this?" she asked eagerly.

"Yes he does, and he agrees with me," said Darcy. Elizabeth looked across at her father. He was watching Darcy with interest and delight. He had never suspected this side of his reserved son-in-law's nature, even as he had come to know him better and found him more amiable, as Elizabeth had promised he would.

Later he would confide in Elizabeth his immense pleasure at finding Darcy expressing such noble sentiments. This was surely the man she had learnt to love. "I know now why you were prepared to defend him so passionately, when I expressed some disquiet. He has certainly shewn he is a man of compassion and principle, Lizzie, one after your own heart, eh?" Her pride and satisfaction at hearing her husband's words had been boundless. Having her father acknowledge his generous nature was especially pleasing. It was a side of

Darcy's character she had known for many years. It had given her much happiness; it was just very satisfying to know that others in her family acknowledged it, too.

The sound of a carriage drawing up heralded the arrival of Colonel Fitzwilliam, somewhat earlier than expected. He was made very welcome, by everyone and particularly Caroline. The bliss of the lovers, who had been apart for almost an entire week, was clear to be seen. They were left undisturbed in the sitting room for a while, before Mrs Gardiner went to remind them that dinner was served.

There was much news to hear and a great deal to talk about during and after dinner, but for Caroline and Fitzwilliam—nothing was more urgent or important than the joy of being together again. But equally, they were also deeply committed to the social and political goals they had set themselves, and their energy enthused others around them. Darcy had agreed to assist with the initial funds for their school at Kympton, and the Parish Council, of which Mrs Tate was a member, was making a hall available to them. The parents of the children who were going to be the first pupils at the school worked hard to complete the repair and refurbishment of the school house. Caroline, who had already obtained a promise of books from Georgiana, was delighted when Mr Bennet offered to contribute a number of items from his own library. "We shall soon have an excellent collection," she boasted, as her infectious enthusiasm drew everyone around her into helping with her project.

Some days later, as she watched her daughter set off on an errand of mercy, to take food and clothing for a family in the village whose father was out of work, Mrs Gardiner wrote to her niece, telling her of Caroline's work for the school and the children of the area:

> *Dearest Jane,*
>
> *I do not have all the words to express what I feel about my dear daughter. Just seeing her so content and so full of plans makes me the happiest mother in the world. Colonel Fitzwilliam has become a member of our family to the greatest extent possible, so that we shall truly feel that when our Caroline is married, we are gaining another son, not losing a daughter. Jane, dearest, what pleases me most is their generosity. At a time when almost everyone is busy pursuing their own selfish pleasures and ambitions or chasing more and more money, Fitzwilliam and Caroline*

seem determined to help as many people as they can. Nothing is too much trouble, if a poor family or a sick child can be comforted. Your uncle and I help them in every way, happy to encourage this wonderful spirit of charity and kindness. Today, they are off collecting to help buy the slates and chalk and other things they need to start next month—when Elizabeth will open the school at Kympton, the first for infants in this village. It will be such an important day for the people of the village; I cannot tell you how happy we are that our little girl is doing so much to help the children.

Mr Darcy and Elizabeth are her greatest supporters, with several donations in cash and kind from Pemberley towards the fund for the school. I give thanks every day for the happy circumstance that took us to Pemberley that summer and brought Elizabeth and Mr Darcy together; they are so perfect a couple, I cannot believe that either would have been happy with any other partner.

Your uncle and I are well. We hope you and Mr Bingley will be able to come down to participate in our little function, next month. With Colonel Fitzwilliam standing for Parliament, we expect the newspapers will take an interest. The Review has had two items already.

Do give our love to Bingley and the children; I trust they are all well.

God bless you all, my dear,

Your loving Aunt, etc.

CHAPTER FIFTEEN

Tides of change

T HE YEARS BETWEEN THE Coronation of King George IV in the summer of 1821 and his unlamented death in 1830 were filled with opportunities for change, which many European nations grasped and Britain, through an excess of inertia and a lack of leadership, missed. As nations large and small in Europe moved restlessly under the yoke of old style conservatism, struggling to change first one system and then another, in England the populace watched with increasing revulsion the absurd antics of the Georgian Court and the Parliament, which seemed to leave them stranded, as the tides of change receded.

The government appeared to lurch from one crisis to another, with no sign of a steady hand on the wheel of the ship of state. The high Tory faction that dominated the government had set their faces firmly against reform, reacting to even the mildest demand for change with repressive measures like the infamous "Six Acts." Meanwhile, the Whigs and other Reformists like Cobbett and Hunt struggled to be heard above the noise emanating from the Court, where the best efforts of all the King's men were concentrated upon his determination to rid himself of his unwanted Queen.

And all this while, more and more "gentleman farmers" were enclosing and enlarging their manors, with little thought for the families they had displaced.

In the big cities of London, Liverpool, Birmingham and Manchester, the working poor were housed in monotonous, grimy tenements, while the unemployed and sick begged or stole to survive on the streets. Across the nation, contradictions brought out the agitators and Reformers. Improvements in trade and transport brought prosperity to a new middle class in the cities, but half a day's journey away, across the green meadows and hillsides stained black with slag heaps and scour, there was deepening despair.

Amidst this national pall of unease and gloom, like a burst of summer sunshine on a bleak North Country morning, Caroline Gardiner and Colonel Fitzwilliam were married, in one of the happiest occasions the district had seen in many years. Caroline made a beautiful bride in a gown of the best French lace and silk her father could buy, and the Colonel in his uniform cut a very fine figure indeed. Caroline had warned all members of her family that they were not to weep. "This is my wedding day, and you are all to be as happy as I am," she had declared, "no one is allowed to spoil it with tears." Which was all very well, until it was time for the happy couple to leave, when Caroline embraced her mother and father and burst into tears. Young Emily, who had been her bridesmaid, followed suit, and soon a number of cousins and aunts were reaching for their handkerchiefs.

Caroline had grown from a rather pert and self-possessed little girl into a graceful and lovely young woman, with the intelligence and poise that a woman in her twenties might well envy. A credit to her parents, whose encouragement had played a big part in her development, she had also been advantaged by the very open, liberal environment of their home, where the children had always been encouraged to participate in family discussions and meet adult visitors, whenever it was appropriate.

She, like her brothers and sisters, had a pleasing sense of decorum quite beyond her years, which had been apparent in her model behaviour during the period of her romance and engagement to Colonel Fitzwilliam. Yet, they were so sincerely and openly devoted to one another, as to cause their friends to remark that neither would have been happy with any one else. Their long engagement, which had caused comment in some quarters, had only served to enhance and deepen their very genuine love. When they drove away, in an open landau, with most of the village wishing them well, no one could have doubted they were witnessing the start of a happy marriage.

Even Mrs Bennett, who had been heard to remark, on an earlier occasion, that she did not approve of big differences in age and long engagements for couples— even she was seen to dab her eyes and blow her nose as she wished the pair a long and happy marriage. She then proceeded to congratulate her brother and his wife on their daughter's excellent match. "Caroline has done very well, Brother," she said, as they moved indoors, "the dear Colonel used not to be such a good catch, being only a younger son. I recall at the time of Jane and Lizzie's weddings, saying to my sister Mrs Philips, that it was a great pity he had no fortune, for he was such a well-mannered and charming young man and could have married anyone he wanted. But, dear Lord, he certainly has done well for himself after his stint in the colonies," she said, somewhat carried away by her enthusiasm.

Mrs Gardiner, now her son-in-law's greatest supporter, spoke up. "Colonel Fitzwilliam's fortune is not merely the result of a stint in the colonies, Sister, he has worked very hard to invest his money wisely, and, as Mr Gardiner will agree I am sure, he is a most valuable and active partner in his business." Mr Gardiner, realising that his wife's sensitivities had been upset by his sister's usual tactlessness, intervened to wholeheartedly defend Fitzwilliam. Mrs Gardiner added pointedly, "Of course it is satisfying to know that he is very comfortably situated now, but, Sister, I am sure you would agree that our greatest comfort must come from knowing that Colonel Fitzwilliam is a perfectly honourable and trustworthy gentleman, whose devotion to Caroline is unquestioned. Indeed, no sooner were they engaged than he proceeded to endow Caroline with considerable assets; despite the protestations of her father, he would not be deterred. We cannot think of anyone else we know to whom we would so gladly entrust our daughter's happiness."

Mrs Bennett appeared to open her mouth and then shut it again, quickly. It seemed she had thought better of making any further comment. Elizabeth and Jane, who had come into the room in time to hear the tail end of the conversation, could only shake their heads and sigh with relief that their husbands, who were still outdoors, had been spared their mother's opinions. "Oh Lizzie, I do wish Mama would not upset Aunt Gardiner," said Jane, taking her sister aside, "She is going to miss Caroline and can do without further aggravation." Elizabeth shrugged her shoulders, "You know what Mama is like. Nothing will stop her from saying whatever comes into her head." Jane had resolved to take Mrs Bennet away with her, when they returned home.

"I have already asked Bingley and he has no objection; I shall go and ask Papa. I know Mama had intended to stay with my aunt and uncle, but I do not believe it is fair. I have already stopped her asking Uncle Gardiner whether Lady Catherine had been against the marriage and had stayed away to show her displeasure. I was happy to be able to assure her that Lady Catherine was unable to attend because she was ill."

"In fact," said Elizabeth, "Lady Catherine has met Caroline, and I am assured by Fitzwilliam, his aunt is very taken with her and has invited them to Rosings for Christmas together with James and Rosamund." Jane expressed great surprise.

"Lizzie, you are not serious?"

"Indeed I am. Lady Catherine has probably realised that Fitzwilliam, being the youngest son of her cousin, is extremely fortunate to marry such a beautiful, accomplished, and charming young woman, who is also likely to be very well-endowed. For while, I am told, Fitzwilliam has asked for no marriage settlement, our uncle will insist on arranging for Caroline to have a very reasonable income of her own." Jane promised she would tell her mother as soon as she had an opportunity to do so.

"If only Mama would stop talking, for just a little while," she sighed.

Elizabeth agreed, "She will not cease asking questions and making predictions—it will drive Aunt Gardiner insane." Jane nodded and went in search of her father to make arrangements for their journey. Left alone in the room, Elizabeth experienced a mixture of pleasure and guilt. She was undeniably pleased not to have her mother to stay at Pemberley, even if it was for one night, especially because they were playing host to the Hursts and Miss Bingley, who were returning to Bath on the following day. The prospect of her mother's meeting the Bingley women and spending an entire evening with them was more mortifying than Elizabeth could bear. Yet, she felt guilty that she had allowed Jane to do what was clearly the right and proper thing, in relieving her aunt and uncle and having Mrs Bennet to stay at Ashford Park, instead. That Jane did not appear to feel any degree of strain herself, was a tribute to the stability and equanimity of her sister's nature and the exceedingly tolerant attitude of her husband.

Mr Darcy came in search of his wife and found her looking anxious and uncertain, which was very unlike herself. He inquired and was told, with a sigh, that Elizabeth was wishing she had the same steady, unruffled calmness of her sister Jane. To which her husband replied that, while he thought Jane was one of the most beautiful women he had met and he agreed she had the most steady and gentle disposition, it was she, Elizabeth, with all her faults, who had bewitched him from their very first meeting, and since they were married, he did not think it was fair that she should want to change her nature now. Even though she knew he was teasing her, this ingenious argument so enchanted Elizabeth that, without warning, she warmly embraced him, unaware until she heard their laughter that three of the children had run into the room and were looking on with interest. Darcy laughed too, and said, "Let us go and find Mr and Mrs Gardiner, dearest. When I came in search of you, it was to tell you that they are to dine with us at Pemberley tonight." Seeing her surprised expression, he added, "I thought and I am sure you would agree, my dear, that you would appreciate their company and since they would be missing Caroline, it would be a good idea to invite them to join us."

"Darcy, it is a wonderful idea! At this moment, I cannot think of anything I should like better." So delighted was Elizabeth that it was only the arrival of several other guests that saved Darcy from another public demonstration of her affection and gratitude, but her smile said it all. There was nothing she preferred to having her favourite aunt and uncle at her side, while entertaining Miss Bingley and the Hursts at Pemberley that evening. The respect and affection Mr Darcy always showed them would be, she felt, a salutary demonstration to their guests. That Darcy could have thought of her and of the Gardiners and arranged to please them all so well only reinforced her love and admiration for him. It was the kind of thoughtful gesture, he would freely admit, would not have occurred to him before he met and married her. Now he knew how much it meant to her, he was doubly pleased with his efforts. It would transform the entire evening from a dull and dutiful one into a pleasure for both of them.

The evening proceeded in an entirely predictable fashion, with the Hursts paying much more attention to Mr Darcy than to Elizabeth, and Caroline Bingley's asking so many questions about Pemberley that one would have been forgiven for thinking she had a personal stake in the property. Indeed, so bewildered was Mr Hurst by the extent of Caroline's interest that he fell asleep and snored rather loudly. Fortuitously, the timely interruption enabled Mrs Gardiner to change the conversation and ask Miss Bingley how she liked living in Bath. "Very well," she replied, with a rather false brightness, "Oh, I like it very well indeed. One gets to meet so many people of real quality, and there is always something worthwhile one can attend." Elizabeth glanced at Darcy, who did not appear to be listening, being intent on pouring out some wine. She was, therefore, very surprised when he responded to Miss Bingley's question, addressed, as it was, to Mrs Gardiner.

Recalling that the Gardiners had left London to move to Derbyshire, Miss Bingley had remarked pointedly that they must surely miss the convenience of living close to their business premises in Cheapside. Before either of the Gardiners could reply, Darcy, who had returned with a glass of wine for Mrs Gardiner, intervened in a polite but cold voice, "That is hardly likely, Miss Bingley, since most of the business has moved West to the Midlands, and the port of Liverpool rather than London is fast becoming our chief trading centre." Miss Bingley raised her eyebrows in mock astonishment.

"Why, Mr Darcy, you seem to be exceedingly well-informed on matters of trade," the inflection in her voice suggesting that trade was surely a subject far beneath Mr Darcy's attention. Her attempt to insult his guests infuriated Darcy. He shrugged his shoulders and said, "And why should that surprise you, Miss Bingley? I do not deny it. Considering that your brother and I have been partners in Mr Gardiner's Commercial Trading Company for several years and have been recently joined by Colonel Fitzwilliam, it would surely be far more surprising if I was not," adding, "I confess I had a great deal to learn—Bingley had the advantage over me there." Darcy was too much of a gentleman to remind her that their father had been in trade himself, but the implication was clear. "But Mr Gardiner has been a most patient teacher, and I have found it a most engrossing subject. It is, without any doubt, the key to the future prosperity of our nation," he concluded.

Caroline Bingley was the kind of woman who never seemed to know when to leave well alone. Her attempt to insult the Gardiners with references to their background in trade had obviously backfired and angered Darcy into what could only be seen as a rebuke. Elizabeth met her aunt's eyes and knew she was fighting to keep from smiling at Miss Bingley's embarrassment. She remembered well a similar incident in this same room, when on a visit to Pemberley before her engagement to Darcy. Miss Bingley, who was also a dinner guest, had tried to humiliate her with a reference to Wickham and had hit the wrong target, upsetting Georgiana instead. On that occasion, too, she had stupidly angered the very person with whom she was trying to ingratiate herself.

Miss Bingley tried again, "But what made you choose Derbyshire?" she asked, this time, turning to Mr Gardiner, who began to explain that his wife was born and raised in the county. Once again, Mr Darcy intervened quite deliberately, "Mrs Gardiner and I had the good fortune to grow up not five miles from each other in what we both agree is the best of all counties in England," he said casually, and as Elizabeth and her aunt and uncle listened, hardly believing what they were hearing, he went on, "I was aware of Mrs Gardiner's great attachment to this district; we had spoken of it often and of the family's hopes of returning to the area, which was why I suggested that Mr Gardiner take a look at Oakleigh Manor, when it came up for sale. As for the rest, I am quite sure Mr and Mrs Gardiner will gladly tell you how happy they've been since moving there." As the Gardiners nodded and smiled agreement and Elizabeth could barely conceal her delight, Miss Bingley's confusion was complete. Despite the best efforts of the kindly Mr Gardiner, who tried to keep the conversation going, there was little more for Caroline to say. Mercifully, Mr Hurst snored again, and as if on cue, the footman brought in the candles. The Hursts and Miss Bingley decided it was time to retire; they had to make an early start, but not before they witnessed an affectionate leave taking between Elizabeth and Darcy and Mr and Mrs Gardiner, with promises to meet again soon.

Once their guests had retired, Elizabeth said not a word to her husband on the subject of Miss Bingley's humiliation, intending to let the matter drop, believing that would be his wish too. She was therefore more than a little surprised when Darcy said quietly, "You can stop pretending now, Lizzie; you may laugh if you wish."

Elizabeth did laugh but not at Miss Bingley's discomfiture alone; she was also laughing at herself, "And to think that, when I first met you, I thought you had no sense of humour," she said. Darcy smiled, permitting himself a small degree of satisfaction. He knew that despite her reticence, Elizabeth was delighted with what had transpired that evening. Recalling the many occasions on which Miss Bingley and her sister had either insulted or patronised Elizabeth, before she became his wife, Darcy was happy to have been able to even the score. Standing at the window beside him, Elizabeth thought of Caroline and Fitzwilliam. From the bottom of her heart, she wished them happiness. That they loved each other dearly was not in doubt. If they could find within themselves deeper sources of that joy, they would be happy indeed.

As if reading her thoughts, Darcy remarked, "If Fitzwilliam and Caroline are as happy in five years' time, as we are tonight, they can count themselves truly fortunate. Do you not agree, my dearest?" And of course, she did.

～

The birth of a son to Georgiana and Francis Grantley, in the spring of 1822, took Darcy and Elizabeth to Oxford, for his baptism. At the University, the movement for reform was gaining support, despite the draconian laws enacted to muzzle dissent. A new generation of writers and artists had joined the political agitators in calling for reform. These were more liberal minds with dreams of democracy and equality. The poets Shelley, Keats, and Byron were replacing Wordsworth, whose conservatism was regarded by the young as a betrayal. They, like Pushkin, Balzac, and Victor Hugo, who dominated the European scene, used their artistic reputations in the political struggle. The Greek war of independence fired their imaginations with romantic, often unrealistic aims, for which some Englishmen were ready to die. It was an exciting, if uncertain, time to be alive.

Dr Grantley and his charming young wife had around them a circle of artistic and academic friends, whose company, far from overwhelming young Georgiana, had served to stimulate her interest in a range of new ideas and activities. In addition to singing and playing the harp and pianoforte, Georgiana began to take an interest in teaching music. She expressed a hope that she might, one day, find time to study how to teach young children to perform and appreciate music. Elizabeth and Darcy continued to be amazed at the blossoming of her once shy and diffident character. "If anyone had told me two or three years ago that my young sister would host a soirée with such aplomb, I would not have believed them," he declared. Elizabeth agreed and added, "What is most pleasing is the way she seems to enjoy it all so much." Darcy believed that Georgiana was responding to the environment in which marriage to Francis Grantley had placed her. "The richness of experiences offered by such a centre of artistic and intellectual activity is a very exciting prospect, even if one is not directly involved. Georgiana is clearly enjoying it."

The Grantleys frequently attended chamber music concerts and operatic recitals with the Continis, with whom they had developed a particular intimacy. On this occasion, they invited Elizabeth and Darcy to accompany them and spent a most enjoyable evening with the Italian family, who had a sumptuous villa at Richmond, as well as their town house in Portman Square. Their sincere affection for Georgiana was quite obvious. Rich gifts of plate and crystal had arrived for her wedding, and now her son was showered with presents.

The Continis travelled frequently to Europe, and from them, Darcy and Elizabeth learned a great deal about events taking place there. The French appeared to be teetering on the edge of chaos, with revolution followed by monarchy, followed by further revolution, while in their native Italy, liberal, nationalistic movements had been crushed, and young patriots were looking for new leaders.

The Continis had a serious interest in music and were keen to endow a scholarship for the study of English music. They pointed out to Darcy and Elizabeth that much of the music being performed and composed in England was German in character. The Court had extended its patronage to composers like Bach, Handel, and Mendelsohn. "All very wonderful musicians but not very English," said Signora Contini.

"Who is composing or playing English music?" asked her husband. It was a question that did not admit of an easy answer, because if the truth were told, apart from the country people, who held to their old traditions, those who would be a part of the "elegant society" sought to cultivate the style of European art and manners.

Dr Grantley and Georgiana invited Darcy and Elizabeth to consider the proposition of allowing such a scholar to spend a part of the year at Pemberley using the resources of the library, with its collection of art, literature, and music, to study and compose. "Have you a particular person in mind?" asked Elizabeth, interested enough to want to know more.

"Yes, indeed, " replied Dr Grantley, "there are two likely candidates at least; one is a very talented young theology scholar, who also composes and helps with the choir, and the other is an older man—already in Holy Orders, but keen to study and compose sacred music."

Georgiana pleaded, and Elizabeth knew it would not be long before Darcy acceded to her request. There was hardly any occasion on which he had refused his young sister anything.

Elizabeth made her own contribution with a comment that such a person might be a good influence upon Cassandra and William, who were approaching an age when more formal teaching in music than their mother could give them was needed.

It was clear that Darcy was going to allow himself to be persuaded. He raised no objection and listened most attentively to all they had to say. Finally, he said, "Well, Francis, we will leave the selection in your hands, but I shall insist that Elizabeth have the final say on who it will be, after she has met them. Since the person you choose will live in our neighbourhood and be a frequent visitor to Pemberley, which is our home, I must insist on it." It was generally felt that this was a most reasonable condition, and so it was agreed that a selected scholar would start work in the Autumn. Lodgings would be arranged for him at Kympton, where the curate's house lay vacant.

This was the manner by which a young theology student, Mr James Courtney, came to live in the village of Kympton, worship at the church, and ride over to Pemberley each day. He was the first endowed scholar of English music to work at Pemberley.

The people of the parish of Kympton were delighted. The arrival of a young, active man, even if he were only a student of theology and not a proper curate, as they said, would add interest to their church activities, which, since the departure of the last curate at Kympton, had depended upon the generosity of the incumbents of neighbouring parishes. They hoped that young Mr Courtney would use the opportunity to do something for their parish, which had felt rather neglected since the living fell vacant. Mrs Gardiner, who together with her daughters had put a great deal of work into the little school at Kympton, was doubly pleased to discover the special interest that James Courtney had in music, since the school could do with some help.

As for his work at Pemberley, both Darcy and Elizabeth welcomed him and urged him to apply to the housekeeper for any assistance he may need, but so overwhelmed was he by the wealth of material he found and the quality of the collection, that he would scarcely leave the library all day. Mrs Reynolds complained that he hardly ate the food that was set out for him in a little ante-room, so engrossed was he in his work. Quiet and studious James Courtney was a very keen scholar indeed.

❦

The Summer of 1822 saw many children born to the families, whose stories are recorded in the Pemberley chronicles: to Kitty and Huw Jenkins, twin daughters named Elizabeth Anne and Maria Jane; to Kitty's friend Maria

Lucas, now Faulkner, who already had a daughter, Katherine, a much longed-for son, Daniel. News also came of the fourth child born to Lydia and Wickham, another son to bear his father's not particularly distinguished name. By now, even Mrs Bennet had grown bored with Lydia's confinements and could not be persuaded to travel to Newcastle for the event. She claimed to Jane that she was tired of the rattling coach and the dusty roads, but Elizabeth and Jane agreed that their mother was more probably tired of prattling and wailing grandchildren, who had long lost their novelty for her.

The happiest news of all came in the Summer, when it was confirmed that Mr and Mrs Gardiner would soon be grandparents. Caroline, who had spent a good deal of time helping Fitzwilliam with his campaign to collect the petitions for reform, had not admitted, even to herself, that she longed for a child. Yet, when after almost two years of marriage, she was still childless, her cousins could not fail to see the longing in her eyes as she played with their children.

The news that she would be a mother in the Autumn brought a great rush of joy to all her family and friends. For her husband, whose ambitions she had supported while she hid her own disappointment, it was a special time of happiness. The love and loyalty she had so selflessly given him, he repaid tenfold, and they appeared to have that special talent for sharing their happiness around, with a bright, infectious optimism, born of conviction and hard work. They looked forward to their child as to a blessed gift.

But, even in the midst of life, we are in Death.

Two unrelated events happened almost at once, changing the hopeful mood of the Summer of 1822 to one of sadness and, in some quarters, despair. The suicide of Castlereagh, now the Marquis of Londonderry—an aristocratic statesman and a patriot, a man more loathed than he deserved to be—was probably the lowest point in the nation's descent into political chaos. Fitzwilliam brought the news. He had been in London, lobbying for the repeal of the Anti-Combination Laws enacted at the height of the Napoleonic wars, when repression was accepted as a necessary evil. Calling at Oakleigh to see his in-laws and collect his wife, who had spent a few days with her parents, he appeared grave-faced and not at all himself.

Caroline, who had helped with preparing some of his material, asked quickly if anything was amiss. She feared he had been unable to see anyone in the Parliament. Was it disappointment, or, worse, had he been refused a hearing?

Passionately involved in the struggle to repeal the laws that prevented work-ing men from forming associations or unions by declaring them to be illegal, Fitzwilliam had gone to London to meet with men like Francis Place and the Radical Joseph Hume, but to his great consternation found the place in chaos, as the news of Castlereagh's death spread like wildfire through Westminster and the city. It seemed inconceivable that such a distinguished man, apparently at the pin-nacle of his career, should take his own life. The news, when Fitzwilliam succeeded in breaking it gently to Caroline and her parents, shocked and horrified them. That a man who had devoted so much of his life to the practice of government and diplomacy should die in such a manner was impossible to comprehend. Widely hated, especially by the younger Radicals, the Foreign Secretary had yet been, in the last few years, a peacemaker, working hard to prevent another conflagration in Europe—as the Greeks fought for their independence from Turkish tyranny.

Fitzwilliam told of the confusion that reigned in Westminster. "No one could understand his motives, unless it was the agony of frustration and a kind of personal rage against the world," he said, still rather shaken and welcoming the respite afforded by the Gardiners, whose wholesome goodness and consis-tency contrasted with the anarchic atmosphere of the city he had left behind.

Later that year came worse news, with the drowning of the poet Shelley in the Aegean Sea. He had gone with fellow Romantic Byron and others to help the Greeks in their struggle and was lost at sea. Caroline wept, when the news came. She, having transferred her loyalty from Wordsworth to Shelley and Keats, was distressed to find that they were so short-lived, dying tragically, within a year of each other. It seemed as if the young lives of those who could be called upon to fight for reform and enlightenment were being wasted.

"Can you not see that we are losing the best?" she cried, when Elizabeth, who loved her young cousin dearly, sought to console her.

"I can, and I share your sorrow for their passing, dearest Caroline, but remember there will be others. Fitzwilliam is sure that the mood is changing; people are demanding change. It must come." While her cousin's words and presence served to comfort Caroline, they did not convince her that circum-stances were about to improve. From her experience of helping Fitzwilliam over the last two years, she knew how difficult the political struggle could be. For a while, it seemed she would be inconsolable, and her parents worried about her health. But Nature reasserted her own power.

Later that year, when in the final month of Autumn her son was born, the change in Caroline was so remarkable that it was difficult to believe she had been so despondent but a few months ago. Her mother's support and excellent common sense, combined with the unswerving love and care of her husband, brought her through a difficult birth, and soon she settled into a comfortable domesticity, from which she had apparently no desire to be emancipated—for some years at least. A daughter, born a year later, brought even greater delight, and it was hardly possible to recall that this thoroughly contented young woman with her delightful children was the same girl who had wept inconsolably for Keats and Shelley.

Darcy permitted himself a little smugness, "I did urge you not to worry too much, Lizzie. I was certain that Caroline's innate good sense would reassert itself," he said, and Elizabeth had to admit he had been right. Fitzwilliam, meanwhile, continued his campaign, working with the Reformists and the Whigs to defeat the Tories, whose disreputable and discredited government hung on for as long as they could.

It was only after the death of George IV, unlamented and despised, and the accession to the throne of William IV, the Sailor King, in 1830, that matters of reform came to the fore again. The old Iron Duke's government was tottering. Many businessmen, who had joined up with the Reformist Whigs, Lords Russell, and Durham in an unlikely alliance, begged the Tories to throw him out. Despite their distrust of the Whigs, the working class Reformists Cobbett and Place, as well as the middle class leaders like Brougham, had no alternative but to accept the assurance of Lord Grey, who vowed to fight the next election on the issue of Parliamentary reform.

Fitzwilliam and his supporters, who were out daily collecting signatures for their petitions and money for their campaign, sought "Power for the People" in Westminster and in their local districts. But it was a fair bet that they would have to wait rather longer for it than the forthcoming election.

None of this appeared to worry Caroline, whose devotion to her husband's cause was total. "Collecting signatures for Fitzy," was as much a part of her domestic life as looking after her children or helping her charities.

With both her children and frequently her younger sister Emily, she would set out from home in her pony trap to carry the message to the denizens of Matlock, Lambton, Kympton, and Ripley, clambering up rocky paths to reach farmhouses and fording streams to get the information to isolated cottages and often stopping at markets and fair grounds to distribute pamphlets or collect signatures. Her enthusiasm surprised her mother and her cousins, but her father, though he said little in public, was obviously proud of the tenacity and courage of his daughter.

The Gardiners regarded themselves as a family blessed with many gifts, especially with regard to their children. If there was a smidgen of disappointment, it related to Robert, whose somewhat lacklustre personality contrasted with the charm of his sisters and older brother. When Mr Gardiner regarded Caroline, however, he felt he was completely compensated for any minor dissatisfaction he might experience with any of his other children, by the sense of purpose, the energy and sheer delight she seemed to bring to the whole business of living. It infected and enthused everyone around her and gave her a lustre that set her apart.

Marriage to Fitzwilliam had broadened Caroline's horizons and afforded her access to a new, exciting world of social and political causes, which she gladly embraced. What astonished her family and friends was her ability to throw herself into all of these activities, while remaining a warm and loving woman, whose husband and children had the best of her care and love at all times.

Elizabeth and Jane, whose happy marriages were the product of much less hard work and a good deal more comfort and leisure, never quite understood what motivated their young cousin. But they had no doubt at all of her happiness.

CHAPTER SIXTEEN

And time, perchance, to start anew

MR DARCY AND ELIZABETH had not expected to be in Kent again in the summer of 1830. They were to have joined the Bingleys, whose children were firm friends of Cassandra and William, in a tour of the Cotswolds, when two events, unrelated and quite unpredictable, had intervened to force a change of plan.

In late July, King George IV died. While his demise was hardly a matter for lamentation, it did necessitate the presence at Westminster of Fitzwilliam, who was standing for Parliament in the General Election that would surely follow. Since it was hardly fair that all three of Mr Gardiner's partners in business should be away at once, plans had to be rearranged. Jane and Elizabeth, who had been looking forward very much to the holiday together, were disappointed but had hoped a postponement would suffice until, not ten days later, there came the news of the untimely death of Mr Collins. While he had never been a man for whom she could feel anything above mild contempt, Elizabeth was deeply shocked because of the effect his death would have upon her dear friend Charlotte. Darcy had broken the news to her in the very early hours of the morning. A message had been received from Rosings, the express rider having ridden overnight, and Darcy's concern was written all over his countenance, when he gently woke his wife. "Dearest, we have some grave news," and as Elizabeth sat up, afraid that it concerned her father, whose health had caused some anxiety last Winter, Darcy held her and told her that Charlotte's husband had died, suddenly, the previous evening. Elizabeth's reaction was instantaneous, "Oh my God! poor Charlotte, I must go to her at once."

Darcy, who had anticipated her wishes, had already sent a message to Lambton informing the Gardiners and requesting their help with the children. Elizabeth rose and set about making preparations for the journey.

For most of the long drive, broken only to change horses and take refreshment, apart from the detour to Oakleigh with the children, Elizabeth was silent. Her face betrayed the feelings of guilt and sorrow that afflicted her. Her unhappiness stemmed, not from any feeling of great loss at the death of Mr Collins, but more from the realisation that, while she had frequently remarked quite cruelly upon the odd behaviour of the man her friend had married and shared her critical observations with others, now he was dead and Charlotte would be left to fend for herself, without the security that marriage to Mr Collins had brought her. On one occasion, her unhappiness was so plainly written upon her face that Darcy reached out and took her hand, hoping to offer comfort but succeeded only in releasing a flood of tears. "Poor Charlotte, whatever will she do now? What will become of her three girls?" she cried, "How will they live and where?"

Darcy understood her concern and tried to reassure her. "I cannot believe that they will be left unprovided for. There is no doubt that Lady Catherine has a very high regard for Mrs Collins, and I believe she is especially attached to young Catherine. She is not an entirely uncaring person and will certainly not turn them out of the parsonage at Hunsford before appropriate accommodation is found for them. It is a valuable living, and my aunt will take time to find a suitable replacement for Mr Collins, who was also her personal chaplain; that will surely afford Mrs Collins time to make what arrangements may be necessary for herself and her daughters," he explained.

Elizabeth was not so sanguine. Her more intimate knowledge of the Lucases gave her much cause for concern about her friend's future. "But where will they live? I cannot believe that Sir William can afford to have them all at Lucas Lodge. He has been much less active in business since his illness last year, and I do believe he has intimated to Papa that his eldest son, who is now away in India, expects to return to the house. Should he marry soon after, there will be no question of Charlotte and her children continuing at Lucas Lodge." Elizabeth sounded so distressed that Darcy was genuinely concerned that she might make herself ill with worry. Speaking even more gently than before, he sought to assuage her anxiety with argument.

"Dearest Lizzie, I understand completely and share your concern, but I cannot believe that Charlotte and her daughters will be left destitute. While Mr Collins may have been somewhat ridiculous in his manners and pompous in his speech, there is plenty of evidence that he was well able to obtain advantage for himself and his family. Please, my love, let us wait until all of the facts are known, and then, I promise that if there is need to help Mrs Collins and her daughters, in whatever way is appropriate, it will be done. I shall speak to my aunt, if necessary; I give you my word, Elizabeth, your friend will not be left helpless."

So determined and sincere were his words that Elizabeth, who knew she could believe him implicitly, was sufficiently reassured to allow her to regain her composure, as they turned into the lane that ran along the boundary of Rosings Park, leading directly to the parsonage at Hunsford. Her Ladyship's regard for Mrs Collins was apparent even as they alighted. A manservant had been sent to meet visitors and assist them as they arrived. Elizabeth hurried indoors to find a parlour maid, also from Rosings, serving tea.

Charlotte and her three daughters, in deep mourning, rose to meet them, and as the two women embraced, tears stained their faces. All three girls were redeyed with crying. While Catherine, the eldest, who was now fifteen, tried valiantly to keep control of her feelings, as she stood with her mother, young Rebecca's lip trembled as Elizabeth put her arms around her, and little Amelia-Jane, who was only nine, hid her face in her mother's skirts and sobbed. So affected was Darcy, that he seemed quite unable to resort to the usual formalities that obtained on such occasions, and bending down, he gathered the little girl into his arms to comfort her. Even Charlotte, in her grief, could manage a smile, and Elizabeth's love for him almost caused her to weep again, for she alone knew how deeply he was affected and how sincerely he cared.

Later, she knew he would assist in any way possible, when there had been time to talk to Charlotte of practical matters. For the moment, she had no doubt of his concern for her friend and her three children, left without the husband and father they had hoped would provide for their future. As others arrived to commiserate and console, Elizabeth moved to help without fuss, wherever she could. Lady Catherine's generosity, a form of "noblesse oblige" no doubt, extended to providing one of her smaller carriages with a driver for Charlotte's use and baskets of food and drink, which had been delivered to the kitchen. It was left to Elizabeth to organise the servants and look after the needs of the children, so as to spare Charlotte.

Meanwhile, Darcy drove on to the inn, a short distance up the road, where they would stay the night, having arranged to meet with the Bingleys before the funeral, for which preparations were afoot at the church. Later, he called on Lady Catherine and spoke with her manager at Rosings, where he learned that Mr Collins would receive the ultimate accolade of being laid to rest in a part of the family estate reserved for good and faithful retainers. Darcy did not doubt that Mr Collins would have been gratified indeed, to be so honoured by his patron.

Returning to the parsonage in the late afternoon, through the familiar woods, he found Elizabeth wandering somewhat aimlessly amidst the trees in almost the exact spot where many years ago, he had waited for her, intending to hand her a letter which he had hoped would exonerate him of charges laid at his door by George Wickham.

The Darcys had been invited to Rosings following Georgiana's wedding, which Her Ladyship had approved of sufficiently to let her rehabilitate her once-favourite nephew and his wife to a level of acceptability. However, they had never had the occasion to walk in this part of the grounds. Meeting there now brought a rush of nostalgia.

Silently, they held hands, each remembering but reluctant, in the face of the solemn reason for their present visit, to speak of their memories. Still, so attuned had they become to each other's thoughts and feelings over the years of marriage, that words were scarcely necessary, as they walked slowly back to the parsonage. As the footpath widened to meet the lane, Darcy spoke, "I have seen Lady Catherine. You need have no fears, Lizzie, it is just as I thought; Mrs Collins will receive a small annuity as well as any accumulated savings her husband had set aside. Perhaps best of all, Lady Catherine has endowed young Miss Collins, who is her goddaughter, with a sum sufficient to provide her with a good education and a small income. In fact, she appears to have been quite generous. My aunt is genuinely distressed at the death of Mr Collins, especially as it happened when he was inspecting with her a newly restored window in the chapel. He suffered a sudden seizure and collapsed, and though her own doctor was called immediately, Mr Collins was found to have died almost instantly. I am told Lady Catherine came to the parsonage herself, to break the news to Mrs Collins."

Elizabeth, astonished by his account of events, was silent as Darcy continued, "As for their accommodation, they can stay at the parsonage for as long as they need to make alternative arrangements; my aunt is in no hurry to replace Mr Collins. The rector from a living in the South of the estate will visit Rosings and provide services at the chapel. However, if after the funeral, you would like to invite Charlotte and the girls to spend some time at Pemberley, it may help them to come to terms with their loss in less painful surroundings."

Though Elizabeth had remained silent during this elucidation of Charlotte's circumstances, she was certainly not unmoved by it. It was a clear demonstration of her husband's thoughtfulness and consideration even for those outside his own circle of family and friends. She had been pondering, as she wandered the groves around Rosings, the injustice of Charlotte's fate—bereft as she was of the man she had married for some small security from poverty—the man Elizabeth had scorned but who had given Charlotte a comfortable home and loving daughters; it was a turn of fate Elizabeth could not begin to comprehend. Darcy had set her heart at rest, at least for the immediate future.

As they reached the stile over which he helped her into the lane, she embraced him with warmth and expressed her gratitude, "Thank you, thank you, my dear, dear husband. Whatever would I do without you?" she said and was rewarded with a smile that reminded her of his response, the first time she had admitted to him, on the road between Longbourn and Meryton, that her feelings for him had undergone a complete change since his first, disastrous proposal at Hunsford. They had, by now, reached the house and found waiting outside the carriage that had brought Sir William Lucas, Maria, and her family. Not wishing to intrude upon them, they walked on towards the inn, where Charles and Jane were expected to join them by nightfall. There had been no time to call on them; a rider was sent from Pemberley, with a hurried note bearing the distressing news and advising of the arrangements for the funeral.

When they arrived, Jane was almost sick with the strain of the journey and anxiety for Charlotte and her children. Bingley, who helped her to the room upstairs, looked tired and worn himself. Unused to personal grief since the death of his parents many years ago, he could barely cope with the shock of mortality. Jane was so tender-hearted that she could almost suffer with Charlotte the grief she was sure their friend must feel.

Elizabeth, aware of her sister's sensibility, proceeded quickly to reassure her with Darcy's account of his meeting with Lady Catherine. Jane was still deeply sad for Charlotte, but at least it seemed there would be no question of financial privation to follow.

"It does seem, dear Jane, that Mr Collins possessed rather more good sense than we credited him with, I should say I credited him with, for I recall you were never as ready as I was to condemn him," said Elizabeth. Jane dabbed her tear-streaked face again.

"Dear Lizzie, all through the journey from Ashford, I have suffered such remorse for all the unkind things we have said of poor Mr Collins. I could not believe he was dead and dear Charlotte and her three girls left to fend for themselves." Elizabeth hastened to reassure her, "Hush, Jane, there is no need to worry. Mr Darcy assures me that Charlotte and the girls will be looked after."

Unlike Elizabeth, Jane had never censured Charlotte for her decision to accept Mr Collins. She appreciated that Charlotte, who was almost twenty-seven at the time, had few options open to her if she did not marry, and while Mr Collins was surely one of the silliest men she had ever had the misfortune to meet, Jane could find little wrong with the manner in which he lavished care and attention upon his wife and family. That he was obsequious and excessively deferential to his patron, Lady Catherine, and exceedingly pompous in his expression of his own brand of morality seemed to Jane to be extraneous matters, which may have caused some amusement to observers but did not materially damage his family. Indeed, she pointed out, it now transpired that his attentions to Lady Catherine may have resulted in greatly alleviating the tragic consequences for his family of his own demise.

Elizabeth, despite her reservations, had to admit that this was probably true. It was neither the time nor the occasion to say it, but she knew that however straitened her own circumstances had been, she could never have countenanced marriage to Mr Collins.

As she prepared for the funeral, Elizabeth wondered whether she may not, one day, come to look upon present events as merely another turning point in Charlotte's life, rather than the dreadful tragedy they seemed to be at this moment. Charlotte had always been able to ride calmly over the rough as well as the smooth waters of life. Elizabeth was certain she would do so again. She was, however, sufficiently sensitive to Jane's feelings to keep her thoughts to herself.

After the funeral, which was suitably solemn and full of high sentence, and a mournful little gathering at Rosings, where a tribute was paid to the faithful service given to Lady Catherine and her household by the late Mr Collins, the families repaired to the parsonage at Hunsford.

There, among her friends and family, Charlotte put aside her black bonnet and veil and served tea and biscuits in the parlour. Her face was grave and pale, but she was calm and collected as she slipped into her household routine and her daughters likewise, all but little Amelia-Jane, whose eyes were still red with weeping. "She was her father's favourite," Charlotte remarked, as Jane tried to coax the child to eat a biscuit. Elizabeth was touched. She had not believed Mr Collins would have had a favourite child, so full of correctness and pompous moral rectitude had he seemed whenever they met. Could he have had hidden depths of feeling, as a parent? "He spoilt her," Charlotte continued, "I think he was trying to make amends for the disappointment he expressed so openly, when she was born. He had wanted a son, you see, Lizzie," said Charlotte, as usual, putting it all into perspective. Jane and Elizabeth nodded, both unable to make any response. It was not the picture of Mr Collins they had had.

Later, as they prepared to leave, Elizabeth and Darcy extracted from Charlotte a promise to visit them at Pemberley. It was a promise Charlotte would find no difficulty in keeping, so grateful was she for the support and kindness of her two childhood friends and their husbands, for whom she had a good deal of respect.

She agreed to come to them just as soon as she had completed the formalities and attended to all her obligations at Hunsford. "Lady Catherine has been very kind. She has said I can take all the time I need and has offered me the help of her manager for the paperwork. But, I am anxious to get it done as soon as possible, Lizzie; I shall not outstay my welcome," she said firmly.

"Then you must come to us, dear Charlotte," Elizabeth said, "And bring the children. Cassy longs for the company of a little girl; it will do all of us good."

"We can promise you a peaceful Derbyshire Autumn," added Darcy, and Charlotte, despite her dark widow's weeds, smiled.

"It is always so peaceful at Pemberley; I love it above all other places. Thank you both for your kindness. Yes, I shall be with you, soon."

Returning to Derbyshire, they found the Fitzwilliams in a state of high excitement, engaged most assiduously in the campaign for the election they knew was coming. There was much activity at Oakleigh also, because Richard, the Gardiners' eldest son, was expected home from Paris, where he had completed his studies to become a physician. Caroline and Fitzwilliam, well aware of his strong social conscience, were eager to involve him in their campaign for reform, while his parents simply longed to have him home again, after almost two years in France.

Following the death of King George and the defeat of the Tory government led by the Duke of Wellington, the Whigs, pledging reform, had won the support of the powerful merchant and middle classes. Reformists, who had found new inspiration in the exciting developments in Europe, particularly in France, supported the Whig proposal as a good start, though it did not give them even half of what they wanted. Compared to the achievements of the bloodless Paris Revolution, of the "three glorious days," which brought the downfall of Charles X, the Whig's proposals for change had seemed to provide little, but Fitzwilliam explained, "They were the best they could get and would whet the appetite of the middle classes for electoral reform."

Lord Grey was promising a Reform Bill which would change the electoral system and give a share of power to the men who, through industry and trade, were building the wealth of their nation. Hitherto, Parliament had been dominated by the aristocracy and the landed gentry: it was time for the rest of the people to assert their rights, too. This became the catchcry of Fitzwilliam's supporters, as they organised meetings and street parades. They knew only an election and a new Parliament could deliver a genuine Reform Bill. While no women could vote and most ordinary people, who did not own land, were shut out of the Parliament, Caroline and her husband believed that getting information into the homes and hands of the working people would pay dividends in the future.

To their amazement, Darcy and Elizabeth returning from a visit to the Gardiners, found Caroline in a tiny pony trap, with her two children and her sister Emily beside her, handing out pamphlets outside the inn at Lambton. There appeared to be a great deal of interest, as people stopped to ask questions, and Caroline, obviously well-schooled by Fitzwilliam, had all the answers down pat. "I cannot believe it," said Elizabeth, "she used to be so shy."

Darcy laughed, "She'll have Fitzwilliam run for the Ministry, mark my words. She may be little, but she has one of the brightest minds of any young woman I know. Mr Gardiner confessed to me that he was sorry Caroline had not chosen to go into the business. He believes she is far smarter than Robert. He's very proud of her." Elizabeth had to agree that her young cousin was surely the bright light in her family. Emily was studious and quiet, with a nice sense of humour, but without the distinctive charm of her elder sister, and Robert, though a polite and good-looking young man, seemed not to be filled with enthusiasm for anything at all. There was an unfortunate flatness about his personality that discouraged all but the most superficial engagement. Caroline, on the other hand, was always enthusiastic about any task she undertook, her fine eyes sparkling as she threw herself into her work, whether she was collecting donations for the poor or signatures for petitions. There was no doubt that her husband benefited to a great degree from the charm and grace that came so naturally to her. It was an advantage that many ambitious young Parliamentarians would have given a great deal to acquire.

Her brother, Richard, who, while he was not the eldest, had the advantage of height and weight over both his sisters, had remained something of a mystery to all but his immediate family. By the time the family moved to Derbyshire, he was at boarding school, and while his younger brother ventured no further than Cambridge before moving into his father's business, Richard had decided he wanted to be a physician. So single-minded was his pursuit of this ambition that he excelled at his studies in Edinburgh and was recommended by his masters to study further in Paris, where he soon lived up to his earlier promise.

Now, he was coming home with plans to practice, not in fashionable London or Bath, but in Birmimgham.

"Why Birmingham?" asked Elizabeth, for she knew her aunt had hoped he would return to live at home and work in the district.

"That was exactly my question, Lizzie," said Mrs Gardiner, confessing she was disappointed, but her son had made up his mind, as his reply, which she removed from her pocket book and gave Elizabeth to read, made quite clear.

In answer to his mother's query, Richard wrote:

Because, my dearest Mama, they need doctors in Birmingham, where no one wants to treat the working people. In Derbyshire, you have at least some good surgeons and a hospital. The ordinary people of Birmingham have nothing. If they are too poor to get a doctor, they simply die at home. I have been greatly privileged by my education, and I feel I must give something back to the people who need help. But have no fear, Mama, you will have me at home as often as you wish, when I am not working, Oakleigh is where I shall lay my head. You may soon tire of having me around. Dear Mama, a friend, who has worked with me these last two years, is also coming to England. He is Paul Antoine, the youngest son of a family I have come to know well. He will join me in my practice and work as my assistant. I am sure you will like him very much. His mother was English, but sadly, she has died, and this will be his first visit to England in ten years. He is rather shy; I hope we can make him welcome. I know you will. I long to be at home with all of you.

Your loving son,
Richard.

It appeared to Elizabeth, as she handed back the letter, that her aunt had already accepted that her son would work where he wanted. She was clearly happy he was returning and grateful that he had no plans as yet to leave the family home. Mrs Gardiner loved all her children, but there was never any doubt that Richard was the very apple of her eye. She was exceedingly proud of his achievements and, fiercely loyal, would not criticise his decision, even though she was disappointed with it.

Elizabeth was convinced that once Richard was back among them, his mother, having been converted by her son to his point of view, would become his greatest advocate. Already she spoke warmly of the unselfishness that must surely have influenced his decision, a sentiment that Darcy and Elizabeth could only endorse, even though they had some reservations about its wisdom.

Some days later, Fitzwilliam and Caroline were dining at Pemberley. When Elizabeth revealed Richard's plans to work in Birmingham, Fitzwilliam's response to the news was very different to hers. He pointed out that

Birmingham, with its famous Political Union for Reform, led by Thomas Attwood, was fast becoming a centre for the Reform Movement. "It is an excellent place for a clever young man like Richard to work. He will not only come into contact with many of the working people and their families, he will understand their problems and be able to press for reforms that would help alleviate their misery. Believe me, Lizzie, they need him far more than do the middle class matrons of Derby." Elizabeth was unwilling to let that barb pass, and a riposte was on the tip of her tongue, when Caroline intervened to soothe her irritation. "Dear Cousin Lizzie, do not let him tease you. For shame, Fitzy," she chided and continued, "What he really means is Richard is not just a good physician; he will be a doctor with a conscience and an understanding of the need for changes in places like Birmingham. He will be able to use his influence with the local councillors and Members of Parliament to help those who will otherwise have no one to speak up for them. Am I not right, Fitzy?"

The endearing sobriquet, which no one else was permitted to use, softened Fitzwilliam's countenance and brought a smile to the faces of both Darcy and Elizabeth. Fitzwilliam nodded, admitting his wife was right and what was more, she had expressed his ideas far more succinctly than he had done, but Darcy did add a cautionary note. "I am quite sure Richard will work hard at helping the sick people of Birmingham, and I have no doubt at all of his sincerity of purpose, but he will need more than his physician's skills to convince the councillors to spend any money on a hospital. I believe they have resisted all efforts to improve the conditions at the cottage hospital that provides such inadequate care for the poor, and they cannot be persuaded to pay for an extension to the schoolhouse. I wish him well, but I fear he faces an uphill struggle."

After dinner, the conversation turned inevitably to the election and the promised Reform Bill. Fitzwilliam was certain that Lord Grey would keep his word. Darcy was not so sure. He pointed out that the Whigs were every bit as "aristocratic" in their attitudes as the Tories. "There are no great democrats among them," he warned, adding that the Whigs were used to having their own way too.

But Fitzwilliam was reassured by the increasing dependence of the Whigs upon a new constituency—the middle class. They, together with the educated professional and academic representatives, were bound to press harder for reform, and he was convinced that Lord Grey would not betray them. Amidst mounting political tension, into which Fitzwilliam and his supporters were inevitably drawn, the year drew to a close. In London, a storm was brewing over the intransigence of the Tory Lords on the first Reform Bill presented by Lord Grey, and there was every appearance of fresh elections being called, which would be fought on the issue of reform.

Charlotte Collins, delayed by the need to visit her late husband's relations prior to leaving Kent, arrived at Pemberley in Autumn. Tired of the controversy, Elizabeth welcomed the arrival of her friend, knowing her to be quite uninterested in matters political. It would be refreshing to discuss domestic and family matters again, as she was sure they would need to, if they were to help Charlotte.

Charlotte brought only her two younger daughters, Rebecca and Amelia-Jane. Catherine, now a young lady of sixteen, had been invited to stay on at Rosings for Christmas. It was a privilege that Charlotte, who had refused the same invitation for herself and the rest of her family, was happy to let Catherine enjoy. "I appreciate the value of Lady Catherine's patronage," she explained to Elizabeth, "And while I could not accept it for myself, I felt Catherine could only benefit from the experience; she is a sensible girl and will not let it go to her head. She knows that we cannot hope to match the kind of style that Lady Catherine can afford, so she will enjoy it while she can but not hanker after it later, I think." Elizabeth was sympathetic.

"I am certain of it, Charlotte," she said, "Your girls are a credit to you. I cannot believe any one of them can be misled into foolishness by lavish displays of wealth, however enticing they might seem." Charlotte turned to her friend and smiled.

"No indeed. Eliza, you know my circumstances better than anyone. When I tell you that I have turned down a generous offer from her Ladyship because I thought it was not appropriate for me to accept a paid position in her household, you will understand that I have not forsaken my principles for money and circumstance." Elizabeth was surprised, and this increased to amazement when Charlotte revealed that Lady Catherine had offered her a position as her paid companion on an income that would supplement her annuity, while in addition, a cottage would be provided for her and her daughters on the estate. "It was a kind and generous offer, but I knew I could not accept. I was embarrassed to refuse; there was no other course open to me," she said, smiling apologetically,

"I said I felt I had to be close to my father, whose health is poor, at least until my elder brother Frank returns from India. Her Ladyship was not happy. She has asked me to reconsider, and I feared I had annoyed her, but then she invited my Cathy to spend Christmas at Rosings. I believe the Fitzwilliams are expected, too. I had no desire to vex her Ladyship; I agreed at once."

"Was Cathy happy to stay?" asked Elizabeth.

"Yes, she is very grown up for her age and enjoys using the music room and library where she is permitted to read and practice the piano. Lady Catherine is quite partial to her and has always taken an interest in her."

Elizabeth realised what a struggle it must have been for Charlotte to turn down Lady Catherine's offer, lucrative and tempting as it must have been. Tea was served, and they were joined by Darcy and Mrs Gardiner, who greeted Charlotte with affection and kindness. Charlotte, having thanked them and passed on Lady Catherine's compliments to her nephew, sat down to talk of her plans for the future. She was frank and honest, as well as practical in her outlook, as she had always been even in the days when she, together with Elizabeth and Jane, had been growing up in Meryton. Charlotte spoke quietly of her plans. There were not many alternatives available to her and her young family. She could go to her father at Lucas Lodge, but it would be only a temporary arrangement. Her brother, Frank, was returning from India in the Spring, and he was engaged to be married. There could be no question of her staying on afterwards. "There will be no room for two women at Lucas Lodge," she said, firmly if a little sadly.

Elizabeth felt for her. Lucas Lodge had been her home for almost thirty years; soon she would be a stranger there. But Charlotte was as ever practical and wanted advice about investing her husband's savings for the benefit of her two younger daughters. For herself, she could live thriftily on her annuity, but she wanted to do something with her life. She was forty-three and in excellent health. She could not be idle, she said. "I would like to start a little school," she said brightly, "for young ladies, who would like to learn how to acquire some basic social graces, who need guidance in etiquette, manners, decorum, that sort of thing." Elizabeth, who had not imagined such a possibility for Charlotte, was at a loss for a reply, but Mrs Gardiner spoke up with alacrity.

"I think it is an excellent idea, Mrs Collins. Unfortunately, young women today receive very little guidance on these matters, unless they have good governesses or friends in the right social circles. Many families with sufficient means have no one they can trust to tutor their daughters. Your little school, if I am right in thinking you mean to provide a live-in place rather like Mrs Barton's establishment at Oxford, would serve a very useful purpose."

"Do you think there would be many such families in Meryton, Aunt?" asked Elizabeth.

"Not in Meryton, no, but in Derby or even in Kympton, I am sure there would be many middle class families from the surrounding areas who would welcome it. Your connections with Rosings, and indeed with Pemberley, would be considered a great advantage, Mrs Collins," she said, and Charlotte was pleased to have her plan taken seriously. Darcy, impressed by Charlotte's determination and Mrs Gardiner's encouraging remarks, suggested that they might meet with Mr Gardiner the following day to discuss it further.

"Mr Gardiner is, without doubt, the best businessman I know; I am confident he will give you excellent advice, Mrs Collins. I would recommend that you consult him before you make any decisions." Mrs Gardiner invited them to join her family at dinner on the following day, when Charlotte could consult her husband. Mr Gardiner was almost as enthusiastic as his wife, with a little added caution on the question of investment and leases. He agreed that there certainly were several hundred families in the neighbouring districts all over the Midlands, recently rich, merchant and professional families, who wanted desperately to secure an entré into society for their children, if not for themselves.

"Their rough diamonds could do with some polishing," he said, "so they could move more easily in society. Your little establishment, Mrs Collins, and others like it, could help them gain a degree of acceptance."

"Do you believe people would pay to have their daughters schooled in social arts and graces?" Charlotte asked, with some trepidation.

"My dear Mrs Collins, people will pay for anything if they are convinced they are getting value for their money. It will be your task to convince them, and I'm sure you will," he replied, with his usual air of amiable confidence.

Elizabeth and Darcy exchanged glances, and Elizabeth saw, in her husband's expression, the reason why the two men had become such firm friends. Her uncle's total openness and honesty, together with his complete lack of pomposity or self-importance, had attracted Darcy's attention right at the start of their acquaintance many years ago, and ever since, the relationship between them had grown stronger. Darcy retained enormous respect and affection for both Mr and Mrs Gardiner, and on this occasion, it was easy to see why.

The concern and interest they showed in Charlotte's plans for her future and that of her daughters were matched only by the generosity with which they gave of their time to assist and advise her. Charlotte herself was delighted, requesting assistance with finding a suitable property to lease in Kympton or across the county border in Nottinghamshire. Mr Gardiner, a modern, practical man, was full of admiration for the courage and determination of Mrs Collins and said he would be delighted to assist, in any way. Charlotte was grateful indeed and thanked all of them for their help and advice, especially Mr Darcy and the Gardiners. Without their help, she knew she could not have achieved much at all.

When she left a week later to join her father for Christmas, she left Rebecca behind at Pemberley. She was the same age as Cassandra and a little younger than Emily. The three of them had struck up a friendship that over the years would become as close as their mothers.

Watching the carriage drive away with her mother and Amelia-Jane inside, Rebecca remarked in a self-consciously grown up voice, "Amelia-Jane still needs looking after. I think Mama knows I am grown up enough to be on my own." Elizabeth smiled and put her arms around her.

"Of course she does, but Becky, you know you are not on your own; we are all here for you," but she knew in her heart exactly what the child had meant. Acutely aware of the position in which they were all placed since their father's death, the two older girls had understood that they had to play their part. Their mother's example had set a high standard, and it was clear that Rebecca was determined to live up to it.

❧

Richard Gardiner arrived home in time for Christmas. With him was his friend, Paul Antoine, a young man with exemplary manners and a gentle European charm, not often seen in Derbyshire. The Gardiners, who had met many émigré families in London, during and after the war years, welcomed him and lost no time introducing him to their family and friends.

While everyone was making a huge fuss of Richard, now a fully qualified and accredited physician, the ladies young and old were more intrigued by his friend. He was good-looking, though he had none of the rugged handsomeness of Richard. His fine-featured face was sensitive, and his expressive eyes and dark hair were quite distinctive. His voice and manners were pleasing without appearing to be artificial or contrived, and when he joined a group, at dinner or cards, his conversation was so natural that no one was ill at ease in his company. By the time Monsieur Antoine had met most of the Gardiners' circle of friends, it was universally agreed that he was one of the most agreeable young men they had met in many a year. Part of his charm stemmed from his apparent ignorance of the reasons for his own popularity. Never being boastful or demanding attention, he seemed always to be most appreciative of any recognition.

Emily Gardiner, to whom it fell, whenever her brother was busy, to entertain Paul Antoine and accompany him to social occasions, found him very easy to converse with and had no difficulty finding interesting things to do and places to visit with him. His natural interest and her own obliging nature combined to make for a very easy association. When she brought him over to Pemberley, where he was shown over the house and its grounds, he was completely captivated and pleaded to be allowed to return and see more of the library, which was of course, Emily's favourite part of the estate.

Since James Courtney, the theology student, had returned to Oxford for the vacation, Emily obtained permission for Paul Antoine to spend some time there, for which privilege he was very grateful indeed. For Emily, this was a special pleasure, since her love of the library and art collection at Pemberley increased each time she visited there. When Monsieur Antoine proved to be a keen art lover, with a talent for sketching, Emily was delighted and promised that in the Spring she would show him the best views on the Pemberley Estate, so he could sketch to his heart's content.

At Christmas, when the families gathered at Pemberley, Jane, who was always sensitive to romance in the air, remarked that Monsieur Antoine, whose looks and manners she deemed to be impeccable, and Miss Emily Gardiner had spent almost all evening together; they had certainly danced more frequently than any other couple.

Warning her sister against jumping to conclusions, Elizabeth agreed that they had and indeed they did dance very well together. European dances like the waltz had long since invaded English ball rooms, but, while they were popular in London, it was different in the country. Richard, having spent two years in Paris, was quite an accomplished dancer while amazingly, Paul Antoine seemed less confident and needed persuasion to take the floor. When he did, however, there was no doubting his ability, so light was he on his feet, so easy to follow that every young lady wished he would ask her next. Alas, he insisted on being an exemplary guest, dancing with Elizabeth, Mrs Gardiner, Caroline, and Emily, before he approached any one else.

By the end of the evening, Jane was excited at the prospect of a real romance developing, but Elizabeth was unsure. She had also been observing the pair and Emily, while she was obviously enjoying herself, appeared not to be at all conscious of anything more extraordinary than a very pleasant friendship. Elizabeth said as much to her sister, "I cannot work it out yet, Jane. Either Emily is being very cautious, or she isn't interested in him, as a romantic prospect," she said, puzzled. Jane smiled, "I cannot believe it to be the latter, Lizzie. He is such an appealing young man. As for being cautious, if she isn't careful, she may find she is in danger of breaking his heart. Honestly, Lizzie, the young man looks deeply in love with her, already."

Emily Gardiner did not know quite how to describe her feelings about Monsieur Antoine. It was the very first time that she had taken an interest in any of her brothers' friends, though she had met many of them throughout their schooldays. Paul Antoine was different in many ways. He was French, or at least half French, which meant he had a tradition of natural courtliness in his approach to all women, young and old. She had noted with approval the unaffected pleasure he seemed to take in conversing with her mother or her cousins when he was seated next to one of them at dinner. Even when there were several younger women in the party, he showed no particular preference for them.

Emily had noticed that he often returned to her side on these occasions and would fall quite naturally into step with her when they were out walking but put that down to the easy friendship that had grown between them rather than any partiality on his part. When he complimented her on her mastery of a particularly difficult piece of music, which he had begged her to play for him on a visit to the music room at Pemberley, she was pleased but convinced herself that similar praise from any one would have been as welcome.

She did not deny that he possessed qualities which she admired. For the first time, she had felt herself able to talk to a man who regarded her as a companion, not just a partner for dancing or a game of cards or a presentable woman to escort to the theatre. He appeared genuinely interested in her opinions on various matters and had several of his own, which he shared with her in exactly the same way that he discussed them with her brother or her father.

It was, for Emily, who had been accustomed to the segregation of women in much of social intercourse, a delightfully new experience, and she was enjoying it. She was also totally unaware that their friendship had been the subject of speculation for several weeks, among their mutual friends and her family. Had she guessed it, it is likely she would have been very surprised, for in her own mind, there was no more than the genuine enjoyment of a novel friendship, such as she had never before found with any of the young men of her acquaintance.

Chapter Seventeen

To make the nations free

THE TUMULT OF FIFTEEN months of political agitation brought a wave of social upheaval that washed over England and flowed into the lives of many of her people. Following an historic election, which gave the Whigs an unassailable majority in the Commons, Lord Grey was as good as his word, pushing through his Reform Bill in the teeth of entrenched opposition from the Lords. They delayed its passage, conniving with each other and occasionally, even with the King's men, to the point where they almost destroyed the elected government.

King William appeared to vacillate at first but soon realised after a bitter Winter of discontent during which public rage and uproar brought Britain to the edge of chaos, that Parliamentary reform was essential, if the nation was to hold together. After some weeks of teetering on the brink and much machination, the Lords caved in, and it was as if an almighty sigh of relief went up all over the land.

Fitzwilliam and Caroline had been in London during the last crisis ridden days. When it was over, they returned as if from a battle, bearing their trophy— a copy of "The Bill," declaring it to be a modern Magna Carta. The abolition of the system of rotten boroughs, which had corrupted the Parliament, was a victory for the people, whose protests had forced the King and his peers to listen, they claimed.

Mrs Gardiner who had had charge of her two beloved grandchildren, Isabella and Edward, while their parents were in London, asked if Caroline and Fitzwilliam would take a holiday, now it was all over.

"It isn't over," said Fitzwilliam, to her surprise, "Indeed, it is only the beginning. Now we have a reformed Parliament, we must proceed to press for an extension of voting rights and the abolition of slavery."

Caroline added her voice. "It will never be over as long as young children work long hours in factories and down the mines, Mama. I am pledged to support their struggle." Mrs Gardiner agreed that the exploitation of children was a vile practice, but sadly, neither she nor her husband could see any possibility of a change; now that the men of industry had more, not less power in the Commons, they were hardly likely to pass laws that cut into their profits by outlawing child labour. But Caroline, as always, remained hopeful, determined that she would start a campaign to "get the babes out of the mines and into school."

Fitzwilliam revealed that Caroline had already taken the opportunity of a chance meeting at a social function to take up the matter with the influential Lord Althorp who, though he was initially surprised by her question, had assured her the interests of the children were foremost in his mind. It was a matter, he promised, he would address very soon, through a law to regulate hours and conditions in the mills.

Fitzwilliam had been taken aback when Caroline had told him of her conversation with Lord Althorp, but he was soon reassured, when the man himself congratulated him on the intelligence and charm of his wife. Quite obviously, her venture into social issues had done her husband no harm at all. Darcy and Elizabeth heard the story from Mr and Mrs Gardiner, when they, together with Bingley and Jane, dined at Pemberley the following Saturday. "You could have knocked me down with a feather," said Mrs Gardiner, "but Caroline was not at all overawed by the great man. She felt that he, as one of the most influential and able members of the new government, would surely be the best person to lobby on such an important matter." There were incredulous gasps from Jane and Elizabeth, but Darcy laughed and said, "She is right, of course. Not much good haranguing some obscure backbencher with little or no influence in the cabinet." He reminded Elizabeth of his prediction that with Caroline beside him, Fitzwilliam would go far. Bingley agreed, adding, "Her charming manner will protect her from giving offence, where others might, should they attempt such advocacy, with less than Caroline's sincerity." Mr Gardiner, who could barely conceal the pride he felt in his young daughter, intervened briefly to assert that no one who knew Caroline could ever doubt her complete sincerity of purpose.

"Do you believe she is sufficiently ambitious for Fitzwilliam, to put up with the vagaries of political life?" Elizabeth asked. Darcy replied, "It is not a question of ambition. I do not believe she is unduly ambitious for her husband; well, not any more than he is himself. But, each time I speak with her, I cannot help feeling that Caroline wants to change the world. She sees injustice and wants to do something about it—whether it's the children of the poor, who must work in the mills and get no education, or the widowed women who have nowhere to go in their old age but the poorhouse—after a lifetime of service. I believe she sees opportunities to draw attention to these examples of suffering in our community. That cannot possibly do Fitzwilliam any harm with his constituency." Mr Gardiner agreed, but his wife expressed the hope that their daughter would not wear herself out with political work.

"I can see her, a child in her arms and another at her side, talking passionately to anyone who will listen about the evils of child labour. I know she appears to have boundless energy, but I fear she works too hard," she said, voicing a mother's concern. What none of them knew was that the only thing that could slow Caroline down was about to be announced to the family. She had been keeping it a secret these last few weeks.

In the Summer of 1833, Caroline was to have her third child, and with characteristic dedication, she would turn all her efforts to being a devoted mother, just as she had with her two older children. When Mrs Gardiner was told the news on the following Sunday, she was so delighted she ordered the carriage and set off with Emily for Pemberley, where she could break the news to both Elizabeth and Jane. With their husbands out riding, the sisters were indulging in their favourite pastime—reminiscing and planning for the future. Mrs Gardiner's unexpected arrival added the only missing ingredient to their discussion, the humour and wise counsel of their favourite aunt. Her news gave everyone much pleasure.

Over tea in Elizabeth's private sitting room, they recalled the numerous occasions on which they had been similarly engaged and wondered at the way they seemed always to find harmony and agreement, rather than discord. "I do believe there has not been a cross word exchanged between us, ever," said Jane, rising to go to her little Louisa, who could be heard complaining loudly in the nursery. Elizabeth smiled and exchanged glances with her aunt, who protested, "Dear Jane, I cannot believe that you would ever exchange cross words with anyone, much less with your sister and me." Marriage had not changed Jane. She remained sweet-natured and patient, almost to a fault, so that all her children, whom she loved dearly, got their way with her. Mrs Bennet frequently warned her against spoiling them, but there was no need. All three of them so closely resembled their parents in disposition, there was never any fear of their being spoilt. Furthermore, they had the incalculable advantage of being the beloved children of a happy union.

Elizabeth claimed she was less fortunate than her sister, since her children were not as amenable as Jane's. With both parents being of an independent disposition, it was hardly surprising that their children were similarly endowed. In matters relating to their education, she had had no success at all in organising their lives. Sixteen-year-old Cassandra had refused absolutely to go away to school at Oxford, content to be taught by Georgiana's governess, while all efforts to persuade William, who was almost fifteen, to attend the boarding school in London chosen by the Bingleys for his cousin Jonathan had come to naught. Darcy had tried to speak firmly to young William and insist that he, at least, try a year at College before he decided against it but was disadvantaged by the fact that he had permitted Cassandra to have her own way. "If Cassy doesn't have to go away to school, Papa, why should I?" asked William, reasonably, arguing that he was doing very well with his tutor and didn't think Jonathan's school could do him any good at all. "I do not wish to be forced to drill and play stupid games. I would rather study music and literature with Mr Clarke and ride or play cricket in Derbyshire, than go away to boarding school in London." The boy was so determined that short of ordering him to go, his father, who detested domineering, bullying men himself, had no arguments to change his mind. Elizabeth was disturbed by the refusal of both her children to do what she had expected they would do, but like Darcy, she was unwilling to provoke a confrontation that would do more harm than good.

It was true that Cassandra had succeeded in persuading her father that her education was not going to be enhanced by a year at Mrs Baxter's establishment. She was already, at sixteen, an extremely intelligent and well-read young woman, with opinions of her own and a tendency to emulate her mother's witty style of comment. "Truly, Mama, I cannot believe that I would add anything to my understanding by spending a year or two with Mrs Baxter. If you wish me to spend some time at Oxford in the future, I should prefer to accept Aunt Georgiana's invitation to stay with her. She and Dr Grantley would be far better companions for me at Oxford, than Mrs Baxter would. I should learn so much more from them. Do you not agree?" Elizabeth could hardly disagree. Her attempts to persuade her daughter that there was something to be gained from a resident school fell on deaf ears, and Cassandra replied with a cunning suggestion that took even her mother by surprise. "I know what I should like above anything," she declared, and before anyone could draw breath, she continued, "I should love to learn to cook and shop and run a house just like Aunt Gardiner does. She is the best, Richard says, and so does Emily. Now, that would be something really useful for a modern young lady to learn; do you not agree, Mama?" The sweet reasonableness of her argument combined with the complete innocence of her expression as she appealed to her mother and aunt was breathtaking. Elizabeth hesitated, and Mrs Gardiner, whose love of her nieces' children was absolute, was so flattered she could scarcely believe her ears. Sensing success, Cassandra persisted, turning to Mrs Gardiner, with her wide dark eyes and an angelic smile, "Would you teach me, Aunt?"

"Of course I would, but your mother and father . . . ," she got no further. Cassandra hugged first Mrs Gardiner and then her mother, before declaring with a degree of finality, "That's settled then. It is near enough for me to ride over, and if it rained, you could send the carriage for me, or I could stay overnight. Oh, I can't wait to tell William. I'm glad he isn't going to boarding school, Mama, he would have been miserable, and I should have felt very guilty indeed," she declared and danced out of the room and down the long corridor in search of her brother.

Elizabeth shook her head, not knowing quite what to say. Jane remained silent lest anything she said might offend her sister. Only their aunt was prepared to speak, but so partial was she to Cassandra, that she could do no more than offer some small comfort to Elizabeth. "Dear Lizzie, you must not worry, I know my Caroline and Emily were greatly advantaged by their time with Mrs Baxter, but remember, they did not have the benefit of the background that you and Mr Darcy have given Cassy here at Pemberley. We lived in Cheapside, and your uncle and I felt the girls needed to get out into a more cultured environment for a year or two. Cassy is quite right to point out that she would do better to visit Georgiana at Oxford, than spend time with Mrs Baxter. I do not mean to criticise Mrs Baxter, she is an educated woman and a most conscientious teacher, but knowing Cassy, I can see that she would be very bored within a week." Jane agreed wholeheartedly, and Elizabeth had to accept that her daughter was probably going to get her own way, again.

"Do you really mean to teach her to cook and manage a household?" she asked, and her aunt smiled.

"I most certainly do, and I think she will enjoy it, too," she said, not knowing exactly how she was going to organise her home to accommodate young Cassy, until Emily came to the rescue.

"Since I am here at Pemberley most of the week, Cassy can have my room, whenever she stays over," said Emily, who had been rather quiet throughout the discussion.

"Are you sure you will not be inconvenienced?" asked Elizabeth, anxious that Cassandra's plans should not disrupt the Gardiners' lives. Emily assured her she was happy to let Cassandra use her room. She herself had a pretty suite of rooms at Pemberley, opposite the schoolroom, where she used to teach William and Cassandra when they were little. She enjoyed the privacy it afforded her. She worked in the library and the music room and taught the children at Kitty's infant school; it was a busy life. She always went home to Lambton on Saturdays and returned to Pemberley on Mondays. It was an arrangement that suited everyone rather well.

Meanwhile, the lives of other members of the family had moved on. Robert Gardiner lived almost permanently in London, where he looked after the legal side of his father's business. Robert had wanted to study the Law. Unsure that his son had the will to spend enough time on the business, Mr Gardiner had recently employed a very able business manager. This meant that Robert had more time to study, but reports from London did not suggest that he was doing very much study at all.

Richard, on the other hand, having completed very successfully a gruelling course of medical study in Edinburgh and later Paris, had purchased a practice in a part of Birmingham, which badly needed his services. Assisted by his friend Paul Antoine, he had furnished the modest consulting rooms and hung up his shingle.

There was no shortage of patients from aging men and women suffering from ague or pleurisy to babes in arms with croup or quinsy; they all came hoping to be healed by the new doctor. The doctor from whom he purchased the practice used to work two days a week at the district's cottage hospital, and Richard had been happy to take over the work. He soon realised that there were twice as many patients to be seen at the hospital as at his rooms. Often he worked late and didn't get any dinner before returning to the lodgings they rented in town.

When Mrs Gardiner found out, she decided that it would not do at all. "If you do not eat proper meals, you will soon be as sick as your patients," she said and proceeded to make arrangements to go to Birmingham with Emily and Mr Gardiner to set things right. The first thing to do was to get them better accommodation as well as board, in a house, rather than rented rooms. A business acquaintance of Mr Gardiner's had a couple of rooms and a sitting room to let in his house. These were inspected and pronounced suitable, and arrangements were made for the provision of meals. When they returned that evening, Richard and Paul were astonished at the appearance of the place, with new curtains and a fire in the grate.

"It is," said Richard, "almost like home, except it is Birmingham!" Having extracted several promises including a pledge that they would return home every fortnight, the Gardiners left.

Emily noted that Paul was thinner and paler and hoped he was not being overworked. Her parents glanced quickly at each other, and Mrs Gardiner said she had also noticed his pallor, though she had put it down to the fact that the weather was still cold in Birmingham. "I am quite sure he will get some colour back in his cheeks in Summer," she said, and because Emily was silent, they assumed she had agreed. In fact, she did not agree but kept her counsel, intending to speak to her brother when he next came home.

Charlotte Collins, with the continuing help of the Gardiners and some advice from Elizabeth and Emily, had taken a lease on a modest house in the district of Mansfield in Nottinghamshire. Set in pleasant grounds, with access to a large park, part of the estate of Lord Mansfield, who was her landlord, the house was ideal for her purpose. Charlotte was grateful for the help of Mrs Gardiner and her husband, who provided her with introductions to several families in the area, leading to many enquiries and ultimately five young ladies, who wished to enrol at her establishment.

Whether she would make a success of it was left to be seen, but she certainly did not shirk any of the hard work that was necessary. Her own daughter Rebecca, who had literary ambitions, and young Emily Gardiner were available to help and when Elizabeth suggested a conducted tour of Pemberley and afternoon tea on the terrace for her young ladies, Charlotte was delighted. "It will be an added attraction, Lizzie; there are not too many people, outside your circle of family and friends, who will have such a wonderful opportunity to see Pemberley and have tea on the terrace," she said with great satisfaction.

Meanwhile, the two infant schools at Pemberley and Kympton had been established with the help of Mr and Mrs Darcy, Mr and Mrs Gardiner, and the respective parish councils. In each case, the lack of assistance from any level of government was criticised as a national shame by Fitzwilliam, who, as the Member of Parliament for the area, vowed to press the matter at Westminster. The editor of the *Matlock Review* wrote another strong editorial on the need for a national school system, but it fell on deaf ears again, as it had on two previous occasions. There was, as yet, no political will to take up the cause of education for the children of the poor.

When Caroline's child, a boy they named David, was born, there was a family celebration, and the entire village turned out for the christening at the little church. They were proud of their new member and his family. Fitzwilliam had by his sincerity and passion for reform convinced many who were as yet without the franchise, being neither landed gentry nor middle class merchants, that he would genuinely represent their cause. That his wife was as natural and easy with ordinary working people as she was with the rich and famous merely added to their satisfaction.

As the nation settled into a new era with a new government, their lives seemed as if they were settling into a familiar pattern, too. If there were storm clouds over the horizon, hardly anyone was aware of them yet. Mr and Mrs Gardiner were so proud of their children and grandchildren they were loathe to admit of any disappointments, lest it may seem a reflection upon one of them. Yet, the absence of their youngest son Robert from most family gatherings was causing some comment and consequently much heartache for his mother. While she had no notion of the extent of Robert's problems, Mrs Gardiner had hoped that whatever it was that troubled her son would be easily cleared up by Mr Gardiner when, on receiving a letter from his business manager, he decided to go up to London for a few days. But, on his return, the news he brought was far from good, and even the usually cheerful and optimistic Mr Gardiner appeared grimfaced.

After dinner, when they were free of the servants, he revealed that young Robert was in trouble. "He is in debt and cannot pay his creditors," he said, looking and sounding truly miserable, as he detailed the problems besetting their son. "He seems to have fallen into rather dissolute and irresponsible company. I gathered from a couple of his friends that he had lent a friend a large sum of money to pay a gambling debt." Seeing his wife's look of alarm, he added quickly, "No my dear, it is not what you think; Robert himself does not gamble, but he appears to keep the company of some singularly unattractive characters who do, and they have taken advantage of him." Despite her husband's reassuring words, Mrs Gardiner was so distressed, she could barely speak. When she did, she was confused. "What is to be done? How will he be found, and what will happen to him?" she cried. Mr Gardiner held up a hand, "Well, first we shall have to find him. I have made some enquiries, and I hope to enlist Fitzwilliam's help. He knows London well," he said. "Then, I shall need to discover how much is owed and to whom. It could be a considerable sum, or he would surely have come to us. Finally, I shall have to make good the money and release him from this dreadful obligation."

"But, Edward, if it is a very large sum, how shall we find the money?" Mrs Gardiner asked anxiously. Her husband was unwilling to go into the matter in too much detail.

"Bear with me, my love, once we know what we are dealing with, I shall explain everything. Meanwhile, I must see Fitzwilliam, after which I shall go to Pemberley and talk to Mr Darcy."

"Mr Darcy! Must he know all our troubles, too?" his wife asked, unhappy at the thought and apprehensive about Darcy's reaction.

"He must, we are partners in business, and if I am to undertake a course of action that may cause me to leave my business for a while, my partner is entitled to know the reason. Besides, my dear," he added, "I value his advice." Mrs Gardiner toyed with the idea of accompanying her husband but decided against it. It was very late when Mr Gardiner returned, accompanied by two of the stable hands from Pemberley. Darcy had insisted; times, he had said, were difficult, and it was sensible not to take risks. Mrs Gardiner went eagerly to meet him, and seeing how exhausted he looked, she almost wept. However, when he had explained their plans, she was content to trust his judgement.

The following morning, Mr Darcy rode over to Lambton. Fitzwilliam had already arrived. Without delay, they set off in Mr Gardiner's carriage. Mrs Gardiner, who had not come downstairs, but watched from an upstairs window, felt tears sting her eyes. That one of her children, even poor, shy Robert, should have caused so much trouble was sufficient to break her heart. Yet, Mr Gardiner had insisted that Robert had not done anything dishonourable. There was no hint of embezzlement or false pretences involved, simply an unwise transaction from which he could not extricate himself. The uncertainty was hardest to bear. If only there was someone with whom she could share her fears. She wondered whether she could take the pony trap and drive to Pemberley.

Even as she pondered, shortly after breakfast, of which she ate very little, her wish was granted. The sound of a carriage coming up the drive sent her to the window, and to her great joy, there was Elizabeth, alighting from one of the smaller Pemberley carriages. Mrs Gardiner flew to the front door, and as her niece entered, she was enveloped in an embrace. "Oh Lizzie, if you knew how much I've been longing to see you." Aunt and niece embraced again and sat down to tea before withdrawing to Mrs Gardiner's room to talk in private. Elizabeth knew very little except that Robert was having "money troubles" and Darcy and her uncle were going up to London to help him. When her aunt told her all she knew, Elizabeth was quite shaken. "Do we know who it is Robert borrowed the money from and for whom?" she asked. Her aunt did not know. She knew only that it was to help a friend pay his gambling debts. Elizabeth, her mind going back to the dark days of Lydia's elopement, wondered at the coincidence of events. "There is no question of Robert raiding the business, Lizzie, that at least is certain. Your uncle has told me that he has seen Mr Bartholomew and been assured that there have been no monies drawn out at all by Robert, save his monthly wage." Her aunt was still very distressed, and Elizabeth tried to calm her.

"You must not distress yourself like this, dear Aunt, I am sure Darcy and my uncle will find Robert and settle this unfortunate business. I cannot believe that Robert could knowingly enmesh himself in such a scheme. Surely he must have been deceived." Each mention of Robert or the predicament in which he now found himself seemed to turn the knife in her aunt's heart. Elizabeth decided to take her out for a drive. It was, for her, the panacea for all ills, and she persuaded Mrs Gardiner that she would feel better for it, too.

They drove many miles before realising they were both tired and thirsty. The inn at Lambton, which held so many happy memories for them, offered both shade and refreshment. Taking advantage of its hospitality, they spent a quiet afternoon, during which Elizabeth succeeded in bringing her aunt to a state of acceptance, in which she grew calmer and more confident that Robert could be found and his creditors satisfied. It was a question of knowing where to look, and with Darcy and Fitzwilliam to help, Mr Gardiner's task would surely be easier. As the afternoon grew cooler, they returned to Oakleigh, to find a carriage from Pemberley in the drive. Emily had come for Elizabeth. William had been taken ill, and Mrs Reynolds had sent for the doctor. Elizabeth was immediately eager to return to Pemberley, and Mrs Gardiner went with her, planning to stay overnight. Fortunately, William's illness turned out to be severe indigestion rather than a life threatening disease, but with a summer storm brewing in the Northwest and clouds swirling in from the Peak District, Elizabeth was glad indeed to be home.

Mr Gardiner and Darcy returned late on the following day, having left Fitzwilliam in London with Robert. While the news they brought was not all bad, it was still unlikely to bring much joy to poor Mrs Gardiner, who had spent a wretched night, watched over alternately by Emily and Elizabeth, who were themselves exhausted with worry and lack of sleep. Later, after they had eaten, Mr Gardiner, his voice heavy with unhappiness, detailed the action they had taken. Robert had been contacted by Mr Bartholomew, and on being assured that his father was not enraged at his behaviour, but rather was seeking to help him extricate himself from his unhappy predicament, he had come forward. Advised by both Mr Bartholomew and Mr Gardiner's lawyer that he had best lay all his problems on the table, he had finally made a clean breast of it.

A year or more ago, Robert had been grateful for the friendship of Viscount Lyndsey, one of three sons of a famous family around town, whose attractive sister had seemed to favour him. Through them, Robert had obtained entry into social circles that he had never moved in before and had soon found himself somewhat out of his depth. In an effort to please his friend and retain the favour of his charming sister, Robert had advanced him money to pay several small debts. At first, the monies had been repaid as Viscount Lyndsey appeared to win at Baccarat and Roulette, but a few months ago, he had demanded a sum well beyond Robert's modest means. Urged on by his friend and his sister's tearful appeals, Robert had used his father's credentials to borrow the money, which he handed over at a club, in the presence of two friends. That was the last he had seen or heard of either the Viscount or his charming sister. Under pressure to return the money and with nowhere to turn, Robert had pawned most of his possessions to pay a part of his debt and fled his rooms. Conscious of the disgrace he could bring upon his family and the consequent damage that might inflict upon his father's business, the young man, whose culpability was a consequence more of weakness than criminality, had gone into hiding.

Alerted by Mr Bartholomew, Mr Gardiner had initially gone to London to make enquiries, and so the entire matter had been exposed. "But what is to happen to Robert, now?" asked his mother, unable to hold back her tears. Mr Gardiner proceeded to explain that the debt had been cleared and the depredations of the Viscount and his tribe left in the hands of lawyers. "As for Robert, he is heartily sorry for the trouble he has caused. He was too ashamed to return home with us; he will stay in town, with Fitzwilliam, until all the arrangements are made for his departure for Ceylon."

"Ceylon!" this was too much of a shock for Mrs Gardiner, and even Elizabeth rose to remonstrate that surely this was an extreme step.

Her aunt looked as if she would faint, but Darcy intervened to explain gently and carefully, "Indeed, Mrs Gardiner, it is an excellent opportunity for Robert. You are aware, I am sure, that Fitzwilliam acquired property in Ceylon, when he was out there some ten years ago. I believe he has some Coffee and Cocoa plantations and spice gardens, as well as shares in a gem mine. These enterprises are managed by an excellent trading house, a British firm with very good credentials. An opportunity exists in this same firm for a young man to go out to Ceylon and be trained in the management of such enterprises."

Mrs Gardiner, despite her complete faith in Darcy's judgement, could not cope with the suddenness of the decision and the immense distance between England and this tiny island in the Indian Ocean to which, she felt, her son was being banished. Understanding her anxiety, Darcy explained further, "Fitzwilliam has never regretted going out there and the colony is more peaceful and far further advanced today. It will soon be an important British naval base and a vital trading centre for us in the East." Mr Gardiner intervened to say how important it was for Robert to get away from London and the circle of dissolute and irresponsible young men and women he had fallen in with.

"A few years away, working for a living with some industrious young men would surely bring out the best in him," he said, "I know he has both goodness and talent, which he has had no opportunity to develop. London today provides little incentive for a young man like Robert—it's run by the toffs and their ilk."

Despite the logic and plain good sense of their arguments, Mrs Gardiner remained inconsolable at the prospect of her youngest child's being sent many thousands of miles across the seas, to a life among strangers. Later, on his return, Fitzwilliam himself would spend time with his mother-in-law trying with examples of his own experience to calm her fears. For now, it was heartwrenching to see the pain she suffered.

That night, after the Gardiners had left and Darcy, tired out himself, had retired to bed, Elizabeth wrote to Jane, detailing the events of the past week:

When you have read this, dearest Jane, you will understand the shock and sorrow we have all felt at this most unhappy turn of events. Our dear aunt is quite distraught, and it is only the intervention of Darcy and Fitzwilliam that has allowed for some solution to be found to the problem of Robert's future. Fitzwilliam's contacts with one of the largest trading houses in the East have afforded Robert an opportunity for a new career. I can understand how wretched our dear aunt must feel, she still regards Robert as her "little boy," but Uncle Gardiner is convinced that it is the right course and will benefit Robert. Darcy is also certain that no good can come of Robert's continued stay in London, where he may well fall into the clutches of his "friends" again . . .

Since he appears to have no taste for public life and has little to show for his legal studies, there are few alternatives open to him. We can only hope that for his sake and that of our dear Uncle and Aunt, it will all come right in the end.

Jane's answer came sooner than expected.
She wrote:

Dearest Lizzie,
This is but a short scrap of a note, but it comes with good news that I am

sure will cheer you all. On receiving your letter about poor Robert, I read it out immediately to Bingley. Lizzie, would you believe that Mr Bingley's cousin, Frank, is himself employed with the same trading firm to which Robert is now engaged? He has been out in Ceylon these last twelve months and is expected home on holiday next Christmas, when he expects to marry Miss Evelyn Forster, to whom he has been engaged, since before he went to the colonies.

Bingley is writing to him directly to advise of Robert's planned arrival, and he has informed our Aunt and Uncle of this most fortunate circumstance. Robert will be assured of support and friendship, and I am sure this will go a long way to set our poor aunt's heart at rest. I am, as you are, saddened by what has occurred, especially because of the consequences it has had for Aunt and Uncle Gardiner. It is difficult to think of young Robert's causing so much heartache; he was such a shy little boy. Dearest Lizzie, do you not pray that our boys will be spared such misfortunes as they grow up? I do, each night and day, whenever I see Jonathan and William, for I cannot think how I would bear it, should such a thing befall one of them. But I must not run on so, or you will be angry with me. Dear Lizzie, it is only because I love them so, and I am sometimes afraid to be as happy as we are. I feel undeserving, and when such dreadful things happen as have befallen Robert, I fear that it may be my turn next, for why should I be spared? Forgive me, Lizzie, I know it is foolish, and you will surely scold me in your next letter. I am sure that I deserve it, too.

Your loving sister,
Jane.

Elizabeth shook her head and mused as she put away her letter. "Oh Jane, how little you know your own goodness, to think yourself undeserving of happiness. There is surely no one in the world I know, who deserves happiness more than you do, and I thank God that you are so richly blessed." Elizabeth went upstairs promising herself that when next she saw her sister, she would spend some time convincing her that her joy was not undeserved. Jane above all others deserved every blessing. When Darcy found her in their bedroom, she showed him Jane's letter and had the satisfaction of seeing a smile light up his face. Clearly, they were both agreed that it brought good news. Darcy was delighted with Jane's news about Bingley's Cousin Frank. "This will make it much easier for Mrs Gardiner to accept Robert's departure for Ceylon. Your uncle intends to take the family to London to spend a few days with Robert, before he sails. Fitzwilliam and Caroline will be there for the Parliamentary sittings, so there should be quite a reunion. I've invited them to use the house at Portman Square."

Elizabeth's smile declared her gratitude. The suffering of her dear aunt over the last week had seemed to age her. Mrs Gardiner was a loving and conscientious mother, and she could not believe that one of her children could have fallen into such an error. She blamed herself. Elizabeth had suffered with her.

Darcy, sensing her feelings tried to comfort her. "I know you feel badly for your aunt and uncle, my dearest, I appreciate how deeply they have been hurt, but they are not to blame in this unfortunate matter." Darcy's voice was serious as he explained, "Young Robert, unlike Richard and Caroline, seems less equipped to deal with the deceptions of the world in which we live. He has erred, not because he is innately bad, but because he has been too ready to believe well of his friends. It is they who are culpable. Robert's sins are errors of judgement. He is very young and will learn from this; I am sure of it." Elizabeth knew how well her husband loved the Gardiners and hoped with all her heart that he was right, for their sake.

As for Jane's comments regarding Jonathan and William, Darcy was much less serious as he dismissed her fears about them. "I know of no reason to doubt my belief in the good sense and integrity of Jonathan Bingley. His character is more formed than his father's was at the same age, and believe me, my love, the reports I have of him are uniformly excellent. He is only seventeen but has the maturity of one many years his senior. Jane has no cause for concern."

"And what of William? Have you a similar confidence in him?" Elizabeth asked, her voice betraying some anxiety about his response. She need not have been concerned. Darcy's response had all the warmth and sincerity she could have wished for.

"My dearest Elizabeth, William is our son. Why would I not have confidence in him? He is fifteen, still a child, a sensitive and intelligent boy with much talent yet to be developed. His tutor, Mr Clarke, is well pleased with his work and Georgiana speaks very highly of his progress in music. He does not have Cassandra's independence of mind yet; she is so like you, Lizzie; but I have no doubt he will learn from her example." He knew her love for William was the very centre of her life. Darcy drew her close as if to confirm his part in that relationship. Their love had grown, ever since they had learned to share it without false pride or reservation, and flowed through to their children. Cassandra found them thus, when she came in to ask permission to accept an invitation to join the Gardiners on their expedition to London to farewell Robert. Permission was granted without question, and as she hugged them both, Cassy added, with a little grimace, "William was invited, too, but he would not miss his music lesson."

"Well, at least your father and I will not lack company," said Elizabeth. She looked forward to a quiet week at Pemberley with only her husband and her son for company. It was a week she would recall many times over, during the following years.

Later, Robert Gardiner, having spent a delightful week with his family, sailed for Ceylon and a new life.

CHAPTER EIGHTEEN

"As steady ships strongly part the waters . . ."

T WO EVENTS BROUGHT THE families together in the late autumn of 1833. The first occasioned much happiness, when they gathered for the christening at Ashford Park of Sophia Bingley. Not long afterwards, they were called together again on a more sombre occasion, when news came of the death, from severe pneumonia, of Mrs Bennet. Her daughters, Mrs Bingley, Mrs Darcy, and Mrs Jenkins, accompanied by their husbands, their elder children, and Mr and Mrs Gardiner, travelled to Longbourn, where the Bennets had lived with their only unmarried daughter, Mary, and a modest household staff. No sooner had they arrived and seen their father, whose sobriety of attire and countenance was more evidence of his respect for convention than an indication of his emotional state, than they became involved in arrangements for the funeral.

Their sister Mary was understandably less able to cope, having nursed their mother through a short but exceedingly trying illness. Mr and Mrs Gardiner, invaluable as ever, took upon themselves most of the formal responsibilities, leaving Jane and Elizabeth to attend to their father's needs, while Kitty assisted Mary. Later that day, arriving posthaste from Newcastle accompanied by her husband and all of her children was Mrs Wickham. On arrival, she appeared scarcely able to support herself and was far too distressed to be of any assistance to her sisters. Repairing immediately to her former bedroom, where she sent for Kitty to minister to her needs and those of her younger children, Lydia seemed to take it for granted that she could now take her mother's place in the household. Elizabeth and Jane found very little to sympathise with in their sister's excessive show of grief. Like their Aunt Gardiner, they had some reservations about her protestations of filial affection, and if their father's reaction was any indication of his feelings, he must surely have had his doubts, too. Thanks to the hospitality of Sir William Lucas, they were all comfortably lodged overnight and did not suffer the embarrassment of having to put up with either or both of the Wickhams at dinner.

The funeral at the village church was attended by a large number of people, testimony to the many friendships the family had made in the district over the years. Following the funeral, Jane and Bingley were anxious to return home to their family, but both Elizabeth and Kitty stayed on to support their father and Mary for a few days. To their surprise, they discovered that Lydia had made similar plans. Ensconced in her mother's boudoir, in deep mourning, Lydia made much of the extremely long and tiring journey she had made and a similar one that lay ahead. It was plain from her hints of how much it had all cost, that she hoped to be reimbursed by her father. "Surely, Lizzie, you realise what it has cost to come all this way and buy mourning clothes for all the children," she said pointedly. It would have been to no avail to argue that there had been no call to bring all the children, much less have them attired in formal mourning clothes. Elizabeth and Jane had decided that it was sufficient to have their eldest children pay their respects to their grandmother; yet Lydia's entire brood had trailed behind her and Wickham to the church, attired in formal black. It had been quite a theatrical performance. Lydia, now in her thirties, looked increasingly like her mother and had adopted a remarkably similar manner of self-dramatisation. Elizabeth was loathe to leave her father in such a situation and was extremely relieved when Kitty decided to extend her stay by a week and help Mary and her father get the household settled. It was very good of Kitty to volunteer her time and was an indication of how much she had changed from the rather feckless self-indulgence of her youth under Lydia's influence.

Elizabeth's relief was somewhat short-lived, however, when two days later they stopped off at Lambton and were astonished to hear from Mrs Gardiner that the Bennets' housekeeper, Mrs Hill, had confided in her that Lydia intended to return to Longbourn permanently! Sarah, Mrs Bennet's chamber maid, had confirmed that Mrs Wickham had hinted at a similar possibility, urging Sarah to stay on at Longbourn against her return. Elizabeth was aghast at the prospect, chiefly out of concern for her father. He had found it sufficiently difficult to cope with Lydia's excesses as a silly young girl fifteen years ago; how, she wondered, would he put up with her now, together with all her rather boisterous children? "And what of Wickham? Does he propose to move to Longbourn too?" Elizabeth asked. Mrs Gardiner had no answer, except to suggest that perhaps Mr and Mrs Wickham were happier apart than together! Returning to Pemberley, Elizabeth, still disturbed by her aunt's news, wrote immediately to Jane, detailing the gist of the story and asking for her sister's advice:

> *Can it be true, dear Jane, that Lydia proposes to impose upon poor Papa, while Wickham remains at Newcastle? It seems to me to be an impossible situation. I am at a loss to understand how it can even be contemplated. Aunt Gardiner believes that Lydia is making use of the opportunity afforded by Mama's death to get herself a more comfortable situation at Longbourn, pretending to want to move there to "look after" Papa. She will, in truth, be feathering her own nest and simultaneously driving our poor father out of his mind. Oh Jane, this is such an undesirable development, and yet I am unable to think how it may be stopped . . .*

In desperation she begged her sister to suggest a course of action that may be undertaken, but if the truth were known, she had not a great deal of confidence that one could be found.

The letter was never sent. Hardly had Elizabeth completed it and taken it down to be despatched, when an express arrived at the door. It was from Jane. Standing in the hall, where it had been handed to her, Elizabeth opened it and was astonished to read her sister's hastily penned note:

> *Dearest Lizzie,*
> *Since we parted after Mama's funeral, something very disturbing has happened. I have this morning received an express from Kitty detailing a most unpleasant encounter between herself and Mary on the one hand and our sister Lydia on the other. Kitty writes that Lydia, while packing in prepa-*

ration for their departure last Sunday, declared her intention to return in Spring "to look after Papa and keep an eye on Longbourn for Henry." It appears that Wickham and Lydia have decided that since the death of Mr Collins has resulted in Papa's retaining Longbourn, their son Henry, being a few weeks older than our Jonathan, is his natural heir. Upon this basis, Lydia intends to place herself in a position to make doubly sure of his inheritance by moving to Longbourn, while Papa still lives. Kitty and Mary are exceedingly unhappy, and Kitty writes that they would like to acquaint Papa with Lydia's intentions but have not been able to do so, as he still keeps very much to his room.

Elizabeth's fury was palpable as she threw the letter down on the table and cried out, "It's outrageous! How dare they impose themselves on poor Papa, the insufferable creatures?" Hearing her voice, Emily, who was descending the stairs from the library, came swiftly to her side. Elizabeth handed her Jane's letter. With Darcy away for the day at the Camden Estate, Elizabeth felt she had no alternative but to go directly to Lambton to consult her uncle and aunt.

There was no time to lose. The prospect of the Wickhams' moving into Longbourn, the awful thought of what this would mean for her father and her sister Mary, who had no where else to go and would therefore be forced to remain as some kind of drudge for Lydia and her family, was too horrible to contemplate.

Leaving a note for Darcy, Elizabeth with Emily for company drove to Oakleigh Manor. The Gardiners were delighted at her unexpected visit, but their delight soon dissipated as she showed them Jane's letter. Mrs Gardiner, in spite of having some hint of Lydia's intentions, was still shocked by the impudence of her approach. "How could they be so totally selfish and so uncouth with it?" she lamented, "I can hardly believe what I am reading here." Elizabeth was steely eyed and very angry.

"My dear Aunt, I do not put anything beyond Lydia and Wickham. I am unwilling to believe that this is something for which Lydia alone is responsible. I am certain that Wickham has urged her on. They are both thoroughly selfish, thoughtless of others, and ruthless in advancing their own material advantage. They will stop at nothing to get what they think is their due."

"But is their interpretation of the process of the entail correct?" asked Emily, who had some doubts about the basis of Lydia's claim. Her father shook his head.

"I am not convinced it is. My own understanding is that once the estate remains with Mr Bennet, which it has with the death of his cousin, it is his to dispose of in his will. However, we shall need to have that confirmed by an attorney. But Lizzie, I cannot believe that your father is unaware of this possibility. Perhaps, I could contact him myself and discover how he sees it," he suggested.

Usually, Elizabeth would have been content to agree. She trusted her uncle's judgement implicitly. But on this occasion, her concern for her father and younger sisters was overwhelming. She declared her intention to travel with him on the Wednesday, having first informed her father of their impending visit. She returned with Emily to Pemberley, to prepare for the journey. It was not something she undertook with any pleasure so soon after travelling to Longbourn for the funeral, but her sense of outrage at the unseemly behaviour of the Wickhams overcame her reluctance.

When Darcy returned that evening, Elizabeth had to acquaint him with the details of the wretched conspiracy being hatched by the Wickhams. The severity of Darcy's expression, as his face darkened on hearing the news and reading Jane's letter, left her in no doubt of his response. Like her, he believed that Wickham was the instigator of Lydia's plan, and he certainly agreed that the couple were capable of any stratagem, adding his weight to her opinion that they had to be forestalled at any cost. "There is surely no truth at all in the notion that the entail would extend outside the family. Unless it was specified in a codicil to the original document, your father, with whom the property now remains, is entitled to bequeath it to any member of his family he chooses." Gratified by his support and genuine concern, Elizabeth begged him to accompany them. At first, Darcy was reluctant, unwilling to interfere in what was strictly a Bennet family affair, until his wife pointed out that since they did not seek to benefit themselves or their children, they, rather than Jane and Bingley, whose son Jonathan might be a potential beneficiary, should feel free to act. Darcy, albeit reluctantly, agreed.

Their arrival at Longbourn on the following Thursday, a grey late November day, had been preceded by an express from Elizabeth. Kitty and Mary came out to greet them with the news that Mr Bennet was in the library, with his attorney, Mr Grimes. Kitty added that they had succeeded in informing their father of Lydia's intention of returning in the Spring, to which he had merely retorted, "Oh no, she is not."

"Since then, he has had Mr Grimes over twice, and today, we are all to go in to the library, when Jonathan arrives," said Mary, with her usual air of gravity.

"Jonathan?" Elizabeth was surprised at this new turn of events.

"Yes," said Kitty, "Papa sent an express to London, asking him to be here today. He is expected at any time now." Darcy and Mr Gardiner both appeared pleased, confident that it meant Mr Bennet was not only aware of the Wickhams' plans, but had probably acted to forestall them already. Darcy was particularly relieved. He had not wished to appear as if he was giving his father-in-law advice on the proper disposal of his property. Presently, Mr Bennet came out to greet them and invited them into the library, where they were introduced to Mr Grimes. Refreshments were served as they waited for Jonathan Bingley. He arrived a little later than expected, a tall young man of seventeen, with the good looks of his mother and the amiable manners of his father, Jonathan greeted everyone with affection and apologised for being late.

What followed surprised them all. Mr Grimes, authorised by his client Mr Bennet, confirmed that Mr Bennet was changing his will in relation to the disposal of the Longbourn Estate, which had reverted to him with the death of Mr Collins, who would have been the inheritor under the entail. Hitherto, this property had been willed to his daughter Mary, with life interest to his wife. But the untimely death of Mrs Bennet had necessitated a change, Mr Grimes explained. While there would be no change in the disposition of any monies which were to be divided among his daughters, Longbourn would be left to his grandson, Jonathan Bingley, with life interest to his daughter, Miss Mary Bennet, for as long as she remained single. Should she choose to use a part of the property to conduct her music teaching, she was welcome to do so. Jonathan on his eighteenth birthday would take over the management of the Longbourn Estate, and later, it would be his to do with as he saw fit—rent, lease, or occupy.

When Mr Grimes had finished speaking, Mr Bennet had something to say, too. He had wanted to be fair, he said, because all his daughters were married except Mary. They had husbands and homes, where she had none save Longbourn, which had very nearly not been theirs at all. But, since Fate had decreed that it was to remain in his hands, he had disposed of it in the fairest way possible. He had chosen his grandson Jonathan to manage and ultimately inherit the property, because Jonathan was the son of his eldest daughter, he added mischievously.

Elizabeth and Darcy could barely conceal their delight, but young Jonathan was truly amazed. He appeared to be unsure whether he was ready for the responsibility the inheritance would place upon him. He admitted he had a great deal to learn. But his grandfather reminded him gently that he did not need to worry just yet. Putting an arm around Jonathan's shoulders, he reassured him, "You can take your time learning, young man; I intend to be around for a while yet. But I am sure when the time comes, you will do us all proud."

Mary, not usually given to emotional displays, wept with happiness as Jonathan assured her that she would always be looked after and if she needed any help with establishing her music school, he would do whatever he could. Elizabeth saw in his gentle words the same generosity and kindness that had always set his mother apart.

For Mary, the dreadful prospect of being a housekeeper for her sister Lydia's family had held only terror. Now, as the unpleasant vision receded and she could see her future more clearly, she was truly grateful. She embraced her sisters and thanked her father, promising that as long as he needed her, she would be at Longbourn to look after him. It was the kind of family occasion for which Elizabeth was singularly unprepared. Her family had engendered few strong relationships or deep loyalties, except that which had always existed between her sister Jane and herself.

Frequently, she had suffered mortification at similar family gatherings, as the vulgarity and ignorance of her mother, her Aunt Phillips, or Lydia had been exposed to scrutiny. But, this time, she felt real pleasure at being there to witness the restoration of a sense of responsibility and fairness among them. She was happy that her father had demonstrated good judgement and common sense and pleased with her younger sisters' concern for each other. She was especially proud of her nephew Jonathan and wished his parents had been present on this occasion.

That Darcy was with her was a matter of particular satisfaction to Elizabeth. Although it was a subject they had promised never to mention, since his ill-advised proposal at Hunsford and the letter that had followed her rejection of it, Elizabeth had in the past been embarrassed by members of her family in his presence. This time, she was immensely proud of them.

Since Mr Gardiner had business in London and Jonathan was also returning to the city, Darcy and Elizabeth decided that they would spend a few days there before returning to Pemberley. It had been a long while since Elizabeth had spent time in London. She had grown so contented with her surroundings in Derbyshire and the convenience of having all her favourite family members within an easy distance from her, that she saw no reason to travel to London, unless there was something very particular to attract her there. Her increased interest in the running of the house and the estate gave her much to do, and she never missed the bustle and glitter of the city. She did, however, enjoy the great wealth of music and theatre available there and indulged her passion for them whenever they were in London.

The Continis, who continued to be firm friends, sometimes made up a party with Georgiana and Francis Grantley, and on these occasions, Darcy and Elizabeth would join them for dinner and an evening at the theatre or at one of the popular concerts by famous musicians from Europe. If Parliament was sitting and Fitzwilliam was speaking on a matter of significance, he would invite them to come in and hear him. Caroline faithfully attended and would urge her mother and Elizabeth to accompany her. Despite her lack of enthusiasm for politics, Elizabeth could not resist the pleadings of her young cousin.

This time, the Fitzwilliams were in London celebrating the passage of two momentous bills that the colonel predicted would change the face of Britain and Europe. The first abolished slavery in all British territories, ending the vile trade in human beings that had enriched many and brought misery to millions more. The second, the measure promised by Lord Althorp, when the Whigs won their great victory in 1830, was the Factory Act, which placed limits on the hours that could be worked by women and children and began for the very first time a process of factory inspections, by which the government could enforce the law on behalf of the workers it sought to protect.

Fitzwilliam and Caroline, who had campaigned for both reforms, were ecstatic, particularly because it set Britain apart in Europe. When they dined together at the Darcys' house in Portman Square, Elizabeth took the opportunity to acquaint them with recent developments in the family, including the latest news from Longbourn. As they gathered in the drawing room after dinner, young Jonathan received congratulations and some teasing about becoming the squire of Longbourn, a title he was loathe to acknowledge. "I have no intention of thinking about it," he declared, "since my grandfather is in extremely good health and the Longbourn Estate is unlikely to require a new squire for many years yet. But, I shall be spending a great deal of time learning to manage the place well."

Darcy and Fitzwilliam expressed their confidence in his ability to do just that, pointing out that he had already learned much from his father, who was doing an excellent job at Ashford Park.

Elizabeth, writing to her sister, could not fail to mention her favourite nephew:

Dear Jane,

If I had one regret, it was that you and Bingley were not present to witness the graciousness and kindness of your son. Papa was so very proud and spoke with great affection of his grandson. All present were agreed that Jonathan acquitted himself with distinction, showing a degree of maturity quite unexpected in one so young. Dear Jane, you would have been very pleased with your boy. I know I do not need to say this to you, dear Jane, but both Darcy and I are delighted that Jonathan is to become Papa's manager and will ultimately inherit Longbourn. Kitty and I are agreed that no better person can be trusted to look after it than Jonathan. His assurances to Papa and Mary were so sincere, they brought tears to their eyes, and even I, unsentimental as I am, could not deny that I was moved. There are not many young men in society today, who feel so deeply for those older and less fortunate than themselves . . .

Apart from this genuinely happy circumstance, I am able to report also, that the Wickhams have been thoroughly routed and their impertinent plans lie in tatters. Papa, on hearing the merest whisper of it from Mary and Kitty, had immediately set Mr Grimes to work to prevent such a catastrophe from occurring. Darcy and Uncle Gardiner are of the opinion that Papa had been considering the disposition of the Longbourn Estate ever since the death of poor Mr Collins but had not wanted to upset Mama by changing his will while she was still alive. Her sudden death and the Wickhams' unseemly haste in declaring their intentions had obviously brought about a swifter response. I confess I may be prejudiced in my judgement, but when we met at Mama's funeral, I did not find young Henry Wickham an attractive or likeable young man, and I am thoroughly pleased that he is not to play any role in the future of Longbourn. He has too much of his father's swagger and very little of his ability to please, which if you recall was the quality that originally promoted him in our own estimation, when he appeared in Meryton all those years ago. Perhaps this is a good thing, in that Henry will have less ability to dissemble, lacking the smooth manner which had so many people, and I include myself, sorely deceived by his father.

To pleasanter subjects now, dear Jane, Papa and Mary will join us at Christmas as will Georgiana and Dr Grantley. We are eager to see you and Bingley and the children. Charlotte and the girls will be with us too, so we shall have many opportunities for really good long talks together, and there is so much to talk about. I am looking forward to it.

Your loving sister,

Lizzie.

Returning to Pemberley was always, for Elizabeth, a moment to look forward to. As the carriage reached the point where the road, emerging from the surrounding woods, provided a most compelling view of the handsome stone building that was now her home, she unfailingly caught her breath at the beauty of the prospect. Adding to its natural attractions, was the felicity of her life within it—the peace that it brought her in an era of national ferment, the gentle care and loyalty she received from the staff, her own family—the happiness she had found with Darcy and their two beloved children. Pemberley had become a symbol of all this. Even now, in the midst of Winter, it was her warm and secure home.

Alighting from the carriage, Elizabeth looked around and was surprised not to find Emily or Cassandra anywhere in sight. Untroubled, but mildly curious, she asked after them. Mrs Reynolds' face had not betrayed her anxiety, but when she spoke, her voice trembled. "I would have told you when you had come indoors, Ma'am. There has been a nasty accident in the valley; a coach has gone off the road into a gully near Kympton, and many people are said to be injured. Miss Gardiner and Miss Cassandra have gone to help. They've taken Jenny and a couple of the men with them," she said, and despite her best efforts, could not hold back her tears.

Elizabeth went indoors immediately and asked for more information. Darcy had already spoken with the stable hands who had first heard the news. One of them had witnessed the accident and had ridden over to Lambton to get help. "Could you see who they were?" Darcy asked, and the lad replied that they were obviously travellers from outside the district, unfamiliar with the hazards on the roads around here.

"There was ice and slush on the road, Sir. The wheels must have skidded as they came around the big bend above the gully." Within half an hour, Elizabeth and Darcy had set off with a couple more men and emergency supplies, to see if anything more could be done to help. They arrived at the church hall at Kympton to find it buzzing with activity. Clearly, most of the passengers who had been rescued had been brought into the church, out of the cold, where they were being plied with hot drinks, while their less fortunate fellow travellers, who had suffered injuries, had been carried into the vestry, where to her surprise Elizabeth found Richard Gardiner and Paul Antoine tending the wounded, with Emily, Cassandra, and Jenny in attendance. The Gardiners were there with blankets, bandages, and tea, or something a little stronger for those who had need of it. Mercifully, no one had been killed, but several of the children had suffered bruising and were now very cold indeed. The rest of the afternoon was spent transporting the wounded to the district hospital, several miles away.

As it grew dark and the threat of sleet or worse became imminent, Darcy decided that the seven remaining travellers could not be allowed to spend the night in the draughty church hall. Some of them would probably need further treatment. Having consulted Richard and Elizabeth, he sent a message to Pemberley to have beds prepared in the old nursery wing, for those who would be brought in, as well as food for the travellers and others who had helped, working in the cold all afternoon.

Richard, who had been working without rest for several hours, was delighted that his patients would soon have hot food and warm beds. He was, however, rather more concerned about his loyal assistant, Paul Antoine. Emily had noticed that Paul had been running back and forth from the church hall to fetch and carry and help Richard as he struggled to treat the wounded and calm those who were panicstricken. In spite of his warm clothes, he looked cold but seemed not to notice. When she stopped him with a bowl of hot soup, he had thanked her profusely, but having only taken a couple of mouthfuls, he had rushed away to attend to a frightened child. Richard sought out Elizabeth and confided that he was worried about Paul and asked if she could take him back to Pemberley with her. Elizabeth agreed at once.

It was late and very cold when the last of the travellers had been transported to Pemberley, where rooms, beds, blankets, hot water, and food had all been made ready for them. The men and women and a couple of young children had no idea who their benefactors were, but they were grateful indeed for this timely succour. Had they not been promptly rescued and sheltered, they may well have caught their deaths of exposure. As it happened, Richard, who quite by chance had been at his mother's house in Lambton, had been called by Darcy's man, and his prompt attention had probably saved their lives.

That night, exhausted, but well-pleased with his work, he used the opportunity to broach the subject of a cottage hospital for the area with Darcy. "It is of no use to expect either the government or the council to do anything. The only hospital is many miles away, and as you can see, in a real emergency, the victim could die before he gets there. It was just by chance that I was here to help them," he said. Darcy was interested. He had always believed that a community needed hospitals, schools, libraries, and similar facilities situated locally. They were the heart of any society. The success of the infant schools at Pemberley and Kympton had proved him right. He promised to talk to the other landowners in the area, especially Sir Thomas Camden, and give Richard an answer by Christmas.

"There is one problem," said Darcy, "we would need a doctor resident in the area, would we not?" He was pleasantly surprised when Richard said, "Build us a hospital; you shall have a resident physician, I promise."

"Do you mean you would move from Birmingham?"

"Indeed, I would, sir," said Richard, surprising and delighting his mother, "I went to Birmingham because they needed a doctor. There was work for me there. They have a district hospital at which I work, on two days a week, as well as running a very busy practice. If I had as much work here, I would gladly move."

"That," said Darcy, "sounds very much like an offer I cannot possibly refuse. If I can get Camden to agree, I might hold you to that promise."

Emily came in to say that Paul had a high fever and should be sent to bed. Richard rose immediately and followed her upstairs, while Elizabeth, who longed to ask her aunt many questions, remained silent. When Richard returned, his face was very grave. "Paul is very ill. He must not be moved. Cousin Lizzie, may I stay overnight? I am very reluctant to leave him like this."

"Richard, of course you must stay. In any event, some of the travellers may need your help too; think nothing of it. Darcy can lend you some clothes. Meanwhile, is there anything we can do for Paul?" Elizabeth asked, eager to help. Richard shook his head.

"No, it is mostly exhaustion from working all afternoon in the cold. He is not very strong." Emily appeared very troubled too, but Elizabeth noticed that her brother spoke softly to her for a while, and she seemed to be calmer thereafter.

Fortunately, the following week brought clearer if not exactly warmer weather, and all of the travellers who had suffered mainly bruising and exposure recovered and were able to return to Matlock and resume their interrupted journey.

Paul Antoine, however, remained at Pemberley on the orders of his friend and physician. Emily seemed to take great pleasure in his company and in carrying out all the strict instructions her brother left for the care of his patient. Paul himself was the most undemanding of patients, always being grateful for the care that was lavished on him and appearing to improve with each passing day. Emily was sure that the warmth, comfort, and good food at Pemberley were hastening his recovery. Elizabeth was even more certain that the identity of the carer had as much to do with Paul's progress as the care he received.

During the time he spent at Pemberley, Elizabeth discovered the particular charm of this unassuming, gentle, young Frenchman. She could, by observing Emily and Paul together, see how much they enjoyed each other's company, but she could not say with any certainty that there was a deeper level of affection between them. Emily's commitment to ensuring that Paul recovered from his illness and was assisted to become stronger and healthier was paramount. Try as she might, Elizabeth could find no evidence of a romantic attachment at all. It left her even more bewildered, and she was determined to seek some explanation.

It would soon be Christmas, and for all the good fortune they had enjoyed, it did not look as if the family would have as enjoyable a celebration this year as before. Though no one had been killed in the coach accident on the Matlock road, it had frightened a great many folk, and there was a general lack of merriment around.

When the families gathered on Christmas Eve, three of the children in the choir failed to arrive, being suddenly taken ill with croup. It was a bitter blow to Cassandra, who had taken over organising the children's party from Georgiana. Elizabeth was disappointed but, despite this, determined that they would enjoy their Christmas together. At least, they were not snowed in, as they had been a few years ago. Pemberley was a large house, but it had been well-designed for comfort in all types of weather. It was not difficult to engender a warm and cheerful atmosphere for the festivities on Christmas Eve and the days that followed, and the families as they gathered filled the house with laughter.

Jane, Charlotte, and Elizabeth had the pleasure of seeing their children meet and mingle as friends, in the same way that their mothers had done. Amelia-Jane, Charlotte's youngest, who was not quite fourteen, insisted on teaching William the latest dance from Europe—the polka, which he declared was more like a barn dance.

Jonathan and Emma Bingley were without doubt the handsomest young couple dancing, but Richard Gardiner and Cassandra Darcy drew many admiring comments too.

By the end of Boxing Day, when the festive food was cleared away and the big front room glowed with the light of candles and the warmth of a huge log fire, Elizabeth felt everything was right with her world. The voices of the children rose in song as their parents sat together around the room. William and Cassandra played and sang a charming French carol they had been practising all week and received many compliments for their performance. Sitting beside his wife, Darcy put an arm around her, and Elizabeth caught her sister's eye across the room and smiled. Jane, surrounded as usual by her beautiful family, made a blissful picture.

Elizabeth felt a niggling little doubt creep out of a corner of her mind, a reminder of Jane's persistent unease—the obsession with "not deserving such happiness." But, annoyed with herself for letting it in to spoil her pleasure, Elizabeth pushed it away.

Darcy caught the merest flicker of irritation as it crossed her countenance, "Is something wrong, Lizzie?" he asked, sensing that she was uneasy. Elizabeth smiled serenely and shook her head.

"No, dearest," she said, "nothing is wrong, nothing at all," she replied, as the voices of the children singing the lovely Coventry carol filled the room.

Chapter Nineteen

And why has happiness no second Spring?

WHEN ELIZABETH AWOKE TO a cold grey morning, she did not stop to consider whether it was some ill-omen for the day to follow. She was sufficiently familiar with the changeable nature of Derbyshire weather in January to be grateful that it was not pouring with rain.

The previous evening had been a particularly pleasant one. Before most of her guests left, Elizabeth had successfully broached an idea upon which she and Emily Gardiner had set their hearts. They had planned to hold a Harvest Fair at Pemberley, to provide an opportunity for the tenant farmers, farm labourers, and their families to sell their garden produce, display their individual skills and crafts, and help their community at the same time.

Jane had suggested that it would also be a good opportunity to celebrate the "coming out" of three young ladies, who would all be seventeen that year—Emma Bingley, Cassandra Darcy, and their friend Rebecca Collins. Especially if Mr Darcy could be prevailed upon to give a ball in their honour, it would surely be an occasion for a great family gathering. Bingley, who was still most enthusiastic about dancing, keeping up with all the new European dances, declared it to be a splendid idea.

Plans were immediately afoot for a variety of activities to be organised for the fair and the ball that would follow, after Mr Darcy agreed to the ball, for how could he refuse in the face of such universal approval? The younger members of the family insisted that there had to be a "magic show" and "fortune tellers" at the fair, while others saw opportunities to benefit their favourite causes. Kitty and her husband decided they would collect donations in cash and kind for their school, while Caroline thought it would be an ideal occasion to get more signatures for the People's Charter for Universal Suffrage, which was gaining popularity around the country. Colonel Fitzwilliam warned that if Elizabeth did not exercise some control, the Pemberley Harvest Fair may begin to rival the scale of the celebrations after Waterloo!

Undeterred by such mischievous cynicism, Elizabeth, Emily, and Caroline were determined the event was going to be a great success. "You may laugh, Fitzy, but I think it is going to be a wonderful occasion. People will come from miles around, and we shall remember the day for many years to come," predicted Caroline with confidence.

Elizabeth was delighted with their response and thanked Darcy for having agreed to the idea in the first place. She knew how much he valued his privacy at Pemberley and was grateful he had agreed, without complaint, to let it be invaded. "I know that you will feel put out by having all these people tramping around the grounds, dearest, but I do believe it is in a very good cause," she said, apologetically. Darcy insisted that he would not be put out at all.

"You need not apologise to me, Lizzie. I am perfectly happy to have the grounds of Pemberley used for the benefit of our community. Pemberley is at the centre of that community, and I think we should play our part. I think it is an excellent idea, and I am sure it will be a great success." Elizabeth was genuinely surprised by his apparent enthusiasm, but she responded quickly, "I do hope so. Of course, there is a lot of work to be done, and I shall need to organise a team of helpers. I am so glad you are in favour of it; I was afraid you might be set against the whole idea."

Darcy smiled, "Oh, I may well have been, some years ago, before my selfish, thoughtless ways were so thoroughly exposed and severely dealt with. But as you know, my dear Lizzie, I am now a reformed man." She could hear the ironic humour in his voice, and her own response acknowledged it.

"I do know it, and I hope that reformed man knows he is more loved than anyone in the world, because he is quite the kindest and most generous person

I have ever known." Darcy fairly beamed with pleasure but, pretending to be embarrassed by the extravagance of her declaration, he teased her, "Hush, Lizzie, have a care or I may have such a high notion of my virtue, that I shall become insufferable all over again, and all your good work will have been undone!" Even as she laughed, Elizabeth wondered how she had ever found him insufferable. There remained little similarity between the man who had walked into the Assembly room at Meryton with a hauteur she had deemed to be intolerable and the husband she loved so dearly. His approval meant everything to her, and his encouragement of the undertaking bestowed upon it a special distinction.

Unfortunately, the following morning—which by breakfast time had lived up to its promise, turning even colder with sleet falling on the hills behind the house—brought Elizabeth's surge of pleasure to an abrupt end. Shortly after breakfast, Darcy and Mr Gardiner had driven out to Kympton, leaving Mrs Gardiner and Emily with Elizabeth, when an express was delivered to the door. When the maid brought it to Elizabeth, she thought it was nothing unusual. "It's from Lydia," she said. Emily and Mrs Gardiner exchanged glances, expecting it to contain the usual request for help with her post-Christmas bills.

But, when Elizabeth had read it quickly through, she threw it down with a cry of pain, tears welling in her eyes. Mrs Gardiner left her seat beside the fire and flew to her niece's side. "Why, my dear Lizzie, what is it? What has happened? Is it bad news?" Elizabeth could barely speak.

"No," she said bitterly, "it is not bad news—it is just bad!"

"Why? What does she say?" asked her aunt. Elizabeth spoke with difficulty, as if her feelings were choking her.

"Lydia accuses us—Darcy and me, of manipulating Papa's will, so that her son, Henry Wickham, is deprived of the chance to inherit Longbourn."

Mrs Gardiner gasped. "This is outrageous," she said. Emily went further. "How dare she? What right has she to suppose such a thing?" She reached for the letter and as she read it, grew angrier by the minute, until her mother urged her to read it aloud. Emily complained that Lydia's handwriting was so poor she could hardly make it out. Finally, she began to read:

> *My dear Lizzie, you will probably not welcome this letter, but it will be no*
> *worse for you and Mr Darcy than the communication I have received this*

day, from Mr Grimes, Papa's attorney. I have never met him, but I imagine him to be a most disagreeable man, judging by his horrid letter. He informs me that in order to spare me and my family any further disappointment of expectations based upon speculation rather than fact regarding the disposition of the Longbourn Estate—fancy all those long, difficult words— he has been asked by his client (by which he means Papa!) to advise me of the following. He then informs me that Papa has named Mr Jonathan Bingley as his manager, when he attains his majority, and heir to the Longbourn Estate on Papa's death, with life interest to Miss Mary Bennet, as long as she remains single. What a joke! All I am to look forward to is my share of whatever monies are left to be divided between us after Papa's death, but Mary will have all of Longbourn! Lizzie, you could have knocked me down with a feather! Jonathan to be Papa's manager! Why he is not yet eighteen. And why, when my Henry is older than Jonathan and is Papa's eldest grandchild, does he ignore him? As for Mary, what will she do with that large place? Wickham and I believe this is all your doing—you and Mr Darcy. Wickham says it is exactly the kind of thing Mr Darcy would do, just as he edged Wickham out of a most valuable living at Pemberley, after old Mr Darcy's death. Lizzie, it is not right. As you know well, Jonathan will inherit Mr Bingley's fortune, which we hear has grown considerably of late. Why then should he have Longbourn, too? It is selfish and greedy. I shall write to Jane and Papa. They must see that my two boys also need help to get on in life. Henry could manage Papa's estate and live at Longbourn, while he did it. I could run the household for both of them. There would be plenty of room, Mary does not need more than a couple of rooms, and Papa spends most of his time in his library. Lizzie, I hope you and Mr Darcy realise what you have done to my poor children. Perhaps if you were not quite so rich, you would have understood how difficult it is for those of us who have insufficient money and no inherited wealth. I hope Papa and Jane see how unfair they have been to us and our children—especially Henry. I have to say that having felt his coldness towards us when we were at Longbourn for dear Mama's funeral, I do not expect much sympathy from Papa. Perhaps Jane will be more helpful.

Yours etc.

Lydia Wickham

Mrs Gardiner, who had sat aghast as Emily read the letter aloud, appeared to have been struck dumb. Emily went to Elizabeth and put her arms around her cousin. "Oh dear Lizzie, do not pay any attention to Lydia. She is both stupid and ignorant. This is a cruel, vicious letter, which betrays her complete lack of decent feeling," she said as she tried to comfort her.

Elizabeth, who had wept as Emily read the letter, sat up and blew her nose. "You are quite right, Emily, Lydia is stupid, but this letter is not her own work. It is Wickham's doing and shows his vicious nature; he still persists with his attacks upon Darcy and by association, myself, with all those lies about being edged out of his valuable living, and now there is this nonsense about our part in denying Henry his inheritance! Mr Grimes has made it very clear that Longbourn is now Papa's to leave to whomever he chooses and he has chosen Jonathan—of all his grandsons. Now, we have not objected on William's behalf, nor has Kitty. So why should Lydia?" She could scarcely hold back her tears of rage.

"Dearest Lizzie," said Mrs Gardiner, who had recovered some of her composure, "Can you not see that Wickham and Lydia are furious because their wretched little plan has gone awry? They wish to blame you; it is just their dreadful way of being revenged upon Mr Darcy and yourself."

Elizabeth nodded, appearing a little calmer but still sufficiently angry to wish to sit down immediately and pen letters to her father and sister Jane, warning them of Lydia's complaints. As soon as they were written and sealed, she had them despatched by express, after which tea combined with sympathetic understanding from her aunt and Emily helped considerably to improve her spirits. When Darcy and Mr Gardiner returned, nothing was said about the letter before and during dinner.

After the Gardiners had left and Elizabeth and Darcy had retired to their apartments, she handed her husband the letter, apologising as she did for its dreadful contents. She was uncertain of his response—expecting anger. But as Darcy read it, he laughed out loud and declared, "Elizabeth, dearest, is it not good to know that Wickham has been so soundly beaten? This letter, filled with rage, betrays him and proves how right your father was to have acted as he did," he said, smiling broadly, obviously delighted with the prospect of Wickham's defeat.

Bewildered, Elizabeth asked, "Are you not angry about all those lies?"

"Angry? Of course not. Why should we be angry? We sought nothing for ourselves and our children. We were happily present to witness your father declare clearly his wishes for the disposition of his estate. This squalid letter proves what I have always believed; I do not accept that this is all Lydia's doing; Wickham was behind it, it is his type of devious trick, and it gives me immense pleasure to see him comprehensively routed." Darcy sounded genuinely pleased, and despite the hurt she had felt at Lydia's cruel words, Elizabeth's humour began to improve.

In the days that followed, letters received from her father and Jane reassured her that the Wickhams' effort to disrupt their peaceful lives had failed. Neither Jane nor Mr Bennet appeared at all perturbed by the threat of incurring the wrath of the Wickhams. Both of them reassured Elizabeth that they would deal with any approach from Lydia very swiftly indeed. Elizabeth was relieved and soon decided that Darcy was right; the Wickhams were best ignored.

When Richard Gardiner returned to Oakleigh from Birmingham, he found two invitations waiting for him. The first, which he considered an honour, was to address a group of churchmen, public officials, and landowners, who had heard good reports of his work in Birmingham and wished to try something similar in Derby. Lord Derby was said to be interested in improving the housing and health of his tenants, and the possibility of obtaining his assistance for their scheme had excited the worthy citizens of Derby and the editor of the *Pioneer* newspaper, which had long campaigned for better health care and schooling for the children of the area, with little success. Having despatched a letter of acceptance, Richard took up the next letter, an invitation to dine at Pemberley, which he expected would be pure pleasure. The note from his cousin Elizabeth suggested that he might wish to stay overnight, since there were some matters to discuss, "about the hospital and other things besides." She went on:

Cassy and William have also begged me to remind you to bring along the copy of the composition by Mr Mendelsohn you apparently promised to pick up for them. They have talked of little else since attending his concert in London. I cannot believe that either of them will have sufficient skill to play the grand "Capriccio Brillante," but they are determined to attempt it.

Since his sister Emily had, as was her usual practice, returned to Oakleigh to spend a few days with her parents, Richard found himself dining with Darcy, Elizabeth, and Sir Thomas Camden. There was plenty of interest in the work Richard was doing in Birmingham, where in a very short time, he had transformed a rundown clinic into a children's hospital. Much of the inspiration and funds had come from his friend and assistant Paul Antoine, who had been determined to spend some of his own money on renovating the old place. When he mentioned the invitation to speak to the influential citizens of Derby, Sir Thomas was most impressed. "It looks as if they mean business," he said.

"Perhaps we are finally beginning to make people understand the importance of decent housing and health care in a community," said Richard, pointing out that they had waged a hopeless battle for many years with very little success. Darcy was quick to agree.

"I have always believed that we cannot build a strong nation if the people who do the most difficult jobs—the farmers, miners, mill workers, and such are housed in unsanitary conditions, with no schools or hospitals. Fitzwilliam has been campaigning for the recognition of this need for years, and so has Sir Thomas through his newspaper, but unfortunately, neither the old Tories nor the present government seem prepared to spend the money, because it will mean higher taxes on the middle classes, who support them."

"And form a large part of their new majority in the Commons," said Richard. Elizabeth, who had been listening in silence, asked, "Would it not be worthwhile making a start ourselves? If the community set the example and began work on a hospital, could we not then persuade the government, through our local members, for support to continue the work?"

"Indeed, Cousin Lizzie, that will be the burden of my message when I go to Derby next week. If we can show that there is a need and make a start locally, I believe we can push the government for support. On the other hand, if we do nothing but complain, we will achieve nothing." Darcy nodded, smiling as he agreed.

"You are quite right. There is nothing better calculated to capture the attention of a Member of Parliament than a large group of his constituents involved in an undertaking that benefits their community. It fills him with a desire to be associated with such good works. We shall have to ensure that we extract a price for this association with a noble cause."

"Well, it will cost either money or votes," laughed Richard.

"Indeed," said Darcy, who then proceeded, to Richard's great delight, to announce that Sir Thomas Camden and he had agreed to donate the land and initial costs for the building of a cottage hospital for the area. "There is a fair-sized block of land at Littleford, on the boundary of the Pemberley Estate and the Camden property, served by a lane that comes directly off the road that goes through to Bakewell and Lambton. It used to be quite a prosperous farm, tenanted by a farmer, who died last year. He had no family, and the place has been vacant for several months. I think it is well-situated for your purpose—being both private and accessible by public road."

Sir Thomas intervened to add that if there was a need to use some of the adjacent land on his side of the boundary, it would present no problem, and furthermore, his steward would be able to organise a group of builders, labourers, and artisans who could work on the building, once the plans were ready. "There are several men in the area who are not fully occupied—there is not very much work around, and they would welcome the money," he said. Richard was almost speechless with delight and could not thank them enough. As they rose to move into the drawing room, he said to Elizabeth, "I can hardly believe what I have heard. This is excellent news. I cannot wait to tell Paul; he will be delighted."

Elizabeth had been waiting for just such an opportunity. Having first asked after his friend's health and been assured it was improving, though slowly, she continued, "Richard, there is a matter I must discuss with you." Her voice indicated the seriousness of her concern, and Richard was immediately attentive, thinking it involved the health of some member of the family or household.

"What is it, Cousin Lizzie? I shall be happy to help in any way."

"It is not help I need, Richard; rather it is information, for I am quite bewildered by a certain situation which I am unable to understand. I need to ask you to be completely honest with me. Will you?" Richard, still unaware of the core of her concern, looked more puzzled than ever but, convinced of its seriousness agreed immediately.

"Of course."

"Well then, when Cassy and William go off to the music room, I shall follow them, leaving Darcy and Sir Thomas in here. Please come with me; we can talk undisturbed there." After coffee was served and the gentlemen settled into comfortable chairs by the fire, as Elizabeth had predicted, William and

Cassandra went to the music room, carrying the music Richard had brought them. Richard could tell from his cousin's expression that she was worried, but he had no idea what was causing her anxiety.

Elizabeth's first question took him completely by surprise. "Richard, are you aware that your friend Paul Antoine is falling in love with Emily?" Before he could respond, she continued, "For many months now, I have observed him in her company, both here and elsewhere; so frequently are they together whether by coincidence or design, I cannot say, but it is quite clear that they are very partial to one another. Neither of your parents has said anything to me, but I shall be astonished if they are unaware of it." Richard's face betrayed both his surprise and some obvious distress. Elizabeth expected him to respond, and when he did not, she persisted, "Richard, I have asked you for the truth, because I must know, if only because I dearly love your sister and feel responsible for her since she lives here at Pemberley. Please tell me, what is the true situation? I am convinced they are in love or soon will be. Has Paul confided in you? What are his intentions and his prospects? If they marry, how will they live?" Richard hesitated for a moment before he spoke.

"They cannot marry," he said, in so firm a voice that Elizabeth was shocked into asking, "What do you mean? Is there some impediment?"

"Yes, and they are both aware of it. They may well care for each other; I am sure they do, but they both know there is no question of marriage." Richard's face and voice were so grave that Elizabeth feared to ask her next question.

"Why? What has he done?" she had dreadful visions of the young Frenchman as a fugitive from justice perhaps.

"Nothing," replied Richard, "Paul has done nothing wrong. But he cannot marry Emily or anyone else, because he is ill; he is dying of Tuberculosis and unlikely to survive the next Winter." This time, Elizabeth was quite unable to speak. She sat down on a couch at the far end of the room, her mind racing wildly, glad of the distraction of William and Cassandra's trying to make music at the piano. She had known that Paul was not very strong. He was pale and had seemed to cough so much recently, but Tuberculosis had never entered her mind. When she spoke, her first thought was for Emily.

"Does Emily know all of this?"

Richard nodded gravely. "Yes, she has always known, and so have my parents," he explained and went on, "I lived with Paul's family when I was in

Paris, completing my medical studies. They treated me as if I was their own son. Paul was studying too—to be an apothecary. Even then, he had signs of a weak constitution, and it was deemed that he was not strong enough to study medicine, though he was certainly intelligent enough to do so." Richard's voice was low, and Lizzie strained to hear him, "When his father died, he left most of his fortune to Paul; his sisters were all well-married and settled in the country. His mother, who herself had a very delicate constitution, begged me to look after him. She knew that Paul was not only in poor health, he has a kind and unsuspecting nature which may easily fall prey to crooks and charlatans. I promised her that I would do everything I could, not just because we were as close as brothers, but also out of appreciation for their kindness and generosity to me. Not very long afterwards, I had completed my studies and was preparing to return home, when Paul's mother died. Being quite alone in Paris, he asked if he could accompany me to England and work as my assistant. He asked for no salary; he has plenty of money of his own and offered to pay for a share in the practice."

Elizabeth asked, "And at this stage did you know he had Tuberculosis?"

"Certainly not. At that stage, he appeared to have a recurring respiratory problem, but that is not uncommon in Europe. Some months after our arrival in England, however, when his condition did not improve, I took him to see a colleague in Harley Street, and my suspicions were confirmed. He has a form of Tuberculosis—not the galloping consumption that afflicted Keats, but a slow death sentence nevertheless."

"Is there really no cure?" asked Elizabeth, shaken and incredulous. Richard shook his head, his voice sad, "If there were, many more lives would have been saved."

He proceeded to list a number of illustrious persons who had succumbed to the disease, from the young daughter of King George III to the great German composer Karl Maria von Weber, who had thrilled English audiences during a triumphant tour only to die shortly after he returned to Germany. "And of course, there are thousands of ordinary men, women, and children dying of this same affliction in England," said Richard.

"And is there nothing to be done to help them?" asked Elizabeth.

"Very little when they live as most poor people do in unsanitary and crowded conditions, undernourished, and overworked."

"What about Paul?"

"There is no cure for him, but we can do several things to prolong his life and make him comfortable. Fresh air, exercise, nourishing food, friendship and good company will all help. He did improve considerably last Summer, but since that accident on the Matlock Road, when he worked with me to help the travellers, he has not been able to shake off the severe cough he got as a result of the exposure."

"And your mother, father, and Emily all know about this?" asked Elizabeth, still incredulous.

"Indeed, they do. Surely you do not believe that I would have allowed my family, my sister in particular, to remain in ignorance of the truth? How could I? It was quite plain that they liked him; he is a most attractive and likeable young man. Indeed, my mother loves him like a son. She will do anything to help him, but she knows there is nothing we can do for him except to give him all the affection and care we can, for as long as he needs it." Elizabeth was concerned for Emily, who spent so much time with Paul.

"Can she be in any danger of infection?" she asked.

"Not unless she is careless, and I have instructed her well on the precautions she must take. She is healthy, strong, and sensible, which is her best protection," Richard explained, adding that Paul himself was very careful not to place others at risk, particularly children. "You must understand that he will not visit Pemberley again, because he does not wish to place William and Cassy in any danger, nor will he visit the Fitzwilliams because of their young children. That is his decision. When he can no longer live on his own, I shall get a professional nurse to care for him; I would never place him in an institution."

Elizabeth was so shocked by Richard's revelations as to make a swift response impossible. Her anguish heightened by the belief that Richard must have judged her to be hard and insensitive, she apologised for having broached the subject as she had done. "I am most sincerely sorry, Richard; I knew nothing of this. Had I known, I would never have questioned you as I did." Richard tried to put her at ease.

"Please do not distress yourself, Cousin Lizzie, how could you have known? You were quite properly concerned for Emily."

"Yes, and I did not spare a thought for Paul. I am truly sorry."

Her contrition touched Richard, and he reassured her, "I see now that I should have told you and Mr Darcy, but for Paul's sake we did not wish to tell too many people. Once the news got around, there was bound to be a change in the way people regarded him, and that would have caused him even more pain. Emily made me promise to keep it secret until she was ready to tell you herself."

Elizabeth realised that Emily would probably have done so soon. She asked Richard's permission to tell her husband.

"Of course. He must know why Paul will not be visiting Pemberley."

"And can you say how long it might be?" Elizabeth could not bring herself to utter the dreadful words, yet he read her thoughts. "No one can tell with any certainty," he said, "A great deal depends on his ability to fight the disease. The weather is important, too. If we have a bright, warm Summer, it will help him. A cold, wet one, and he certainly will not see out the year."

Later that night, Elizabeth told her husband of her conversation with Richard. After the initial shock and expressions of sorrow, Darcy was silent and thoughtful. When he spoke, it was with a suggestion. "I shall tell Richard tomorrow that should he need a place for Paul to stay, where he could be cared for conveniently, he is welcome to use the house at Littleford, on the property we have donated for the hospital. It is a clean and comfortable place and would probably suit them well. A couple of our men could help with the daily chores. It's the very least we can do." Elizabeth was struck by his compassion and concern. Noticing her distress, he put his arms around her to comfort her. "I know how you must feel, Lizzie. I am truly shocked and saddened, but we cannot begin to understand their sorrow. There can be no situation more tragic than theirs. I can only wonder at their selflessness. I doubt I should have been able to bear similar misfortune with such courage." Elizabeth agreed, adding quietly, "How little we know even those closest to us. I have known Emily since her childhood, yet never did I dream that she was capable of such deep feelings and so much fortitude."

The following morning, after breakfast, Mr Darcy walked with Richard to the carriage that was waiting to take him to Lambton. Before they parted, he advised Richard that he could use the house at Littleford for Paul, whenever he wished to move him from Birmingham. "I am truly grieved by this news, Richard, both for your friend Paul and for Emily, who has become so much a part of our family here at Pemberley. It grieves me that she has suffered alone and we, in our ignorance of this unhappy situation, have been unable to help in any way. I want you to know that if there is anything I can do, if we can assist you in any way at all, you must feel free to ask. As soon as you wish to use the house at Littleford, my manager will see that it is made ready, and any help you require will be provided, for as long as it is needed." Expressing his profound gratitude for the generosity of his host, Richard declared that he would like to move Paul out of Birmingham as soon as possible.

"Birmingham does him no good at all; it's too polluted and crowded. The air here is fresh and sweet; exactly what he needs. Moreover, Paul will be most enthusiastic about the hospital, and if I can persuade him that I need him here, to keep a watch on the project, it will give him something to do." Having expressed his gratitude once again, Richard departed, eager to acquaint his mother and sister with the excellent news about the hospital as well as Darcy's generous offer of the house for Paul. In spite of his sadness about his friend's condition, Richard felt his spirits lift as he contemplated Darcy's kindness. Having spent much of his adult life studying in Edinburgh, London, and Paris, Richard had not had the opportunity to become closely acquainted with Mr Darcy, depending largely upon the judgement of his parents, whose affection and praise for him were unqualified. His own observation of Darcy's actions on the day of the accident to the coach and his present compassionate behaviour confirmed this. For his part, Darcy, who had felt deeply unhappy on hearing the news about Paul Antoine, was glad to be able to help.

Later that week, Elizabeth went to Lambton to visit her aunt. It was apparent that Richard had told his mother about his conversation with Elizabeth, because the two women hardly needed words to express their feelings. Both had been through much soul searching and agony, and it was not easy to speak of the concerns they shared. But they had too much affection for each other to let anything come between them. Elizabeth's own love for Emily and her aunt's unhappy sense of helplessness in the face of her present sorrow brought them together. Mrs Gardiner was contrite, "I am sorry that you were left in ignorance for so long, my dear Lizzie; it was only that Emily would have it so, and since it was not my secret to divulge, I could not speak of it to you, even though I have longed to do so, many times." Elizabeth, whose affection for her aunt far outweighed any unhappiness she may have felt at being excluded from her confidence on this matter, assured Mrs Gardiner that she understood perfectly well

Emily's wish to have as few people as possible made aware of Paul's illness and her own feelings for him. As Darcy had pointed out, in such circumstances, the knowledge that a wide circle of family and acquaintances, not all of whom were equally sympathetic, were privy to a situation of which they had not the fullest understanding could be unbearably harrowing. Elizabeth told her aunt that she above anyone knew how a person's misfortunes could be magnified and used by others to denigrate an entire family. She recalled Mr Collins' unpleasant little letter gloating over Lydia's elopement and its consequences for the rest of her family. Clearly, Emily would have been anxious to avoid anything similar.

Having spent sufficient time to reassure her aunt of her love and willingness to help at any time, if help was needed, Elizabeth left to return to Pemberley, where she sought out her cousin Emily, finding her in her favourite spot, an alcove at the far end of the library. She had a book of poems in her hand and a notebook on the desk in front of her, but it was quite plain that she had not been reading or writing at all, for her eyes were red with weeping, and her note paper was covered with meaningless scribbles. When Elizabeth approached her, she tried vainly to smile but failed as her feelings spilled out with her tears. Elizabeth put her arms around her and held her awhile, "Emily dearest, I have just come from seeing your mother. I know from her, and from Richard, how things are. Please do not blame your brother; it was I, in my ignorance of your situation, who questioned him on Saturday night and demanded to be told the truth. It was concern for you, my dear Emily, that led me to ask him. I was afraid you would be hurt," and as Emily shook with the violence of her sobs, Elizabeth went on, "I did not know how much pain you were suffering already. I am sorry, Emily; I did not mean to pry or intrude upon you."

When she was able to speak coherently, Emily reassured her cousin that she had not resented her concern. Richard had made it clear that Elizabeth's motives in asking had been completely estimable and free from censure. Emily felt she owed Elizabeth an explanation for not having confided in her earlier, but it was for Paul's sake, she said. They had not wanted him to be conscious of the curiosity and, even worse, the pity of everyone he met. Elizabeth took her cousin's hands in hers and asked very gently, "Do you love each other, Emily?" Emily's voice was quiet but very firm.

"Yes, we do. But we also know the consequences of our present situation. Oh Lizzie, I know I could help him, but there is so little time," she said, and again, she could not hold back her tears. Elizabeth struggled with her own feelings as she held her cousin close. It was plain to her that while the young couple may have spoken of their feelings to each other, Emily was in no state to speak of it to anyone else. Embracing her once more and assuring her that she was always available, should Emily need to talk or sit with her, and praying for some comfort for both of them, Elizabeth left, still feeling helpless and unhappy.

Some days later, Emily came to Elizabeth to ask if she could borrow some linen for the house at Littleford, since Richard had written to say he was bringing Paul home on Saturday. Not only was Elizabeth happy to oblige, she insisted on taking Emily to the house in her carriage, where they accomplished a great deal, working together as they prepared it for its new occupant. The loving care with which Emily performed all the little tasks was not lost on Elizabeth; she also had a more fatalistic composure, which made Elizabeth's heart heavy with sadness.

A month or so after Paul Antoine moved into the farm cottage at Littleford, Richard, with the help of an architect from Derby, produced a plan for a simple cottage hospital. The necessary approval and paperwork having been obtained by Mr Darcy's manager, Mr Grantham, building was planned to begin in the Summer. Paul had been overjoyed at the news of the generosity of Mr Darcy and Sir Thomas Camden, whose donations of land, materials, and labour had made Richard's dream a reality. He was excited to be present when the first sod was turned, even if there was no certainty that he would still be there when the hospital welcomed its first patient. Unwilling to admit defeat, he made Emily promise that she would cut the ribbon on the day. It was a promise she gave without question.

❦

While Spring had promised much and delivered little, being alternately wet and windy or windy and dry, Summer arrived in a blaze of glorious sunshine, which summoned everybody out of doors. Darcy, Elizabeth, Cassandra, and William left for an extended holiday in the Lake District. It was a journey undertaken mainly because Elizabeth had declared that she could not believe it was possible for anyone to live so close to such an area of renowned natural beauty and not visit it. "I can no longer make excuses when every stranger I meet tells me of the magnificent beauty of the Lakes, but I am dumb for never having seen them. I feel such a barbarian!" she had complained.

"We cannot have that, can we, Papa?" said William, appealing to his father, who had agreed at once. "Certainly not, William, if your Mama must see the Lakes to complete her happiness, we must and shall go there, this Summer."

And so in May, they set off for the Lakes, making a virtue of necessity and taking the opportunity to have new plumbing and other vital conveniences installed at Pemberley while they were away. Bidding goodbye to Mr and Mrs Gardiner and Richard, with whom they dined the day before their departure, Elizabeth left the addresses of the inns at which they proposed to stay and begged her aunt to write with all the news from home. She was particularly keen to hear of Emily and Paul.

Elizabeth had written also to Jane, who had been prevented from joining them at dinner because of the indisposition of her two youngest children:

Dearest Jane,

We missed you at dinner yesterday and were exceedingly sorry to hear that little Sophia and Louisa are unwell. I pray it is nothing serious and they will soon be themselves again. We leave tomorrow for the Lakes. Only a small party with Darcy, myself, the children, and my faithful Jenny, who refuses to entrust me to unknown ladies' maids in Cumbria, of which she speaks as if it were a veritable wilderness. Save when she has travelled with me, Jenny has never left Derbyshire, and though a pleasant and intelligent young woman, she still believes that, everywhere outside her home county, men are vile and not to be trusted!

Would it not have been wonderful if we could have taken this holiday together? I do miss our long lazy afternoons and have promised myself that next Summer, we shall all travel to Surrey or Hampshire or some such pleasant spot, where the children will safely entertain themselves, Darcy and Bingley will fish, ride, shoot, or play cricket, while you and I allow ourselves some really long talks together. I shall think of you at the Lakes and look forward to a letter or two while I am away. Dearest Jane, I do miss your letters, now you are so busy with your little ones.

My love to Bingley, my favourite nephew, and all my lovely nieces.

Yours etc.

Elizabeth looked forward to their tour of the Lakes with a greater degree of anticipation than she had felt about any other recent activity. She had confessed to Jane that, on her last visit to London, she had been bored except for the excellent recital by Mr Mendelsohn they had attended with Signora Contini and had longed only to return home.

Wondering at her own sense of excitement, which easily exceeded that of her daughter Cassandra, she reasoned that it was probably due to the disappointment she had felt, when many years ago, their plans for just such a tour had been curtailed due to Mr Gardiner's business commitments. And yet, it had been that very disappointment that had resulted in their being in Derbyshire and more particularly at Pemberley, when its owner happened to return a day earlier than expected. The rest, of course, was history.

Elizabeth and her aunt had often speculated about the possibilities. But Mrs Gardiner, like Jane, had insisted that some things in life were inevitable, and she was confident that Darcy and Elizabeth were so clearly right for each other that they would have met and married anyway. Elizabeth was not so sure and never ceased to thank her aunt and uncle for their part in bringing them together.

On that last occasion, the excursion was to have helped her overcome some degree of disappointment in her estimation of a certain officer of the militia, whose engagement to Miss Mary King had astonished her. Then she had hoped that mountains, rocks, and lakes would bring her fresh life and vigour. Almost twenty years later, with the confidence that a happy marriage and loving children gave her, she was setting off full of life and vigour, looking to enjoy the glories of a place whose beauty had become a lure for many travellers.

Travelling North from Matlock, their journey took them through Yorkshire, which had been a route preferred above the ancient and hazardous one from Lancaster across the treacherous sands of Morecambe Bay at low tide. Their driver regaled them with hair-raising tales of coaches disappearing in the quicksands and careless travellers lost in the fog or engulfed by the rising tide.

William, who was of an age when a touch of a danger seemed to add zest to any activity, wondered aloud why they had not chosen the "cross-sands route." "Would it not have been so much more exciting, Mama?" he said wistfully. Neither his parents nor the driver of the carriage were prepared to agree with him. Cassandra pointed out, with some sarcasm, that she had thought the purpose of this excursion was to get to the Lakes and enjoy their beauty, not to be drowned or sucked into the quicksands before reaching them.

Elizabeth felt a little sympathy for her son; his elder sister had a quick wit and a sharp turn of phrase, which she occasionally used to put her young brother in his place, yet William, being of a gentle disposition, never ever retaliated. "William is so much like Jane," her Aunt Gardiner had commented, "such a steady, sweet nature," and Elizabeth could not but agree. On this occasion, she felt compelled to enter the conversation on his side, "There will be plenty of exciting things to do when we get to the Lakes, William. I promise we shall not spend all our days looking for Mr Wordsworth's favourite places." Darcy caught her eye and, understanding her purpose, added that he was looking forward to some fishing and boating on the Lakes and unless he was very much mistaken, there were some exciting hills to climb as well. William, who was easily pleased, agreed that he was looking forward to all of that, but it might have been fun to be able to regale Mr Clarke and Mrs Reynolds with a terrifying tale of being lost in a fog amidst the quicksands of the estuary, at which prospect everyone laughed, including Jenny, who was Mrs Reynold's niece. William was a great favourite with Mrs Reynolds, a fact not lost on the rest.

Stopping whenever they needed rest or refreshment, while the horses were fed and watered, or staying overnight at an inn which took their fancy, they travelled at a leisurely pace from the dales of Yorkshire into Cumbria. The children were especially intrigued by the dry stone walls that seemed to wind in and out of valleys and over steep craggy mountains, in the teeth of the wind, quite different to the friendly green hedgerows that formed the boundaries of farms in the Midlands and the South of England. Passing through Lonsdale and Kirkby on the border of Cumbria, they proceeded to Kendal, which had grown into an important market town with its cobbled yards and busy inns, filled with coaches and people travelling either for business or pleasure.

A good turnpike road which made travel safer and cheaper brought hundreds of tourists into the district. Many of those who came were attracted by the idyllic word pictures of this part of England drawn by the poets—Coleridge, Southey, Keats, and the father of them all—William Wordsworth. Unlike her cousin Caroline, whose passion for Wordsworth had undergone a radical change upon discovering he had joined the Conservatives, Elizabeth still found great pleasure in his poetry. A wellworn copy of his *Lyrical Ballads* accompanied her on this journey, during which, she promised herself, she would read from it whenever she felt in a mood to do so. Unfortunately, like all the best laid plans, such promises could not always be kept, as Elizabeth found when they reached the inn beside Lake Windermere, where they were to stay a few days.

That night, she wrote to Jane, in an unusually poetic frame of mind:

It was twilight, and the setting sun lit up the sky as it sank behind the hills, while the quiet lake lay like a dark silken sheet before us. Only the swallows wheeling around over the water seemed awake, as all around the darkness gathered everything into its arms. Now, I thought, if ever there was a time to read some lines of Wordsworth, now was the time. But alas, dear Jane, it was too dark to read, and my book of poetry lay in a bag at the bottom of a pile of luggage on the footpath. The children, especially William, were tired from travelling, and Jenny was anxious to get their luggage into their rooms, before it was completely dark. Darcy had gone to see the landlord, and there was no one to share with me this magical moment, my first glimpse of that special quality that the Lakes have above every other part of England. How I wished for you or Caroline to share my mood. My Cassandra is very keen on her music and would rather sing than read poetry. I have some hope for William, though. I have been reading Keats and Wordsworth to him recently, and he is much more receptive. Better still, he can draw and has promised to do some sketches of our most favourite places, so I shall have some souvenirs of our tour.

Later that night, when they had dined and retired to bed, Elizabeth told her husband of her missed "poetic" opportunity. Sympathetic, but not without a hint of mischief in his voice, he promised that, on the morrow, he would seek out the exact spot where Wordsworth composed the lines about Lake Grasmere, and she could take her book of poems and read to her heart's content.

And when the day dawned bright and clear, with the sun making the water glint like cut crystal, Darcy was as good as his word. Fortunate for having been in the area before with a touring party from Cambridge, he recalled that the places of pilgrimage for lovers of Wordsworth were Grasmere and Rydal Water, rather than Windermere, which was the most popular of the Lakes and therefore, frequently, the most crowded.

So it was to the Vale of Grasmere and tranquil Rydal Water, which lay at the northernmost end of Lake Windermere, that they went, and there, indeed, it was both appropriate and possible to lie in the shade and read poetry that had been inspired by this quite magical place, hidden for centuries amidst the mountains and valleys of ancient Cumbria. The two lovely Lakes, linked by the river Rothay, were the centre of an exquisite scene, and in whichever direction one looked, a prospect of great beauty opened up before one's eyes.

They had brought a picnic and spent all day in such happy pursuits that when the sun slipped behind the hills and Jenny reminded them it would be best to get back to the inn, nobody wanted to leave. There was still light in the sky, and William and Cassandra begged to be allowed to stay a little longer. William was completing a sketch, and Cassy just could not bear to leave the sound of water slipping over the stones. "It was so much like music," she said. Neither Darcy nor Elizabeth had the heart to refuse.

Returning later to the inn, they found it filled with a party of travellers, rather noisily celebrating a successful fishing expedition. Windermere, for all its beauty, was too popular to be attractive to them. The following morning, they moved on, to Grasmere, where they found very acceptable lodgings, within walking distance from the Lakes. It is not necessary to relate in detail the pleasures of the next six weeks that so engrossed their little party; none of them felt the time pass other than too swiftly.

The Summer days slipped by, whether fine or occasionally wet, with visits to a myriad of places. There were the curious, tiny "Dove Cottage," where William and Dorothy Wordsworth used to live when they first settled in the area and the sad little graves of two of Wordsworth's children, Catherine and Thomas, in the churchyard, reminding one that life here was not all beautiful vistas and rustic romance. On many lovely days, all their daylight hours were spent on or beside the water, at Grasmere, Coniston, Derwentwater, or over the far side beside Lake Buttermere, and each found something of the magic that had enchanted thousands of travellers and held in thrall artists and poets alike. They clambered up craggy hills, walked miles in the woodlands and meadows, and read poetry as they picnicked beside the waters of tumbling streams and placid lakes. Mysterious, ancient stone circles like the one at Castlerigg left them as much amazed as the natural phenomena—monuments to men and women who had inhabited these mist covered mountains and hidden valleys many centuries ago.

Everywhere they went, around each deep bend in the road, a new vista opened, enticing them to stay longer. William had become absorbed in sketching places they visited, and his sketchbook was filling up with pictures of lakes, bridges, boats, dark fells, and sunlit valleys—all souvenirs of this splendid summer. Elizabeth and Darcy enjoyed the close companionship with their children, even more than the sights and sounds of the Lakes. It was a rare and precious thing, and they treasured it.

In the penultimate week of their holiday, Elizabeth and Cassy declared that they needed new boots, since theirs were completely worn with walking, and Darcy suggested a day in Kendal, well-known for its rustic entertainment. The offer was accepted immediately, for they had all heard from their hosts of the excellent country fair at Kendal and were keen to visit it.

Returning from Kendal to Ambleside, they found several letters which had been sent on from their lodgings at Grasmere. Seeing hers were from Jane and Mrs Gardiner, Elizabeth begged to be excused from a walk after dinner to the Lake, where the end of a boat race was to be followed by country dancing and fireworks. Darcy, noting how eagerly she had opened up Jane's letter, smiled to himself. Fireworks offered no competition to a letter from Jane.

As William and Cassandra set off with their father for the ferry wharf, Elizabeth curled up in a large, comfortable chair and settled down to read her letters. Jane's letter was, happily, full of news. She wrote:

> My dearest Lizzie,
>
> I have had yours, written at Windermere at the start of your tour of the Lakes, for almost two weeks, and I am sincerely sorry for this delay in replying. I have no excuse to offer except that we have been very busy, and instead of sending off a scrap of a note, I decided to wait for a day when there would be sufficient time to write you all the news. Today, everyone is away at a cricket match. Bingley and Jonathan are both playing, and Emma has gone along with some friends in the neighbourhood to cheer their team. It means I have the day to myself, and my first thoughts were of you, out there enjoying the beauty of the Lakes. I hope this finds you still at Grasmere, which I am told is very peaceful indeed. My informant is Caroline Bingley, who together with Mrs Hurst has just left for Bath after spending a few days with us, on their return from London, where they had

attended a wedding. It was not as trying having them because we did not have to be concerned with our brother-in-law, Mr Hurst, whose gout has rendered it impossible for him to travel to London. While I am sorry he suffers with the gout, I have to confess I was relieved he was not with them.

Back to Caroline and the Lakes—she declared that she had spent two weeks there some years ago. While she found it "peaceful," she admitted to being bored with the "endless panorama of mountains and water and no one of any quality about." I do long to hear your response, dear Lizzie. I gather from your letter that you are unlikely to be similarly bored.

Charlotte Collins has just this week returned to Mansfield, having spent a fortnight with us together with her two girls. Catherine, her eldest, is still at Rosings. Charlotte says her godmother and namesake, Lady Catherine, has invited her to stay on as a companion to Miss de Bourgh. While Charlotte will miss her, I think she sees it as an opportunity not to be missed and has prudently consented. Her own endeavours are bearing much fruit. She has seven young ladies at Mansfield, who will finish in November, with seven others starting next Spring. She has neither the room nor the capacity to take in more. Rebecca, she says, is very helpful. She wants to be a writer for the newspapers—and has been sending work away to several publishers— including the Matlock Review *but is happy to teach Charlotte's young ladies in the meantime. Rebecca says they are eager to learn and especially love to read poetry, write pretty letters and verses and such things. It amazes me Lizzie that we got on without such tutoring at all.*

But, Lizzie, my favourite young person has to be our goddaughter, Amelia-Jane, who is almost fifteen and already the loveliest young girl you could hope to meet and with such a sweetness of disposition, too. Bingley gave a party for the two Misses Collins last Saturday and Amelia-Jane was remarked upon by everyone present. Unfortunately for all the gentlemen who wanted to dance with her, since she is not yet "out," her mother did not permit her to accept invitations except from Jonathan and Richard, who she said "were almost like her brothers." There were many disappointed partners, to be sure, but Charlotte is very protective of her girls, understandably, seeing she has to bring them up on her own. She has, however, promised that Amelia-Jane may spend Christmas with us, while Charlotte and Rebecca go to Lucas Lodge.

Dear Lizzie, we have had so many visitors this Summer—Caroline and Fitzwilliam have been here on their way back from London—all very excited with their achievements. Caroline could hardly stop telling us about all the hard work Fitzwilliam had been doing with this Reform Group, who are trying to improve conditions for working people and get everyone the vote.

Bingley swears that if women could vote and stand for Parliament, Caroline would be at Westminster herself! Oh Lizzie, how this couple have given the lie to those who thought they were unsuited, because she was too young for him. I have rarely seen a marriage in which two people loved, encouraged, and appreciated each other more . . .

There was more, with details of several domestic and personal matters, all of which Elizabeth greatly enjoyed, glad that Jane had waited to write at length. She was still smiling when she opened up her aunt's letter, and on glancing at it very quickly, as she was wont to do, she was struck by the difference between the two.

As much as Jane's letter had been filled with the sweets of Summer, leaving her sister thankful for the happiness Jane and her family enjoyed, Mrs Gardiner's brought an immediate feeling of unease. The letter, not obviously seeming gloomy or despondent and certainly not conveying any specific bad news, appeared strained and difficult to read, quite unlike her aunt's usual style. She also wrote of her daughter and son-in-law and their pleasure at the success of Fitzwilliam's campaign to give more power to local councils, but Elizabeth was unconvinced; the letter lacked enthusiasm. To the extent that she could read between the lines, Elizabeth felt her aunt, whom she knew well and loved dearly, was trying to conceal some anxiety or unhappiness, but her letter betrayed her.

She wrote:

I am almost sorry that Caroline and Fitzwilliam are back and my darling grandchildren are gone to Matlock with them. I really do love having them with me; especially when your uncle is away on business, they are my chief source of happiness. Oh Lizzie, I do miss them.

Some good news followed. They had heard from Robert again—he had met with Mr Bingley's cousin Frank, who had helped him settle down and find his feet in the colony. He liked the work and had already made some friends. He did not like the hot weather but was looking forward to going up country where it was much cooler. Elizabeth could sense that her aunt was very pleased with Robert's news. But of Emily, there was hardly any news, save to say she was busy at Pemberley. Elizabeth searched eagerly for information about Paul. There was none. In the final paragraph, there was a line about Richard's moving from Birmingham to take up work in Derby, and almost as an afterthought, there followed the news that he was going up to London with Paul, at the end of the week. Elizabeth checked the date of the letter—it was almost ten days old. She wondered why Richard was taking Paul to London. She was certain that there was something her aunt had not revealed.

The letter unsettled her. They had less than a week of their tour left, and Elizabeth was now eager to return home. She sensed there was something wrong and wanted to be back home to see, hear, and do whatever she could. She realised that the situation was one over which she had very little control, but she hated being miles away. She longed for news of Emily and was disturbed by the fact that her aunt had written nothing of her state of mind or Paul's health. Elizabeth felt a pressing need to be back at Pemberley.

Bewildered and uneasy, she was in a very different frame of mind, when Darcy, who had left her reading Jane's letter, returned. He was surprised by the change in her, and when she showed him Mrs Gardiner's letter and admitted her feelings of unease and anxiety, he tried at first to reason with her, arguing that if anything serious had occurred, they would have been informed by express. Yet, aware that she was unconvinced and remained unhappy, he suggested that they leave a few days early. "I know we had planned to go on to Penrith, but there is nothing very remarkable to be seen there; if we left tomorrow and travelled via Kendal, we could reach Pemberley at least two days earlier than planned." Elizabeth thanked him with tears in her eyes, grateful for his understanding and his efforts to alleviate her concern. "It will bring you no pleasure to spend any more time here, when your heart is no longer in it, my love," her husband explained. "I can see that you are troubled, and nothing will do but to return home."

Elizabeth was concerned that the children may be disappointed to be going home early, but having spoken with them, Darcy returned to reassure her. "Cassandra has grown a little tired of travelling around and is yearning for the comforts of home."

"What about William?" she asked, "Is he not upset?" Darcy shook his head.

"William has no preference and on hearing that you were anxious to return early, although I have not divulged the reason for your disquiet, he was immediately in agreement that we should leave at once," he said, to her great relief.

With adverse weather forecast for the morrow, it seemed by far the most sensible thing to do. Preparations for their journey were speedily put in train, and just a day later, they were on the road to Derbyshire and home.

CHAPTER TWENTY

The grinding agony of woe . . .

TRAVELLING AS EXPEDITIOUSLY AS possible and breaking journey only for rest and meals, they reached Pemberley by midafternoon on the day following. Though Darcy had taken the precaution of despatching an express announcing their change of plan, Mrs Reynolds seemed unusually perturbed, and Elizabeth was immediately aware that all was not well.

While a bustling crowd of servants and stable lads unloaded luggage and led the tired horses away, Elizabeth, ignoring the activity around her, sought out Mrs Reynolds. She hardly needed to speak, for Mrs Reynolds held in her hand a letter, folded over and sealed. Elizabeth could tell from the writing it was from Emily. As she took it, she looked at the housekeeper, "What is it, Mrs Reynolds; what has happened?" Mrs Reynolds ushered her into the sitting room, where to her surprise, she found her sister Kitty, waiting. Kitty's tense expression did not fill Elizabeth with confidence either. She was convinced that something was very wrong indeed. "Please, why will one of you not tell me what has happened? Kitty, what are you doing here? And where is Emily?" she demanded.

Mrs Reynolds left the room to follow William and Cassandra upstairs. It was plain to her that the sisters needed to talk alone. Kitty urged her sister to read Emily's letter first, but Elizabeth was adamant, "Not until I know what has happened to her. Where is she, Kitty? You must tell me." Finally, Kitty realising that it was useless to argue, said, "Emily is in Italy—or at least, she should be there by now."

"Italy? Good God! What on earth is she doing in Italy?" Elizabeth was astounded.

Kitty begged her to open Emily's letter and read it.

"I know she has explained it all; please, Lizzie, do not distress yourself unduly. No harm has come to Emily—as you will see when you read her letter, it was a decision she took entirely of her own free will." By this time, Elizabeth had opened up the letter. As she read it, she was so bewildered and shaken, she was forced to sit down.

Emily's letter was written in plain, undramatic language. In terms that would have sufficed if she were informing Elizabeth that she intended travelling to Lambton or Matlock to visit her mother or her sister, she explained her actions:

My dearest Cousin Lizzie,

When you read this letter, I shall be in Italy, with Paul. Please do not be angry with me, for it is not as you fear. I shall be travelling quite respectably, with my husband, who must move to a warmer, drier climate immediately. The physician in Harley Street, who saw Paul ten days ago, insisted that he had no hope unless he did so. Richard will tell you more if you wish to have more medical information. When I heard the facts, I decided that I would go with Paul, to ensure he is properly cared for, but I knew it was neither wise nor seemly that I travel alone with him. I decided, therefore, that we should be married, by special licence, and travel as hus-band and wife. This would not only afford me protection as we travel, but it would protect my family and yourselves from any malicious gossip.

I told Richard and my dear parents of my decision. I cannot help it, dear Lizzie, that Mama is unhappy. I suppose I would be, too, if it had been my daughter. But Richard and Papa have been very helpful. Richard has arranged our travel and lodgings. There is no problem with money, Paul has sufficient for both of us, but Papa insists I must have my own as well. Paul himself was, at first, quite adamant that I must not "sacrifice" myself, as he quaintly put it, but I have persuaded him that it is what I want to do, because, dear Lizzie, I love him dearly and want to look after him for however little time we have left. I could not bear to have him locked away in some dreary hospital, where we would have no way of reaching him.

Kitty will explain how the wedding was arranged, with Dr Jenkins very kindly performing the ceremony and dear, kind Mrs Reynolds help-ing me prepare for the journey. She has found a good, middle-aged woman, who will travel with us. Mrs Brown is familiar with Paul's con-dition, having helped me care for him at the cottage in Littleford. Papa is also to send a manservant to accompany us, to help with Paul, and be our general protector.

I think that is all I have to write, except, my dear Cousin, to beg your forgiveness and understanding, that I have taken this step without wait-ing to ask your advice. Please understand, there was so little time, and as I said to Richard, I am all of twenty-six, albeit somewhat less experienced in the ways of the world than my brothers and sister.

But of one thing I am absolutely certain, I love Paul very much, too much to let him die alone in some hospital. My love would have been worth little, and I could not have lived with myself or faced my God, had I not done whatever I was able to do for him, when he needed me most. We are both sensible people and know well what lies in store. I pray we have the strength to help each other through it. Please, Lizzie, all I ask is that you understand and pray for us.

Your loving cousin, Emily.

When Elizabeth finished reading the letter, her face was wet with tears. As she sat unable to speak, Darcy entered the room with Richard, who, like Kitty, had arrived, alerted to their early return by Mrs Reynolds.

Elizabeth's instinct was to go at once to her aunt and uncle, but Richard would not let her. "No, Cousin Lizzie, you must not go now. You have been trav-elling for almost two days; you are tired and already upset by the news; you are not in a state to be of any help to Mama. Perhaps tomorrow . . ."

"But Richard, do you not think your mother needs me?" Elizabeth asked.

"I am sure she does, and I know she would welcome a visit from you, but I do not believe you should undertake the journey now."

Darcy agreed, "Richard is right, Elizabeth. Besides there are things with which you need to acquaint yourself. You will want to talk to Mrs Reynolds,

Kitty, and Doctor Jenkins as well as Richard, before you go to your aunt and uncle." Elizabeth could not deny the commonsense of his argument and reluctantly agreed to postpone her journey to Lambton. After dinner, Kitty and her husband returned home, but Richard stayed on to explain how it had all come about. Elizabeth wanted to know everything, and Richard alone had all the answers, for he had been his sister's confidant from the outset. Arriving from Birmingham, a week before he was to start work at the clinic in Derby, he had been troubled by Paul's condition. In spite of the warm Summer, he was still pale and very breathless.

"I insisted that we see my colleague in Harley Street at once, and it was not a moment too soon. He said, quite categorically, that Paul had no chance at all, unless he left England and moved to a warmer, drier climate. He recommended southern Italy—he has sent other patients there and they have benefited quite remarkably. Some have enjoyed prolonged periods of reasonably good health. Paul himself accepts the inevitable. While he was not happy to go, he agreed when I said I would accompany him and see him settled there. He can afford comfortable accommodation and a local servant or two." Elizabeth was impatient to know how and when Emily became involved. "Almost as soon as we returned from London," he replied.

"She insisted on knowing every particular. At first, she was distraught and wept a great deal. Then, she went away and came back about two hours later with her mind made up. She had it all planned—the special licence, the travel arrangements, everything. They were to be married, so she could accompany Paul and look after him in Italy." Darcy, who had said little, intervened to ask, "How did Mr and Mrs Gardiner respond to Emily's decision?" Richard's answer was not entirely what they expected.

"Mama was most upset. It was not a question of being unsympathetic, because she has always liked Paul and treated him as one of the family. She was afraid for Emily and did not wish her to go. She even suggested that I should go with him; I was a man and a doctor, she said; it was right and proper that I should go. But Emily's resolve could not be shaken. I have never seen her so determined about anything before. Nothing any of us said would change her mind," he explained.

"And Mr Gardiner?" Darcy prompted, knowing how difficult such a situation would have been for him.

"I think I was most surprised by my father. He listened to everything Emily said, and when he realised how determined she was to go, he simply asked about the practical arrangements for their journey and lodgings; he even decided to send one of his servants to accompany them," Richard sighed and added, "I think Mama was deeply shocked. She had hoped he would support her and try to dissuade Emily, but, as Emily reminded me, she is twenty-six. Caroline had been permitted to become engaged to Fitzwilliam when she was but fifteen—not much more than a child. How could they tell Emily she had no right to do as she chose at twenty-six?"

"But surely, there is no comparison, Richard. Emily must be aware, as we all are, that there is no future in this tragic marriage." Darcy's voice was as grave as his countenance. He wondered whether Emily's natural kindness had perhaps blinded her to the hopelessness of their situation. But Richard was quite sure that Emily understood perfectly the consequences of her decision.

"Emily was well aware of the facts about Paul's health, from the outset. I ensured that she knew everything, as soon as I discovered it. She knows there is no hope of recovery, not even with the best care in the world. She accepts that. But, she loves him and wants to be with him to bring him some happiness and comfort until the end. Paul was reluctant at first, much as he loves her, but she persuaded him."

"And the wedding, how was that arranged?" asked Elizabeth.

"Dr Jenkins and Kitty were splendid. They arranged it all. It was a simple ceremony with just the family. Bingley and Jane were here, of course. Caroline and Fitzwilliam came direct from London. But, everybody agreed Emily looked beautiful, and if you had seen them, you would have thought they were a happy couple with a lifetime of married bliss ahead of them; it was quite astonishing," he said. They had left the following day, by private coach; Richard had accompanied them to ensure that everything was in order.

"Where are they now?" asked Elizabeth.

"They have taken a house outside Rome—it has to be near enough for the doctor to reach them regularly," Richard explained.

"Will it really help him?" she persisted.

"Oh yes, it will probably extend his life by several months. Better still, the weather will enhance his enjoyment of it. The sunshine and the dry, fresh air will all help. It will certainly be better for him than the Midlands in Winter."

Richard's voice betrayed his feelings, despite his attempt to remain as detached as possible. Paul was his friend as well as his patient. Now, he was also his brother-in-law.

The following morning, at breakfast, Cassandra and William, who had heard whispers from the chambermaid on the previous night, were told of Emily's marriage and some of the reasons behind it. They asked a few questions, and after straightforward and truthful answers from their parents, their responses were quite remarkable. Cassandra declared that Emily had done something very brave and noble—an unselfish gesture of true love. William agreed, though he could not quite understand why the weather in Rome was better for Paul than the weather in Derbyshire or Bath. He hoped it would mean that Paul might recover but added that he would miss Emily very much. Elizabeth was more than a little surprised. Their reactions, uncomplicated by adult priorities and social prejudice, were in sharp contrast to her own.

Discussing it later with Darcy, she confessed to being disappointed in herself. "I wonder, my love, am I becoming hard and unfeeling?" she asked, and as he regarded her with astonishment, explained, "I should have been feeling, like Cassy, that Emily's has been a brave, selfless act—an example of true love. Yet, I see only the recklessness and the possible pain that must surely follow, not just for her, but for all her family and especially her parents, who must feel bereft. I know she is twenty-six and had every right to decide for herself, but I cannot help wishing I had been here to advise her." Darcy looked very grave indeed. Elizabeth knew that expression—it was almost always a sign that he disagreed with her. His voice, however, was gentle when he spoke.

"I am particularly pleased that we were not here, Elizabeth, and that Emily was able to make her decision untroubled by opinions and advice, however well-meant, from either of us. I should not have liked to feel that we had placed any more strain upon a young woman, who felt that the most important thing in her life was to bring some affection and comfort to a man she loved, when, as she says in her letter, he needed her most."

"But Darcy, you cannot believe that she has done the right thing by marrying Paul, when he is dying? Surely, there were other ways of helping him? I know she loves him, but must she blight her entire life to give him some temporary comfort?" Even as she spoke, Elizabeth could have bitten off her tongue. She heard the harshness of her words and regretted them immediately. Darcy heard it too, but he knew her too well to assume that she had meant them. He realised it was the consequence of her anxiety and concern for Emily, whom they both loved. Turning to her, he spoke with a degree of gentleness that precluded any hint of censure, "Elizabeth, that question is neither fair nor worthy of your generous and loving nature. I know you too well to accept that you believe what you have just said. Nevertheless, let me try to answer your concerns."

They were standing beside a window in their private sitting room, overlooking the park. Elizabeth continued to gaze out on the sunlit scene, as he spoke, unable to trust herself to look at him. "Lizzie, when we chose to marry, both you and I defied the judgement of others, including my aunt and your father, each of whom had reservations based upon their perceptions of our characters and conduct. We had no thought except that we loved each other. Nothing else mattered. How then, can we censure Emily for following her heart, as she has done? Consider also this, she has not acted rashly in any practical sense, Richard assures me Paul has a considerable inheritance, which will ultimately be Emily's. Indeed it had been so willed—before their wedding. If we consider his character and background, they are without stain. Richard speaks highly of him, and I cannot imagine that a single objection would have been raised, had he been fit and well. Surely, Elizabeth, if we marry promising to love in sickness and in health, there can be no criticism of what Emily has done, on the grounds that the condition was known to exist? She has acted as she has done with only the noblest of motives. What would we say of a man who abandoned his partner on discovering she was similarly afflicted? Would we not find him worthy of severe condemnation?" Elizabeth was silent, her mind in turmoil as she heard the strength of his arguments and the compassion in his voice. He spoke quietly, but there was a level of gravity that compelled attention.

"My only reservation flows from the sorrow she will bear when he dies, but that is a choice Emily has made. She has accepted that the sorrow she must endure, when he is gone, is part of the love they both share now, while he lives. It is not for us to sit in judgement over her, my dearest; rather we should endeavour to support and help them in every way possible." Elizabeth knew he was right. She, above all, had fought prejudice and small mindedness and, through her own marriage and that of her sister Jane, seen her proud belief in the primacy of character and principle vindicated. Darcy, whose greatest strength lay in the consistent integrity and decency of his character, was reinforcing her own deeply felt beliefs and drawing her back to them.

Grateful for his intervention, she turned from the window and looked up at him, noticing how age had changed his countenance. The hard, determined chin and fine features still dominated his face, but the dark eyes were gentler, and the lines of many years' experience had mellowed his expression. While strength and determination still prevailed, the hauteur had long gone, and in its place were respect and compassion for others, as well as a generosity of spirit that never failed to delight her. Reaching for his hand, Elizabeth spoke from the heart. "You are quite right, my love, I should never have believed that I had any right to be censorious of Emily's actions, based as they were on totally unselfish love and devotion—which are surely blessed virtues. If Emily never loves another man in all her life, she will still have the memory of the love she shares with Paul, for however short a time. None of us, least of all myself, with my reputation for independence, has the right to criticise her. I have you to thank for showing me, albeit in the kindest possible way, how very wrong I was. I am sorry."

Darcy drew her to him and held her close. He was deeply touched but not surprised by her contrition. Knowing her well, he understood her reasons and loved her honesty and sincerity in acknowledging it. It was her affection and concern for Emily and her parents, for whom both of them cared so deeply, that had brought her first, seemingly insensitive, response. Yet, Elizabeth, herself capable of deep love and loyalty, could not deny the pre-eminence of such unselfish love as Emily had shown, over any material consideration. So completely did she accept her husband's account of the situation that she worried about her ability to comfort her aunt, whom she expected to find still grief-stricken over Emily's marriage and in dire need of consolation, when they travelled to Lambton on the following day.

To her surprise, they found the Gardiners far more composed than they had anticipated. Seeking a reason for their equanimity, Elizabeth did not have to look very far or wait very long. While the maid was getting tea and cakes, and Mr Gardiner invited Darcy to walk down to look at a new vehicle he had acquired, Mrs Gardiner took Elizabeth upstairs, where she produced a letter, closely written in Emily's own hand. Posted in Rome, it was addressed to Richard but plainly intended for all of the family.

Having first thanked her brother from the bottom of her heart for all he had done to help them and asked his forgiveness for having caused him and her "dear parents" so much grief, she proceeded to write in great detail of the arrangements that had been made for their accommodation, the generosity and kindness of their Italian neighbours, and not least, the difference the warmth and constant sunshine had made, within only a week of their coming, to Paul's spirits.

She wrote joyously of her happiness at being able to be with him:

How I wish you could see us in summer clothes, enjoying the fresh air and this wonderful Italian sun. I am determined that we shall be as tanned as our neighbours, Signora Cassini and her children, by the end of summer. They look so beautiful, brown as berries and ever so healthy. Tomorrow, being Sunday, after they return from Mass, we are to go with them to Anzio, which is on the coast. The Signora has promised to bring along a picnic, and we are to have a day by the sea! What bliss! Their grandmother, who lives with them, makes the most delectable ice confection—a type of sorbet with fruit—and she has begun to spoil us by bringing some over each time she prepares it for her family. Paul has won her by declaring, quite truthfully, that it is the best thing he has tasted in years. Oh Richard, I must not forget, the doctor from the hospital called yesterday. He is quite pleased with Paul's condition and has recommended that he takes a short walk each morning, after breakfast. I am to go with him in case he becomes overtired, in which case, I must hurry home and send Jack with the little curricle to fetch him. I do not believe, however, that this will be necessary. He is looking and feeling so much better already.

Dearest Richard, Papa, and Mama, I cannot finish without saying again how I wish I did not have to cause you so much sadness. I am so happy here, but for the fact that I know I have caused you pain. That is my only regret. Please try to think of me as Paul's wife, and you will under-stand that I had no other choice but to be with him at this time. I hope and pray that we might see each other again soon, but that is really in the lap of the Gods. Paul sends his love and asks you to remember to feed the birds at Littleford. He worries that they may go hungry in Winter.

Your loving and very grateful sister, etc.

Whilst Elizabeth read the letter, her aunt had sat beside her, and when she had finished, they were both tearful, but this time they were tears of relief, even happiness. As they embraced, she held her aunt tight and said, "Oh my dear Aunt, how much you must have gone through!" Her aunt smiled and took her hand.

"And I did not have my dear Lizzie's shoulder to cry on." Elizabeth remembered well how much comforting she had once sought and received from her aunt. Downstairs, the gentlemen had returned to the sitting room, and tea was served, as the ladies joined them. Elizabeth, with her aunt's permission, let Darcy read Emily's letter. She had no doubt at all that he had been absolutely right. In his own conversations with Mr Gardiner, Darcy had reached the same conclusion, although he forbore to say so.

Returning to Pemberley, Elizabeth found waiting for her another piece of evidence, if more were needed, to convince her. A letter from Jane, which had been addressed to her at Grasmere, had arrived a week later, having gone on a circuitous journey through the Lake District, before being redirected to Pemberley. It had been written the day after Jane and Bingley had attended the wedding of Emily and Paul. Even allowing for the eternal optimism of the Bingleys and her sister's complete inability to speak other than well of anyone, until there was flagrant evidence of malice or worse, the letter was confirmation of everything that Kitty, Richard, Darcy, and Dr Jenkins had said.

Jane, after an initial admission to feelings of disquiet, based upon her fear that Emily had so little hope of a long and happy marriage—which was Jane's preferred state of life—could not say too much about the selflessness of their cousin. She wrote:

Emily looked beautiful in a simple white gown with a posy of roses from the Rectory garden. Her compassion and love shone through, as they made their vows. No one could doubt how deeply they cared for each other. Oh, Lizzie, I wish you could have been here to see them—it was such a beautiful experience, even for us who have been married many years, it brought tears to my eyes . . .

Bingley and I had been very surprised when we first received a letter from our Uncle Gardiner, inviting us to attend, but then Richard arrived to explain why it was happening in this way. We have been so busy with the children and Bingley's work on the farm, that we did not know the seriousness of Paul's illness. Of course, I had always believed them to be in love and was more convinced of it, each time I saw them together.

Dear Lizzie, I know Aunt Gardiner is very upset; with Robert gone to the Colonies and now Emily in Italy. But, as I said to Bingley, just to see the joy on their faces and know how much they care for each other is sufficient to make one happy for them. I cannot help getting rather tearful each time I recall what Richard has told us about Paul's health and the likelihood that he may not live long. Bingley knew a young man in London, who went to Rome because he had Tuberculosis. He lived for several years and only passed away because he could not give up drinking, which hastened his death. I am hopeful that Paul may also be helped by the salubrious climate in Italy, to live a good deal longer than is presently expected.

Ever the optimist and always the one to look at the brightest of all available possibilities, Jane helped to improve Elizabeth's spirits quite considerably. She also spoke at length with Kitty who, together with her husband, had been convinced of the sincerity and, more importantly, the justification of Emily's wish to marry and care for the man she loved. When Elizabeth asked if they had thought about the possible danger to Emily of infection, Dr Jenkins had replied that they had, and in talking to her, he had asked Emily if she had considered it. Her reply, that hundreds of doctors and everybody else who tended the sick, at home or in a hospital, took the same risk and it was a chance she would gladly take for Paul, had only served to demonstrate her devotion to him.

"It was," said Dr Jenkins, "the kind of selfless love one hopes to see once or twice in a lifetime, in my calling. It is what priests preach with little hope of seeing it practised. I felt privileged to be able to help; I did not feel I had the right to question her further."

Kitty, whose understanding had matured tenfold since her marriage to Dr Jenkins, had told her sister of a talk she had had with Emily, as they made preparations for the wedding. "She was so happy, Lizzie. That was what made it so wonderful. It was as if she was looking forward to years and years of happy married life. Never a word of complaint about the unfairness of it all, that is how I would have felt, but not Emily. Before leaving, she thanked everyone, even the servants, and of course, we did get the Children's Choir together to sing two of

her favourite hymns. Everyone was in tears, but Emily was smiling. Poor Aunt
Gardiner, I was afraid she would faint, she looked so pale, but Richard was won-
derful. He got everyone together, and after the wedding breakfast, he and
Colonel Fitzwilliam packed us all into two big carriages, and we drove out to
Dovedale. It was such a lovely day. Emily had tears in her eyes, but she was still
smiling," said Kitty, obviously overwhelmed by the experience.

For Elizabeth, it was difficult, if not impossible, to retain any of her original objections after all these accounts. It remained for her to do just one thing
more, and later that evening, sitting at a table in the music room, while William
and Cassandra practised at the piano, she wrote to her cousin:

> *My dearest Emily,*
>
> *Since our return from the Lakes, I have had your letter, spoken with
> Richard and your parents and with Kitty and Dr Jenkins, as well. If I
> were to say that I was not surprised, even shocked, by the news of your
> marriage, I would be untruthful, and I know you would not wish that. I
> was both shocked at the news and distressed at being away, so I had no
> means of sharing what I am sure were difficult days for you. However,
> despite that obvious handicap, I have, I believe, gained sufficient knowl-
> edge from several sources, to feel able to write as I do. Mr Darcy and I have
> also talked at length about you and Paul, and your wish to marry and care
> for him is surely an act of great devotion. I pray that your devoted care and
> the warm Italian sun will help him greatly.*
>
> *Dear Emily, I cannot say if I would have had the courage to do as you
> have done. But let me say how much we love you and want you to be
> happy. We wish both of you much joy together and pray for Paul's improv-
> ing health. Your mother has let me read your last letter to Richard, which
> seems to prove that sunshine, fresh air, and love combined in equal parts
> are an excellent medication for the body as well as the spirit. Do write
> when you can. We all love you and pray for you. God bless you both,*
>
> *Your loving cousin,*
> *Lizzie.*

Throughout the Summer and into Autumn, letters were received from
Emily, which recounted warm happy days and slow but steady improvement in

Paul's health. They gave Elizabeth and Darcy as well as Mr and Mrs Gardiner, with whom every scrap of new information was eagerly exchanged, a good deal of comfort. However, Richard warned Elizabeth against being carried away with Emily's good news. "It often happens with this wretched disease," he explained, "It appears to withdraw for a while, and the patient rallies strongly, but it always returns, often with redoubled vigour." Seeing disappointment written all over her face as he spoke, he was immediately contrite, "Oh my dear Cousin Lizzie, I am sorry. I ought to have been more sensible of your feelings. I was just speaking as a physician." Elizabeth, though saddened, was glad of the truth. But she was also concerned about her aunt.

"Do not tell your mother what you have just said to me, Richard. She places great store by the good news she hears from Emily." Elizabeth pleaded, and Richard agreed.

"I know Mama is very pleased with Emily's reports of Paul's improving health, and I must confess I have not had the heart to tell her the truth. But, I have hinted to my father that they should not be too optimistic. I hope to travel to Italy in November, and I shall bring you an accurate report when I return."

Listening to him, Elizabeth wondered at the fine young man he had become. She recalled the cheeky lad, who used to play Hide and Seek at Longbourn, often leaving his quieter little brother behind and defying all attempts to find him. Now, at twenty-five, an esteemed member of the community, he was a very personable and popular young man, a physician with a social conscience and an eligible bachelor!

On this occasion, he had arrived early, to collect Cassandra, who had promised to help at a Charity Concert organised by his sister Caroline. With a lively sense of humour and a naturally engaging manner, he was very much in demand by his sister, whose chief concern was organising her husband's reform campaigns. Her goodlooking, well-spoken brother was an asset and a useful ally at these gatherings.

They were all due to dine with the Fitzwilliams that evening, and Cassy, who looked very fetching in her new bonnet, wondered aloud whether there might be music fit for dancing. To which Richard replied, "If you wish to dance, Cassy, I can absolutely guarantee there will be music." As they were getting into Richard's curricle, Elizabeth reminded him that she was counting on his help for the Harvest Fair in October, especially now they were without Emily. After assuring her that he would not miss it for the world, Richard took the vehicle down the drive and across the park, watched by Elizabeth and William.

Turning to her son who was standing in the sunlight, his honey coloured hair tousled, his blue eyes squinting at the bright light, Elizabeth asked if he had not wanted to go, too. William was not interested, "No, Mama, I owe Mr Clarke an essay on the Lake Poets, which I must finish today, and I do want to get in some practice on the new Mozart sonata, before Mr Goldman arrives for my lesson tomorrow." His mother teased him, "Oh you poor dear, how hard you must have to work at all the things you love, mind you do not wear yourself out," she warned. William laughed and embraced her, before running upstairs, leaving her smiling as she saw a maid taking up a tray of food, which would surely sustain him for most of the morning.

Elizabeth's easy relationships with her children brought her deep contentment and happiness. William, whose sensitive, quiet nature had initially made it difficult for his father to reach him, had been drawn out by his mother, and in the last few years, the three of them had become good companions. Cassandra's bright nature and ready sense of fun and William's sensitivity were treasured equally and enjoyed by their parents, who never left them in any doubt of their affection. It was something that Darcy had missed as a child and Elizabeth had been determined to give her children in full measure.

❧

The week before the Harvest Fair and the Pemberley Ball was one of the busiest in all her life. Elizabeth could not recall having so much to do and being so much in demand ever before. With only Caroline and Cassandra to help her with organising both functions, she had reason to be extremely grateful for the superb training and efficiency of the staff at Pemberley.

Jenny, her personal maid for many years, had recently been married and was beginning to take over responsibilities as housekeeper from her aunt, Mrs Reynolds. She had worked with Elizabeth throughout the past fortnight on a host of details for the dinner and the ball, while her husband, who was Darcy's chief Steward, was in charge of all matters relating to the fair. Elizabeth had not fully realised the level of interest the first fair at Pemberley was likely to raise in the community. Tenants, craftsmen and women, and farm labourers from Pemberley and the Camden Estates, as well as those from further afield—Lambton, Matlock, and Bakewell—had all wanted to participate, and there were thus numerous stalls and tents set up in the lower meadows, with trestle tables upon which were laid a myriad of articles proudly displayed. Everyone who had something or some skill to show and sell was there with woodwork, toys, tools, basketware, farm produce in plenty, honey, jams, pickles, preserves, as well as baskets of fruit, flowers, and vegetables from their home gardens. There were even a few paintings of the Peak or Dovedale, together with colourful knitted rugs and fine embroidered linen.

When Caroline, as the popular wife of the local member, opened the fair, the buying was brisk, and the visitors most enthusiastic. Everyone seemed pleased especially as the weather, which had been pleasant enough for most of the week, improved on the day to produce a final burst of Summer in the middle of Autumn, adding a somewhat unreal quality to the occasion. Elizabeth, feeling a little tired by midafternoon, returned to the house and found Darcy upstairs, looking out on the scene from a window in the library that afforded a most picturesque view of the meadows. She joined him, pointing out that the distance lent a storybook quality to the hive of activity down there. As they watched the figures scurrying around, they played a game—picking out individuals by their gait or dress. Caroline was easy to spot as she and her children flitted from stall to stall, and it wasn't difficult to recognise Richard and Cassandra, the latter in a much-loved hat, smothered in yellow roses, as they emerged from a tent carrying two rather unwieldy baskets of apples across to a trestle table. Halfway across, Cassandra tripped and dropped her basket, spilling its contents all over the grass. Richard hastened to help her, solicitously examining her foot and ankle, to assure himself that she had suffered no injury. Though they could hear not a word of their conversation, both Elizabeth and Darcy could not help smiling as they watched and noted his concern and her smiles of gratitude. As they collected their apples and went, this time, with Cassy keeping a firm hold of Richard's arm, Darcy asked, apropos nothing at all, "How old is Richard?"

"He will be twenty-six, soon after Christmas," Elizabeth replied. Nothing more was said on the subject, and after resting awhile, they went downstairs again and out into the late afternoon sunshine, where the fairground was slowly emptying as most people loaded up their carts and made their way home.

Later, Elizabeth watched as her daughter persuaded first her friends and then her cousin Richard to join in the country dancing, which was in progress on the lawn. "Now there is a man with a big heart," said Fitzwilliam, to Elizabeth. Mrs Gardiner, sitting beside them commented, "Cassy has been very busy all day, and yet she does not seem at all tired. Indeed, she looks livelier and more vivacious than ever in that pretty new gown." Elizabeth touched her aunt's hand and asked, "Do you think, dear Aunt, that there could be some special reason for this liveliness and vivacity?" Hearing something of the old archness in her niece's voice, Mrs Gardiner looked quickly across at her, but she was prevented from answering by the arrival of William, who had stoutly refused to dance. Like his father, who had on a famous occasion in Meryton surprised Sir William Lucas with the laconic comment that, "Every savage can dance," William found it a boring activity and rarely participated unless he had a particularly pretty or amiable partner.

As the sun sank behind the hills, a cool breeze sprang up and reminded everyone that it was indeed Autumn. Many people came to thank Mr and Mrs Darcy for their hospitality and the opportunity to sell their wares. Mr Gardiner, seeing that his wife was looking rather tired, suggested that it was time to leave, but not before he had heaped lavish praise upon Elizabeth and Darcy and everyone involved in the day's success. "I have to say, it has been a splendid day, Elizabeth. I am sure you will have requests for a repeat next year," he predicted. Darcy agreed, adding that Sir Thomas Camden had offered to host the fair next year.

"What an excellent idea," said Mr Gardiner, expressing what appeared to be the general view.

The family returned to the house, and Elizabeth suggested an early night. Charlotte and her two younger daughters were expected the following morning.

That Pemberley was meant to be a venue for a grand ball was not in any doubt. Its gracious proportions and beautiful grounds, its exquisite furnishings and accessories, all combined to provide an ideal setting. Sadly, its present Master had no taste for dancing and did not give many balls.

This occasion, however, was quite another matter, being in honour of three young ladies, who had all recently turned seventeen. No expense was spared to make it perfect for them. Jenny Grantham and a team of Pemberley staff together with hired help had spent many days getting all the arrangements right. Menus had been meticulously planned, and the best of everything—linen, chinaware, and crystal—brought out of storage to grace the tables. Vases and baskets of flowers filled the corners of every room, and hundreds of candles waited for twilight to be lit. Not one, but two, groups of musicians were to provide music—chamber music before and during dinner with music for dancing afterwards.

Earlier that morning, hearing the sound of music floating through the house, Elizabeth had entered the music room, and seeing William's golden head bowed over the instrument, she had felt, suddenly, unaccountably, sad. He looked lonely and vulnerable. He was determined to master a difficult passage in the composition and repeated it until he had it right. Elizabeth knew he would love to be a concert pianist; he had told her so when he was twelve. But would it ever do for the future Master of Pemberley? Would not everyone say it was frivolous self-indulgence for a young man in his position not to undertake a serious education?

As he concluded playing, Elizabeth applauded. William turned and, delighted by her appreciation, came over to her. "William, that was good. Mr Goldman will be pleased," she said.

"But I suppose there is no hope of Papa's permitting me to take it up seriously—as a career, I mean?" he asked, tentatively.

"Have you ever tried asking him?"

He shook his head and ran his fingers through his already unruly hair. "I am too afraid—not of Papa, afraid of being refused, I suppose. I just want to keep hoping."

"Is it what you really want to do?"

"More than anything in the world, Mama," he said, sounding so totally sincere and serious that Elizabeth felt a tug on her heart that made her promise to speak to Darcy, after all the festivities were over.

"Perhaps we could suggest that you study music seriously, maybe with a more advanced teacher for two years, and then, if you did not wish to pursue it further, you would still be young enough to take on something else," she said.

"Such as managing Pemberley?" William quipped, with a sardonic smile. As he returned to the piano, she asked, "Will you play the new Mozart sonata for Papa and me, sometime?"

He smiled, and his face lit up with pleasure, "Of course, I'd love to. Do you think it will help to persuade him?"

"It may well do. In any case, it is a beautiful composition, and I am sure he will enjoy hearing you play it. Your Papa has an excellent appreciation of music."

He came back to her and suddenly, impulsively, hugged her as he used to do when he was a little boy. "You are the best mother in the world," he declared. "Thank you."

Touched, Elizabeth embraced the boy, then begged him not to be too long. "I do need your help with Charlotte's girls, and they will be here soon," she said and gently shut the door behind her.

That evening, Elizabeth took great care with her clothes and hair, selecting her gown and jewellery. It was a very special occasion. As she was completing her toilet, Cassandra came in to ask if she could borrow some of her mother's jewels to set off her new gown. Her hair had been styled in the fashionable Grecian mode, and she had an extra glow of excitement that presaged something; her mother was not yet certain what it was.

As she helped her select earrings and a necklace, Elizabeth asked, casually, "And has any gentleman asked you to reserve the first dance tonight?" She had expected an evasive answer, so it surprised her when her daughter laughed and said, "Oh yes, Richard has, for the first and the second and quite a few more." Seeing her mother's face, she added, "Mama, I fear I have fallen in love with him. I did not mean to, but there it is." Elizabeth raised her eyebrows.

"Indeed? And what is the cause of your fear?"

"That Papa would not approve, which would really break my heart."

"And why should he not approve?" asked Elizabeth, quite unable to comprehend the logic of this argument.

"I do not know, Mama. Richard is the most intelligent, handsome, kindest man for hundreds of miles around. Why on earth would Papa object? But Richard seems to be anxious too."

"I cannot imagine why," said her mother, "And since Papa has not had the opportunity to do one thing or another, it hardly seems fair to assume he would disapprove." Then deciding to defer the discussion, she added, "in any event, that is a matter that will arise only when Richard decides to ask your Papa's permission, and we are not there yet. For tonight, my love, I suggest you enjoy yourself, but do be discreet."

"Oh I will, Mama, I do not wish to spoil anything, and neither does Richard."

That night, as they watched the dancers, Jane and Elizabeth let their imaginations wander at will. There were several handsome couples; Jonathan was dancing with Rose Fitzwilliam, Becky Collins danced often with young

Anthony Tate, who was now editor of the *Review,* and Emma Bingley, without any doubt the most beautiful girl at the ball, was never short of partners.

It was, however, Richard and Cassandra who caught their eye and caused Jane to comment that she hoped Darcy had prepared his speech, because he was surely going to need it very soon. Elizabeth had never been able to conceal anything from her dearest sister and found herself repeating her conversation with her daughter.

Jane, remembering many unhappy, anxious days and nights spent wondering about the intentions of the men who became their husbands, smiled as she acknowledged that the younger generation was so much more open with their affections. "It is plain to see that Richard and Cassy are in love, and while there is no lack of decorum in their behaviour, they do not appear to wish to conceal their feelings. When I think of the unhappiness we suffered, I rejoice that our children will be spared such wholly unnecessary grief. Bingley and I have often regretted the long months we spent apart, being miserable, each ignorant of the other's feelings." Elizabeth agreed wholeheartedly and was only prevented from replying at length by her husband's arriving to claim her for the next dance. She always enjoyed dancing with him yet could not resist taking the opportunity to tease him a little by trying to draw him into a conversation as they danced.

"Have you noticed how well Cassandra looks tonight?" she asked.

"I have indeed, she's looking very elegant," he replied, and then added, "But if my observation of young Doctor Gardiner is worth anything, I may have to begin preparing an answer to that question that all fathers of beautiful young women have to ponder."

"And have you thought what your answer will be?" his wife asked.

"What would you like it to be, Lizzie?" he teased. She was determined that he should give her an answer, first.

"It is you who will have to give him an answer. What is it to be?"

Darcy smiled. "If you are content to leave it to me, I shall have no difficulty at all.

Richard is perhaps the most eligible young man in the district, and I cannot think of anyone more suitable for Cassandra. He is mature and responsible, with a sound career, and she seems to have a good deal of affection for him. Has she told you she means to accept him?" he asked.

"Not in so many words, but she isn't likely to refuse him. They've been inseparable these last three days; they obviously enjoy each other's company and do not seem to mind who knows it," she replied.

Darcy smiled and, like Jane, commented upon the open acknowledgement of affection that characterised the younger set. "If she accepts him, I can see no reason to refuse permission, provided they are willing to become engaged and wait until she is eighteen." Delighted with his answer, Elizabeth longed to tell her sister and would have gone to her immediately, had there not been a sudden burst of applause from the dancers on the floor. William, for the first time, was leading a partner into the dance, and it was Charlotte's youngest girl, Amelia-Jane, who was acknowledged by everyone to be the prettiest of the three Collins girls. William's fair good looks, a striking contrast to his partner's dark beauty, complemented Amelia-Jane's graceful figure, as they went down the line of the dance. Elizabeth's cup was full to the brim. Much as she loved her daughter and took pride in her achievements, it was her young son, now almost seventeen, who always made her heart race with joy. Because she had never had a brother, the birth of William had brought a new dimension to her life. He had, with his gentle affectionate nature, added considerably to the sum total of her happiness.

When Darcy left her to join Bingley and Fitzwilliam, she found Jane on the stairs and immediately proceeded to share her secret. The sisters, after twenty years of marriage, had lost nothing of their sense of fun, and it was in conspiratorial whispers that they shared their information. Jane declared that there was no doubt in her mind, having observed the couple, that Richard intended to propose tonight. "Lizzie, they have never left each other's side, except to dance with a cousin or a sister, and though they have been very discreet, I could swear I saw them slip away during the polka."

Just then, the musicians struck up a waltz, and apart from a few intrepid couples, the floor was left to the younger dancers, whose mastery of the light swirling steps was watched with envy and admiration by many. Jonathan, having claimed young Amelia-Jane, joined Richard and Cassandra and a few other couples on the floor, as the dance that had taken Europe by storm, and was the rage in the assembly rooms of London, invaded Derbyshire. When all the dancers finally left the floor and the weary musicians put away their instruments, it was late.

As they went upstairs, Elizabeth looked in vain for Cassandra. She had half expected her to bring her some news, but she had disappeared. Only after the last carriage had left and the remaining guests had retired, was there a gentle knock on her door. Pulling her mother out into the cold corridor, Cassandra whispered the news that Richard was expected early on the morrow. "He is going to ask Papa," she said, "but he wants to tell his parents first." Elizabeth embraced her daughter and assured them they had no need to fear her father's objections; there would be none. "Mama, do you think we shall be as happy as you are?" Cassy asked wistfully, to which her mother had only one reply, and that was given with all the assurance that she could muster.

"If you are as sure of your feelings as we were when we married, I have no doubt of your happiness. Are you?" she asked. Cassandra's voice was quite firm, "Oh yes, Mama, I have always adored him. He says he has loved me for years but was reluctant to declare it until he was settled in his profession. Tonight just seemed to be the perfect time." Elizabeth smiled a wry smile, recalling how much difficulty Darcy had had with getting the words and timing of his proposal right. Richard had obviously had no such problem.

The sun rose on a day as pretty, if a little cooler, than the one just past. The debris of the ball had been cleared away by a small army of servants, and the early risers had already ridden out to enjoy the fresh Autumn air in the park. Elizabeth, having told Darcy to expect Richard, had decided to spend a little longer in bed than usual and was still not fully awake, when Cassy bounded in, all dressed up and eager, urging her mother to rise and dress for breakfast. Elizabeth sent her away, but she returned half an hour later, to declare that Richard had already arrived and was in the morning room with her father. "Papa was just returning from his ride in the park with Mr Bingley, when Richard arrived," she said, "so you must go down." Elizabeth recalled the day, some twenty years ago, when Bingley, impatient to propose to Jane, had ridden over from Netherfield, almost before anyone at Longbourn was awake. He'd had to sit alone in the parlour, and poor Mrs Bennet had been thrown into complete confusion, while her daughters raced around upstairs, getting suitably dressed for their very welcome, though untimely, guest. Elizabeth sought, however, to calm her daughter's anxiety, "Cassy, my darling, it is your father that Richard is here to see. Afterwards, they will want to see you, and when they do, you must be ready. I shall come downstairs to hear the good news before breakfast." Cassy seemed unconvinced, but later, Elizabeth was proved right, when her father called her in to give them his blessing, by which time Elizabeth and William had come downstairs in time to wish the happy pair even greater joy.

At breakfast, where they were joined by the Bingleys and Charlotte's family, it was agreed that this was too good a day to spend indoors. The engagement and pleasant weather were justification for a picnic, and soon preparations were afoot, while Richard and Cassandra decided to drive to Lambton, to tell the Gardiners their good news, before returning together for the picnic in the park.

As the family gathered that afternoon, on one of those magical Autumn days, when golden light filtered through the leaves creates a dream-like atmosphere, happiness reigned.

For Elizabeth and Darcy, the engagement of their daughter to Richard, the son of the Gardiners, who were their dearest and most trusted friends, was a match made in heaven. Elizabeth could not imagine anything that could possibly spoil this perfect day.

A repast fit for the occasion had been prepared and carried down to the picnic spot in baskets. Elizabeth had picked the prettiest spot in the park, shaded by ancient oak and elm trees, within sight of the stream, where they'd had many picnics but none as special as this, nor in such congenial company. The afternoon slipped by very slowly, in a kind of post-harvest haze, quite unlike the hectic days of Summer. Most of the guests declared they had too much to eat; some fell asleep, while the newly engaged couple strolled away for a quiet walk in the woods. Elizabeth and Darcy were too comfortable to want to move just yet, but after a while Jonathan and William stood up and announced they would walk to the house, following the stream, and Edward, Caroline's son, joined them.

Some time later, Jane made to rise, and this prompted a more general movement, as Bingley rose to accompany her. A sudden gust of wind caught Elizabeth's scarf and made her shiver as the oak leaves, russet and brown, showered down around her. Helping her up, Darcy said, "That was the first really cold gust of wind we've had all day," and Caroline, putting on a wrap, agreed.

"I'm afraid it looks as though our glorious Autumn weather is finally ending." It was a remark she would recall again and again. Another cold gust, more leaves rustled down onto the grass, and everyone was ready to go indoors.

As they approached the house, walking in groups or as in the case of Mrs Gardiner and Jane, driven in a little phaeton, Jonathan was standing in the drive, with a young man not much older than William. Elizabeth did not recognise him, nor did Darcy. But young Isabella Fitzwilliam did. "It's that horrid Lindley fellow, Mama, his father has a farm at Bakewell, and they breed horses. They enjoy showing off."

"I wonder what he wants," said Elizabeth.

Isabella obliged again, "They ride down by the river; I have seen them there together. He has probably come to show off a horse. Tom the elder brother is a real wild one, always racing the horses along the roads and jumping the hedgerows." Still, puzzled, Elizabeth looked around for William.

She called out to Jonathan, "Jonathan, is William with you?" but before he could reply, the Lindley boy moved right out into the drive and answered for him, "William and Edward have ridden up into the woods with Tom, my brother."

"What?" Elizabeth could not believe her ears.

"What horses are they riding?" Darcy asked, and the boy replied with a degree of boastful pride, "Why ours, of course. We were taking them out for a gallop. They wanted a ride." On hearing his words, Elizabeth flew to her husband's side.

"William doesn't ride unfamiliar horses; he is not at ease with them and makes them nervous and skittish!" she cried.

By this time, Richard and Cassandra had come up and joined Jonathan, who was looking very anxious indeed. Darcy, meanwhile, had asked for a couple of horses to be saddled up. He was going after them, with one of his men. Caroline and Fitzwilliam, who had lingered by the lake, arrived in time to hear Darcy call out to one of his stable hands, "We had better take along an extra horse." Caroline was bewildered and worried; she had not heard where Edward had gone and with whom. She appealed first to Elizabeth and then Jane for information; neither could satisfy her. Jonathan confessed to being unhappy about William's and Edward's riding Tom's horses, but he had not been able to dissuade them in the face of so much encouragement from the Lindley brothers.

"They were in the saddle and gone in no time at all," he said, worrying that they had not yet returned, in spite of repeated assurances from Lindley that they would be all right, because "Tom is the best rider in the county." Bingley, an excellent rider himself, was less worried, "I expect they'll be back soon," he said, but all the women were troubled, none more than Elizabeth, who shivered as the wind rose. Cassandra ran upstairs to get her mother a warm wrap, as

Richard followed Darcy to the stables, asking to be allowed to accompany them. "In case there has been some trouble, you could do with a doctor," he said, and Darcy, clearly relieved, agreed.

Minutes later, with the North wind gusting more strongly, they were saddled up and gone, leaving behind an anxious group to straggle into the house. The sun was setting on a scene that had changed utterly in the space of an hour; a day filled with happy optimism had ended in a mood of apprehension—even dread.

CHAPTER TWENTY-ONE

No coward soul is mine

A S THE TIME CRAWLED by with no news, and darkness fell, shrouding the house, the small group of mainly women and children had either fallen silent or spoken in whispers, standing about or crowding together by the fireplace in the saloon, as if to draw comfort from each other.

Bingley and Colonel Fitzwilliam paced restlessly in the hall, while Mr Gardiner, his face heavy with concern for the two boys, sat with his wife, trying desperately to give her hope. Not knowing made matters worse; the uncertainty adding another fearsome element to their waiting. The two women most afraid—Elizabeth and Caroline said little. Gripped by cold fear, they sat together holding hands and occasionally failing to suppress an impatient cry as more time passed without result. Jane, ever the loving and caring one, tried to urge them to take some refreshment and was rebuffed. "How could one think of food?" scoffed Caroline, turning abruptly away, and even Elizabeth, always sensitive to her sister's gentle, good nature, covered her face with her hands, unable even to contemplate it at such a time.

Jenny, whose anguish matching that of her mistress showed in her harrowed face, busied herself getting the younger children upstairs, fed, bathed, and bedded down. When there had been no news from the search party for over an hour, Mrs Gardiner wondered aloud whether someone else should not go out after them. Fitzwilliam and Bingley had been discussing just such a proposition and were about to walk down to the stables for their horses, when Will Camden, who had been silent all evening, spoke up, "It will be of no use for any one unfamiliar with the woods, to go out there at night. It would be too dangerous. But if one of you will follow me, I am willing to go. I know these woods well." Fitzwilliam immediately agreed, and the two of them set off for the stables, leaving Bingley back at the house.

They had only been gone a few minutes, when Jenny was heard calling from upstairs, where, with Mrs Reynolds, she had been keeping watch at a window that offered a clear view of the drive. "There's someone coming up from the bridge," she called, and in a trice, Elizabeth and Caroline were at the front door, with the others close behind. As the horse approached, it was clear there were two men—Jack, the groom, was riding, with the stable hand walking beside the horse. The women at the door rushed out into the cold and surrounded them. Their desperate questions came all at once, creating a babel of sound; neither of the men was able to answer. It was Jenny's husband, John, who intervened and got the men inside first, and as the others followed them in, he asked the groom, "What is it, Jack, tell me, where is the Master, and what has happened to the lads?" The young stable hand was sobbing, and even the groom's face was contorted with shock. They were cold. A hot drink helped as they sat before the fire, and then, slowly, painfully, the tale was told.

There had been a dreadful accident. On one of the bridle paths in the woods, a horse had stumbled and fallen, breaking a leg and tripping up the animal following, which then appeared to have lost its footing and rolled into a gully with its rider, young Master Edward. As a scream came from Caroline, the boy broke down, and the groom had to take up the tale. Both horse and rider had been killed instantly. It had taken over an hour to rescue the boy, but to no avail. He must have been dead at least an hour before they had found him. Elizabeth stood by, panic-stricken, unable to ask about her son, as Caroline's heart-rending pain filled the room, and her mother rushed to her side. Then Jenny, feeling Elizabeth's anguish, asked, "And Master William?" The groom shook his head as his tears fell.

"It seems his horse must have bolted, because Master William had been thrown on to the path, striking his head as he fell. Dr Gardiner was with him the instant we found him, and so was my Master; the doctor tried everything he knew, but he passed away within a few minutes of our finding him. Oh Ma'am, I am so sorry. I feel it as if he were my own. It would never have happened with one of our horses!" he cried. Elizabeth turned away and wept, her body shaking with the violence of her grief. As they asked more questions, and the terrible tale unfolded, it became clear that only Tom Lindley had survived, with a broken leg to show for it. Reaction ranged from anger and rage to despair, as the entire family contemplated the loss of two of their dearest and best. Caroline and Elizabeth embraced and wept together. They were comforted by Jane and Mrs Gardiner but remained inconsolable. Mr Gardiner, despite his pain, persisted with the questions.

"Where are Dr Gardiner and Mr Darcy?" he asked. He was told that they had contacted the authorities at Matlock and were waiting for a vehicle to transport the children's bodies, which had been carried up to the roadway. Jack could not contain his grief and sobbed all through his story. The stable hand sat on the floor, his head in his hands, unable to believe what he had seen. He was the son of one of the farmers, born on the estate; in all his life, he had not experienced anything like the tragedy that was unfolding at this moment. The sound of approaching horses and a cry from Elizabeth alerted them to the arrival of Richard and Darcy. As they came indoors, Mr Darcy, his face dark and drawn, went directly to his wife, embraced her as she sobbed, and took her upstairs, where she could vent her grief in private. Jane helped Fitzwilliam and Mrs Gardiner take Caroline to a room that had been prepared for them, where she continued to weep for hours, despite the efforts of her family to comfort her.

In spite of her pain, Elizabeth was determined to discover exactly what had occurred. Though her husband tried to persuade her to rest awhile, she would have none of it, asking about every particular of the accident that had taken her child's life, wanting most of all to know if William had suffered much pain and had he recognised his father, when they found him.

In answer to the first, Darcy said that to the best of Richard's knowledge, it was unlikely William had suffered much; the fall and consequent blow to the head would surely have caused him to become unconscious, a state from which he had appeared to emerge only fitfully, when they had found him. To her second, more difficult question, Darcy answered truthfully, but with great sorrow, that William had not spoken at all, but, when Richard was tending him, appeared to recognise him. When his father had held him as he lay on the grass, Darcy had kept hold of his hand until he had closed his eyes for the last time. Darcy honestly believed that his son had known him then and was comforted by his presence. For Elizabeth, every detail brought more tears, and one burst of grieving was so passionate that Darcy feared she would injure herself. Going out of the room, he sought out Jenny and Jane and begged them to sit with her awhile.

Meanwhile, Mr and Mrs Gardiner, feeling for both their daughter and their niece, were torn between the two of them but not wanting to intrude upon Darcy and Elizabeth, contented themselves with waiting in the long gallery until Darcy emerged. He saw them and went to them at once. He had spoken with no one since his return an hour or more ago. The Gardiners warmly embraced him and expressed their sorrow, and Darcy acknowledged their shared agony, for had they not all suffered terribly tonight.

They asked after Elizabeth, and on being told that Jane was with her, Mrs Gardiner asked if she may go in to her, too. "Please do, I am sure Lizzie is longing to see you," urged Darcy, who then walked to the end of the gallery with Mr Gardiner and stopped as they reached the point where the portraits of the two Darcy children hung alongside the splendid painting of his sister—Georgiana and his favourite portrait of Elizabeth—in a striking emerald green gown. While Cassandra's portrait had captured her vivacity, William's was characterised by a pensive expression, with a half smile on his lips. Even at fourteen, there had been a special quality about him, which his mother had recognised as she encouraged his interest in music and art.

Unlike Edward Fitzwilliam, who was occasionally wilful and difficult, William's was a gentle, sensitive nature. That he should have been destroyed in the pursuit of crude excitement, urged on by a stranger to ride a horse he could not possibly have known well enough to control, was the supreme irony. Standing before the portrait, Darcy was silent, heartsick with sorrow. Mr Gardiner stood a few paces behind him, unwilling to intrude but keenly feeling his pain.

Charlotte Collins approached; she seemed deeply shocked. Her family had survived the death of Mr Collins, a husband and father, but the death of a child, one as dearly loved as William, was inconceivable to her, and she felt their loss deeply. Her obvious distress moved Darcy, who had always held her in high esteem. "If there is anything I can do, Mr Darcy, please let me be of some use.

Eliza and you have been so good to us, I cannot bear to stand by and see your pain. Rebecca and I are here and ready to help in any way."

"My dear Mrs Collins—Charlotte—I thank you from the bottom of my heart and on behalf of Lizzie. Your kindness is truly appreciated. Perhaps if you would speak with Mrs Reynolds and Jenny, they will know exactly what needs doing, and I am sure they would welcome your help, as would Lizzie. Please go to her," he said, quietly. She held his hand in hers for a moment and saw the tears in his eyes, as she turned and walked away. Charlotte, whose goodness of spirit had permitted no hint of envy, had rejoiced when her best friend had married Mr Darcy, even before she learnt how remarkably happy their marriage was. Since then, she had herself personally seen the generosity and kindness that Elizabeth had spoken of, and on the death of Mr Collins, she and her children had been recipients of it. That such a tragic blow should have befallen them seemed to her to be deeply unfair. All night long, the women kept vigil with their bereaved sisters and friends. Hardly anyone slept, except fitfully, from sheer exhaustion.

Early the next morning, the dark carriage bearing the undertakers arrived, beginning the funeral procedures that must move inevitably to their awful conclusion. Caroline and Elizabeth wanted only to see their sons, but that had to wait until the formalities were completed and their bodies could be prepared and laid out at last. Ironically, all the exciting promise of their young lives being snuffed out, their mothers could look forward only to this last dreaded encounter with their beloved children. Stunned and incredulous, Elizabeth contemplated how swiftly the days of bright, unalloyed joy had ended, bringing home a bitter harvest of tears.

Some days passed before arrangements for the funerals were complete. Friends and relations around the country had to be informed and allowed a reasonable time to attend. Mr Bennet and Sir William Lucas came, despite their advancing years, making the long and uncomfortable journey. Mary and, surprisingly, Lydia, but not Wickham, came with them, the latter having travelled overnight from Norwich, where they now lived. Lady Catherine sent words of sympathy; William had found favour with her at an early age, but she was prevented from attending by her daughter's illness. Her emissary, Charlotte's daughter Catherine travelled in style, arriving in one of the best carriages from Rosings, attended by a personal maid and escorted by Lady Catherine's librarian.

Many of the Gardiners' friends and Fitzwilliam's political colleagues attended, and the church was filled to overflowing, well before Dr Grantley, who had travelled from Oxford with Georgiana, arrived to conduct the service. Georgiana's distress was almost as great as that of her brother and sister. William had been a special favourite of hers. Men and women from the villages and estates in the neighbourhood had come to stand along the roads and fill the churchyard at Pemberley, where several generations of the Darcy family had been buried. Here, in illustrious company, the two young cousins would be laid to rest, before a vast number of mourners.

Arriving at the church, unexpected, having travelled all the previous day and through the night was Emily Gardiner. Elizabeth and Darcy caught sight of her as they were leaving the church. She ran over to them, and her face crumpled as she and Lizzie clung together. "Emily, dearest Emily, when did you arrive?" asked Elizabeth, when she could speak.

"Richard sent me an express as soon as it happened. I had to come."

"And Paul?"

"He insisted that I leave at once. The servants and Signora Cassini will look after him for me. But Lizzie, my dearest Cousin, what can I say?" her eyes filled with tears, which spilled down her cheeks. "William and Edward, both our beautiful boys, gone! Why? I have not ceased to question, but I can find no answer."

Darcy and Elizabeth were touched by her heroic journey, by coach from Italy and packet boat across to Dover and post again to Lambton, where Richard had met her and conveyed her to the church. She had slept little and eaten hardly at all, until she reached the inn, waiting impatiently to get to Pemberley, desperate to reach her sister and cousin and discover how this terrible thing had happened. She wanted, too, to comfort them, knowing how much it would be needed. Her own sorrow, suffered for the most part alone, except for the constant support of her brother Richard, had prepared her for sharing their grief. That she continued to carry in her heart the grinding agony of caring for a dying husband gave her a sensibility which Jane, whose life had been, mercifully, free of such pain, could not know, even though her tender heart was filled with compassion for her sister. Shared sorrow created a bond deeper than shared happiness, it seemed, and Elizabeth found herself looking for Emily again and again, to sit with, to talk to and weep with, when she could no longer hold back her tears, as thoughts and feelings welled up inside and overwhelmed her.

There grew quickly between the two women a relationship born of their understanding of each other's sorrow, seeming to eclipse even Elizabeth's most tender bond with her sister. In spite of their deep affection and Jane's efforts to console her bereaved sister, Elizabeth found it difficult to accept that her own life had been shattered, while Jane's remained complete and secure, untouched, it seemed to her, by the harrowing sorrow she had suffered. Unreasonably, unfairly, she would contemplate the fact that all Jane's children were safe and well, while William, her only son, was dead. Elizabeth made no excuses for her feelings; they left her heart sore and miserable as the inexplicable waste of his young life seared her with often unbearable pain.

There were times, when they could all share happy memories, some more recent than others, but Elizabeth clung to those precious memories of William she shared with her husband. None was more tender than the week in the late Summer of 1833, when most of the family, including Cassy, had gone to London to bid farewell to Robert. Darcy, Elizabeth, and William had spent a near-idyllic week together, fishing, riding, walking in the woods, and picnicking at Dovedale and Brush Farm. During so many matchless days, a closeness had grown between them, untrammelled by the need to be available to anyone else. Darcy had considerately given Mr Clarke the tutor a week off—to visit his mother. Nothing had happened to spoil their time together. Elizabeth recalled an incident for Emily, "I can still hear his laughter as he helped me ford a stream in Dovedale, and then quite accidentally, he claimed, let me slip into the shallows, getting my feet and petticoats wet. Even Darcy joined in, enjoying my embarrassment, but then, seeing how uncomfortable I was, William was most contrite. He apologised, fussing over me, offering to dry my shoes. By the time we had reached the top of the stream, I was quite dry but kept up the pretence of discomfort. When he discovered this, he almost threw me in again!" She was laughing, at the memory, but suddenly there were tears in her eyes, and she grew silent. Emily put her arms around her cousin and held her close.

"I know how you feel, dear Lizzie. There are times, after Paul has gone to bed, that I go round to Signora Cassini and talk to her about the good times, and when I weep as I almost always do, she holds me like this." Reminded of her cousin's continuing agony, Elizabeth was deeply sorry; she felt ashamed at having ignored Emily's sorrow, while indulging her own. "I am sorry, Emily, I have been selfish, making you share my pain, when all the while, you carry the

burden of your own. Tell me, how is Paul? Has the doctor given you hope?"
Emily smiled and in a very quiet voice replied, "We are determined to have a
very good Christmas this year, because the doctor does not expect Paul to see
another." Elizabeth was speechless that Emily, in the full knowledge that her
husband was dying and every day away from him was a day lost from their life
together, had stayed on at Pemberley to help her cope with the loss of William.
She could not believe that such kindness was possible or indeed, that she
deserved it. "My dearest Emily, you must return at once. I shall speak to Darcy
directly. We cannot keep you here, while such a terrible possibility hangs over
you both. Paul needs you," she cried, ashamed not to have enquired sooner.
Emily assured her that she had intended to leave at the end of the week but had
delayed to mention it. She took from her pocket a letter she had received from
Paul. He wrote that he was being well cared for. He sent his sincere sympathy
and love and suggested that Darcy and Elizabeth spend some time in Italy this
winter and "stay at the villa which overlooks the river—just a short walk from
us. It is quiet and comfortable and has been vacant since the end of Summer."

"You could travel to Rome and Florence, there are many splendid places to
visit, and it will be much warmer than England," Emily added, encouragingly.

Darcy and Elizabeth had discussed going away at Christmas. There
would be no festive celebrations at Pemberley, this year. Italy was certainly
worth considering. When she left, Emily pleaded with them to visit, not only
promising a "quiet and loving Italian Christmas" but adding that it would
make Paul very happy indeed to see them again. It was this last remark that
fixed their decision to go.

Two weeks later, when Richard and Cassy were dining with them, Elizabeth
broached the subject. "We intend to visit Italy in December; Emily and Paul have
suggested it. We shall take a villa close to where they live and hope to travel to
Rome and Florence. Will you join us?" Richard, who had intended to go in
November but had been unwilling to leave Cassandra at such a time as this, welcomed the suggestion. But Cassy, who had found that the loss of her brother had
also isolated her from her parents, whose grief had often excluded her, seemed
unsure. The deaths of William and Edward on the day of her engagement to
Richard had shattered her happiness. Except for Richard, she had, for the most
part, suffered alone. Darcy, sensing her reservation, intervened gently, "Cassy, I
know we have neglected you. We have taken advantage of Richard's kindness

and let him share your sorrow, keeping Emily to ourselves. Perhaps, in that, we have been selfish, but dearest Cassy, William belonged to us all, and we must help each other bear his loss. Your Mama and I need you and Richard. Will you not join us?"

She had been a little withdrawn, hurt at being left out of their grieving. Now, her father's words, spoken so quietly and sincerely, reached right into her heart. Looking across at her mother, she saw the pain in her eyes and could do no less than embrace them both and promise, "Of course I shall. We shall both go with you; Richard knows that Paul is not likely to see another Christmas—Emmy told him so," she said. Richard agreed.

"We must go, we owe it to Paul and Emily, as well as to ourselves," he said, pointing out that Emily had not spared herself when, on receiving news of the deaths of William and Edward, she had set out, with Paul's blessing, for Pemberley, to help her family bear their sorrow. "Now, having bravely borne her own burden for nigh on a year, she needs us to help her carry it through Christmas, for Paul's sake." After he had spoken, no one had any doubt that they had to go.

And so they did, leaving two weeks before Christmas, escaping the cold of England for Italy. For the very first time since Elizabeth had first visited Pemberley and then returned as a young bride, she left it without a backward glance. For years she had not been able to leave it without turning back to look at the house she had come to love, before they took the bend in the road, where it was lost from view. This time, she wanted only to get away from the place, which held so many memories of her lovely, gentle, lost son. Pemberley would never, ever be quite the same again.

Reaching Italy, they were met by Emily and Paul, with great warmth and affection. Their Italian neighbours, a large, friendly family, lost no time in coming over and making them feel welcome.

❧

The villa they had rented boasted a spectacular view, comfortable accommodation, and two live-in servants, who would keep them fed and cared for. Hospitable and caring, they wrapped their visitors in an atmosphere of warmth and comfort. Elizabeth was very glad they had come.

Despite the attractions of the high art and culture of Rome, most of their first two weeks were spent with Emily and Paul. Finding Paul looking remarkably stronger than he had been in England, they had to force themselves to remember Richard's warning of the intractability of this disease and Emily's words to them at Pemberley.

After Christmas, during which each had carried their own private grief, they decided to follow Paul's advice and do some touring. While Darcy and Richard had both travelled previously in Europe, neither Elizabeth nor Cassandra had ever been outside of England. There was, therefore, a special pleasure in sharing the unique treasures of Italy with them. Winter was not popular with touring parties, and this afforded them easy access to many places which would have been too crowded in Summer. Returning from time to time to their villa, to stay in touch with Paul and Emily, they set out on short journeys and did some sightseeing, wandering at will, and lingering wherever they found something of particular interest.

However, when she wrote to Jane, Elizabeth's letter was filled, not so much with accounts of the grand monuments and ancient architecture of Rome, but with the peace and comfort they had enjoyed with Emily and Paul and the kindness of the generous Signora Cassini and her family.

Believing her sister was owed some explanation, she wrote:

> *My dearest Jane, if you wonder why it is I have not written at length about the divinely beautiful paintings of da Vinci and the frescoes of Raphael and Michelangelo, it is because I know these beautiful works of art have a longer lifespan than the human beings around us. I look at Paul, dying inevitably, while Emily uncomplainingly expends her life caring for him, and I think of our William and Caroline's Edward—gone from us almost before there was time enough to know and love them—and I cannot become too excited about great art, which will surely outlive us all. However, everyone tells me Florence is not to be missed, so it is to Florence we go next week. I shall complete this letter while we are there and tell you all about its treasures.*

When the letter continued, however, it dealt, not with the fine art treasures of Florence, but with the unhappy news of a sudden and unexpected deterioration in Paul's health.

Since writing the above, dear Jane, we have spent a few days in Florence, which is so truly spectacular that I must contain my enthusiasm until we meet, for something has occurred that is taking up all of our time and attention.

We returned from Florence to find Emily very concerned that Paul had developed a fever. His Italian doctor is puzzled, and Richard cannot understand it either. Paul had shown no signs of a patient in whom the disease has staged a resurgence. He seems fit and is in good spirits; Richard wants to call in a physician from Rome to obtain another opinion, but my dear Sister, I confess I am not very hopeful. Paul has a pallor which is very concerning. Emily's constant hope is that he is cheerful and eats well. She believes these are good signs, that he is successfully fighting the disease. I wish I could agree with her, but it is difficult to do so, even though the patient himself remains uncomplaining and optimistic. Darcy agrees with me and has decided to extend our lease here for another month, so we can be here if Emily needs us. Which means, it will be March, at least, before we return home. I do look forward so much to seeing you again, my dearest Sister. Please forgive this short and unsatisfactory letter. I promise to make up for it when we return to England, when I shall stay awhile with you, before travelling to Pemberley. God bless you,

Your loving sister,
Lizzie.

When it was time for Richard to return to England, to start work at the hospital in Derby, Elizabeth would not leave Emily, and Cassandra decided she would remain with her parents. It was as if they were afraid to leave for fear that they would never see Paul alive again. His unfailing appreciation of their presence and Emily's loving care was almost too painful to bear. Some weeks later, as the first buds of Spring began to burst, making each dawn a new beginning, Paul Antoine died peacefully in his sleep. Emily had found him very early in the morning and called Signora Cassini, who sent her eldest boy up to the villa to give Darcy and Elizabeth the news.

When they got down to the house, the Signora and Emily had already laid him out properly and sent for the priest, the doctor, and the undertaker, in that order. With a little help from her neighbours, where she needed help with the language, Emily made all the arrangements for the funeral and the disposition of Paul's things afterwards.

When, after the funeral, which only one of his sisters attended, the will was read, it was to Emily, his beloved wife, that he had left everything. A property in France, an orchard with a farmhouse, and a not inconsiderable sum of money were hers, with just one request—that she donate on their behalf sufficient money to Richard's hospital at Littleford to build a facility for the care of young children, in memory of Edward and William. Now Emily understood why he had wanted so badly to have the lawyer from Anzio return last week for further instructions.

Elizabeth, who felt she owed Emily her sanity, for her support at the time of William's death, was immensely grateful to have the opportunity to be at her side. She felt she had much to learn from her cousin, as she noted the quiet calm that enveloped her as she went about her tasks, preparing for their departure, and said as much to Darcy and Cassandra. But, Darcy realised it was not a simple matter of learning. As he explained to Cassy, "The difference is one of acceptance, Cassy. Emily knew of Paul's illness from the outset. She accepted it. Oh, I know, she may have hoped and prayed for a miracle, but Richard had told her the truth. When, she decided to marry him, she carried that acceptance into her marriage; she loved him and cared for him, but she knew it would not be for long; it was going to end, quite soon."

He tried not to sound as if he was preaching to her, but she was clearly interested enough to listen attentively. "With your Mama, it was different. When William was born, he was the son she had longed for. He was fit and healthy, and she had never contemplated his death at such an early age; he was the boy who was going to grow up and become her hero. What is worse, his sudden, violent, meaningless death makes it even harder for her to make sense of it. She cannot understand why it had to be his turn, that night."

"Does she still scream with rage at the unfairness of it?" Cassy asked, and her father nodded, "Yes, sometimes, when it gets too hard to bear and I can find no answers for her." Darcy hoped that returning to England with Emily would help them all and especially Elizabeth to accept, however reluctantly, that William was gone. He recalled how she had raged against the unseen powers that had decreed that William and Edward had to die that night. Her question was always the same, "Why did it have to be William and Edward? Why not Tom Lindley, the reckless show-off, the one who had caused it to happen, by turning up with his wretched, skittish horses and taking them, like some medieval tempter, luring them away from an innocent family picnic to their deaths? What right does he have to be alive, while our gentle, innocent William and dear, little Edward are dead?" It was a question Darcy could not answer. Nor would he try with pointless platitudes to assuage her grief.

Emily, by her selflessness, had shown them a different type of love, and her grief reflected this difference. Her example of courage and true generosity of spirit had been an inspiration to him. He fervently hoped that it would help Elizabeth, too. He knew there had developed a rare closeness between them and prayed for it to continue, for there was no doubt Emily's singular strength could help raise Elizabeth from the mire of her grief. Cassandra surprised him by suggesting that the loss of William was all the more catastrophic because it meant Pemberley had lost its male heir. Darcy remonstrated, dismissing her concern, "It is not of any significance, Cassy; since the estate is not entailed, if we had no sons, you would inherit Pemberley, when your Mama and I are gone." Cassandra was not convinced.

"That is not how it is meant to be, Papa. In any event, I shall be Richard's wife, with our own place to run. There has always been a Master of Pemberley. It will not be the same, and Mama knows it." Darcy sighed and let the discussion lapse. It would be best to let things take their course, since they were returning to England with Emily, who may be staying on at Pemberley. She had spoken of taking up teaching at the school and working with the choir again. Richard would need someone to help him with the hospital at Littleford, she had said, and she would offer her services if they needed any help at the school at Kympton. She pointed out that there were a great many things to do in the community, and she thought Caroline would appreciate some help, too. Emily seemed determined to devote her energies to doing everything she could possibly find.

Darcy, understanding her desire to keep busy, wished with all his heart that Emily might draw Elizabeth back into the life of the community at Pemberley. His own inclination was to continue the work they had undertaken to improve the estate and build a community for all of the people in the district. In that aim, Elizabeth had been his greatest supporter, but now he feared she might retreat into her private grief, turning her back on Pemberley, rejecting it as the scene of her greatest sorrow.

CHAPTER TWENTY-TWO

The dower of
inward happiness

O N RETURNING TO ENGLAND, Emily hastened to her parents at
Lambton, while Elizabeth went, as she had promised, to Jane at
Ashford Park. It had been several months since the two sisters had
met. Their greeting was warm and affectionate, while tears filled their eyes as
they embraced. With Bingley and Darcy in London on business, they looked
forward to the time they would spend together.

Before her visit to Italy, Elizabeth's inability to control the bitter grief that
kept welling up inside of her, each time she encountered the security of her sister's family, had distressed them both. But Jane, far from being insensitive to her
sister's feelings, was careful not to add to her anguish. She strove to shield her
from aggravation and pain. Overcoming her impatience to acquaint her sister
with everything that had happened while she was away, Jane set aside trifling
matters and related only significant news. Even this was done with discretion
and care. Once Elizabeth became aware of these matters, however, she was quite
determined to know everything. When Jane had hinted in a letter at Christmas
that Emma was spending a great deal of time in London at the invitation of the
Wilsons, a family with whom the Bingleys were well-acquainted, Elizabeth had
assumed that Jane had been missing her daughter. The possibility of an imminent engagement had never occurred to her.

Now, it was revealed that David, the younger of the two sons of the Wilsons, both of whom were in Parliament, had proposed to Emma and been accepted! The speed with which it had come about had surprised everyone, Jane said, though it did appear that the two had been inseparable for most of the previous month. The engagement was soon to be announced at a gathering of both families, in London.

While this news came as a complete surprise to Elizabeth, it was less astonishing than that which followed shortly after. No sooner had it been revealed than she demanded to be told every detail. Jane explained that soon after Darcy and Elizabeth had left for Italy, Charlotte Collins and her two daughters had been invited to spend Christmas at Ashford Park. "It was really Jonathan's idea, Lizzie," she said. "He thought they would be lonely at Mansfield, where except for their immediate neighbours, they knew few families. They were hardly likely to be invited to Lord Mansfield's Christmas dinner! Mr Bingley and I agreed, hoping it would save Charlotte from the embarrassment of waiting upon an invitation to Lucas Lodge."

Elizabeth understood. "I do believe her new sister-in-law keeps the household on a very tight rein," she remarked.

"Indeed she does; Charlotte was there last October, and by her account, she was not eager to repeat the experience," said Jane.

"And what was Jonathan's interest?" prompted Elizabeth. Jane held up a hand, as if to ask for time to explain. It was quite an astonishing tale.

"Well, they came to us, and over Christmas the young people spent a good deal of time together. Lizzie, I could swear that I did not notice any special attention paid to one or the other of the girls, but by the time we were preparing to go to London in the New Year, Jonathan was exceedingly keen to take Amelia-Jane to the *Review* and the Richmond Ball. Bingley claims he noticed nothing at all, but Caroline Bingley alerted me to their being a great deal together, while we were in town. I must confess that I was not inclined to pay much attention to her, but Lizzie, you would not believe it, they were engaged within the month!" Elizabeth agreed that she could hardly believe it.

"But my dear sister, Amelia-Jane is not yet sixteen!"

"Indeed she is not. I have asked Jonathan if he is sure of his feelings as well as hers. He assures me he loves her and it is what they both want." Seeing Elizabeth's sceptical expression, Jane hastened to add, "But Lizzie, let me say that, since then, I have been most impressed with young Amelia-Jane. She is sensible beyond her years, when I think how trying Kitty and Lydia used to be. Charlotte has been an exemplary mother to all her girls. They are uniformly accomplished and perfectly well-behaved. Amelia is helpful and obliging, with not a trace of frippery or flirtatiousness about her. She sings, paints, and plays the piano, as well as sews her own clothes. Jonathan assures me that she reads a good deal, too, so as to improve her mind, in which she is encouraged by her sister Rebecca, who as you know, is very well-educated," said Jane, adding, "But Lizzie, as she is still very young, we have asked that they wait awhile, which neither seems to mind; Bingley says it would be best they are quite certain of their feelings, since Jonathan means to stand for Parliament in the future," Jane explained.

To Elizabeth, this piece of news was a source of even greater amazement. As far as she could recall, young Jonathan Bingley had hitherto shown no interest in public life at all. "Jonathan for Parliament! Is this the Wilsons' doing?" she asked. Jane shook her head.

"No, Lizzie, it is the result of the persuasive efforts of Mr Anthony Tate," she said, adding with rising excitement in her voice, "but thereby hangs another tale. Oh Lizzie, there is so much you do not know, so much that has happened while you were away."

"So it seems, pray do tell me, Jane, what is Mr Tate's involvement?" Elizabeth asked, her curiosity thoroughly roused.

Jane was almost apologetic as she explained, "Lizzie, I know I should have written something of this to you, but it seemed hardly appropriate to be talking of trifling things like love affairs and engagements, in the midst of the pain that you and Emily had to endure. I tore up so many letters." "Oh Jane," said Elizabeth, knowing well her sister's tender heart, as she went on, "Lizzie, you do recall that Charlotte's second daughter Becky has been something of a writer?"

"I was aware that Becky Collins was a scribbler, I know that she wrote some poetry—none of it very remarkable, mind," replied Elizabeth, remembering some material she had seen in Rebecca's hand.

"Well, throughout last year, she has been writing pieces for the *Review*, of which Anthony Tate is the editor, using the pen name Marianne Laurence." Elizabeth's raised eyebrows indicated some surprise, which increased as Jane continued, "She has since moved from Mansfield to Matlock, where she lives at the home of Mr Tate's mother, Therese Camden, and now, she is as good as engaged to Anthony."

Elizabeth exclaimed, "Good heavens, Jane, all these engagements in such a short time! Are they not a little sudden? What does poor Charlotte say?" Jane smiled, a little amused at her sister's reaction.

"Well, Lizzie, I am sure Charlotte understands that these things can sometimes come upon one, quite unexpectedly" she replied, as if to remind her sister of Charlotte's own very precipitate engagement to Mr Collins, many years ago, some twenty-four hours after he had been turned down by Elizabeth.

For the first time since William's death, Jane saw her sister laugh, her eyes bright as she recalled that fateful day at Longbourn and all that had flowed from it. "You are quite right, as usual, dear Jane. I am sure Charlotte would understand perfectly well the importance of seizing the opportunity. Besides, I am being presumptuous in making judgements. If all these young people wish to become engaged, why should they not? Now, tell me, are the wedding dates fixed?"

"No," said Jane, suddenly serious again. "Except for Anthony and Rebecca, who plan to marry in the Spring, the others must wait at least a year. It will not be proper for anyone in our family, so soon after . . . ," and as her voice trailed away, Elizabeth, understanding her drift, went to her at once, and they embraced as the tears they had not shed together for a very long time fell freely. Jane wept as she spoke, "Lizzie, if you only knew how deeply I have felt for you. Yet I did not know how to reach you. I was afraid I would hurt you by speaking of it, though I longed to share your sorrow." She could not contain her grief, "William meant so much to all of us. Bingley has never ceased to rage against the fates that let it happen, and Jonathan has nightmares and blames himself for not stopping the boys from riding out that day." This time, it was Elizabeth who, seeing how keenly Jane had felt their separation, reached out and held her sister close.

"Dear Jane, how I have missed you. But Jonathan is not to blame. There were others, who should never have intruded upon us on that day. They are culpable, not Jonathan, no more than Darcy or Colonel Fitzwilliam or myself. Jonathan must not blame himself. I cannot believe that Caroline or Aunt Gardiner would say any different." Her voice shook, though she remained strong, determined to reassure her sister.

Jane assured her that neither the Gardiners nor Caroline had blamed Jonathan, but he still felt responsible. Being the eldest, he felt he should have done more to stop his young cousins' foolish escapade. "He misses them, Lizzie, especially William, and I am sure that this sudden passion for Amelia-Jane is due, at least in part, to the loneliness he feels," said Jane, her lovely face saddened by the memory. "I feel that Emma, too, has become engaged sooner than I ever expected, in an attempt to overcome those terrible feelings—losing first William and Edward, then Paul, only a few months later. Oh Lizzie, it has been such a terrible year for us all," she cried.

Later, as they took tea together, they talked of how it had been when they were both young girls and their lives had hardly been touched by sorrow. A disappointment here, some gossip there, what were they but mere pinpricks, compared to the recent tragedies they had suffered? As they talked, Jane told Elizabeth of Anthony Tate's wooing of Rebecca Collins and the link that had led to Jonathan's friendship with her sister, Amelia-Jane. "She would be visiting Rebecca, when Jonathan was calling on Anthony to discuss their political plans," she explained, adding, "You see, Lizzie, Mr Tate, who now owns the *Tribune* as well as the *Review,* intends to throw the weight of his newspapers behind a campaign to elect some younger men to Parliament. They say Mr Peel is building up the Conservative Party and the Whigs need fresh talent to bring against him. Mr Tate sees Jonathan as a likely candidate."

"And is Jonathan inclined to agree to this scheme?" Elizabeth asked.

"He says he wants to. Bingley thinks it is a good idea, too. He says it is time for the middle classes, who are creating Britain's prosperity, to be better represented in the Parliament." Elizabeth could not disagree with this sentiment; she had heard it espoused frequently, by both Darcy and her uncle.

"And what of your dear Emma and her Mr Wilson?" she asked, wanting to know more about her niece's engagement.

"Emma and Mr David Wilson are to marry in the Autumn, while Jonathan and Amelia-Jane will wait until the following Spring, when she will be seventeen," Jane explained.

"And, tell me, Jane, are you pleased about Emma's engagement? Is this Mr David Wilson the right man to make my lovely niece happy?" asked Elizabeth, knowing how rarely her sister spoke ill of anyone but concerned that she had not sung the praises of her future son-in-law to any great extent. Jane smiled and said she thought most young people today decided matters for themselves and if Emma was going to be happy with David Wilson, then she, Jane, was very happy for her. "Do I detect some uncertainty here?" asked Elizabeth, sensitive to every nuance of her sister's voice. Jane was immediately defensive.

"No, Lizzie, you must not think that. Bingley and indeed Jonathan have nothing but praise for both brothers, but I have always preferred Mr James Wilson, probably because he reminds me of Bingley. He is quite the nicest young man, with the best manners I have seen in many a year. He is sensitive and good humoured, never opinionated or boastful. Not since that summer when Mr Bingley first came to Netherfield, have I met so amiable, modest, and pleasing a young man as Mr James Wilson," she declared, leaving her sister in no doubt that Emma was marrying the wrong Mr Wilson—at least from her mother's standpoint. The comparison of Mr James Wilson with her beloved Bingley was the highest possible accolade.

"And Mr David Wilson? Is he not amiable and well-mannered too?" demanded Elizabeth.

"Of course, and he is intelligent and personable as befits his position. But James is my favourite. However, it is Emma's choice, and she is in love with her Mr David Wilson, so, Lizzie, I shall have to be content."

When Mr Darcy, who had been conscientiously catching up on his business commitments, returned with his brother-in-law, he was relieved to find Elizabeth and Jane as close as ever again. Their affection for each other was the very heart of their relationship. He knew they both drew strength and love from each other and had feared for Elizabeth, if she had not been able to restore the precious bond between them. For his part, difficult as it had been for him to bear his own burden of grief, while extending his sympathy to Caroline and Fitzwilliam, whose agony could not have been less than their own, he had strengthened his resolve to help his wife by his own example. His compassionate and ardent nature enabled him to help her deal with the profound grief they felt at the loss of William—without always feeling bereft and desolate. While it was not easy, he found he could often guide her to a calmer state of mind, where she was more amenable to consolation and comfort.

By the time Elizabeth was ready to return home, Emily, too, had restored her own relationships with her parents and her sister Caroline. She had decided to remain at Pemberley and help Richard manage the hospital at Littleford.

There was much to be accomplished, with funds to be raised, furniture and linen to be purchased, as well as staff to be hired. Increasingly, Elizabeth found herself being drawn back into the activities of the community that had once been the centre of her life at Pemberley. Richard was very grateful for her help. The involvement of the Mistress of Pemberley in any charitable project guaranteed success. The hospital at Littleford needed her patronage, and Elizabeth gave it gladly. Caroline and Rebecca meanwhile, were campaigning for a permanent library for the area, using the newspapers and council meetings to do it. The need for young women to have access to good reading material was a cause célèbre for the popular writer known as Marianne Laurence, who wrote extensively on the need for education for women. Emily needed no prompting to join their campaign.

Emma Bingley's wedding in the Autumn of 1835, a month short of the anniversary of her cousin's death, was the first such celebratory occasion that Darcy and Elizabeth had attended all year. The young couple were surrounded by a host of friends from London, and their distinguished professional connections afforded Mr and Mrs Darcy a chance to remain in the background, for once. Missing William terribly, they longed only to be away from the celebrations. They would never be free of these painful moments. Gradually, they would learn to live with them, but not yet.

~⋎~

That Winter brought another, not entirely unexpected sorrow, when Mr Bennet, who had never quite recovered from the shocking death of his beloved grandson, seemed suddenly to lose interest in holding on to life and, in his sleep, let it slip gently away. It was a hard blow for all of them, especially Jane and Elizabeth, but Darcy, who had grown to respect his father-in-law, whose dry wit was always at the ready to take down the presumptuous and stupid in society, regretted his untimely passing more than anyone knew. Mr Bennet's appreciation of the library and grounds at Pemberley had led him to spend quite a few Summers there, and a warm, easy relationship had developed between them.

Only Elizabeth, who had found him browsing in the library, idly looking over the piles of familiar books her father used to read, picking up titles and finding short scribbled notes in his hand among their pages, knew how much Darcy would miss her father.

Sir William Lucas, too, was frequently unwell, and Charlotte was afraid he may not live to see her Rebecca married. He did but did not survive long afterwards, succumbing to a respiratory complaint from which he had suffered for many years.

The deaths of these two neighbours—old friends, brought home to everyone a quite remarkable irony, upon which Elizabeth made a wry comment. "Do you realise, Jane, that despite our mother's dire predictions about Mr Collins and Charlotte's throwing her out of her home, it will now be their daughter, young Amelia-Jane, who will one day be the Mistress of Longbourn, as a consequence of her marriage to your Jonathan, who is Papa's heir!" Jane confessed that she had thought of it, and the sisters laughed together, remembering their mother's outrage at the prospect of Charlotte Collins in her place at Longbourn. Things had certainly come full circle. Both Bingley and Darcy, who had a high regard for Charlotte and her children, whom she had raised with courage and principle, ventured to suggest that it was a fortuitous turn of events.

"I think Mrs Collins deserves some good fortune," said Bingley. Darcy agreed it was an excellent outcome, "It seems like poetic justice to me," he said, "especially since it was the foolish Mr Collins who was denied his entailed inheritance."

Elizabeth, despite her affection for Charlotte, could not resist remarking that, "with two of her daughters very satisfactorily married or about to be, and her eldest enjoying the patronage of Lady Catherine de Bourgh, Charlotte's cup must be close to being full, if not quite running over!" Everyone laughed, and Jane had to chide her sister for her sardonic comment, but she enjoyed it all the same. It was good to hear the laughter in Lizzie's voice again.

❧

In the Spring of 1836, Mr Darcy, sensitive to Elizabeth's sadness following her father's death, embarked upon a project to engage her heart, while taking her away from Pemberley for a while. He was offered by chance, and decided upon an impulse, to take out a year's lease on a property on the Albury Downs, not far from Guildford, where he and Mr Gardiner had important business contacts.

Happily situated, amidst rich farmland and wooded valleys, Woodlands included a house, not much larger than Longbourn but a good deal more comfortable, being a low, sheltered building, set well back in ample gardens. The meadows below the house sloped away towards a winding river, which cut its way through the chalk hills and downs. As far as the eye could see, the prospect was pleasing and peaceful. From the Albury Downs, superb views stretched across the county—a landscape of woodlands boasting ancient yew trees, green fields, apple orchards, and meadows filled with wild flowers and butterflies.

It was, Elizabeth wrote to her sister Jane:

> *. . . a source of soothing balm for the weary heart; it is just exactly what I needed, at this dreadful time.*

She made no attempt to deny the seductive quality of this beautiful place, nor its appeal to her grieving soul. Reasoning that increasing business commitments in the area and his desire to be of greater use to Mr Gardiner rendered it convenient, Darcy took the opportunity to spend what became an idyllic few months with Elizabeth, in the loveliest part of southern England.

At Pemberley, he had once found her weeping over the sketchbook that William had filled with memories of the Lakes, while on another occasion, after dinner, she had sat at the instrument to play one of his favourite compositions but, unable to control her tears, had fled the room. Darcy had hoped a change of scene would help. After they had been at the farm for some weeks, with only a few of their personal staff from Pemberley, Darcy, seeing how happy and relaxed Elizabeth seemed to be at Woodlands, asked whether she would like him to purchase the property for her. When she seemed bewildered by the suggestion, he explained, "If I thought, my dearest, that it would increase your happiness by some small quantum, if it would mean that I could see you heal the wounds you carry a day sooner, I would gladly sell the house in London and invest the money here, to help us get away occasionally, from the memories that crowd around us at Pemberley," he said earnestly. Elizabeth was deeply touched both by his gesture of concern and the love from which it clearly flowed. During the terrible days and weeks after William's death, she had been grateful indeed for his strength and support, but much more did she welcome the warmth of his love. But, grateful though she was for his recognition of the pain she had suffered, Elizabeth did not seek to run away from Pemberley.

She acknowledged with tenderness his concern and determination to help her but made her own wishes quite clear. "I have no desire, my love, to flee from the memories that surround us at Pemberley. It is our home, it was William's home, and he loved it. I see him everywhere—in the park, by the river, where he used to ride, and all over the house. I hear the music he used to play running through my head all the time. One Sunday morning, I came in from the garden and heard the Mozart sonata he was practising on the day of the Pemberley Ball, echoing through the house, the same piece he promised to play for us. I raced up to the music room, but of course, it was only in my head, or perhaps it was in my heart; whichever it was, it will be always with me. I know I shall have to learn to carry my memories of William wherever I go, but I will not turn my back on Pemberley. It is our home, and to it we must return."

Darcy explained that he had hoped only to provide her with an alternative place to heal the terrible wounds they had both suffered. She smiled and assured him she had already begun to heal with his help and that of Jane, Emily, Jenny, and all their dear friends. "And do not think, dearest, that in the midst of my sorrow, I have been unaware of yours, nor that I have been so insensitive as to imagine that only I suffer the days and nights that wring out one's heart. I also know how much Pemberley means to you. I know how you have tried to build a community there. I want to share that, too. Much as I have enjoyed these weeks of peaceful idleness in this lovely place, and I thank you with all my heart for bringing me here, it has been a wonderful respite, I do want to go home." Darcy responded with warmth and gratitude, holding her close.

Elizabeth then showed him the letter she had written to Jane, which concluded:

It is, without question, the prettiest, sweetest part of southern England, and I should love to have us all spend a gentle Summer here, for I am sure you will like it exceedingly well, and so will Bingley. I shall speak to Darcy and if the owners will consent to let it again next year, we shall all be here together. Perhaps, after your Jonathan and Amelia-Jane are married, it may be time for us to get away from the bustle and crowds and spend the rest of the season here, for, dear Jane, it is a veritable heaven on earth.

He smiled and said, "What a good idea, my dear; I shall make some enquiries directly."

Convinced she was right, they returned to Pemberley, and in the late Autumn, their son was born. They called him Julian Paul, and Emily was his proud godmother. The delight of both parents at the birth of their child was shared by almost everyone in the district. All who knew the family had keenly felt their loss and had hoped to see them regain some of the joy that had departed with William on that dreadful night. Pemberley, as one of the great estates of the county, had always been the centre of the district's prosperity. When the estate and its family flourished, so did the men, women, and children of the surrounding farms, parishes, and towns. At forty, Elizabeth was grateful for this child; her young cousin Caroline, who had been delivered of a daughter in Summer, still longed for a boy to assuage the pain of losing Edward. Elizabeth knew that nothing, not even this dear little boy, could do that for her. The memory of William burned too brightly. Unlike William, Julian was dark like his father but with his mother's bright smile and pleasant nature. His birth had brought them joy this Christmas. For the first time since William's death, there was at least a genuine reason to celebrate.

Mrs Gardiner, who came with Jane to visit Elizabeth and her son, brought the news that James Courtney, the Oxford scholar, who had worked at the Pemberley library some years ago, was back, as the new curate of Kympton. Having completed his theological studies and taken Holy Orders, he had applied to Mr Darcy for the living with the recommendation of Dr Grantley, and it had been granted. Elizabeth knew of his appointment but was unaware that he had arrived already.

"Everyone is delighted to have him back. He was a most active and hard working young man, when he was only a scholar. He worked so hard at the school that Caroline thought he ought to return as a teacher," said Mrs Gardiner, adding that Emily had liked him very much indeed. Jane offered the information that Mrs Gardiner had already decided that the Reverend James Courtney must be invited to Christmas dinner at Oakleigh Manor, when he could meet the rest of the family. Sensing, rather than hearing a plan developing, Elizabeth added a note of caution, "Dearest Aunt, do have a care. I know how much you long for Emily to be happy, but she felt the loss of Paul very deeply and may not be ready to entertain the thought of any one else, just yet. We all want her happiness but, believe me, there is little to be done when Death puts a nagging ache into every crevice of your heart and mind. There is no room for anything else. That has been my experience; I do not doubt that it will be no different for Emily. That she has such compassion for others, is not an indication of the diminution of her pain, but of the greatness of her heart." Mrs Gardiner, moved by her niece's heartfelt advice, agreed that she would do nothing to push her daughter; she was a wise and sensitive woman. "But I do hope, Lizzie, for her sake that something will come of it," she said, "I cannot bear to see the sadness in her eyes. She deserves some happiness."

Jane agreed, "Emily, above all others, deserves a share of happiness. She has been there for every one of us, whenever we needed help or comfort. All the children love her, and yet, she has none of her own. It is not fair, Lizzie." Elizabeth could not hide her feelings. "The world, dear Jane, is not fair," she said. "How else would our dear Edward and William be lying in the churchyard, while the wretched Lindley boys win prizes in the Derby Horse Show?" Her bitterness surprised even her sister and aunt, who knew and loved her dearly. It did not, however, relieve her grief; both aunt and niece fell silent, as she wept.

Emily, meanwhile, threw herself into everything that needed doing—the choir, the school, the hospital, the campaign for the library, even a promise to help Fitzwilliam resurrect the Chartist petitions! But Fitzwilliam, now thinking of handing over the reins to Jonathan, had begun to lose interest in active Parliamentary politics. The deaths of both his hero, William Cobbett, and the famous "Orator" Hunt, whose speeches had resounded in his ears, had signalled for him the end of a great political era. Many reforms he had campaigned for had been achieved, though not in full measure, he would freely admit.

Since Edward's death, he had felt impelled to spend more time with Caroline and the children. The birth of their little daughter Rachel simply increased his desire to remain at home, rather than fight political battles at Westminster. He looked to settle down at his farm at Matlock and lead a quieter life, helping Mr Gardiner with the business and enjoying his family. Grateful for the love and unfailing loyalty Caroline had given him, Fitzwilliam hoped he could give her the support and love she deserved. Caroline, still energetic and determined to work with the rest of the women to achieve their goals, involved Emily and Rebecca in her campaigns. Whether it was education for girls or shelter for the destitute, they were active and vocal on every available occasion.

Rebecca, Caroline, and Emily brought so much vigour and conviction to their work, and with the backing of the Tate newspapers, they were so successful at getting things done for the district and its people, that folk were beginning to make jokes about getting the vote for women and putting them into Parliament. Their work had caught the attention of some quite distinguished persons too, who had written to congratulate them on their success. There was no denying that they were an excellent team.

❧

Early in 1837, the death of King William IV brought a very young Queen to the throne of England. It was regarded as a most auspicious moment in the nation's history. The Victorian Age had begun, and there was a new excitement abroad. Indeed, the entire country seemed to lift itself out of its malaise. Art, music, and literature were thriving, trade and commerce were profitable and growing, and though several social goals were still distant, there was hope of change and improvement, predominantly because the Parliament had been forced to act as an instrument of reform for the community, dealing with social issues as well as economic and political matters. No longer dominated by the landed gentry, it had begun to represent more of the people of Britain, and more importantly, it had begun to listen to them and act for them.

Jonathan and Amelia-Jane were married and settled in the area he hoped to represent. He had been persuaded to stand in Fitzwilliam's seat in the election of 1838, which was expected to see the rise of Mr Peel's new Conservatives.

Writing to Jane, who was spending some time in London with her daughter Emma, Elizabeth commented:

> *Dear Jane, We are all agreed, that Jonathan will make a particularly good candidate; he seems to enjoy making speeches, and his Amelia-Jane is very good at playing the aspiring member's wife. He is intelligent and handsome; she is charming and dutiful. Colonel Fitzwilliam predicts that they will make a formidable couple at Westminster.*
>
> *Charlotte has always been a practical woman, able to see an opportunity and use it, without appearing mean or grasping. She has obviously bequeathed the same useful quality to her daughters. All of the Collins girls have made the best of any favourable opportunities that have come their way.*
>
> *You will be pleased to know, dear Jane, that the Tates—Anthony and*

Rebecca—have made a firm friend of Emily, whose work for the school and the hospital has gained her an enviable reputation for service in the community. Their newspapers readily promote the many good causes she has espoused; it is clearly a mutually beneficial association. As for the Reverend James Courtney, who has renewed his pleasant association with the parish of Kympton, he seems to find time to assist with many of the projects undertaken by Emily and Caroline in the parish. Our dear aunt is exceedingly pleased and still hopeful. She is right, of course. He is a good man, and Emily deserves someone like him. Richard is particularly appreciative of his pastoral care among the poor and the sick, who are flocking to the hospital at Littleford, in increasing numbers.

Do give my fondest love to Emma and tell her I would like very much to see her beautiful house in London, of which you have sent us such a charming description in your letter. Unfortunately, Julian is too little to travel to London yet, so I must wait patiently until later in the year, to visit my dearest niece. Darcy and I hope to see you and Bingley soon; do not stay away too long.

Your loving sister,

Lizzie.

For Elizabeth and Darcy too, life had been returning to normal. Their pride and satisfaction in their daughter were matched now by delight in their son. That Julian would ever replace William was unthinkable. His bright presence had been etched into their lives, and his memory could never be replaced by any other child, however delightful. Nevertheless, they were grateful for the simple joys that Julian brought them. He broke the long silences and filled the empty corners that might otherwise have held only sorrow. Now, Pemberley had another child's voice echoing down its corridors and flowing out into its sunlit gardens, helping to lift the pall of grief that had descended upon the house.

Later that year they purchased "Woodlands," having received what both Darcy and Mr Gardiner declared was an excellent offer. Elizabeth agreed that the farm was worth keeping in the family; it was after all the place where her heart had started to heal. Not surprisingly, it came to be known in the family as "Lizzie's Farm" and was the venue for many happy family gatherings.

But it was in the Autumn of 1837 that the marriage of Cassandra Darcy to Dr Richard Gardiner finally restored some of the magic that had fled from Pemberley, on that fateful evening, some three years ago. It was a very special wedding. There was universal agreement on that score, nowhere more than in the hearts of the two families, thus united.

The Darcys and the Gardiners found their greatest joy in the union of their two beloved children. Richard and Cassandra, having loved each other deeply for many years, had proved themselves by their constancy, their unselfishness, and their shining example of service to their families and community. Now, they were ready to make that best of all possible unions, a marriage of both hearts and minds.

Once again, Shakespeare's lines were spoken, "Love is not love that alters when it alteration finds," as they were married by Dr Grantley at Pemberley, on a day very much like the one on which Darcy and Elizabeth had been wed almost twenty-five years before.

As if to compensate for the dread filled memory of the day on which they became engaged, a day forever blighted by the deaths of William and Edward, their wedding day had a special brightness, like a peal of bells across the land, heralding a perfect morning. As the wedded couple left the church and insisted on walking, rather than riding in a carriage, down the drive from the church, through the assembled party of family, friends, and wellwishers, their happiness seemed to spread like ripples on the water, out into the churchyard and across the grounds of Pemberley.

Standing with their parents on the steps of Pemberley House, before they went in for the splendid wedding breakfast, Richard and Cassandra knew they were part of a great tradition, one they respected and served gladly. Mr Darcy's pride in his beautiful daughter was matched only by the regard and affection he felt for Richard. Had he chosen a son-in-law himself, he would not have found one he could have loved better. Elizabeth, sustained by the love of her husband and family, looked with singular happiness upon her daughter and son-in-law, seeing in them a new generation, to whom Pemberley, with its fine traditions, may be safely entrusted.

Some weeks later, Elizabeth was writing to her Aunt Gardiner, who was holidaying in France with Emily. Legal requirements of Paul's will had necessitated a visit to the farm she had inherited, and Emily had felt it afforded an ideal opportunity to take her parents with her.

Having given her aunt all the usual domestic news, Elizabeth found herself in a reflective mood. Only with Jane and her aunt could she be as open with her innermost thoughts. She wrote:

You will recall, dear Aunt, how highly we regarded Pemberley, when we first visited here in that summer many years ago? It was the very pinnacle of perfection. I shall never forget my first impressions of a place so special, it stood like Camelot in a romantic park, on the far side of a glistening lake, a haven from reality, where vulgarity and evil would not dare intrude upon those so fortunate as to reside here.

Do you not recall how you and my uncle teased me about Pemberley? I seem to remember that you were absolutely certain that the Mistress of Pemberley would be no one known to any of us. How often have we enjoyed recalling those words; Darcy particularly likes my uncle's remark about the "Master of Pemberley being a disagreeable fellow." I do not dare reveal that I was in complete agreement with that sentiment at the time! Seriously, though, to me then and when I first came to Pemberley as Mr Darcy's wife, it represented an escape from the ugliness, the embarrassment of Meryton society—a refuge from the petty irritations that so beset us at Longbourn.

Well, dear Aunt, will you be very surprised to learn that my impressions of Pemberley have undergone a significant change over the years? I do not mean to suggest that its great beauty or its appeal have in any way altered, or that my appreciation of them has diminished, but that I have found here not a refuge, but a different reality, which I have learned to enjoy.

I have learned from my husband that the reality of Pemberley requires a level of involvement and responsibility. It is the heart of his commitment to this place and all the people who live and work here. I have found too, that I no longer fear the memories of our dear William, which surround us here. They are a part of our lives now. When you return to England, you

must come to Pemberley and let me show you how well I have gathered up
the pieces of my life. I warrant, you will be proud of your niece.

While it had not been easy, Elizabeth acknowledged that she and Darcy had learnt to live with their memories, just as they had learnt and in many private moments expressed sincerely to each other the folly of the arrogance and pride, which had caused so much hurt and almost cost them a lifetime of shared happiness.

Pemberley, for all its grace and prosperity, could never promise them freedom from sorrow or disappointment. It did, however, promise a place of peace and beauty, a home like few others, where Elizabeth, Darcy, and their family had given and received great love, happiness, loyalty, and friendship, in full measure. Here too, they had found the strength to survive great suffering.

Surely, these were rich blessings, indeed.

END OF PART TWO

An epilogue . . .

My dearest Becky,

As I stand by my window, and look out over the park at Pemberley—
dear, beautiful Pemberley, my home for so many years—it is truly difficult
to believe that tomorrow, I shall go from this beloved place. Yet that is what
I shall do, going first to my parents' home at Lambton and then, on
Saturday morning, to the village church at Kympton to be married to
James Courtney. I know you will all be there to see me take my marriage
vows and wish me happiness.

Dear Becky, I feel as if a whole life, not just a chapter, is ending for me.
My life as part of this wonderful family, with whom I have shared so
much, is over, and I am moving on. Though, as the wife of the curate at
Kympton, I shall still be a part of this community, I shall no longer be at
the heart of it, for Pemberley and its people are really the great, strong heart
of our community.

I know I shall weep tonight, when Mr Darcy and my cousin Lizzie
drive me over to Lambton and say goodbye. Much as I love my own family, I have shared less of the joy and agony of life with them than I have
with Elizabeth, Mr Darcy, and Cassandra, and they have shared my pain
and sorrow as no one else has done.

I have been, dearest Becky, a most fortunate creature, for it has been a privilege and a joy to have been in the circle of this family at Pemberley, entrusted with the confidences of these people whom I dearly love. Through my personal and intimate position at Pemberley, I was able to chronicle their lives and mine, as well as their joys and sorrows. The stories of the Pemberley Chronicles are theirs, not mine. I have not attempted to embroider and colour the facts. I have merely observed people and noted incidents as they happened. As you will see from my journals, which I have sent to you, together with the chronicles, I have made my observations, but I do not sit in judgement over those whose lives I have shared. All this and the rest of the material I have gathered together over many years, I am sending you for safe keeping. The reason is that I have decided, as the wife of the curate of Kympton, who may be privy to private material about the lives of many people, it would not be seemly that I continue these chronicles.

The same constraint would not apply to you, since writing is your profession. So, if at some future date, you feel inclined to continue the labour of love I started, you must feel free to use any or all of my material. All I ask is that you remember that these are the stories of real people, whom I loved dearly, and that you tell them with a modicum of affection and understanding. I had hoped to place the manuscript of the completed chronicles in the family's collection at Pemberley, and to this end I had obtained permission from Mr and Mrs Darcy. Since we spoke last Sunday, I have written to them, acquainting them with my intention of passing all this material on to you.

Dearest Becky, I owe you a debt of gratitude for your help and friendship, especially in those terrible months after Paul's death. I know we shall see a good deal more of each other once I am married to James Courtney and settled at Kympton, for there is much work to be done in our parish. But, dear Becky, then I shall no longer be "little Emily," as I have been to many of you, but Mrs Courtney, the curate's wife. There lies the difference. Thank you again and God bless you.

Your loving friend,

Emily

Pemberley House. October 1840.

Postscript

Emily Courtney, née Gardiner, formerly widow of Monsieur Paul Antoine, married the Reverend James Courtney, curate of Kympton, in 1840. She led a long and happy life, devoted to her husband and children—Elizabeth, William, and Jessica, all of whom grew up to be talented and distinguished members of the community.

Her son William, a handsome gentleman if ever there was one, having shown an early love of music, became a celebrated organist and conductor. Elizabeth, her eldest daughter, married into a distinguished family, while young Jessica emulated her mother's example in serving the poor and teaching at the school.

Mrs Courtney was much loved throughout the parish for her charity work and community service and was honoured by the Queen for her work with the children of the poor.

But, she never put pen to paper again. All the documents, letters, notes, diaries, and memoranda, as well as the opening Prologue to *The Pemberley Chronicles* and several half-finished drafts of chapters, were sent to Rebecca Collins, who remained her close friend and confidante. The material was subsequently bequeathed to her daughter, Josie, who in turn passed them on to me. They comprised a rich and fascinating memoir—too good to be locked away in an old chest forever. The generosity of the Pemberley families of Julian Darcy, Cassandra Gardiner, and their children has given me the opportunity to complete the work begun by Emily a generation or so ago, with their blessing.

For the sake of continuity, I have used Rebecca's maiden name as my *nom-de-plume*, mainly because I feel that is how Emily and her beloved Pemberley family would have preferred it.

For while they may have been somewhat uneasy with the thought of a stranger looking around their family home (now a national treasure), reading their letters, and trying to chronicle their lives, there would be fewer reservations with Becky Collins, the daughter of Charlotte, Lizzie's closest friend.

To Lizzie, Jane, Charlotte, Darcy, and all those other wonderful people whose stories inspired *The Pemberley Chronicles*, and to "dearest Jane," their creator, my heartfelt thanks.

RAC

Appendix

Readers will need no introduction to the cast of characters from Jane Austen's *Pride and Prejudice,* some of whom I have borrowed for these Chronicles. There are, however, some newcomers, many from the next generation, who have been introduced into the Chronicles. Below is a list of those characters for the benefit of readers who may need an *aide memoire:*

Cassandra Darcy and William Darcy – children of Fitzwilliam and Elizabeth Darcy of Pemberley.

Jonathan and Emma Bingley – eldest son and daughter of Charles and Jane Bingley.

Caroline, Emily, Richard, and Robert Gardiner – children of Mr and Mrs Gardiner and cousins of Jane and Elizabeth.

Catherine, Rebecca (Becky), and Amelia-Jane Collins – daughters of Charlotte and Mr Collins.

Dr Francis Grantley – of Oxford, friend of Mr Darcy, later husband of Georgiana Darcy.

Dr Huw Jenkins – rector of Pemberley, later husband of Kitty Bennet.

Anthony Tate – publisher of the *Matlock Review,* later husband of Becky Collins.

Paul Antoine – a friend of Richard Gardiner, later husband of Emily
 Gardiner.
The Camdens – a neighbouring county family, close friends of the Darcys.

Acknowledgements

Quotations have been used from William Shakespeare; William Blake; Emily, Charlotte, and Anne Brontë; Charlotte Smith; and the Song of Solomon. The author acknowledges a debt of gratitude to all these sources, which are in the public domain, and, of course, chief of all to Miss Jane Austen herself, whose characters have been "borrowed" with love.

Thanks to Ms Claudia Taylor, librarian, for help with much of the research.

A very special thank you to Beverly Farrow of The Pink Panther, who on a fine Sydney afternoon in 1997 had the initiative and courage to take on the first publication of this book and whose encouragement was vitally important to the success of the enterprise.

About the Author

A lifelong fan of Jane Austen, Rebecca Ann Collins first read *Pride and Prejudice* at the tender age of twelve. She fell in love with the characters and since then has devoted years of research and study to the life and works of her favourite author. As a teacher of literature and a librarian, she has gathered a wealth of information about Miss Austen and the period in which she lived and wrote, which became the basis of her books about the Pemberley families. The popularity of the Pemberley novels with Jane Austen fans has been her reward.

With a love of reading, music, art, and gardening, Ms Collins claims she is very comfortable in the period about which she writes, and feels great empathy with the characters she portrays. While she enjoys the convenience of modern life, she finds much to admire in the values and worldview of Jane Austen.

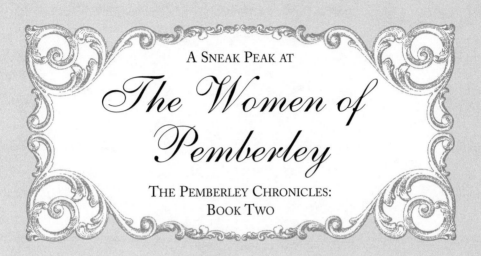

A Sneak Peak at

The Women of Pemberley

THE PEMBERLEY CHRONICLES:
BOOK TWO

E lizabeth was happy to be going home to Pemberley.

The Summer of 1847 was almost over. It had been a particularly pleasant Summer, spent only in the company of those she loved most.

A month or more had been taken up with travelling in the Cotswolds with Jane and Charles Bingley and their two younger daughters, Louisa and Sophie, followed by several weeks at Woodlands—the farm in Sussex—where they had been joined by Elizabeth's Aunt and Uncle Gardiner.

The farm, which Darcy had purchased for her, had become an absorbing hobby. She had come to cherish it as her own little corner of England—"a veritable paradise," as she had once described it to her sister Jane. Happily situated on the Albury Downs, its proximity to the town of Guildford, where Darcy and Mr Gardiner had established business contacts, was an added advantage.

With the help of a small, handpicked group of staff from Pemberley and the tenant farmers, who worked a part of the land, Elizabeth had transformed the grounds and refurbished the interior of the house. Informal elegance and comfort were now its most striking features.

The family and their closest friends, who were the only visitors she would ask to Woodlands, enjoyed the delightful intimacy that it afforded them and many happy weeks were spent there. Both Darcy and Elizabeth had already acknowledged that it had made a significant difference to their lives, left desolate after the death of their son William.

"I am very glad I let you persuade me that we needed Woodlands," Elizabeth said, as they took a last look before leaving, recalling her first reaction to his suggestion that he should purchase the farm.

"Indeed," her husband replied, "so am I. Judging only by the pleasure it has brought us, it must be one of the best investments I have ever made. Do you not agree, my love?"

"I certainly do and thank you very much for it," she replied.

They both understood how much the place meant to them.

Julian, still reluctant to leave the horses in the meadow, was finally persuaded to join them in the carriage, and they were soon on their way. It was to be a leisurely journey, breaking for the night at Banbury in Oxfordshire, but Elizabeth was keen to be back at home.

Returning to Pemberley after some time away was always a pleasure.

This time there was a special occasion, too, for they were soon to celebrate the christening of their first granddaughter, Elizabeth Jane, along with Julian's eleventh birthday.

Arrangements for the celebration had been meticulously planned in advance and left in the capable hands of Jenny Grantham—their housekeeper—and her husband, who was Darcy's manager.

Pemberley had not hosted such a gathering for quite a while and Elizabeth was anxious, but Darcy had complete confidence in their staff. "I have no doubt at all that John Grantham and Jenny will manage very well indeed. You have no need to worry, my dear," he said, and Elizabeth had to agree.

"Indeed, I do not. I realise it is foolish of me to be so anxious when everything has been so carefully planned. Jenny wrote last week that Mrs Reynolds is quite determined to emerge from retirement for the occasion, so I know nothing could possibly go wrong."

The following morning, they left Banbury after breakfast and Julian, plainly keen to be home, was rather restless and kept hanging out of the window. As they turned into the park, however, he sat down and was as good as gold.

Familiarity had not dulled Elizabeth's appreciation of Pemberley. The old stonework burnished by the afternoon sun, the wooded hills clothed in rust and gold, and the inviting soft green lawns aroused in her the same response of heightened excitement she had always felt as they approached the house.

Darcy helped her out—he understood and shared her feelings. Julian had already raced away in search of his dog.

Jenny Grantham came forward to welcome them. She had matured from the days when she had been Elizabeth's maid and was regarded by her mistress with both affection and respect. Her loyalty was without question.

"Welcome home, ma'am," she said, her face lighting up with genuine pleasure.

It was with a great deal of regret that she had agreed to relinquish her role as Elizabeth's personal maid and accept the honour of succeeding her aunt, Mrs Reynolds, as housekeeper of Pemberley. Young Susan, whom she had then trained with great care, held her in awe.

Still, Jenny jealously guarded her own privileged position—being always the first to greet her mistress, accompany her upstairs, and acquaint her with the latest news while she took a welcome cup of tea.

As Darcy had predicted, there were no problems—all arrangements were proceeding smoothly for the celebrations at the week's end. Jenny assured Elizabeth that it was all in hand. She had worried in vain.

Later, after the weary travellers had bathed and rested, she would return to discuss the details of the occasion with her mistress.

Much as she loved her little farm, Elizabeth was very happy to be home. Pemberley was very much the centre of her life.

Two letters lay on her writing desk, having arrived too late to be sent on to Woodlands. The first, from Charlotte Collins, brought news from Rosings, where Charlotte had been visiting her eldest daughter Catherine, who continued as companion to Lady Catherine de Bourgh and her daughter, Anne. What had appeared at first to be a matter of convenience for the de Bourghs had actually turned out to be quite advantageous for Miss Catherine Collins. Despite a seemingly impenetrable carapace of snobbery, Lady Catherine, it seemed, had taken a liking to young Miss Collins—her goddaughter—who was treated more as a member of her family than a paid employee and benefited considerably from being within the social circle at Rosings.

Charlotte's letter, served to confirm this:
She wrote:

My dear Eliza,

You may be surprised to receive a letter from me, since we are to see you very soon at Pemberley.

I had thought to leave the news I have to give you until we met, but Catherine, ever conscious of the niceties of etiquette, was adamant that I should write advising you that she is engaged to Mr Harrison, the parson at Hunsford.

Elizabeth had only met Mr Harrison once at Rosings and, while he had seemed pleasant and tolerably well spoken, he had not impressed her with his rather prosaic sermon in church. She agreed with Darcy that he was an improvement on Mr Collins. At the very least, Mr Harrison seemed able to conduct himself in society without appearing ridiculous, and that was a singular advantage. And, as Elizabeth said later to her sister Jane, Catherine was almost thirty years old and seemed unlikely to receive a better offer.

Charlotte was clearly pleased; her letter continued:

Lady Catherine de Bourgh has expressed her approval of the match, much to my relief, and has generously offered to host the wedding breakfast when they marry next Spring.

I am not sure that I should accept. I feel quite strongly that my daughter should be married from my home. But there is the matter of Lady Catherine's continuing kindness and generosity to her.

It may seem ungracious to refuse, and I am anxious not to upset her ladyship. She has been excessively solicitous and good to Catherine, since the death of Mr Collins.

Dear Eliza, I am very keen to discuss this question with you and have the benefit of your opinion.

Catherine and I look forward to seeing you and Mr Darcy on Saturday.

Yours etc.

Charlotte Collins.

Mr Darcy came into the room just as she had finished the letter, and

Elizabeth was so excited telling him Charlotte's news and discussing his Aunt Catherine's amazing generosity that she quite forgot about her second letter.

Darcy was of the opinion that Charlotte should have no compunction in accepting Lady Catherine's offer to host her daughter's wedding at Rosings. "Lady Catherine is very attached to Miss Collins—and since her own daughter is, sadly, an invalid with little or no chance of being married, this is probably an opportunity for her to play a role she has always coveted," he declared. Elizabeth was inclined to agree.

"It is not as if Lucas Lodge is available to Charlotte," she said. "With the deterioration of her relationship with her sister-in-law since Sir William's death, I cannot imagine she would want to approach her."

"Indeed not," said Darcy, "and since they are to continue to live at Hunsford, they may as well be married there." The logic of this argument was so clear that Elizabeth resolved to use it to set Charlotte's mind at rest when she arrived at Pemberley.

On returning to her sitting room, Elizabeth found her second letter, unopened and lying on the floor where it had fallen.

She could not recognise the unfamiliar handwriting, which was quite strange, though not ill-educated. It was also well sealed, in the manner of a confidential communication. When she had it open, the contents—two closely written pages—puzzled her even more. Turning quickly to the last page, she checked the signature, which made no sense at all, since she knew no one by that name.

However, on reading the letter, Elizabeth was so astonished at the news it contained that she had to read it over again.

The writer, a Mrs Brewerton from Norwich, was writing, she claimed, on behalf of Mrs Lydia Wickham, who was too distraught to put pen to paper.

The writer, identifying herself as "a neighbour and family friend of the Wickhams," wrote that Mr Wickham had been seriously injured in an attack upon him by a former officer of his regiment. Though she seemed reluctant to give any details, it appeared that the assailant had borne a grudge, which he had carried with him for some years, and on meeting Wickham unexpectedly at a club, he had attacked him most violently, putting him in bed with a number of bruises and a broken arm.

While Mrs Brewerton appeared to be quite sympathetic towards Lydia and her children, she did not seem to waste any of her concern on Wickham himself, leaving the impression that the punishment meted out to him may have been well deserved.

> *We are all very shocked and sorry for poor Mrs Wickham, who is quite bereft. I have taken the liberty of writing to you, Mrs Darcy, because I am aware she has no parents to help her and only fair weather friends, who may buzz around her socially, but are unlikely to be of much help at such a time as this. She appears not to have much in the way of savings, either.*

Mrs Brewerton, who seemed particularly well informed about the state of the Wickhams' domestic and financial affairs, wrote.

Elizabeth sighed. No doubt, she thought, Lydia, with her usual lack of discretion, must have regaled her neighbour with all the details.

Shocked and embarrassed, for she had a fair notion of the reason for the attack on Wickham, she hurried out to find Darcy. When she found him in the gallery, she also found herself somewhat tongue-tied and had to be satisfied with handing him Mrs Brewerton's letter with very little explanation—so mortified was she by the situation.

Darcy had to read the letter through twice before the full import of the words sank in.

Watching him, Elizabeth saw expressions of bewilderment, anger, and exasperation chase each other across his countenance. The look of resignation that finally settled upon it suggested that nothing he heard about the Wickhams surprised him any more.

When he finally handed it back to her, Elizabeth asked, reluctantly, if there was anything that could be done.

Darcy shrugged his shoulders, and replied, "Probably not, and even if there were, intervention by us may not be welcome. Wickham has always had a degree of arrogance quite out of proportion to his capacity. He may well resent an offer of assistance. In any event, we do not know who his assailant was and how the attack came about."

Elizabeth was silent, not knowing how to respond, as he went on, "However, it seems to me your sister Lydia and her children may need some help while he spends the next few weeks in bed!"

Elizabeth, who over the years had never failed to marvel at Darcy's generosity to the undeserving and frequently ungrateful Wickhams, wondered aloud how she could help Lydia—especially in view of the celebrations at Pemberley, which would occupy most of her time.

Darcy was quick to reassure her, "You need not worry about it, Lizzie. I shall send young Hobbs over to Norwich with some money. Perhaps you could write a note in reply to this Mrs Brewerton and one to Lydia, which he could take with him.

"I shall ask Hobbs to make some discreet enquiries about the circumstances of this assault. Wickham may well have brought it upon himself—he has always had a reckless streak. I cannot believe it was entirely unprovoked."

Elizabeth hastened to agree and thanked him for what he proposed to do. "I'm sure you are right. Wickham has probably failed to pay a debt or outraged this man in some way," she said.

"Whatever the cause, Lydia and the children cannot be left to the charity of neighbours," he said and went away to find Hobbs, having both agreed that they would not speak of this matter to anyone but Jane and the Gardiners.

Later that night, as they prepared for bed, Elizabeth thanked her husband again. "It is truly kind of you to help them, dearest; I am sure they do not deserve it."

Darcy sighed, "I know they do not, my dear, but the children are hardly to blame for the stupidity of their parents. Moreover, whatever I do is for you, Lizzie, for your peace of mind; you know that to be true, do you not?"

"I certainly do, but I know also that your generous heart discounts the hurt that you have suffered at the hands of this wilful, incorrigible couple, and you continue to help them. I am grateful and I, too, worry about her children, I do not deny it; but Darcy, I am so ashamed…" Her voice broke, and she wept.

He would not let her continue, putting his arms around her. He was very gentle but firm. "My dear Lizzie, you have nothing to be ashamed of. Wickham and Lydia are as far removed from you as they could possibly be. You are not responsible for them and need never apologise on their behalf. I cannot forget that it was my reluctance to speak out and expose his true character that permitted Wickham to present himself to you and all of your acquaintances in Hertfordshire as he did. Had I done what I should have and the truth were known, your sister's disastrous elopement may never have happened."

With her knowledge of Lydia, Elizabeth was not quite so sure, but said nothing as he continued.

"While I have no desire whatsoever to meet Wickham, and will avoid any dealings with him, I shall do whatever I can to help your sister and her children. I realise that they would be in a parlous state indeed without some help from her family. He appears to remain as wasteful and feckless as he always was, and her lack of understanding compounds their problems.

"Lizzie, I have spoken of this to your uncle, Mr Gardiner, and he agrees with me. Indeed, he helps Lydia quite regularly," he said, hoping to comfort and reassure her. As she had often done in the past, she accepted his judgement and was content.

The following day, on a mild Autumn morning, the Bingleys arrived, early as usual. While the gentlemen were out talking to Darcy's manager, Mr Grantham, Elizabeth took Jane upstairs and showed her Mrs Brewerton's letter.

Jane was even more shocked than her sister had been.

"Oh! Lizzie, how could he be so reckless, so lacking in self-control?" she cried, even as she agreed that some help had to be sent to Lydia and the children. Jane would, as she had done many times before, send Lydia some money out of her own income.

When Elizabeth explained what Darcy had done, she praised his generosity. "Lizzie, to think that for a while we actually believed all the vicious lies that Mr Wickham told about Darcy—and yet he is such a good man. We must surely have been blind!"

Elizabeth had the grace to blush even after all these years.

"We were—at least I was, Jane, blinded by prejudice and my desire to believe what Wickham, who was flattering me at every turn, was saying about Mr Darcy, who had hurt my vanity. I well recall that you were never so quick to condemn him."

LOOK FOR *THE WOMEN OF PEMBERLEY* IN APRIL 2008

"With three decades of cancer [...] vinced than ever that the reci [...] mind-body fitness, a life-affirmi [...] to chemotherapy when needed, precise lab studies tailored to determine the appropriate nutrients and herbs for each individual, and quite significantly, a diet of anti-cancer foods. For anyone confused or uncertain about what to eat, Verne Varona's splendid work is a must. *Nature's Cancer-Fighting Foods* should be read by anyone concerned about this dreaded illness."

"*Nature's Cancer Fighting Foods* is a lifesaver. Not just for cancer candidates, but for anyone who wants to eat sanely in a world where convenience and efficiency have taken precedent over health. It's filled with crucial information and is actually fun to read." —ALAN ARKIN, actor

"With a wealth of both practical and theoretical information, this exhaustively researched and clearly written book is a must-have item. And it's not just for those concerned about cancer, but for the library of anyone interested in the effects of food on health."

—ANNEMARIE COLBIN,
author of *Food and Healing and Our Bones,*
and founder of the Natural Gourmet Cookery School

CONTINUED . . .

"I personally have heard Verne lecture on how the food you eat impacts every aspect of a person's life. His presentation had a real effect on changing my diet because not only was it true but his method of presentation was excellent. Everyone reading *Nature's Cancer-Fighting Foods* will also benefit from his wisdom."

—ARTURO S. RODRIGUEZ,
president of United Farm Workers of America

"*Nature's Cancer-Fighting Foods* is a much-needed resource for combating the growing cancer epidemic. In a user-friendly way, Verne Varona provides specific, research-based dietary information that empowers readers to begin their own personal program for optimum health."

—HYLA CASS, MD,
author of *The Addicted Brain and How to Break Free*

"If you have the inspiration, this book is an excellent, unbiased source of information that can help you on your healing journey."

—BERNIE SIEGEL, MD,
author of *The Art of Healing*

NATURE'S CANCER-FIGHTING FOODS

Prevent and Reverse the Most Common Forms
of Cancer Using the Proven Power of Whole Food
and Self-Healing Strategies

REVISED, UPDATED, AND EXPANDED

Verne Varona

A PERIGEE BOOK

A PERIGEE BOOK
Published by the Penguin Group
Penguin Group (USA) LLC
375 Hudson Street, New York, New York 10014

USA • Canada • UK • Ireland • Australia • New Zealand • India • South Africa • China

penguin.com

A Penguin Random House Company
Copyright © 2014 by Verne Varona

PERIGEE is a registered trademark of Penguin Group (USA) LLC.
The "P" design is a trademark belonging to Penguin Group (USA) LLC.

ISBN: 978-0-399-16289-3

The Library of Congress has cataloged the Rewards Books edition as follows:

Varona, Verne.
Nature's cancer-fighting foods / Verne Varona.
p.   cm.
Includes index.
ISBN 0-7352-0176-5 (paperback)
1. Cancer—Diet therapy. 2. Cancer—Prevention. I. Title.
RC271.D52 V37   2001
616.99'40654—dc21

PUBLISHING HISTORY
Reward Books trade paperback edition / June 2001
Perigee revised trade paperback edition / May 2014

PRINTED IN THE UNITED STATES OF AMERICA

10   9   8   7   6   5   4   3   2   1

Text design by Pauline Neuwirth, Neuwirth & Associates, Inc.

In loving memory of my mother and father,

Sara Irene Hertzovitz

and

Carlos Enrique Varona

CONTENTS

Tribute   ix

Foreword   xiii

Introduction by Mark Scholz   xv

1. Ten Essential Keys for Taking Control of Your Total
   Well-Being   1

2. Eating Habits, Food Quality, and Cancer Prevention   41

3. Nutrition's Top Trio: Carbohydrates, Fats, and Proteins   52

4. Phytochemical Superheroes and Amazing Antioxidants   82

5. Meat, Dairy, and the Vegetarian Option   95

6. Balancing Our Acid–Alkaline Chemistry   111

7. Increasing and Strengthening Immune Function   130

8. Practical Strategies to Eliminate Sugar, Fat, and Overeating   148

9. Detoxifying Your Body, Naturally   177

10. Cancer-Fighting Supplement Strategies   199

11. Food for Healing   220

12. The Healing Kitchen: Healthful Ways for Preparing
    and Cooking Nurturing Food   252

13. Salud! Nutritious, Delicious, and Easy-to-Make Recipes   274

Ingredient Glossary   323

Resources   329

References   332

Acknowledgments   352

Index   357

He that conceals his grief finds no remedy for it.

—Turkish Proverb

Brooklyn, 1965

NOW you see her, now you don't.

She was just there laughing and making me, her 13-year-old, a sandwich, and suddenly I'm standing in a dark room before her casket waiting for that frozen, lifelike face to come alive and tell me it was all just a cruel joke.

But it wasn't.

My beautiful, youthful mother with long red hair and an infectious smile had succumbed to a 3-year battle with cancer; taken at the prime of her 35 years of life, leaving behind a grief-stricken husband and three children, two of whom were too young to comprehend the meaning of death and to deal rationally with their perceived abandonment.

Just two weeks earlier, while watching early evening television in our two-story Brooklyn duplex, a jarring thud echoed from the upstairs. Dashing up to the top landing of the stairs, I was instantly benumbed by the sight of my mother lying unconscious, her body convulsing on the blue-green tweed carpet, white foam spilling from her lips. It was a living picture that would be forever imprinted in my mind and heart.

My instinct pushed aside shock and took command as I struggled to pull her from the hallway into the bedroom and onto the bed. I called the ambulance and then, putting aside dread and confusion, returned to her bedside. I held her tightly and pleaded through my tears that she not die; there were children who loved and needed her, more pictures to paint, dances to learn, and life to live.

Outside our home, the flashing red ambulance lights illuminated the faces of shocked neighbors as they milled and murmured in the darkness. The paramedics worked quickly, prepared an IV, and radioed their dispatcher. I held my mother's hand. Racing into the dark with sirens blaring, the reflective blur of streetlamps and traffic lights passed across my face.

Two weeks had passed since that ride to the emergency ward; 14 days filled with school, homework, and endless self-imposed household chores, all done by reflex in an effort to keep my mind and heart detached. During a quiet dinner, my stepfather updated me on my mother's "improving" condition. She had been moved to room 506, a semiprivate room, with a grand view of Central Park and was, "doing well." When I asked to visit, he urged patience, adding that she "might be home . . . soon." He punctuated that sentence with a quick smile. Having been an actor as a child and early teen, I was keen on recognizing deception in speech or appearance. I decided to secretly visit my mother and see for myself.

The following morning, in an effort to appear older, I dressed up for school: dark suit, white shirt, tie, and polished shoes. "Class picture," I told my stepfather. Remaining on the bus as it passed my school, I traveled to the end of the line and transferred to a subway headed for the city.

Waiting on the outdoor station platform for a train that would take me from sleepy suburban Brooklyn into the pedestrian jungle of Manhattan, I heard a salsa tune blaring from someone passing by with a radio. Hearing my mother's favorite music transported me back to an earlier time when I had come home unexpectedly from school during a lunch break. My mother didn't hear me enter because the sounds of salsa filled the house.

From the living room archway beside the door, I spied her dancing around the room, moving with an uninhibited and natural rhythm. Suddenly, she turned, noticed me, and began to laugh like a mischievous child caught playfully jumping on a bed. "Come here," she said with a smile, "Let's learn some salsa." And, for a few timeless moments in the light of a sun-drenched room filled with the echoing sounds of Tito Puente, she patiently taught me to salsa, holding my hands, leading and twirling me, pretending to ignore my two left feet. When the music ended, she applauded my attempt.

I entered the hospital cautiously and slipped by the visitor check-in desk, past the "Children Under 14 Not Admitted Without an Adult" sign, and raced up the steps in the emergency stairway. Once on the fifth floor, I passed the nurses' station to enter the room corridor. The area reeked of an odor I'd never forget: a mixture of strong disinfectant and medicine coupled with the sounds of coughs, moans, and the steady electrical pulse of life-support machines.

Each room looked the same; anonymous faces on broken bodies with drip bottles and oxygen feeds from green tubing that kept death in the distance—at least for the present. My eyes searched every room, but still no sign of the face that for 13 years had loved and nurtured me. She was supposed to be in 506. Could I have missed her?

I ran back to 506 and surveyed the room from the doorway. Light filtering through half-closed venetian blinds had cast linear shadows across an empty bed.

Stripped of sheeting, the bare mattress was a visual testimony to all that is mortal and temporary—here today, gone tomorrow. I panicked. Questions overwhelmed me: Had she been in that bed? Did they move her? Was I too late? While I was in mid-thought, my field of vision registered a bed across the room in the opposite corner where, beside a web of intravenous lines, monitors, and pumps, a young woman lay propped against several pillows, staring blankly at the ceiling.

It was my mother.

Her once vivacious and optimistic presence had been consumed by the ravages of sickness and radiation treatment, leaving her weak and unrecognizable. Her hazel eyes, which once gleamed so brightly, were now lifeless, darkened orbits.

Years of memories flooded my mind. She was a gifted dancer, painter, and poet who had struggled through a devastating divorce with graceful resiliency and natural fortitude, guided by an unfaltering faith. She had a compassionate nature, deep sensitivity, and a playful sense of humor.

I understood that her illness was considered *terminal*—from the Latin *terminus*; a word meaning "finishing point; of an end; resulting in death." But the child in me refused to accept the crushing reality of a life without her; the one person always available to confide with my deepest thoughts, the one who always managed to solace my fears, and the one I could depend on for unconditional love.

There I stood, frozen, numbed by a naive hope that gradually dissolved into anguish and guilt: I had not recognized my own mother.

Of all things changeable and unsettling, the one thing now painfully clear and certain was that nothing would ever be the same.

My mother died one week later.

Over the following 35 years, I lost numerous other family members, including my natural father, to cancer and a variety of degenerative diseases. They died painful, disabling, and traumatic deaths. Helplessly, I watched their weight and appetite decrease as life ebbed away. Beneath a tough exterior, I still carried my boyhood fear of the same fate, reasoning that if most of my family became sick, surely my turn was inevitable.

Repeatedly, I asked myself the same questions: What factors caused them to become sick? What, if anything, could prevent me from becoming sick? Are we all just victims of some mysterious destiny or do we really have a choice in creating healthful, meaningful lives for ourselves?

At that moment, I made myself two promises: a promise to find a natural way to be well and a promise to learn from the mistakes of my family members so their deaths would not seem in vain. I discovered a renewed strength in thinking of their short lives as a lesson in what *not* to do or how *not* to live. If I couldn't save my mother, I could certainly try to save myself, and as a tribute to her memory, give myself permission to experience the life she could not live.

Over the years, the pursuit of a healthful life has been my quest; a formidable journey of learning through education, observation, and experience.

What did I learn?

I learned that growing older does not have to mean sickness, senility, or incapacitation. I learned about alternate therapies that might have saved, or extended, my mother's life had these been more widely known in 1965. And I learned things that have undoubtedly saved my own life. For more than 40 years, I have dedicated myself to sharing this informationthrough counseling and lecturing.

Now, with this revised and updated edition of *Nature's Cancer-Fighting Foods*, I share it with you.

—Verne Varona

New York City, 2014

SOME people wonder if diet is relevant for cancer patients. I myself was in that group until about 15 years ago. Back then I had a patient whose prostate cancer relapsed after surgery and whose prostate-specific antigen (PSA) level was steadily rising. For you who don't know, an increasing PSA level in the blood accurately reflects the growth rate of prostate cancer. Rather than starting the hormone blockade medications that I had recommended, my patient told me his plan was to initiate a stringent diet designed by someone I had never heard of before, Verne Varona.

Back then I had no faith in diet. So I expected that the PSA level would keep rising in a steady fashion as it had in previous months. Lo and behold, almost immediately my patient's PSA stabilized and remained unchanged for several years. He also lost a significant amount of weight, which initially made me concerned. The weight loss, I later learned through subsequent experience, is a common pattern with effective anticancer diets.

Results like these have made me a believer in Varona's approach. Being a curious scientist as well as a physician, I decided to go back and review the blood tests in the patients who were following Varona's approach. I discovered that their blood sugar levels were consistently reduced *even when they were tested right after eating.*

Blood sugar levels are well known to have a major impact on cancer growth. Glucose functions like gasoline, fueling all the cells in the body. Cancer cells are especially greedy for sugar because growing cells have a great need for energy. This is dramatically illustrated by PET scans. PET scans detect radioactive sugar, which is injected into the patient's bloodstream, to locate tumors throughout the body. Cancer cells use the glucose so quickly that they light up brightly on PET scans within ten minutes after the sugar is injected.

There is another reason cancer cells require vastly more glucose to survive and proliferate than normal cells. They run on a primitive and inefficient energy metabolism called *anaerobic glycolysis*, which burns sugar in the absence of oxygen. Because cancer cells are extraordinarily inefficient, they require 8 *times* more glucose than normal cells.

So I have become a believer in the anticancer power of an appropriately structured diet. However, as it turns out, knowing the correct diet is only half the battle. *Sustaining* proper eating patterns over time can be an even bigger challenge.

Part of Varona's genius is his profound insight into the *psychology* of healthy eating. Rather than demanding immediate abandonment of our lifelong habits, his book gently guides us down a pathway of step-by-step changes that are practical and manageable.

You will find *Nature's Cancer-Fighting Foods* to be a treasure trove of wisdom and clarity. Varona understands the partnership between our body, which is affected by the eating choices we make, and our spirit, which depends on our thinking, our relationships, and our faith. His wisdom will empower you to make important life-saving changes in your eating habits and enable you to sustain those healthy eating patterns over the long haul.

—Mark Scholz, MD

Medical Director, Prostate Oncology Specialists Inc.,
Marina del Rey, and Executive Director,
Prostate Cancer Research Institute, Los Angeles

What You Need to Know About Cancer Prevention and Reversal

The only difference between a healthy person who never gets a cancer diagnosis and a sick person who does . . . is that the former has a healthy body and strong immune system, while the latter does not . . . the goal for any cancer prevention or treatment program is to avoid those things known to cause cancer, and to create the healthiest possible body with an optimally functioning immune system.

—Dr. David Brownstein

The Most Important and Intimate Relationship You Have

We all have relationships we value. Whether they are with family, friends, or associates, we devote an enormous amount of time cultivating and nurturing them. In turn, these people support and help us grow.

Of all the relationships we develop in this lifetime, the most important and intimate relationship we have is the one with our own body. It is the physical residence in which we live and the home of our psyche and spirit.

If you're at home in your own body, in control of its functions, and familiar with its rhythms, you cannot help feeling a deep sense of well-being. But many of us avoid thinking about our bodies or are simply not aware of the potential power we have over the direction of our health. Feeling disconnected from our own power can foster a distinctive sense of loneliness.

We avoid thinking about our bodies because they sometimes behave in ways that seem mysterious. If you're tired, do you understand why? What if you can't fall asleep, suffer from indigestion, or have trouble thinking clearly? In all likelihood, the body doesn't give us immediate clues about *why* those things are happening.

To unravel the mystery of the body is to understand how it works and thus become sensitive to any signal of dysfunction. By experimenting with the way you nourish your body, you'll come to know what works and what doesn't. You'll become more intimately familiar with its strengths and its limitations.

Nature's Cancer-Fighting Foods

In this book I offer a simple and wholesome approach to transforming your health through the power of ordinary, everyday food. My plan is based on the premise that affordable, natural foods have powerful medicinal value, which is an accepted notion in the healing traditions of many cultures. In the last 25 years this approach has been repeatedly validated by medical research throughout the world.

Certain foods can have an impact on your health in numerous ways. Through good nutrition, bowel function and energy levels can be regulated. Specific dietary habits can increase the amount of beneficial intestinal flora, the bacteria that help synthesize nutrients and regulate blood sugar. There are even foods that help minimize or control tumor growth.

Immune function is maximized by eating foods that increase the activity of natural killer (NK) cells that fight off invasive microbes, such as harmful viruses and bacteria. By careful selection of foods and elimination of nonsupportive foods, you can significantly reduce inflammation and pain. Various other nutrients help reduce the cell-damaging actions of dangerous free radicals, the unstable molecules that afflict the core genetic material of your body's cells.

Nutrition can prevent, halt further progression of, and in some cases even reverse cancer. A statement of that kind might have been controversial a few years ago. Now there's ample research offering documented evidence that cancer and the environment—including everything you eat and breathe—are intimately related. Large population studies have shown that certain kinds of cancers are far more prevalent among some groups of people than others, largely due to the individuals' dietary habits. In lab experiments, researchers have observed tumors that are caused by or proliferate because of specific components in diets high in animal proteins. Even at a cellular level, scientists are seeing how certain food components have an immediate and direct impact on the way living cells either remain healthy or suffer irreversible damage.

Much of the information in this book is drawn from ongoing research conducted in prestigious medical facilities. That research is pointing to some inescapable conclusions. Nutrition has preventive power. It also can even have redemptive power—the ability to stall or reverse the damage that has been done.

When I work with clients one on one, I review their diets in great detail before providing nutritional counseling. When they experience positive health transformations in a short period of time, they invariably ask, "Why didn't my doctor tell me about this?"

At the heart of the problem is the eroding doctor–patient relationship. Not so long ago, our physicians knew us and our medical problems. They knew when our children were born, about our work and marital conflicts, and how we dealt with pain and loss. Today it's a vastly different story. In fact, consider yourself fortunate if your doctor can even pronounce your name, let alone know your medical history. Some of the blame for this might have begun with the managed-care revolution of the 1980s, which was a well-intentioned effort to increase medical care and control costs. One result, however, was the demise of any kind of meaningful doctor–patient relationship. Today, the standard office appointment with a primary care physician runs 6 to 10 minutes, long enough for doctors to ask about their patients' symptoms and then mechanically scribble a prescription. This point-and-shoot approach defines generic symptomatic treatment.

One study found that doctors interrupted their patients on average within 23 seconds from the moment they began explaining their symptoms. More alarming, in 25 percent of visits, doctors never even asked patients what was bothering them. Another study looked at 34 physicians during more than 300 visits with patients. The researchers noted that physicians spent an average of only 1.3 minutes conveying crucial information about their patients' condition and treatment and most of the provided information was far too technical for their patients to understand.

Although many medical schools are beginning to wake up to the critical importance of nutrition and have expanded their curriculums accordingly, the emphasis on nutrition remains anemic. In a series of surveys reported by the *American Journal of Clinical Nutrition*, 99 of 106 schools that were queried required some form of nutrition education; however, only 32 schools (30%) required a separate nutrition course. On average, medical students received barely 23 hours of nutrition instruction during their entire medical school term. Of all schools queried, only 40 schools required the minimum 25 hours of instruction as recommended by the National Academy of Sciences. Most instructors (88%) expressed the need for additional nutrition instruction at their institutions.

It is not surprising that modern medicine has put little emphasis on prevention. Disease prevention offers meager profit. It's certainly more profitable and expedient to authorize a sophisticated diagnostic test than it is to educate someone on a preventive diet and lifestyle. A 15-minute MRI scan can cost $800 to $2,000. A physician could hardly justify charging this much for a 10- to 15-minute chat on illness prevention.

For too long, doctors have been busy chasing and treating symptoms without aggressively seeking causes. Often alternative therapies are dismissed because of a lack of scientific validation.

There's something seriously amiss about waiting until all the research is in, when the real issues of politics and finance may be in the operating agenda. The reality of this possibility can be unnerving. Neal Barnard, president of the Physician's Committee for Responsible Medicine and author of *Foods That Fight Pain*, writes:

Of course, it is a very different story when a research study favors the use of a new drug. Then the drug company will hire a public relations firm, pay for massive mailings to physicians, and advertise in medical journals. The company will sponsor medical conferences that highlight the role of the drug and pay speakers to discuss it. Drug companies, motivated by potentially millions of dollars in profits, are skilled at getting a busy doctor's attention. But no industry makes money if you stop eating a food that causes your migraines. No surgical supply company makes a cent if you open your arteries naturally through diet and lifestyle. A pharmaceutical company's bottom line does not improve if you use natural anti-inflammatory foods instead of expensive drugs. And without the PR machinery paid for by industry, some of the most important findings never make their way onto a doctor's desk. Patients with arthritis, migraines, menstrual cramps, or even cancer who ask their doctors what they should be eating to regain their health get no answers, simply because no one has brought new information to the doctor's attention.

Habits Die Hard

Of course, knowing *how to* change your diet and *doing* it are two different things. There's no guarantee that you would suddenly stop eating junk food—as we almost gleefully call it—even if a doctor declared unequivocally that it would increase your risk of certain kinds of cancer by 20 or 30, or even 40 percent.

For the best example of failure to change habits, just look at the research on smoking. There are thousands of well-publicized studies showing the health risks of smoking, warnings on packages, and mountains of publicity, yet millions of people are still lighting up every day. The number of new smokers continues to increase and the number of smokers who have quit is still fairly small. Richard Hurt, professor of medicine and director of the Nicotine Dependence Center at the Mayo Clinic in Rochester, Minnesota, says that two public policies have had significant effects on smoking cessation: increasing the price of cigarettes and creating smoke-free workplaces. "They reduce the number of cigarettes that people are smoking, usually between three and five cigarettes less per day for heavier smokers," he says, and "increase the chances of a smoker stopping smoking."

In a similar way, our addictions to favorite goodies can hold us hostage to familiar foods, even when clear evidence directs us to follow a more healthful path. I suggest to my clients that they think of dietary change as a short-term experiment; this way of framing the changes often eases the fear that they are permanently giving up foods that are familiar or comforting. You may find that your craving for junk foods disappears and you feel better without them, which makes saying good-bye fairly effortless. So think about the short term when you're making a change, viewing it as an experiment.

While getting educated can motivate us to make positive changes, the ultimate test is simply how our body responds. Our own convictions are truly enforced not by theoretic argument but by the experience of change.

Facts of the Matter

In our search for effective cancer prevention and cancer-fighting techniques—whether in conventional medicine or in nutritional and holistic approaches—we know we're up against a powerful foe.

More than 40 years have passed and more than $1 trillion have been spent since President Richard Nixon's war on cancer began with the National Cancer Act in 1971, yet the situation facing most people with cancer still remains dismal over 40 years later:

+ According to the American Cancer Society, nearly 2 million people are diagnosed with cancer every year.
+ Conservative statistics indicate that 1,500 people die from cancer every day.
+ Cancer is the cause of 1 of every 4 deaths in the United States.
+ In the early 1900s, 1 in 20 people developed cancer.
+ In the 1940s, 1 in 16 people developed cancer.
+ In the 1970s, 1 in 10 people developed cancer.
+ Today, 1 in 3 people develop cancer.
+ In 1992, a statement signed by 68 pominent national experts in cancer prevention, carcinogenesis, epidemiology, and public health released at a February 4, 1992, press conference in Washington, DC, stated, "Over the last decade, some five million Americans died of cancer and there is growing evidence that a substantial proportion of these deaths was avoidable."
+ Between 80 and 90 percent of all cancers occur as a result of poor nutrition, bad habits (smoking, alcohol, etc.), chemical ingestion, and other environmental factors, according to the National Academy of Sciences, the National Department of Health and Human Services, the Cancer Institute, and the American Cancer Society.

According to the Centers for Disease Control and Prevention (CDC), more than 1.66 million new cancer cases were diagnosed in 2013. Cancer death rates are not falling. America's 40-year war on cancer has been a farce. This may explain why so many Americans have resorted to innovative, nontoxic alternative therapies, such as anticancer diets, herbs, supplements, vitamin drips, and vaccines in an effort to take personal control and management over their healing. Our modern diet of refined foods laden with chemicals and deficient in nutrients is currently thought to be the greatest single contributor to cancer development. According to the World Cancer Research Fund, you can reduce your risk of cancer by up to 40 percent just by lowering fat and consuming a higher percentage of wholesome vegetable foods.

Because research has established these common risk factors for cancer, it should naturally follow that many of these cancers can be eliminated or substantially reduced in number, by changing dietary and lifestyle patterns. Most cancers have a 10- or 20-year interval between their carcinogenic stimulus and the initial appearance of a developing tumor. So the foods that you're eating today, in addition to other lifestyle habits, are likely to influence, by the nature of their chemistry and how they influence your cellular condition, the direction of your health a decade or two from now.

Although it is true that the incidence of some cancers is decreasing, it is particularly disconcerting that we are seeing a rise in hormone-related cancers. These are cancers of hormonally sensitive tissue which, in men appear in the prostate and testes and in women show up in the breast, uterus, ovaries, and cervix. Not only is the incidence of these cancers more frequent than a decade ago but statistics also show that these cancers are occurring earlier in people's lives.

Five of the most common cancers—lung, breast, stomach, colorectal and prostate—were practically unheard of before the early 20th century. Population studies have revealed that the escalation of cancer parallels the development of industry and chemical technology. The more developed a country, the higher its cancer ratio. As per capita income increases, so does the incidence of cancer. In the short space of only two generations, 10 million new chemicals have been invented and randomly released by the thousands into our environment. Many are known to be carcinogens (cancer causing), poisons that we inevitably end up ingesting through food, air, and water, and a good number of these are easily avoidable.

Bad Influences and Good Agents

Carcinogens are not new kids on the block. They exist in nature and even in common health-promoting foods but rarely present a problem because our body has unique mechanisms to help detoxify them. It's only when our body's defenses are vulnerable, as a result of a compromised immune system, that the risk of developing cancer sharply increases.

One prominent factor for this increase is how certain intestinal bacteria can activate substances such as bile and ingested fats to mutate into carcinogens that linger within our body. Over time, these carcinogens initiate cell division and change the surface of the colon in a way that eventually leads to cancer. The DNA of a normal cell appears to be permanently altered into that of a cancer cell anxious to divide.

In the last 20 years, a staggering amount of scientific information has clearly demonstrated that certain compounds in foods provide significant protection against cancer and can slow, interrupt, or even reverse its development. Many of these compounds have been shown to stop normal cells from becoming rebel cancer cells, and some can actually revert cancer cells back into normal cells.

Specifically, the natural plant substances known as phytochemicals or phytonutrients (*phyto* means "plant"), have been shown to have particular disease-fighting potency. These phytonutrients are often depleted in the processing of packaged, canned, and frozen foods. And you simply can't rely on getting necessary phytonutrients delivered in supplement form. Commercial supplements lack the varied natural compounds found in whole foods. However, whole grains, vegetables, beans, and fruits can provide a genuine feast of cancer-fighting substances.

> **NUTRITIONAL SUPPLEMENTS JUST** cannot compete with Mother Nature. They are isolated and concentrated compounds, and do not contain the array of synergistic nutrients that are available from natural whole foods. There are estimated to be over 40,000 phytonutrients, yet only a small fraction of these nutritional elements have been discovered. Further, the calcium matrix of magnesium, silicon, vitamin K, inositol, L-arginine, boron, vitamin C, copper, zinc, manganese, vitamin D, and numerous trace minerals make calcium more absorbable to the human body, so it is somewhat simplistic to think we can *replace* natural phytonutrients with supplements. One orange alone is believed to contain over 170 phytonutrients! One of the marketing seductions for selling supplements is the emphasis of quantity over quality—getting higher doses of single nutrients. While some supplements can support good health, there is no replacement for what exists in a plant-based diet. Eating a wide variety of vegetable colors ensures a variety of phytonutrients.

A Self-Healing Primer

First and foremost, this is a book about the healing power of food. It is not within the scope of this book to exhaustively detail numerous alternative treatments, environmental concerns, stress management techniques, relationship conflict, or the role of faith, other than to mention that the healing puzzle consists of many pieces. I touch on these subjects in Chapter 1 to provide you with a context for how these issues can work in concert when you start to make more healthful choices in the way you feed yourself.

It is interesting that many of the measures we can take to reduce cancer risk resemble the way most humans lived over 150 years ago. In the 1800s, people were more physically active, had less exposure to toxins, and consumed fresher, better-quality foods. That changed with the advent of labor-saving and food-processing technology.

In attempting to stall, reverse, or prevent cancer, *Nature's Cancer-Fighting Foods* offers a practical formula for achieving four health strategies that serve as a foundation on which additional therapies (conventional or alternative) can be constructed.

- ✦ **Strengthen blood quality:** This is accomplished through the daily consumption of a wide variety of nutritious plant-based whole foods. These foods include whole grains, grain products, beans, vegetables, sea vegetables, fruits, quality vegetable oils, nuts, seeds, and small quantities of animal protein (optional). Minimizing foods high in acid residues contributes to maintaining valuable alkaline mineral storages, which optimize our digestion and cellular functioning.

- ✦ **Strengthen immunity:** This strategy involves reducing sugar and minimizing fat and unnecessary chemicals, which have an enormous impact on our immune system's health. Learning to regulate exercise and sleep are also crucial steps. In addition, I suggest proven immune-enhancing supplements and herbs. Although most books on cancer recovery focus on supernutrients, my emphasis is on strengthening the immune system to guide healing.

- ✦ **Regulate blood sugar:** The nutritional plan in this book is designed to stabilize blood sugar. Ultimately, this will allow you to have more control over your physical and emotional health. A Swedish study found that high blood sugar levels, which produce excess insulin, are linked to pancreatic, endometrial, breast, urinary tract, and melanoma cancers, among other varieties. Blood sugar swings have also been linked to numerous inflammatory conditions, such as heart disease, diabetes, and arthritis.

- ✦ **Improve your body's natural detoxing ability:** The balance among carbohydrates, fats, and proteins in our diet and the quality of the food we eat dramatically influences our body's natural ability to detoxify. The plan in this book strengthens the organs

of elimination (intestines, liver, kidneys, lymph, and skin), thus
promoting better circulation to make our detoxification process
more efficient, consistent, and less of an effort.

These four factors constitute the blueprint for strengthening immunity
and preventing cancer. One mouthful at a time, the power of good food
offers us an essential key for transforming our health and the health of
generations to come.

So Many Theories, So Little Time

The late-comedian George Burns once said, "Too bad all the people
who know how to run the country are busy driving taxis and cutting
hair." This applies equally to nutrition: Everybody seems to have his or
her own theories, and everybody seems to have passionate convictions to
support them.

Obviously, there are many dietary paths that can lead to a healthful
destination. My 40 years of personal and professional experience have
convinced me that there exists no one dietary solution for all of our ills.
Practically speaking, our needs are far more complex and often require a
flexible, individualized approach.

There are as many impressive case histories that support a raw foods
approach as there are that recommend a whole foods, multicultural approach. Some people just don't do well on a vegetarian path and, initially, may thrive better with small quantities of quality animal protein.
The factors that determine a healthy dietary approach have to do with a
person's genetic makeup, upbringing, lifestyle, former diet, and current
health condition. A successful dietary plan, one that allows you to experience noticeable benefits and feel comfortably committed to following
consistently, might be difficult to maintain without considering these
factors.

Although we may have similar organic functions and needs, we are
still biochemically unique. Our strengths, weaknesses, nutritional pro-
files, and habits vary distinctively. A body builder, office worker, messenger,
athlete, and homemaker all require different and changing percentages
of nutrients and food groups (fats, sugars, and protein). Therefore, a
one-size-fits-all approach to healing is naively simplistic. It might sound
good on paper, but in the real world, your dietary and healing needs are
best when individualized.

Nature's Cancer-Fighting Foods Plan

The Nature's Cancer-Fighting Foods Plan is built on offers seven positive principles:

+ **Short- and long-term benefits:** You'll immediately notice positive changes in your bowel function, sleep quality, energy level, and mood. Over the long term, you'll find increased immunity, better blood chemistry, control of weight and cravings, and more emotional stability.

+ **Sensible nutritional and lifestyle theories:** The theory behind making whole grains, beans, and vegetables primary foods is based on our physical design (long intestine, carbohydrate-digesting enzymes in our saliva, predominantly vegetarian tooth structure) and makes logical sense from a biochemical, historic, and ecological perspective. The principles of eating primary foods that grow in your environment (or, at least, latitude) and of eating in a way that minimizes acidity are sound and practical principles that appeal to nutritional and intuitive wisdom.

+ **Track record:** Observe any culture that has had a developed agriculture, and you will see the primary foods of whole grains, beans, and vegetables. These simple yet abundant foods have been staples for over 10,000 years. With individual and local flavors added, you can still enjoy these primary foods in almost any ethnic restaurant.

+ **Scientific support:** According to several studies from the Harvard Medical School, eating whole instead of refined grains substantially lowers total cholesterol, low-density lipoprotein (LDL, or bad) cholesterol, triglycerides, and insulin levels. Among the studies that support this theory are the following:

  - In the Harvard-based Nurses' Health Study, women who ate 2 to 3 servings of whole grain products (mostly bread and breakfast cereals) each day were 30 percent less likely to have a heart attack or die from heart disease over a 10-year period than women who ate less than one serving per week.

  - In a study of more than 160,000 women whose health and dietary habits were followed for up to 18 years, those who averaged 2 to 3 servings of whole grains a day were 30 percent less likely to have developed type 2 diabetes than those who rarely ate whole grains.

- A large 5-year study among nearly 500,000 men and women suggests that eating whole grains, but not dietary fiber, offers modest protection against colorectal cancer.

The benefits of whole grains continue to be discovered and are enjoyed by millions who actively include whole grains in their daily diets.

✦ **Sound nutritional advice:** The grains that nonindustrial populations consumed came straight from the stalk. As a result, this carbohydrate package was rich in fiber, healthy fats, vitamins, minerals, plant enzymes, hormones, and hundreds of additional phytochemicals. Even after the introduction of milling, there was still vitamin B nutrition in the starch; however, valuable and plentiful nutrients were lost as a result. This is not a matter of a single beneficial nutrient; the healthful characteristics of whole grains come from the entire package, in which a number of nutritional elements work together in a complex matrix.

The soluble fiber in whole grain helps lower cholesterol levels, while the insoluble fiber helps push waste through the digestive tract. Fiber may also trigger the body's natural anticoagulants and, in doing so, helps prevent the formation of small blood clots, which can cause heart attacks or strokes.

✦ **Affordability:** With the right strategies and a little planning, it's possible to enjoy healthful, whole food inexpensively. Concentrate on purchasing local, unprocessed foods and on preparing meals at home. Your food will be more healthful, tastier, and more affordable.

Ideally, ingredients that make up a healthful diet should be available to everyone, not just those who can afford exclusive preparations. Although some medicines and supplements may enhance health, it is also possible to nourish the body with inexpensive and easy-to-find foods. If supplements are used, they should be taken in addition to eating a nutritious, healthful diet.

Here is some simple supermarket math to demonstrate the value of whole foods:

- A 1-pound bag of brown rice sells for $2.00 and provides 10 side servings—that's 20 cents a serving.
- A 42-ounce container of store-brand old-fashioned oats

sells for $3.99, and provides 30 servings—that's 13 cents
a serving.

- A can of store-brand vegetarian beans can be purchased
  from $1.45 to $2.25 per 12- to 15-ounce can.

  Generally, vegetables are affordable and don't carry the high
  manufacturing price tags you find in processed foods that are
  loaded with sugars, coloring, and chemicals.

- **Satisfaction:** We have to enjoy what we eat. If our food tastes
  like medicine all the time, the fun factor and joy of new or familiar tastes are lost in the discipline of healing, and this can grow
  old quickly. Fortunately, our body and taste buds are resilient
  and soon become accustomed to natural whole foods, which offer
  a healthy variety of satisfying tastes and textures. It's important
  to appreciate the food you're eating. It shouldn't be something
  you have to put up with. I've seen clients on so-called healing
  diets who approach their meal preparation and dinner table as
  if they were about to have gum surgery. This attitude can make
  the simple act of eating an unnecessarily stressful event—hardly
  conducive toward good digestion, healing, or long-term commitment.

Ultimately, the best judge of my program will be your own experience, not studies, theories, or blind loyalty. Your personal experience will
determine whether you can keep to the program's guidelines.

The Nature's Cancer-Fighting Foods Plan is an opportunity to transform your health. Its flexibility, which allows you to shift programs
according to individual circumstances, changing needs, or a desire for
variety, prevents you from falling into the all-or-nothing trap.

> If we are to effectively prevent cancer, we will have to
> change our diets and our smoking habits; we're also
> going to have to clean up our environment, change
> industrial processes, and do any number of things
> that will be difficult, expensive, time-consuming, and
> intrusive.
>
> —John Bailar III, biostatistician and former editor
> of the *Journal of the National Cancer Institute*

1

Ten Essential Keys for Taking Control of Your Total Well-Being

Work like you don't need the money,
Dance as though no one is watching you,
Sing as though no one can hear you,
Love as though you have never been hurt before,
Live as though heaven is on earth.

—Anonymous

Loving the Life You Lead

Jim entered my seventh-floor office and closed the door behind him. In his mid-60s with a laborer's physique, he had a commanding presence, contrasted by a remote, indifferent demeanor. His deep blue eyes and the weathered skin that framed them quickly surveyed the panoramic view of the Hollywood Hills. Then, with a quick glance, he eyed me from head to toe as I extended my hand to greet him.

"Hi, Jim, good to meet you," I said.

He nodded his head, dropped the questionnaire he'd filled out on my desk, and offered a firm, but obligatory handshake as he stood for a moment taking in the city view from my window.

"Make yourself comfortable."

"Easy for you to say," he muttered, settling into a chair.

Suddenly, I was feeling defensive.

"What made you say that?"

"I'm the one with the cancer, right?"

No doubt in my mind, this was going to be a challenging session. Because Jim had refused conventional medical treatments, my job was to provide some education on available alternatives along with some dietary suggestions supported by the physician who had referred him to me. I began with the questionnaire. Based on his curt answers, I thought questioning him further might provide more insight into his character and lifestyle.

But to no avail, Jim was mostly unresponsive and negative to my questions. He disliked his job (sanitation); hated Los Angeles; felt stuck in a "hopeless marriage"; and occupied most of his time working, sleeping, and late-night tavern hopping with his buddies. He drank to excess, frequently spent his days hung over, and made cursing the world around him a pastime.

When I asked him about his two sons, he called them his "parasites."

"It's always, gimme, gimme, gimme with them," he said. He had zero hobbies ("maybe fishing, once in a while") and no interest or time to develop any.

I put down my clipboard.

"I'm wondering *why* you're here. How can I help you?"

He shifted uncomfortably in his chair. You would think I'd asked him to jump out the window.

"Well . . . they're telling me I'm gonna die, and . . . uh, I'd prefer to live, if you know what I mean. It's very simple—what kinda question is that?"

"I'm wondering what's really important to you? What is it that you *have* to live for? Where's the meaning? If everything is so bleak and negative, which is the impression I'm getting from you, I can't help wondering what will *motivate* you to do the work necessary to heal so you can live longer?"

The redness around his neck began to spread toward his face. He suddenly stood, pushed the chair aside, and walked to the door. He put his hand on the doorknob, turned to me, and gave a two-finger salute, resembling a Cub Scout, but it reminded me more of a gesture tough-guy actor James Cagney made in a 1940s gangster movie before exiting a door and taking three bullets.

"I think this session is over," he announced.

I immediately stood, and looked him square in the eye.

"Look, I've seen a lot of people pass through these doors with some pretty serious conditions. And, truth is, a good number of them died, *but* there *have* been some, with very complicated and life-threatening conditions, that were able to experience extraordinary healings despite physicians giving them a death sentence. And it happens to *exceptional* individuals—it's not the norm. I believe they were exceptional because they were on fire to live—they had a passion to enjoy their lives. They committed themselves to making healthier choices, from redefining their spiritual and philosophical beliefs to changing their attitudes about their relationships, their work, their diet, their living spaces, and on and on.

"They viewed their disease as an awakening toward developing deeper values for life. In the face of death, they discovered ways to make each moment count without walking around feeling like they got the short stick, blaming others, pitying themselves, or thinking negatively that the glass is always half empty instead of half full. And, from all of this they discovered a renewed passion for living—one that made them more whole in character and more grateful in their attitude and cleansed from the toxicity of self-loathing, anger, and hopelessness. The real tragedy I see, in what I do, is not that life ends so soon for many but that so many wait so long to begin it. Hope is where healing begins."

He leaned against the door, his hand still clutching the handle, ready to bolt. I could tell the committee in his head was at work, considering, resenting, judging, processing. He surveyed me again from top to bottom, pausing at my shoes, then took a breath and saluted me again with that two-finger wave.

"Thanks for the speech—nice shoes."

He turned and slammed the door behind him.

FIVE YEARS LATER. I was one of the keynote speakers at a popular health convention in Seattle. After the talk, I spent about 10 minutes answering questions from audience members. When the last person left, I turned to pack my materials but glanced back to the vacant chairs. I noticed one man still seated in the shadows. I called to him and asked if he had a question for me.

He rose slowly and walked toward the stage. Within 5 feet I realized he looked familiar, but still couldn't place his face. He stopped at the edge of the stage and gave me a two-finger salute. Suddenly, my mental Rolodex began spinning: Why do I remember that salute? He smiled at my recall.

He looked fit, well dressed, and had a friendly calm.

"How are you?" I ask.

"*Exceptionally* well," he said through a smile.

I sat on the edge of the stage.

"I remember you now. Tell me, what happened since?"

He smiled, thought for a moment, then told me that his impulse during our consult was to wring my neck because my questioning had irritated and confused him. A friend had taken him to a men's support group, and there, finally, in the safety of other men revealing their vulnerability with personal issues, he broke down and said he was tired of being "a stone, not allowing myself to feel or enjoy my life." Through diligence and patience with therapy, Jim realized that for the longest time he had felt out of control with his body and stuck in a dead-end job and a loveless marriage; he had stopped making time to positively challenge himself or just enjoy life. The support group inspired him not only to make career and health choices but to improve his familial relationships. He started to believe in himself again.

"One day I finally asked myself, What's really important? Making more bucks? Looking for more things to complain about? What did I want to do with whatever life I had left in ways that I hadn't?"

"And . . . ?" I asked.

"Got an amicable divorce, sold my house, moved up to Seattle, qualified for a loan, and bought, of all things, a trolling boat! That was a secret dream of mine since I'd been a teen. Well, I started chartering it out, and soon I was able to buy another boat. Five years later, I now *own* two boats, they pay for themselves—*and* my employees, and I get to fish whenever I want! Hell, I even have my two *parasites* come help me during the summer! And in my big backyard, guess what I got?"

"A new pool?"

"Nah, I got the ocean, who needs a pool? I'm building my own boat! From scratch! Mahogany hull, inlaid ebony, the works!"

I asked the status of his tumor and if any more were diagnosed. He drew a smile and said: "Me and that little tumor get along just fine—I don't bother it, it don't bother me. I'm a lucky guy. I thank God every morning when I look at the sun."

I smiled, being a former resident of the Pacific Northwest. "Not too much sun around here, Jim."

He grinned, radiating positive conviction, and said something that, to me, was a perfect summation of a half-full attitude: "Man, these days I see sun *wherever* I look."

A mere six months after our initial appointment, Jim had created a new life in a new city, challenging himself on every level, remaining vulnerable, and focusing diligently on his goal of healing. He studied, talked to survivors, renewed his spiritual faith, and made every effort to reduce his stresses. The benefit of that work stood before me, radiant, positive, and vital.

The Privilege of Choice

There is but one thing that cannot be taken away from us and that is our attitudes. It is in the realm of our attitudes that we can shape our salvation.

—Viktor E. Frankl

One familiar word that is underestimated for its role in healing is *choice*. Our lives revolve around the many choices we make on a daily basis. Choice determines the quality of our lives, presenting the opportunity to empower or enslave, to create safety or challenge, to invite love or loneliness. Through the perspective we choose, we can uncover a primary and powerful tool for self-healing.

Our reactions to events, tragedy, and the surprises that everyday life brings are based on our personal philosophy of life. That personal philosophy can be designed to give our lives richer meaning, enabling us to better cope with situations beyond our control.

Over 3,000 years ago, the I Ching, also known as the Book of Changes came out of China. The basis of the I Ching philosophy is that every aspect of life is in a constant state of change. At any given moment, some aspects of our lives are falling away and others are taking shape. The ancient Chinese endeavored to master emotional resiliency by accepting rather than fearing change.

One key to developing such resilience is by asking yourself relevant questions, such as, What could be another meaning behind this difficult situation I'm facing? and What can I learn from this experience? Discovering the value in our suffering can sometimes minimize emotional trauma. But suffering can be devalued only by appreciating the natural compensation of whatever we've gained in exchange.

When my father died at age 51 from liver and kidney failure, I allowed myself to grieve. Then, at some point, I chose to view this loss differently; I could not have my father back in the way I wanted, but I could draw on his memory, find inspiration in what he'd taught me, and honor his life by taking care of my own and in ways that he neglected to care for his. I decided that it would be a more healthful option for me to honor his memory by experiencing life as he could not, as opposed to remaining wounded and wearing my loss as an unresolved trauma.

My father's death gave me a renewed gratitude for life and the inspiration to live with a deeper sense of reverence. This idea of adopting a *value perspective* for things that happen to us gave me a new way to accept change.

Hidden Opportunities in Disguise

If you are distressed by anything external, the pain is not due to the thing itself but to your own estimate of it, and this you have the power to revoke at any moment.

—Marcus Aurelius

Attaching a symbolic significance to sickness, such as viewing it as a life-changing challenge or an awakening, causes you to pay more attention to self-care and make more healthful choices. Learning to see your illness as an opportunity can help you discover more meaning in your life. Although this attitude might do little to eliminate pain immediately, unlike blame and the accompanying stress that goes along with it, this is an attitude that promotes calm and patience. A positive attitude does not mean the repetitive mouthing of trite affirmations but entails completely changing your perspective. Ultimately, changing your viewpoint is foundational for healing.

We can override fear and be more resilient when we change our perspective to view difficulty as a challenge. We find ourselves automatically more aware of the present moment and separate from thoughts of what might happen in the future. It is usually when we are absent from the present moment that we become vulnerable to fear.

A cancer client once told me, "When I think about my past, I become very angry for the way I abused myself. If I think about my future, I get depressed because I might not have a future."

"What does that leave you?" I asked.

Without missing a beat, he replied, "The present! The difference between us is that I have an idea when I might die, whereas you don't have a clue when you'll die. It makes me value each moment more, as I never have before. I had to nearly die to learn how to live, so I feel more alive now than ever, just being present. I've noticed that whenever I'm unhappy, it's usually because I'm stuck in the past or future."

Self-healing begins with a conscious commitment to make choices that will affect you positively and bring you closer to your ultimate goal of living a healthy, passionate, and rewarding life. Every health-supporting choice you make strengthens your muscles of self-empowerment that may have long atrophied; choosing to love when you want to hate, choosing to nourish when you want to abandon, or choosing to be physically active when you're inclined to stagnate. By exercising positive, self-supportive choices, you will see that real transformative healing power is not an external acquisition but something that initially originates within you.

> There is no journey to healing. Healing is the journey.
> —Greg Anderson, *Healing Wisdom*

The way to healing begins with an inspired will to make more conscious and healthful lifestyle choices that can lead to a renewed balance of body, mind, and spirit. The first order of business is to consider the areas of our lives in which we feel incomplete, those we've neglected and that may need some attention.

In this relatively young field of conventional Western medicine, we've only recently recognized that healing efforts must be personalized and patients *must* feel a semblance of control, of being able to make their own choices, and of not feeling pressured by experts who insist on doing it all for them.

Our hope for healing begins when we commit ourselves to understanding the primary factors contributing to our disease. Were there dietary factors that made us more susceptible? What psychological issues have we ignored that have now evolved into a source of continuous stress? What faith factors can we strengthen to provide us with spiritual support?

There is no one-size-fits-all solution or universal cure because illness is more than a simple assault by a virus, bacteria, or cancer; illness can be fed and bred by any number of factors, including our psychological state and stress.

"It's so confusing," admitted a friend with cancer who had just returned from an exposition trade show of cancer alternatives. "Everybody is hawking a different solution. Whom do you trust when so many people all claim they have the answer?"

"That's a good question," I sympathized.

"But I want an answer, not an agreement," came the frustrated reply.

"That's also the problem: How *can* there be just one answer?"

Who Survives?

When we look at the data on those who have survived life-threatening illness, we see a vast number of successful options that do not fit into any pat formula; one individual's saving grace might be another's road to demise. I've seen many clients focus on one promising solution with a compulsion that borders manic, often resulting in bitter disappointment.

Based on what I have observed over 40 years of counseling and teaching, there doesn't seem to be one specific method of healing. We're all unique in character, dysfunction, and physical condition so one-dimensional formulaic approaches often miss the larger picture and end up exploiting people who are emotionally vulnerable.

There are many "selves" we have to consider; from physical, spiritual, and psychological to the subdivisions within each of these categories. This collective embodiment of selves reminds me of those of Russian *matryoshka* nesting dolls, each one a fragment smaller than the other and all of them fitting within a larger doll. Just like the dolls, our selves are layered and interdependent. True holistic healing should nurture each one.

Clinical research and anecdotal testimony have repeatedly shown that the 10 most common characteristics shared by cancer victors are the following:

A call to meaning
Positive attitude
Good, balanced nourishment
Active, healthful lifestyle
Stress reduction
Humorous perspective
Love
Emotional expression
Strong sense of faith
Gratitude

These traits can have a powerful healing influence. After reading the descriptions of these traits in the following sections, consider what areas you might need to emphasize for a more comprehensive healing approach.

A Call to Meaning

> It's not that some people have willpower and some people don't, it's that some people are ready to change and others are not.
> —James Gordon, director of the Center for Mind-Body Medicine, Washington, DC

Having a sense of meaning strengthens the will to live and the spark to rise out of bed each morning. Self-healing individuals appear energetic, present, and enthusiastic. They personify the Greek word *enthousiasmos*, "having the God within." Few books have had the sustaining impact of Viktor Frankl's moving *Man's Search for Meaning*. Written in the mid-1900s and based on his experience as a prisoner in four different Nazi concentration camps, Frankl's book has been endlessly quoted and referenced in literary works. He developed his theory of logotherapy (Greek: *logos* means "meaning") as a modern and positive approach to the mentally or spiritually disturbed personality. Logotherapy, according to Frankl, "stresses man's freedom to transcend suffering and find a meaning to his life regardless of his circumstances."

Logotherapy views responsibleness as the very essence of human existence. Responsibility implies a sense of obligation. Obligation, according to Frankl, can be understood only in terms of a meaning—the specific meaning of a human life.

Human species have the unique distinguishing trait of being able to question life and seek meaning. Frankl considered the search for meaning as "the greatest need humans have." It could be argued, as Sigmund Freud established, that the sex drive is one of the most powerful human needs, but as powerful as this need might seem, individuals have been able to live fulfilling and happy lives without sexual fulfillment.

In contrast, it is a rare individual who can say he or she has led a happy and satisfying life without a sense of purpose and meaning. When imprisoned in concentration camps, Frankl observed that many survivors were individuals with a strong sense of purpose. Their purpose sustained their will to live. Frankl's books and subsequent life work centered on this theory.

Mohandas K. Gandhi spent more than 2,300 days in prison and endured numerous self-imposed fasts to bring attention to his beliefs. Pioneering nonviolent political resistance by such acts, he initiated many social reforms and eventually won political freedom for India. What defined Gandhi's life? It was a commitment to his principles with an unwavering conviction. His purpose consistently sustained him.

Whether such convictions are found through religion, social work, or political reform, dedication and purpose are healthy, as long as they aren't taken to the extremes. In Japan, for example, a cultural emphasis on loyal and dedicated work has resulted in longer workdays than ever before. While a passion for work is admirable, this extreme pace is resulting in *pokkuri byo* (sudden death) and *karoshi* (death from overwork). Modern Japanese citizens have experienced elevated stress levels, fatigue, and suicide as well as a breakdown in the family structure and the rise of numerous addictions. "Everything in the extreme changes to its opposite," confirms a Japanese axiom.

MEANING IN YOUR LIFE

Discovering meaning in your life should not be limited solely to a personal, internal purpose, but should include purposeful work and a devotion to a cause or something that stirs your passions.

PERSONAL MEANING. Family and friends offer us the opportunity to love, to be loved, to belong, and to feel a sense of need. These relationships present us with a core family. Same-gender friendships offer us someone to mirror our own growth and provide unique support. My senior clients often lament that the loss of friendships, either from death or sickness, contributes to their deepening sense of isolation.

MEANINGFUL WORK. Our work of choice should ideally provide us with a sense of passion and challenge. If we are bored, bitter, or indifferent about the work we do, it becomes an exclusively money-oriented task, and we eventually begin to resent the amount of time and energy it demands. You may not be doing the work you love but your present job may be a temporary stop on your journey to find something that offers more personal fulfillment. This perspective gives us more coping ability.

HAVING A CAUSE. When we have a cause, we feel motivated and encouraged to make a deeper commitment to action. Some people commit themselves to a cause with a fanatic devotion when they may have less meaning in other areas of their lives. Their cause then becomes a substitute for deep multilayered friendships and camaraderie or for a satisfying and fulfilling career. While causes can enrich one's life, a more profound quality of meaning comes from the human relationships in which we allow ourselves to love and be loved.

In Japanese, the literal definition of the word *ikigai* is "a reason to get up in the morning" or a reason to enjoy life. The Japanese believe that the discovery of *ikigai* creates satisfaction and meaning to life. The long-lived Okinawans feel *ikigai* is essential for survival; it stimulates centenarians to ignore the concept of retirement and instead to stay active, teaching martial arts, offering sage counsel to others within the community, or passing down traditions from their ancestors.

Throughout the world, different cultures have ritual ceremonies and traditions that fostered a greater sense of meaning for their seniors; researchers have concluded these rites contributed to the high longevity rates in these populations. In many cultures, the elderly were considered an integral part of the community. For example, in Sardinia, seniors lived in extended-family homes well into their hundreds, taking part in chores, conversations, and celebrations with a gusto that belied their years. They did not shuttle aging family members to rest homes to live unproductive lives in lonely isolation and be ignored.

MEANING OF LIFE ITSELF

Discovering that life itself is meaningful creates a deeper sense of meaning. At the foundation of most religious thought is the idea that a guiding force, God, or a creator, makes for a more purposeful existence rather than one that focuses only on personal meaning.

When we are young we believe that meaning ends with the common comforts of life, and we are not mature enough to visualize the larger picture. A truly spiritual perspective embraces what we cannot see with our modern pragmatism and analytical minds, recognizing the physical as well as the invisible, the energetic world. This is the basis of prayer, visualization, and faith. They are all a part of the energetic realm. Just as acupuncture taps into our body's energy to stimulate healing, we can rely on the energies of the world to provide a more complete healing.

Although the immediate goal may be to heal, finding a renewed perspective becomes part of our framework of individual purpose. That purpose can be to have a more meaningful life, with smaller goals becoming the completion of individual steps that lead to deeper meaning.

PURPOSE AND GOAL

> Many persons have a wrong idea of what constitutes
> true happiness. It is not attained through self-
> gratification but through fidelity to a worthy purpose.
> —Helen Keller

There is a distinct difference between the words *purpose* and *goal*. Purpose is not simply a goal, but a concentrated action that is physically manifested. We strive with a sense of purpose to accomplish; however, goals are desires that have a beginning and ending and that we engage in by choice.

A clear purpose stimulates our motivation to live and gives us the perspective to judge whether other choices we are confronted with support our larger purpose. Cancer survivors typically demonstrate a passionate purpose for living. They frequently talk about not having time to be ill and express a value for living they did not have before their diagnosis. Often their diagnosis has stirred a deep awakening that magnifies the will to live and love.

Whether your purpose for a deep sense of meaning in life is about enjoying the bliss of each day, helping others, having a religious focus, contributing to society in some way, becoming self-actualized, or pursuing a passion for the creative arts, it will guide, nourish, and sustain you.

Positive Attitude

> You can be upset because rosebushes have thorns or
> you can rejoice because thorn bushes have roses.
> —Anonymous

I once had a Japanese philosophy professor who had a unique way of explaining the purpose of life. He'd draw a circle to represent the world place an infinity sign on each side, with arrows pointing to and from the globe. At the top of the picture, he'd write the word *picnic* in capital letters.

Using this diagram, he'd explain his philosophy of life as a long journey that we take from the infinite world to the earthly world and then back to the infinite. He'd emphasize that our time on earth, an 80- to 90-year cycle, is really but a blink of time, compared to the 3.2 billion years of evolution that brought us here. He would say that our short stopover was merely a rest period; a brief picnic to be enjoyed before moving on. After all, picnics are supposed to be happy times. Why not consider your time here on earth as a picnic?

Philosophy teachers, yoga gurus, and New Age self-help motivational speakers tell us to live our life in the spirit of play, which at first sounds a bit silly and abstract. However, the *spirit of play* means maintaining a greater flexibility in character, being able to abandon ourself to spontaneity, and nurturing a positive demeanor in the face of things that cannot be changed or that go against our expectations. Like children at play, we become focused in the present moment, awake, absorbed, and amused.

When I first heard this life-should-be-play aphorism over 40 years ago, I dismissed it as simplistic happy-face philosophy. It was entertaining to muse on but seemed absurdly superficial. Over time, as I matured and counseled many disease survivors, I began to see the value of a life-as-play mind-set. This practice makes us less prone to stress, can create a deeper appetite for life, and is an important element that contributes to our healing.

Many years later I read a quote by psychologist Eric Fromm: "Man is the only animal for whom his own existence is a problem he has to solve." I recalled the words of my Japanese professor, and suddenly they had renewed meaning. Maybe life, this brief stopover on an infinite journey, *should* be more like a picnic.

A personal philosophy offers us life guidance and plays an essential part in our restoration of health and day-to day happiness. The basis of a personal philosophy is formed from our own self-reflection and continued education. Our attitude and daily behavior clearly reflect our personal philosophy. The character of our personal philosophy is based on how we've redefined values and the commitment we've made to ourselves to maintain what we believe.

Our personal philosophy determines how we respond to loss, happiness, love, obligations, death, and risk. It colors the various causes we support, our spiritual beliefs, the depth of our friendships, and how we care for ourselves.

We continually develop our personal philosophy by questioning what we experience and by a personal sense of accountability in what we say and do and how we react. Our personal philosophy is nurtured by our beliefs and values—how we feel about justice, ethics, compassion, forgiveness, faith, self-reliance, and humor. We must learn to define who we are and what we believe.

In his book *Super Immunity*, author Paul Pearsall reports the results of

Elmer and Alyce Green's examination of 400 cases of spontaneous remission in cancer patients. He defines *spontaneous remission* as "all of a sudden the disease went away and we have no idea why, and we didn't seem to do anything to make it go away based on our treatment." The Greens "found only one factor common to each case they examined. All these people had changed their attitude prior to the remission and, in some way, had found hope and become more positive in their approach to the disease."

The work of creating a personal philosophy that defines our daily behavior is the work of living a conscious life, a life in which value is demonstrated by the example we set with an honest acceptance of our individual limitations. A personal philosophy can enhance our self-esteem and, in the process, grace our life with abundant meaning. The consistent practice of self-reflection and self-examination and owning our personal opinions, not just those we have mechanically adopted from parents, peers, and educators allow us to resonate in a higher level of consciousness, one that has a higher value for self and self-care.

Taking responsibility for your own healing requires you to establish good communication and honest partnerships with your caregivers and medical professionals. They become your team—and a team works together for a common goal, which is why we call it teamwork. If your doctor claims he or she is in charge, treats you with an air of condescension, does not answer your questions, and offers evasive and indirect answers, then that doctor is clearly not being a cooperative team member and should be told so.

From the very beginning patients must establish their need to know, ask why, and make sure to agree only if they understand the available choices and treatment side effects and effectiveness. Sherrie Kaplan and Sheldon Greenfield, executive codirectors of the Health Policy Institute at the University of California, Irvine, determined that "the average patient asks fewer than four questions in a fifteen-minute meeting with the doctor, and one of those queries includes, 'Will you validate my parking?'"

Creating a personal philosophy can also help you avoid negative interactions with health professionals who may have your best interest in mind but who offer unsatisfying therapy choices that you might decide to refuse. You must remember that the therapy you undertake, whether it is conventional, alternative, or both, is ultimately *your* choice.

Your personal philosophy should demand behavior from others that supports your recovery. This means you'll need to communicate to care providers, friends, and family the kinds of behavior that work best for you. This does not mean to develop extreme expectations for everyone you interact with but means communicating your needs, as you become aware of them, to those within your friendship or recovery circle.

One client I spoke with from a small town in the Midwest finally told her family to either support her adventure in healing or risk losing her respect and friendship. They would tease her about the affirmations she'd post on her refrigerator, joke about her "birdseed breakfasts," and make distasteful faces when she prepared her "mud color" health cocktails. She recounted:

> I decided that I felt like a stranger in my own home, hiding out, not being comfortable doing my yoga in the living room because they'd joke and call me a "Mahatma." That state of constant discomfort I found myself in felt so contrary to healing. I finally laid down the rules about what upset me, what I wanted, and why such behavior was not supportive. I'd never spoken out before. It was so empowering for me to take responsibility for what I wanted. It made me realize how uptight I'd become in my own home! My home is supposed to be my sanctuary, not another source of stress. Eventually, I realized their comments reflected their fears and anguish about me, and maybe even their own fears about their mortality, but regardless, it was behavior that just didn't make me feel good. Now, I come first.

MAKING MOMENTS COUNT

Many years ago a client named Harry recalled an encounter with his oncologist. Harry, 80, was a feisty Southerner, an ex-longshoreman, and a self-confessed hard-drinking, hard-living kind of guy. He had an exceptional disposition and a strong will to live. At some point in the conversation, the physician told Harry that his case of colon cancer was incurable and there was a high probability that he'd die within a year. Harry became livid. He could not believe the insensitive audacity of this physician to categorize him in a statistical group. Harry recalled the encounter to me very clearly: "I stormed out of that clinic with smoke coming out of my ears—madder than hell. I mean, tell me it might be painful, or the odds might not be all the great, but jeez, don't take away my hope, man. Tell me it'll be 'challenging,' but don't give me that graveyard face and suggest I 'get my affairs in order.' People are not statistics, you know . . . the guy had nerve."

Harry did live out the year. In fact, he died nine years later, at the age of 89, in his sleep.

Our attitudes about life and the way we approach its challenges evolve from a personal philosophy that is constantly being revised. The value of a personal philosophy is in how it helps us balance our lives with confidence and faith.

With a personal philosophy, we can have, for whatever amount of time, a life worth celebrating, a life worth healing.

Good, Balanced Nourishment

A short history of medicine: I have an earache.

+ 2000 BCE—Here, eat this root.
+ 1000 CE—That root is heathen, say this prayer.
+ 1850—That prayer is superstition, drink this potion.
+ 1940—That potion is snake oil, swallow this pill.
+ 1985—That pill is ineffective, take this antibiotic.
+ 2000—That antibiotic is artificial, here, eat this root.

THE THREE E'S

The Three E's make up the blueprint for your dietary healing plan: educate, experiment, and evaluate.

EDUCATE. Educating yourself, asking pertinent questions and getting answers, is the first step for adopting a healing plan.

From the Internet to books and the experience of others, learn more about your dietary approach. You'll have more mental comfort that your nutritional needs are being met and more confidence that you can make a positive difference in your health.

Don't ignore your intuition; get a sense of what feels right to you. Intuition is an inner voice that speaks clear and succinctly. The more you recognize it, the more you'll be able to benefit from its advice. Listen, because it speaks to you constantly.

The self-healing character is a resourceful one and has to become his or her own best advocate. This type of individual will research opinions and therapies, find out their drawbacks, investigate case histories, attend support groups, read the pertinent available literature, and talk to fellow patients. Become computer literate; if you're not, push through the fear and learn.

We can no longer hide behind ignorance or fear of technology when machines are becoming more user-friendly and educational help is available from numerous sources. Be careful of assuming that everything you read about alternative medicine on the Internet is true (and the same goes for ad copy touting numerous "natural" products and healing services). The cancer market is aggressive, blatantly assertive, and, in many cases, profit motivated. Check your sources carefully, do searches for product reviews, and beware of breakthrough claims in ad copy.

EXPERIMENT. Experimenting with diet and lifestyle changes is the most practical way to gauge your progress. Consider this an intensive one- to two-month adventure in self-care. I've had clients undergo monthly blood work for their different conditions and observe tumor marker levels, blood pressure, sugar levels, and nutritional panels for positive differences. This can be motivating and helpful, unless you find yourself living entirely, as physician and author Bernie Siegel put it, "between office visits," stressfully worrying about whether your treatment is working. In this case, your vigilance becomes self-defeating because stress levels alone can aggravate sickness.

I often suggest that clients keep records during their dietary experiments, noting bowel changes, energy levels, sleep quality, mood, appetite, weight, digestion, cravings, and questions. This short-term focus of one to two months is easier and more positive than thinking long term forever. Your motivation is stronger because the experiment is designed to evaluate your particular response, based on your developing sensitivity for a relatively short experimental time.

EVALUATE. Evaluation means that after a time of one to two months you should be able to determine the merit of your changes. Have you seen a positive change? Do you feel better, more vital? The reality here is that the short term usually determines motivation for the long term. If you had constipation in the past and now after a month of dietary change, find you are consistently regular, you'll obviously stick with the changes that keep you regular. It takes more than good philosophical reasoning or documented studies to inspire change. The most sensible reason for following a healthful diet and lifestyle plan is because of the benefits it can bring to every area of your life.

Food that we consume is absorbed through digestion to become chemically part of our blood, which nourishes all organic functions. What we cannot digest becomes waste. If we stop eating, eventually we die. We can eat poor-quality food and hasten that process or eat natural whole food in balanced proportions and maximize our health and longevity.

How we nourish our blood is a foundational way to prevent or reverse disease. This is done not simply by special nutrients but by eating in a way that helps our elimination system to detox more effectively every day and by eating in a way that naturally enhances our immune function.

About 65 percent of all cancer-related deaths have been related to faulty diet. The elements of good nutrition can support healing in four ways: good nutrition, immune support, strengthening digestion, and regulating eating habits.

Quality, balanced *nutrition* provides a foundation for good health, a resilient immune system, improved circulation, cellular oxygenation, mental clarity, reduced blood acidity, and more endurance and vitality. The topic of nutrition embraces the following categories:

✦ Vitamins
✦ Phytochemicals
✦ Herbs
✦ Fiber
✦ Minimizing acidic foods
✦ Minerals
✦ Antioxidants
✦ Carbohydrate, fat, and protein balance
✦ Water
✦ Sodium and potassium balance

It has been documented that two dietary factors can stimulate growth of tumor cells: an excess of simple sugars and the estrogen-like compounds resulting from excessive dietary fat. Many books on diet and cancer suggest that nutritional deficiency forms the basis of degeneration. I disagree. It is not deficiency in most cases that hinders our health, it's excess, and we have a good variety of excess in our Western diets—excesses of fat, sugar, protein, and food chemicals, for example. These are all factors of excess that can accelerate disease, increase insulin production, and hinder healing.

Most books focus on the quality issue. The labels *pure*, *natural*, *organic*, and *unprocessed* refer simply to food quality. There is ample research supporting the health benefits of sticking with organic foods, and generally, the more processed a food, the less healthful. However, what's been overlooked in this quality battle is the balance factor. Specifically, this means:

✦ Focusing on whole foods (as opposed to refined)
✦ Balancing fats, complex carbohydrates, and proteins
✦ Paying attention to the amount of food consumed

Our *immune system* can be bolstered by numerous nutraceutical supplements as well as good-quality nutrition. It's also important to reduce our intake of sugar, alcohol, fat, and dietary chemicals. Besides diet, our immune system is strengthened by our lifestyle habits, such as getting enough rest and exercise, not eating before going to sleep, and reducing stress.

"You are not what you eat, but what you digest" goes a popular saying. Our ability to absorb and synthesize nutrients from food into cellular compounds for growth and renewal is based on more than just having good *digestion*. First, it is based on a physical condition that is uncompromised by drugs. Our digestion improves when we consume a minimum of acid-producing foods, develop nonstressful eating habits, restore our beneficial intestinal bacteria, and eat quality, nourishing whole foods.

Five simple *eating habits* can increase our assimilation of nutrients:

✦ Thoroughly chewing food allows more of its surface area to be exposed to the alkaline enzymes in our saliva.
✦ Eating in a calm environment helps digestion and the flow of digestive juice.
✦ Getting a greater variety of nutrients (more vegetables, beans, grains) increases nutrition.
✦ Eating less allows the food eat to be more effectively assimilated.
✦ Avoiding drinks with meals means the nutrients will not become diluted.

Food is the foundation of any healing plan. Understanding what to eat and what to avoid and learning how to prepare food and make more healthful choices when dining is essential. Without food, we cannot survive. With good balanced food, we can thrive.

Active, Healthful Lifestyle

It matters not how long you live, but how well.

—Publilius Syrus

Our lifestyle is the way we live our life, including how much we exercise, the quality of our environment, and the manner in which we organize our time (balancing responsibilities and priorities), our self-care habits, and our creative expression. Living a healthful lifestyle means we consciously create time for everything that matters most. One simple way to do this is by making a list of everything you need to do as well as another list of everything you would like to do for each day.

Consider what's most important to accomplish. What are the things that create stress for you and are they avoidable? How can you become better organized so that you can make some time for activities that are creative or give you pleasure? Finding such time is an essential step to a healthful lifestyle.

Sometimes lists of things to do can seem endless: family time, meal planning, shopping, cooking, cleaning, children's activities, exercising, time with your loved ones, and more. The only way to accomplish your goals without losing your mind is by becoming well organized and developing a schedule. Delegating, for all you perfectionists, is also an important strategy.

Failing to do this results in a subtle but ever-present stress, which is clearly not a healing influence.

On the other hand, living by endless chore lists can also drive you crazy because you'll begin to feel controlled and stressed by self-imposed deadlines. So the trick here is to find a balance between what is essential and what contributes to your healing.

PHYSICAL EXERCISE

Much research has concluded that consistent exercise not only reduces the risk of cancer but offers mood elevation; weight loss; deeper sleep; increased energy; a healthier sex life; strengthened and toned joints, ligaments, and muscles; and an enhanced flexibility and endurance. Exercise is also a natural catalyst for improving blood and lymph circulation, adding an improved quality of life.

Three popular studies, among many, confirm the cancer-protective effects from regular exercise.

A study involving more than 25,000 women conducted at the University of Tromso in Norway found a 53 percent reduction in the risk of developing cancer in those women who exercised most frequently.

Another study of more than 17,000 Harvard alumni, aged 30 to 79, found that vigorous activity was associated with a significant decrease in the risk of developing colon cancer. Highly active individuals (energy expenditure of more than 2,500 calories per week) had half the incidence of cancer than those who expended fewer than 1,000 calories per week.

A 23-year research project called the Copenhagen Male Study found that regular exercise helps prevent intestinal cancer. The researchers followed 5,000 men, who were divided into four exercise groups (ranging from those who exercised very little to those who exercised frequently). From this study, physicians concluded that moderate physical activity strengthens our immune function and therefore helps prevent intestinal cancer from developing.

Think of exercise as another essential way of nourishing your body, making blood flow more efficiently and delivering much needed oxygen to hungry cells.

CREATING A HEALTHY EXTERNAL ENVIRONMENT

Your surroundings directly influence your health. It is a fact that we are inundated with chemical toxins in and out of our homes; cleaning solvents, air fresheners, perfumes, cosmetics, and building products, as well as furniture that constantly throws off its chemical gases (known as outgassing). Fumes are absorbed into our bodies from the air through our respiratory system, and substances are absorbed through skin and hair follicles into our blood. These chemicals have a negative impact our lung, liver, and lymph health. Whatever you rub on your skin or spray in your hair, eventually ends up in your bloodstream.

In fact, the plethora of toxic chemicals that surround us seriously compromise our ability to regain our health.

The chemical hazards we are exposed to every day may not be completely avoided, but they can be minimized in a threefold way: We can strengthen our natural filtration systems in the body to help discharge these toxins, we can consume certain foods that bond to toxins and remove them, and we can educate ourselves to identify and avoid toxins when possible.

Making your home more ecofriendly with wisely chosen natural products can make a significant difference. By avoiding plastics and using untreated wood, air and water filters, natural-fiber carpets, and safe cleaning products, you'll be on your way toward rejuvenating your external environment.

Stress Reduction

> One of the symptoms of an approaching nervous
> breakdown is the belief that one's work is terribly
> important.
>
> —Bertrand Russell

It is well known that stress and negative emotional states can accelerate cancer progression. Problems at work, traumatic events such as the death of a family member, and frequent emotional strain can stimulate stress hormones, such as cortisol, and diminish the function of our immune-fighting white blood cells.

Researchers at Ohio State University College of Medicine and Comprehensive Cancer Center reported decreased DNA repair in highly distressed people who have difficulty coping with problems. Some studies have shown an increased incidence of breast and prostate cancer with consistently high levels of stress.

A natural defense substance known as secretory immunoglobulin A (SIgA) is compromised by stress hormones and makes the digestive tract more vulnerable to breakdown. This is one of the reasons colon cancer has been associated with periods of consistent high stress. Since our digestive tract is home to three-quarters of our immune cells, good intestinal health is foundational for self-healing.

When we are under challenging circumstances, our bodies release a hormone from the adrenal glands called cortical hormone (cortisol) along with a number of its sister chemicals. (The group of cortical hormones are often referred to as *stress hormones*.) These hormones attempt to reestablish the body's internal homeostasis. When cortisol levels are normal, the hormone has a positive influence on our bodies, but when they at a consistently high level (as with chronic stress), negative effects become manifest.

POSITIVE CHARACTERISTICS OF CORTISOL
+ Helps glucose metabolism
+ Regulates blood pressure
+ Stimulates the release of insulin to balance blood sugar
+ Helps immune function
+ Manages the body's inflammation response

NEGATIVE CHARACTERISTICS OF CORTISOL

+ Diminishes cognitive responses
+ Elevates blood pressure
+ Can cause hyperglycemia (blood sugar imbalance)
+ Decreases muscle tissue
+ Reduces thyroid activity
+ Leads to bone mineral loss
+ Lowers immune function

This last item, a lowered immune function, can cause a systemic in-flammatory response in the body. This results in slower wound healing and more abdominal and stomach fat. Excess weight in the abdominal area has been associated with heart attack and stroke.

Cortisol is known to interfere with fatty acid distribution, thereby accelerating atherosclerosis—a thickening of the artery wall, which nar-rows the path of blood flow. High levels of cortisol have also been linked with depression.

The formula for keeping cortisol levels balanced and under control, beyond diet, is learning to relax using any one or more of the many known stress management techniques, including meditation, regular execise, yoga, self-hypnosis, guided imagery, journaling, breathing ex-ercises, intimacy, singing, playtime with children, and creative pursuits.

THE CREATIVITY INGREDIENT

Whether you paint portraits, paint walls, fashion auto mounts with junk parts, or fit pipe, the need for daily creative play is an indispensable part of how we heal.

The same can be said for competitive sports, exotic travel, and intri-cate 1,000-piece jigsaw puzzles (that, at times, can make you want to pull your hair out). Such agreeable challenges, according to stress re-searcher Hans Selye, are considered to provide healthy stress.

Do you have to be an artist to be creative? Of course not! Creative play is any structured or unstructured activity in which you can freely and sponta-neously challenge your intuitive, artistic, logical, impulsive, or imaginative skills; it allows you to tap into a universal bank of inspiration and create something that keeps you blissfully absorbed in the present moment.

I've seen the renewal of hobbies and creative pursuits bolster confidence and wellness in a number of clients. When individuals are less mobile, I recommend creative activities such as sewing, ceramics, workshop carpentry, journal writing, intricate puzzle assembly, and model making.

Allowing yourself to become thoroughly absorbed in creative work grounds you in the timeless present, where you are immune to distraction. During such times, you are full of life, savoring each moment with alert focus and a precision driven by passion. Timeless moments are periods that repair, inspire, and heal.

Humor as Medicine

> After 12 years of therapy, my psychiatrist said
> something that brought tears to my eyes. He said,
> "No hablo inglés."
>
> —Ronnie Shakes, comedian

I was once asked to visit a former neighbor named Edgar who was nearing the end of his life. His wife requested an appointment urgently. I began asking questions, which she interrupted, saying: "We don't want any more information or advice, Edgar just likes you and a visit would be good for him. You always made him laugh, and that's the medicine he needs right now."

I immediately agreed to this heartfelt invitation. Later that evening, while chatting with Edgar there was an awkward lull in conversation as often happens with end-stage sickness. It was then I noticed a pile of videos of the British comedian Benny Hill beside the bed. When I asked, Edgar confessed to being a devoted fan. Then, remembering a memorable episode, I asked him about the skit in which Hill portrayed a news anchor who had forgotten his glasses and was having great difficulty reading the teleprompter. Edgar couldn't remember the episode, so I acted it out for him. Squinting at the imaginary teleprompter, I recited: "There is conflict today in Hugo's Saliva—oops, sorry . . . that's Yugoslavia!"

Edgar nearly blew out his oxygen tubes with laughter, inspiring both his wife and me to laugh along with him. It took a long time for us to get back to normal . . . and even when I left the room, Edgar was still laughing.

Several months later, I ran into Edgar's wife in the local market. She looked at me and smiled through an expression of sadness. I knew Edgar had died about a week after I saw him and had sent her a condolence card. She told me that after my visit, Edgar couldn't get the Yugoslavia joke out of his head. She recounted that barely an hour before he died, she had asked him if there was anything she could do to make him more comfortable. Edgar nodded and beckoned her closer to him. She put her ear next to his mouth and in a faint whisper, he said, "Hugo's saliva!" They laughed together, and soon Edgar closed his eyes and passed.

THE HEALING POWER OF HUMOR

A sense of humor, either sharing laughter or being able to laugh at ourselves, has proven to be a powerful emotional coping tool. A humorous perspective that celebrates irony or appreciates the futility of everyday life helps us not to take ourselves so seriously and eases our navigation through turbulent waters.

Humor places us in the immediate moment where there exists no future or past but only a focused awareness of the vital present. Our body loves what humor does: from enhancing immunity to improving oxygen flow and helping discharge carbon wastes to improving numerous internal chemical responses.

Medical research has verified how humor positively affects our body. Laughter promotes the release of natural neurotransmitters known as endorphins and serotonin. These neurotransmitters have the power to improve our mood and reduce pain. The effects of laughter are the same as those we experience from other positive stimuli, such as exercising, engaging in sexual intimacy, and witnessing something that makes us happy. Other research focusing on laughter revealed the following:

+ Observations of individuals viewing filmed comedy segments revealed elevated salivary immunoglobin A (IgA), a substance known to defend our bodies against certain viruses.
+ Laughing increases our respiratory and heart rates, fostering better circulation and increased oxygen levels. It also gives our facial and abdominal muscles a much needed workout.
+ Laughter may help the body discharge toxins more effectively. Tears produced in reaction to emotions (happy or sad) contain more concentrated levels of proteins and toxins than tears caused by other stimuli, such as from mincing onions.
+ Laughing increases serum cortisol levels, which in turn increases our immune system's disease-fighting cells. Humor acts as a natural stress reliever, and it is almost impossible to maintain muscle stress while laughing.

Humor can also help change the way we view challenging circumstances. When we are faced with events in daily life over which we have little control, a sense of powerlessness can often result in depression and frustration. By developing a humorous perspective, we discover ways to minimize the feeling of helplessness. The power of humor can transport us from feeling the heavy burden of unrelenting stress to experiencing a fleeting yet gracious moment of joy. Such a moment has a deep value for healing, because it provides a scale to measure the degree to which we are stressed. Often, we are insensitive to how much stress we actually carry in our hearts and bodies. Humor, the ability to laugh with others and to laugh at ourselves, is a cardinal ingredient for self-healing—the vitamin H that we require daily.

Love

> One word frees us from all the weight and pain of life:
> That word is love.
>
> —Sophocles

The new science of how our psychology is directly linked with our nervous and immune function is called *psychoneuroimmunology*, and early research has documented how personal relationships have a direct influence on the activation of our immune systems. The love we share in familial, personal, and primary relationships is directly connected to our ability to heal. It is an old but true adage that our ability to love others is usually in direct proportion to the degree that we can love ourselves.

For some who may be deficient in self-love and unable to reach out, emotional rejection fosters a deep and constant vulnerability. This inevitably evolves into a growing alienation fed by an unexpressed fear that something may be wrong with us.

We may also define ourselves by such rejection, become overly self-critical, and develop a low-level depression. This negatively affects our physiology and our emotional self-worth. It also keeps us from engaging with others.

The fear of rejection can be paralyzing because it makes us behave cautiously. Remaining indifferent is one defense because it makes us feel safe. But it's not safe. It keeps us outside the loop, passive observers of the life around us. And even in the company of others, we still feel alone.

A survey of more than 10,000 men with cardiovascular disease found a 50 percent reduction in the frequency of chest pain (angina) in those who saw their wives as supportive and loving.

Letting go of certain relationships that have proven to be non-nurturing and consistently stressful can also improve immunity. Although the letting go may initially result in added grief and even negative physical symptoms, in the long term, the freedom from stress will inspire a renewal of purpose and personal growth, helping you rediscover an increased capacity for loving, caring, nurturing, and self-awareness.

Love is fundamental to our survival and can provide a deep and profoundly fulfilling experience. The act of giving and receiving love is prime nourishment for our body, mind, and spiritual well-being.

THE MEDICINE OF LOVE

David McClelland of Harvard Medical School demonstrated the power of love to make the body healthier through what he labeled the "Mother Teresa Effect." He showed students a documentary film of Mother Teresa ministering to the sick at her center in India in the loving and gentle way she was known for. McClelland measured the levels of IgA in the students' saliva before and after they viewed the film. He noted that the students' IgA levels rose significantly, even in those who considered Mother Teresa too religious or who thought she was a fraud.

In another experiment, McClelland asked his graduate students to concentrate on two things: moments from their past when they were deeply loved and cared for by another and a time when they loved another person. The results of this experiment also supported the Mother Teresa Effect.

I once read of a medical conference attended by Ashley Montagu, noted anthropologist and author of books on the subjects of touching and love and their healing effects. Montagu stood before an audience of physicians and nurses and asked a question that dumbfounded everyone: "How can you demonstrate a lack of love on an X-ray?"

The room fell silent. After a moment, Montagu explained that when children aren't loved, they don't grow. The evidence for this is the dense lines that can be seen in X-rays of their bones, indicating periods when love was lacking and growth did not occur.

CAN I HELP YOU?

In addition to helping the intended recipient, the question "Can I help you?" is probably one of the most effective means for initiating a deeper level of self-healing. These four words can give birth to a sense of purpose. Helping others in need can melt cynicism, mistrust, ingratitude, prejudice, and arrogance.

I keep a list of charitable organizations in my office and often suggest to certain clients that they'd benefit by doing volunteer work for one of these groups. On more than one occasion, clients who volunteered recounted how the experience opened their hearts; one client revealed, "[It] allowed me to put aside my own pain and offer love."

Helping others takes you out of yourself, allowing you greater ease in making personal connections. Even if you feel you don't have love in your life, you can always find love in your heart to give to others. Paradoxically, giving love will fill you with love.

THE PRACTICE OF LOVE

The body does not lie. It is extremely vulnerable to the subtleties of our emotional states. This was summed up by St. Augustine: "Resentment is like drinking poison and hoping the other person dies." We are all physically vulnerable to emotional stresses. Until we are willing to summon the emotional courage to express ourselves with love and compassion, our healing remains compromised.

To love requires that we transcend the fear, jealously, grief, and despondency in our own lives. It doesn't always have to feel good to take a loving action when our impulses might be otherwise. In fact, it can feel uncomfortably artificial, but part of the decision to be a more loving person lies in the commitment to choose more loving actions. The expression of love is an act of faith; faith that sees love as the final victor. Such actions feed on each other and open the heart deeper.

The real work of loving begins with loving yourself; giving yourself the opportunity to heal, to forgive, to laugh, to hope, to recover gratitude, and to love again and again and again.

Emotional Expression

> The best strategy for handling a feeling, any feeling, is to accept it as it is (without trying to fight it directly in any way) and go on about doing what life presents us to do. The feeling, in time, will pass and be replaced by some other feeling. No feeling lasts in its intensity forever.
>
> —David K. Reynolds, *Even in Summer the Ice Doesn't Melt*

The human distinction of being able to express feelings can do much to minimize negative effects that emotional conflict has on our body. While everyone has feelings, not many know how to express them in a civil, communicable way that allows for resolve and satisfaction. It is a more common coping strategy to suppress anger, hurt, and fear.

The problem with suppression as a habit is that at some point, bottling up feelings becomes intolerable; you become prone to having those feelings burst out with a vengeance when they can no longer be suppressed. In this state, emotional upsets can easily be triggered by what may seem the most insignificant circumstance.

The remedy is to learn when to identify when you are hurt or provoked and, if the circumstance is appropriate, to express your feelings then, or soon after, instead of waiting, suppressing, and trying to pretend it was nothing.

It has been said by many a therapist that anger, in many cases, is a form of aged hurt. There are many people walking around who think they have anger issues, when in fact they are harboring aged and unexpressed hurt that has transformed into anger.

It has also been noted in gender studies that men often, as a result of cultural influence and gender distinction, express their fears as anger because expressing fear for a man has typically been viewed as a feminine trait.

Although there are many psychological theories about emotions and their expression, the bottom line is that it is important to express your feeling promptly when someone you care about criticizes you or says something hurtful. Often, in an effort to not rock the boat, we devalue our feelings, suppress them, or find ways to distract ourselves. This, however, is clearly not a healthy strategy because suppression elevates stress hormones, which, as we've seen, has a negative impact on healing.

Does this mean that you have to express every little feeling? No. Only those that matter to you, and with people who matter.

EVERYDAY EMOTIONAL LIFE

Emotions of conflict, anger, hurt, and fear are best expressed as soon as possible. They have a way of distracting you from the present moment. If you are on the receiving end of a personal criticism and feel offended, it would be in your best interest to express how you feel at that moment. The problem is that we can easily feel so overwhelmed by our reaction that it becomes difficult to immediately analyze exactly what we are feeling.

Here's a good way to determine when a feeling should be expressed: If you cannot hear anything else the person is saying to you as he or she continues to speak because you are still harbor feelings from the hurtful comment, you then need to say something about how you're feeling. If you fail to do this, you'll end up pretending that you are present while growing increasingly irritated.

Expressing your feelings is not as simple as it sounds and requires emotional courage to identify conflicted feelings. But, similar to a muscle that has not been exercised, at first expressing such feelings seems uncomfortable, but with practice it becomes easier as you do it and results in better communication, more honest interactions, and of course better health.

EMOTIONS: A TRADITIONAL CHINESE MEDICAL PERSPECTIVE

Traditional Chinese medical theory considers the body to be an energy conduit, much like a battery whose entire technology is useless unless nourished by a current. The Chinese say that our life force or inner energy flow (*chi* in Chinese) governs the health and vitality of our body similar to a battery current. An impeded energy flow can produce emotional and physical problems, in the same way that water flowing from a garden hose slows to a trickle after a section of hose is bent or kinked. The goal of many traditional Chinese medical treatments—such as cupping, moxibustion, acupuncture, and acupressure—is to disperse any blockages for the purpose of promoting a stronger flow of energy.

In Chinese medicine, specific emotions are considered to be connected to specific organ systems. Although it is natural to experience a gamut of emotions, frequently feeling negative emotions could be a sign of physical imbalance. The reverse also applies; suppressing emotions over a long period of time can manifest itself as disease in a particular organ or set of organic systems.

Chinese medicine has a distinct way of relating to the cycle of emotions. For instance, in what is known in Chinese medicine as the five-element cycle, it is said that anger will counteract grief. A traditional Chinese doctor dealing with a patient who has inconsolable grief might attempt to make that patient angry as a way to diminish grief. A memorable story I once heard in class was one of a female patient who was heartbroken over being abandoned by her boyfriend. It had been months since she'd heard from him, and she'd become reclusive, weak, and numb with grief. Her parents had tried many different remedies, but to no avail.

Finally, they took her to a famous Chinese doctor, who after hearing her story decided that her overwhelming grief could only be diminished by inspiring anger. He told her that he had seen her boyfriend just the week before with another woman and they were laughing at a café and obviously enjoying each other's company. The young girl became angry and suddenly felt foolish for grieving. Her anger seemed to breathe a new life into her and suddenly she was seized with energy and a desire to change her life.

It is a healthy characteristic to feel a range of emotions, but being stuck in a one particular emotion is thought to be a hindrance to healing. Similar principles can be found in cultural folk medicines throughout the world, from those of the Kung people of the African Kalahari Desert to Native Americans.

One of the most common emotions that negatively affect healing is the feeling of being out of control. It brings up anger, fear, and worst of all, hopelessness. The sense of being out of control is strong when you have a life-threatening disease. I've recognized this thinking pattern in clients who have make comments such as "I feel like no matter what I do, those cancer cells are dividing and no one seems to know what to do except for extreme therapies that weaken my immunity and bring back the cancer later. It just feels hopeless."

I am always very concerned about this type of client because, as pragmatic as it may sound, this is not always true and continuing to think this way does not help the situation. Therefore, those on the healing path need to take account of all the important areas in their lives in which they may feel a lack of power and an inability to express that emotional frustration.

There are three elements to behavior: what we do, what we think, and what we feel. While having a terminal illness can foster a sense of powerlessness, remember that healing *can* happen—you can prepare for the worst, but expect the best. If your physician says, "We've done all we can," believe him! But, remember: They've done all *they* can—now investigate alternatives and do what *you* can.

Real change is a matter of perspective, because we almost always have choices. How we feel is not controlled by others or events—unless we choose to do so. Ultimately, the will of the human mind and spirit is far stronger than the body. Make time for new choices, instead of thinking that you "don't have time." When you are clear on new actions to be taken, begin them immediately. Additionally:

1. **Change perspective.** Consider feeling overwhelmed, power-less, or helpless as an opportunity in disguise. See your situation as the chance to regain control of your life.

2. **Keep challenging yourself.** Our brains work at their best when challenged. Learn a new self-help therapy, routine, or sport, or create new goals. Become remotivated.

3. **Take care of your health.** Good sleep helps coping ability, energy, and immunity. Avoid simple sugars, alcohol, and excess animal protein; eat less and eat often to maintain stable blood sugar. Move your body gently, but regularly.

4. **Practice gratitude.** This is defined as thankfulness, count-ing your blessings, becoming aware of simple pleasures, and acknowledging everything you receive. Gratitude transforms your focus from what your life may lack to the abundance that is already present.

THE SIX-STEP FEELING PROCESS

There are many ways to handle emotional upsets. *To process* means "to self-monitor" or become aware of feelings and seek their origins to bet-ter understand them. Processing your emotions means entering a new self-monitoring awareness of what you are feeling, why you may be feel-ing that way, how it may be affecting you, and finding a way to express those feelings for resolve. Here is the Six-Step Process that I use with my clients:

1. **Awareness.** The first step is to become aware of what emotion you are feeling. Just thinking "I'm upset" is not enough. Are you disap-pointed? Angry? Frustrated? Anxious? Further define what you may be feeling to better understand your reaction.

I sometimes give clients a sheet of paper that has a number of cartoon faces, with captions to describe the range of emotional states: angry, sad, fearful, remorseful, loving, guilty, happy, ashamed, lonely, overwhelmed, anxious, bored, depressed, confused, frustrated, cau-tious, and so on. It has proven easier for clients to identify their feel-ings when they had illustrated examples.

2. **Resonance.** How is this emotion affecting you? Thoughts have a tremendous influence on our body chemistry. Give yourself permis-sion to experience your feelings. Allow them to temporarily wash over

you. Notice where you feel tightness in your body. Focus on these places and breathe deeply, permitting your exhalations to loosen the tightness and disperse it outward.

3. **Reason.** Why you are feeling this way? For how long have you felt it? When did it start? What could be the story behind this feeling? Whom are you blaming? What is your part in this conflict? How can this situation be prevented from occurring again in the future? What's the worst thing that can happen in this situation and, if that happened, what then would you do? Most important, what is familiar about this feeling? Can you remember feeling this way in the past, perhaps in your youth? Is this conflict or situation a pattern that's an ongoing theme for you?

4. **Express.** Find a way to express your feelings through writing. Some people have found keeping a journal to be extremely helpful. You don't have to write detailed treatises, just something brief and to the point about how you've been feeling and what you may have realized about this feeling. Frequently, writing about such emotions can allow deeper feelings to surface when you give yourself permission to surrender to the feeling. Write from your heart and not your head. Using simple words in a short paragraph or two can be enlightening. Be direct in your expression without intellectualizing—pretend you're talking to a 5-year-old.

Talking with friends or mentors can also help give you a larger perspective. However, there is no substitute for dealing directly with your feelings by expressing them to the party involved, if possible, to bring about a quicker resolve.

Another valuable way to express important feelings is through a nightly "gratitude" exercise. Each day we are confronted with numerous experiences that can help us recover a deeper sense of gratitude by how we mentally frame them. Before retiring for the evening, try this brief exercise to align yourself with a gratitude mind-set:

> *As you lie in bed, recall the events of your day and find a way to feel gratitude for those experiences. Recall your neighbor's beautiful, fragrant garden, which you passed on the way to work this morning; your son, who sent you a text at work to ask you if you can do something fun this weekend; your boss, who complimented you on a proposal you toiled on; your wife, who made your favorite*

soup for dinner and decorated the plate with colorful vegetables; your father, who called to tell you that he found an old Mustang that he wants to restore and, "by the way, could you help?"; your dog, who jumped in your lap and nudged you for affection.

Remind yourself of your gifts and what you are truly grateful for in your life. Your physical condition may be compromised, but the parts of you that are functioning are still a cause for thanks; your heart continues beating, your lungs process oxygen, your ability to think and feel continues, and your will to live is strong.

Find gratitude for the body that still works for you. Find gratitude for whatever gifts of love and support you have around you. If your health is compromised, feel gratitude for finding alternate paths for healing or for the resources available and your will to recover.

In time, doing this daily exercise will hone the sharpness of your gratitude so it can cut across resentment, negativity, and any sense of hopelessness. This is one of the deepest expressions of feelings.

5. **Get physical.** Activate your body: Go for a long walk, sing, work out, dance, and do yoga or breathing exercises. Find a way to physically destress and clear your accumulated tension. Physical activity can increase your stamina and give you a broader perspective to help you cope with conflict. Do anything physical (except eat!). Being active does not remedy the conflict but makes it more tolerable physically, while strengthening your clarity about what course of action to take.

6. **Share.** "Share it to own it," goes the saying. Talk to a comforting friend who'll listen to your feelings without being compelled to offer solutions or analyze you. Or, if possible, talk to the person who initially brought your feelings to the surface. Although the benefit is found in your opportunity to share, be careful to not create expectations of how you think the other person should or will respond.

Strong Sense of Faith

We've not lost faith, but we've transferred it from God to the medical profession.

—George Bernard Shaw

"Keep the faith" is a catchy phrase that manages to straddle the secular and religious worlds with equal appeal. By degrees, the concept of faith is profoundly significant to both. To the religious mind, faith has moved mountains, walked across water, healed the sick, and intimately communed with the almighty. To the secularist, faith implies loyalty, trust, sincerity, and belief. There are numerous New Age concepts related to faith that have been borrowed from Buddhism, Hinduism, modern psychology, and the *Course in Miracles* that share a sort of universal philosophy. That many of these concepts appear in the texts of different ideologies and religions is a testimony to their universality. The concept of karma (reaping what you sow) is a predominant one. The religiously oriented likely have faith in a supreme being, whereas those with a secular ideology might focus on universal laws that are bound within the framework of karma, compassion, and integrity, and a reverence for the energetic force of nature.

Faith can either be a badge of glory or a rationale for failure. However, failure can also prove a humbling motivator, allowing us to believe that with more faith, more love, and more trust, all things might be possible.

FAITH AND HUMAN WILL

Most folk medicine practices the world over—Indian, Native American, Chinese, African—deal with the healing energy of touch, the energy of the earth, the power of prayer, and the power of creating a healthy vision. Western medicine has its share of stories of faith as well. One of the most popular and much discussed cases involving the mind–body connection is worth noting here because it is a phenomenal example of the placebo response and clearly defines faith in action. Bruno Klopfer, a psychologist, recounted the case of a Mr. Wright, who was admitted to the hospital with a generalized terminal lymphosarcoma involving tumor masses "the size of oranges" throughout his neck, groin, chest, and abdomen. His thoracic duct was so blocked by the cancer that several quarts of milky liquid had to be removed from his chest every other day just to enable him to breathe. Attending physicians presumed Mr. Wright had no more than a week or two to live.

Mr. Wright learned that Klopfer was involved with testing a new wonder drug called Krebiozen and insisted on being treated with it, despite Klopfer's skepticism. Assuming that Mr. Wright would expire before the week's end, Klopfer agreed, and Krebiozen was administered. Much to everyone's surprise, Mr. Wright's tumor masses "melted like snowballs on a hot stove, and a few were half their original size!" Within days, Mr. Wright walked out of the hospital "practically symptom-free." Now, the terminal patient, who barely one week earlier was gasping for his last breath through an oxygen mask, was not only breathing normally but fully active and flying around in his private plane at altitudes of 12,000 feet with no discomfort.

Within two months, conflicting reports began to circulate in the media about the ineffectiveness of the new drug. Testing clinics were reporting no results with Krebiozen. This greatly disturbed Mr. Wright, who began to lose faith in his last hope. After two months of nearly perfect health, he had relapsed to his original state.

Klopfer perceived Mr. Wright's state as an opportunity to test the placebo effect and decided to experiment. He explained to Mr. Wright that the early shipments of Krebiozen had deteriorated rapidly in the bottles; however, he'd be receiving a new superrefined double-strength product within several days. Known only to Klopfer, this new superstrength version of Krebiozen was merely sterile water.

Within days of taking the new, improved version of the drug, Mr. Wright's tumors seemed to magically dissolve faster than after his first treatment. His chest fluid vanished, and once again he was walking effortlessly and resumed flying. He was described as a "picture of health."

However, within a couple of months, a final American Medical Association announcement appeared in the national press, concluding that tests indicated Krebiozen to be a worthless drug in the treatment of cancer. Predictably, within days of this report, Mr. Wright was readmitted to the hospital with all symptoms having fully returned. With his faith broken and his lasting hope shattered, Mr. Wright succumbed to his cancer in less than two days.

His subsequent death was not the result of a negative attitude but of a situation in which a strong belief system, which had been powerful enough to combat cancer, was shattered. After Mr. Wright's death, Klopfer claimed that one of the keys to both the fragility and the power of Mr. Wright's healing response was his "floating ego-organization." Mr. Wright's sense of self was unusually fluid. His greater than normal susceptibility to both negative and positive suggestions as well as his boundless faith in his doctor and the potential of Krebiozen ultimately influenced his healing at both extremes.

SECRETS OF THE IMAGINATION

George Engel, a professor at the University of Rochester Medical Center, discovered that extreme feelings of hopelessness and helplessness, or what he termed the Giving Up–Given Up Complex, produced sudden death. Common examples of this state can be seen in widows and widowers who become sick immediately after the deaths of their spouses, something we commonly refer to as death due to a broken heart.

Engel found hundreds of examples of sudden death in unusual circumstances from newspaper clippings around the world. Examining available information about the psychological status of those people before their deaths allowed him to conclude that an individual's sense of powerlessness and an inability to cope with life frequently led to that person's death. Engel summarized by saying it isn't the circumstances of life, but one's attitude toward these circumstances that seals one's fate.

THE VALUE OF PRAYER

> The most practical reason to examine prayer in healing is simply that, at least some of the time, it works. The evidence is simply overwhelming that prayer functions at a distance to change physical processes in a variety of organisms, from bacteria to humans.
>
> —Larry Dossey, MD, *Healing Words*

When confronting cancer, faith (spiritual or secular) offers us a comfort that originates from our connection to a higher power, or the simple fellowship of others.

Countless stories have been told of dramatic healings resulting from individual and group prayer. I have met hundreds of cancer survivors at conferences at which I've lectured who have attributed their healing to *Course in Miracles* prayer groups, the support of their weekly cancer support groups, visualization meditations, the love of family members, immersion into their passions of creative arts, and to the their devotion to seeing their children grow.

Whether the benefits of prayer come from a compassionate God or are a healing mystery from the collective energy of others, there is great value in the simple act of prayer or focused healing meditation. However, this is not something that has been successfully measured in scientific studies. We should remember that our pragmatic Western culture is matter focused. Despite the new physics and unique ways of measuring energy, traditional Chinese theories about pathways of energy and energy flow are still met with huge skepticism, but researchers have continually failed to identify other biological underpinnings for the success of acupuncture treatment. Nerve connections, hormonal flows, and cellular chemistry have still not been associated with the success of acupuncture.

Medical researchers continue to look for a physical reason why this works, when, in fact, it is purely energetic. This is the same problem with attempting to examine the power of prayer, whether it's to the almighty or if it originates from a group of caring people sending their collective prayers for healing. What we need to understand about healing is that it embraces both the physical and the energetic.

Gratitude

> He is a wise man who does not grieve for the things
> which he has not, but rejoices for those which he has.
>
> —Epictetus

More than any other character trait, gratitude is strongly connected with our mental health. Some research has shown that people who regularly feel and express gratitude share lower levels of stress and depression while experiencing higher levels of happiness.

People who are more grateful seem to possess a stronger purpose in life, have more resources for coping with life's challenges, and tend to seek emotional support from others. Rarely do they blame others or have a need to numb themselves with unhealthy substances. Overall, they also tend to be more positive minded and have a greater capacity for self-care.

Gratitude can best be understood when looked at from both an internal and an external perspective. We can feel an internal sense of gratitude for the reverence of life, the process of daily living, and the gifts we have received that touch us in profound and moving ways.

We can also feel enduring external gratitude for blessings outside ourselves such as loved ones, animals, nature, and a higher power. We may be pleased with our personal work or some life choices that we've made or filled with pride, or even guilt, but we don't express gratitude to ourselves. This makes gratitude a practice of recognizing our smallness, the gifts of others, and how they've positively influenced our growth.

True gratitude means, giving endless thanks, acknowledging everything we've received and seeing it all from a perspective of half-full as opposed to half-empty (wouldn't this be a positive attitude?). The gratitude mind-set reduces stress, makes us happier, makes us more resilient, and bolsters our self-esteem.

A STUDY OF GRATITUDE

Psychologists Michael McCollough of Southern Methodist University in Dallas, Texas, and Robert Emmons of the University of California at Davis conducted a study on gratitude and its impact on well-being. They separated several hundred people into three groups. The first group was asked to maintain a diary about daily events. The second was instructed to write about only their unpleasant experiences. The third was told to keep a daily list of things for which they were grateful.

The results of this study revealed that the daily gratitude exercises produced a higher level of enthusiasm, alertness, positivity, determination, and energy. The gratitude group had reduced levels of depression and stress, and its members were more helpful to others, kept up with daily exercise, and were more successful in accomplishing personal goals.

AUTHENTIC GRATITUDE

There are numerous exercises designed to help you focus on what you have to be grateful for in your life. One has you imagine that all the things you value vanish and as each is returned, you should take notice of the rise in your gratitude level. Whether you express gratitude on a daily basis in a journal, directly to individuals to whom you are thankful, or in a form of prayer or meditation, gratitude informs our personal philosophy and allows us to see the positive aspects of life while appreciating the best in others. This can be a tremendous antidote to depression and negativity. Gratitude, in the face of adversity, offers a calm sense of being that supports faith and endurance in tackling hardship or conflicts.

However, gratitude is best when it's felt unconditionally. If we suddenly feel grateful because of a thoughtful act someone did or because we received a gift, this is a restricted form of gratitude. Real gratitude is a spiritual condition of deep appreciation for positive circumstances or for whatever meaning we can discover from negative circumstances.

As such, it is willful, steadfast, unwavering, and best represented by maintaining childlike qualities of wonder and awe through which we remember to marvel at everyday life.

The recovery of authentic gratitude is a formidable challenge that shows us a higher road to travel, asking us to let go of our judgments and our unmet expectations, surrender our fears and bitter resentments, and cultivate an attitude of thankfulness and joy for everything in our life.

> Gratitude is not only the greatest of the virtues, but the parent of all others.
>
> —Cicero

Eating Habits, Food Quality, and Cancer Prevention

When Yummy Is Not Enough

Over the last 150 years our eating habits have shifted dramatically from consuming whole, natural foods to relying on packaged, processed fare that sacrifices nutrition for convenience and profit. You can almost hear the marketing logic between the lines: "Hey, we're selling you refined food with high sugar content and lots of additives, but don't worry. We've fortified them so you'll get the nutrition you need. We care!"

The changes in our eating patterns and declining food quality have been directly related to the incidence of certain diseases. The following changes have occurred over the last century:

INCREASE REFINED SUGAR; DECREASE WHOLE GRAINS. There has been a tremendous increase in sugar consumption from sources such as refined white sugar, "raw" sugar, honey, maple syrup, date sugar, agave syrup, high-fructose corn syrup, fruits, molasses, and fruit juices. At the same time, there has been a decreased consumption of complex carbohydrates from whole grain, grain products, and beans. Ironically, this deficiency is one of the reasons we crave sugar.

INCREASE ANIMAL PROTEINS; DECREASE VEGETABLE PROTEINS. According to the Earth Policy Institute, meat consumption increased from 44 million tons in 1950 to 284 million tons in 2009, meaning that annual consumption per person had doubled to over 90 pounds. The rise in the consumption of milk and egg protein is equally dramatic. Wherever incomes rise, so does meat consumption. This increased intake of animal-source protein coincides with the decrease of dietary vegetable proteins such as grains, beans, and bean products.

INCREASE SATURATED FATS; DECREASE UNSATURATED FATS. As the percentage of consumption of saturated fat from animal proteins has increased, that of unsaturated fats from vegetable oil sources has decreased.

INCREASE FIBER-ABSENT FOODS; DECREASE WHOLE, FIBROUS FOODS. There has been a dramatic increase of nonfibrous foods in our diets from dairy products, fatty sauces, and refined grain products (flour cereals, breads, pastas, crackers, and so on). This is contrasted by a decrease in unbroken fiber chains from whole grains, vegetable, and fruit sources.

INCREASE ARTIFICIAL ADDITIVES; DECREASE NATURALLY NUTRITIOUS FOODS. We are becoming more reliant on vitamins, minerals, hormones, and other supplements in pill form as we continue to consume nutrient-deficient food from chemically treated soil.

INCREASE SYNTHETIC CHEMICALS; DECREASE NATURAL QUALITY. Synthetic chemicals in the form of fertilizers, insecticides, preservatives, emulsifiers, artificial dyes, and stabilizers have increased, while natural textures, colors, tastes, and odors have decreased. These unnatural chemical additions to our foods compromise our health in the long term, specifically as it relates to liver, kidney, lymph, and intestinal functioning.

INCREASE FAST-PACED LIFESTYLE; DECREASE MEALTIME RITUALS. We have increasingly relied on store-bought prepackaged foods consumed on the run and denied ourselves the benefit of regular, home-cooked meals enjoyed at a leisurely pace. Our current lifestyle does not support physical health or emotional well-being.

Not All the Food News Is Bad

In response to the general decline in food quality, eating habits, and nutrition, there has been a promising trend in the opposite direction. Over the last 40 years, the alternative health movement has blossomed. Since the advent of the supermarket, the shelf space devoted to packaged, frozen, and canned foods far outpaced that given over to fresh produce. Most grocery stores are now evolving to offer expanded produce sections with nonorganic *and* organic varieties, along with bulk items, such as whole grains and legumes. Low-fat meat and diversified seafood sections reveal America's newfound zeal for minimizing the intake of red meats and emphasizing poultry and fish. Where health food specialty items were once relegated to import or dietetic sections, they now have their own aisles and provide increasing competition for more standard and familiar fare.

Nutritional supplements, once found on the shelves of pharmaceutical sections, now merit their own displays. Outdoor farmers' markets offering organic produce have sprung up in every large city. With the national expansion of exclusive natural food markets, our changing tastes have become more than just a trend. But this positive change in eating habits has been embraced by only a very small percentage of the population. Most people lack the knowledge to make more healthful choices and many do not know how to or are too busy to cook. Still others live in areas in which whole foods are generally unavailable.

Making more healthful nutritional choices is not simply about adjusting quality and buying something because it's organic. The way we balance the food groups and complex carbohydrates, fats, and proteins creates the foundation of a healthful diet.

Staple, Supportive, and Pleasure Foods

Staple Foods

A staple food is one eaten with every major meal or at least once daily. A staple shares all or most of the following qualities:

+ Is available throughout the world
+ Is naturally sweet the more it is chewed
+ Is affordable
+ Can healthfully sustain life for short periods of time
+ Can be prepared with great variety
+ Helps regulate blood sugar
+ Has a long shelf life

Whole cereal grains, beans, and vegetables contain abundant vitamins, micronutrients, and long-chain fiber, promote blood sugar stability, and have a naturally sweet flavor. They also have storage capacity (beans and vegetables were dried for winter consumption). These factors easily qualify whole grains, beans, and vegetables as ideal candidates for staple foods.

For more than 10,000 years, whole cereal grains and vegetables were the principle (staple) foods of humans. Traditionally, these plants were revered as the sacred source of life. The Bible does not say "Give us this day our daily chocolate chip cookies." The reference is to whole grain bread as the staff of life.

Every culture that had a developed agriculture cultivated native grains (corn, rice, wheat, barley, millet, rye, buckwheat, depending on the location) along with various types of beans and vegetables.

NUTRITIONAL ANATOMY: "THE DOCTRINE OF SIGNATURES"

Nature marks each growth . . . according to its curative benefit.

—Paracelsus (1493–1541), Swiss physician

"THE DOCTRINE OF Signatures" is an integral part of ancient herbal philosophy as well as Chinese and Indian folk medicine. It was thought that when a food's structure resembles a body organ, this pattern signifies a healing quality for that particular organ system. To a modern ear this might sound a bit silly or contrived, but what's fascinating is that some nutritional science has affirmed these antiquated claims. Some examples:

- **Kidney beans:** Perfectly resemble the human kidney and are considered a healing food for the kidneys.
- **Walnuts:** Look like miniature brains with both left and right hemispheres, upper cerebrums, and lower cerebellums. Even the wrinkles or folds on walnuts resemble the neocortex of the human brain. Our brain is approximately 60 percent "structural fat" and requires high-quality fats such as omega-3s for essential functioning and to keep the brain fluid and flexible. Some studies have linked low consumption of omega-3s to depression and decreased cognitive function.
- **Carrots:** Take a look at the cross-section of a carrot. It resembles the human eye in great detail. The core and radiating lines of the carrot closely resemble the human eye's pupil and iris. It is known that carrots enhance blood flow to the eyes, offer

vitamin A to the rod and cone cells that store it, as well as aiding in general vision function.

- **Celery:** As well as rhubarb and bok choy, among others, celery has a similar structure to the human bone. These green vegetable varieties contain ample natural sodium and calcium, which are also abundantly found in bone matrix.
- **Avocados:** Resemble the female womb and cervix. Their oil content helps women balance hormones. Interestingly, it takes approximately nine months to grow an avocado from blossom to ripened fruit.
- **Ginseng root:** Some varieties of what the Chinese call a "longevity" herb actually resemble the human form, indicating that it can be a good overall tonic for health.
- **Lungs:** The human lung is made up of branches that end deep within the lung and appear like clusters. The lung bronchi are actually small airways that narrow into small bunches of tissue called *alveoli*. When held upside down, the vegetables that most resemble this lung branch and alveoli are broccoli and cauliflower.
- **Onions:** Uniquely resemble body cells. A 2002 UK study found that eating sautéed onions increases the resistance of blood cells to DNA damage.

Generally, vegetables can be classified in three categories: root vegetables (carrots, onions, radishes, parsnips, turnips), ground varieties (all squashes, cauliflower, broccoli, mushrooms, cucumbers), and green leafy vegetables (lettuces, bok choy, kale, collards, mustard greens, endive, watercress, vegetable tops). For many coastal cultures, vegetables from the ocean (also known as seaweeds or sea vegetables) are standard fare, providing essential minerals and cancer protection.

WASTING NATURAL RESOURCES

SOME STASTISTICS TO document how our infatuation with animal protein is ecologically, socially, and economically wasteful:

- Raising animals for food requires huge amounts of land, food, energy, and water and often contributes to animal suffering.

(CONTINUED)

It is a grossly inefficient practice, because while animals eat enormous quantities of grain, soybeans, oats, and corn, they only produce small amounts of meat, dairy products, or eggs in return. This accounts for the 70 percent of grain and cereals that we grow in this country being fed to farmed animals for their meats and byproducts.

- It takes up to 13 pounds of grain to produce just 1 pound of meat.
- Even fish on fish farms must be fed up to 5 pounds of wild-caught fish just to produce 1 pound of farmed fish.
- Industrially, it takes more than 11 times as much fossil fuel to make one calorie from animal protein as it does to make one calorie from plant protein.
- It takes more than 2,400 gallons of water to produce 1 pound of meat, while growing 1 pound of wheat only requires 25 gallons. You can save more water by not eating a pound of meat than you do by simply not showering for six months!

Supportive Foods

Supportive foods complement the staple foods. Animal protein has been used by most traditional cultures as a condiment, consumed infrequently and in small quantities.

Each organism's body has been designed to process certain kinds of food. Carnivorous animals, for example, have sharp pointed teeth to make meat easier to tear apart for quicker entry into the stomach, where strong secretions can dissolve high amounts of protein immediately, and a shorter intestinal length, which allows meat acids to be discharged and not acccumulated. By contrast, humans' blunter teeth are more for grinding and mashing whole grains and vegetable fibers, not tearing. Our saliva is more chemically alkaline, which is an ideal solution for initiating prompt carbohydrate digestion. Stomach secretions are less potent, and the 30- to 32-foot intestine provides an environment in which meat acids can ferment, particularly if not countered by fibrous vegetables and grains, which, like a sponge, soak up the acids and help carry them out of the body.

Fruit is also a supportive food. However, while it may be rich in vitamins and fiber, it is still a concentrated sugar and best eaten in moderation for optimum health.

Pleasure Foods

The category of pleasure foods can be misleading. For healthy individuals, a pleasure food is any food they feel like eating—from a sirloin steak to chocolate cake! There should be no restriction for the individual in good health to enjoy anything *in moderation*.

Unfortunately, most of us don't practice moderation, nor we are encouraged to do so in this supersize culinary landscape. We aren't aware of the actual content of what we are eating—the hidden fats and sugar that can put on the pounds and compromise our well-being. I've found that the inclusion of this category helps tame the rebel in my clients. If being told that a small volume can be permissible on occasion, people will tend to be less indulgent than if it were prohibited entirely. This changing category can also suffice as a "nonguilt" percentage where one can eat more flexibly, if generally healthy, during social occasions and celebrations.

Cancer: Detection Versus Prevention

The war on cancer in this country has been focused mainly on detection, so much so that it has become our method of prevention. Medical organizations and the media routinely publicize the benefits of early cancer detection by promoting self-examination as if it were a method of prevention.

It's true that the detection techniques, which are constantly being revised and developed, have saved some lives, particularly if a tumor can be removed before it spreads.

A cancer cell is an out-of-control rebel setting its own course of gradual multiplication in any organ, gland, or body system. It continues to divide until it invades other parts of the body. This process of spreading is called *metastasis*. Cancer devastates the most important part of the cell, the DNA, which controls the cell's ability to function. Nearly 75 percent of the cancer's growth occurs before it can be medically detected. This rate of growth is slow, but progressive, often taking 15 to 25 years before appearing noticeable.

The only logical and immediate line of defense is to employ a self-healing lifestyle with a diet focused on reducing the possibility of developing or nurturing cancer cells. Prevention is still the only approach possible to win the war on cancer. This does not mean that you have to deprive yourself of everything that you like, but that you must moderate indulgences and make consistent educated food choices.

Cancer and Diet

The National Cancer Institute estimates that 80 to 90 percent of cancers originate from environmental causes, which include diet and tobacco smoking. Poor diet encourages the growth of cancer cells. It has also been documented that certain foods will increase the volume of hormones that elevate the risk of cancer. Cancers such as breast, uterine, ovarian, and prostate are directly associated with an excess of sex hormones.

A number of foods carry carcinogens that can stimulate the production of free radicals, which are reactive atoms with unpaired electrons. When they form within our cells, they damage cellular functioning.

Cancer rates have increased more slowly in countries that follow traditional diets made up of complex carbohydrates and little animal protein and fat.

The most common cancers that have been specifically linked to diet are those associated with sex hormones and those that involve the pancreas, liver, colon, esophagus, and stomach. Dietary factors also influence many other cancers as well.

The China Project

Much of the research on diet and cancer can seem conflicting. Therefore, the most reliable and promising research comes from population studies that look at a wide variety of dietary and lifestyle patterns. One of the best population studies associating faulty diet with cancer is the China Project (CP), which was conducted by Campbell and Junshi in the 1980s. The CP surveyed dietary disease patterns in 6,500 Chinese citizens from 65 counties (100 from each county). The discoveries of the CP have vigorously challenged and altered existing conceptions about nutrition and health.

According to Campbell:

> The China Project offered a rare opportunity to study disease in a precise manner due to unique conditions that exist in rural China. Approximately 90% of the people in rural China live their entire lives in the vicinity of their birth. Because of deeply held local traditions and the absence of viable food distribution, people consume diets composed primarily of locally produced foods. In addition, there

are dramatic differences in the prevalence of disease from region to region. Various cardiovascular disease rates vary by a factor of about 2-fold from one place to another, while certain cancer rates may vary by several hundred-fold. These factors make rural China a "living laboratory" for the study of the complex relationship between nutrition and other lifestyle factors and degenerative diseases. As a result, the China Project is the first major research study to examine diseases as they really are, multiple outcomes of many interrelated factors.

Compared with the standard American diet (SAD), Chinese diets are much lower in fat (generally accounting for 6 to 24 percent of calories), much higher in dietary fiber (10 to 77 grams daily), approximately 30 percent higher in caloric intake, and substantially lower in foods of animal origin. Chinese diets contain 0 to 20 percent animal-based foods, whereas American diets typically consist of 60 to 80 percent animal-based foods.

The China Project findings reveal dramatic differences associated with cancers of the breast, ovary, uterus, and prostate. These cancers are aggravated by dietary fat and higher levels of reproductive hormones, brought on by eating meat, sugar, and dairy products typical of Western diets.

The average Chinese ratio of dietary fiber intake was 3 times that seen in Western diets. The CP reported that "consistent reductions in cancers of the colon and rectum were found with higher intakes of these various fiber fractions."

Statistics indicate that 1 out of every 36 men in America will die from prostate cancer. Chinese men have one of the lowest rates of prostate cancer death in the world—approximately 1 in every 100,000. Although not conclusive, it is well known that testosterone can be a triggering factor in prostate cancer, and dietary animal protein can stimulate testosterone production.

Other Findings That Should Change Appetites

There have been numerous other studies that support the conclusions of the CP, the bottom line being that *diets high in fat, protein, and calories but low in fiber increase the risk of cancer.* Here are some other findings that show the impact diet has on cancer:

✦ Seventh-Day Adventists who follow a vegetarian diet have a 30 percent lower prostate cancer mortality rate than the general population of California.

✦ The China Study documented that the incidence of prostate cancer is directly related to the overconsumption of dairy products, eggs, and meats.

✦ In a case-control study at Roswell Park Memorial Institute, high milk consumption was found to be associated with a higher risk of breast, mouth, colon, stomach, rectum, lung, bladder, and cervical cancer, relative to no consumption of milk at all.

✦ According to the *Medical Journal of Australia*, any level of alcohol use can be a cause of cancer, and there is no evidence that there is a safe threshold of alcohol consumption for avoiding cancer.

✦ According to the American Cancer Society, alcohol may raise levels of estrogen, a hormone important to the growth and development of breast tissue, increasing the risk of contracting breast cancer.

✦ The Million Women Study, which followed 1.3 million women for an average of 7 years, found that about 13 percent of cancers—affecting the breast, mouth, throat, rectum, liver, and esophagus—could be linked to alcohol. Women who consumed the most alcohol were the ones most likely to get cancer, but even one drink a day increased their risk.

✦ Animal fats seem to pose a greater threat than vegetable oils. Researchers at New York University compared the diets of 250 women with breast cancer to those of 499 women without cancer from the same province in northwestern Italy. Both groups consumed a good deal of olive oil and carbohydrates. The striking difference with the cancer patients was the volume of animal products consumed. Those who ate a greater amount of meat, cheese, butter, and milk had about 3 times the cancer risk of those who did not.

✦ When animal proteins are heated, they produce cancer-causing chemicals called *heterocyclic amines*. Although they have been known to occur in beef, it was not until a report by the National Cancer Institute in 1995 revealed that the same phenomenon occurs in chicken. However, depending on the method of cooking, chicken can contain up to 15 times more carcinogens than a well-done hamburger or grilled steak.

PROTECTING YOUR COLON

THE PRESENCE OF bile acids in the colon is a factor in cancer development. Bile acids are released by the gallbladder into the first part of the small intestine (duodenum) to emulsify fats and then flow into the small and large intestines. Unfortunately, bacteria in the digestive tract change bile acids into cancer-promoting chemicals called *secondary bile acids*. The bacteria that causes these acids is stimulated by a meat-based diet.

On the other hand, vegetarian-based diets do not produce harmful bacteria in digestion. A higher consumption of grains, vegetables, beans, and fruit is directly related to lower rates of colon cancer. Plant roughage, devoid of animal protein complexes, bonds to toxins while moving food through the intestine quickly. The fiber absorbs and dilutes bile acids, altering the quality of intestinal bacteria to a less harmful one.

A healthy diet is crucial not only for anyone wishing to prevent colon cancer but also for individuals already diagnosed with colon polyps, intestinal growths that can become cancerous. One study from the Cornell Medical Center experimented with dietary bran for patients with recurring polyps. Within 6 months, the polyps had become smaller and fewer in number.

The benefits of whole grains, beans, vegetables, and fruits come from abundant long-chain fibers that absorb toxins and expand to keep the intestinal tract clean and free of harmful bacteria.

While there are obvious environmental factors that can instigate a variety of diseases, our best defense is to create strong immune systems that will make us less susceptible to other negative influences. Choosing better food quality, understanding how to balance food groups, and creating more healthful lifestyle habits are integral to building and maintaining good health.

Nutrition's Top Trio
Carbohydrates, Fats, and Proteins

Here we have the great irony of modern nutrition: At a
time when hundreds of millions of people do not have
enough to eat, hundreds of millions more are eating
too much and are overweight or obese.

—Marion Nestle

IN 1825, Jean Brillat-Savarin wrote what has become one of the most
popular food quotes: "Tell me what you eat and I will tell you what you
are." And today, given what we know about the design and function
of the human digestive system, we know scientifically the truth of this
statement.

The food we consume, initially broken down in the mouth and mixed
with salivary enzymes, goes through various stages in the digestive process before it is finally absorbed in the small intestine (gut). Substances
that cannot be absorbed, such as indigestible fiber from whole foods,
eventually become discarded through the bowel as waste.

The job of digestion is to break down the three basic macronutrients—
carbohydrates, fats, and proteins—into smaller particles so our bodies
can absorb as much nutrition from them as possible. This process of
absorption happens along the 30-foot length of the digestive tube.

By the time the mostly digested food arrives in the small intestine, it has been reduced to a nutrient-filled liquid that's absorbed into the bloodstream through villi. The villi, tiny nipple-like protrusions that line the walls of the small intestine, absorb nutrients from the liquified food and transport it directly into the blood. This food then becomes part of the blood, affecting blood chemical quality and body fluid chemistry, and providing energy and nutrients for our physical needs and cellular functioning.

Because the average life span of a red blood cell is 4 months, the chemical quality of *your current blood is a reflection of your eating habits for the last 4 months.* This is important to understand in healing because true healing begins as your blood chemistry changes. As blood chemistry changes and continues to nourish other parts of the body, muscle cells begin to change, then organ cells, and eventually bone and nerve cells, functioning so that every 7 years we get a complete cellular renewal.

On some diet plans, you may eat well for a period of several weeks; however, you'll need at least 4 months of consistently good eating to really change your blood chemistry and improve immunity and cellular health. Healing regimes that tout a quick "cleanse" of several days' duration merely clean out a very small portion of the large bowel and do little to change or strengthen blood quality. A 4-month period of disciplined dietary habits sets an ideal foundation for your healing.

Carbohydrates: Fuel for Your Body

> When asked about the commonly held idea that ancient people were primarily meat-eaters, the highly respected anthropologist Nathaniel Dominy, PhD, from Dartmouth College responded, "That's a myth. Hunter-gathers, the majority of their calories come from plant foods . . . meat was just too unpredictable." After studying the bones, teeth, and genetics of primates for his entire career as a biological anthropologist, Dr. Dominy, states, "Humans might be more appropriately described as *starchivores*."
>
> —John McDougall

Carbohydrates are intricately manufactured by plants as a way of storing energy from the sun and provide us with most of the energy we require for everyday functioning. For some people, the word *carbohydrate* sounds like a swear word that needs to be expunged from the nutritional lexicon.

The truth is simple, yet complex.

The simple fact is that your body requires a constant supply of carbohydrates for all of its metabolic activities, particularly neurological. There are two basic types of carbohydrates, some with very simple molecular structures (*simple sugars of one to three molecules*) and others with more complex forms (*complex sugars containing thousands of molecules*). For the body to utilize carbohydrates (generally known as sugar), it must break them down into the simple sugar known as *glucose*. Glucose is the only form of sugar that is transportable in the bloodstream. It is also the sole source of energy for the brain. A lack of glucose, or of oxygen to burn the glucose, could result in permanent brain damage.

Digestion of simple sugar is analogous to tending a fire. You can use newspaper, which has a quick burning effect and thus the fire has to be constantly fed, or you can use wood, which is slower to start but will burn for longer periods and thus provides a consistent and longer-lasting heat.

This is the story of carbohydrates: Some burn quickly and some burn slowly. Quick-burning carbohydrates (simple sugars) are usually sweet to the taste, lose most of their flavor when chewed, and promptly flood the bloodstream with sugar, elevating hormonal levels, producing potentially harmful anaerobic bacteria, reducing oxygen, and leaving a residue of strong acidity.

Among the most common simple sugars are white and brown sugar, honey, maple syrup, molasses, fruit, alcohol, rice syrup, barley malt, milk sugar, agave syrup, dextrose, high-fructose corn syrup, and maltose. Because the blood can maintain only approximately 2 teaspoons of sugar at a time, any more than this is converted into a large, branched molecule called *glycogen,* which is stored in liver cells. When the liver's 60- to 80-gram storage capacity is reached, the sugar must be converted into fat and stored in the body tissues—a fact that sweet lovers find endlessly annoying.

Complex sugars, on the other hand, are found in whole grains, grain products, beans, and vegetables. They are the hardwood of carbohydrates, burning slowly and evenly, while regulating blood sugar so that it's neither high nor low, and providing consistent energy.

However, whole grains have become rare in most modern culinary styles. Brown rice, for example, has a seven-layer covering that contains minerals and healthy fiber that shield the inner carbohydrate, known as white rice. Before the widespread use of husking machines, this was the original whole grain of Asia (there are over 160 varieties of whole rice). Today, the white rice you see in Japanese restaurants is highly polished brown rice stripped of these important layers; thus it's a simple carbohydrate that gets rapidly absorbed and tends to elevate blood sugar. It is not a whole food or a healthful food.

Whole grains, with their covering intact, provide necessary fiber and are known to lower the risk for cancer, heart disease, hypertension, diabetes, and numerous digestive problems. Unlike simple sugars, whole grains might initially taste somewhat bland, but when thoroughly chewed, they impart a subtle sweetness that can be satisfying and easy on digestion.

The Whole Grain and Nothing but the Grain . . .

To combat heart disease, diabetes, obesity, and cancer, we have been repeatedly advised to eat plenty of whole grains. But, how do we determine which foods provide whole grains and which only appear to do so. Bread, pasta, bagels, cold breakfast cereal, muffins, cookies, and instant oatmeal have their ultimate origins in whole grains. However, they are no longer considered whole grains. They are grain products made from whole grains. Bury a bagel and it will not sprout a bagel tree. This distinguishing difference is sadly still misunderstood.

When the packaging on a loaf of bread says "Made with Whole Grain Goodness!," unsuspecting consumers feel a false sense of security. Actually, this is a marketing strategy. If we grind whole wheat and make bread from the resulting flour, we'll have unrefined whole grain bread. But when the flour is refined by taking out the bran, we end up with common white flour, from which we can bake ordinary white bread. Further refinement gives us cake flour, which has even less nutritional value.

Maximum nutrition comes from whole grains and not simply grain products. Breaking down the grain structure to make flour particles allows the wheat to be more quickly absorbed into the bloodstream than would, say, whole wheat berries. In some sensitive individuals, refined flour enters the blood just as quickly as simple sugar. In fact, refined grains are high on the glycemic index, a rating system that measures how quickly blood sugars rise after eating a particular food.

BRIEF HISTORY OF WHOLE GRAINS

**Behold, I have given you every herb-bearing seed, which
is upon the face of all the earth, and every tree, in which is
the fruit of a tree yielding seed; to you it shall be for meat.**
—Genesis 1.29

EVERY GREAT CULTURE cultivated rice, wheat, barley, oats, rye, corn, or buckwheat. Frequently, these plants were worshiped as a sacred source of life.

In Will Durant's books on world history, the dietary habits of different societal groups have a fascinating similarity:

- The Babylonian civilization, established thousands of years before the birth of Christ, produced a healthy variety of grains, peas, beans, fruits, and nuts. Meat was rarely used; however, fish, being more affordable and available, was eaten occasionally. Small quantities of goat products along with grapes and olives supplemented their diet.
- North of this civilization lived the near-vegetarian Assyrians, whose fields were ripe with wheat, barley, millet, and sesame. Meat eating was limited to the aristocracy, though fish were occasionally taken from the Tigris River.
- Throughout India, rice, peas, lentils, millet, vegetables, and fruits were considered staples; all meats were limited to the wealthy. In the south, predominantly, the cuisine was made more flavorful by the addition of numerous spices.
- Dominating the vast terrain throughout China were fields of millet, barley, wheat, and soybeans as well as paddies of numerous rice varieties.
- In Japan, which has limited land space, agriculturalists still managed to grow more than a hundred varieties of rice, buckwheat, small beans (adzuki), and seaweeds, which were eaten both fresh and dried.
- Despite living in a harsh mountainous region, ancient Greeks grew barley, from which they made porridge, flatbreads, and cakes, usually mixed with a small amount of honey. Olive oil, goat products, beans, peas, cruciferous vegetables, lentils, on-

ions, garlic, figs, grapes, and wine were regularly consumed as supporting foods.

- Originally, the Roman diet was similar to that of the Greeks, but as the empire declined, meals (at least for the wealthy) became legendary rituals of prolonged feasting at which diners ate richer foods and a higher percentage of animal protein.
- For the past 5,000 years, the chief crop of Mexico has been corn (known as maize) and, later, rice (introduced by Spanish colonizers in the early 1500s). Besides numerous beans, tomatoes, onions, peppers, and small amounts of meats, Mexicans enjoyed a wide array of vegetables, fruits, and coffees. The cow was unknown before the arrival of the Spaniards. Until then, the largest animals consumed were wild turkeys. Lard, used extensively in modern Mexican cooking, is a recent addition, as is cheese, which you'll find in many bean dishes. As food refinement has increased, oils and dairy fats have taken a more prominent place in the Mexican daily diet.

The common thread to the dietary habits of these traditional societies is a regular consumption of whole grains and vegetables with beans and bean products as primary protein sources. Unfortunately, when grain refining (aka polishing) was introduced, valuable fiber, minerals, and vitamins were sacrificed. This fostered a pattern of food manipulation that continues to the present. It has been pointed out that many of the subsequent food additions in modern cultures (dairy, fat, protein) to these once-traditional diets are the result of a compensatory attempt to make meals more filling and nutritionally satisfying and as a way of buffering dietary acids.

THE OATMEAL STORY

For most people, the word *cereal* usually brings to mind a visual of boxed breakfast cereal. The kind you soak in milk and top with lots of fruit. But not so. Common breakfast cereals are merely flour products. The once-whole grain has been through processing, which transforms it into particles and then into grain products.

Cereal grains go through different styles of processing. Although whole grains are preferable for a healthful diet, cut and rolled grains are also acceptable. However, powdered forms of grain (flour) are

(CONTINUED)

recommended only as a minimum percentage of dietary grain products. They are less satisfying, and in some individuals, they can increase blood sugar because they are relatively quickly absorbed.

What we know as oatmeal is available in a number of forms:

- Whole oat groats
- Steel-cut oats
- Precooked rolled oats
- Instant rolled oats
- Powdered oat bran

WHOLE GRAINS HAVE three essential parts: bran, germ, and endosperm. To be classified as a whole grain, the entire grain must still be intact, not just the endosperm, as is the case in refined grains. By removing the germ and the bran, refined grains lose most of their original healthful benefits.

Intact whole grain retains more nutritional benefits than does processed grains. One of the primary benefits of whole grains is their high fiber content. A diet that is rich in fiber has been proven to reduce certain cancers (specifically colon cancer), combat diabetes, reduce digestive problems, and even reverse heart disease. The rich balance of vitamins and minerals in whole grains helps the immune system to remain healthy and responsive.

Whole oat groats can take 1.5 hours to cook. When they're cut with a sharp-bladed machine they become steel-cut oats, which cooks in half that time. If whole groats are rolled flat, and presteamed, they are called rolled oats, which typically cook in 10 to 15 minutes. When rolled oats are broken up, they become instant oats, which can be cooked quite quickly. But, it doesn't stop there. When oat bran is stripped of its outer layers and powdered, it becomes powdered oat bran, a which requires absolutely no cooking and is usually taken as a fiber additive to the morning meal.

Because the word *meal* literally means "grain," any form of oats can be called *oatmeal*. Generally, I recommend whole or steel-cut. Regular rolled oats cook more quickly and offer variety, and the instant variety can work in a pinch for a fiber source when traveling. This is what restaurants usually serve. So the term *oatmeal* can actually refer to several different forms of oats, which can be cooked until soft.

CONCERNS ABOUT GRAIN PHYTATES

I've seen some dramatically exaggerated online articles that claim whole grains are killing us because of their gluten and phytic acid content. Although it is true that some people have gluten intolerance, this can be remedied by avoiding whole grains containing gluten (see "Nongluten Grains," on page 221).

Phytates (and phytic acid) are antioxidant compounds found in whole grains, legumes, nuts, and seeds. The main concern about consuming foods that contain phytates is that they bind to certain dietary minerals such as iron, zinc, manganese, and, to a lesser extent, calcium, thereby slowing their absorption and leaving us mineral deficient and with increased cellular acidity.

However, the presence of phytates in foods really isn't the major concern that some individuals claim it to be. According to current research, the dangerous ramifications of phytic acid are overblown. In fact, there are numerous studies that demonstrate manifold *benefits* of phytic acid. First, they have anti-inflammatory effects and, in laboratory research, have helped normalize cell growth and stopped the proliferation of cancer cells, even improving the effectiveness of chemotherapy. Phytates may also help prevent cardiovascular disease and lower a food's glycemic load.

If you are concerned about phytates, try soaking short-grain brown rice in water overnight, which diminishes the phytates by 30 to 40 percent. Phytates can be reduced by cooking, chewing (adding more alkalinity to food from saliva), and the moderate use of sea salt. Many cultures soaked, sprouted, and fermented their grains, all of which reduce the phytic aid.

If you are eating a diet rich in whole grains, beans, and vegetables (especially mineral-rich green leafy varieties), sea plants, and beans, you are usually consuming enough minerals to render the phytate fear a nonissue.

WHAT ARE WHOLE GRAINS?

Strictly speaking, whole grains are cereal grains with their bran intact. They have seven layers of protective fiber that lock in hundreds of nutrients. There are more than a hundred versions of whole grains. As long as you eat unrefined grains and limit your intake of flour products, you can enjoy all the nutritional and cancer-fighting benefits of these wholesome foods.

Botanically, wild rice and buckwheat are classified as seeds; however, for the sake of simplicity and due to their fiber content, I've included them in the following list of whole grains. I have also included grits, made from dried and milled corn.

+ Brown rice
+ Barley
+ Millet
+ Oats (groats, rolled, steel cut, instant flaked)
+ Rye
+ Bulgur (cracked wheat)
+ Quinoa
+ Amaranth
+ Buckwheat
+ Grits
+ Wild rice

THE GRAIN PRODUCT LOWDOWN

In the West, grain products, particularly breads, are the main source of whatever whole grains we consume. Among the products we consume on a daily basis, many of which are misleadingly referred to as whole grain, are bread (including bagels and flatbreads), pasta, muffins, rice cakes, crackers, and corn chips.

The dry texture of bread (especially toasted) or crackers makes an ideal companion with sauces, soups, sandwiches, and spreads (jams, nut butters, and pâtés). Aside from the obvious advantage of convenience, the most appealing factor about the most common types of grain products is their texture, which adds variety to our daily diet.

THE BOTTOM LINE ON TOAST

THERE IS A downside to our affection for toasted bread. Prolonged toasting or baking promotes the formation of mutagens, which can be cancer-causing or -promoting agents. The most common "probable" carcinogen is called acrylamide. Aside from being a chemical used in certain industrial processes, such as in making paper, dyes, and plastics, in treating drinking water, and found in wastewater, acrylamide is also found in small amounts in some consumer products, such as caulk, food packaging, and some adhesives, as well as cigarette smoke. It is also found in certain starchy foods during high-temperature cooking, such as fying, roasting, and baking.

Acrylamide has shown a tendency to increase the risk of several types of cancer when given to lab animals (rats and mice) in their drinking water. While the doses of acrylamide used in these studies have been as much as 1,000 to 10,000 times higher than the common levels that people find in foods, it is still difficult to know if these results would apply to people as well. Therefore, it might be safest to minimize our exposure to substances that we've seen grow animal cancers. This is not to say that you should *never* eat toasted bread. It can supplement a meal, but should not replace the need for whole grain that is not broken into flour particles.

Eating ground whole grains (or beans) in the form of flour increases the available calories and the tendency to store fat because the fiber is removed during processing. Fiber contains virtually no calories, so its removal increases calorie concentration. Flour, specifically refined flour, causes a greater rise in blood insulin levels during digestion than do whole grains, which actually stabilize blood sugar.

Because individual tolerances often vary, no hard-and-fast rules can apply when it comes to eating flour products. Some people are temporarily energized by them, whereas others may exhibit allergic symptoms, including fatigue. The best choice if you want to eat bread is to choose unyeasted whole grain varieties made without stabilizers, conditioners, chemical preservatives, sweetenings (sugar, molasses, honey), and food coloring. Real bread shouldn't taste like a sweet roll!

Pasta appears to be a popular second to bread products but here, too, you may wish to avoid the more refined varieties and instead cook soba, artichoke, brown rice, quinoa, or whole wheat noodles.

FIVE GOOD REASONS FOR EATING WHOLE GRAINS

For the individual on a healing path, particularly for someone with cancer, whole grains are indispensable to health. Each of the following effects of eating whole grains ties into a foundational healing plan:

REGULATES BOWELS. Ensuring bowel regularity means that you reduce the amount of time that toxic bacteria remain in your intestine. This creates less of a burden not only on the intestines but also on the liver. The fiber that comes with whole grain, commonly referred to as roughage, is actually the indigestible part of the carbohydrate.

The outer covering of the grain absorbs water in the digestive tract, making the stool bulkier as it sweeps along the intestinal walls to be discharged. A bulkier stool passes much more quickly through the digestive tract, lowering the body's exposure to carcinogen-contain foods (and lowering absorption through the gut). When carcinogens are bound to the stool, they do not have time to ferment within the intestine.

Often, when people first begin to eat more whole grain and consume fewer foods and substances that stimulate bowel function (caffeine, sugar, tobacco), they complain of being temporarily constipated. In the beginning, you may experience several days of sluggish bowels as they become accustomed to purging themselves without the help from stimulants. Within days, however, you'll be amazed at your body's adjustment to whole grain, and you'll notice a new regularity in a way you've probably never experienced. The net effect of this is to feel lighter, more energetic, and physically renewed. This has a positive effect on both your disposition and the absorption of nutrients.

STABILIZES BLOOD SUGAR. One of the most important healing aspects of eating whole grains is how it helps maintain blood sugar levels. Keeping blood sugar regular is a wise healing strategy because this can reduce inflammation, minimize sugar cravings, and maximize energy and mood. The complex sugar chains in the molecular structure of whole grains break apart slowly and gradually raise blood sugar in an even and consistent manner. This process creates more endurance energy and a mental calm unlike the wide swings created by simple sugars, which release stress hormones, create physical tension, and initiate the development of arterial plaque. Swings in blood sugar can stimulate strong cravings for simple sugars.

PROVIDES A SOURCE OF VITAMINS B AND E. Whole grains provide a number of trace minerals and vitamins, especially from the B and E groups. The bran covering of whole grains contains many essential B vitamins, such as niacin, B_6, pantothenic acid, riboflavin, and thiamin. These water-soluble vitamins are essential for immune health, cardiac strength, DNA health, skin and eye health, red blood cell development, and gum health. The B vitamins protect us from diseases (beriberi, and pellagra), lower cholesterol, and prevent depression. They are essential for the building and maintenance of body tissues, for promoting the appetite, and for the formation of certain hormones.

Vitamin E is well known for its valuable antioxidant properties that help neutralize free radicals, which have been shown to produce tissue and cellular damage. Vitamin E also aids the circulatory system by helping the blood clot more effectively, helping the body produce red blood cells, and easing chronic respiratory problems.

DISCHARGES TOXINS. Dietary fiber from whole grains is divided into two groups: insoluble and soluble fiber. Both bind (aka chelate) with the body's harmful toxins, cholesterol, and fat (from which estrogens are made) to remove them from our system via the bowel. Removing excess fat before it enters your bloodstream keeps estrogen formation low. This is a positive quality because estrogens can stimulate the growth of abnormal cells, which eventually leads to the growth of cancer cells. Known cancers that are stimulated to grow from estrogen excess are breast, uterine, fallopian tube, vaginal, prostate, and ovarian, as well as head and neck cancers.

DECREASES CRAVINGS FOR SUGAR AND FAT. Given their nutritional value and stabilizing influence on blood sugar, whole grains will automatically reduce your cravings for sweets and fatty foods. This is done in two ways: First, via blood sugar. Whole grains aid the blood in maintaining a more even blood sugar level, creating less desire for sweets because their gradual breakdown consistently feeds the blood with complex sugars for fuel. The most important point about foods that turn to sugar is their rate of absorption. Grains break down slowly and gradually. Second, the gradual and regular feed of sugar as it is released during the digestion of whole grains also helps reduce the actual craving for simple sugar. These factors reduce sugar cravings and make your change of diet less of an effort; you'll need less willpower to avoid foods that are not health supportive.

Fiber: Friend or Foe

When missionary surgeon Denis Burkitt returned to Britain after working with native African peoples, he compared the pattern of diseases in African hospitals with those found in Western populations. One of his conclusions, that many of the Western diseases that are rare in Africa are caused by diet and lifestyle, led him to write *Don't Forget the Fiber in Your Diet*, which became a bestseller. A key aspect of his theories was based on his observational research about the length of time it took food to travel through the digestive system.

Burkitt concluded that constipation and intestinal cancers were rare in traditional African societies due to the heavy fiber content of their natural diet. The Africans he studied had active lifestyles and lived chiefly on whole grains, vegetables, beans, and fruits with modest amounts of low-fat animal proteins. Transit time from mouth to bowel discharge was approximately 17 hours.

The general promotion of high-fiber diets was, however, tempered for a time by the discovery of role of phytates, antioxidant compounds found in the fiber of whole grains, legumes, nuts and seeds, and numerous other plant foods. Nutritional researchers warned the public to avoid phytates because of their ability to bind to certain dietary minerals and decrease the breakdown of proteins. This conclusion came from studies in which raw wheat bran (a concentrated source of phytates) or baked goods high in wheat bran were given as a primary source of dietary fiber. However, these warnings have little relevance for vegetarians or whole grain eaters whose intake of dietary fiber comes from a variety of cooked, raw, and processed sources.

For those concerned about phytates, the following recommendations will enhance the breakdown of phytates:

- Soak beans overnight and discard the water before cooking in fresh water.
- Roast nuts before eating.
- Sprout seeds and legumes and use in salads and on sandwiches.
- Cook cereals (you can also soak cereals for several hours before cooking).
- Add a pinch of sea salt (per cup) when cooking any type of cereal.
- Eat fermented foods, such as tamari (natural soy sauce), miso, and tempeh.
- Eat mineral-rich green leafy vegetables with cereals.

One the positive side, phytates are considered an iron watchdog because they bond to excessive iron elements and carry them out of the body, protecting susceptible individuals from iron overload. There is some research that links excessive stored iron to cancer development. Additional research suggests that phytates can also provide benefits by regulating the absorption of glucose from complex carbohydrates.

The World Health Organization (WHO) explained the effects of fiber and phytates on the availability of minerals from plant foods:

Studies from the eastern Mediterranean region suggest that very high intakes of unleavened bread, where the cereal phytate has not been destroyed by the endogenous phytase in the grain, eventually leads to problems of mineral absorption. However, this seems to be a problem of food preparation rather than of the diet as such. In human physiological studies, exchanging full-grain cereals for refined starches low in fiber does not lead to calcium, zinc, or iron malabsorption, because the whole grain provides an additional intake of the minerals that compensates for any reduced mineral availability. Oxalate-rich foods such as spinach do, however, limit mineral absorption.

The WHO study recommends up to 54 grams of fiber daily as a healthy limit.

Fiber is best consumed from whole foods (long-chain carbohydrates). A diet of whole grains, grain products, vegetables, beans, and other plant foods will supply abundant fiber and will not compromise your mineral status.

RESEARCH ON FIBER AND CANCER

- A 1977 study that examined women who ate a low-fat, high–complex carbohydrate diet over a 2-year period, found positive changes in breast tissue composition, which was linked to a reduced risk of developing breast cancer.
- A National Cancer Institute study that examined the different roles nutrients play in cancer prevention and tumor inhibition revealed that dietary fiber inhibits cancer by binding to chemical carcinogens and removing them from the colon.

Sweet News with a Bitter Taste

In the early 1900s, two-thirds of carbohydrate consumption in the United States came from complex sources, such as whole grains, grain products, and vegetables. Today, only half of all carbohydrates consumed come from these sources. Since 1990, Americans have consumed more than 150 pounds per person of natural sweeteners annually. Add noncaloric sweeteners to that number, and it leaps to 165 pounds. Most simple sugars are highly concentrated, and herein lies most of the problem. For instance, approximately 3 feet of sugar cane is industrially processed to create 1 teaspoon of white sugar. The average piece of coffee shop cherry pie (about an eighth of a pie) contains nearly 10 teaspoons of sugar. Add one large scoop of ice cream (5 tablespoons of sugar), and you now have a grand total of 15 teaspoons of sugar! So through the efforts of modern technology, we can, in the course of about 6 minutes, consume 45 feet of concentrated sugar cane and call it a little snack.

Honey, regardless of its quality, is also a very concentrated food. Just 1 teaspoon of honey is equivalent, in sugar concentration, to approximately four medium apples. Maple syrup is even more concentrated: To make 1 gallon of maple syrup, you have to boil 35 to 40 gallons of tree sap. If you've ever squeezed oranges to make juice, you already know it takes three to four oranges just to fill a small cup. It's important as a health safeguard to consider the degree of concentration of certain foods that you consume daily.

WHAT HAPPENS TO SUGAR IN THE BODY?

As anyone who has a passion for donuts will confirm, an excess of sugar easily turns to fat in the body. But it's not just the fat content in donuts that's responsible for putting on pounds. (Low-fat foods may contain a low percentage of fats, but the amount of sugar added to make the food more palatable ends up producing the very condition that consumers are trying to avoid in the first place: weight gain.)

Excess sugar eventually affects every organ in the body. Sugar excess, beyond what your body can immediately use, is stored in the liver as a form of glucose called glycogen. If the liver storage capacity (60 to 90 grams of glycogen) is exceeded, the liver could swell. This can happen simply by eating too much fruit! Some evidence for this exists in medical literature, which has shown that fruit sugar causes liver cells and the endoplasmic reticulum (a part of the cell that transports proteins) to take up water and swell. This disturbs, and ends up compromising, the cell's natural detoxification functions.

With the liver at maximum storage capacity, excess glycogen is returned to the blood in the form of fatty acids. These acids are taken to various parts of the body and stored, first in the most inactive areas such as the belly, buttocks, thighs, and breasts. Excess fatty acids are then distributed among the active organs, such as the heart and kidneys, hindering their function in the long term.

THE WRATH OF SUGAR

There are many debilitating conditions that excessive sugar can create or, at the least, aggravate. While we have all heard about the dangers of fat, in many cases the problem is an excess of sugar that turns to fat, fostering acidity and triggering immune breakdown.

Excess sugar leads to many degenerative conditions. Most notable are mineral deficiency, an increase in anaerobic intestinal bacteria, inflammation, tooth decay, obesity, *Candida albicans* fungus, heart disease, diabetes, irritable bowel syndrome, gallstones, and tumor growth.

The solution to sugar cravings is first to understand what our basic nutritional needs are and then how to adapt them into our lifestyle so we can enjoy natural sweet treats without developing an addiction. We do not require simple sugar as a dietary nutrient, which it is not, anyway. There is no recommended daily allowance (RDA) for sugar. It is strictly a food that we eat for pleasure.

THE HIGHS AND LOWS OF BLOOD SUGAR

A TYPICAL FOOD diary: You eat breakfast at 8:00 a.m. About 2 hours later (10:00 a.m.) you take a sweet break at work. Next, you have a noon lunch (with dessert) followed by another sweet break at 3:00 p.m. (perhaps you drink a cola). After work, at 5:00 p.m., you join your colleagues for liquid sugar (aka alcohol, a distillation of sugar) during the aptly named happy hour. About 2 hours later, you have dinner (with another dessert); by 9:00 p.m., however, you find yourself indulging in "prime-time snacking." Finally, before you go to bed, you're into the kitchen eating several tablespoons of ice cream or enjoying a lifelong ritual of milk and cookies.

What you've done is continually tease your blood sugar throughout the day—elevating it and making it drop, over and over until you finally drop into bed and call it a day. The consequences are mood swings, weight gain, tumor growth, immune weakness, mineral deficiency, lack of mental clarity, and, most notorious, a lack of energy and fatigue.

(CONTINUED)

The simplified molecular structure of sugar allows it to become absorbed into the blood almost immediately upon leaving the mouth and entering the esophagus. If blood sugar becomes too low or too high, the result is you risk putting yourself into coma. Fortunately, we have several natural blood sugar regulators to prevent this from occurring. One of those is the pancreas, which produces two hormones, a sugar hormone and an anti-sugar hormone (insulin). When the blood sugar level falls dangerously low (from not eating for a long period, or from intense and consistent exercise), the pancreas secretes a hormone that signals the liver to release its stored sugar. This immediately regulates blood sugar. However, if the sugar level is driven too high (from eating too much sugar), the pancreas secretes insulin, which automatically lowers sugar levels. So while our pancreas is very busy either way, the liver also has to work extra hard as the final regulator.

This constant rise and fall of blood sugar levels is the root of many a problem, especially with respect to immune weakness and systemic inflammation.

Making Sense of the Glycemic Index: The Politics of Blood Sugar

"Pasta makes you fat."
"Eating carrots can be just as bad as eating refined sugar."
"A 2-ounce serving of noodles has the same effect on blood sugar
   as a chocolate bar."

If you've ever heard these confusing claims and scratched your head in bewilderment while feeling overwhelmed with the new science, you're not alone.

In the mid-1980s, researchers at the University of Toronto developed the glycemic index (GI) as a tool for helping diabetics control their blood sugar levels. Today, the GI is used in sports performance and weight management and as a barometer for evaluating health.

Essentially, the GI ranks carbohydrate-based foods by the degree they elevate blood glucose and insulin levels. Carbohydrates with a high GI score tend to increase these levels quickly. The lower the GI number, the slower the absorption rate, keeping these levels more steady.

The GI score is based on a 50-gram carbohydrate portion, such as 1¼ cups of rice and 2 medium apples. The degree to which blood glucose rises after eating the food in question is compared to that seen after eating 50 grams of table sugar, which is given a GI score of 100. It is the difference between the two levels that determines the food's ranking.

Oatmeal, for instance, has a glycemic index of 49, which means oatmeal produces a 49 percent increase in blood glucose compared to straight glucose (which causes a 100 percent increase). Foods that score above 70 are classified as *high glycemic*. Foods that rate below 55 are classified as *low glycemic*.

Scientists conclude that the most important factor in predicting glycemic ranges is the surface area of the food. The more finely a food is ground or the more refined a food is, the higher its glycemic rating because grinding increases a food's surface area. Foods with a small surface area typically have a low glycemic index.

GLYCEMIC LOAD

There is another rating system used to determine the response of blood glucose to the carbohydrates consumed. The glycemic load (GL) uses the glycemic index as well as the actual amount of carbohydrate (that is, the serving size) to determine the overall effect that a carbohydrate-containing food has on blood sugar and subsequent insulin values.

The GL is a more efficient rating system than the simple GI because it factors in the actual *amount* of carbohydrate that is being consumed as well as the food's glycemic index score. (The GI is not always practical because you might not consume exactly 50 grams of carbohydrates during one meal.)

The glycemic load is calculated by multiplying the number of carbohydrates in your food by the glycemic index. Then that number is divided by 100. Therefore, a boiled potato might have a high glycemic index score but it has a lower glycemic load than a chocolate candy bar. Despite the fact that a chocolate candy bar might have a GL of 26 and an ordinary potato a GL of 17, the candy bar produces a higher rise in blood glucose than the potato even though the size of the candy bar might be less than half of the potato.

Glycemic loads of greater than 20 are considered high, and loads of less than 10 are low.

AVOIDING THE HEADACHE OF FIGURING OUT GLYCEMIC RATINGS

Many experts are labeling bananas, carrots, brown rice, millet, corn, sweet potatoes, rice cakes, parsnips, and apricots as sources of bad carbohydrates and recommending that we avoid them because of the speed with which these carbs are converted into glucose according to the glycemic index.

If this were true, and we were evaluating foods only for their glycemic index, it would mean that ice cream and potato chips are as healthful as lentils and superior to brown rice and carrots. Many researchers were quick to point out that the glycemic index was a serious oversimplification. How we prepare food, the volume consumed, whether we use salt or oil in our preparations, and the combinations of food we eat all influence our glycemic index.

For example, rice cakes are usually assigned a glycemic index of 78 to 82, making them a high glycemic food. However, add a thin spread of any nut butter (peanut, almond) and the oil content helps drop that score into the 50s.

Other studies showed, however, that although adding fat and protein to carbohydrates (as many protein-oriented diets recommend) produces a flatter glucose curve by slowing absorption, it has no such effect on an individual's actual insulin response. In addition, high-fat, low-glycemic foods (buttered potatoes, potato chips, ice cream) impaired glucose tolerance in the subsequent meal.

Although both the glycemic index and the glycemic load offer valuable information on how carbohydrates influence blood glucose levels, the glycemic load is simply more practical because it looks at the total carbohydrate load as opposed to single values.

Most of these calculations feel overwhelming, but the benefit of the glycemic classifications have helped draw attention to the fact that refined (and even some unrefined) flours can elevate blood sugar and frequently result in fatigue, sweet cravings, excess acidity, and so forth. The importance of including whole complex carbohydrates (brown rice, barley, oats, quinoa) into the daily diet, instead of only refined grain products, has been one of the most valuable benefits of glycemic index research.

If you're following the Nature's Cancer-Fighting Foods program, you need not worry about calculating, cross-referencing, or keeping track of your glycemic scores, since you are eating foods in mixed combinations that end up creating a balanced and moderate blood sugar wave, without the highs and lows.

The Carbohydrate–Cancer Connection

Cancer cells feed directly on blood glucose, similar to fermenting yeast. The concept that sugar feeds cancer is often ignored in standard dietary recommendations for cancer patients. For the millions of patients currently being treated for cancer, few are offered specific advice or guidelines for using healing nutrition, beyond being told to eat good food or "a balanced diet." Cancer sufferers could achieve major health improvements and more positive disease outcomes if glucose levels were controlled. Eliminating refined sugars and adopting a whole foods approach combined with quality nutritional supplements and regular exercise are critical components for cancer recovery.

Otto Warburg, a 1931 Nobel laureate in medicine, first discovered that cancer cells have a different energy metabolism than healthy cells. Warburg found that malignant tumors frequently show an increase in anaerobic (without air) glycolysis—an abnormal process that uses glucose as the primary fuel—generating large amounts of lactic acid as a byproduct. Although all cells feed on sugar, cancer cells have voracious appetites for glucose and are the first to use sugar. The lactic acid generated from sugar metabolism must be transported to the liver for processing and discharge. This acid lowers the pH in cancerous tissues and results in physical fatigue from liver stress due to the amount of work required to clear the lactic acid buildup. As a result, larger tumors tend to be more acidic.

The goal is to return the body to aerobic (oxygen-using) metabolism as quickly as possible and to achieve an alkaline tissue pH (between 6.4 and 7.0). This state of alkalinity is threatened not only by sugar excess but by fat excess as well. One of Warburg's conclusions was that an alkaline environment *discourages* cancer growth (see more about the acid–alkaline balance in Chapter 6.)

Because a cancer cell's metabolism is very inefficient (extracting only about 5 percent of the available energy in the food supply and from the body's own calorie stores), the cancer is wasting energy. This is one reason cancer sufferers become tired and undernourished. This vicious circle increases body wasting, leading to death and explaining why almost 40 percent of cancer sufferers die from malnutrition (called *cachexia*, or wasting away).

When cancer patients are given a feeding tube, 70 percent of the calories in the total parenteral (TPN) solution administered intravenously is in the form of glucose. Unfortunately, these high-glucose solutions are a poor choice of nutrition and could very well be fueling tumor growth. A more nutritionally balanced IV solution would combine low glucose levels with a broad spectrum of nutrients, such as amino acids, vitamins, minerals, lipids, and other essential nutrients. Such a solution would allow patients to build strength and would not feed the tumor.

Among European health professionals, the "sugar feeds cancer" concept is well acknowledged. This is evident from the Systemic Cancer Multistep Therapy (SCMT) protocol, developed in Germany by Manfred von Ardenne in 1965. SCMT injects patients with glucose to suddenly increase blood glucose concentrations, which in turn lowers pH values in cancer tissues by way of lactic acid increase. This procedure intensifies the thermal sensitivity of the malignant tumors and promotes the rapid growth of cancer cells, which is necessary for the next step of hyperthermia. Patients who are in that rapid state of cancer growth are then given whole-body hyperthermia (107°F core temperature) to further stress the cancer cells, which is then followed by chemotherapy or radiation.

One of the most popular studies, originally done is 1975 and since duplicated numerous times, had human volunteers ingest 100-gram portions of simple sugars from sucrose, fructose, honey, and orange juice. Within a 3-hour period, these sugars significantly impaired white blood cells' ability to engulf bacteria and perform immunity functions for up to 6 hours. In a healthy individual, this can be managed. But in an individual with multiplying cancer, it is as if the soldiers had suddenly left the fort, making the body more vulnerable to increasing cancer activity.

Fat: The Dietary F-Word

Our love affair with dietary fat has complex social, sensorial, lifestyle, nutritional, and psychological grounds, making it difficult for us to reduce it as a food group in our diets.

Our ancestors did not have the luxury of being able to process huge amounts of oil from seeds and nuts. For example, it takes 14 to 16 ears of corn to produce just 1 tablespoon of corn oil—we're talking about a basket of corn, not something we'd easily polish off in a meal. We were simply not designed to tolerate such high amounts of oil a single serving.

Fat holds in the taste of food. It has a chameleon quality that absorbs flavors without imparting its own. It's a common ingredient in our favorite fast foods: french fries (which contain 80 times the fat found in a baked potato), chicken-fried steak, battered and deep-fried fish, commercial salad dressings, hash browns, fried eggs, ice cream (with nuts), and so forth.

Once fat leaves the stomach, it takes 3 hours to finish being digested. Once fat enters the first section of the small intestine, bile salts are released from the gallbladder to emulsify the fats before they travel through the intestines for absorption. Given this long time frame for absorption, fat provides a sense of fullness, of solidity, of a stick-to-your-ribs satisfaction. Fat also has a stabilizing effect on blood sugar, which makes it a common food to eat in place of sugar because it can sometimes delay cravings. The smooth texture and lack of fiber make it similar to baby food; no doubt there is some association with fat (particularly dairy fat) as a comfort food.

About Fats

Fatty acids are the building blocks of fats. It is only through the mechanics of modern industry that we are able to extract huge amounts of oils from seeds and nuts. As mentioned earlier, it takes more than a dozen ears of corn to obtain just 1 tablespoon of corn oil. A typical order of fast-food french fries can contain more than 2 tablespoons of very poor refined oil that has been overheated and used throughout the day, which forms free radicals that can injure our tissues and weaken our arteries and heart. Research has shown that meals with a high oil content can suppress immune function and increase the spread of cancer growth.

All naturally occurring fats have varying amounts of saturated, monounsaturated, and polyunsaturated fatty acids. Although the average Western diet contains a combination of these types, for many years there has been an emphasis on saturated fats. Saturated fatty acids are usually found in animal products such as whole milk, cheese, butter, egg yolks, beef, lamb, and pork. Polyunsaturated fatty acids occur in high levels in vegetable oils, including corn, sesame, safflower, sunflower, soybean, and cottonseed. Monounsaturated fatty acids can be found in olive, canola (rapeseed), peanut, and avocado oils as well as in nuts and seeds.

Highly saturated coconut and palm oils, are a common ingredient in processed foods. Early studies in which animals were fed hydrogenated coconut oil that was devoid of any essential fatty acids determined that coconut oil was a plaque builder and injurious to heart tissue. However, recent research has proved otherwise, with numerous claims of antimicrobial and anticarcinogenic benefits. Yet the value of coconut oil still has to be determined with certainty.

Rethinking Olive Oil

The diet of the Mediterranean cultures features olive oil, which because of its monounsaturated fatty acids (MUFAs) has been considered heart healthy. It is touted to lower the risk of heart disease, total cholesterol, and low-density lipoprotein (LDL) cholesterol (the "bad" cholesterol) levels and to normalize blood clotting.

Yet recent research from University of Maryland School of Medicine researcher Robert Vogel found that eating bread dipped in olive oil caused forearm arteries to constrict, suggesting cellular damage. Japanese researchers have also shown that monounsaturated fat caused elevated blood sugar and triglycerides in rodents that were predisposed to diabetes.

Caldwell B. Esselstyn Jr., a former surgeon, researcher, and clinician at the Cleveland Clinic, convincingly argues that a plant-based, oil-free diet can not only prevent and stop the progression of heart disease but also reverse its effects. Esselstyn began his research with a group of patients who joined his study after traditional medical procedures to treat their advanced coronary conditions had failed. Within months of following a plant-based, oil-free diet, their angina symptoms eased, their cholesterol levels dropped significantly, and they experienced a marked improvement in blood flow to the heart. Twenty years later, most of Esselstyn's patients are still following his program and remain "heart-attack proof."

Regardless of the type of fatty acid you consume, it's worth remembering that all fats can be potentially harmful if excessively eaten. Diets high in any kind of fat (with the exception of fish oils) have been associated with cancer. Research with native Greenland Inuit populations has shown that the oils in cold-water fish lower serum triglycerides (blood fats) and can prevent blood clotting. This finding has spawned an entire industry of fish oil supplements being hawked to consumers for cardiovascular health and blood clot prevention. However, fish oils do not effectively lower the levels of LDL. There have even been some studies that reveal fish oil supplements can actually increase LDL cholesterol.

Fish oils have long been thought as cardiovascular protective, but this has recently come into question. A review of 20 studies covering nearly

70,000 participants has found no statistically significant evidence that omega-3 supplementation (referred to as fish oil supplements) is linked to lower risk of heart attack, stroke, or premature death.

With all the conflicting opinions and contradictory research on oil consumption and supplements, the wisest and safest choice seems to be the less the better.

Oxygen Bandits

The sole purpose of the 11 to 14 breaths we take every minute—more than 17,250 breaths a day—is to obtain oxygen. Our lungs process this oxygen and send it via the circulatory system to all body cells, whose function depends on this fuel. (The brain can be irreversibly damaged if it is deprived of oxygen for only 4 minutes.)

As you inhale, millions of oxygen molecules attach themselves to red blood cells and travel to cell structures by way of the arteries, arterioles, and capillaries. In the narrow capillaries, the oxygen molecules disengage from the red blood cell and pass through the capillary wall to enter cells. In exchange, cellular waste (carbon dioxide) enters the capillary, attaches itself to the red blood cell, and hitchhikes to the lungs, where it is discharged through exhalation.

The best way to upset this flow of red cells is by consuming a fatty meal. Fat, by various mechanisms, makes the blood sticky. In digestion, fats are broken down and emulsified into small droplets called *chylomicrons*. Different from other nutrients, such as glucose and amino acids, which are carried directly to the liver via the bloodstream, fats are absorbed into the lymphatic system, a slow-moving auxiliary circulation to the blood system. The lymphatic system bypasses the liver and empties the fat into the blood. Then the heart pumps the fat throughout the body. The bottom line: Consuming an excessive amount of fat means a bloodstream full of fat.

Fat coats the cells and makes them bond together. The cell sticking, or clumping, traps them. When red blood cells clump together and slow the general circulation, we have rouleaux formation or red blood cell aggregation, often described as sticky blood cell syndrome. This gumming of red blood cells prevents oxygen molecules from entering the cells. The result is oxygen deprivation.

Timothy Regan at the cardiovascular research laboratory of Wayne State University College of Medicine studied the way a high-fat meal prohibited oxygen supplies to the heart tissue. Healthy volunteers without a history of heart trouble consumed a high-fat meal. At peak levels of fat in the blood, the oxygen uptake by the heart was reduced by 20 percent.

Because cancer cells will thrive in a deoxygenated environment, any substance that diminishes cellular oxygen can foster the growth of cancer cells. Excess sugar is stored as a fatty substance, so in effect, a high-sugar diet would also cause oxygen reduction.

Cancer Risks with a High-Fat Diet

It has been found that a diet high in oil content can suppress immunity and promote the growth and spread of cancer.

China, Japan, and Singapore, where the majority of people consume a low-fat diet, have the lowest incidences of breast cancer globally. Countries that consume a higher percentage of fats, such as England, Scotland, Wales, and Finland, have greater incidence of breast cancer. Finnish women on high-fat diets showed higher estradiol (one of the most powerful natural forms of estrogen) levels than did Asian women—and a higher degree of breast cancer. In the United States, 1 in 8 women (just under 12 percent) will develop invasive breast cancer over the course of her lifetime. We know from research that a high-fat diet can increase estradiol by 30 percent. Many breast tumors are fueled by estrogen.

Although estrogens are normal and essential hormones for men and women, the higher the level of estrogen, the higher the chance of stimulating certain kinds of breast cancer. On high-fat diets, estrogen levels increase; on low-fat diets, they decrease. This pattern is also found in prostate cancer. Men who consume diets that emphasize animal proteins tend to have more testosterone and higher levels of estrogen when compared with men who eat less animal protein and fat. Usually, men consuming a low-fat diet are taking in a higher amount of fiber. The advantage of a high-fiber diet is that the fiber bonds to sex hormones, helping discharge them from the body before they can become reabsorbed within the intestine and recirculated in the body.

Dozens of animal studies have shown that a high-fat diet stimulates the growth of cancers. One such study published in the *British Journal of Cancer* found that a 15 percent low-fat diet, strictly followed for two years, lowered estradiol levels by 20 percent.

Animal fats seem to be a bigger problem than vegetable oils. Paolo Toniolo, of the New York University Langone Medical Center, compared the diets of 250 women who had been diagnosed with breast cancer to

499 women who were cancer free; all women were from the same province in northwestern Italy. Both groups consumed identical amounts of olive oil and carbohydrates. The distinguishing factor among the cancer patients was that they had eaten more meat, cheese, butter, and milk. Among the women who consumed more animal products there was a 3 times higher cancer risk compared with the other women in this study.

The power of a vegetarian diet can be undermined by the inclusion of milk, cheese, and other dairy products. According to some studies, lactoovovegetarians (vegetarians who eat milk and egg products) have a cancer risk that is comparable to meat eaters. Although these vegetarians may have been avoiding meat, they were consuming considerable amounts of dairy products that, like meats, contain animal fat and are devoid of fiber.

However, vegetable oil is not exempt from blame entirely. Vegetable oils have shown to affect estrogen levels while increasing cancer-causing free radicals. More than substituting deep-fried onion rings for fried chicken, the wisest preventive, as well as the healing choice, is to eliminate, or dramatically reduce, animal protein and consume a minimum amount of vegetable oils.

Protein Propaganda

I have lived temperately, eating little animal food, and not as an aliment, so much as a condiment for the vegetables which constitute my principle diet.

—Thomas Jefferson

The word *protein* usually conjures instant associations with meats, dairy food, and most recently protein powders. There was a time when people believed they could never get enough protein. In the early 1900s, Americans were advised to eat more than 100 grams of protein daily. When I was in high school during the 1960s, there wasn't a coach worth his salt who didn't advise varsity athletes to boost their protein. "Get that steak in before the big game!"

Weight trainers went a long way to perpetrate the meat–protein association. In my late 20s, I went to a famous West Coast bodybuilder's gym for an evaluation. The owner, a well-known 1950s muscleman who had graced many a muscle magazine cover, looked at my thin body and said, "If you want muscle, ya' gonna haf'ta eat a lotta meat!" He also wanted me to drink a protein drink he had developed that contained four to six eggs. This was the dietary core of his training protocol. I asked, in my youthful naivete, whether it was really necessary to eat that much animal protein. His face scrunched up. I watched the words "Don't be stupid!" fly from his lips as he leaned close to me with his biceps an inch from my nose. "See this?" he said, pointing to his bulging biceps. "Meat! Workin' out, rest, and clean living! That's it! You wanna healthy body? You gotta work for it." (In a sad but ironic turn of events, this champion body builder later succumbed to colon cancer.)

Although there are many myths surrounding protein, the idea that protein is vitally important is not one of them. It is a crucial component of every cell and most of the chemicals necessary for life. We build the proteins in our bodies from amino acids, which are provided from the protein in our diets. Protein is essential for blood vessels, skin, bones, muscles, cartilage, lymph, hair, digestion, enzymes, antibodies, and some hormones. Hundreds of other bodily functions depend on protein. However, this does not mean we must have a high amount of protein to sustain these functions.

Sources of Protein: Animal or Vegetable

The most recent recommendations for protein intake for adults from the World Health Organization and the Food and Agricultural Organization of the United Nations suggest 0.5 gram of protein per kilogram (2.2 pounds) of body weight. So for instance, an adult weighing 150 pounds (70 kilograms) who is functioning in normal working conditions would require about 35 grams of protein daily. A person on a wholly vegetarian diet, consuming between 2,100 and 2,600 calories of a variety of foods daily could be ingesting between 65 and 80 grams of protein, or close to 200 percent of the WHO recommended amount. A person on a standard meat-inclusive diet generally consumes 100 to 120 grams of protein daily, which is 300 to 400 percent above the recommended level!

The protein that I most recommend comes from vegetables, such as beans and bean products. For certain clients (particularly those who are on or are coming off of chemotherapy or radiation), I will sometimes recommend small quantities of animal protein, typically from fish.

For clients who are used to a high-fat and high-meat diet, I suggest a gradual transition to a lower-fat and lower-protein diet, which is most beneficial in the long run. Sometimes, just the small amount of oil used in a lightly sautéed dish or the oil from a sprinkle of nuts as a garnish on grains satisfies an individual's craving for fat. However, clients diagnosed with advanced cancers and on conventional therapy often require a greater amount of protein. Because cancer patients may have trouble digesting a large amount of beans, I recommend a gradual increase in beans along with a slow decrease in animal protein, which often proves easier on digestion and absorption.

I have observed that clients with cancer who are on very strict macrobiotic diets with little or no oil are rarely satisfied with their meals. They constantly crave a variety of other foods, frequently overeat, lose muscle mass, and inevitably became depressed by their diminishing body image, equating it with the progression of their cancer. This doesn't negate the effectiveness of a macrobiotic whole foods approach; however, it does point to the need to individualize a dietary program and maintain some flexibility.

The bottom line: Dietary guidelines depend on a person's previous diet, daily energy demands, and individual physiology and disposition.

Pervasive Protein Poisoning

Excess protein has been linked with osteoporosis, kidney disease, urinary tract calcium stones, and some cancers. In 1982, the National Research Council introduced the link between cancer and protein in its report *Diet, Nutrition, and Cancer*, stating:

> Results of epidemiological studies have suggested possible associations between high intakes of dietary protein and increased risk for cancers at a number of sites. . . . In addition because of the very high correlation between fat and protein in the diets of most Western countries, and the more consistent and often stronger association of these cancers with fat intake, it seems that dietary fat is the more active component. Nevertheless the evidence does not completely preclude the existence of an independent effect of protein.

Since the publication of this report, further research has confirmed the link between high protein consumption and cancer and has shown us that the standard Western diet includes far more protein than we need or is safe.

Research by Willard J. Visek of Cornell University suggests that one of the problems associated with protein breakdown in the body is an excess of ammonia. Cell culture experiments reveal that this excess of ammonia slows the growth of normal cells more than that of cancer cells.

Ammonia has also shown that it can alter the character of RNA, which is the cell's regulator of protein production. In addition, it changes the rate at which thymidine is used for DNA, the cell's genetic material. These qualities of protein metabolism make cells less able to protect themselves from infection and from malignant transformation that is stimulated by ammonia excess. Visek believes that cells inside the human body act the same way as they do in laboratory tissue cultures. Cells in the body are exposed to ammonia whenever protein is broken down. The higher volume of protein consumed, the greater the possibility of producing damaging quantities of ammonia.

Excess protein also increases the chemical compound uric acid, which is produced by the body as a result of the breakdown of purines in protein metabolism. Proteins are nitrogen-based. Since the body is unable to store excess protein, it is broken into amino acids, which enter the bloodstream. These amino acids are converted through a process (deamination) that occurs in the liver to other usable molecules. This process converts nitrogen from the amino acid into ammonia, which is converted by the liver into urea, in what is known as the urea cycle.

Urea is a compound made up of nitrogen, ammonia, carbon dioxide, and water. Normally, urea, or uric acid, gets filtered from your bloodstream by the kidneys and is then flushed out of the body via the urine; however, when too much uric acid accumulates in your body, you are at risk for a condition known as *hyperuricemia* This high intake of purine-containing compounds can cause kidney abnormalities, such as kidney stones and, potentially, kidney failure.

The National Kidney and Urologic Diseases Information Clearinghouse states that uric acid–based kidney stones are likely caused by persistent systemic acidity, which results from a diet rich in animal proteins. Therefore, reducing animal protein intake and getting more protein from plant sources can help reduce the risk of uric acid–based stones. In addition, uric acid can cause gout, a form of arthritis, by forming crystals that accumulate in the joints and cause inflammation.

Excess protein forces the body to mobilize minerals such as bone calcium to neutralize increasing acidity from protein's breakdown products. When the kidneys eliminate these breakdown products, the mobilized calcium goes with it.

Richard B. Mazess of the Bone Mineral Laboratory at the University of Wisconsin studied a group of 217 Alaskan Inuit living on a high-protein diet of fish, marine mammals, and caribou. The Inuit consumed up to 3 times the amount of protein as the average American. By the age of 40, individuals who ingested this excessive protein had caused enough calcium loss to reduce their bone density by 10 to 15 percent compared to those in the same area eating reduced levels of protein.

Although fat is portrayed as the underlying cause of cancers in men, protein has a definite role. Populations that eat meat on a regular basis seem to be at an increased risk for colon cancer. Researchers believe that the fat, protein, natural carcinogens, hormonal excess, and the absence of fiber in meat all play significant roles.

Beans have been noted to lower bile acid production by 30 percent in men with a tendency toward elevated bile acid. Bile acids are necessary for proper fat digestion but in excess have been associated with causing cancer, especially in the large intestine. Case-control studies showed that pinto and navy beans were effective in lowering bile acid production in men at high risk for elevated levels.

Optimum Protein Needs

+ Eat a wide variety of plant foods that provide protein without depending on animal sources: beans, bean products (tempeh, tofu, natural soy sauce, miso), whole grains, and vegetables.
+ Limit the daily intake of protein to only 12 to 15 percent of the total calories ingested; excess protein can turn into glucose and then become stored as body fat.
+ Reduce or eliminate the many types of animal protein that contain high percentages of fat, which can be responsible for numerous disease conditions.
+ Boost athletic performance with effective and clean-burning complex carbohydrates; some athletes require increased total calories as a result of increased energy expenditure.
+ Moderately increase protein intake if you are extremely active or are undergoing conventional cancer therapy (chemotherapy, radiation).
+ Minimize animal protein while transitioning to a plant-based diet.

The Nature's Cancer-Fighting Food Plan includes a varied diet of whole grains, beans, and vegetables that contain all the essential amino acids you need (see Chapter 11 for details). In the past, we were advised to eat certain bean and grain combinations to create complete proteins. Nutrition experts now agree that this type of food-combining strategy is unnecessary in an individual meal because a varied diet of grains, beans, and vegetables can meet all protein needs within the course of a day.

4

Phytochemical Superheroes and Amazing Antioxidants

Don't eat anything your great-grandmother wouldn't recognize as food.

—Michael Pollan

Showdown on the Cellular Frontier: Antioxidants Versus Free Radicals

While oxygen is considered vital to life, scientists are also finding it could contribute to aging and illness. When bananas develop dark spots or an apple turns brown, it's a result of the natural process of oxidation, which happens to all cells in nature, including those in our bodies. Antioxidants help protect us from the damage of oxidation and are found in whole grains, vegetables, beans, fruits, and nuts. When oxygen is metabolized, or burned, by the body, the cells can form byproducts called free radicals.

Free radicals are not political upstarts, but are atoms or groups of atoms with at least one unpaired electron. This makes them highly reactive. They are called "free" because they are missing an essential molecule. Free radicals will rob a molecule from somewhere else to satisfy their need, possibly injuring the cell structure, deteriorating the cell's DNA, and laying the foundation for the development of disease.

This process is helped along by external toxins, such as cigarette smoke and air pollution, which are considered free radical generators. Pesticides and toxins in our food and drink and excessive alcohol consumption also contribute to the development of free radicals. Such cellular damage is known to contribute to the aging process and the development of numerous diseases, including cancer.

On a positive note, free radicals also promote beneficial oxidation, which produces energy and kills bacterial invaders. Sometimes the body's immune system purposely creates them to neutralize viruses and bacteria. However, environmental and dietary factors make controlling free radical development more difficult. Antioxidants are the natural elements that keep these radicals from taking over.

Antioxidants to the Rescue!

Antioxidants protect cells from damage by neutralizing free radicals. To date, the best sources of antioxidants are fruits and vegetables. In 1999, scientists from Johns Hopkins University in Baltimore compared the diets of 123 people over an 11-week period. During the first three weeks of the study, participants consumed varying amounts of fruits, vegetables, and dairy products. Some groups ate up to 4 servings of vegetables and fruits each day.

Scientists measured the ethane levels in participants' breath. This measurement indicates how well the body neutralizes harmful free radicals. The study's conclusions revealed that the participants consuming the most vegetables and fruits had the lowest breath ethane levels. Lead study author, Edgar R. Miller, claims such an antioxidant-rich diet protects the body against cancer and heart disease.

The most popular antioxidants are vitamin C, vitamin E, and beta-carotene (converted by the body into vitamin A). Carrots, broccoli, sweet potatoes, cantaloupe, melons, and apricots are particularly high in beta-carotene. For vitamin C, eat dark leafy greens, such as kale, mustard greens, garden cress, turnip greens, broccoli, cauliflower, Brussels sprouts, etc. For vitamin E, eat nuts, almonds, sunflower seeds, avocado, squash, pumpkin, carrots, parsnips, quinoa, olive oil, fish, tofu, etc.

Eating these foods is an effective and natural way to prevent DNA damage from free radicals and keep cancer from developing.

The Phytochemical Superheroes

There are hundreds of plant chemicals known as phytochemicals found in whole grains, beans, vegetables, fruits, nuts, and seeds. These chemicals protect plants from disease. These biologically active compounds have also been proven to help defend the body from disease and aging. Some phytochemicals have shown promise in inhibiting tumor growth, while others stop the chain of events that lead to cancer, heart disease, diabetes, and hypertension. Phytochemicals can have antioxidant properties (to protect against harmful cell damage), anticancer properties (to prevent the initiation and growth of cancer), and antiestrogen properties (for improved libido, better mental health, arthritis prevention, and better cardiac health). Consuming a whole foods diet (whole grains, vegetables, beans, fruits, nuts, seeds) will provide a wide mix of phytochemicals (phenolic compounds; terpenoids; pigments; and other natural antioxidants such as vitamins A, C, and E), as well as some nonnutritive substances that have been associated with prevention and/or treatment of chronic diseases such as heart disease, diabetes, hypertension, and cancer. At last, the wisdom of eating your vegetables has been documented.

PHYTOCHEMICAL SOURCES

THIS TABLE LISTS the vegetable sources of key phytochemicals and nutrients.

PLANT FAMILY	TYPES	PRIME NUTRIENTS
Whole grains	Barley, brown rice, buckwheat, millet, oat, rye, quinoa, wheat (including bulgur)	B vitamins, soluble and insoluble fiber
Legumes	Adzuki, black bean, chickpea, lentil, pea, pinto bean, soybean	B vitamins, fiber, protein
Alliums	Chive, garlic, leek, onion, scallion, shallot	Anticancer elements, heart-disease fighter
Leafy greens	Bok choy, collard, endive, kale, lettuce, root vegetable tops (turnip, beet), Swiss chard	Calcium; iron; magnesium; vitamins A, B, and E
Cruciferous	Bok choy, broccoli, Brussels sprout, cabbage, cauliflower, rutabaga, sprouts, turnip, watercress	Calcium, iron, magnesium, vitamins A and C

PLANT FAMILY	TYPES	PRIME NUTRIENTS
Umbelliferous	Carrot, celery, cilantro, fennel, parsley, parsnip	Beta-carotene, vitamins A and C
Cucurbitaceous (gourd family)	Cucumber, muskmelon, pumpkin, squash, watermelon	Beta-carotene, fiber, iron, phosphorus, vitamins A and C
Convolvulaceous	Sweet potato	Potassium, vitamins A and C
Solanaceous (nightshade family)	Capsicum, eggplant, pepper, potato, tomato	Potassium, vitamins A and C
Fruit	Apple, apricot, banana, orange, peach, pear	Fiber, potassium, vitamins A and C

The specific manner in which plant compounds help combat disease is still being researched, and the molecular structures are equally as complex. Some may work as antioxidants, others as enzyme inhibitors. Current scientific research has identified approximately 14 different classes of phytochemical compounds. With names like isoflavones (found in soy and other beans), sulforaphane, lycopene, lutein, xanthene, anthocyanin, isothiocyanates, allium, glutathione, beta-carotene, quercetin, carotenoids, and glucosinolates, they sound more like *Star Trek* terminology than substances that are fast becoming the new research frontier in the battle against America's deadliest diseases. The most researched class of phytochemicals is the phenolic group, including monophenols, polyphenols, and flavonoids, which are found in most cereals, vegetables, and fruits.

Phytochemical Cancer Prevention Research

For the more academically inclined, the following data, based on a variety of research studies, support the benefits of consuming phytochemicals to prevent and fight cancer:

✦ While fruits and vegetables are often mentioned as the cancer-prevention twins, scientists at the Fred Hutchinson Cancer Research Center in Seattle think vegetables are the only group that can aid in warding off cancer. Based on the results of a study on prostate cancer prevention in the January 2000 issue of the *Journal of the National Cancer Institute*, they found that a diet rich in vegetables seems to reduce the risk of developing prostate cancer by nearly 50 percent. This was especially helped by vegetables of the cruciferous variety (their flowers have four petals suggestive of a cross), such as broccoli, cabbage, and Brussels sprouts. The popular notion of tomatoes being extremely protective against cancer was debunked in the study. Fruits did not offer any preventive advantage.

"We found no protective effect at all from fruits," said Alan Kristal, an investigator with the center's cancer prevention research program. While their study looked only at prostate cancer risk in 1,230 middle-aged men, Kristal said a growing body of evidence from other studies of diet and cancer indicates the same effect may hold true for other cancers as well. "We think it's all in the vegetables," he said. "Go ahead and eat fruit as well," Kristal remarked, "but do it because it tastes good."

✦ An early 1990s study that spanned five years and cost $20 million examined the anticancer potential of plant foods. Researchers concluded that the foods highest in anticancer activity are garlic, soybeans, cabbage, ginger, licorice, and the umbelliferous vegetables (carrots, celery, cilantro, parsley, and parsnips). Foods with a modest level of cancer-protective activity are onions, flax, citrus, tumeric, cruciferous vegetables (broccoli, Brussels sprouts, cabbage, and cauliflower), solanaceous vegetables (tomatoes and peppers), brown rice, and whole wheat. Other foods found to contain a measure of anticancer activity are oats, barley, mint, rosemary, thyme, oregano, sage, basil, cucumber, cantaloupe, and berries.

✦ Some have claimed that phytochemicals may be diminished in the process of cooking. However, research has shown that most of the compounds are heat stable and are not significantly lost in hot water. Although vitamin C might be reduced through cooking, carotenoids and indoles (found in broccoli) may actually be increased.

✦ A complete variety of phenolic compounds are contained in whole grains, vegetables, herbs, and fruits, so that you may be ingesting as much as 1 gram of phenolic compounds per day. These compounds can influence the quality, digestibility, and stability of foods by acting as flavorings, colorants, and antioxidants.

✦ Glutathione S-transferase (GST), a cancer inhibitor, is stimulated by the phthalides in celery seed, the sulfides in garlic and onions, the dithiolethiones and isothiocyanates in broccoli and other cruciferous vegetables, along with the bitter liminoids in citrus, and the curcumins in ginger and tumeric.

✦ Flax has also been shown to be an extremely rich source of lignans, which have been shown to be anticarcinogenic. The lignan metabolites bear a structural similarity to estrogens and can bind to estrogen receptors to inhibit the growth of estrogen-stimulated breast cancer.

✦ Soybeans have shown very high levels of numerous compounds with established anticancer activity. These compounds include phytates, protease inhibitors, phytosterols, saponins, and isoflavonoids. Soybeans are thought to be a contributing factor to the low incidence of breast and prostate cancers in Japan. Chinese citizens who regularly consume soybeans and/or tofu have only half as many occurrences of cancer of the stomach, colon, rectum, breast, and lung compared with those citizens who rarely consume soy or soy products. Decreased prostate cancer has also been observed in Hawaiian men of Japanese descent who regularly consume grain (rice) and bean products (tofu, tempeh).

✦ Whole grain is not without its powerful phytochemical members, containing ample amounts of plant sterols, phytases, phytoestrogens, tocotrienols, lignans, ellagic acid, and saponins. These powerful substances reduce the risk of cardiovascular disease and cancer. Of particular importance is that the active phytochemicals are concentrated in the bran and the germ, confirming that the health benefits of grains truly come from eating grains in their whole form. The refinement of whole wheat illustrates this point clearly: Refinement causes a 200- to 300-fold loss in its phytochemical makeup.

Raw Versus Cooked?

Research has shown that the vitamins and minerals in raw vegetables may be much less available to the body than those present in cooked vegetables. Cooking carrots can enhance carotenoid absorption by as much as 500 percent. This also holds true for other vegetables rich in phytochemical carotenoids.

A study released in the June 1999 issue of *Scientist* reported that cooking and mashing vegetables increases carotenoid absorption from 4 to 20 percent. By softening the plant's cells, cooking allows for better intestinal absorption of these nutrients. Carotenoids, such as the beta-carotene in carrots, the lutein in yellow peppers, and the lycopene in tomatoes are all known to offer cancer protection. Steaming broccoli increases its glucosinolates, which may help fight cancer. This doesn't mean you should avoid raw vegetables but rather be sure to get a mixture of cooked vegetables into your daily diet.

To someone with irritable bowel syndrome (IBS), raw food might be an invitation for pain. Foods that have not had their roughage softened by the element of heat can create digestive discomfort in someone with compromised conditions. For someone who is anemic, liberating needed nutrition from deep within the vegetable cellulose fibers requires heat. The elderly often find raw food equally irritating if not nutritionally deficient, so the recommendation to eat a daily salad doesn't apply across the board.

Steaming, quick boiling, and light sautéing increase the antioxidant levels in vegetables. The researchers of the previously cited 1999 study theorized that this is due to the "softening of the vegetable cell matrix where valuable nutritional compounds are bound."

Unfortunately, sloppy science prevails in the raw-food movement. Extreme advocates for a raw diet mistakenly conclude, and in black-and-white tones, that all cooked foods are bad. This is simply not true. It is true that food cooked at extremely high temperatures, especially fried or barbecued, forms toxic compounds and many nutrients diminish. Overcooking can also reduce some of the important water-soluble vitamins (vitamin C and the B vitamins) that we require on a daily basis. According to Mark Fuhrman, writing in his newsletter, "Healthy Times":

> Every living cell makes enzymes for its own activities. Human cells are no exception. Our glands secrete enzymes into the digestive tract to aid in the digestion of food. However, after they are ingested, the enzymes contained in plants do not function as enhancements or replacements for human digestive enzymes. These molecules exist to serve the plant's purpose, not ours. The plant enzymes get digested by our own digestive juices along with the rest of the food and are absorbed and utilized as nutrients.
>
> Contrary to what many raw-food websites claim, the enzymes contained in the plants we eat do not catalyze chemical reactions that occur in humans. The plant enzymes merely are broken down into simpler molecules by our own powerful digestive juices. Even when the food is consumed raw, plant enzymes do not aid in their

own digestion inside the human body. It is not true that eating raw food demands less enzyme production by your body, and dietary enzymes inactivated by cooking have an insignificant effect on your health and your body's enzymes.

Only a minimal amount of nutrients are reduced by common forms of cooking, such as simmering. Some nutrients are even made more absorbable. These nutrients would have been absent from the diet if the vegetables had been eaten raw. Cooking can also destroy some of the harmful antinutrients that bind intestinal minerals and block the utilization of nutrients.

The very destruction of these antinutrients actually increases digestive absorption. Some forms of cooking, like steaming, break down the cellulose from plant fibers, altering the plant's cell structures. Therefore, less of your own stomach enzymes are required to digest the food, instead of more. Conversely, roasting nuts and baking cereals reduces the availability and absorbability of protein.

The traditional act of cooking also significantly improves the digestibility or bioavailability of starchy foods such as tubers (potatoes, yams), squashes, grains, and legumes through the process of gelatinization.

Some roots, seeds, stems, and leaves contain natural toxins that can be eliminated through cooking. According to Andrew Weil, moist raw beans and sprouts, especially alfalfa, are actually high in the natural toxin canavanine, which can damage the immune system. Ordinary button mushrooms may contain agaritine, which is a natural carcinogen. Even celery has its dark side: It tends to produce psoralens, compounds that sensitize the skin to the harmful effects of ultraviolet radiation in sunlight. While our body's immune system can often flush these toxins out, a system that is overly taxed can become significantly weakened.

Enzyme Loss?

A dubious claim from hard-core raw-food propagandists is that cooking heat destroys valuable enzymes. The fallacy that's promoted here is that the fragile, heat-sensitive enzymes held within the plants we consume catalyze chemical reactions that occur in humans and aid in food digestion. However, this is simply not true.

Cooking sometimes alters plant cell structure so that nutrients become more susceptible to our own body's digestive enzymes (such as by gelatinizing starch, destroying antiamylases, or antiproteases). As a result, in many cases, cooked food actually requires less enzyme action for digestion than raw food.

The raw-food movement's notion that our body has a limited enzyme potential and therefore requires a large part of our food to be uncooked is, according to much research, idealistic fiction. Digestive enzymes in food are exactly how they're described: a supportive step for digestion.

Naturally, enzymes can help, whether they're inside or outside the body. Examples of enzyme activity occurring outside the body are the ripening of fruits, sprouting of grains and seeds, pickling, or the aging of meat. These are forms of external food processing that numerous cultures have practiced for thousands of years to naturally improve digestion. Cooking can be considered an act of digestion in this regard.

How Much Should We Eat?

The following recommendations are generalized, but worthy of making a daily goal. Additional details and vegetable lists are provided in Chapter 12.

+ Eat enough to maintain a healthy and consistent weight.
+ Eat a variety of vegetables from the leafy green, root vegetable, and ground/round groups. Make sure your selection is colorful and prepared in a variety of styles, including raw. For those prone to any kind of stomach acidity, anemia, irritable bowel syndrome, or ulcers, raw foods can be quickly boiled or lightly steamed to soften them for better digestion, while remaining crisp and vitamin rich.
+ Eat a minimum of 3 cups of vegetables daily.
+ Enjoy fibrous seasonal fruits, such as apples, apricots, pears, and peaches, which are usually lower in sugar content, several times daily, if craved. Individuals prone to fatigue, gas, mineral deficiency, or sensitive to acidity are encouraged minimize their fruit intake. Fruit juice, a concentration of sugar minus the fiber, is not recommended. It is better to eat the whole fruit. In cases of digestive weakness, fruit can be slightly cooked into compotes or baked to reduce acidity; in such cases, fruit might be better avoided during healing.
+ Make soup once or twice a week. Soup can last several days and will satisfy the most finicky of palates (see Chapter 13 for recipes).

BURDOCK: THE GARDEN PEST YOU'LL LEARN TO LOVE

NATIVE TO EUROPE and Asia, burdock now grows wild throughout the United States, thriving in backyards, overgrown fields, and parks. Its leaves, which grow up to two feet, are large and heart shaped. Its carrot-like root is dark brown.

Burdock stimulates the flow of bile by improving liver function. Anything done to aid liver function will improve blood quality and overall health. Another detoxing bonus is burdock's diuretic properties. It contains a compound called inulin, which is believed to enhance immunity by encouraging white blood cell activity. A 1984 study in *Mutation Research* showed that burdock protected cells exposed to carcinogenic chemicals from mutations, which can lead to cancer. A 1996 study published in *Pharmacology Letters* found that burdock extract has antiviral—in particular, anti-HIV—properties.

Recommended by herbalists and used in numerous cultural folk medicines, burdock is generally considered to be a blood cleanser and is an essential ingredient in many herbal cancer formulas. It was a staple in Japanese monasteries, where monks were given side dishes to increase stamina.

With a mild, earthy flavor, burdock can be added to soups and stews and combines well with sweet vegetables such as carrot and onion. It can be purchased in many natural food stores as well as in Asian markets. The Japanese call it *gobo*.

The Five-Factor Rx for Veggie-Phobia

> I do not like broccoli, and I haven't liked it since I was a little kid and my mother made me eat it. I'm president of the United States, and I'm not going to eat any more broccoli!
> —George H. W. Bush, former U.S. president, 1990

When former President George H. W. Bush made national front-page news with his broccoli statement, he opened up a controversial public dialogue on America's love–hate relationship with this frequently maligned vegetable. News media debated the topic for days, nutritionists rallied with defensive assertions on broccoli's abundant value, and broccoli growers sought to capitalize on this negative publicity with a positive spin and all-out campaign.

Overnight, Bush became the poster boy for vegetable haters throughout the country. I recall seeing a news cartoon that had an adult restaurant diner pushing away a broccoli plate; the caption read: "If the president won't eat it, I won't either." However, this is the tip of the veggie-phobia iceberg. The average American eats only about 1.5 servings of vegetables per day and less than 1 serving of fruit per day.

A recent survey of American eating habits showed that only 1 in 11 Americans met the guidelines for eating at least 3 servings of vegetables and at least 2 servings of fruit per day. This survey also pointed out that 1 in 9 Americans had not eaten any fruit or vegetable the day they were polled, and 45 percent reported eating vegetables but no fruit that day.

Vegetables have played such a small role in most of our diets, chiefly due to a lack of education. Most people still think that french fries, a tomato, and some lettuce on a sandwich should suffice as vegetables, when it is a far stretch to think that this is sufficient vegetable fare. The importance of vegetables in the daily diet has only recently been emphasized, and we lack the skills for selection, preparation, and cooking. Here are five simple ways to create greater appeal and enjoyment of vegetables:

REDUCE CONSUMPTION OF REFINED AND SIMPLE CARBOHYDRATES. The frequent eating of concentrated sugar lessens the desire for and taste appeal of vegetables. A child who loves his soda pop won't get excited about eating squash, just as an adult who consumes a bowl of ice cream has little inclination to eat turnips afterward. The solution? Eat less sweets and stick to small amounts of fruit, fruit juice–sweetened treats, and natural syrups and malts (barley malt, rice syrup, or maple syrup).

EAT MORE VEGETABLES. Consume a wide variety of colorful vegetables on a daily basis. Make vegetables more familiar to your taste buds. Different cooking styles also create a greater sense of texture and variety in meals. Try vegetables steamed, raw, water sautéed, baked, or added to soups to avoid boredom.

AVOID EATING BETWEEN MEALS. While it might be a good general suggestion to eat more frequently throughout the day, allow 3 to 4 hours between meals. Constant snacking can reduce the desire for vegetables.

CHEW YOUR FOOD. This might sound insulting, however, few of us really chew our food. We gulp and wash food down. Watch people eat for 5 minutes in a restaurant, and you'll see diners virtually inhaling their food. Are you any different? Being carbohydrates, vegetables begin their digestion in the mouth. When chewed thoroughly, they impart a natural sweetness that lingers.

LEARN TO COOK. Believe it or not, this can be invaluable. I'll never forget my first garden and the joy at being able to go into the backyard, pick some carrots and greens, and then go prepare them. When you don't have access to a garden, visit the local farmers' markets, talk with the growers, and buy fresh, quality vegetables whenever possible. After taking a short cooking class and learning the basics, I'd invite friends over as a weekly ritual and cook a meal. Learning simple food preparation can take the fear out of cooking, make your food more enjoyable, and reduce the compulsion to eat out all the time. Cooking at home is also easier on the budget and, as a bonus, increases your sense of self-worth.

The Vegetable Rainbow

It is an integral part of Asian cooking to consider that the visual preparation of food offers satisfaction of our psychological appetite. This term implies the physical arrangement of foods in various colors to inspire the visual appetite. Considering the variety of plants available to us, different pigments in our food not only lend unique health benefits but also enhance the sensory enjoyment of our eating experience.

There are approximately 200 known plant pigments in our food. Contained within these pigments are over 800 flavonoids, 450 carotenoids, and 150 anthocyanins. Plant pigments protect us from disease by combating free radicals to offer protection from oxidative damage and stimulate immune function.

Some marketing techniques would like potential consumers to believe that phytochemical and antioxidant protection can be delivered exclusively via supplements. The long-term benefits of supplementations are currently unknown, requiring further confirmation from large-scale intervention trials. We do know that regular consumption of natural phytochemical superheroes (whole grains, vegetables, legumes, and fruits) produces substantial health benefits. While some of these foods have high levels of antioxidants, many of them are thought to act synergistically. Therefore, a pill or potion may exert a different physiological effect in the body from that of naturally occurring phytochemicals.

At this point, the safest and most economical advice is to depend more on consuming real foods in their whole form. But the key in doing so with gusto and enthusiasm is to try a greater variety of vegetables.

From root varieties (carrot, onion, turnip, radish, parsnip) to ground plants (squash, cabbage, cauliflower) to greens (chard, collard, kale) to sweet vegetables (carrot, corn), the combinations can be plentiful, satisfying, and delicious. Adding more vegetables cooked in different ways not only ensures better health and easier healing but reduces cravings for sweets while adding a welcomed variety of tastes and textures.

Meat, Dairy, and the Vegetarian Option

Until recently, many eyebrows would have been raised
by suggestion that an imbalance of normal dietary
components could lead to cancer and cardiovascular
disease. . . . Today, the accumulation of . . .
evidence . . . makes this notion not only possible, but
certain. . . . (The) dietary factors responsible (are)
principally meat and fat intake.

—Gio B. Gori, deputy director of the Division
of Cancer Cause and Prevention,
National Cancer Institute

For the Love of Meat

Americans love their meat. A leading hamburger chain advertises "billions and billions sold." Many males take an unquestioned pride in identifying themselves as meat-and-potatoes men, associating themselves with staple-food character qualities that are basic, simple, and solid.

However, despite America's love affair with meat and the meat industry's intensive marketing efforts, the necessity of meat in the daily diet is being given serious reconsideration by leading scientific evidence.

There is no question that modern society's dietary habits are excessive when it comes to animal protein. The average American eats approximately 70 grams of animal protein daily from a total protein intake of 107 grams or more. Compare this with the daily protein intake in Asia of 56 grams of protein, of which merely 8 grams might be from animal sources. While beef consumption has dropped by more than 13 percent over the last 230 years, Americans are still eating nearly 65 pounds of red meat per person annually. Recent publicized reductions in red meat consumption have been compensated by an increased intake of poultry and fish. Still, hamburger is America's favorite single source of fat.

According to Jeremy Rifkin in *Beyond Beef*, the average middle-class American consumes more than 2,000 pounds of grain each year, but four-fifths of that grain is consumed indirectly by eating grain-fed animals. Essentially, we now consume our grain through a "beef processor." In contrast, Asian adults consume only 300 to 400 hundred pounds of grain per year and most it is eaten directly.

Each year the average American family eats half a steer, a whole pig, 100 chickens, 556 eggs, and 280 gallons of milk products. Using these estimates, over an entire lifetime, the average American eats the flesh of 15 cows, 211 hogs, 900 chickens, 12 sheep, thousands of eggs, hundreds of gallons of milk and ice cream, and hundreds of pounds of cheese and butter. We are, literally, eating the farm.

Meat and dairy products provide the most significant source of dietary fat for Americans. Because of this, their impact on dietary-related cancers cannot be ignored. Combine this with the common American habit of adding additional fats and oils to our dishes, and you now have a potent recipe for cancer development, most notably breast, ovarian, prostate, and colon.

A 1992 Hawaiian study found that animal fat and protein, especially from sausage, processed cold cuts, beef, lamb, and whole-milk dairy products was associated with the highest rates of breast cancer.

Meat excess is also cited as a factor in escalating glandular cancers because its lack of fiber contributes to increased hormone levels by reducing the fecal excretion of estrogen. Higher childhood protein levels have been cited as a primary reason for early menarche (the first menstruation), increased body weight and height, and breast cancer. Historically, high protein levels have been inversely associated with longevity.

The connection between excessive protein intake and osteoporosis has been well established. In a nutritional report posted on a popular website, Michael Klaper takes a stronger position for the elimination of animal protein in the diet:

> If you are not convinced that animal foods cause osteoporosis, consider this: the ethnic group on the planet with the worst osteoporosis is the Eskimos, who live up in the Arctic. They eat all this fish, and all this seal meat, resulting in excess amounts of protein racing through their bloodstream. They have horrific incidences of osteoporosis from the steady drain of calcium from their bodies. . . . You're not doing yourself a favor if you think, "well this chicken and fish is lower fat food. It looks white, it's not red and bloody, so it's cleaner." Kid yourself not: animal muscle is animal muscle. It doesn't matter if it flaps a wing, moves a shoulder, or wiggles a tail. Animal muscle is essentially the same stuff from species to species. It all contains essentially identical amounts of protein and fat, very little carbohydrates and lots of cholesterol. Researchers have done studies taking people eating red meats and changing their diet to one consisting of fish and chicken. Surprise! Their cholesterol levels did not drop a bit. There's no reason that they would—the only difference between chicken/fish and beef is the color of the meat. Changing the color of the meat does not change the amount of cholesterol in the meat. . . . We are evolving as a species. What our caveman ancestors ate is of little importance to us now. The question is what is the best diet for modern human beings? Medical literature is clearly showing that the less animal fat and animal protein you put in your system, the healthier you are going to be.

Eating an excess of meat can also lead to high iron storage and may increase cancer as well as heart disease risk. One factor that might account for why men, who tend to eat greater volumes of animal protein, are more susceptible to heart disease than women is the type of iron found in meat and absorbed by the human intestine.

Comparing chicken to beef yields some surprising nutrient percentages: 3.5 ounces of broiled lean flank steak is calorically 56 percent fat and 42 percent protein, and contains approximately 70 milligrams cholesterol. Light and dark chicken with the skin is calorically 51 percent fat and 46 percent protein, and has 88 milligrams cholesterol. They are nearly identical. According to *Bowes and Church's Food Values of Portions Commonly Used*, chicken breast without the skin is calorically about 20 percent fat and chicken franks have fully 68 percent of calories from fat. Most processed chicken runs between 30 and 60 percent of calories from fat.

A Historical Perspective

In his book, laboriously titled *Report on the Effects of a Peculiar Regimen on Scirrhous Tumors and Cancerous Ulcers* (1809), William Lambe made a then-novel association between increased meat consumption and cancer development. Eighty-three years later, a *Scientific American* article made the bold assertion that cancer was "most frequent among those branches of the human race where carnivorous habits prevail."

In 1907, the *New York Times* reported on an interesting study that contrasted the eating habits of numerous ethnic groups in the Chicago area. The Irish, Scandinavians, and Germans were described as heavy meat eaters with high cancer death rates. By contrast, the Italians and Chinese, who relied more on grains (polenta, rice) and grain products (pasta, noodles) and lower meat consumption, had lower cancer rates. This study included 4,600 cases over a 7-year period, which began in 1900.

Writing in his 1916 book, *Notes on the Causation of Cancer*, Rollo Russell stated that cancer death rates were highest "in countries that eat more flesh."

During World War I, cancer rates fell significantly. Ironically, during these times of economic belt-tightening and diminished food production, meats and fats were scarce. In Denmark, the death rate from non-war-related disease was reduced by 34 percent.

During World War II, similar statistics were noticed, and by this time, documenting such information had become more sophisticated. The millions of European women who were forced to reduce their intake of meats and fats owing to the war had, in the process, also greatly reduced their risk of cancer and heart attack. This effect lasted until a full 7 years beyond the end of the war.

Questioning Meat Quality

> Much meat, much malady.
>
> —Thomas Fuller, *Gnomologia* (1732)

Putting aside evolutionary, nutritional, philosophical, moral, sociological, agricultural, and economical reasons for drastic meat reduction and/or elimination, is the issue of quality—quality in regard to the way it affects the human organism as well as its effect on the quality of our environment.

Pesticide, bacterial, and viral contamination are too frequently present in the meat Americans consume. With increasing industrialization and changing farming practices, meat, poultry, fish, and dairy products now account for between 60 to 80 percent of the pesticide and organochlorine chemical residues in the American diet. This warrants serious consideration.

Organochlorine is a family of industrial chemicals heavily used in modern farming. Within the umbrella of this chemical compound group, PCBs and dioxins are known to be potent immune system poisons. Fortunately, only 10 percent of pesticide residues in our diets come from grains, vegetables, beans, and fruits. Just changing your diet to a higher percentage of whole natural foods will help minimize your exposure to these powerful carcinogens.

Bacterial contamination of the national meat supply is a growing concern. In 1906, Upton Sinclair penned his now-famous novel *The Jungle*, which shocked Americans with its detailed descriptions of the filthy conditions in slaughterhouses; unfortunately, unsanitary conditions have still not been eliminated. When the media reports people getting sick from contaminated meats, the U.S. Department of Agriculture points its finger at the victims and food preparers, blaming them for faulty storage or inadequate cooking.

The evidence of bovine leukemia in American cattle herds is another concern. Viruses have been discovered in the milk and meat of affected cattle, but it is thought that they are killed through cooking. Although there is no evidence that humans can contract cancer from viruses found in meat, a greater concern is the long-term effects of exposure—for example we may see a gradual reduction in the resistance to lymphoma (a type of lymphatic cancer) in humans who have relied on meat and dairy for years.

Bovine growth hormone (BGH) is a genetically engineered hormone that when injected into dairy cows, increases milk production by as much as 25 percent. However, it has a tendency to cause infections, which demand antibiotic treatment. The residues from these antibiotics then show up in milk products and are absorbed into our bodies by ingestion.

Finally, although more disease connections are inevitable, there is the dreadful condition of bovine spongiform encephalopathy (BSE), frequently referred to as mad cow disease. It first made an appearance in England during 1985. This spreading contagion necessitated killing more than 120,000 cows and destroying their bodies by incineration, as required by British law.

This issue of meat quality only compounds the argument for the immediate reduction, or elimination, of animal products from the daily diet. Trying a three-month dietary experiment with reduced animal protein can show very positive and noticeable benefits. More than any research, this kind of personal test can provide the most enduring motivation for a permanent change of habit.

Meat Eating and Cancer Research

Available current nutritional research has consistently concluded that plant-based diets provide cancer protection, whereas animal-based diets have the potential to stimulate and nurture certain cancers.

We have learned, repeatedly, that it is not necessary to depend on animal sources for our protein needs. Organic (ideally) plant sources (grains, beans, and bean products) are equivalent in quality to animal sources yet are lacking the contaminated elements of saturated fat, hormones, excess cholesterol, bacteria, viruses, pesticides, and numerous other harmful substances, such as GMO foods, particularly corn products. The following are highlights of this research:

+ The Seventh-Day Adventists are a religious group that strictly avoids smoking and drinking. Approximately half of its members do not eat meat, while the remaining half consume meat, but in a reduced quantity. Long-term studies on the group show that the incidence of breast cancer is 2.5 times greater among non-Adventist meat eaters than among the Adventist women. Similarly, vegetarian non-Adventist women also show a reduced level of breast cancer, but this changes to a grimmer picture of a cancer increase when the women consume eggs and milk (ovolactovegetarians). The recurring conclusion of many studies focusing on a link between breast cancer and fat is that there is a positive relationship with animal fat and protein consumption but not with plant fats.

+ In a large study on the meat–cancer connection, Takeshi Hirayama of Japan followed a group of 122,000 people for a number of years. Women from this group who consumed meat seven or more times each week had a nearly 4 times greater chance of developing breast cancer compared with women who consumed meat a maximum of one time per week. It was established that those with an intermediate consumption (two to four times per week) were 2.55 times more likely to develop breast cancer than the low-consumption group. The same trends were shown in studies focused on egg, butter, and cheese consumption.

✦ The digestion of meat produces strong carcinogenic substances, particularly deoxycholic acid in the colon. Powerful carcinogens are created when deoxycholic acid is converted into clostridia bacteria in our intestines. It has been established that meat eaters generally have greater amounts of deoxycholic acid than vegetarians, which accounts for their higher rates of colon cancer.

✦ There is some evidence regarding carcinogen production in cooked meat products. Charred meats, in particular, carry polynuclear aromatic compounds such as benzopyrene, which is a known carcinogen. As mentioned earlier in the chapter, there is also evidence that many meats carry viruses that can be killed by thorough cooking, but this line of thought warrants additional research.

✦ Regarding the development of colon cancer, researchers who analyzed and tested human feces claimed that they could distinguish the feces of meat eaters from those of vegetarians by their smell. They reported that the stool of meat eaters smells far stronger and more noxious than that of non–meat eaters. This is due to putrefying animal bacteria to which the colon is subjected for long periods of transit times.

✦ A diet high in animal fats will increase the concentration of saturated fat and arachidonic acid compared with individuals on a vegetarian diet. This concentration alters the types of fatty acids available to tumor cells and increases their growth rate. Some evidence to support this is found in studies that show vegetarian diets associated with decreased tumor growth and longer tumor induction.

✦ Hawaiian researchers published a case-controlled, multiethnic population study that examined the role of dietary soy, fiber, and related foods and nutrients on the risk of endometrial cancer. (The endometrium is the mucous membrane lining the uterus.) The researchers found a positive association between a higher level of fat intake and endometrial cancer as well as a reduction in risk for endometrial cancer with a higher level of fiber intake. They also found that a high consumption of soy products and other legumes was associated with a decreased risk of endometrial cancer.

The bottom line seems to be that you should reduce, if not eliminate, consumption of animal-based proteins to prevent cancer and to maximize health.

If you wish to keep animal protein in your diet, safer choices are deepwater, low-fat fish and occasional small amounts of hormone free, freerange lean fowl. Ideally, you would eat this protein in small quantities and without added oil (steam, bake, or poach) along with an abundant amount of a variety of colorful vegetables.

In certain cultures, meat dishes are often accompanied by pungent-tasting vegetables (such as radishes, ginger, scallions, onions, leeks, watercress, parsley, and chives) that assist in the breakdown of fats. Certain herbs, such as mustard, dill, and horseradish perform the same function. In addition, meat dishes may be served or prepared with sodium—a small addition of sea salt, soy sauce, miso, or pickle. You can find evidence of this in culinary cooking styles that add sauerkraut to meats (German), offer a ginger–soy sauce dip and grated white radish with fish dishes (Japanese), and classic combinations of meats and vegetables such as liver and onions (continental cooking).

Questioning Dairy Food

I will no longer drink the milk from cows or consume products made from that milk. Cow's milk is a superbly engineered fluid that will turn a 65 pound calf into a 500 pound cow in a year. That is what cow's milk is for. Unfortunately, it has the same effect on human beings.

—Michael Klaper, MD

Dairy marketing has gone from Elsie the friendly cow to celebrities wearing milk moustaches and justifying dairy consumption because of its calcium content. Along with bumper stickers that remind us "Milk Makes Better Lovers" and "I Brake for Cheese," the dairy industry's attempt to refocus dairy as a primary food is rapidly becoming pointless as the scientific case against milk and other dairy products grows stronger, validating its reduction, if not elimination.

Terry Shintani, author of *The Hawaii Diet* writes:

Why is dairy food recommended by many experts as a "daily requirement" in this country? Scientific studies are showing that dairy isn't the wonder food it was once touted to be. But there is so much money to be made that even the federal government, under the influence of commercial interests, promotes diary. This is done despite scientific information that dairy fat promotes heart disease, that dairy protein is the leading cause of allergies in this country, and that dairy sugar (lactose) cannot be digested properly by seventy percent of the adults in the world.

The basic dairy product, whole cow's milk, contains high percentages of fat, cholesterol, and protein and is low in carbohydrate and has no fiber. Popular products made from whole milk are cheese, cottage cheese, yogurt, butter, buttermilk, skim milk, kefir, ice cream, whey, cow's milk–based baby formulas, and evaporated milk.

Think about this for a moment: Milk is a food that is ideally designed for the growing nutritional needs of calves. Modern humans now have a unique distinction of being the only species that drinks milk after they are fully teethed—and from another species! We don't simply drink it for occasional refreshment; we've made it into a principal beverage.

Comparing the fiber, cholesterol, and macronutrient (protein, carbohydrate, and fat) content of dairy products to meats reveals similar percentages of each and qualifies milk to be redefined as "liquid meat." Dairy products, like meats, are fat-laden foods. Therefore, an excess of these foods can produce similar diseases found in meat-eating societies.

While the focus of this book is on cancer prevention, additional conditions with which excessive dairy consumption has been associated include osteoporosis, diabetes, pesticide residue, antibiotic-resistant bacteria, leukemia virus, vitamin D toxicity, iron deficiency, infant colic, constipation, childhood ear infections, colitis, enlarged tonsils, obesity, multiple sclerosis, and food allergies.

Dairy Products and Cancer Research

When pediatrician Russell Bunai was asked what single change in the American diet would produce the greatest health benefits, his response was brief and unequivocal: "Eliminating dairy products."

The following discussion focuses on research that is part of the growing body of evidence that links excessive consumption of dairy products to numerous cancers, tumor growth, and immune dysfunction.

OVARIAN CANCER

Ovarian cancer rates parallel dairy-eating patterns throughout the world. The milk sugar, lactose, is broken down in the body into another type of sugar, called galactose, which is further broken down by digestive enzymes. In a Harvard study, Boston gynecologist Daniel Cramer and colleagues observed that when dairy product consumption exceeded the enzymes' capacity to break down galactose, a buildup of galactose in the blood occurs, which is thought to affect a woman's ovaries. Many women have particularly low levels of these enzymes. When these women consume dairy products on a regular basis, their risk of ovarian cancer can be triple that of other women. Yogurt and cottage cheese seem to be of the most concern because the bacteria used in the manufacture of these products increases the production of galactose from lactose.

Publishing in the *Journal of the American Medical Association*, John Snowden, epidemiologist at the University of Minnesota's School of Public Health, summarized a 20-year study of diet and ovarian cancer: "Women who ate eggs . . . three or more days each week had a three times greater risk of fatal ovarian cancer than did women who ate eggs less than one day per week." Similar to other female cancers, ovarian cancer incidence rises not only with egg consumption but also with the consumption of any form of animal fat.

PROSTATE CANCER

Prostate cancer has also been linked to dairy consumption. This is thought to be related to an increase in a compound called insulin-like growth factor 1 (IGF-1). Although a certain amount of IGF-1 in the blood is normal, high levels have been linked to increased cancer risk. IGF-1 is also found in cow's milk and has been shown to occur in increased levels in the blood of individuals who consume dairy products on a regular basis. Other nutrients that increase IGF-1 are also found in cow's milk. Another study showed that men who had the highest levels of IGF-1 had more than 4 times the risk of prostate cancer than those who had the lower levels. According to a review published by the World Cancer Research Fund and the American Institute for Cancer Research, at least 11 human population studies have linked dairy product consumption and prostate cancer. In the United States as a whole, the incidence of prostate cancer is reportedly related to consumption of dairy products, eggs, and meat.

The findings of the 13-year Physicians' Health Study, which involved 20,855 male doctors aged 40 to 82, showed that men who consumed lots of milk, cheese, and ice cream are 30 percent more likely to get prostate cancer than those who had less dairy in their diet.

BREAST CANCER

Breast cancer is commonly called a hormonally driven disease. The body's hormones, primarily estrogen, stimulate the growth and development of a breast tumor. High-fat foods can encourage increased estrogen levels that are readily absorbed back into the body. Research has shown that higher levels of estrogen are typically found in women who eat fatty foods typical of American dietary staples of meats, dairy, and excess oil. In a case-control study at Roswell Park Cancer Institute, high consumption of milk was found to be associated with a higher risk of breast cancer—as well as cancers of the mouth, stomach, colon, rectum, lung, bladder, and cervix—relative to a dairy-free diet.

In a report in *Cancer Research*, Ronald Phillips concluded that the evidence is now overwhelming: Vegetarian diets strongly reduce the incidence of breast, uterine, ovarian, colon, and many other cancers.

NON-HODGKIN'S LYMPHOMA AND LUNG CANCER

A study published in the journal *Nutrition and Cancer* linked the risk of non-Hodgkin's lymphoma with excessive consumption of butter and cow's milk. Some medical research suggests that animal proteins, specifically dairy proteins, play a featured role in the development of this cancer of the immune system. Continuous overstimulation of the immune system by dairy proteins may eventually lead to the weakening of immune function. In addition, excessive levels of a milk protein called beta-lactoglobulin were discovered in the blood of lung cancer patients.

Human Body Design and Function

Our physiological design offers several indicators for what should constitute our basic diet. Our evolutionary history reveals that humans developed predominantly as herbivores (plant consumers) and not as carnivores (meat consumers). Human salivary glands secrete carbohydrate-digesting enzymes into the mouth, where carbohydrates begin their initial break-down. Our tooth structure is largely made for grinding, and we lack the very sharp canines found in carnivorous animals, used for tearing meats into smaller pieces. While we have very limited ability to eat meats (having four canines in the normal human mouth and 20 molars, but still nothing resembling the canine teeth of true carnivores such as dogs), our dental anatomy reveals that animal protein is best as a minor supplement, *if* included at all. In addition, carbohydrates begin their digestion in the mouth, and not the stomach. Clearly, this is sensible reasoning that we are far better equipped to digest carbohydrates as primary foods than animal proteins. This is one of the reasons thorough chewing is always emphasized for people who eat whole grains.

Anatomically, the human is vastly different from that of natural carnivores such as cats and dogs, whose shortened intestinal length guarantees quicker bowel transit times. The contrasts are not only structurally different but functionally as well: Our bowel walls are deeply puckered and pouched, whereas theirs have smoother surfaces that are free of these pouches. The length of human intestines varies from 25 to 29 feet and resembles a winding mountain road full of angular turns; carnivore intestines are from 7 to 9 feet and are structured like a chute, without angular turns. In the moist and warm environment of the human intestine, the putrefaction tendency is greater if meats are present at a higher percentage. Also, carnivore intestines have a great capacity to discharge the large amounts of cholesterol that their diet contains, whereas human livers can process and excrete only a limited amount of dietary cholesterol, leaving our tissues to deal with remaining amounts.

Human saliva has carbohydrate-digesting alkaline enzymes that are absent from carnivores. Finally, the carnivore's stomach acids (for concentrated protein breakdown) are more powerful than human digestive secretions.

It is clear, that the human physiological design is not suitable for large volumes of animal protein, despite in-vogue diet-book theories, enzyme benefits, megaconglomerate food recommendations, or Paleolithic references. We have become too dependent on animal protein as a staple food. Historically, aside from Arctic Inuit populations and some African and Middle East nomadic tribes, meat has *never* been a staple food.

The Vegetarian Option

The word *vegetarian* has an interesting origin. First coined in 1842 from the Latin *vegetus*, it means "one who is sound, whole, fresh and lively." If you are choosing to become a vegetarian or plan to at least experiment with a plant-based diet, the following suggestions might make this choice easier and help produce better results. They also apply to individuals who simply want to reduce the amount of animal protein in their diets.

THE RIGHT AMOUNT OF DIETARY SODIUM. Sodium and potassium have a complementary relationship in the blood. As you increase the amount of vegetables you eat, it is best to have a source of good-quality sea salt to use in small amounts or use fermented products, such as natural soy sauce (tamari) and/or soybean paste (miso), which contain good-quality sea salt. Macrobiotic vegetarians tend to oversalt their food, which leads to increased thirst, overeating, craving sweets, tendency toward irritability, and, in more severe cases, elevated blood pressure. Whether an individual can benefit from a salt-free vegetarian diet largely depends on his or her previous diet. Someone with a dietary past heavy in meats, salt, and/or cooked foods initially does well on a diet high in raw food and that's low in, or even free of, salt. However, this is for the short term. Over the long term, a no-salt diet often results in fatigue and meat or sugar (stimulant) cravings.

REDUCE SIMPLE SUGARS. Vegetarians, tend to use too many simple-carbohydrate products such as fruit juice, honey, maple syrup, barley malt, rice syrup, and molasses. When consumed in excess, these products have been shown to cause blood sugar instability, fatigue, and mood swings. They also suppress immunity, compromise mineral values for neutralizing the acids they create, and can increase cravings for salt or meats. Overconsumption of simple carbs can easily esclate into an addictive cycle: You're fatigued, you crave something sweet as a stimulant, you eat the sweet, your blood sugar swings, and you find yourself fatigued again. For numerous reasons, vegetarians are *more* sensitive to the negative effects of acid-producing sugar.

USE MODERATE AMOUNTS OF NONANIMAL OIL. The transition to a low-fat and low-sugar diet often results in what is perceived as meat cravings. Increasing vegetable proteins (beans or bean products) and adding 1 to 2 teaspoons oil to the diet daily can make the difference between a satisfying meal and one that leaves you with mysterious cravings. For cooking, use olive, sesame oil, or sometimes coconut oil; for dressings, use either of these or a small amount of flaxseed oil. For men, flaxseed oil, particularly in regard to prostate cancer, is to be avoided. Researcher Charles Myers showed that flaxseed oil causes a 300 percent increase in the growth of prostate cancer cells. "It is the most powerful stimulus we know of for prostate cancer cells," he said in his newsletter *Prostate Forum*. Some research has shown that flax oil can increase prostate cancer cell growth; however, flax ground into a meal and used as a food condiment does not have this effect. Most often, vegetarians experiencing these cravings overeat to compensate for the lack of fat and reduced protein in their diet.

BE AWARE OF POSSIBLE DEFICIENCIES. The most common deficiencies about which vegetarians are warned are vitamin B_{12} and healthy intestinal bacteria, which assists us in absorbing nutrients. There is questionable benefit to the value of B_{12} supplements. Some sources claim that the B_{12} pills contain cannot be effectively broken down and might even have an anti-B_{12} effect. Some fermented foods (miso, tempeh, and tamari) contain trace amounts of B_{12}. However, the degree of their bioavailability is still questionable. Because actual deficiencies such as these are rare, it might be a good idea to have blood work done to determine if you are deficient before attempting to treat any symptoms with sublingual supplementation. To promote the constant renewal of healthy intestinal bacteria, it may be appropriate to take probiotic supplements and a B-complex supplement with all the B factors, especially if you are now taking or have repeatedly taken antibiotics. All B factors taken together have a more positive synergistic effect. When your gut bacteria (flora) are compromised, as a result of antibiotics, it becomes difficult to synthesize the vitamin Bs from your food.

INCLUDE A VARIETY OF VEGETABLES AND WHOLE GRAINS. To ensure the best opportunities for healing, consume a wide variety of whole grains, bean and bean products, sea vegetables (for minerals), other vegetables (including leafy greens), small amounts of vegetable-based fermented products, and fruits.

CHEW THOROUGHLY. Grain digestion begins in the mouth, temporarily stops in the stomach, and resumes again in the duodenum before nutrients are absorbed into the blood in the small intestine. All too often, while we'll change the quality of our food, we hold on to old habits of rushing through meals as if the food were being inhaled. Thorough chewing ensures better assimilation of nutrients, less acidity, and regulated bowel function.

AVOID SIMPLE SUGAR AND COMPLEX SUGAR COMBINATIONS. I've heard a complaint from clients over the years who dine in natural food restaurants: "The meal was great, but I had bad gas for the next 24 hours. Frankly, it's not worth it." There's a very simple reason for this: Simple sugars digest quickly, whereas complex sugars are broken apart more gradually. Clients will order a healthful grain, vegetable, and bean meal and then enjoy a dessert immediately afterward. Within 10 minutes, there's a fireworks demonstration in their intestines. Such gas attacks have several causes:

+ Eating too much
+ Eating a dessert too soon after a complex sugar meal
+ Eating unsalted beans or an excessive amount of beans

If you must eat dessert, save it for later! A small amount of hot caffeine-free tea after a meal can often soothe cravings for sweets and make for a satisfying meal closure.

CONSUME WHOLE GRAINS EVERY DAY. The need for whole grains is important. I've met many vegetarians who don't know the difference between whole grains and grain products. An excess of processed grain products can result in fatigue, sugar cravings, and sometimes allergic reactions, presumably due to the mixing of yeast, sugar, and refined flour, which can negatively affect blood sugar and contribute to body fluid acidity. (For more on whole grains versus refined grains, see Chapter 3.)

Three Vegetarian Pitfalls

Choosing to eat a predominant amount of plant foods is not simply a matter of steering clear of foods that are animal in origin. In addition to selecting good-quality food, we need to be mindful of the balance factors: a food's relative acid-to-alkaline ratio, the food's wholeness, and the food's fat and sugar content.

CONCENTRATED SUGAR. Check for ingredients such as white and brown sugar and the numerous other forms of refined sugars. Look for concentrated sugars such as honey, corn syrup, agave, and fructose. Use sweeteners infrequently and in small amounts, and choose less refined sugars such as barley malt, rice syrup, fruit juice, and maple syrup.

REFINED FLOURS AND GRAINS. Limit your consumption of refined grains, such as white rice, white flour, couscous, flour (grain product), breakfast cereals, and wheat germ. Sometimes you can mix a portion of these in with whole grains. For instance, for my Asian clients who long for their familiar white rice, I recommend 70 percent brown rice with 30 percent white rice, which gives them the health benefits and lets them enjoy a familiar taste.

PLANT FOODS HIGH IN FAT. High-fat plant foods include coconuts, avocados, olives, nuts, seeds, soybeans, tofu, and vegetable oils. Many of these products can be included in the your diet, but in *limited* amounts. Try to keep the overall fat percentage of your diet below 15 to 20 percent of your total daily calories.

So What's Left to Eat?

A client once commented, "Everything I like and have been eating all my life is suddenly bad for me. So what's left?"

For those desiring optimum health and noticeable benefits, it would be prudent to severely limit meat, dairy, and simple sugars or eliminate them altogether. Sometimes, just eating a little bit or simply reducing the amount of these foods can foster cravings for more, which escalates your daily eating into a battle of willpower. This can be enormously stressful. At best, an 85 to 90 percent reduction in these foods will still produce noticeable positive results, so if complete elimination proves too difficult, the alternate is to eat less of these foods and to eat them less frequently.

Fortunately, there is an almost unlimited variety of health-promoting foods that can easily satisfy many tastes and make up for missed foods. In the process, you'll happily discover that your cravings for foods that are not health supportive or that are part of your daily habit are noticeably reduced.

While there are other reasons for cravings (discussed in the next chapter), one key is to make sure that you are eating a greater variety of foods and using different cooking styles, which contributes to having more diverse textures that nourish and satisfy.

6

Balancing Our
Acid–Alkaline Chemistry

Life is a struggle, not against money, power, or
malicious animal magnetism, but against hydrogen
ions.

—H. L. Mencken

In the Ocean of the Body

All living things depend on water, and that life consists of an intricate series of chemical reactions that take place in the body's fluid medium. However, one of the most important factors in the chemical makeup of these fluids is the concentration of hydrogen ions and hydroxide ions, which define the quality of our acid–alkaline chemical balance within blood and body fluids.

The lifeblood of primitive sea life was the ocean. Biologists theorize that as evolution progressed, early sea organisms began to evolve in ways that eventually contained their watery environment within them, making it their own and creating a fluid flow that surrounded their cells.

Commonly called "the sea within us," circulating blood acts as the body's portable ocean for two main reasons: its salinity and its microorganism content. Carrying nutrients and oxygen, the blood gives life to all tissues. As a partner to the nervous system, blood is the source of all communication between the remote parts of the body, delivering nutritional elements and essential hormones that keep tissues and cell networks harmoniously functioning.

The body has several types of fluids that nourish and sustain cells. Extracellular fluid, the fluid outside of our cells, is separated from the intracellular fluid, the fluid inside of our cells. As primitive life forms evolved into more developed species, the extracellular fluid became further divided into the circulating blood (known as plasma, in which our red blood cells float) and the fluid that is outside of the blood vessel walls (known as the interstitial fluid, which fills the spaces between the body's cells). Across the walls of our smallest blood vessels (capillaries) there is a continuous exchange of fluid between the interstitial fluid and the blood plasma, which mixes with the extracellular fluid.

Therefore, blood quality also influences the quality of the acid–alkaline balance of our body fluids. Although the blood can deal with too much acidity via various protective buffering systems, other body fluids end up bearing the brunt of acid excess.

This balance of acid and alkaline chemistry in the body's fluids and blood is critical for controlling health and healing. Typical American diets, heavy in sugar, animal protein, fat, and chemical additives, are highly acid producing and set the stage for inflammation, mineral deficiencies, fatigue, and immune weakness, which in turn makes us more vulnerable to disease, particularly cancer. Acids also happen to be a constant waste product of the body's natural metabolic process, putting a burden on our liver and kidneys. Unless properly eliminated, these toxins accumulate in connective tissues and organs, leading to premature aging and numerous disease conditions.

Cancer, Acidity, and Immunity

There are a number of scientific studies indicating that cancer patients have reduced immune function. In extensive lab work, researchers have shown a marked decrease in the number of total lymphocytes and helper T-cells and a decreased helper-to-suppressor cell ratio. These findings in diminished immunity reveal a direct influence in cancer progression.

This is one reason many cancer researchers believe in stimulating immunity in cancer patients.

Current research shows that cancer cells feed directly on blood glucose, like a fermenting yeast organism. Elevating blood glucose in a cancer patient, a process that causes acidity to rise, has been compared to adding gasoline to a smoldering fire.

Recent European studies have shown that regardless of the cancer type, the cellular environment that nourishes and develops cancer cells plays a significant role in influencing how the disease may progress. This has been demonstrated in numerous studies that show that the incidence of cancer recurrence was reduced dramatically when patients underwent various therapies that strengthened their immune system compared with doing nothing.

One of those therapies that has attracted strong press is the baking soda procedure promoted by former Italian physician Tullio Simoncini. This therapy of using a strong antacid solution (12.1 pH) as a cancer therapy is actually not his creation.

According to James Ewing, "in 17th century Germany, chemical conceptions of cancer held sway, and cancer was attributed usually to an excess of acid, to be treated with alkalai." Cancer advocate, journalist, and author Ralph Moss wrote in a blog post:

> Tumors tend to exist and thrive in an acidic environment. One of the key reasons for this is the so-called Warburg effect, i.e., the production of lactic acid by cells breaking down glucose through glycolysis. Prof. Ian Tannock and his colleagues at the University of Toronto have written: "Solid tumors have been observed to develop an acidic extracellular environment." This "is believed to occur as a result of lactic acid accumulation produced during aerobic and anaerobic glycolysis." . . .
>
> At the University of Arizona, Robert J. Gillies and his colleagues have demonstrated that pre-treatment of mice with sodium bicarbonate results in the alkalinization of the area around tumors. This "enhances the anti-tumor activity" of two anticancer drugs, doxorubicin and mitoxantrone, in two different mouse tumor models. . . .
>
> In March 2009, the same group reported that bicarbonate increases tumor pH (that is, makes it more alkaline) and also inhibits spontaneous metastases.

Factors That Influence Acid and Alkaline Chemistry

The state of acid–alkaline balance reflects the condition not only of the blood but also of the internal body fluids, most of which are slighty more alkaline than acid. In this case, "balance" indicates a weak alkaline state, closer to the middle of the acid–alkaline scale. Four factors chiefly influence this balance:

1. The acid–alkaline ratios of the food we consume
2. The amount and consistency of our daily movement and exercise
3. How we respond to and deal with the emotional conflict of daily stress
4. The influence of our environment (air and water quality, chemical exposure)

The way the human body is affected by an acid–alkaline imbalance is through its chemistry. The chemistry of our blood and body fluids rules our health and immune function. That chemistry is evaluated by a measurement called the pH scale. One end of the scale is acid, the other is alkaline. While most of our body fluids are slightly alkaline, the stomach contains very strong acids. The pH evaluation of different food categories allows us to make more healthful and safer choices in what we eat and drink.

The pH Factor

We carry nearly 10 gallons of fluid inside and outside the cells of muscles, bone, and the brain, within the bloodstream, urine, saliva, digestive fluids, and spinal fluid. And our health depends on the quality of these internal body fluids, which bathe cells and organs, aid digestion, and help us eliminate the body's waste products. Our diets, our lifestyle habits, and the way we manage everyday stresses determine the quality of this fluid.

Body fluids have differing levels of acid and alkaline, which is expressed in terms of pH (power of hydrogen), which indicates the relative acidity or alkalinity of a solution. Generally, the liquid environment of the body, with the exception of the stomach, is predominantly alkaline.

pH

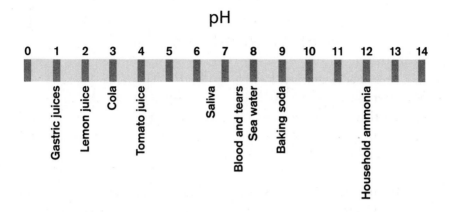

We measure pH on a scale of 1 to 14, with 1 being the most acidic and 14 being the most alkaline (also called *basic*). The pH of the blood is considered a good indicator for the pH of the organs and tissues. It is generally thought that to maintain good health, the blood pH must be slightly alkaline, existing between a fine margin of 7.35 and 7.42 on the pH scale.

The slightest deviation in either direction beyond this narrow margin could actually prove fatal. If the blood pH falls below 7.35, the result is a condition known as acidosis, which can lead to central nervous system depression and a slowing of the heartbeat. Consistent acidity impairs the enzymatic reactions in cells and overloads the lymphatic system, which inhibits the body's natural detoxification process. Severe acidosis, where blood pH falls below 7.00, can result in a coma and eventual death.

If the pH of the blood rises above 7.45, the result is alkalosis. With severe alkalosis, the nervous system becomes hypersensitive and overexcitable, creating severe muscle spasms and convulsions, which, in extreme cases, can be fatal.

Online and in various books you can find assorted pH charts that get very specific about the exact pH of certain vegetables and fruits. I believe that most of this is confusing and contradictory. I would simply advise looking at the acid–alkaline factors in more general terms and setting the focus on reducing stronger acids and stronger alkaline substances from our diet. This will automatically move your dietary balance to a more moderate midpoint without the need to do calculations that make meal planning complicated and restrictive. Here's the general view of where food categories fit into the acid–alkaline scheme:

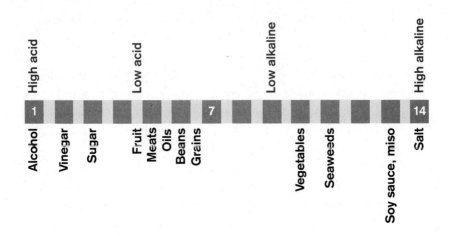

Damage from Extreme pH Imbalance

If the pH of our body fluids, particularly intracellular and extracellular, consistently measures more acid or more alkaline, our cells risk becoming poisoned by their own toxic waste, eventually no longer able to carry out simple biochemical tasks and finally dying. Other examples are how acid rain can wipe out a forest and how alkaline wastes pollute lakes and streams, extinguishing all life within.

Extreme pH can also destroy body tissue, slowly corroding the 60,000 miles of our arteries and veins, much like acids can literally dissolve marble. If allowed to continue, consistent acidity can disrupt all cellular functions, diminish mineral status and weaken heart tissue. Eventually, plaque lesions and microscopic tearing begin to appear throughout the arterial and venous framework.

Extreme pH can also adversely affect the neural firing of brain activity, make blood pressure irregular, and potentially cause different types of arrhythmias. Over time, extreme pH can create more vulnerability to heart attacks. Although it may go unnoticed, or even undetected for years, extreme pH can lead to the progression of cancer, diabetes, and numerous degenerative diseases.

Problems associated with consistent acidic pH in blood and body fluids include the following:

NUTRITION

✦ An acidic condition hinders antioxidant activity and encourages free radical oxidation.

✦ A lowered muscle pH leads to a decrease in muscle permeability, causing nutrients to become blocked from entering the cells. Nutritional absorption, from food or supplements, becomes compromised.

✦ Cellular adenosine triphosphate (APT), a chemical used in cells for energy transfer, is decreased in production, resulting in mood, stamina, and energy changes. Fatigue is a common sign of excess acidity.

IMMUNITY

✦ Excess acid hinders the breakdown of food within the small intestine, particularly in the area known as Peyer's patches, linked with longevity, which produce lymphocytes to assist in maintaining immunity. Excess acid weakens the production of these lymphocytes and affects their absorption.

✦ An acidic condition decreases the beneficial bacteria within the intestine and hinders the absorption of the entire B vitamin group.

✦ Fatigue, from failure to remove acid waste within and around the cells, is one of the most common problems resulting from excess acidity.

PREGNANCY

✦ During pregnancy, the fetus takes priority in getting necessary alkaline nutrients. This is one reason babies are born with relatively high levels of alkalinity. During sleep, the mother loses a good deal of alkalinity to the baby's developing mineral needs, making her condition more acidic. Japanese doctors, describing this phenomenon as the reason behind morning sickness, claim that women can become more susceptible to morning sickness by having previously eaten foods high on the acidic scale.

PSYCHOLOGY

✦ Symptoms of hyperirritability are common to acid states, including mood swings, learning disabilities, hyperactivity, agitation, and violent temper.

ARTHRITIS

✦ Many different forms of arthritis, including gout, are attributed to acid accumulations in the joints. In Japanese studies, cartilage and joint damage stem from accumulated acids around, and in, the joints. Such accumulations make it more difficult for the blood to discharge acidic wastes from these sensitive areas. Reducing acid intake and bringing healthier, more balanced blood to these areas of pain through skin brushing and hot soaks offer hope for alleviating pain and possibly reversing arthritic symptoms.

ORGANS

✦ The heartbeat can be altered by acidic wastes that diminish tissue oxygenation. A moderate alkaline system creates ideal regularity.

✦ Excessive acidic wastes create labor for the lungs, hindering their natural function of ridding the body of carbon dioxide.

✦ All nourishment assimilated by the intestines enters the blood and is then carried to the liver. The burden on the liver is greater when acidic blood wastes are excessive.

✦ In addition to regulating blood sugar, the pancreas produces alkaline enzymes and sodium bicarbonate. The physiological functions of the pancreas are designed to reduce excess acidity. To create optimal blood sugar balance, the pancreas requires less acid and more alkaline foods.

✦ Of all organs, the kidneys, which work ceaselessly to maintain blood alkalinity, probably take the brunt of damage from acid wastes. Research has shown that kidney stones are composed of waste acid cells and mineral salts that have become bonded in an albuminous (waste acid) substance. Reducing the intake of acid-forming products increases the likelihood of avoiding kidney stones.

✦ Toxins cannot be thoroughly removed via the kidneys, liver, and intestines. This creates greater susceptibility to infections and headaches.

BLOOD PRESSURE

✦ Japanese physician Kancho Kuninaka relates high blood pressure to an excessive acid condition. His explanation: "With a higher blood pH, the heart has less work to do. The viscosity of a high blood pH is so low that the heart does not need to pump as hard. The calcium ions in a higher-alkaline condition dissolve plaque and arterial wall buildup, creating a larger area for blood flow. It is well known that if a patient takes several deep breaths immediately before a blood pressure measurement, the reading will be lower. This happens because acid blood pH is temporarily reduced by exhaling carbon dioxide and taking in more oxygen."

MUSCLE AND SKIN

✦ The integrity of the connective tissue weakens, causing a loss of tone and texture to skin and hair, contributing to a more aged look.

✦ Athletic performance decreases as ammonia levels and lactic acid build, limiting muscle efficiency (contraction and expansion of muscle tissue) and the availability of oxygen to ravenous cells. With lowered blood pH, hemoglobin has a decreased ability to bind with oxygen and delivers less to the cells.

SLEEP

✦ With increased acidity, the quality of sleep becomes affected. Patients with high acidity need more sleep to compensate for poor-quality sleep. Difficulty in awakening is often a sign of excess acidity.

LYMPH SYSTEM

✦ The body has about an equal number of lymph vessels as blood vessels and more than 600 lymph glands. The amount of lymph fluid we have is three times as much as blood, and this fluid has the dual function of transporting nutrition to the cell and removing acid waste products. Lymph flows best in an alkaline medium. However, if the lymph fluid is acidic, its movement becomes slowed, creating dryness and forming microscopic adhesions throughout the tissues. Acid wastes reach the tissues through lymph and blood toxicity. The scope of this problem can be responsible for numerous conditions, from inflamed nodes to lowered immunity and bowel irregularity.

How Sugar Produces Acidity: The Myth of Alkaline Fruits

Simple carbohydrates are made up of small numbers of sugar units that get absorbed into the blood immediately on contact with the mouth. Before you can say Yum!, it's already entered your blood and with lightning speed is distributed to body cells and lymph. This is where the problem begins; the change is so rapid that sufficient supplies of oxygen are not readily available to completely burn the sugar. This is why so-called alkaline fruits, in most cases, actually acidify the blood. This is another reason to be weary of some of the more simplistic information written about acid and alkaline food balancing.

Refined sugar, the empty nutrient food, has been stripped of virtually all minerals and vitamins. The minerals that have been eliminated were essential for the building of tissues, for nervous system functioning, and for blood filtering. Without a constant renewal of iron and sodium elements from this powerfully concentrated nonfood, the blood cannot take up sufficient oxygen, and metabolic waste products fail to be neutralized and eliminated.

The result is a bloodstream burdened with various acids (lactic acid, butyric acid, pyroracemic acid, acetic acid, carbonic acid). As acid levels in the blood rise, a general drowsiness and sluggishness occurs—typical symptoms of sugar's carbonic acid toxicity. Therefore, the result of sugar metabolism in the human body is acid forming. This is the beginning of a systemic inflammation response.

Often, you'll hear the argument that unrefined simple carbohydrates (honey, maple syrup, rice syrup, barley malt, raw brown sugar, evaporated organic cane sugar, molasses), unlike refined white sugar, contain some minerals that can help balance sugar's acidity.

Don't bet on it.

First, clever marketing concerns have managed to hoodwink the general public—especially the natural food–buying public—into replacing ordinary sugar with organic evaporated cane sugar (or cane juice), advertising it as natural. They are emphasizing the quality issue here ("Organic!"), but the chemical truth is that sugar is sugar is sugar. Evaporated cane sugar, for whatever its existing mineral content, is still a simple carbohydrate and highly acidic. You might consider it sugar in a tuxedo.

While honey might also contain *some* alkalizing minerals to suggest that it is alkaline forming, chemically its concentrated sugar content, in the long run, becomes acidic in the human body. The same applies for maple syrup, barley malt, corn syrup, agave syrup, and other sweet concentrates. Natural, quality sweet syrups with some mineral content such as barley malt, rice syrup, maple syrup, and molasses are generally more healthful choices when you want a sweetener; however, they can still be very acid forming. For cancer conditions, these foods are not healing and should be strictly limited to the infrequent social occasion at best.

The Most Common Acid-Excess Problem in the World

Typically, the word *acid* is associated with negative physical conditions: acidosis, heartburn, acid accumulation in the muscles (lactic acid excess) that plagues athletes, acid breath, and the digestive disorder gastroesophageal reflux disease (GERD).

It's no wonder that acid-blocking medications are the third top-selling type of drug in the United States today. Two other drugs that are used to treat reflux disorder, Nexium and Prevacid, are among the world's best-selling drugs. Combined, they have totaled $8.5 billion in annual sales.

Today, with acid conditions so prevalent, pharmaceutical recommendations are given like candy for most acid symptoms, and some are even available without a prescription (such as Prilosec). The message being conveyed by pharmaceutical companies is that we can eat what we want and shouldn't worry about acid-causing foods, because we can always rely on a pill to make us feel better.

Unknown to many, there's a double-edged sword to using acid-blocking medications. Your body actually *needs* stomach acid to remain healthy because acid is necessary to aid in protein and food digestion, to activate digestive enzymes in the small intestine, to keep bacteria from growing in the small intestine, and to help us absorb essential nutrients such as calcium, magnesium, and vitamin B_{12}.

There's also substantial evidence that taking these medications can weaken digestion, create vitamin and mineral deficiencies, and foster problems such as irritable bowel syndrome, depression, and more. A *Journal of the American Medical Association* study found that chronic use of acid-blocking drugs can lead to osteoporosis symptoms and an increase in hip fractures because blocking acid prevents calcium absorption (and other minerals, as well as trace minerals) required for bone health.

Clearly, we need to discover the real causes of reflux and heartburn and *rely on eating foods that don't leave strong acid residues*. This means, to really avoid this problem, we need to make sustaining dietary and lifestyle changes, instead of simply treating annoying symptoms with alkaline medications that neutralize acids. It is no secret that an excess of fried food, caffeine, soda, alcohol, spices, tomato-based foods, citrus, and chocolate can be probable culprits in most acid-related conditions, as is overeating in general, eating late at night (just before bed), or being overweight or having unresolved stresses.

These are the most well-known causes behind acidity excess. But we need to understand some fundamentals of acid and its neutralizing partner, alkaline: how they work together, the result of their excesses, and how we can achieve some state of healthful balance to help to heal or avoid disease.

Acid–Alkaline at Work

How the mechanism of acid–alkaline balance works is probably one of the most puzzling, misunderstood, confusing, and controversial areas of nutritional science, which may be why it's not an established part of most health and wellness practices. The original acid and alkaline research was published during the 1930s, and since then scant scientific validation has been presented.

A number of medical researchers and physicians have begun to turn their attention to acid–alkaline balance in the body, including Lynda Frassetto, a professor of medicine in the division of nephrology at the University of California at San Francisco. Frassetto is an internationally recognized authority on the connection between health and pH levels. Frasseto has published papers on regulation of acid–base balance in healthy and aging people and on the dietary influences of acid–base balance in healthy people and those with diabetes. Much of her work has been about connecting chronic low-grade acidosis directly to numerous health problems.

If we cannot maintain an alkaline condition of body fluids, we will not be able to maintain a healthy cell condition. When our cells are not healthy, our organs become sick and body fluids become more acidic and toxic as weakened cells transform into sick cells. Eventually, this develops into a variety of degenerative conditions. The normal pH for all the tissues and fluids in the body, except the stomach, centers around neutral or slightly alkaline. The following chart shows the different pH levels within the body.

DIGESTIVE SYSTEM	
Saliva	6.50–7.50
Stomach fluid	1.5–3.50
Duodenum fluid	4.20–8.20
Pancreatic fluid	8.00–8.30
Liver bile	7.10–8.50
Gallbladder bile	5.50–7.70
Small intestine	6.50–7.50

ELIMINATION SYSTEM	
Urine	4.80–8.40
Feces	4.60–8.40
MISCELLANEOUS	
Blood	7.35–7.45
Spinal fluid	7.30–7.50

Your Body in Protection Mode: Buffering Systems for Reducing Acids

Whatever the source of acidity we accumulate, the body has an innate wisdom that serves as an automatic protection against the onslaught of extreme pH. This system protects us by instantly reducing, or buffering, acid accumulations when they rise in the blood.

The alkalinity of our body's mineral storage is one of the ways that we neutralize acid excess, taking it from a strong acid and reducing it to a mild one; however, this comes at a price. During this automatic process of buffering acids, valuable minerals become diminished—minerals that come predominantly from our bones—and can make us susceptible to developing osteoporosis.

A saving grace is that this process can be minimized by reducing foods that are extremely acidic, such as meats, sugars, dairy, alcohol, vinegar, and caffeine. Healthier dietary habits can eventually replace these lost mineral sources from natural foods, such as whole grains, beans, vegetables, fruits, and herbs, and the moderate use of sea salt and some naturally fermented foods.

Our body is designed with seven powerful buffering systems that work to convert strong acids into lesser ones, as a way to naturally normalize blood and body fluid pH.

+ **Bicarbonate buffers:** Work in blood, tissue fluids, lymph, and kidneys.
+ **Phosphate ammonia buffer:** Works with blood pH and the kidneys.
+ **Protein buffers:** Work within the fluid around the cells (intracellular).
+ **Electrolyte buffers:** Work in blood, lymph, and the fluid within and around the cells.

✦ **Low-density lipoproteins:** Work in blood, lymph, and the fluid around the cells.
✦ **Hormone buffers:** Work in the blood.
✦ **Water:** Works in all body fluids.

Demystifying the Acid and Alkaline Controversy

The table below lists the most common acid–alkaline arguments made by practitioners of both alternative and conventional medicine. It also includes a summary of Nature's Cancer-Fighting Foods' perspective:

ALTERNATIVE MEDICINE	CONVENTIONAL MEDICINE	NATURE'S CANCER-FIGHTING FOODS
Claims that acid blood instigates and promotes degenerative diseases.	Disregards blood pH, saying the blood is always alkaline and that acid and alkaline are relevant only in kidney disease or in cases of extreme acidosis.	The claims made by both types of practitioner need more study. It is true that the blood is always alkaline, but at what cost? With the introduction of acids, the blood immediately alkalizes itself with minerals borrowed from the body's reserves (bone and body fluids). The blood remains alkaline only because buffering systems are working. According to biochemist and 1931 Nobel Prize winner Otto Warburg, "The prime cause of cancer is the replacement of the respiration of oxygen in normal body cells by a fermentation of sugar." In recent years, it has been demonstrated that cancer cells can actually grow in the body almost with only the energy of fermentation. This continuous and concentrated form of acidity is foundational for cancer development.
Claims acid foods create acid conditions.	Says all foods leaving the stomach are acidic, so no food can change this solution. Claims that the blood protects us from acid–alkaline imbalances.	It is a fact that simple sugars are digested and become absorbed through the mouth, tongue, and throat, before even arriving in the stomach. Acid ions also move through blood vessels to influence the chemical balance of our body fluids. This can happen before food even enters the acidic environment of the stomach. It is also true that the blood carefully monitors and controls acid–alkaline levels, keeping them in a safe range, but it is at the cost of needed minerals and trace minerals from the bones and body fluids as well as valuable enzymes. While the blood may be balanced, the body fluids are not, and this is where disease begins.

Caffeine and Cancer

Caffeine is a worldwide socially sanctioned addictive habit. By conservative estimates, humans consume more than 4 billion cups of caffeinated drinks a day. Americans alone consume over 100 billion cups yearly without a second thought or understanding the debilitating effects that caffeine addiction can cause. The potency of caffeine is only realized when one attempts to kick the habit. A wide range of painful and fatiguing withdrawal symptoms make this a very difficult habit to change.

Research shows that a high caffeine intake can increase the chance of developing larger tumors. Scientists involved in caffeine research suggest that those who frequently consumed a large number of caffeinated drinks were more at risk of getting a form of breast cancer, which accounts for a third of all cases. While researchers do not understand the precise mechanism of how caffeine influences cancer, they believe that an excess of caffeine could affect how tumors grow and flourish.

A 10-year study led by Ken Ishitani and Tokyo Women's Medical University followed 38,432 women to determine caffeine's effect on cancer. Study volunteers, all aged 45 years or older, were asked to provide their dietary details, including the amount of caffeine they regularly drank. Over the decade, 1,188 of the women developed breast cancer. The findings concluded that drinking more than four cups of coffee a day increased the risk of the cancer by 68 percent.

It was shown that a high-caffeine diet also increased the possibility of tumors growing larger than 2 centimeters by 79 percent. These larger tumors are more difficult to treat than smaller ones.

Ishitani remarked: "These findings indicate that caffeine consumption may affect breast cancer progression, and such an effect may be independent of the (sex hormone) oestrogen. More research is needed to understand why caffeine had this effect on breast cancer."

Coffee Chemistry

> Though caffeine is generally considered to be a safe product provided it is taken in small quantities, it may still be considered a poisonous substance regardless of the amount ingested.
>
> —David M. Mrazik

There are more than 100 acids in green and roasted coffee that contribute to indigestion and a variety of health problems caused by excess acid pH. Among these many acids, caffeic acid, positively known as an antioxidant, may also be a carcinogen. The net effect of this combined quantity of coffee acids, consistently taken on a daily basis, including decaf, can potentially weaken the body's alkaline status.

To neutralize these acids, our bodies require calcium, among other minerals, as a buffering agent. Coffee acids can deplete available calcium, forcing it to be excreted through the kidneys. This expends calcium reserves, thereby increasing the risk of osteoporosis. It is estimated that one cup of coffee deletes over 25 milligrams of calcium!

Decaf consumption paints a nastier picture: The chemical solvents used in extracting the caffeine content remain as a residue that shows up in your cup. Even the Swiss-water process, which exposes the beans to a hot-water bath, leaves behind oils and acids.

The U.S. Food and Drug Administration (FDA) estimates that a 5-ounce cup of coffee can contain anywhere from 75 to 155 milligrams of caffeine, noting that percolated coffee represents the low range and drip coffee the upper range. Black tea contains approximately 50 to 60 milligrams of caffeine and green tea 30 to 40 milligrams. Some sodas, particularly orange and yellow varieties, may contain around 55 milligrams per 12-ounce bottle.

Coffee depletes available calcium by excreting it through the kidneys. This expends the calcium reserves of coffee drinkers and increases their risk of osteoporosis. In an accumulative sense, coffee drinking is a major mineral leech.

The acidic nature of coffee stimulates hypersecretion of gastric acids within the stomach. Even decaffeinated coffee has been shown to increase acidity, and to a greater degree than either regular coffee or caffeine alone. However, both caffeine and coffee stimulate gastric acid secretion while raising serum gastrin levels. In sensitive individuals, this could lead to digestive ulceration and inhibited protein digestion. Also, because caffeine acids are absorbed into the blood, they increase blood acidity, drawing minerals from numerous other body sources to buffer the excess acid.

Although few of the findings are conclusive, medical research has linked caffeine consumption to fatigue, mood swings, premenstrual syndrome, hypertension, fertility problems, birth defects, irregularities in heart rhythm, anxiety, panic attacks, irritable bowel syndrome, migraine, tremors, restlessness, tension headaches, joint pain, lower back pain, fibrocystic breast disease, and insomnia and other sleep disorders.

If you are a devoted coffee drinker on the healing path, my recommendation is to gradually reduce your caffeine intake over the course of several weeks so that you are ingesting no more than ¾ to 1 cup per day. Then, over a period of another week or two, gradually eliminate coffee completely, experimenting with natural caffeine-free teas. This is an effortless way to wean yourself and usually won't leave you with headaches or fatigue.

Indicators of Elevated Acid Levels

A coated tongue is a visible indicator of excess digestive acidity. In many cultural folk medicines, as well as in conventional medicine, tongue examination is an important method of internal diagnosis. A skilled physician of traditional Chinese, Indian, or Tibetan medicine will examine the structure, flexibility, coating, texture, moistness, and color of the tongue. According to the color, thickness, and location of mucus, a coated tongue reveals the condition of an individual's systemic balance. While it's natural to have a thin, almost clear coating on the tongue, a thick white coating or white tinged with a greenish-yellow color might indicate the following:

+ Overeating (eating beyond capacity)
+ Eating prior to bed (within 2 to 3 hours before retiring)
+ Excess dietary sugar
+ Excess dietary fat
+ Overworked digestive system

While a sudden inflammatory skin reaction may be the result of an allergy symptom, pimples, skin eruptions, or canker sores of the mouth and tongue are more often considered signs of excess acidity. These problems are usually dealt with symptomatically by topical medicines, saltwater rinses (alkalizing), tongue scrapers, and so on.

These solutions are only a temporary fix because the cause of such problems is rooted in the blood and body fluids.

Measuring Your pH

How does one determine an acid or alkaline condition? Through blood work? Saliva tests? Hair analysis? Muscle resistance testing? Urine quality?

Most current diagnostic tests show the acid wastes present in the body fluids of urine, saliva, or blood. The problem with such tests is that they don't read how much acid waste is within the cellular fluids because as acids they are constantly being removed as waste products. While it might be possible to measure the relative acid or alkalinity of some body fluids, it is rare and more complicated to evaluate the acid or alkaline quality of body tissues such as skin, organs, glands, muscles, ligaments, and arteries.

The tissue quality of these structures is the real determining factor of our health. *When acid wastes are not eliminated, they become reabsorbed through the colon, get filtered through the liver, and end up being rereleased into the general circulation.* In this case, you're recirculating waste as opposed to cleansing and rejuvenating.

Measuring the blood for acid–alkaline variations is not reliable or useful because the blood will almost always maintain a working alkaline status. When acid is introduced into the blood, alkaline minerals from other parts of the body (digestive fluids, bones, and so on) are immediately mobilized to maintain a crucial pH level of 7.35 to 7.45. The body just cannot tolerate increasing acidity of the blood. It must be alkalized. To do this, the body goes on an alkaline-borrowing spree, indiscriminately and immediately. To get an accurate acid–alkaline reading from a blood test would require taking blood samples at numerous intervals throughout the day and only after eating one particular food—a costly, exhausting, and unreliable process.

Testing acid–alkaline levels with litmus paper (saliva) or urinalysis sticks (urine) can be assumptive, simplistic, and misleading. Saliva or urine is not reflective of your overall acidity. Such arbitrary and unpredictable testing does not read the cellular fluid or tissue quality of skin, organs, glands, muscles, ligaments, arteries, and other vessels. It can yield only a partial evaluation. The best barometer for evaluating your general acid–alkaline levels is your overall well-being.

Practical Advice for Acid–Alkaline Balance

A whole food, plant-based diet of whole grains, vegetables, beans, and small amounts of fruit, nuts, seeds, and natural teas is the one of the most effective ways to achieve acid–alkaline balance. Small amounts of quality animal proteins, if you are in a dietary transition, or other foods can be included to satisfy cravings or for special occasions. Overall, the most significant change you can make to achieve a better acid–alkaline balance is to reduce extremes (refer to chart on page 116).

You don't need to consult complicated charts listing individual acid and alkaline food values, perform complex calculations, or worry about exact food balancing.

The problem with acid and alkaline charts is that they all seem to be very different and detail endless lists of foods to eat in order to "balance" acidity. Truth is, you don't really balance acidity—you minimize it. Consuming extremes only continues to lead to extreme cravings, which become very difficult to overcome, especially when it comes to salt, animal protein, and sugar.

The hallmark of health has always been moderation. Therefore, eating closer to the middle of the food acid scale is always the safest and most balanced bet.

7

Increasing
and Strengthening
Immune Function

Man lives in a sea of micro-organisms; the immune
system is his license to drive.

—Robert Good, MD

Natural Immunity:
Our First Line of Defense

This chapter on immunity will address the different ways our immune
function can be weakened and strengthened. The dietary link, the effect
of emotional and physical stress, and certain genetic factors influence our
immune response, the quality of our health, and our ability to heal. In
terms of physiology and medicine, *immunity* refers to a state of lessened
susceptibility to injury by microorganisms and certain poisons formed
by animals, plants, or artificial means. The state of *natural immunity* is accomplished by the still somewhat mysterious immune system that comprises many types of microscopic cells, molecules, organs, and tissues,
including the lymph nodes and vessels, spleen, bone marrow, thymus
gland, and tonsils.

Unlike other systems of the body, it is not composed of a single organ per se, such as the liver or heart, nor is it a series of channels, such as the digestive or lymphatic systems. In an operational sense, it is a system, but one without a recognized physical presence.

The immune system is the body's first line of defense against the onslaught of foreign substances. Its main objective is to locate, disable, and digest any disease-causing invader through its army of white blood cells, which has widespread access throughout the entire body. It is our primary defense from not only infectious agents, bacteria, and viruses but also from malignant abnormal cells that have cancer-forming potential.

In fact, cancer can be considered an immune disease because it is the immune system's function to monitor the body, recognize precancerous cells, and consume them, eventually dissolving them with powerful cellular enzymes. This occurs in each of us on a daily basis. When someone's immune defenses have become weakened, there is a possibility of precancerous cells multiplying, which increases the probability of cancer progression.

Truth be told, the body is under constant attack. Air, food, water, animals, people, and the environment continually overwhelm us with bacteria, viruses, and other microorganisms. Some of them can aid our health, but others pose a threat.

Understanding how the immune system works and the various negative and positive influences that compromise it can help determine the best natural strategies for bolstering immunity to support health or recovery from sickness. While the germ theory initiated a revolution in medicine at the time of its discovery, it conversely encouraged the attitude that the body was simply a passive recipient of disease. Because a weakened immune system makes us more vulnerable to sickness, it is now recognized, that the body is not as much a victim of disease but an accomplice.

The immune system is the most sensitive of body systems to toxic exposure. At the same time, it is very susceptible to dietary influence, which might be due to the fact that 70 percent of the immune system surrounds the intestinal tract, conveniently helping protect you from toxins produced during digestion.

And, to support immune function, the body has five additional avenues that offer protection against disease organisms or substances:

+ **Skin:** As the body's main physical barrier to all kinds of infection, the skin secretes antiseptic substances that reduce the chances of potentially dangerous organisms from entering the body.

✦ **Stomach:** Acid secretions of the stomach along with digestive enzymes help minimize unwanted potentially dangerous organisms.

✦ **Lymph:** The lymph circulation cleanses the blood fluid through its interaction with immune cells in the tissue linings of lymphatic channels as well as in the lymph nodes.

✦ **Liver:** The many detoxification abilities of the liver minimize the toxicity of numerous compounds and drugs.

✦ **Intestines:** Dietary fiber and vegetable matter enter the intestines and absorb toxins, which are then discharged as a bowel movement, helping to reduce toxin levels within the blood.

Cells with Pit Bull Appetites

In the 1980s there was a popular video game called Pac-Man, in which quick-moving circles with large snapping mouths gobbled invading attackers in the form of little dots. Pac-Man would roll along, engulf an entire dot in its large mouth, and voilà: enemy vanquished! Presumably, the enemy was eaten, dissolved, and digested, never again to stand in the way of that fearless, rolling Pac-Man—until you'd deposit a quarter for another round.

Simple game. Simple strategy. And quite similar to the general workings of your immune system.

Immune cells actually occupy every part of the body—the eyes, nostrils, skin, lungs, and lining of internal organs. With watchful senses, they stand guard to protect us from anything foreign to the body that could pose a threat. Some immune cells guard the lining and blood vessels of specific organs, while others circulate through the body looking for action via the lymph fluid.

Lymph fluid circulates within a separate network from the circulatory system and consists of a pale, thick fluid made chiefly of fat and white blood cells. Many of our immune cells are headquartered in the lymph, on alert status to be dispatched, via the lymph circulation, to the location of threat.

Interconnected by way of the lymphatic vessels, the immune system includes four key organs: lymph nodes, thymus gland, spleen, and bone marrow.

Combating Immune-Related Disease

Until relatively recently, the accepted method of dealing with immune-related diseases was chiefly to focus on killing the invader, whether it was a bacteria, virus, or cancer cell. In the last 20 years, this approach has become less popular and alternate strategies designed to support the body's immune system are now more universally accepted because maintaining the health and vitality of our immune systems is more a matter of nutrition and lifestyle factors than simply destroying invaders. Modern medicine has spent billions of dollars in the last 25 years for antibiotic, antiviral, and antifungal medicines and to decreasing results. If this invader-killing approach was as effective as medical marketing would have us believe, there would be far fewer deaths from infections. Statistics have shown just the opposite.

A survey of all deaths in the United States between 1980 and 1992 revealed a shocking 58 percent rise in deaths from infection. A sixfold increase occurred in those between the ages of 25 and 44, and this is only partly due to the increased number of deaths from HIV infection. Deaths from respiratory infections increased by 20 percent. Poor immunity makes us more susceptible to many debilitating conditions. But in progressive nutrition, the focus for enhancing immunity targets different ways to stimulate immune function. Previously, the alternative approach for treating cancer focused on nutritional factors. Now, the role of supernutrients has taken a backseat to dietary strategies that awaken our immunity, so the body reacts defensively in a self-healing manner. The first order of business for immune enhancement is to eliminate the factors that weaken immunity.

The two main factors responsible for weakening immunity are diet (simple sugar consumption, alcohol excess, strong acids, and toxin exposure) and lifestyle (getting adequate rest and reducing stress to manageable levels). Once we adjust these weakening factors, we can then begin to strengthen immunity with nutrition, mushroom and herbal therapy, and physical and energetic therapies (acupuncture, Qigong, massage).

PASSING IMMUNITY TO BABY

DURING THE FIRST 8 weeks of a child's life, the immune system is still developing. It has not dealt with the gamut of pathogens it will face in

(CONTINUED)

the future, and at this time, the baby's system is at its most vulnerable; it can easily be overcome by the most common of microorganisms. This is one of the reasons physicians generally recommend the newborn be kept in seclusion for up to 8 weeks as the immune system continues to develop and strengthen its ability to ward off pathogens.

One of the best ways a mother can positively influence the health of her newborn is via breast milk. The first milk produced by mother after birth is called colostrum. It is a powerful source of immune-enhancing proteins that ready the infant's immune system for living in a world full of ever-present microorganisms. In addition, breast-feeding can reduce the potential of food allergy, which can have a debilitating impact on the immune system.

The Biochemistry of Stress

One of the symptoms of an approaching nervous breakdown is the belief that one's work is terribly important.

—Bertrand Russell

In the 1950s, researcher Hans Seyle first introduced the concept of stress. His classic work, *The Stress of Life*, coined the term *general adaptation response* to explain that stress is an unavoidable state because it is the body's adaptive response to any demand made of it.

Seyle was actually investigating a hormonal substance that originates from the ovaries. The now-famous experiment he performed was to inject one group of rats with the ovarian substance and another group with a placebo. Several months later, he noticed some strange changes in the rats that had received the ovarian extract: They had developed ulcers and weakened immune systems.

Initially Seyle considered that these changes were the result of the hormone shots. However, his mind was changed when the rats that were receiving the placebo shots had developed the same ulcer and damaged immune system symptoms. Rethinking his methodology, Seyle finally realized that the only common factor affecting both groups of rats was the daily shots, which both groups of rats clearly did not like. Their negative resistance to these shots was so strong that Seyle had to physically hold the rats down to give them the shots as they writhed and attempted to run away. What was becoming apparent was that this discomforting experience was producing a negative physical result.

Seyle conducted other experiments in which he duplicated unpleasant conditions for his rats by holding them down for specific periods throughout the day, plunging them in cold water, and so on. Eventually, Seyle realized that the emotional stress the rats were experiencing had been resulting in negative changes in their physiology. Their intense emotional reactions somehow triggered a stress response system.

The biochemical effects of stress orchestrate multiple glandular reactions. As hormone levels are forced to increase as a stress response, *immunity is turned off,* growth and repair functions cease, and reproductive functions come to a halt. At the same time, blood sugar levels elevate, the heart rate speeds up, and blood begins to concentrate in the lower extremities, preparing the body for its flight-or-fight response. The physical translation of this reaction is a *greater susceptibility to sickness, prevention of recovery from illness, and a diminished libido.*

There is no doubt that daily life stresses can be consuming, in terms of the focus of our attentions, sense of joy, energy needs, and peace of mind. The right diet, supplement program, discipline, and will to live can be seriously undermined by the presence of constant stress. Reducing stress and finding renewed perspectives to keep from becoming overwhelmed by their presence is an integral part of the health equation.

Hope for Helplessness

> I was going to buy a copy of *The Power of Positive Thinking*, and then I thought: What the hell good would that do?
>
> —Ronnie Shakes, comedian

Another form of common stress that is particularly harmful is called *learned helplessness.* This condition is brought about by constant exposure to uncontrollable stressors—specifically, finding oneself in a painful or very uncomfortable situation from which there seems to be no hope of relief or escape.

The experience of being captive in a hospital is somewhat of a paradox. Assume, for a moment, you have entered a hospital (root word: *hospitality*) for some kind of operation. In the safe confines of the hospital you really have little control over what you can eat, when you can eat, what you will wear, when you will sleep, or even whom you may see. You are regularly given mediation, interrupted by visiting rounds of nurses or doctors, and must listen to the collective and constant sounds of other patients whining, moaning, or dying.

Psychologically, it feels as if you have surrendered control. In this situation, it is no small feat to keep from feeling victimized as you watch your faith waver, and find yourself nursing a sense of hopelessness. Such feelings can exert a profound negative influence on immune function.

The patients who manage to regain their health in hospitals are usually considered the *difficult* ones; they ask questions, request test interpretations, eat selectively or have food brought in, and personalize their rooms by adding decorative elements that offer a familiar sense of home. A highly significant study published in 1979 revealed that cancer patients who were rated as less cooperative by doctors and nurses lived longer.

Much of the research on learned helplessness has been done with animals, specifically rats that have been exposed to a number of repetitive electrical shocks or loud noises. At some point the rat is placed into a different cage where it could control the shocks: It could move to another side of the cage to avoid the shock or remain in place and continue getting shocks. Researchers even wired a warning bell to alert the rat that a shock was coming. Despite all of this and the fact that freedom from shocks was just a crawl away, the rat remained immobile and continued to receive shocks. However, when a rat that had not been subject to previous shocks was placed into the same cage, it quickly learned how to avoid the shocks.

Why was the first rat unable to learn the same lesson, especially considering that it had already experienced the physical trauma of being shocked repeatedly? Call it "rat belief" or "rat misconception," but the first rat *believed* that it was powerless. Absorbed in such negative thinking, it merely collapsed and didn't even attempt to seek safe ground. This example is a definitive picture of learned helplessness in action. Conclusively, the animals that had learned helplessness were much more likely to become sick, develop immune breakdown, and finally succumb.

On a human comparison, feeling that you have lost control around you can bring on similar negative physical consequences. Numerous studies have associated higher occurrences of heart disease and cancer with people who consistently feel they have little control over their work. According to Martin Seligman, a researcher who documented the effects of learned helplessness in his book *Learned Optimism: How to Change Your Mind and Your Life*, proposes that people can learn to be more optimistic and in control by changing their basic assumptions to a more upbeat, empowered view. Optimism is redefined not as a state of mind but as a reflection of daily action.

Cancer, Emotions, and Stress

Stressful influences are those events, activities, or interactions that exceed an individual's ability to comfortably cope. Research has shown that a wide range of stresses, from losing a spouse to facing a tough examination, can deplete immune resources, causing greater susceptibility to disease, including cancer. When American psychologist Lawrence LeShan examined more than 400 cancer patients, he discovered that a phenomenally high 72 percent of these patients had experienced the loss of someone close to them in a short period before the onset of their cancer. In contrast, only 10 percent of comparable people without cancer had suffered such a loss.

In another study examining emotional and psychosocial factors affecting cancer patients, it was determined that the "inability to express emotion, particularly in relation to anger" is a very valid factor contributing to the progress of cancer. In many cases, what really prevents us from the expression of feelings is not only the fear of consequences but the inability to articulate what we're actually feeling.

Brain physiology is thought to directly influence the immune system by telegraphing its messages down nerve cells. Networks of nerve fibers have been found that connect to the thymus gland, spleen, lymph nodes, and bone marrow. Some experiments have also shown that immune function can be altered by actions that destroy specific brain areas.

Substantial evidence has shown that individuals overwhelmed by severe depression, and the resulting stress, exhibit a greater tendency to fall ill or die prematurely than do people who do not suffer from depression. A 20-year study of 2,000 middle-aged American men demonstrated that those with depression had twice the risk of developing a fatal cancer in later years, aside from other medical risk factors, including smoking and a familial history of cancer.

Depression, like stress mechanisms, is associated with chemical changes in hormone levels in the blood. Typically, depressed people get less sleep, consume more alcohol, exercise less, often smoke tobacco, and frequently use more drugs, either therapeutic or recreational. These behaviors strongly manipulate immunity function.

Compelling evidence for the association between stressful life events and ensuing breast cancer was noted in a study from King's College Hospital in London. Women who had a "suspicious but (at that point) undiagnosed lump in their breast" underwent a psychological interview before a biopsy analysis. The outcome revealed that the women who had experienced severe life events during the preceding 5 years had a high probability of being diagnosed as having breast cancer instead of a benign lump or no disease. Nearly half of these women who had experienced emotional trauma turned out to have breast cancer, compared with less than a fifth of those whose biopsy results proved negative.

Defining the Type C Individual

From all the research existing on stress, immunity function, and cancer, a general personality profile has been identified that scientists are calling the Type C individual. Similar to the established Type A coronary-prone behavior pattern, Type C is an evolving profile but currently comprises the following characteristics:

+ Suppresses strong emotions, especially anger
+ Lacks assertiveness and frequently complies with the wishes of others
+ Avoids conflict and is overly concerned with what might offend others
+ Exhibits a calm, outwardly rational, and unemotional approach to life
+ Obeys conventional behavior norms and radiates niceness
+ Self-sacrifice attitude (martyr syndrome) and stoicism
+ Tendency to experience feelings of helplessness or hopelessness

It is not surprising that repeated psychological stress can accelerate cancer and thereby shorten survival times. Some research at Guy's Hospital in London found that high stress heightens the risk of relapse in women who had been operated on for breast cancer. Women dealing with bereavement issues, job loss, or other consistent events determined to be stressful were 5 times more likely to have a recurrence of breast cancer than women who had not experienced such stress.

For all the damage we can do to our immune function with repressed emotions, hopelessness, and general pessimism, such effects can be, as numerous studies have proved, reversed. A major contribution on mental states and cancer comes from research by David Spiegel and his colleagues at Stanford University, whose conclusions reveal that a high-quality social environment can dramatically improve a cancer patient's mental and physical state, prolonging his or her survival. Spiegel and his team discovered that women with advanced breast cancer survived twice as long when they took part in psychological therapy, which improved their social environment.

Negative Influences on the Immune System

The adult body produces approximately 126 billion neutrophils (white blood cells) on a daily basis. Normally, over 25 billion are patrolling the blood and another 2.5 trillion are headquartered in the bone marrow. Over 10 trillion lymphocytes are housed in the lymph tissues. The need to feed these hungry warriors good nutrition is essential for maintaining good immunity.

Nutritional deficiencies decrease a person's natural capacity to resist infection and its aftermath and decreases the overall functioning of the immune system. Poor nutrition adversely affects all aspects of immunity, including T-cell function, other cellular-related killing, the ability of highly specialized defender "B" cells to make antibodies, the functioning of the complement proteins that clear pathogens from our bodies, and phagocytic capacity (ability of the white cells to engulf invading microorganisms).

The following is a nutritional overview of what we know enhances or inhibits immune health:

+ *Vitamin A* can inhibit the growth and development of cancer. Vitamin A deficiency decreases the number of plasma cells that produce antibodies. Some recommendations run as high as suggesting 15,000 to 20,000 IU (International Units) per day; however, long-term supplementation can lead to liver toxicity. Some research suggests that even 10,000 IU per day can increase the risk of fetal abnormalities in pregnant women.

+ *Vitamin C* is an antioxidant nutrient that offers protection to the cell. As an antihistamine, it has a detoxifying action on histamine, which has been shown to weaken immune function. There is reasonable evidence that shows vitamin C can aid many immunological functions. It is found in high concentrations in white blood cells (10 to 80 times greater than plasma levels), mostly in the lymphocytes. Deficiency of vitamin C can also reduce the normal inflammatory response.

+ *Vitamin E* is an antioxidant that protects the fat (lipid) ingredients of cells, including cellular membranes. Vitamin E works in conjunction with the mineral selenium. A deficiency of vitamin E can lower immune resistance by reducing white blood cell numbers and the antibody response to invading toxins. A lack of vitamin E also weakens delayed hypersensitivity reactions, a vital immunological response to cancer, parasites, and chronic infections. While vitamin E is a powerful intracellular antioxidant and protects the white blood cells from being broken apart by free radicals, large doses (over 600 IU) have been shown to inhibit immune response.

+ *B vitamin* deficiencies, particularly of B_1, B_2, B_6, pantothenic acid, and biotin, inhibit antibody production. Reduced amounts of folic acid and B_{12} have also been shown to weaken immune defenses. A deficiency in pyridoxine reduces antibody volume and decreases white blood cell functioning.

+ *Zinc* deficiencies cause a decrease in the strength of certain white blood cells known as T killer cells and natural killer cells. Zinc is also an essential trace mineral element for immunity and plays a featured role in immune maintenance.

+ *Iron* deficiencies reduce phagocytosis, the process in which lymph cells engulf microorganisms.

+ *Copper* deficiencies reduce T-cell populations, causing immune depression.

+ *Selenium* is necessary for the regular functioning of one of the body's most critical antioxidants, glutathione peroxidase, an enzyme that neutralizes cell-damaging free radicals. Reduced selenium can cause a significant decrease in the body's antibody production. Selenium also has the ability to neutralize toxic metals, which can suppress immunity. Vitamin E and selenium work synergistically. A shortage of these two nutrients can decrease the cytotoxic function of natural killer cells.

Although these concentrated nutritional elements are important, the gamut of antioxidants, phytochemicals, whole grain fiber, and daily vegetable protein sources are the basis for maximized functioning of our immune system. Some common foods can inhibit immunity.

For instance, consuming over 100 grams (3 ounces) of simple carbohydrate (table sugar) at one sitting (easily done with a can of soda pop) dramatically reduces the ability of the white blood cells to engulf and destroy bacteria. However, simple carbohydrates are equal-opportunity offenders, and this applies to *all* simple carbohydrates and not just ordinary table sugar, whether it be from glucose, fructose, sucrose, honey, or even the "natural sugar" found in three glasses of orange juice. Overall, research has shown that elevated sugar levels have a depressing effect on immune function.

In contrast, the consumption of 100 grams of *whole* complex carbohydrates (aka starch) yields has virtually no apparent effect on immunity and helps to regulate blood sugar. Requiring barely 30 minutes to begin its immune damage, simple sugar causes a suppressive effect that can last from 3 to 5 hours. Only 2 hours after ingestion, the overall white blood cell activity has shown to be reduced by as much as 40 percent. Obviously, this can be devastating because the defending neutrophil white blood cells make up from 60 to 70 percent of the total circulating white blood cell population. With glucose volumes of only 2 ounces (approximately 75 grams), lymphocyte activity has shown a marked decrease.

If you're an average American, you're consuming a whopping 140 to 150 grams of sucrose every day, and this amount does not include other refined simple sugars, such as fruit juice and honey. The problem is not only sugar intolerance due to concentration but a physical low blood sugar state, which can be immediately triggered by sugar ingestion. Plentiful research has found that low blood sugar levels weaken immune function.

Physician John McDougal recommends the avoidance of animal-based proteins for increasing immune health:

> To avoid autoimmune diseases, such as insulin-dependent diabetes, nephritis, rheumatoid arthritis, and lupus, we should eliminate animal proteins from our diet and the diet of our children. Animal proteins can pass intact through the intestinal wall into the blood stream. The immune system recognizes these proteins as foreign, invading substances, like a virus or bacteria. Our body makes antibodies that attack small segments of these proteins, consisting of a specific sequence of amino acids. Unfortunately, this same sequence of amino acids may be present on the cells of our body. In an effort to destroy the animal protein, the antibody attacks our own tissues, destroying them. This process is known as immunologic mimicry. Plant proteins are unlikely to cause mimicry because they are so structurally different from human proteins. . . . Ingested animal proteins from cows, chickens, pigs, and other animals can stimulate an attack on our own body parts.

A high-fat diet in some experiments has also been shown to impair immunity; however, a deficiency of fatty acids can also significantly contribute to immune dysfunction. Part of the strength of certain foods comes directly from their effect on our immune defenses. For our white blood cells to attack cancer cells, they must recognize that such cells are abnormal. White cell function is dramatically enhanced with minimum fat in the bloodstream. Obesity can alter a variety of immune responses, most commonly the risk of infection and a reduced capacity for the immune cells to be protective.

Associations between food allergy and chronic infections have been documented in a wide variety of studies. Many experts consider allergic reactions to foods as one of the most important (and generally unrecognized) immune-suppressing problems confronting us today. Numerous allergy-related reactions and their resulting effects on immune function warrant attention to determining what foods may put one at risk.

Studies with alcohol show a profound decrease of white blood cell neutrophils after ingestion, even in nutritionally normal individuals. While alcoholics are known to be more susceptible to pneumonia and other infections, a major cause of disease and death among alcoholics is infectious disease.

Chemicals That Threaten Immune Health

The modern reality is that our current society has become highly dependent on synthetically manufactured chemicals. Some research has found that over 600 different chemicals can be detected in our bodies that were not previously detected in human subjects before the early 1900s. This correlates with increases of cancer, stroke, birth defects, and immune, neurological, and reproductive disorders, and the rise of infectious diseases. Our inevitable ingestion of heavy metals, such as mercury, lead, cadmium, and arsenic, is known to cause immunological disorders that are irreversible.

A study of harbor seals that were fed fish with high pollutant levels, showed a correlation with infections and immune system dysfunction. Based on our increasing exposure and inevitable physical degeneration, the term *behavioral toxicology* came into existence during the 1980s.

Additional immune system poisons that we are commonly exposed to include dioxin (a toxic chemical formed in combustion and pulping of paper), PCBs (linked to increased breast cancer rates), chromium, copper, nickel, tin, vanadium, DDT, chlordane, dieldrin, heptachlor, lindane, mirex, toxaphene, other pesticides (carbamates, carbaryl, carbofuran, and malathion), and chlorine (primarily used for dry-cleaning and formed during water treatment).

The source of some of these chemicals can be found in everyday ingredients we use in the workplace, at home, and on our dinner tables as well as in the environment:

+ *Lead* can be found in paint, paint dust, colored newsprint, soil, and water. Rice and vegetables cooked in lead-contaminated water can absorb 80 percent of the lead. Other lead sources may come from food wrapping, canned foods, plastic wire insulation, and even in calcium supplementation and antacids.

+ *Cadmium* accumulates in the soft tissues (particularly the kidney) and is generally found in high amounts in organ meats (especially liver and kidney). Shellfish such as snails, oysters, mussels, shrimp, and crab and some fish have been reported to have high amounts of cadmium. It is also found in cereal grains, root crops, and green leafy vegetables. A common and highly absorbable source of cadmium is cigarettes.

+ *Mercury* is easily absorbed into the body through food and can be frequently found in fish and seafood. The fish we are especially concerned about are predatory fish, such as shark, swordfish, pike, and barracuda (any fish with teeth). These fish have shown repeatedly high levels of mercury and PCBs. Freshwater fish are usually mercury carriers. For those choosing to eat fish, deep-water white fish that is low in fat content (flounder, cod, sole, haddock, red snapper) are better fish choices.

And, there's more; our exposure to organic solvents (paint thinner, petroleum distillates, and cleaning products), drugs, medications, pesticides, cosmetics, and certain vaccinations all take a toll on immune health. The evolving research and declining health of our immune systems warrant a serious look at what we tolerate and choose to be exposed to in everyday life.

Maximizing Immunity

Lifestyle Factors

AVOID TOBACCO. The list of destructive factors behind smoking grows continuously. Smoking creates irregular blood sugar patterns, taste and fragrance insensitivity, diminished lung function, circulatory inhibition, blood toxicity, hormonal fluctuation, and decreased oxygenation to cells and more, all of which negatively influence immunity. Smoking has been linked to coronary heart disease and respiratory cancers. You cannot freely enjoy something that wreaks such biochemical havoc.

GO TO BED BEFORE MIDNIGHT. This will help you obtain a minimum of 6.5 to 7 hours of restful sleep. Your body produces its peak amount of the sleep-related hormone, melatonin, at around 2:00 a.m. Ideally, you should be in a deep sleep by that time. Poor sleep can diminish the number of disease-fighting natural killer (NK) cells in the blood. When a group of volunteers were denied half of their usual sleep times for a single night, levels of NK cells, which help fight off viral infection such as the flu, dropped by 30 percent and remained low until the volunteers were able to get a normal night's sleep. In a landmark 1993 study at the National Institute of Mental Health, biopsychologist Carol Everson found long-term sleep deprivation caused fatal blood infections in laboratory rats.

Even a small amount of sleep loss over one night can weaken immune function. A *Science News* study of 23 healthy men aged 22 to 61 were deprived of 4 hours of sleep for one night. The following day, their NK cell activity plummeted to 30 percent. A good night's sleep the following night restored the cells to normal status.

MAINTAIN AN EMOTIONALLY SUPPORTIVE EMOTIONAL AND SOCIAL NET-WORK. The mind and body interact in many ways to influence immunity. The emerging field of psychoneuroimmunology is full of conclusive data on the positive influence that love, nurturing, and high motivational states have on immunity. Even pet ownership shows a marked influence on immunity. However, feeling isolated and unmotivated lends toward depressive states. Volunteering, renewing old friendships, making new acquaintances, and connecting with family members all offer a deep sense of belonging and emotional nourishment.

MAKE STRESS MANAGEABLE. There is always stress. In fact, the state of no stress might be considered death. Thus, it's a question of making your stresses *manageable*. Mental stress is one of most debilitating hazards to the immune system. Author Blair Justice has documented many research studies that show stress-induced illness is real and contributes to numerous diseases. Justice clarifies that it's simply not just external sources of stress *but rather how each person reacts to stress.* Physiologically, negative reactions increase the adrenal gland's secretion of hormones, especially the corticosteroids and catecholamines, which inhibit white blood cells and accelerate thymus shrinkage. The common result is reduced immune function, leading to a propensity for infections, cancer, and other illnesses.

PRACTICE DAILY RELAXATION THERAPIES. A whole host of therapies have proven effective for relaxing, immunity enhancement, and restoring vitality. Yoga, meditation, tai chi, biofeedback, Qigong, worship, chanting, guided visualization, massage, and breathing practice can all be effective therapies. Find a group, class, book, video, or private instructor to introduce you to a particular therapy so you can begin practice.

EXERCISE MODERATELY BUT CONSISTENTLY. Moderate exercise can significantly benefit the immune system by causing short-term increases in white cell count and minimizing the occurrence of common infections. However, strenuous exercise can do just the opposite—it can result in immune suppression and increase the risk of infections. It has been documented that exhausting activity temporarily reduces the immune system's defense frontlines for several hours after exertion. Heavy acute or chronic exercise is also associated with an increase in the occurrence of upper respiratory tract infections.

Dietary Factors for Enhancing Immune Function

REDUCE OR AVOID ALCOHOL. Alcohol, a fermented sugar product of great concentration, has been shown to increase susceptibility to infections in animals. Alcoholics are also known to be more prone to pneumonia and other infections. A study of human neutrophils (white blood cells) revealed a severe drop in their activity after alcohol ingestion, even in people who had tested nutritionally normal.

REDUCE FAT INTAKE. The American diet, filled with meats, dairy products, and refined foods, is at the root of a deficient immune system. Some of the most detrimental foods in the Western diet are polyunsaturated fats (vegetable oils) and animal fats. While we do have certain requirements for essential fatty acids, they can be obtained from foods and supplements. The diet that best supports optimal immune function is a low-fat, complex carbohydrate–based diet.

AVOID OR MINIMIZE SIMPLE SUGARS. Based on the fact that as little as 3 ounces of sugar can reduce immune function to nearly 50 percent for a period of 1 to 5 hours, major restriction of simple carbohydrates is advised. Choose small amounts of fibrous fruit for sweet cravings as opposed to the concentrated source of sugar available from juice. If your commercial beverage contains high-fructose corn syrup, steer clear. This is a very poorly absorbed sugar source that is not intestinal friendly.

MINIMIZE ANIMAL PROTEIN. Research from fat, protein, digestive, and toxicity studies have established that animal protein, if included in the diet, should be considered more of a side dish than a staple food, and consumed less frequently. When including animal protein in a meal, complement it with abundant vegetables.

EAT WHOLE GRAINS, VEGETABLES, AND BEANS. The nutritional wealth and detoxifying effect of whole grains, vegetables, and beans in the body make these whole foods excellent choices for daily fare.

TRY NEW FOODS. The healthy bacterial quality of fermented foods (miso), sea salt, and the mineral richness of sea vegetables (seaweeds) offer adventurous palates expanded nutrition, greater toxin discharge from the body, and additional immune protection.

AVOID OVEREATING. "Quantity changes quality," goes the saying. In excess, anything can be toxic. Overeating burdens not only digestion but the detoxifying action of our liver, which can be considered a frontline defense for maintaining good immunity.

ALLOW TIME TO DIGEST THE EVENING MEAL BEFORE SLEEP. Evening is usually a restful time when we wind down before retreating for the night into a restorative sleep that prepares us for the energy demands of the following day. Lying down after eating can weaken the door between the stomach and esophagus (esophageal sphincter) as a result of stomach acids saturating and compromising its seal. This is one of the causes behind acid reflux disorder. If you're digesting most of the night, chances are that your sleep will be disturbed, immunity impaired, and energy, along with mental clarity, during the subsequent day will be compromised

Immune-Supportive Supplements

Nothing can substitute for the power of quality whole food as a daily nutritional source; however, some supplements have been shown to boost immune function and in certain individuals with low levels or poor assimilation, can be beneficial. Immune-supportive supplements can be used to enhance immunity:

◆ *Essential fatty acids* are required for the production of prostaglandins (hormone-like chemicals that stimulate immunity)

◆ *Vitamins A, B, C,* and *E* are generally available from dietary sources but can be enhanced with modest supplementation.

◆ *Zinc, copper,* and *selenium* have clearly been established as necessary for healthy immune function.

Immune-Supportive Herbs

Herbal support for enhancing immunity is becoming recognized as a valuable healing resource. Because it is not within the scope of this book to provide detailed descriptions of immune-boosting herbs, I recommend two books I have found to be especially thorough: Donald R. Yance Jr. with Arlene Valentine, *Herbal Medicine, Healing and Cancer* (Keats Publishing, 1999) and Joseph Pizzorno, *Total Wellness* (Prima Lifestyles, 1996).

The following herbs and fungi are known to contain strong immune-boosting qualities:

Astragalus
Ashwagandha
Aloe vera
Cat's claw (uña de gato)
Garlic
Ginseng (*Panax* and Siberian)
Goldenseal
Echinacea
Cloud fungus (PSK)
Maitake, reishi, and shiitake mushrooms

We are relearning and scientifically documenting what ancient peoples have known all along: that mind and body are inseparable and that to move health forward we must unify the fragments. How we nourish ourselves, how we relate to others, our personal perceptions, and the manner in which we live on a daily basis are all important strategies toward restoring health or as a part of any healing protocol.

8

Practical Strategies to Eliminate Sugar, Fat, and Overeating

He who makes excuses, accuses himself.

—French proverb

Will Power and His Band of Excuses

Many people, despite having all kinds of information in their heads about health, cannot stick to a healthful diet. Why is this?

From my observation, the key to eating healthfully consistently is *not* about having more nutritional information any more than it is about having a private chef prepare everything you need and spoon-feed you. Dietary awareness in this country is definitely increasing—most people have heard through the media, government reports, medical studies, and countless books, that whole grains, vegetables, beans, and fruits are good for you and that we've relied too heavily on animal proteins, dairy foods, and sugar. In reality, the most common reasons people offer for their dietary transgressions are the following:

Excuse. I just have weak willpower.

Real reason. It might feel as if you had an overwhelming urge that should be defeated by using your will; however, cravings or the inability to remain on a diet has very little to do with willpower. You might have to remind yourself, once in a while, why you're doing what you are because the desire to eat what everyone else is eating or the way you used to eat might seem more convenient or comforting. But in the long run, it's not. And it probably has a lot to do with whatever condition you may be battling, either as a cause or as an aggravating factor. If you are following a balanced way of eating, in which the foods consumed offer variety, taste appeal, good nutrition, and some degree of familiarity as well as supporting the regulation of your blood sugar, it is doubtful that you will have strong cravings. These factors are what make it easy to dismiss the idea of craving. However, if you're eating irregularly and experiencing lowered blood sugar (when sugar becomes more physically appealing) or restricting yourself to one or two bland ways of preparing your food, such as steaming or boiling all of your vegetables, then chances are your cravings will be strong. You will also be frustrated, and sticking to a disciplined healing or dietary approach will prove difficult.

Following a structured plan that you implement with gradual changes will make it easier to stick to your health goals. In the end, it's about being more organized and aware of the subtle and not-so-subtle factors that can sabotage your dietary planning. It is being fully aware of the steps you need to take and why you are doing this in the first place.

Excuse: It's not that bad for you.

Real reason: Minimizing the negative effects of certain foods may be a justification for not following through or for intentionally giving up on a dietary plan. At the same time, keep in mind that bad is relative. It's just too general a statement to make good sense. For some, a certain food or habit might not be all that bad, but if it's not really supporting you, it's best avoided—for now.

You want to avoid thinking in extreme black-and-white terms of good and bad. For some, eating dessert every day might not be a good thing right now. Maybe later, you can widen your diet and be more flexible.

Chronically categorizing everything you do and eat on an extreme scale might not always be in your best interest. Constant self-criticism will not engender a healthy self-image. You want to judge your choices in a healthier and more positive way.

Excuse: I just wanted it.

Real reason: Pure excuse. This might be all right to hear from the lips of a six-year-old, but I was taken aback when I had a client say, "That hot fudge sundae I had after dinner Tuesday . . . I just wanted it . . . real bad."

There could be many reasons that my client wanted that treat after dinner, but just wanting it was not sufficient. When I reviewed this particular client's dietary record, I saw that for the day he gave into his inner six-year-old, he had a very scant breakfast, no lunch, and due to the afternoon's work demands, ended up not eating until he had returned home for dinner. Since his declining blood sugar from not eating all afternoon did not sufficiently rise after completing dinner, he was not satisfied. Even a second dinner portion did very little to satisfy him. He suddenly realized that he had a craving for something much more concentrated and sweet: ice cream!

"How did it feel to eat this after your dinner, despite being full?" I asked.

"It was heaven—lapped it up like it was the last hot fudge sundae of my life."

That reaction—aside from his obvious love of ice cream—sounded like lowered blood sugar finally being elevated. His craving was, in fact, based more on physiological factors than on some random food preference or craving.

Excuse: Hey, come on; you gotta live a little!

Real reason: This is a common superficial justification from someone who has felt restricted and frequently goes through the frustration of unsatisfied cravings. If you find yourself feeling like this, you may need a more gradual and flexible dietary approach The key to dealing with cravings successfully is learning about balance—not simply balancing nutritional elements like acid and alkaline foods, but the physiological and psychological reasons that make us crave foods that cannot support long-term health. Otherwise, we feel out of control as we try to justify our choices. Secretly, we know we're lying to ourselves. However, learning how and why cravings can derail us is essential in for achieving dietary balance.

HE SAYS, SHE SAYS

I ONCE COUNSELED this macho pro-football jock who had been diagnosed with type 2 diabetes. The physician who referred him to me wanted me to outline a complex-carbohydrate, high-fiber, low-fat diet for him. From his diet records, I noticed that Mr. Jock ate cheese practically every 10 minutes. When I asked him if cheese was something he craved, he looked at me, indignantly, as if I'd asked him to disrobe.

"No," he replied. "I don't *crave* it. I just . . . I, uh . . . *like* it."

It seems that the word *craving* is secretly part of the feminine vernacular. Real men don't crave. They "like." For many men, the word *craving* often implies neediness. Real men don't give in to cravings. They only have likes, that's all . . .

This gender difference in language is quite common in numerous areas; men don't use *intuition*, instead they have a *hunch*. A woman will have little reservation about saying, "I'm *afraid* we're drifting apart." Whereas a man might be more comfortable rephrasing that statement to downplay fear, remarking: "Well, I have some *concerns* about our relationship."

Real men are supposed to be able to handle deprivation. But semantics aside, a craving is a craving and most often, it's a message that your body is broadcasting—an attempt to make some kind of balance.

Internal Memo from the Body Department

Aside from sentimental associations ("Dad, remember how we used to have milk shakes every Sunday? Let's go get some."), most cravings can be attributed to either physical or psychological factors. Recognizing what drives your cravings is the first step toward finding your own balance and creating good health without having to feel deprived.

The process of homeostasis is how the body maintains its most desirable equilibrium. Your body has a number of automatic devices for regulating the fine balance of blood pressure, internal temperature, blood pH (acid–alkaline balance), blood sugar, and hormonal secretions.

A number of our popular consuming passions wreak havoc with homeostasis: Alcohol, sugary foods, tobacco, caffeine, and various drugs all lead to gross imbalances that we attempt to counterbalance in extreme ways. For example, excessive alcohol and refined sugar intake, which steal vital minerals from our bodies, often result in strong cravings for meats and salted foods. Long periods of fasting (skipping meals) frequently give way to overeating. Eating excessive amounts of fatty food can produce fatigue when red blood cells clump and bind the oxygen that they are carrying. In turn this promotes cravings for stimulating foods, such as spices, sugar, or caffeine.

The negative long-term effects, both mentally and physically, of going to extremes carry inevitable consequences. By developing your awareness of the factors that create cravings, you can feel more in control of your body, while acquiring an attuned sensitivity to your needs and body signals.

Craving What the Body Needs

As is well known to farmers, ranchers, and veterinarians, salt cravings are not uncommon among domesticated animals. Animals have been known to roam for miles in search of salt licks. As reported from various part of the world for the past two centuries, some animals develop a distinct craving for bones. Presumably, these animals lack phosphorus and eating bone is an attempt to rectify this deficiency. Experiments with phosphorus-deficient cattle revealed specific appetite preferences for ground bone or bird feces. These appetites disappeared when they were injected with phosphate, indicating a physiological basis for the craving.

Blood levels of calcium and phosphate have a definite influence on feeding behavior. One study showed that calcium-deficient rats had a preference for high-calcium diets. However, on removal of their parathyroid gland, calcium intake increased to as much as 13 times the normal levels but returned to normal with treatment. In a separate study, calcium-deficient chickens ate eggshells whenever available. Not to be outdone, calcium-deficient pigs have been observed licking mineral-rich lime from the walls of their cages. In most cases, these bizarre behaviors are physiologically driven as a way to compensate for nutrient imbalance.

Many pregnant women have strong cravings for certain forms of acidity (tomatoes, lemons, spices, peppers, and so on), which can draw minerals into the blood to neutralize this acidity. While acidity from these foods might not be health-supportive for the mother, the developing fetus is the probable benefactor of the alkaline minerals that the acidity has drawn.

The indigenous Pomo tribe of northern California used dirt in their diet, mixing it with ground corn. Whether this could have been for reasons of tradition, superstition, wisdom, or intuition was not known, but the mineralized (alkaline) dirt neutralized the acid elements of the corn, thus making it easier to digest. A similar practice by some Southwest native tribes used wood ash (carbonized wood is highly alkaline) in their corn cooking water, presumably for the same reasons.

Eight Categories of Cravings

There is very little conclusive scientific research on specific reasons for human food cravings; why you'd sell your firstborn for exotic chocolate, or drive 35 miles for a particular kind of cheesecake. Sometimes, there seems to be no rhyme or reason to our cravings.

The following information is based on my observations over the course of more than 40 years of nutritional counseling, personal experimentation, and the study of available research. I have identified eight general categories of cravings. Each will be discussed in detail along with the specific strategies to aid in eliminating sugar and fat and curbing overeating.

Nutritional
Acid–alkaline balance
Blood sugar–hormonal
Emotional
Genetics
Allergy response
Elimination–detoxification
Expansion–contraction

Your desire for a particular food can be attributed to any one of these categories. As previously stated, cravings are usually the body's way to signal its varied needs. It's important to pay attention to these signals but equally important to recognize there exists a fine line between fueling dietary addictions and just following dietary intuition. Understanding the meaning behind different cravings can liberate you from feeling guilty or out of control with your eating. Self-mastery begins with awareness.

Nutritional

Nutritional cravings can fall into two subcategories: food group imbalance and specific nutrient excess or deficiency.

FOOD GROUP IMBALANCE

The chief food groups are carbohydrates, fats, and proteins. Western nutrition therapy, both clinical and naturopathic versions, seems to have a preoccupation with stressing *quantity* of nutrients or watchdogging calories. The concern is usually about fear of deficiency: Do you have enough protein? Are you getting proper vitamins and minerals? Drinking enough water? These are all valid questions; yet, it seems that most of our problems are usually due to excess and rarely deficiency.

The following chart provides an at-a-glance summary of the sources for carbohydrates, fats, and proteins in modern and traditional diets:

MACRONUTRIENTS	MODERN DIET SOURCE	TRADITIONAL MODEL SOURCE
Carbohydrates	Grain products (bread, pasta) vegetables, fruits, refined sugars	Whole grains, grain products, vegetables, whole fruits
Fats	Meat, dairy, oils, nuts	Vegetable oils, nuts, minimal animal products
Proteins	Animal products, dairy	Beans, bean products, minimal animal products

The most striking difference between the two diets is the amount of refined sugar and meat in the modern profile versus the abundance of complex carbohydrates and reduced animal protein in the traditional profile.

A lack of complex carbohydrates and an excess of simple carbohydrates can create an imbalance that fosters strong cravings for more protein or fat or for overeating. Years of studying client dietary records has convinced me that a substantial reason for these cravings is based on this imbalance.

The lack of whole complex carbohydrate (particularly whole grains) can trigger carbohydrate cravings. We often crave refined sugars and concentrated simple sugars as an attempt to satisfy carbohydrate requirements. However, due to their quick digestion, simple carbohydrates eventually create irregular blood sugar levels. As a result, we are attracted to fat or protein to feel more satisfied, to stabilize blood sugar, and to experience the flavor that fats hold.

The Nature's Cancer-Fighting Foods Plan provides an abundance of mineral- and vitamin-rich whole grains, beans and vegetables, and fruits, offering a more enduring, satisfying nourishment. Automatically, our desire for fat, protein, or overeating becomes reduced.

SPECIFIC NUTRIENT EXCESS OR DEFICIENCY

The second factor in the nutritional category of cravings focuses on specific nutrient cravings based on vitamin, trace mineral, or mineral deficiency.

When I've counseled clients who complain about having milk cravings, I recommend more mineral-rich foods or a mineral supplement, which often eliminates these cravings. Smokers tend to crave foods with vitamin C (usually orange juice, also high in sugar) because their vitamin C levels tend to fall below normal levels. This also ties in with blood sugar, but more about that in category three.

Excess sugar or alcohol (both highly acidic) tend to require minerals in order to be neutralized and made less toxic, so it makes sense that this excess can cause cravings for more salt, pickles, meats (for stored salt within animal muscle tissue), or other alkaline and mineralized foods.

Acid–Alkaline Balance

Opposites attract. This also applies to the chemical qualities of acid and alkaline within different foods.

As mentioned previously, the overall effect of excess acidity, which our modern diet contains in plentiful amounts, is the leeching of minerals from bone, digestive fluid, and blood sources in order to reduce acidity to make it more tolerable for the body's assimilation. If your diet tends to be more acid based (found in high-protein, high-sugar diets; from excess dietary fat; or from regular alcohol consumption), restricting strong alkaline foods is one way of naturally reducing your craving for sugar and assorted sweet foods, as the reduction of alkaline eases our craving (or need) for acids.

Sugar and salt are dietary opposites; the more sugar you consume, the more you're likely to increase your craving for salted foods and meats—which contain salt residues in the animal tissues. In addition, from a nutritional point of view, animal meats, being high in protein, contain no carbohydrate, whereas sugar, being primarily carbohydrate, contains no protein. This probably accounts for why the combination of meat and sugar seems to be at the foundation of the modern Western diet. Fast-food restaurants seem to understand this, leading to the typical menu of burgers, fries, and a milk shake or pie.

One theory suggests fat has a unique buffering effect and makes a comfortable middle-ground food choice to neutralize either extreme. Chemically, fats have the ability to moderately buffer acids, or acidify weak alkalis. Some dairy (salted and nonsalted cheese, milk, butter, yogurt, ghee) and most soybean products (tofu) fall into this category.

Blood Sugar–Hormonal

Our blood sugar state is somewhat like a roller-coaster ride. The highs and lows can be exciting, but at the same time, they can be exhausting and stressful, if not dangerous.

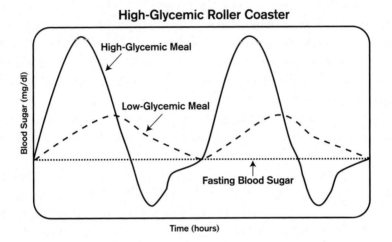

High-Glycemic Roller Coaster

However, blood sugar can be moderated so that these highs and lows are not so extreme. Any extreme fluctuation of blood sugar brings our hormonal system into play, releasing insulin as a balancing mechanism and hormones from the adrenal glands as well. With high and low blood sugar, insulin spurts can have a damaging effect on arteries and trigger systemic inflammation.

During digestion, carbohydrates are broken into simpler tiny units of sugar in the stomach. This sugar can then enter the blood to nourish the cells. Actually, a good portion of a food's simple sugar enters the blood as soon as it touches your tongue! There are a number of hormonal mechanisms that help regulate this process. Blood sugar levels will fluctuate, elevating and descending according to the kind of diet and activity you have. Ideally, for enduring energy, you want a stable blood sugar level. Wildly fluctuating blood sugar levels is one of the most common ways to sabotage your diet and your long-term health.

Hyperinsulism is the result of high sugar volume. Extremely high blood sugar can make you feel suddenly energetic, giddy, and talkative. However, if blood sugar goes unchecked and continues to dive or escalate, you could find yourself in a coma. As a unique form of autoprotection, the body releases insulin from the pancreas, which bonds to the sugar, transports it out of the blood, and stores it in the liver.

If the liver becomes flooded beyond its capacity (approximately 60 to 90 grams), the excess sugar has to be stored in body tissue, and the location of choice is usually in the less active body tissues of our buttocks, abdomen, and thighs, which are areas of prime concern to overweight individuals.

The rapid release of insulin in response to excess sugar can result in hypoglycemia, or low blood sugar. With low blood sugar, fatigue increases as the muscles have less sugar supply for energy. You might also feel negative and irritable. In Chinese medicine, one of the diagnostic indicators of chronic blood sugar problems is consistent darkness beneath the eyes, specifically, close to the inner eye corners.

Sometimes, a low blood sugar condition can be initially mistaken for hypothyroidism because of slowed reaction times and sleepiness. Understanding this can save you much anxiety.

When blood sugar soars, meaning an influx of sugar to the blood, you're likely to suddenly crave salted foods or animal protein. With low blood sugar, it's usually the opposite: You'll crave sweet foods. I've observed that the most common physical reasons for sweet cravings and overeating tend to be from skipped meals, which means long periods between meals, which causes lower blood sugar.

From personal as well as client observation, I suspect that choosing to eat something fatty or fried in place of something sweet is an unconscious strategy to temporarily pacify the sweet tooth. Because fats take nearly 3 hours to leave the stomach, you feel a satisfying sense of fullness given their slow digestion. In addition, fat has a buffering effect on the acid–alkaline balance of blood chemistry. Consuming whole grains, vegetables, beans, and fibrous fruits as main foods will keep blood sugar at a more stable level, increasing your sensitivity and endurance while minimizing cravings.

There could be any number of nutritionally based reasons for cravings. An interesting study from University of Michigan researchers showed that chocolate cravings are not just about flavor but that chocolate actually has a chemically altering effect on brain physiology, similar to opiate drugs. The researchers observed 26 volunteers on a drug called naloxone, which is an opiate blocker used in emergency rooms to stop powerful narcotics (heroin, morphine) from affecting brain tissue. Ironically, the researchers learned that the naloxone ended up blocking the appeal of chocolate for these volunteers. When they were offered different choices of chocolate (popular chocolate bars, M&M's, chocolate-chip cookies), the chocolate seemed about as exciting as raw broccoli.

What this revealed to the researchers was that a strong aspect of chocolate's appeal was in how it stimulated the identical part of the brain that morphine does. Strangely, this puts chocolate in a drug category. Obviously, not a serious one or one that can be fatal, but enough, in some cases, to stimulate addictive tendencies.

Instead of being too focused about missing nutrients, adopt a whole foods approach to eating. In some cases, temporarily adding a multivitamin or multimineral food-based supplement to your eating plan can help balance nutritional factors.

Emotional

Eating can be a nurturing activity. Sometimes, when we feel emotionally deprived, we may automatically turn to eating for this nurturance. It can be a conscious or unconscious attempt to get our needs met. Learning to identify and express emotions is the first step toward stopping this self-destructive cycle.

Psychologically, self-esteem and social value are frequently connected to our physical appearance. The modern concept of beauty, perpetuated by Hollywood images, women's magazines, and men's action heroes, suggests that the ultimate goal is to be thin (or muscular), hard bodied, smooth skinned, young looking, and vital. Considering that less than 1 percent of the population will fit this ideal, it's not surprising that many people are dissatisfied with their bodies. The popular media and its unrealistic portrayal of beauty and chic seduce them with the unattainable. The inability to meet these ideals, in many cases, leads to lowered self-esteem and often results in self-punishing behaviors.

For some, eating is not a nurturing fuel or pleasure ritual. In times of loneliness, stress, and fear, it becomes a convenient drug of choice; a friend, a companion, a comfort, and a distraction from the frustrating, unfulfilling experiences of daily life.

More serious compulsive overeating is characterized by an inability to cease eating when one's physical hunger has been satisfied. Here are some of the most common factors that drive compulsive overeaters:

+ High levels of anxiety and/or shame
+ The preoccupation with and fear of fat
+ Negative body image and lack of acceptance of a normal body
+ Extreme dieting; alternating restrictive periods with binge eating
+ Sensitivity or allergy to specific foods or food groups

While there are many approaches to dealing with compulsive overeating, some therapists recommend 10-minute journaling when the urge to eat—not arising from actual hunger—occurs. To get started, ask yourself questions such as these:

How am I *really* feeling presently?
Has anything happened that has made me feel upset, sad, or fearful?
When I feel these feelings, what do I really need?
What is familiar about these feelings?
When I have felt this way in the past?
When is the first time that I can remember feeling this way?
What can make me feel better other than eating?
Where do I feel discomfort in my body? Shoulders? Jaw? Chest? Abdomen?
If I do eat, how will I feel?
What will I feel if I wait until the next meal?

Recommendations for combating emotional eating include the following:

+ Give up restrictive dieting and eat well-balanced meals.
+ Develop a healthy self-image by focusing on the positive aspects about yourself and others. Think about people whom you admire. Why do you admire them? Realize that physical appearance is a very small part of a person's attractiveness.
+ Get involved in interesting hobbies, creative pursuits, or activities that challenge you and inspire good feelings.
+ Increase your physical activity and focus on the pleasure of movement instead of weight loss, heart threshold levels, or calorie burning.
+ Encourage the healthy expression of your emotions. Learn better ways to articulate how you feel, simply and directly.

HOW DO HORMONES FIT IN THE EMOTIONAL PICTURE?

I'VE HEARD CLIENTS have complained that their physicians make comments such as, "This condition is hormonal and has nothing to do with

(CONTINUED)

your diet." Unfortunately, this is not true and some basic understanding of physiology can clarify this. You cannot separate blood chemistry and hormones. They influence each other. Escalating blood sugar and falling blood sugar both call and bring different hormones into the blood, not only affecting your body but influencing your mood as well.

Many women experience strong cravings for sugar just before menstruation, and this is usually due to having low progesterone levels at that time. Hormones can be powerful initiators of numerous cravings; any diabetic who is insulin dependent must have access to refined sugar in the event of the common occurrence of insulin excess.

Most important, hormones have a powerful influence on mood and emotionality—something handy to remember if you're experiencing a depression and can't find anything to pin it on. It might just be related to a stressed physiology or accumulated acids from the last several days of your eating pattern.

There is an old Chinese saying, "Mind and body, not two." While emotional eating is frequently a symptom of deeper issues, it can be exacerbated by physical factors, such as blood sugar instability, poor nutrition, and inactivity.

The healthiest physical perspective is to view dietary change not as an exercise in deprivation, but as an experiment you've chosen to conduct to test its personal value. When you challenge yourself rather than bend to someone else's rules, the changes you make will quickly prove their positive worth and continually inspire you to remain committed.

If, for example, you begin to stabilize blood sugar levels and can resist eating late at night, you'll inevitably discover that you enjoy deeper sleep, have more energy the next day, and feel a restored sense of hope. The noticeable positive changes you experience will sustain your will to continue. You connect cause and effect. This is the power of an informed choice.

Genetics

True or false: Cravings are your parent's fault. Dad ate sugar by the wheelbarrow and so, what else is a chip off the old block supposed to do? Mom was a compulsive eater, so naturally it's in your genes.

The answer is false—with a bit of true. Many people believe that heredity is the prime factor for many of their ills, addictions, and habits.

In reference to disease, while there might be valid genetic components, what is inherited is a *susceptibility* to develop disease and not the disease itself. It is difficult to separate genetic factors (nature) from the influence of upbringing (nurture or the familial factor) and the environment. But there is little doubt that our habits, including eating, and mannerisms are greatly influenced by the models set by family members

Sometimes, certain cravings you experience might remind you of similar cravings that you recognize in your parents. Or certain foods trigger memories of cherished family celebrations. Usually, such cravings have little to do with biochemical inheritance but more to do with the search for sentimental reconnecting to the past through familiar comfort foods.

Allergy Response

Allergic reactions occur when an offender (food, pollen, dust) interacts with our immune system and produces harmful responses. Among the most common responses, or symptoms, of food allergy are fatigue and sleeplessness. Other symptoms are weakness, headaches, mucous congestion, irritability, poor concentration, memory problems, and depression.

EVERYDAY FOODS THAT CAN CAUSE ALLERGIC REACTIONS

Apples	Eggs	Peanuts
Beef	Green	Pork
Cane sugar	beans	Potatoes
Carrots	Lettuce	Soy prod-
Chicken	Dairy prod-	ucts
Coffee	ucts	Tomatoes
Corn	Oats	Wheat
Chocolate	Oranges	Yeast

Food allergies are distinct from other allergies in that many food allergies can actually foster addiction for the very foods that create debilitating symptoms. The analogy allergists frequently use is one that relates to drug addiction: A heroin addict must use continuously to avoid painful withdrawal symptoms. The risk of cold-turkey withdrawal can be a prolonged ordeal. A continuous dose of the drug keeps the addict symptom free. Food can produce similar reactions. However, the principle difference between food and drug addiction is the degree of severity. I have heard clients say they're climbing the walls for chocolate, but this is figurative, whereas during the ordeal of heroin withdrawal, it's not uncommon to literally try to climb walls.

The worst food addictions are to caffeine, alcohol, dairy products, sugar, and chocolate. In most cases, your favorite treat can often be the one to which you are most allergic. Because a person might be continuously including an addictive food in his or her daily diet, allergy-causing foods can easily go unrecognized.

Two approaches can be used to deal with allergy reactions.

DETERMINE THE OFFENDER AND ELIMINATE OR REDUCE YOUR EXPOSURE TO IT. This is easier said than done. It requires some very simple eating and self-observation, but sensitizing yourself is one of the best ways to figure out the culprit. First, *stop* consuming the most offending items, such as *all* dairy foods, sugar, alcohol, nuts, soy items, corn, and grains with gluten (the best nongluten grains are brown rice, millet, and quinoa). Eat a baseline diet of whole grains, beans, and vegetables for 4 to 5 days. By this time, all of your symptoms should cease and a renewed sensitivity should be established. Now gradually begin adding one former food category per day and note your reaction. Any noticeable nasal congestion, immediate fatigue, brain fog, or skin breakouts (typically, welts or raised red patches) are standard indicators of food intolerance.

STRENGTHEN YOUR IMMUNE SYSTEM TO CREATE GREATER RESISTANCE TO THE FOODS OR SUBSTANCES THAT PRODUCE REACTIONS. There are numerous ways to strengthen immune function, and the chief strategy for accomplishing this is to first refrain from consuming foods that weaken immunity! Such foods are sugar, highly refined foods, alcohol, excessive fats, and exposure to prolonged stress. Another immune-debilitating factor is a lack of rest. Inadequate rest or very late nights have a debilitating effect on immune function. Once the factors of diet and lifestyle are handled and not sabotaging the healthful path, then certain supplements can be added to enhance immunity.

The nutritional supplement, beta-glucan, has been shown to stimulate immune function. Beta-glucans are complex sugars that are found in the cellulose of plants, cereal bran, some seaweeds, the cell walls of bakers' yeast, and certain mushrooms (maitake, reishi, and shiitake varieties).

These exceptional nutrients are considered biological response modifiers because of their ability to activate the immune system. See Chapter 7 for immune-enhancing strategies.

Elimination–Detoxification

Cravings can arise when you are in a cleansing process and have begun to change your diet. Theoretically, as we cleanse our bodies from toxins and foods that are not health supportive, stored toxins from fat tissues dissolve, and it has been suggested that toxins are then released back into the blood for elimination through the liver and kidneys, lungs, and skin. During this time, it's not unusual to crave foods that originate from this storage. While this theory, also known as detoxification, belongs to cultural folk medicine models and the natural hygiene schools of a hundred years ago in western Europe, I've seen clients experience such purgings often enough to recognize that it does have relevance despite the lack of so-called scientific merit.

Some years ago, I heard about a group of businessmen who were involved in undergoing a sauna cleansing process with a natural-hygiene group in the California desert. They spent long periods in infrared saunas, where low heat penetrates deeper into tissue than ordinary saunas, taking 10-minute breaks every hour and continuously hydrating themselves with bottled water. As it turned out, many of these men had been regular marijuana users in their hippie days, but had long abandoned the habit.

Those who had been heavy users, admitted to experiencing a sudden craving for marijuana during the detox sessions. Some claimed they could even taste it in their saliva, whereas others remarked they felt slightly dizzy headed or even stoned.

The individual, a nutrition PhD, conveying this story to me, theorized that the potent THC resins from the cannabis plant had been long stored in the men's fat tissues and due to the prolonged sauna heat reentered the blood, and while circulating through their systems, passed through the blood–brain barrier, triggering the marijuana memory and cravings.

This might best be described as an elimination craving. Generally, such cravings usually disappear after several hours. If the craving lingers, it might be wise to satisfy it in small quantities as part of your growing respect for the body's innate wisdom, providing whatever substance you're craving is legal!

Expansion–Contraction

The craving category of expansion–contraction is based on a concept from traditional cultures, such as Asian medicine, Ayurveda, and Central American folk medicine. These cultures philosophically observed life in terms of opposites and recognized the natural laws that exist between them.

In the natural world, all phenomena exist in opposition and support each other: light and dark, strong and weak, hot and cold, centrifugal force and centripetal force, short wave and long wave, sodium and potassium, animal and vegetable, male and female, and so on. Numerous cultures categorized these differences under specific terminology. In Asia, for example, yin and yang were used to describe these opposite forces. For the sake of simplicity, I refer to these extremes as *contraction* and *expansion*.

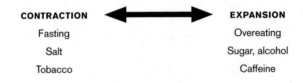

CONTRACTION	EXPANSION
Fasting	Overeating
Salt	Sugar, alcohol
Tobacco	Caffeine

Overeating can produce distension and bloating, which can be physically described as a state of expansion. The opposite of overeating is fasting, a state of gradual constriction. Just as fasting constricts the intestines, eating too much salt has the same constrictive reaction. In fact, people who have a tightened look are often described as salty-looking, like calling an older sailor an "old salt."

Excess dietary salt can create a strong craving for sugar or alcohol. Tobacco users will find that giving up smoking becomes much easier if they eliminate some of the stronger acidic substances (namely, caffeine, alcohol, and sugar) that make tobacco more desirable. The strong alkalinity of tar and nicotine are some of the factors behind these acid cravings, which make them somewhat compatible and makes smoking while drinking alcohol or coffee more desirable. Naturally, there are psychological and reasons of habit that drive certain food and substance behaviors, but by removing strong acid and alkaline elements, the resulting change in body chemistry makes it easier to physically reduce stronger cravings for each extreme.

Handling Cravings for Familiar Foods

Three months into my own dietary change, at the point at which whole grains, beans, vegetables, and fruits had replaced meat, sugar, and dairy food, I began to develop a compulsive craving for chocolate. Not any chocolate, but a particular kind I used to love as a kid and as a teenager: chocolate wafers. I resisted for a while, but eventually, I impulsively bought a package and took it home for a private savoring ritual. That's when I had a realization that took me from disappointment to gratitude: The chocolate wafers didn't taste the same as memory served. I was able to detect strange artificial ingredients that tasted horrible and their high sugar content made them sickeningly sweet.

I've had many clients report similar experiences with foods they previously enjoyed. After a time on their new diet plan, they felt deprived of familiar foods, but when they indulged themselves with the old foods, they realized that their favorite treats no longer had the same appeal or richness of taste that memory held.

As you make whole food dietary changes, your taste buds will sharpen. They will gradually become receptive to the natural quality of complex sugars and the natural sweet taste of fruit. If you return to your old favorites with the anticipation that there's going to be a sensory party, get ready for some heavy disappointment. It's actually a positive sign that your taste buds are becoming sensitized, and this will better guide you to maintain and develop your health with less of an effort. You'll find that you appreciate the natural tastes in whole food and that steering clear of the artificial stuff becomes less of an effort because when you thoroughly chew refined food, the taste, unlike the gradual sweetness from complex sugars, is only pleasant for the first several chews.

Two Factors That Manipulate Cravings

Here are two factors to consider when you have strong cravings. These are foundational and can often influence the kinds of cravings you experience.

OPPOSITES ATTRACT. To better understand why you might be craving what you do and that most cravings are just not random, consider what you ate earlier in the day. This might be a key to why you are craving certain foods. For example, if you had a salty breakfast, like an omelet with a side of turkey sausage, chances are you might crave something sweet a few hours later. If you had pancakes with lots of syrup for breakfast, you might end up craving animal protein or something salted in the next meal, or as a snack. Eating plentiful amounts of salted movie popcorn will have you guzzling cola. If you don't eat for long periods, as a result of falling blood sugar, you'll find yourself tempted to overeat.

TEXTURES AND TASTE MATTER. Try to get specific about what is most appealing from the food you are craving. Sometimes it could be a matter of texture, more than a taste. In traditional Chinese medicine, similar to the classical medicine of India (Ayurveda), there are five essential tastes. Used properly, these tastes will lend a greater sense of variety and balance to your daily meal plan.

THE FIVE TASTES

BITTER	SALTY	SWEET	SOUR	PUNGENT
Arugula	Cooked grain	Carrots	Fermented dishes	Cooked cabbage
Celery	Miso	Cooked onions	Lemon	Garlic
Collards	Pickles (salt)	Corn	Lime	Ginger
Endive	Sea Salt	Fruits	Pickles (tart)	Raw onions
Kale	Sea vegetables	Parsnips	Sauerkraut	Red and white radish
Mustard greens	Sesame salt	Squash	Umeboshi plum	Spices
Parsley	Tamari	Yams		Wasabi
Roasted grain beverage	Umeboshi plum			

There are plentiful combinations with cancer-fighting qualities. The underlying principle here is that these flavors make meals more tastefully balanced and satisfying.

For example, let's say you're making a side dish by steaming collard greens (usually considered a bitter taste). Alone, this might sound fairly boring. However, if you mix together a little soy sauce (salty taste) with lemon juice (sour), you get a mixture of three tastes: bitter, salty, and sour. This creates more taste satisfaction by enhancing flavor and will reduce cravings.

Cravings can also be for certain textures. The basic five textures are crunchy, creamy, dry, liquid, and chewy.

The first time I heard the description of different food textures, I realized why I had such a bread habit. I loved chewy foods that were made from flour. Part of this was for my need (and at the time, a lack of) carbohydrates, but I especially enjoyed my bread with soup, which is of course a popular combination. Something wet, something dry. There's a complementary nature in such opposite textures. You can also see this with Italian dishes that have ample sauces; dry bread is often used to clean the plate.

Opposition in texture is common throughout the culinary world. In Chinese restaurants, if you order chop suey (a combination of creamy and chewy, also called gooey texture), you will usually be given a small order of dry noodles to sprinkle over your food for crunch; for some soups, you are given croutons; the popular combination of yogurt and granola is also a mixture of textures. This combination of textures offers a small sense of the extreme and happens to be, in most cases, very satisfying.

So when you take an inventory of your craving, be aware that sometimes you might just be craving a texture instead of a taste. This can help you narrow the choices of what you might need, allowing you to discover a greater sense of balance in your diet for a more satisfying sense of texture.

Craving Substitutions

Most of the general advice about reducing cravings focuses on nutritional deficiencies and recommends plentiful supplements as a solution.

Because published studies are few, I had to learn through the trial and error of personal experimenting, from peers who developed similar strategies, and from the feedback of many thoughtful and diligent clients who have shared what worked and didn't work for them.

The following are some general substitution guidelines for specific foods and food groups. Remember that the idea is not to feel like you can never have your favorite goodies again. Rather, it's about no longer having to *depend* on them and feeling more in control of what you eat. You don't have to compromise your health for a treat because you'll learn how to avoid the triggers that drive the craving. You might also discover, as I did, that your tastes change. What you once thought was delicious and something you could never imagine *not* having soon becomes something that you no longer desire, enjoy, or depend on.

SUGAR. Enjoy whole fruit, fruit juice–sweetened desserts, and grain-based sweeteners, such as barley malt and rice syrup. Include more sweet vegetables in the daily diet, such as corn, onions, squash, carrots, and parsnips. These can be enormously satisfying.

ANIMAL PROTEIN. If you do not want to give up meat completely, opt for white meat, such as chicken or fish. Choose deep-water, lean varieties of fish in small (3- to 5-ounce) servings, two to three times weekly. And always accompany any dish of animal protein with abundant servings of vegetables.

However, choosing a vegetarian path is preferable, from many points of view, and particularly healing. To do this effectively, you can include a variety of protein-rich beans and bean products such as soybean burgers (tempeh), tofu, and miso. Use a small amount (1 to 2 teaspoons) of olive or sesame oil with these dishes once daily to make the dish more satisfying without adding animal protein.

DAIRY. Dairy cravings can usually be satisfied with foods that supply some fat, protein, and mineral content in combination. Try to eat a daily portion of 1 cup cooked leafy dark greens, sea vegetables (which can be added to soups or bean dishes), beans as a side dish or in soup, and popular bean products (tofu or tempeh). Small amounts of oils or roasted seeds or nuts as condiments can help reduce or eliminate dairy cravings. For milk cravings, try soy, rice, or oat milk, which can be diluted with water to use in cereals or in recipes that call for milk. For ice cream cravings, try any number of the frozen (non–sugar cane) soy ice creams or rice-based ice creams, which can be very satisfying and make it easier to avoid mainstream brands. There are also some pure fruit sorbets that are delicious and made without sugar.

BREAD. A lack of complex carbohydrates in your daily diet might trigger cravings for bread and other flour products. Texture also plays a major role in bread cravings, especially for those whose diets are predominately soft (diets high in pasta, boiled veggies, creamy sauces, and soups, etc.). Having a good variety of textures will make meals feel more balanced and satisfied. Because the use of bread in sandwiches has become the default for lunch and since the breadbasket is ubiquitous at the restaurant table, the key to handling these cravings is in planning to use satisfying substitutions as a way to easily reduce the amount of bread you consume.

CAFFEINE. A formidable challenge for many! While caffeine-containing drinks (particular coffee and tea) often become addictive if consumed regularly, some of the factors that create caffeine cravings are excessive exercise, too much dietary fat, and mineral deficiencies. You can try to stop completely or gradual reduce consumption and replace coffee or other caffeinated drinks with herbal teas or cereal grain, coffee-like teas available at most natural food stores, but this particular process is made easier if done gradually. Be aware that caffeine can appear in many over-the-counter medications as well as in soft drinks.

ALCOHOL. Aside from obvious addiction (having emotional and possible genetic influences), some dietary factors behind alcohol cravings have to do with excessive salt and animal protein in the diet, or possibly a lack of fermented foods. Include a little bit of fermented food, such as vinegar on salads, a small piece of salt pickle with your main meal, or some weak miso paste in soup broth to help with the body's need for fermented foods. These foods provide necessary and rich enzyme nutrients that we need as a catalyst for better food absorption.

For reducing the physical craving for alcohol, reduce red meat, chicken, and fish consumption. Watch the tendency to overeat, by eating more frequently and in smaller volume. Also, it is best to minimize your salt use. Brisk walks or biking (indoor or outdoor), at four to five times weekly is an excellent way to promote good circulation while oxygenating your respiratory system. Seek support, attend meetings, get counseling, and make new goals. Alcohol addiction is not something you can gradually eliminate. It has to be completely avoided, and you should especially take care to avoid salty, high-protein foods, which are a prime culprit in stimulating cravings for alcohol.

Ten Strategies for Eliminating Sugar Cravings

Read each of the following suggestions and notice how they apply to your eating patterns or lifestyle. Reducing your desire or addiction for sugar should not require Herculean willpower. When you become conscious of the physiological and lifestyle factors that stimulate sugar cravings, taming them should make overcoming your sweet tooth a piece of cake—so to speak.

REDUCE SALT CONSUMPTION. We have a definite need for dietary salt from natural sources, such as sun-dried sea salt, but in small quantities. A lack of salt can cause fatigue, stimulate the desire to overeat, and often result in strong cravings for animal protein. However, with the availability of good-quality sea salt, miso paste, tamari soy sauce, and natural pickles, it's very easy to take more than necessary. Thirst, irritability, and a craving for sweet foods are reliable indicators of excess dietary salt.

REDUCE ANIMAL PROTEIN. The propaganda of the U.S. standard four basic food groups was force-fed to the American public in the 1950s along with the myth that animal protein and dairy foods should be dietary staples. This meat-and-potatoes mentality, originally dictated by powerful food lobbies, must be rethought because established research now shows excessive animal protein has a direct connection to colon and prostate cancer. If you wish to continue to eat animal protein, then you need to dramatically reduce the volume to 3- to 4-ounce servings only two or three times per week. If your sugar habit feels out of control, it would be best to completely abstain from animal protein for a while.

REDUCE OVERALL FOOD VOLUME. Overeating can lead to fatigue and sluggishness that make a stimulant like sugar (or coffee) tremendously appealing. Eating more frequently will allow you to reduce overeating with a minimum of effort.

EAT MORE FREQUENTLY THROUGHOUT THE DAY. Not eating for long periods between meals is one of the most common reasons for sugar cravings, especially at night. By skipping meals or waiting long periods between meals, you stop supplying your blood with glucose—the body's primary muscle fuel. Your blood sugar suddenly drops and by the time you finally have a meal, you're already thinking about something sweet before the first bite of the meal. In a low blood sugar state, you're also likely to end up overeating or craving something fatty as a compensation for not eating sugar. Initially, try not to wait more than 3.5 to 4 hours between meals. Planning is the key.

AVOID EATING BEFORE BED. If your body is digesting when it requires long awaited rest, you'll later require more sleep, dream excessively, and find it difficult to awaken with alertness. Good deep sleep results in wide-awake days. Eating too close to bedtime can result in a groggy awakening and with a morning craving for sugar (or caffeine). Eating a light evening dinner at least 2.5 to 3 hours before retiring makes it easier to get the rest your body requires, instead of having to digest while it should be resting.

AVOID SUGAR. This might sound obvious, however, continuing to eat simple sugars results in a continuously low blood sugar state, thus stimulating the need for *more* sugar—and the cycle continues. Even though fruit is a simple sugar, switching to fruit instead of refined or more concentrated forms of simple sugar, is a good first step. Also, when possible, eat the skin of the fruit for the fiber and to slow the passage of sugar into the blood.

EXERCISE MODERATELY, BUT CONSISTENTLY. Daily aerobic exercise will increase circulation and strengthen willpower. Brisk walking, biking, light jogging, and so on naturally increases your sensitivity to the negative effects of sugar. Try to get 20 to 30 minutes of some type of pleasurable exercise at least five times per week. Find joy in this; it should not be a chore.

EMPHASIZE WHOLE COMPLEX CARBOHYDRATES. If your daily diet includes whole grains (brown rice, oats, millet, barley), vegetables (roots, greens, round vegetables, cabbages), and beans as a primary fuel, you'll find that you automatically crave less and less sugar. Emphasizing sweet vegetables, such as carrots, cooked onions, corn, cabbage, parsnips, and squashes, can also add a natural and satisfying sweetness to meals. Introduce some sea vegetables (seaweed) to enhance your mineral status, which can reduce the need for a stimulant.

DON'T SUPPRESS YOUR FEELINGS. You don't have to broadcast *every* feeling—only those that matter and to those who really matter to you. Food indulgence, especially with sweets, is often a convenient way to anesthetize conflicting feelings. Sugar has a unique ability to overwhelm you with sensory pleasure, temporarily providing mental relief from whatever might be stressful. Conversely, simple sugars also hinder energy levels as well as mental clarity, so in the long run your emotional coping ability becomes diminished.

BEWARE OF FAMILIAL AND PSYCHOLOGICAL TRIGGERS. The many psychological associations we connect with food have a powerful influence. Consider the influence of family gatherings, movie rituals, familiar restaurants, and childhood habits. Although these connect us to memories or old coping strategies, sometimes they compromise our health when sensitivity is needed most. Enjoy familial and sentimental food rituals, but do so in the most moderate way possible.

Six Ways to Defeat Your Fat Tooth

Fat—in the form of french fries, deep-fried shrimp, tempura vegetables, pizza, and melted cheese—has become America's dietary obsession. In part, fat's slow digestion time accounts for that stick-to-the-ribs (satisfying) feeling after a rich meal. Here are six general reasons for fatty food cravings.

CARBOHYDRATE IMBALANCE. It's not uncommon for a lack of daily complex carbohydrates to result in sugar or fat cravings. Generally, we'll crave fat to feel more fulfilled with a meal. Fat remains in your stomach for up to 3 hours, whereas sugar gets absorbed as soon as it hits your tongue and on the way down the food tube.

You can combat a craving for excessive fat by eating the three primary foods of whole grains, vegetables, and beans and adding a very small amount of vegetable oil (sesame, olive, and occasionally coconut) to one dish per lunch and dinner. Too much oil has been shown to create arterial problems, so if you're challenged with heart disease, the less oil the better.

EXCESSIVE BREAD AND FLOUR PRODUCTS. Eating too many dry flour products (pasta, toast, muffins, or crackers) can cause cravings for oil or butter. Rarely, does anyone eat bread dry. We dip our bread in olive oil, butter it, or spread nut butters on it. It only stands to reason that the more bread you eat, the more you'll want an oil-based product to spread on it. So if you have a healthy fat tooth, go easy on the breads and flour products. Sometimes, eating a slice of bread with the meal and dipping it into your food is a way to make it more satisfying without the use of added oils.

NEED FOR FERMENTED FOODS. One of my teachers used to claim that oil cravings resulted from intestines that have poor absorption and are not accustomed to digesting whole foods. Some fermented products can help the intestines more effectively synthesize nutrients by offering a source of enzymes that contribute to the growth of healthy gut bacteria. Miso soybean paste, usually used as a vegetable soup ingredient, or minimum amounts of naturally processed tamari soy sauce, tempeh soybean cakes, and even some natural sourdough breads made with a naturally fermented starter, but without yeast, can be excellent forms of fermented foods. As some of these products contain sea salt, be sure to take minimum amounts.

Yeast can contribute to fatigue, among other symptoms, by producing a pathogenic yeast called *Candida albicans*. This single-cell organism is found growing in our bloodstream and organs and is considered a cause for much of the inflammation that disrupts the normal operation of our metabolism.

NEED FOR PROTEIN. Another reason for fat cravings is often an increased need for protein. Because fat usually accompanies protein, it is best to take small amounts of beans or bean or soy products with one or two meals daily to satisfy this craving.

FAT-EMULSIFYING FOODS AND FAT-STIMULATING FOODS. In observing different culinary combinations and from client feedback, I began to see a dietary connection between specific foods that, in combination, were well suited to fat. It only made sense that if you began to restrict these foods, the desire for fat would diminish. This is what I discovered from years of looking at client dietary records and comparing different cravings:

♦ Foods that have a *fat-dissolving* effect are like that old kitchen pot-cleaning tip of adding a bit of salt to an oily skillet to dissolve the oil. Those who have a body with ample fat storage, beneath their skin or within the arteries, might end up craving foods that have a dissolving effect on that fat. While the term *fat dissolving* may sound like a good thing, an excess of such foods can actually increase cravings for dietary fat. People will often go out of their way to avoid fat, yet grossly overeat to compensate. This is counterproductive because any dietary excess can become fat! When I used to counsel in Texas, some clients were very protective about their hot pepper cravings. I noticed that the more cheese and fatty meats they consumed, the more they wanted to include peppers at most meals. When I reduced hot and spicy foods from their diets, reducing fat became much easier.

✦ Foods that have a *fat-stimulating* effect can counter the fatiguing effects of fats and sharpen the senses. It only makes sense that if you're eating in a way that could cause reduced circulation and fatigue, you'd crave pick-me-up foods that stimulate energy. Caffeine and salt are two extreme examples of these foods.

The following chart will help you recognize some reasons for different food preferences. If you eat many of these emulsifying or stimulating foods on a daily basis, you may be *increasing* your desire for fats.

FATS	EMULSIFYING FOODS
Dairy, oils, nuts, meats	Vinegar, citrus, alcohol, mustard, ginger, salt, onions, radishes
	STIMULATING FOODS
	Spices, salt, caffeine, sugar

Vegetables that are considered to be fat emulsifying are onions, scallions, leeks, watercress, parsley, white (daikon) and red radishes, ginger, mushrooms, dandelion greens, burdock root, peppers, and tomatoes. If your diet has been high in fat and animal products, these vegetables are considered to have a detoxifying effect on fat storages in the body. However, eating too much of these foods could cause more cravings for fat, so while they have therapeutic value in terms of reducing fat storages, be moderate.

This idea of food combinations with fat can be seen throughout the culinary world and some of our most popular combinations are often complementary, such as these classics:

✦ Wine and cheese
✦ Alcohol and salted nuts
✦ Tempura (Japanese deep-fried vegetables) and a soy sauce–ginger dip
✦ French fries and ketchup or vinegar (British) with salt
✦ Eggs with salt and pepper or with a spicy sauce (Tabasco)
✦ Coffee with cream
✦ Toast with butter
✦ Meats with salt, onions, mustard, ketchup, or tomato
✦ Cheese enchiladas with spicy green or red sauce
✦ Liver and onions

Each of these food pairs work together in their own unique way, and that's the traditional wisdom behind some of these combinations. When I've counseled people who had strong cravings for fats, this information helped them effortlessly reduce fat cravings, by reducing their typical pairing. Just because certain combinations have tradition behind them does not make them particularly health supportive, or healing.

NEED FOR COMFORT FOOD. Fat is one of the macronutrients often considered a comfort food. Mother's milk has nearly 4 times more fat than protein. It has been theorized that this might be ample reasoning for the comforting effect of fats.

Fat with a sweet taste, as in ice cream, might provide some psychological refuge for us in times of stress. However, in the long run, it could compromise our emotional coping ability, instigating such symptoms as immune dysfunction from sugar excess or allergy response from poorly digested dairy-based proteins. Notably, ice cream, cheese, butter, and warm milk are typical foods associated with comfort, often being cited for their comforting texture. If your attraction to fat does not seem to relate to any of the physical qualities previously mentioned, then it could be a comfort craving, or a craving based on certain psychological associations from the past. Sometimes an occasional indulgence can be highly therapeutic. The real concern is when we eat these foods too often or in high volume.

Six Keys for Handling Overeating

For people in dietary transition, especially to a diet lower in fat and sugar, overeating is a common practice. Here are six key reasons behind overeating and some of the remedies you might seek.

EMOTIONAL EATING. There are many psychological factors that are the basis for overeating or binge eating. If you feel that this is a component to your overeating, first address the physical factors, such as excessive salt, possible nutritional deficiency, low blood sugar, and so on. Second, accept that your overeating might be emotionally based and either seek support or do some research to get a better perspective on what emotional factors could be involved.

EXCESSIVE SALT OR ANIMAL PROTEIN. I've seen the craving to overeat occur with people who begin eating miso and soy sauce and pickles—some of the traditional, salt-based products recommended for their alkaline properties and enzyme benefits. The desire for these new foods once you

begin eating them may be due to a previously high-acid diet that stimulates a continued craving for salt. Sometimes, eating large amounts of
food can be an unconscious strategy to avoid eating sugar. In this sense,
overeating then becomes a compensatory act.

FLUCTUATING BLOOD SUGAR LEVELS. Waiting long periods between
meals can make you ravenous! This is one of most common reasons for
overeating. If you suspect this might be a cause of your overeating, plan
more carefully and eat more frequently throughout the day—not one
continuous meal, but perhaps four to five smaller meals. You'll be less
likely to have a late-night appetite if you plan properly.

INACTIVE LIFESTYLE. Becoming more physically active on a daily basis
can make you more sensitive to the subtle, and not-so-subtle, negative
effects of overeating. If you know you're going to take a bike ride or
long walk, the last thing you'll want to have is a belly full of food to
accompany you. Changing your evening ritual can help as well. If you
normally watch television and snack late at night, consider watching earlier programming and do some gentle stretching, several yoga postures,
sustained stretching just before bed. You'll have a more relaxed and
deeper sleep instead of digesting while you toss and turn, as a panorama
of nonstop dreaming keeps you in a superficial and dissatisfying sleep.

POOR NUTRIENT ASSIMILATION. Poor absorption could be another reason
at the root of frequent overeating. We're not satisfied and so we'll eat to
capacity. The solution to overeating as a result of poor assimilation is
simply experimenting with your diet, not just the random popping of
vitamin pills but the elimination of foods that threaten your vitamin
and mineral status, such as excessive sugar or fat. You can experiment
with adjunctive foods, such as herbs or supplements, as *part* of a more
detailed inquiry into your needs. In more serious cases, a blood panel or
stool sample might reveal more chronic conditions, such as anemia or
parasites, which could, in more extreme cases, be at the root of chronic
overeating. Consistent good nutrition, daily activity, rest, and a wide
variety of foods and cooking styles can help restore intestinal strength
fairly quickly.

INSUFFICIENT CHEWING. I used to have a teacher who claimed overeating was simply due to a lack of thorough chewing. Period. That was his
theory. Based on what I've observed around me, sometimes I think he
was right.

When all is said and done, it still remains that good digestion begins
with the thorough act of chewing. It's not enough to just change our diet;
we have to change our manner of eating. Fat and protein do not digest

in the mouth. They begin their digestion in the stomach and in the following structure, the duodenum. If our diets are high in fat, protein, or sugar, we're less likely to chew thoroughly.

Whole foods have the distinction of beginning their digestion in the mouth. Their taste becomes naturally sweet and fills you up, without filling you out. Most people shovel tremendous amounts of food into their mouths. It's difficult to chew a large volume of food because you become so overwhelmed with saliva that the swallowing impulse is practically automatic. So I suggest small volumes, chewed thoroughly. These lists of generalized craving recommendations should help you recognize what factors are specific to your habits or lifestyle. Sometimes, as Mark Twain said, "eat what you want and let the food battle it out inside," might be appropriate advice. However, when you need tools to aid desired, healthy diet change, you'll find that many of these factors will be of enormous support, by creating better awareness and less need for dietary willpower and discipline strategies.

9

Detoxifying Your Body, Naturally

There is no basis in human biology that indicates we need fasting or any other detox formula to detoxify the body, because we have our own internal organs and immune system that take care of excreting toxins. Your body is designed to remove toxins efficiently with organs such as the kidneys, liver, and colon. You don't need detox diets, pills, or potions to help your body do its job.

—Frank Sacks, epidemiologist, Harvard School of Public Health

Detox Without Drama

I began my natural foods adventure many years ago in southern California. Threw out the white bread, passed on the meat, stopped refined sweets, and began consuming whole grains, beans, and vegetables. At the time, I'd read about fasting and detoxing in a popular health book. It claimed if I were doing things correctly, I would soon be detoxing— discharging all the "poisons" I'd taken or was exposed to over the past years. The fellow at the health food store who recommended the book assured me that this would be the profound life experience that I was seeking, hinting at new spiritual insights, physical rejuvenation, and intuitive revelation, *if* I "pursued the natural path." I was young, impressionable, and eager for change—and the clerk was damn persuasive, so I began my new regime and waited for the detox . . . and waited . . . and waited.

But no detox.

I'd heard and read accounts of people hallucinating, going through food withdrawals that seemed to rival hallucinogenic drug withdrawals, having obsessive dreams about the foods they felt deprived from eating, symptoms of constipation or discharging black tar-like bowel matter, hair loss, reexperiencing childhood sicknesses, and so on.

Yet, for me, nothing.

At the time I didn't realize it, but I actually had been detoxing all along! And this is precisely the central point of this chapter: The body is designed with an automatic and amazing process for natural detoxing. It constantly labors to eliminate undesirable elements from the blood and tissues. These toxic elements are discharged through urine and bowel movements, perspiration, and exhalation (as carbon dioxide). If our transition to a whole food diet is gradual and accompanied by a lifestyle that contains manageable stress, the extreme side effects of detoxification rarely occur.

There are many theories about detoxing, and some of them can sound rather sensational with false and naive assumptions that we can cleanse our body in a few days. This thinking originates from the magic-bullet mind-set that has us believe that salvation lies in pills, instant fixes, exotic touch, or obscure tribal potions. In years of lecturing and counseling, I've met people who seemed to relish the drama of detox; they craved the experience of feeling disabled by the purge of yesterday's bad judgment, as if the suffering of such a discharge were the justified price and the badge necessary to advertise their struggle or transform their health. A therapist friend and former client expressed the opinion that this might just be an unconscious self-punishment strategy for the guilt of previous dietary abuse.

Redemption is never supposed to come easy.

I've heard clients champion with evangelistic zeal (after decades of dietary abuse or addictive bingeing) their need for cleansing:

"I just want to get all the toxins out. *Then*, I'll feel better."
"I'm going on juices for a couple of days, just to *clean out* my system."

"I fast *every* month, just to detoxify."

"Since I've began to eat *pure* foods, my body is getting rid of old poisons."

Generally, the most common detoxification therapies recommend a variety of pills, cleansing herbs, short-term fasts, coffee enemas, and various kinds of sweat therapy from infrared saunas to body wraps to being buried in mud or sand. You might *feel* somewhat cleansed after all this; however, such quick fixes usually do not take into account the changing quality of the blood and the length of time it takes to really begin changing one's health condition on a cellular level. While certain detox therapies *can* offer advantages, the bottom line is that detoxing actually happens on a daily basis, *not* just in the form of a major breakdown.

In fact, you're detoxing as you read this! The liver and kidneys; the digestive, respiratory, and lymphatic systems; and the skin never cease their detoxifying functions.

The Detox Smorgasbord

In recent years, a number of detox approaches have flooded the commercial market and been made popular by numerous celebrities who usually lost some weight, felt better, and then suddenly become spokespeople for these products. Most of the popular detox diets follow a pattern of low-calorie fasting with small portions of fruits, vegetables or vegetable juices, water, and various supplements or herbs.

Generally, the marketing of detox regimes preys on the vulnerability of dieters with standard fear tactics that warn that toxins will kill you, your bowel has been impacted for years with sludge, your lymph system is in vital need of being drained, and only a detox program will clean you out efficiently so you can avoid diseases. Often, the products are unnecessarily expensive and recommended far more than actually necessary, if at all.

In reality, there are no long-term studies available to document the benefits of these products. Most claims are based on sensational emotional testimonials, that show before-and-after comparisons and claims of instant rejuvenation.

The three most popular detox regimes are the liver flush, fasting, and the master cleanse.

The Liver Flush

There are many variations of the liver flush, however, here are the basics: It's recommended to drink two glasses of apple juice every 2 hours for 2 days. At the end of the second day, before retiring for the night, dissolve 2 tablespoons of Epsom salts in water (presumably to soften the stones) and follow that with a half-cup of olive oil. Then, chase it down with some lemon juice. If the thought of vomiting after all of this arises, it's a common reaction. Finally, it's recommended that you retire to bed, and lie on your right side with your knees positioned at your chest. Supposedly, from numerous online postings about the liver flush, this allows the oil to enter the liver much quicker. The following morning (if you can even manage sleep), you'll have a strong impulse to relieve your bowels. During the first discharge, you'll notice green fragments (balls) within the bowel movement. This is supposed to be old stones that have been stored in your gallbladder.

Writing in the British medical journal the *Lancet*, Sies and Booker report on these stones:

> Experimentation revealed that mixing equal volumes of oleic acid (the major component of olive oil) and lemon juice produced several semisolid white balls after the addition of a small volume of a potassium hydroxide solution. On air-drying at room temperature, these balls became quite solid and hard.
>
> We conclude, therefore, that these green "stones" resulted from the action of gastric lipases on the simple and mixed triacylglycerols that make up olive oil, yielding long-chain carboxylic acids (mainly oleic acid). This process was followed by saponification into large insoluble micelles of potassium carboxylates (lemon juice contains a high concentration of potassium) or "soap stones."

In other words, the stones that liver cleansers are so proud of and go to such effort to strain their bowel movements after completing their flushes are, in fact, not gallstones and are the product of the actual oil flush itself! It makes perfect sense, if you think about it. These protocols often involve fasting and then consuming up to a half liter or more of olive oil at one time. That could easily provide the conditions for this sort of reaction to take place. The very sign of success of the liver flush is something that has nothing to do with gallstones and everything to do with the results of the flush itself. Indeed, it's quite clear that, even if you don't have gallstones, if you do a liver flush and then look closely enough, you'll find things in your stool that very much look like gallstones that are really due to saponified oil.

Fasting

Known for centuries to be effective in certain cases of extreme sickness, fasting enjoyed a brief revival in the late 1940s with Norman Walker's *Become Younger* and mid-1960s with health author Paul Bragg's popular book, *The Miracle of Fasting*. Within 3 days of fasting, the appetite begins to wane and holding out for a longer fast no longer becomes an effort. However, fasting is rather extreme and is also known to dump stored toxins in the bloodstream, making it more difficult for your filter organs. In addition, for some with a tendency toward low blood sugar conditions (aka hypoglycemia), fasting can be a dangerous proposition.

The safest fast might be a food-reduction fast, for which you eat half the volume of what you normally consume and don't allow yourself to eat for at least 3 hours before bed. This alone can still yield positive and dramatic health results.

The Master Cleanse

Several celebrities have made the master cleanse diet a household name. Consisting of hot water, lemon juice, maple syrup, and cayenne pepper, the cleanse is recommended for an exclusive period of 10 to 14 days. Again, considering the blood changes in a period of 120 days and chemically reflects what we've consumed during that period, this is really not much of a cleanse, other than to perhaps clean out a portion of the bowel. Still, in my opinion and personal experience, the concentrated sugar content and acidity of the maple syrup and pepper could aggravate a number of conditions and result in promoting inflammation.

Quality Versus Quantity

Detoxing is influenced not only by the quality of the food but also by the quantity. While it is important to make good-quality food choices, it's more than a matter of pure versus impure, natural versus unnatural, or merely emphasizing the concept of quality. Recently, a client with immune problems told me she had been eating "lots of fresh, organic fruit and home-squeezed juice" as a form of self-treatment. I suggested she limit her total sugar content, including fruit, and especially fruit juice, for a 2-week period.

She began to defend her position on the issue of quality; arguing about organics, local organic growers who grow their food with love (instead of "conglomerate apathy"), and the rich mineralized soil where this fruit was grown. I explained that my argument was not regarding *quality*, whether the food was organic or nourished with filtered water or lovingly nurtured, but my concerns were about the *concentration of nutrients* and the *quantity of nutrients* and not simply a solo emphasis on quality.

In this case, my concern was about sugar (fruit sugar), which has a strong systemic acidic influence. Quantity (regarding excess of nutrients, such as simple sugar) in this case overruled quality. There might be some healthful nutrients in a particular fruit, but if the dominant nutrient is sugar, little else matters because sugar's acidity will usually diminish other nutrients, particularly minerals.

In my personal experience and from years of observation, the most success has been achieved when someone takes gradual and consistent steps as a way to ensure consistent and positive change. Otherwise, extreme detoxing can become, in itself, a stress for the body. Sometimes, people can even experience severe detox reactions.

In people who have been fasting, there is a risk that the microscopic kidney filters could contract as intestinal movement (peristalsis) weakens. Additionally, taking foods that produce a constrictive effect in the body (such as the drying and tightening effect from excessive salt) or using remedies that contain an excess of salt (miso, umeboshi, soy sauce) could cause the same reaction of making the bowel sluggish. Suddenly, two of the natural channels of toxin elimination, the kidneys and the intestines, have become compromised.

According to traditional Chinese medicine, a poorly filtering kidney or blocked intestines can force toxins to discharge via the skin. But treating skin discharges topically is merely the tip of the iceberg. It's obviously a far deeper and more systemic issue.

The Detox Blame Game

It is common, especially among the vegetarian, macrobiotic, natural-food, and raw-food groups, to attach the detoxing label to a broad host of abnormal symptoms. Constipation, lethargy, low blood sugar, and skin discharge are frequently considered detox indicators. In most cases, these symptoms are merely the body's reactions to a new diet or signals of imbalance, not indicators of deep healing.

CONSTIPATION. What is casually labeled as detoxing might simply be a lethargic bowel condition that occurs as a result of weaning the body from foods or substances that previously stimulated bowel movements (sugars or stimlants such as prune juice, cigarettes, coffee), and now peristalsis (intestinal contraction) has become restrained. Making sure to consume daily whole grain fiber, eating freqently, and exercising daily can promptly remedy this annoyance.

FATIGUE. Lethargy could be the result of poor assimilation from a new diet, an excess of simple sugar, or a low blood sugar reaction to the absence of foods that previously made blood sugar dance the swings of high and low. To help change these symptoms, eat more frequently, avoid undereating (that is, going too long between meals or fasting), and include whole grains (an endurance food) and vegetables in at least two daily meals.

SKIN BREAKOUTS. Skin breakouts could be the result of a burdened liver and kidneys now made more sensitive to dietary changes or in reaction to a condition of excess acidity, despite the purity of a new diet. Regular rest can bolster immune function. A clean diet that is low in fat with no refined sugar and moderate amounts of fruit, as well as continued consistent exercise, can help beautify skin usually within a week or two.

As long as you're getting regular rest, eating simply, not overeating, and are physically active, any so-called discharge symptoms will occur through the body's many detox systems effortlessly, without drama and pain.

The Body's Natural Detox Systems

Putting physical and personality characteristics and qualities aside, humans collectively share an amazingly well-organized and intricate internal physiology. What we take into our bodies as nourishment, what we breathe, and what gets absorbed through the skin's pores, must go through an elaborate process of breakdown, storage, and discharge.

Food is eventually broken down into tiny energy components that provide fuel for cells. What we inhale also gets absorbed into blood via the lungs and, after becoming part of the bloodstream, is then filtered by the liver and finally thorough an additional filtering process by the kidneys before becoming discharged as urine.

The six filtering factories responsible for body detoxification are the liver; the kidneys; the digestive, respiratory, and lymphatic systems; and the skin.

What we store within the body—and what we eliminate—depends on the condition of these organs and systems, our fat reserves (toxins can find long-time room rental in body fat), circulation, and blood quality.

The Liver: Border Guard of the Body

The liver is like a border guard at the entrance to a country; it's going to scrutinize (and ask for ID from) everything that comes its way to make sure it can be broken down. As one of the most important organs of detoxification, the liver is the largest gland in the body (3 to 4 pounds), and it is also the largest solid organ in the body. Supposedly, it is seven times larger than it needs to be in order to perform an estimated 500 functions. It is also known for its remarkable ability to heal itself. You can cut away nearly 80 percent of the liver and within 2 years it will completely regenerate. You might consider the liver as the body's ultimate workaholic, competing with only the heart and kidneys in accumulating overtime hours.

Some of the liver's most critical daily tasks are:

+ Nutritional breakdown and absorption of food
+ Storage of iron, copper, fat-soluble vitamins A and D, and vitamin B_{12}
+ Vitamin A formation
+ Conversion of dead red blood cells into bile (to aid digestion)
+ Filtering the more poisonous elements from the blood and converting them to nontoxic substances that can be excreted via urine and feces
+ The manufacture of blood plasma (blood liquid) proteins
+ The production of a blood-clotting substances
+ Balancing blood sugar via glucose storage and distribution
+ Production of red blood cells in the developing fetus
+ Formation of numerous antibodies (the basis of our immunity)

Of particular importance is the liver's ability to detoxify poisonous substances in the bloodstream, including the potentially toxic quality of caffeine, nicotine, and alcohol. Foreign substances that cannot be broken down and used by the body are sent to the liver via blood flow for removal or to have the poison neutralized. The liver can add its own mix of chemicals to the digesting material, which aids its breakdown and eventual elimination.

A strongly concentrated substance that cannot be neutralized by the liver can cause permanent damage. This applies to substances such as alcohol and drugs. As a defensive move, the liver replaces its active cells with fatty tissue, giving it a golden-yellow appearance instead of its normal one of reddish brown. Eventually, the liver becomes hardened, shrinks in size, and then becomes cirrhotic. Cirrhosis of the liver can be fatal.

The liver manufactures bile, a dark green material, from used red blood cells; bile stored in the gallbladder is later used in digestion. Bile dissolves fat. A large high-fat meal can trigger the release of bile, which acts like a detergent, allowing fats to be dissolved and eventually absorbed by the intestine.

The liver releases many chemicals it has taken up from the blood into the bile. Some of these potent poisons include arsenic, cadmium, lead, manganese, mercury, and environmental chemicals like DDT (a notorious carcinogen that was banned in the United States in 1972, but is still manufactured and used throughout the world and continually brought to the country via imported goods and air and ocean currents) and PCBs (a family of 209 different synthetic organochlorine compounds designated as carcinogens by the U.S. Department of Health and Human Services and the International Agency for Research on Cancer).

To speed removal of these unwanted chemicals, the liver attaches various proteins and sugars to them so that they more easily bind with bile and are then excreted them into the intestine.

Researchers at Johns Hopkins School of Medicine documented that the natural sulforaphane chemical, abundant in cruciferous vegetables (such as broccoli, cabbage, cauliflower, kale, and Brussels sprouts) can increase the liver's ability to engage in "phase II conjugation reactions," thus helping the body convert chemicals that might be cancer-producing into nontoxic substances that can be excreted. In some studies, animals given a concentrated extract of sulforaphane had a greater resistance to potentially cancer-causing chemicals than control animals.

Unfortunately, although these toxic substances have been released by the liver, they can easily become reabsorbed by intestinal bacteria. Sometimes these bacteria convert bile into secondary bile acids, that make reabsorbing toxins easier.

The saving grace for this potential of reabsorbing toxins is fiber! Whole grain fiber binds to bile and drags it out of the system via the bowel movement.

The Kidneys: Tireless Filtering Agents

The two kidneys are positioned on the back wall of the upper abdomen, behind the liver and stomach. Through the production of urine, they act as filters that clean blood and remove organic wastes of digestion, excess salts, water, and excessive small protein molecules.

Each kidney has basic filtering units called nephrons. The nephrons are tiny networks of tubules that, at a magnification of 100 times, appear like a nexus of human brains. Together, both kidneys contain more than 2 million of these waste-processing structures.

Approximately 99 percent of the fluids removed from the blood by the kidneys are reabsorbed, together with glucose, salts, vitamins, and other substances needed by the body. In this way the kidneys control the balance between acid and alkaline conditions of the body's tissues and the balance between water and salt in the body's cells.

Playing a major role in maintaining the balance of water in the body, the kidneys excrete 1.5 to 2 quarts of urine on a daily basis. Urine contains the products of digestion, uric acid, urea, and creatinine. To accomplish this, the kidneys filter about 48 gallons of blood every 24 hours—close to 4 times the body's liquid weight. This volume amounts to an approximate 1.3 million gallons filtered in a lifetime of 73 years—presumably enough to fill a good-size city water tank. As you read these words, as much as a quarter of your blood is passing through your kidneys for filtering.

Including more water in your diet is necessary but should be based on your diet profile. If you're eating whole natural foods, which tend to be 80 to 90 percent water, we don't have a need for the 8-glasses-daily rule. Given our individual situations—work life, diet, and physical needs—we don't all have the same requirements for fluids.

The need for fluid is actually proportional to the quality of your diet. With a healthy, whole food diet, low or absent of gluten, low in simple sugars, and low in fat and protein, you will require less—perhaps 1 to 2 quarts daily at the maximum. So any liquid recommendation cannot be a hard, fast rule. Obviously, if you're running a marathon, you'll need more water, but liquid requirements must be based on exercise, salt intake, and thirst.

One way to stimulate healthy kidneys is through rest. Staying up late is one of the most common ways to tax the kidneys and the adrenal glands, which are attached to the top of each kidney. Good sleep before midnight helps align your body clock with natural circadian rhythms and regulates your immune functioning.

Excessive fat and sugar are prime culprits for kidney weakening, for creating mucus, and for developing inflammation of the nephrons.

The Digestive System: The Basis of Good Health

The digestive vessel, where digestion and absorption occur, is a layered muscular tube that runs approximately 25 to 29 feet from mouth to anus. Nutrients within food are reduced, through digestive fluids, to compounds tiny enough to pass through the walls of the intestines and into the blood for cellular distribution.

Digestion begins with your first bite, when saliva initiates the breakdown of starch (complex carbohydrate) into smaller units of sugar (simple sugar). We swallow, and the food travels the length of our esophagus into the stomach. The stomach contains more than 35 million glands that produce about 3 quarts of gastric juice daily. Acting as a hollow muscle, the stomach contracts and mixes the food with these juices to produce a pulpy and creamy fluid called chyme.

Gradually, within a 3- to 4-hour period, the chyme leaves the stomach and enters an extension of the small intestine called the duodenum. In the duodenum, bile from the gallbladder and a digestive juice from the pancreas (known as *trypsin*) converge to continue the digestion of the chyme. The chyme ends up in the small intestine, where nutrients pass directly into the blood. What cannot pass, usually fiber, continues to travel into the large intestine, which absorbs water, expands, and becomes discharged as a bowel movement. In a healthy body, this entire trip might constitute an 18- to 24-hour journey, depending on individual metabolism and fiber content in the daily diet.

The six best and most practical recommendations for intestinal health are the following:

◆ **Control your volume:** Overeating taxes the stomach and intestines. Eating less allows our digestive secretions to better function and break down foods for maximized assimilation.

◆ **Don't eat for 3 hours before bed:** As discussed earlier, food remains in the stomach for up to 3 hours. When you lie down after eating, stomach acids bathe the muscle at the bottom of the esophagus (food pipe), which can eventually allow this stomach acid to travel up the esophagus. This very common condition is known as acid reflux. Therefore, evening meals, ideally, should be the lightest meal of the day, thus ensuring good deep sleep and wide-awake mornings. A UK friend told me that an old English aphorism suggests, "For breakfast, eat like royalty; lunch like a commoner; and for dinner, eat like a pauper."

+ **Chew your food:** This practically sounds condescending because everyone chews his or her food, right? Wrong. Primarily, this is because most of the food we eat is doctored to have immediate taste, whereas grain, vegetables, and beans require chewing to bring out their taste. As mentioned, these foods can have an initial bland taste but become sweeter the more they are chewed. The entire purpose of chewing is to allow our alkaline saliva to cover more of the food surface area to expose more of the food's nutrients for better digestion, making it easier for the food to become absorbed when it arrives in the intestine.

+ **Fiber it up!** Consuming whole grains, beans, and vegetables ensures that you are getting the superior antioxidant and phytonutrients your body needs. In addition, fiber stimulates more regulated bowel function and creates a more manageable blood sugar.

+ **Don't drink with meals:** Most people drink with their meals to wash the food down. Frankly, I think this is a moronic theory and makes no sense. If we don't chew our food, yes, it feels better to just gulp some liquid and "wash" the food down and be done with it. However, we are not gulping canines and are endowed with a unique physiology that permits us to extract fluid from our food as we chew. Drinking cold water with a meal can sometimes inhibit digestion for up to 20 minutes, depending on temperature. After finishing a meal, sip some tea, which is a healthier and more satisfying strategy.

+ **Don't exercise on a full stomach:** Yes, sounds like common sense, but it is a common thing to do. In a way, even standing while eating accounts for a type of exercise because the blood that is going to support your stance could be better used for digestion. This also goes for intimate activity. Often a full stomach can press against the lungs and inhibit the deep full breathing required for most activity.

The Skin: Your Body's Largest Organ

With a total surface area of 22 to 25 square feet, the skin is the body's largest organ. An average-size person might shed about 600,000 particles of skin every hour, which amounts to 1.5 pounds yearly. Being a tireless detox mechanism, your body, by 70 years of age, will have shed nearly 105 pounds of skin, an amount equivalent to two-thirds of your body weight.

The skin is a crowded mass of various structures all working to protect our body and facilitate the discharge of toxins. Just 1 square inch of skin, about twice the area of your thumbnail and no thicker than two pennies, contains the following:

+ 645 sweat glands that constantly work to discharge toxins to the skin surface
+ 77 feet of nerves with over 1,000 nerve endings
+ 65 hair follicles that also act as exits from the body for detoxing
+ 97 sebaceous glands (providing lubricating oil for skin and hair) that discharge excesses of fat generated by the diet
+ 19 feet of blood vessels

It is important to remember that whatever you apply topically to your skin, eventually ends up in your liver, lymph, and blood. Considered the regulator of body temperature, the skin helps us discharge internal wastes via the secretion of sweat that contains salt and small amounts of other substances such as ammonia. In total, there are more than 2 million tightly coiled sweat glands in the adult human body residing in the inner layers of the skin. Each of these coiled glands, if unwound, would measure approximately 50 inches in length. As a mathematical diversion, this means that we have nearly 2,000 miles of coiled ducting in our skin, which may give new meaning to the phrase, "It just unravels me to no end."

Exposure to heat brings blood to the skin's surface, creating that lobster-red look you see among sauna aficionados; cold drives blood deeper into the body, creating a pallid, anemic look that in the extreme becomes purple. Both colors—red and purple—represent the extremes of the color spectrum and systemic signs of excessive heat or excessive cold. The traditional practice of alternating a hot sauna with cold dips or showers was designed promote the movement of lymph fluid and stimulate perspiration and the toxins that sweat carries.

Because the skin is a conduit to our blood and tissue fluid, the benefit of many skin therapies was the discharge of toxins, via the pores. For years, the official modern medical position stated that persistent pesticides such as BHC, chlordane, DDT, dieldrin, and heptachlor as well as PCBs could not be eliminated from the human body. It was believed that once those poisons got into your body, you were stuck with them.

In his book *Diet for a Poisoned Planet*, David Steinman documents the results of a program of medically supervised saunas sponsored by Health Med, Los Angeles, that showed how persistent pesticides could be eliminated from the body by prolonged exposure to heat. The program results were widely reported by organizations such as the Swedish Royal Academy of Science, the World Health Organization's International Agency for Research on Cancer, and numerous other scientific and medical groups.

From Native American sweat lodges to Russian baths, many cultures have traditionally used heat therapies that induced sweating for the purpose of cleansing. Hot, wet clay either applied as a full-body coat or made into a mud bath was used much in the same way. A former Japanese teacher of Asian medicine with whom I studied used to recommend deep sand baths in which the individual is literally buried from the neck down in beach sand for several hours to induce the discharge of toxins. He said that traditional folk medicine claimed the sand had great absorption ability and could literally draw out toxins through the skin. Moderate sweating, can also have a detoxifying effect while improving immunity and circulation.

Another traditional recommendation for helping the body to discharge toxins was swimming in salt water or immersion in a salt bath. The strong alkalinity of the salt was thought to draw out and bond to acidic tissues and toxins stored beneath the skin surface. In the last 100 years, Epsom salt (magnesium sulfate) has replaced the traditional salt bath (sodium chloride), both being known for reducing inflammation and drawing out toxins from the skin.

Another technique for strengthening circulation, promoting lymph flow, and causing sweat and thereby the discharge of toxins is the traditional practice of skin brushing, Skin brushing (done with a loofah, brush, or rough towel) is a brisk rubbing of the skin until it becomes slightly red. It is commonly done on dry skin to help exfoliate the top-layer surface.

The Respiratory System: Life from Breath

On the average, humans breathe about 20,000 times per 24-hour cycle. This function of breath is solely dependent on the respiratory system, which includes the nose, voice box, throat, windpipe, and lungs. With every breath, you take air in through your nostrils and mouth, filling your lungs and then quickly emptying them. The mucous membranes of the nose and mouth warm and humidify the air we breathe.

Air is made up of several invisible gases, with oxygen ranking as the most important because body cells require it for energy and growth. Without oxygen, the body's cells die.

One of the waste gases produced when carbon is combined with oxygen as part of the body's energy-making process is carbon dioxide. The lungs and respiratory system allow oxygen from the air to be absorbed into the body, while at the same time enable the body to discharge carbon dioxide through our exhalations.

Respiration is a common term for the exchange of environmental oxygen for carbon dioxide from the body's cells. The intricate process of taking air into the lungs is known as inhalation, or inspiration, and the process of discharging it is known as exhalation, or expiration.

The respiratory system has a unique ability to filter out foreign matter and organisms that enter the nose and mouth from the air we breathe. The pollutants that we breathe in, or cough out, can be dissolved by digestive secretions or consumed by our white blood cells—a specific type of blood cell that's an integral part of our immune system.

Within the lungs, tubes called bronchi branch into smaller bronchi and then even smaller tubes called bronchioles. Bronchioles, with a diameter as thin as a hair strand, end in minuscule air sacs called alveoli. Each lung contains hundreds of millions of alveoli. In fact, it's been estimated that if our alveoli were spread out, they could easily cover the area of a tennis court. It is within the alveoli that the exchange of oxygen and carbon dioxide occurs. According to the Centers for Disease Control and Prevention (CDC), after heart disease, cancer, and stroke, the fourth-leading cause of death in the United States is chronic obstructive pulmonary disease (COPD).

To maximize the health of our lungs, a diet of low fat and low sugar is best for an easier exchange of gases. Aerobic activity increases the circulation within the lung and helps keep its tissues elastic and resilient. Big offenders for lung tissue are the odors of chemical household cleaners, tobacco smoke (direct or secondhand), carbonated drinks, excessive salt use, and alcohol.

The Lymphatic System

The lymphatic system is one of the most vital systems in the body, made up of tissues and organs that produce, store, and carry infection- and disease-fighting white blood cells. This system includes the spleen, bone marrow, thymus, lymph glands, and a complex network of narrow tubes that escort lymph and white blood cells into all body tissues.

While the circulatory system's central component, the heart, works nonstop for our entire lifetime pumping blood, the lymphatic system lacks a central pump. The flow within the lymphatic vessels is unidirectional because of one-way valves that keep the lymph from traveling backward, so its circulation depends strictly on forward movement.

The three essential functions of the immune system are to absorb fatty acids and transport fat into to the circulatory system, drain excess fluid from body tissues, and produce immune cells (also known as lymphocytes).

When lymph fluid circulates through the body, it collects waste products and toxins and discards them through the lungs, bowel, bladder, and skin. With any lymphatic dysfunction, we become at risk for the development of a wide range of illnesses. Signals of poor lymphatic functioning include swelling (or edema), swollen glands, recurring tonsillitis or sore throat, a tendency for infections or viruses, and constipation.

NATURAL WAYS TO PROMOTE LYMPH FLOW

DRY SKIN BRUSHING. Considering that the skin is the largest organ in the body, dry skin brushing invigorates the entire nervous system as well as the circulation, helping move lymph fluid through the vessels so it can discharge toxins from the body.

VIGOROUS EXERCISE. Exercise is a critical component for a healthy lymphatic system. Regular exercise creates vigorous motion in the body, which is necessary for stimulating waste disposal and the flow of lymphatic fluid. Ideally, walking should be brisk and, if possible, in a natural setting, such as outdoors in the open air among trees and grass. I generally recommend a 15-minute walk, five times weekly at the minimum, in one direction; however, you have to return, so it is actually a 30-minute walk. But, it's usually more motivating to think of it as a 15-minute, one-direction walk.

According to *Hole's Essentials of Human Anatomy and Physiology,* "Muscular activity largely influences the movement of lymph through the lymphatic vessels. Lymph, like venous blood, is under low hydrostatic pressure and may not flow readily through lymphatic vessels without outside help. These forces include contraction of skeletal muscles, contraction of the smooth muscle in the walls of the larger lymphatic trunks, and pressure changes associated with breathing."

Considering that the upper body, armpits, shoulders, and neck contain an abundance of lymph nodes, it's best to have vigorous arm movement when walking. For women who wear tight-fitting bras and for anyone who uses commercial deodorants that contain toxic chemical compounds, arm movement generates stronger blood and lymph flow in the upper body, helping carry away toxins.

REBOUNDING. Rebounders are mini-trampolines that have become a popular in-home way to promote lymph flow with very little effort. Each time your foot strikes the pavement surface, gravity helps lymph flow more effectively. When you suddenly stop with your full weight, you create an additional gravitation pull, helping direct lymph flow downward. When you bounce on a mini-trampoline, you are increasing the gravitational pull on your lymph fluid. This gravitational pull is similar to what you feel from a sudden change in car speed or on an amusement park ride. By bouncing up and down, you are in a vertical alignment with your body and its lymph vessels.

For as little as $30, you can usually obtain a rebounder, which typically measures about 4-feet in diameter. Sitting less than a foot off the ground, you simply step onto the trampoline and gently bounce up and down for 12 to 15 minutes. You could be watching television when you do this. I have a friend who has one in her kitchen and uses it while she cooks, waiting for different dishes to finish.

DEEP BREATHING. Deep diaphragmatic breathing is an excellent way of circulating lymph fluid. Take a deep, slow breath and push your belly out as you do so, allowing the breath to expand your tummy; follow this with a long exhalation in which you let all the air that you can out. The pressure of the lungs expanding and contracting also moves our lymph and opens ducts that allow the lymph to reenter the bloodstream by the subclavian veins at the back of the neck. Just doing this for 10 minutes a day will help fully oxygenate the blood while promoting the flow of lymph.

MASSAGE. Lymphatic massage is a gentle technique that is also known as lymphatic drainage. With pressure on the neck, arms, and chest, you can effectively massage and stretch the skin to stimulate lymph flow.

HOT AND COLD TEMPERATURES. Hot and cold temperatures can effectively stimulate lymph flow because they move the blood and lymph fluid deep into the body and to the surface. The safest procedure for doing this is to start with a comfortable shower. Allow warm water to run along your neck and back, then gently increase the heat until it's as hot as tolerable. Thoroughly expose your body to this heat for several minutes, allowing the stream of water to fall over your head, neck, shoulders, back, lower body, legs, feet, and soles. Now, gradually turn down the hot as you gradually increase the cold. Make it as cold as possible. You'll find, if you've thoroughly heated up the body first, that your tolerance for cold will be surprising. Turn the water off and step carefully out of the shower. Pat dry with a towel, and then vigorously brush the skin, bringing the blood flow again to the surface. All done! You'll feel electrically alive and vital!

Eleven Ways to Promote Detoxification Naturally

There are numerous methods for ensuring better internal detoxification; some are complicated and require equipment. The methods detailed here, however, can be easily incorporated into your daily life and will support your body in strengthening its natural detoxing capability. There can also be great value in more strenuous detoxing, such as colonic therapy, fasting, and deep-tissue treatments, but these techniques should be supervised by a health professional and are best preceded by the following suggestions.

ADEQUATE REST. Physical stress produces increased cellular waste and reduces immune capability. Resting restores immunity and enhances the liver's detoxifying abilities. Ideally, in a healthy state, we should not require more than 7 hours of sleep. Thomas Edison got by, supposedly with 4 hours, but he frequently took 20-minute naps throughout the day. When you rest, wearing an eye mask can make your rest feel even deeper because light can make sleep lighter and less restful.

GOOD DIET. Eat good quality food, organic whenever possible, that is low in fat, low acid forming, and low in sodium. Do not overeat. These measures ensure that you are not adding to the toxicity you may already have. Excess sodium can constrict kidney filtering and, in some cases, promote fluid accumulation (edema). Consuming daily fiber from whole grains, beans, and vegetables promotes reliable elimination.

HERBAL SUPPORT. Milk thistle, a powerful liver-specific antioxidant also known as silymarin, has been shown to protect against liver damage during times of oxidative stress, such as after poisoning. In animal studies, a standardized potency preparation of silymarin demonstrated a strong protective effect against poisoning from the amanita (aka death-trap) mushroom. Amanita poison, known to be highly toxic to the liver, is related to increased oxidant stress. Milk thistle concentrate diminished the toxic effects this mushroom would have normally had on the liver. Another popular herb used to strengthen the liver detox function is dandelion root. Popular throughout Italy, the roots are usually roasted and used as a hearty tea that resembles the full-bodied taste of coffee.

DAILY EXERCISE. Moderate, consistent exercise can enhance immunity, promote greater circulation, stimulate intestinal movement, and help discharge carbon wastes via respiration. This adds to an overall positive emotional state and increases will.

SKIN BRUSHING. Skin brushing aids the discharge of toxins through the skin via promoting good circulation. Practice it once daily just before a morning shower.

BREATHING PRACTICE. Any activity that increases the exhalation can be very effective for helping discharge carbon dioxide. Singing, chanting, reading aloud, and breathing exercises all qualify as exhalation therapies. Some of the standard yoga breathing exercises are especially recommended because they focus on the exhalation.

INTESTINAL RUBBING. As a part of a brief morning stretching routine, the deep rubbing of the abdominal surface can help stimulate bowel matter through the intestinal path. Beginning from the right inside hip area of the abdomen, use the fingertips of each hand to rub in counter-clockwise circles on the ascending colon, traveling upward. The pattern can be done in this order: rub in small circles up the ascending colon (your right side), across the transverse colon (just beneath the rib cage), and down the ascending colon (your left side). Then rub in a small circle about 1.5 inches around your navel. Finish with a general free-for-all rubbing. Ideally, there should be no pain when you rub. If this is uncomfortable, you might have mild inflammation and need only look as far as changing your daily diet and food volume to reduce that pain.

MASSAGE. Deep-tissue massage benefits not only blood circulation but the movement of lymphatic fluid through tissue and into nodes as well as the body's inner energy core. The value of touch and passive muscle movement has tremendous energetic healing potential. Some practitioner's focus their practice on lymphatic drainage, a technique emphasizing a deep directional rub on the neck (front and back), shoulders, collarbone, breast, and underarm.

SAUNA. Heat exposure benefits lymph and blood circulation. Additional circulatory and lymph therapies such as salt rubs (rubbing the body vigorously with salt to draw out toxins) and body brushing can be used to great benefit in combination with sauna heat. If you enjoy steam baths, I'd suggest first finding out about if the water source is filtered because the chemicals in the water end up being discharged into the steam, which you'll be inhaling. *Do make certain to check with an appropriate medical practitioner regarding your personal tolerance for any external heat therapy.*

EMOTIONAL EXPRESSION. As another form of inner toxicity, suppressed emotions nurture their own brew of poison. Well documented as a chief source of stress, holding in feelings that we want or need to express is plainly not health enhancing.

BECOME TOXIN SAVVY. The less exposure we have to external toxins, from food and the environment, the more effective our biochemical systems can become in their continuous process of internal housecleaning. Read product labels; avoid long, physically stagnant periods in front of machines; check for radon levels in your home; make sure you surround yourself with ecofriendly home products, filtered water, and possibly air filters; and open windows that send breezes through your home. Educate yourself about natural options to chemicals in hygiene products and throughout your home. Becoming toxin savvy means making healthier choices in what you put into your mouth, on your skin, and in the air you breathe.

AVOIDING WINDY DAYS

AFTER MANY YEARS of trying and failing to convince an older English mentor of mine to try changing his diet, I was pleased when he was finally ready to, as he says, "give it a go." Of course he was ready; he'd just begun dating a woman who was a yoga teacher, health-oriented, and passionate about his need to change. Love had transformed him into a convert.

After the meal at one of my favorite whole foods restaurants, he left me a thank-you message on my voicemail: "First-class meal! Ate like a soldier—maybe more like a pig, but loved it! I could dine like this *all* the time! I can do this, yes I can! Thanks again. Cheers."

Nice message. But, the following morning, I returned home to a second, very contrasting message:

Varona, you can have your food! I've been dog gassy all night. Passed enough wind to fill the *Hindenburg*, and I'll tell you, it's still raging! You should have warned me, lad. I'm afraid to leave the house! How can you eat like this all the time? Won't dare play tennis this afternoon, no sir . . . Call me, will you?

My friend learned his first lesson in food combinations, overeating, drinking with his meals, rushing, and poor chewing.

I've never bought the conventional explanation for gas: the swallowing of air. After 40 years of personal and professional experience, I believe otherwise. Here are eight practical strategies for avoiding gas—and you can thank me later:

- **Volume:** Overeating puts you at risk for increased acidity and subsequent gas. Portion your volume before eating and take your time. You can always eat the remainder later.
- **Simple sugar and complex sugar combinations:** We all have different tolerances, but simple sugars (sugars and fruit) digest much more quickly than complex sugars (such as whole grain) and end up fermenting the slower-digesting grain in the stomach. The result is gas. Until you become accustomed to these foods and have the opportunity to experiment and learn about your own tolerances, it's safest to eat dessert separately, not with the meal, or as long as you can wait after the meal.
- **Bean volume:** I found that when clients began eating beans, they would have an amount just short of a giant fiesta plate— huge portions of beans! Beans have two difficult starches that do not easily break apart in the human intestine, and gas occurs when these starches cannot break down. Generally, in bean cooking there are a number of things one can do to minimize this problem. Here are the four most important solutions for this: Keep the volume down; chew thoroughly; make sure the beans have been cooked with sea salt toward the end of their cooking (about 10 minutes before finishing the dish); and make certain to not eat anything sweet at the same meal you have beans or bean products.
- **Thorough chewing:** The predominant macronutrient in the Nature's Cancer-Fighting Foods Plan is complex carbohydrate (grain, bean, and vegetable). Complex carbohydrates initially

(CONTINUED)

digest in the mouth, but when they arrive in the stomach, they cease digestion, until eventually entering into the next structure, which is an extension of the stomach called the duodenum. Then their digestion resumes. Therefore, it's best to chew these foods well for maximized absorption. Becoming a good chewer does not mean you have to do a slow cow dance with your jaw and take forever at the table. Liquifying food in the mouth means to chew your food well enough so that it almost becomes a liquid. The alkaline enzymes in saliva initiate digestion. If you diligently chew just one meal per week, your chewing will automatically improve with every meal thereafter.

- **Tension:** Our digestive secretions are inhibited when we become upset. At this point it would be better to excuse yourself, take a brief walk, sort out your thinking, and do some deep breathing before returning to the table and attempting to eat. Tension is not conducive to digestion.

- **Drinking with meals:** This might be a minor gas factor but could account for poor assimilation, inadequate nutrition, and residual acidity.

- **Salt:** Certain foods are easier to digest with the alkalinity of sea salt, such as beans and bean products, cruciferous vegetables (cabbage, broccoli, greens), and others. However, this does not mean that your meals should taste salty. Moderate sea salt amounts cooked into the food are the key.

- **Protein and carbohydrates:** Certain people, particularly those who are allergy prone or consume a lot of sweets, often have difficulty combining proteins with complex carbohydrates. In this case, if all else has failed in the preventing-gas department, eat protein (beans) and complex carbohydrates (whole grains) separately—at different meals. So when you have the bean soup, you avoid the grain for that meal and perhaps have a salad or side vegetable dish with it. Eventually, you'll build up a tolerance in order to enjoy these combinations again.

10

Cancer-Fighting
Supplement Strategies

All those vitamins aren't to keep death at bay, they're
to keep deterioration at bay.

— Jeanne Moreau

PICK up any general-interest newsstand magazine, and you'll see numerous advertisements hyping miracle potions that promise everything
from restoring hair growth and improving intelligence to preventing
and reversing cancer. In 1994, Congress passed the Dietary Supplement
Health and Education Act (DSHEA), which in essence deregulated
dietary supplements, permitting them to be labeled and regulated as
supplements (not foods) and thus removing much of the FDA's authority
over their contents and health claims. Since then, there's been a virtual
explosion of health-enhancing megavitamins, magic pills, and cure-all
potions guaranteed to relieve pain, deepen sleep, and boost virility.

The supplement industry, a $25-billion-a-year business, is sustained
by more than 25 percent of the American population who religiously
take daily supplements. National surveys reveal that about half of Americans use dietary supplements. The remaining half either couldn't care
less or walk around overwhelmed by guilt about what they should be
doing to better care for their health.

Do we need supplements? Can they really work as promised? Are they safe?

The answers to these questions are widely debated and not always precise. Even within medical circles, in which pro and con research is reported almost daily, there are very clear divisions of supporters and detractors.

Despite the growing evidence of the benefits of supplements, very little has filtered down to the rank and file of the medical community. Strangely, the average physician still regards food and nutritional supplements with some doubt or considers the supplement issue as an adjunctive therapy to the fundamental or real treatment being drugs and surgery. However, new research has opened the door a bit wider, and now, many physicians concede that pregnant women need folic acid, which has been proven to prevent spina bifida in their newborns. Still, few obstetricians seem to have made the necessary mental connection that healthy living may prevent many other birth defects as well.

This chapter examines conventional, alternative, and traditional folk medicine perspectives on supplements. I offer basic recommendations and detail a supplement-repairing protocol for minimizing the negative effects of chemotherapy and radiation therapy. However, before undertaking a supplement regime, it is essential that you check with a qualified health practitioner regarding possible drug–supplement interactions *and* with a qualified nutritionist for supplement updates, brand suggestions, and specific dosages tailored for your particular condition.

PUTTING THE LIME IN LIMEYS

IN 1747, A major milestone occurred in nutritional medicine when the Scottish navel surgeon James Lind discovered that an unknown nutrient in citrus foods prevented a common disease called scurvy, whose symptoms included spontaneous bleeding, loose teeth, pain, brittle bones, and fatigue. Scurvy was often deadly and had claimed more British sailors than had war injuries. Lind's experiment, one of the first of a controlled clinical nutrition study involving human subjects, provided unprecedented evidence of the curative value derived from oranges and lemons.

Scurvy, recognized from ancient times as a serious disease, was often a deadly problem when fresh fruits and vegetables were not available during harsh winters or during long ocean voyages. Sailors were especially vulnerable to this wasting illness, which afflicted them because the only food given them on these long voyages was hard-tack biscuits and salted meats.

The disease is characterized by frequent hemorrhaging of capillaries in the skin to produce blood spots and structural weakness of cartilage and bone. In the mid-18th century, it became known that the simple addition of vegetables and fresh fruit, particularly limes and oranges, could prevent scurvy. This was the reason that British sailors were nicknamed "limeys." It took until 1928, when chemistry had become more progressive, for a researcher to identify the scurvy-curing substance as vitamin C.

History of the Vitamin–Disease Connection

Throughout history in many societies, diseases were considered to be the work of angry gods, witchcraft, poor air, bad humors (body fluids), family history, poisoning, or simple fate. Yet even 3,500 years ago, ancient Egyptians recognized that night blindness (now attributed to a lack of vitamin A) could be treated with specific foods. The folk medicines of many cultures typically had various herbs and food combinations available to use as remedies.

During the late 19th century, it was discovered that the substitution of unpolished for polished rice, in a rice-based diet, could prevent a disease called beriberi.

In 1906, the British biochemist Frederick Hopkins discovered that foods naturally contained what he called "necessary accessory factors" in addition to the macronutrients of carbohydrates, fats, and protein, along with minerals and water. In 1911, Polish chemist Casimir Funk discovered that the anti-beriberi substance in unpolished rice was an amine (a nitrogen-containing compound). Funk named it *vitamine,* for "vital amine." Soon this term was applied to all accessory nutritional factors. When it was later discovered that many vitamins do not have nitrogen containing amines, the final letter *e* was dropped.

By 1912, scientists Hopkins and Funk advanced their theory of vitamin deficiency, explaining that physical deficiencies of certain vitamins were connected to specific diseases. This was a major finding, prompting extensive animal experiments throughout the early 1900s, when scientists succeeded in isolating and identifying many of the numerous vitamins recognized today.

Today, nutritional medicine is divided in its position on human nutrient requirements. It is plainly evident that free radicals damage DNA, which can lead to premature aging and diseases such as cancer, heart disease, arthritis, and Alzheimer's. Research has shown that vitamins can protect against DNA damage and that amino acids and B vitamins are necessary for the repair and synthesis of DNA. However, while one side proposes optimal nutrition, the other claims adequate nutrition is available from a balanced diet. Exactly what constitutes a balanced diet is still a hotly debated issue.

While many researchers claim that supplements can compensate for deficient soil quality, poor diet, and modern everyday stresses, another fraction claims that only whole foods from organic sources can prevent and treat deficiencies. As the advertising creed of nutritional deficiency rallies support in favor of the supplement argument, the real problem might be more a matter of excess; excess of macronutrients (too much simple carbohydrate, fats, and protein), overall dietary acidity, a lack of activity, and an excess of physical and emotional stress. Supplements, by their very name, should *supplement* our health without creating dependency or supplanting appropriate dietary and lifestyle choices.

THE HARDEST-WORKING NUTRIENTS IN THE BUSINESS

IN THE MIRACULOUS composition of our body, proteins, carbohydrates, and fats combine with other substances to create energy and construct tissue. In the right amounts, they promote normal growth, digestion, mental clarity, and immune function.

Essentially, vitamins and minerals are substances *required in small amounts* to support fundamental biochemical reactions in the cells. However, we don't burn vitamins, so we can't derive energy (calories) directly from them.

Together, vitamins and minerals are called *micronutrients*. A prolonged lack of a micronutrient can potentially lead to a specific disease or condition, which can potentially be reversed when the micronutrient is again provided.

Vitamins are divided into two categories:

> *Water-soluble vitamins:* B vitamins (B_1, thiamine; B_2, ribo-
> flavin; niacin; B_6; pantothenic acid; B_{12}; biotin; and folic
> acid or folate), and vitamin C
> *Fat-soluble vitamins:* A, D, E, and K

At this point in nutritional history, there are 13 known vitamins that the body strives to keep at constant and optimal levels circulating within the bloodstream. The nine water-soluble vitamins are not stored in significant amounts in the body's tissues. The four fat-soluble vitamins are stored within the body's fat tissue.

Surplus water-soluble vitamins are excreted in urine, but surplus fat-soluble vitamins are stored in body tissues and thus can accumulate to toxic levels.

Your body also needs 16 minerals that help regulate cellular function and provide structure for cells, including phosphorus, calcium, magnesium, copper, iron, iodine, chromium, molybdenum, selenium, zinc, chloride, potassium, and sodium.

Supplements as Part of a Healing Protocol

For many debilitating conditions, the moderate use of supplements, along with a whole foods dietary practice, can offer vital healing support. Supplements may benefit the elderly, those in pre- and post-operative care, dieters, smokers, women who are or wish to become pregnant, alcohol drinkers, vegetarians, people on medication or oral contraceptives, and those with chronic illness. However, supplements for the cancer patient can be of particular value, offering enhanced immunity, better nutrition for compromised digestive systems, and support for conventional cancer therapies (surgery, radiation, and chemotherapy).

As long as we depend on foods that are chemically sprayed, processed, refined, canned, frozen, stored, hormonally fed, overcooked, artificially chemicalized, laden with sugar, oversalted, and genetically modified, we run the serious risk of deficiency and increased malabsorption. An attempt to use a supplement regimen to offset these factors is akin to the ice pack analogy: "Allow me to batter you with a 2-by-4 plank, but worry not; I'll give you an ice pack as soon as I am done." It's merely a bandage on a wound that you are aggravating by a poor-quality, unbalanced diet. The only risk in the moderate use of supplements is a potential for psychological dependency and the mind-set that considers them to be a solo therapy. Supplements should support a sound dietary and healthy lifestyle program.

The Cancer Protection Supplement Plan

Antioxidant and nutrient supplements have demonstrated an ability to bolster and reinforce the body's ability to counteract the effects of free radicals, substances that promote tumor growth and weaken immunity. There are other micronutrients and nutritional factors that can help prevent cancer and are essential adjuncts to any cancer therapy.

Antioxidants are chemicals found abundantly in fruits and vegetables. They can also be found in smaller amounts in nuts and grains. Phytochemicals battle specific types of oxygen molecules known as free radicals, which can damage DNA and contribute to the development and spread of cancerous cells.

The common antioxidants are vitamins A, C, and E; selenium; certain compounds in green tea; and the hormone melatonin manufactured by the pineal gland in the brain.

The use of antioxidants in supplement form for cancer prevention and treatment is a controversial and conflicting topic. While some nutritional experts believe that megadoses of antioxidants, including vitamins A and E, offer benefits, some clinical studies have debated the safety of this practice. Some studies have shown that high doses of certain antioxidants can actually *increase* cancer occurrence in certain populations. For instance, smokers who take high doses of beta-carotene tend to be at an increased risk for lung cancer.

Most physicians suggest refraining from taking antioxidants during radiation therapy and chemotherapy because they might protect the very cancer cells that are being targeted. A 2008 study in *Cancer Research* showed that vitamin C supplements blunted the effectiveness of chemotherapy by 30 to 70 percent.

When all is said and done, although there are some positive data suggesting antioxidant supplements can improve the quality of life for some cancer patients, a dietary plan rich in whole foods, such as grains, beans, and vegetables, offers abundant antioxidants in a natural form.

Beta-Carotene

Beta-carotene is a plant pigment found naturally in vegetables and fruits. It has repeatedly proved helpful for the enhancement of natural killer cells and other immune cells against tumors. However, the vegetables containing them may have even more protective effects. One study from Dartmouth Medical School in New Hampshire showed that vegetables are better than supplements in lowering the risks of developing colon cancer. The precursor of vitamin A, beta-carotene can be found in carrots, sweet potatoes, and most leafy green vegetables. It has shown particular importance for women as deterrent to a cervical cancer and for lung protection from smoking and smog exposure.

Vitamin E

As one of the body's key micronutrients for protecting cell membranes and to support the immune system's ability to fight cancer and infection, vitamin E also increases the effectiveness and specific toxicity of chemotherapy agents on tumors and helps protect against radiation treatment toxicity. Vitamin E can be found in dark green vegetables, eggs, wheat germ, unrefined vegetable oils, and some herbs. Researchers claim that the natural D-alpha-tocopherol succinate form may prevent cancer more efficiently than other forms. Often this form can be obtained in a good daily multiple-vitamin supplement. Approximately 400 IU of vitamin E daily, as a minimum, is generally recommended.

Coenzyme Q10

Also known as ubiquinone or ubiquinol, coenzyme Q10 (CoQ10) is the spark that fuels energy production in every cell in your body, including your heart, which is your body's biggest energy user. It is an antioxidant that supports cellular function, enhances immunity, and protects the heart. It is one of a family of brightly colored substances, called quinones, that appear abundantly in nature and are essential for generating energy in living things that depend on oxygen. While the body produces small quantities of CoQ10, our natural levels diminish with age. High concentrations of CoQ10 exist in fish (particularly sardines), soybean and grapeseed oils, sesame seeds, pistachios, walnuts, and spinach. The quality of the CoQ10 is just as important as the quantity.

There are only two real choices for coenzyme Q10: ubiquinone and ubiquinol. Both are forms of coenzyme Q10; the word *ubiquinone* means "the ubiquitous quinone." Ubiquinone, the oxidized form of CoQ10, is the more commercially available type. The less expensive brands of CoQ10 are most likely in the oxidized ubiquinone form. If the label doesn't specifically mention which form of CoQ10 the product contains, it's most likely ubiquinone. The preferred form is ubiquinol, a reduced form of CoQ10, relatively new to the commercial market and far more expensive to produce. Ubiquinol is an antioxidant that neutralizes free radicals and decreases cellular damage. Ubiquinone does not have this antioxidant effect.

The general recommendation is 200 to 300 milligrams daily. It is best absorbed with some type of fatty food.

Modified Citrus Pectin

Some animal studies found that modified citrus pectin (MCP) helped reduce the spread of prostate, breast, and skin cancer. Animals with these types of cancer that were fed MCP showed a much lower risk of their tumors spreading to the lungs. One study examined the effects of MCP on lung metastases from melanoma cells.

Researchers then injected mice with melanoma cells. In the mice that were also given MCP, significantly fewer tumors spread to the lungs than in the mice that did not receive the drug. When lung tumors did develop in the mice treated with MCP, the tumors tended to be smaller than those that formed in untreated animals. These studies appear to show that MCP makes it difficult for cancer cells that break off from the main tumor to join together and grow in other organs.

Dosages vary for MCP; however, a standard of 800 milligrams three times a day is commonly recommended. See your personal health professional for suggested dosages.

Vitamin B Complex

The vitamin B complex includes vitamins B_1, B_2, B_3 (niacin), and B_6; folic acid; and pantothenic acid. Together, they act as a biochemical support system to accelerate chemical reactions as catalysts, regulate overall energy metabolism, and help regulate proper nervous system functioning. B vitamin deficiencies can inhibit the immune system's natural ability to destroy cancer cells. It has been observed that pantothenic acid and vitamin B_6 inhibit tumor growth. Specific deficiencies of B_6 have been shown to depress T-cell activity and antibody resiliency as well as inhibit tumor growth, particularly in liver cancer. Folic acid has also been shown to inhibit development of chemically induced tumors. Growing evidence indicates that B_3, also known as niacin or nicotinic acid, can increase the efficacy of conventional cancer treatment. Food sources of B vitamins are dark green leafy vegetables, brewer's yeast, wheat germ, whole grains and grain products, and various animal meats. Generally, a daily dosage of 50 milligrams of a vitamin B complex supplement is sufficient. Any excess of vitamin B beyond the body's actual needs is generally discharged through the urine, resulting in a bright yellow color.

Vitamin C

Vitamin C has proved foundational for a healthy immune system. Vitamin C limits free radical damage to DNA that may lead to cancer. The natural killer (NK) cells of the immune system are active only when they contain large amounts of vitamin C. Because one study found that vitamin C enhanced leukemia in some human leukemia cell lines, patients with leukemia should be cautious about taking large doses. The National Institutes of Health branch of the Office of Dietary Supplements asserts that approximately 70 to 90 percent of vitamin C is absorbed at moderate intakes of 30 to 180 milligrams per day. However, at doses above 1 gram per day, absorption of vitamin C falls to less than 50 percent and absorbed, unmetabolized ascorbic acid is then excreted in the urine. Vitamin C can also be found in green leafy vegetables, broccoli, green peppers, and numerous other vegetables and fruits.

Vitamin D

Classified as a hormone, vitamin D has antitumor qualities. It has been shown to increase the number of vitamin A receptors on cells, stimulate the reversal of cancer cells back into normalized cells, and randomly induce cell suicide (apoptosis) in cancer cells. Some Australian research has indicated that vitamin D could offer protection from prostate cancer. There is strong research that indicates vitamin D plays a role in the prevention of colon, prostate, and breast cancers. Most typical recommended dosages range from 750 to 3,000 IU daily, although, in cases of extreme deficiencies as determined from blood workups, up to 5,000 IU is typically recommended.

Selenium

Selenium is considered an important trace element for its strong synergistic effects with vitamin E, enhancing its cancer-fighting potential. According to biochemist Gerhard Schrauzer, selenium is often deficient in cancer patients. Studies show that people who consume lower amounts of selenium typically have an increased risk of developing cancers of the colon and rectum, prostate, lung, bladder, skin, esophagus, and stomach. This essential nutrient is found in vegetables, fruits, and some nuts. Recommended dosage in supplement form is 70 to 100 micrograms per day.

Calcium

Essential for bone and tooth development, blood clotting, and cellular metabolism, calcium offers protection against colon cancer. A 19-year prospective study revealed that calcium deficiency was associated with an increased risk of colorectal cancer. Sufficient amounts of calcium can be obtained from dark green vegetables and sea vegetables as well as from various nuts, seeds, sardines, and salmon. Your need for calcium depends on several factors, from what can be seen through blood work to kidney health (a previous history of kidney stones often warrants less or no calcium) and any tendency toward bone loss. General World Health Organization (WHO) recommendations for daily calcium intake is approximately 500 to 1,000 milligrams.

Magnesium

Helping maintain balanced blood pH and the synthesis of RNA and DNA, magnesium offers cancer protection and can be found in various fish, green vegetables, whole grains and grain products (particularly brown rice), legumes, and most nuts. Eating ample sources of this mineral can often be sufficient; however, in the case of lowered blood value levels, increased magnesium might be necessary. The current RDA for magnesium is 300 to 420 milligrams. Forms of magnesium that dissolve well in liquid are more completely absorbed in the gut than less soluble forms. Some studies have found that magnesium aspartate, citrate, lactate, and chloride forms are better absorbed and tend to be more bioavailable than magnesium oxide and magnesium sulfate.

Iodine

Iodine, a trace element, has been shown to offer protection against breast cancer. It's required for cellular energy metabolism and the growth and repair of all tissues. Iodine is found abundantly in seafood and common sea vegetables, such as dulse, nori, wakame, kelp, and others. Seaweed is an ocean vegetable that is quite foreign to most Western kitchens. A side dish of these nutrient-rich foods two to three times weekly proves a powerful healing food. Nori, the green sheet seaweed that is used as a wrapper on sushi has entered the Western gastronomical experience and can be purchased in major supermarkets in the Asian or gourmet section or in natural food markets. Dulse, a reddish-brown thin sea vegetable, is a native of the U.S. Northeast and coastal Ireland and Scotland; it can be tastefully added (in small quantities) to bean soups, vegetable dishes, and even vegetable soups. It may be an acquired taste, but one that you'll grow to enjoy quickly. The RDA for iodine is approximately 150 micrograms.

Zinc

Zinc, known for its protective qualities against prostate cancer, is a necessary factor in RNA and DNA formation and for enhanced immune function. Good sources of zinc are whole grains, seafood, beans (notably soybeans), sunflower seeds, pumpkin seeds, eggs, and onions. The onion and radish families, in particular, offer abundant nutrition and helps keep the blood thin while bolstering circulation. The RDA for zinc is approximately 15 milligrams daily.

Omega-3 Fatty Acids

Omega-3 fatty acids are a type of unsaturated fatty acid that is present mostly in fish oils, although present in smaller quantities in a limited number of vegetable foods. Reliable sources of omega-3 fatty acids exist in salmon, mackerel, haddock, cod, and sardines; vegetable sources are flaxseed, flaxseed oil, and walnuts. Some studies have shown that essential fatty acids can inhibit breast cancer.

A $20 million study underwritten by the National Cancer Institute in 1990 found that flaxseed oil reduced the growth of breast cancers and metastases in laboratory animals when compared to cancerous growth in animals receiving corn oil. This study determined that the strong anti-cancer quality of flaxseed was due to its high lignan content.

However, flaxseed oil was not recommended for men because some medical research suggests that flaxseed oil might actually promote the growth of prostate cancer cells. The actual flaxseed with its fibrous outer covering is, however, recommended for men. Researchers have discovered that lignans can bind to estrogen receptors in the body and diminish the cancer-stimulating effects of estrogen on breast tissue. Recommended amounts of flaxseed oil for women vary from 1 to 2 teaspoons per day; men can use ground seeds as a condiment. When taking capsules, the average amount recommended is 1 to 3 grams daily.

Curcumin

Curcumin, the active anti-inflammatory ingredient of the widely used Indian spice turmeric, is a member of the ginger family. It has been used in traditional healing formulas for centuries in both Ayurvedic and Chinese medicine. Present research has made curcumin one of Western medicine's most researched ancient medicinal herbs.

+ According to scientists at the University of Kansas Cancer Center and Medical Center, "curcumin inhibits the growth of esopha-geal cancer cell lines." The results of the study are promising and timely, given that esophageal cancer is the eighth most common type of cancer in the world and the sixth most lethal.
+ In 2011, researchers at the University of Texas MD Anderson Cancer Center found that curcumin had a unique ability to dif-ferentiate cancer cells from normal cells and create apoptosis (cell death) in cancer cells only, while promoting better cellular health in noncancerous cells.
+ A study from Zheijiang Provincial People's Hospital in Zheiji-ang, China, showed that curcumin is capable of inducing apop-tosis within triple negative breast cancer (TNBC) cells. TNBC has defied conventional therapy.

Research from the Ludwig Maximilian University in Munich pub-lished in the journal *Carcinogenesis* explains how curcumin inhibits the development of metastases in prostate cancer tissues and other cancer lines as well. Dosages vary because curcumin's absorption is poor. Up to 12 grams daily have been well tolerated. The average cancer recommendation is a dosage of 3.6 to 4 grams. You can also sprinkle ground turmeric on food dishes such as whole grains, beans, soups, salads, and stir-fry vegetables.

Chlorella

Chlorella contains the highest chlorophyll level per ounce of any plant. It also rates high in protein (nearly 58 percent), carbohydrates, all of the B vitamins, vitamins C and E, amino acids (including all nine essential ones), enzymes, and rare trace minerals. Western medicine has largely ignored chlorella; however, Japanese scientists have been researching its benefits since the atomic bombings of Hiroshima and Nagasaki. In *Cancer Therapy*, Ralph Moss writes, "Japanese scientists studied *Chlorella pyrenoidosa* as a biological response modifier. Since chlorella does not directly kill cancer cells, the scientists concluded that its effects were caused by boosting the immune response." In one Japanese study, scientists placed lab mice on a chlorella regimen for 10 days and then injected the mice with three strains of cancer.

According to Moss, "over 70 percent of the chlorella-strengthened mice did not develop cancer, while all of the untreated mice died within 20 days." Protein rich and with plentiful amounts of immune enhancing factors, chlorella also bonds to and helps the removal of numerous systemic toxins. You can access the benefits of chlorella by taking only 1 or 2 teaspoons of chlorella powder once or twice daily. Using the small pill form, approximately 20 to 30 pills make up about 1 teaspoon of powder.

Garlic

Documented studies have shown that people who consume plentiful amounts of garlic are less likely to develop common cancers. There is also some evidence that garlic may be helpful for cancer in conjunction with conventional cancer treatments. Depending on how garlic has been processed, it has been shown to contain significant immune-boosting abilities. In addition, there are certain substances that naturally exist in garlic that suppress cancer cell growth, particularly breast and lung cancers.

There are also some studies that show eating garlic decreases the risk for colorectal cancer and stomach cancer. However, similar benefits were not found with popular garlic supplements. Prostate cancer research of Chinese men has shown that both eating garlic and garlic supplements decrease the risk of prostate cancer. A study conducted in the San Francisco Bay Area found that pancreatic cancer risk was 54 percent lower in people who ate larger amounts of garlic, compared with those who ate lower amounts. Garlic can be used by minicing up several cloves and adding to cooking. Recommended dosages are 4 grams daily, approximately 2 cloves.

It just might be worth alienating those within breath range for the promise of garlic's benefits.

WHEN MORE IS *NOT* BETTER

VITAMINS CANNOT REPLACE food. In fact, vitamins are best assimilated after ingesting food. Vitamins help regulate metabolism, convert fat and carbohydrates into energy, and assist in forming bone and tissue. However, vitamin-mineral supplements shouldn't substitute for a healthful diet. High doses do not usually offer extra protection but do increase the risk of potential toxic side effects.

For example, taking large amounts of vitamin D can indirectly cause kidney damage, whereas large amounts of vitamin A can cause liver damage. Even modest increases in some minerals can lead to imbalances that limit your body's ability to use other minerals. Supplements of iron, zinc, chromium, and selenium can be toxic at just 5 times the RDA. Virtually all nutrient toxicities stem from high-dose supplements.

Here are some miscellaneous facts about vitamin excesses and the imbalances they can cause:

- High amounts of calcium inhibit absorption of iron and other trace elements.
- Folic acid can mask hematologic signs of vitamin B_{12} deficiency, which if untreated can result in irreversible neurologic damage.
- Zinc supplementation can reduce copper status, impair immune responses, and decrease high-density lipoprotein cholesterol levels.
- High doses of vitamin E can interfere with vitamin K action and enhance the effect of Coumadin (an anticoagulant drug). Over 25,000 IU per day can cause headaches, dry skin, hair loss, fatigue, bone problems, and liver damage.
- A study of 22,748 pregnant women found that women taking more than 10,000 IU preformed vitamin A had a greater risk of giving birth to babies with cranial neural crest defects.

- Iron supplements intended for other household members are the most common cause of pediatric poisoning deaths in the United States.
- Excessive zinc and vitamin C has an antagonistic effect on copper levels.

Supplement tolerance and figuring individual nutritional needs are still very young sciences and not set in stone. The problem with isolating key nutrients, which is done by common standardization processes, is that it diminishes the natural and complex matrix of many inherent trace nutrients that synergistically aid in our assimilation and cellular use of these nutrients. Also in question is whether it is necessary to take steady daily supplements as opposed to irregular consumption (such as four days on, three days off) in an attempt to keep nutrient dependency at a minimum. At best, an on-and-off prescription might offer a greater sensitivity to what works and what doesn't and at the same time keep the body in a positive state of change. Ultimately, the answer is not in research but in results. And this is best determined through additional study, personal experimenting, and self-evaluation.

The Limitations of Chemotherapy

It's a mistake to think that the war on cancer can be won with treatment.

—John Cairns, Harvard School of Public Health

Chemotherapy is the systemic use of anticancer drugs and still a conventional treatment for treating cancers. While its short-term usefulness in some cancers has, in some cases, been shown helpful (acute lymphocytic leukemia, Hodgkin's disease, testicular cancer, ovarian cancer, and a small number of rare tumors), suggesting it as a standard across-the-board therapy for the majority of cancers, particularly advanced carcinomas, is still highly debatable. Often the actual benefits might amount to only weeks or months and not years of survival.

Unfortunately, the trade-off for this extended time is accompanied by life-threatening side effects and a dramatic decrease in the patient's quality of life. It can make cancer patients nauseated, fatigued, and depressed, requiring them to spend more time in clinics and hospitals than any dying person might choose at his or her own will. But it won't banish cancer. Some aspects of medical prognosis and treatment are uncertain. Not chemotherapy treatment.

One reason why chemotherapy drugs have poor response rates is because solid tumors have a unique method of growth. As tumors develop, their need for nutrients increases. In an effort to meet this demand, the tumor issues a hormonal signal for new blood vessels to grow toward it. Since this is a very quick process, the new formation of blood vessels tends to have holes in its lining that range in size throughout its length. These spaces can measure from 200 to 400 nm (nanometers). While small enough to prevent bleeding, they are still large enough to allow fluid and blood particles—mostly proteins—to leak into the tumor. Since the blood vessels around the tumor's periphery are normal and do not leak, the osmotic pressure within the tumor is actually greater than it is outside the tumor. So now you have solid tumors growing inside a balloon where the pressure inside that balloon is greater than it is outside. Unfortunately, chemotherapy treatments cannot penetrate this physical barrier adequately, and as a result, end up attacking healthy organs and tissues, where there are no such barriers. According to Ralph Moss, a leading researcher in the field of both conventional and alternative treatments for cancer and author of *Questioning Chemotherapy*, chemotherapy "reduces the likelihood of benefiting from other promising nontoxic, nutritional, or immunological treatments." This can occur by damaging the bone marrow and different organ structures, which diminish a patient's chance of benefiting from promising treatments that depend on strong immunity and constitutional health. Moss claims there is no proof that chemotherapy extends life for the majority of patients. According to him, for a minority of tumors—Hodgkin's disease and testicular cancer being two examples—chemotherapy can extend life, but for the majority it does not. In fact, when Moss suggested to an oncologist (who had previously been critical of Moss's work) that chemotherapy of solid tumors, especially in disseminated disease, shows no proof of working, the oncologist replied by stating: "I'd go further than that. I'd say that there is proof—proof that it doesn't work."

Anyone considering chemotherapy would be better informed by diligent research of chemotherapy's effectiveness pertinent to their diagnosis before considering it as an automatic choice. For instance, how many cases of this kind of cancer have been helped or cured? Is it possible to speak to patients about their experience with chemotherapy? These are but two important questions worth asking your physician.

Recent studies have identified the official cancer war as a "qualified failure." According to John Cairns, chemotherapy drugs, the most recommended conventional therapy for cancer, *helps no more than 5 percent of patients who receive them.* The toxic and lethal chemicals of chemotherapy blanket many healthy cells with molecular damage and can result in cell mutation. In doing so, the risk of future cancers is initiated.

Sometimes painful surgical procedures used to remove cancerous growths can also spread cancer. Because most tumors have their own blood circulation, cutting into the area could free tumor cells to move into otherwise healthy tissue, thereby risking future cancers.

In an often-unquestioned ploy for cancer prevention, early detection (mammography screening for breast cancer) or drug treatment (chemoprevention: giving women who are asymptomatic a powerful drug like tamoxifen and suggesting it can prevent breast cancer) is frequently recommended.

Prevention was also the rallying cry behind performing double mastectomies on women who did not actually have cancer but who supposedly were at familial risk of someday developing cancer. Efforts to engage in true prevention, such as cleaning up the environment, stopping big-industry pollution, changing our fast-food eating habits, and more aggressive allocation of funds to explore alternatives have typically been overlooked or devalued.

Minimizing Chemotherapy and Radiation Toxicity

While most of the following suggestions have not been evaluated with the rigorous attention of randomized clinical trials, they are, however, known to stimulate immunity, promote the body's internal cleansing function, and enhance nutrition. Fortunately, they do not have any of the negative side effects attributed to chemotherapy. *Note that these recommendations and dosages should be further researched and thoroughly discussed with your nutritionally oriented health practitioner.*

+ **Malabsorption problems:** A multiple-vitamin and mineral supplement is highly recommended to counteract the negative effect chemotherapy has on nutrient absorption.
+ **Nausea:** Some research has shown that *N*-acetylcysteine, an amino acid–like supplement that has demonstrated strong an-

tioxidant activity, may reduce nausea and vomiting caused by chemotherapy. Using fresh ginger root daily, a few days prior to chemotherapy, reduces nausea associated with the drug treatment. Ginger has long been promoted for stomach upsets, ranging from motion sickness to morning sickness during pregnancy. Recommended dosage: approximately 1 teaspoon of fresh ginger juice per day. You can add small amounts of the finely sliced root to your cooking, or finely grate the ginger and then squeeze the fresh juice into different dishes.

+ **Mouth sores:** Chemotherapy often leaves patients with painful mouth sores, known as mucositis. According to double-bind research, the topical application of 400 IU of vitamin E, has proved helpful. If sores are inflamed but not open, gargling saltwater can also be of aid.

+ **Enhancing the effect of chemotherapy:** Antioxidants, such as vitamins A, E, and C, are known to increase the effectiveness of chemotherapy. Scientists in Luxembourg, who were researching the herb turmeric, described its main chemical component, curcumin, as antitumoral, antioxidant, and anti-inflammatory. They found that curcumin not only helped to alleviate some of the side effects of chemotherapy but was also able to slow the growth of cancer cells.

+ **Folic acid warning:** The chemotherapy drug methotrexate interferes with folic acid (B vitamin) metabolism. Cancer patients taking methotrexate should not supplement with folic acid beyond the recommended 400 micrograms usually found in multivitamin preparations without first discussing this with their oncologist. Typically, oncologists will recommend leucovorin (a form of folic acid) after methotrexate is used to counter any side effects.

+ **Heart damage:** Some chemotherapy drugs (Adriamycin, also known as doxorubicin) may damage heart tissue. A number of antioxidants are capable of reducing this toxicity. In particular, CoQ10, has been found helpful in recommended daily dosages of 120 to 200 milligrams. In animals, vitamin C has been shown to provide protection at recommended dosages of up to 2 grams per day. This dosage must be based on individual tolerance. One immediate symptom of intolerance or too high a dose is loose bowel function. Vitamin B_2 supplementation may also protect the heart from damage when taking the anticancer chemotherapy drug Adriamycin.

✦ **Liver damage:** The ripe seeds of milk thistle, which have been used to make herbal remedies for centuries, contain the antioxidant silymarin, which is thought to be responsible for milk thistle's helpful effects in protecting the liver. A recent study, published in *Cancer*, the journal of the American Cancer Society, found milk thistle helpful for treating liver inflammation in cancer patients who receive chemotherapy. The study showed that milk thistle could allow patients to take potent doses of chemotherapy without damaging their liver. Clinical studies have investigated using milk thistle to treat liver damage from cirrhosis (from alcohol) or toxins (such as mushroom poisoning) with positive results. Despite limited study data, the herb is often used for the treatment of liver problems associated with chemotherapy. Recommended dosages range from 300 to 500 milligrams. (Some studies have shown a slight inflammatory tendency from too much milk thistle, so make sure to have qualified supervision.)

✦ **Hair loss:** There is some anecdotal evidence that hair loss as a result of Adriamycin can be reduced by taking elevated amounts of vitamin E, up to 1,600 IU per day. Nutritionally oriented physicians generally recommend at least 800 IU of vitamin E to patients taking Adriamycin.

✦ **Magnesium loss:** The chemotherapy drug cisplatin frequently leads to depletion of magnesium. Taking an excess of magnesium (dosages as low as 350 to 500 milligrams per day) can cause diarrhea. In addition, people with kidney disease should not take magnesium supplements without consulting a physician experienced in nutritional matters. Cisplatin toxicity can be reduced by taking glutathione; however, this must be given intravenously by a physician.

✦ **Palm and sole pain:** The drug fluorouracil can sometimes cause pain on the skin of the palms and soles. It has been suggested that 200 milligrams daily of vitamin B_6 can eliminate this pain.

Creating Your Supplement Program

A supplement program cannot be universal. Everyone has different tolerances, needs, and responses. In short, when it comes to supplements, my feeling is, less is better. I've known people to take over a hundred supplements. It should be remembered that supplements are a branch of alternative medicine that is constantly being researched and developed. A current sample cancer-fighting supplement protocol might contain the following core supplements:

Multiple vitamin-mineral (vitamins A, C, D, and E, plus calcium, magnesium, selenium, and zinc)
B-Complex (with folic acid)
Curcumin
Coenzyme Q10
Modified citrus pectin
Maitake/reishi mushroom (beta-glucan source)
Chlorella (algae powder)

The Choice of Chemotherapy

No one can make the decision to begin, maintain, or stop chemotherapy treatment other than you. If a client tells me that chemo is recommended by his physicians, I will ask a number of questions:

What do *you* want to do? Is this *your* choice?
Have you investigated the recommended drugs?
Are you aware of the side effects of those particular drugs?
How long is the suggested protocol?
What kind of prognosis is your doctor giving you with these medications?

In the face of uncertainty and overwhelming emotion, it sometimes feels easier to just do what you're told, despite what might be your own intuitive stance to resist. However, sometimes we are unaware that what we perceive as intuition ("I have a feeling . . .") can also be disguised fear, so asking questions to yourself is the best way to qualify whether this is really a preferred choice. I encourage clients to become more proactive in their pursuit of healing; to ask relentless questions, to do their own diligent research, and not be intimidated by what seems to be an onslaught of negativity from friends, family, or medical professionals who condemn alternative approaches without really knowing much about them.

One client of mine recently described his physician's response when he asked for suggestions on how to minimize chemotherapy's debilitating effects. "Drink Kool-Aid," the doctor suggested. "It'll take the edge off of it." Apparently unknown to this physician, soft drinks immediately weaken immune function due to their high sugar content, which paralyzes white blood cell function and quickly makes body fluids more acid, compromising mineral status and inhibiting immune function.

Clearly, research, increased education, and making immediate and sensible changes in diet and lifestyle is a foundational move for recovery.

11

Food
for Healing

THE focus of this chapter is to introduce whole foods in a gradual way that you will find inspiring, healthy, and compatible with your healing goals. You'll find an explanation of essential whole foods and the merits of each, the benefits of the Nature's Cancer-Fighting Foods Plan, as well details of three specific food plans, with an overview of daily serving strategies.

Food Categories and Guidelines

The following lists present foods within the guidelines of the Nature's Cancer-Fighting Foods Plan. Later, the specifics for each cancer-fighting program will be outlined in detail.

Grains

The whole grain category consists of whole grains; cracked, ground, and rolled grains; and grain products.

WHOLE GRAINS

Amaranth

Barley

Brown rice (short, medium, long grain)

Buckwheat groats

Millet

Quinoa

Sweet brown rice

Teff

Wheat, spelt, or kamut

Whole oats

Wild rice

CRACKED, GROUND, OR ROLLED GRAINS

Bulgur wheat

Corn grits

Cracked wheat

Oat flakes

Polenta

Rolled oats

Steel-cut oats

WHOLE GRAIN PRODUCTS

Chapati and tortillas

Crackers and flatbreads

Flours (whole wheat, buckwheat)

Mochi (pounded sweet rice)

Pasta

Popcorn

Rice cakes

Rye flakes

Yeasted and unyeasted bread

MINIMIZE OR AVOID

Natural breakfast cereals—only for Transitional Diet*

Refined grains (white rice) and flours (white flour)

Sweetened flours with oils, artificial coloring, preservatives, conditioners, and so on

---

NONGLUTEN GRAINS

FOR THOSE WITH gluten sensitivities, there are a number of whole grains that do not contain gluten. In the last 10 years, we have learned that healing can be maximized in many cases simply by limiting or eliminating gluten. This is not an across-the-board recommendation; in some people, however, gluten hampers healing by creating intestinal inflammation, diminished nutrition, and weakened immune function.

The following grains are gluten-free:

(CONTINUED)

---

* Familiar boxed breakfast cereals are part of the Transitional Diet and are usually eaten with almond, soy, or oat milk and fruit. While there might be emotional comfort in this familiar kind of breakfast, it is not particularly energizing or nutrient rich.

Rice, as a whole grain, is rich in fiber, niacin, and several other B vitamins as well as some key minerals. When brown rice is processed into white rice, its seven layers of covering are lost, along with many of its valuable nutrients. As such, it ends up being a pure starch. Rice has been bred to survive and thrive in a variety of adverse conditions, leading to hundreds of varieties available today. Short-grain brown rice is the heartiest and contains more flavor.

Quinoa is a very small grain (technically, a fruit seed) similar to amaranth and buckwheat. Originating from cereal grass, quinoa is not really classified as a grain. It's one of the best quick-cooking sources of vegetable protein because it is rich in folic acid and contains all the essential amino acids as well as some minerals. It comes in tan, black, and red varieties and each variety has a slightly different flavor and texture. Quinoa is frequently mixed with other grains and used in stews and salads.

Millet is a small round yellow grain with a slightly sweet taste that has been used for the past 5,000 years in China and is still considered a staple food. Like many grains, it is low in lysine, so it is not a complete protein. However, it's an excellent source of magnesium and other minerals and contains B vitamins. Millet works well as a soup or stew ingredient, usually added about 20 minutes before it's ready to serve. When thoroughly cooked, it clumps together, making it easier to slice once it cools and an excellent choice for polenta, loaves, and croquettes.

Wild rice offers a more superior source of protein than most whole grains because it contains a good amount of the amino acid lysine. Wild rice is also high in many minerals and several B vitamins. It has a unique nutty flavor and a satisfying chewy texture. Blending well with other varieties of rice, it makes a nice complement for pilaf dishes. Real wild rice has defied domestication, which means that most of the wild rice sold in American retail markets is from hybridized versions grown in rice paddies throughout Minnesota and California. However, there are several online sources of native wild rice cultivated by Native American tribes and are worth purchasing in bulk.

Buckwheat groats are botanically classified as a fruit seed but often labeled a grain. It cooks in under 15 minutes. It is also a complete protein, rich in iron, selenium, and zinc and a good source of B vitamins. You can cook them as is, sprout them, or even roast them. If you buy it already roasted, it's known as kasha—from an old Russian translation. With its eastern European roots, kasha is often stuffed in cabbage rolls, used for croquettes, and added to marinated salads. It's most famously used to make kasha varnishkes, a dish of sautéed onions, kasha, and bowtie pasta.

Amaranth is a tiny, slightly nutty-flavored grain that cooks in under 12 minutes. It was cultivated throughout South America. Amaranth is a complete protein, containing more iron than most grains and a healthy source of other important minerals. It can be cooked on its own or in combination with other grains, such as in pilafs or as morning porridge with dried fruits and coconut.

Teff is the staple grain of Ethiopia. Aside from using teff as breakfast porridge, it is more commonly made into a yeast-risen spongy flour pancake called *injera*. This soft Ethiopian flatbread is traditionally used to grab bean and vegetable side dishes. Because of teff's micro size, it is impractical to refine because its nutrients lie concentrated in the germ and the bran. Teff contains good-quality protein, but similar to most whole grains, it lacks lysine. High in fiber, iron, and several B vitamins, teff is a valuable source of calcium and other minerals. It has a mildly sweet flavor and comes in two varieties: dark and ivory. Fully cooked within 20 minutes, it goes well with a wide variety of vegetables, seasonings, other grains, and fresh or dried fruits.

Oats are a complete protein, high in fiber, thiamin (vitamin B_1), and minerals. They offer a number of documented health benefits, from helping lower cholesterol and reducing blood pressure to preventing heart disease and cancer. Pure oatmeal does not contain gluten. Unfortunately, most oatmeal brans in the commercial market today are not so pure; they often contain oats that have

(CONTINUED)

been cross-contaminated with small amounts of wheat, barley, or rye. *Because these grains are known to contain gluten, this cross-contamination might make using oats risky for some individuals on a gluten-free diet.* Oats have proved helpful for insomnia, stress, anxiety, depression, and many other health problems. They make a tasty and satisfying breakfast cereal that can be cooked alone, with another grain, or with coconut, cinnamon, or whatever dried or fresh fruit might be available.

Eat Your Vegetables!

Vegetables are a frequently misunderstood and commonly abused food category. First, I think our national sugar addiction is one of the main reasons we need to include more vegetables on our plates. If you are accustomed to a simple sugar source every day, then discovering the naturally sweet taste of vegetables has little appeal, since simple sugar easily overwhelms our taste sensors. Give a child some ice cream and then ask him if he'd like a side dish of broccoli. That answer is predictable.

However, eating less sugar and consuming more vegetables can make us more sensitized to their subtle tastes—especially if we have a plentiful variety. In addition, the mild alkalinity of vegetables helps neutralize acids obtained from other foods in our diets. But we need to learn how to properly cook vegetables beyond simply boiling them to mush. There are a number of healthful cooking styles that preserve taste and texture and that can make them far more appealing. These unique styles of cooking will be discussed further on in this chapter.

The five categories of vegetables are root and ground-surface vegetables, leafy greens, miscellaneous, sweet vegetables, and nightshade vegetables.

ROOT AND GROUND VEGETABLES

Acorn squash	Chive	Leek
Beet	Corn	Lotus root
Burdock	Cucumber	Onion
Carrot	Eggplant	Parsnip
Celery	Fennel	Pattypan squash
Celery root	Garlic	Red radish
(celeriac)	Kabocha squash	Rutabaga

Salsify	Sweet potato	(daikon)
Scallion	Turnip	Yam
Summer squash	White radish	Zucchini

LEAFY GREENS AND CRUCIFEROUS VEGETABLES

Arugula	Chinese cabbage	Kohlrabi
Bok choy	Collard greens	Mustard greens
Broccoli	Daikon greens	Red cabbage
Brussels sprouts	Dandelion greens	Romaine lettuce
Butterhead	Endive	Spinach
lettuce	Escarole	Swiss chard
Cauliflower	Green cabbage	Turnip greens
Chinese broccoli	Kale	Watercress

MISCELLANEOUS VEGETABLES

Artichoke	Mushrooms (all	Snap pea
Ferns	varieties)*	Sprouts (all
Green bean	Plantain	varieties)
Green pea	Snap bean	Wax bean

SWEET VEGETABLES

The sweet vegetables category is made up of vegetables that become naturally sweet with cooking. They are used in combination with whole grains or to make delicious additions or bases for soups and exclusively grouped here for their distinctive sweet taste, which can help with sweet cravings and to balance more bitter tastes from other vegetable categories.

Butternut squash	Corn	Onion
Cabbage	Daikon radish	Parsnip
Carrot	Kabocha squash	

NIGHTSHADE VEGETABLES

The nightshade category is made up of vegetables that, for select individuals, may have a systemic inflammatory effect. For those

---

* Mushrooms are technically fungi but included in this list because they are commonly used as garnish or side dishes. Mushrooms are a good source of B vitamins, such as riboflavin, niacin, and pantothenic acid, and valuable minerals such as selenium, copper, and potassium. Fat, carbohydrate, and calorie content are low.

with arthritis, this could encourage pain and additional swelling. Although clinically unproven by large-scale studies, thousands of individuals have discovered that eliminating nightshades from their diets had an almost immediate pain-relieving effect on joint pain and promoted better flexibility. Norman Childers, author and founder of the Arthritis Nightshades Research Foundation, collected over 50 years of testimonies from individuals who reversed arthritic pain by eliminating this group from their diet. While a good percentage of people may not be negatively affected by nightshades, it's worthwhile to eliminate this category for a 4- to 6-week period and then eat them again to gauge if their absence has made a difference for you in terms of achy joints, hip pain, fatigue, or cravings.

Eggplant
Green and red pepper
Potato
Tomato

Fearless Beans and Bean Products

Far more than a simple meat substitute, beans contain such valuable nutrition that recent dietary guidelines suggest we triple our current intake from 1 to 3 cups per week.

Comparable to meat in terms of caloric content, beans contain two characteristics that account for feeling fuller and more satisfied: fiber and water content.

Just 1 cup of cooked beans (approximately two-thirds of a can) provides around 12 grams of fiber—almost half the recommended daily dose of 21 to 25 grams per day for adult women (30 to 38 grams for adult men). Conversely, meat contains no fiber. This difference accounts for meat being digested more quickly than bean protein. Low in sugar, beans do not cause insulin spiking, and they promote endurance and better digestion.

Beans are also rich in phytochemicals, nutritional elements that meat clearly lacks. Beans contain valuable antioxidants, which is a class of chemicals that help reduce cell- and artery-damaging free radicals in the body.

Having a known reputation for instigating intestinal gas, bean digestion can be helped with longer cooking times, by consuming lesser amounts, and with the use of salt in cooking after they've softened; careful food combining also helps. For example, do not consume sweet food (fruits or sweet desserts) at the same meal with beans.

The reason for this suggestion is that simple sugars from fruits can ferment the slower-digesting complex sugars in beans, so it's best to wait a little while before diving into a dessert when your meal contains a bean dish. Some natural food companies put small amounts of seaweed in their canned beans (typically, kombu), which does not alter the bean flavor but helps the digestion of beans due to the mineral content of the seaweed. One of my favorite seaweeds to use in cooking beans is dulse. I add a healthy pinch to the beans after the water has initially boiled and allow it to cook with the beans.

BEANS

Adzuki bean
Anasazi bean
Black-eyed pea
Black turtle bean
Chickpea
   (garbanzo
   bean)

Great white
   northern bean
Kidney bean
Lentil (green,
   brown, red)
Lima bean
Mung bean

Navy bean
Peas (whole,
   split, green,
   yellow)
Pinto bean
Soybean

BEAN PRODUCTS

Soy milk (sugar-free)
Tempeh
Tofu (fresh or dried)

MINIMIZE OR AVOID

Canned beans with sugar, coloring, artificial preservatives, added meats, oils, and so on

Sea Vegetables

It's not a very glamorous picture. Hear the word *seaweed* and you immediately picture slimy green stuff, encrusted with sand, creepy-crawly shells, and assorted ocean debris. Not a very appetizing thought.

While such a picture might be the stuff of an average dirty beach washup, the real picture is one of numerous sea vegetable varieties with varied shapes and rich colors ranging from deep emerald green to shiny black. Most of the world's coastal cultures ate vegetables from the ocean, while inland cultures often stored and prepared them from the dried form.

Offering the broadest range of minerals of any food, sea vegetables are an excellent source of the B vitamins folate, riboflavin, and pantothenic acid and also contain magnesium, iron, calcium, vitamin A, iodine, and fiber. The low calorie count supports weight management: 10 sheets of nori, used for wrapping sushi, have just 22 calories!

Most important, seaweed contains significant amounts of lignans, beneficial plant compounds with cancer-protective properties. Lignans have been shown to inhibit angiogenesis, or blood cell growth. Angiogenesis is the process that not only gives fast-growing tumors growth nourishment but sends cancer cells out into the bloodstream, promoting metastases to other areas of the body. In fat cells, lignans have been shown to inhibit estrogen synthesis just as effectively as some of the drugs used in cancer chemotherapy.

Sea vegetables are excellent sources of omega-3 fatty acids and contain a form of fiber that can bind steroids and carcinogens. Extensive research has documented their ability to cleanse and detoxify the body, extracting wastes and toxins from our tissues to be discharged by our eliminative organs. Modern research claims that seaweed has at least 60 times the nutritional potency of land-based vegetation. It is a fact that cultures with seaweed-eating traditions show far less obesity, diabetes, Alzheimer's disease, and other degenerative diseases.

A 2011 study featured in the American Chemical Society's *Journal of Agricultural and Food Chemistry* reviewed over 100 studies on the nutritional benefits of seaweed and noted that seaweed proteins could serve as better sources of bioactive peptides than those in milk products. Bioactive peptides are known for reducing blood pressure and increasing cardiac health.

SEA VEGETABLES AND CANCER PREVENTION

Numerous studies have linked sea vegetable consumption to reduced cancers and tumor inhibition:

+ Several studies have shown that the consumption of brown seaweed, *Laminaria*, is directly related to a lower incidence of breast cancer.
+ Other sea vegetables have also been demonstrated to be protective against other forms of cancer.
+ A processed product frequently sold in health food stores made

from the sea vegetable wakame has been demonstrated to result in regression of lung cancer in laboratory animals.

✦ Studies at McGill University in Montreal showed that the alginic acid in sea vegetables bound to toxins in the body, including heavy metals, through a process commonly known as chelation.

✦ Studies at the Harvard School of Public Health discovered that animals fed only 5 percent of their diet in kelp (kombu) showed resistance to laboratory-induced cancers. In animals that already had cancerous tumors, kelp-fed groups showed partial and, in some cases, complete, tumor regression.

You might not be aware of this but you've probably been consuming a small amount of sea vegetables for years, as essential ingredients in many popular foods often unmentioned on commercial labeling. There are a variety of sea vegetables (generally known as seaweeds), with the most popular and easily available being nori, dulse, wakame, kombu, arame, and hiziki. As mentioned, the wrapper around sushi is called nori, and the seaweed you see floating around your miso soup in a Japanese restaurant is usually wakame. Nori and dulse are the quickest to cook and can be used in many dishes, from soups and rice to stews and salads.

Introduce some sea vegetables in your cooking. Instead of beginning with a concentrated dish, add a small portion of dulse to a bean soup. Cook up a little arame with your next soup or stew or vegetable dish. Try a half sheet of nori crumbled up and added to a grain dish. Get adventurous!

SEA VEGETABLES (AKA SEAWEED)

Agar-agar (used for gelatin dessert)	Hiziki	Sea cress
	Kelp	Sea palm
	Kombu	Wakame
Arame	Nori	
Dulse	Ocean ribbons	

Six common sea vegetables are widely available from health food stores and markets:

✦ **Nori:** A greenish sheet seaweed that is commonly wrapped around rice in making sushi rolls. It can be bought already toasted and used as a crumble in soups and side dishes, or as a condiment.

✦ **Kombu:** I usually refer to this as Asian bay leaf, because it is used in much the same way, as an addition to soups and bean dishes, or baked and ground up to be used as a condiment for mineral-deficient conditions.

✦ **Wakame:** A pretty green-colored, light-tasting sea vegetable somewhat similar to spinach and frequently used in soups. In some markets, you can purchase it dried, which is great for traveling and makes a nice, hearty instant-soup mix.

✦ **Hiziki:** A thick hair-like sea vegetable, richly black with 10 to 12 times the amount of calcium as contained in an equal 100-gram serving of milk. It is usually combined in Asian cuisine with sweet vegetables (onions, carrots, and cabbage) to reduce its sea flavor.

✦ **Arame:** A kinder, gentler, and thinner version of hiziki. It's lighter, less seaweedy tasting, and usually enjoyed without complaint. It's often mixed with carrots, onions, cabbage, or squash for added sweetness. An Asian family I used to live with frequently made a baked dough roll containing cooked arame with onions and roasted almonds. I had to practically beg for the recipe and to this day make it for friends and family.

✦ **Dulse:** A popular northeastern Canadian, Scottish, and Irish sea vegetable. It has a very distinctive strong taste and is frequently used as a dry condiment. I've included it in various soup recipes and green or corn dishes with very enthusiastic responses.

MINIMIZE OR AVOID

Many commercial seaweeds sold in Asian markets are often processed with preservatives, MSG, or chemical coloring. Check label ingredients before purchasing. In some commercial brands, the seaweed is chemically dyed. It helps to hold the package up to the light and note if the edges of the nori seem to have purple hues. If so, it may be from artificial coloring.

Nuts and Seeds

While you may have heard that you should minimize eating nuts and seeds because of their high fat and caloric content, these amazing foods contain heart-healthy unsaturated fats, and offer a satisfying sense of variety and texture for most eating plans.

Containing protein and fiber, nuts and seeds are also rich in many protective antioxidants including vitamin E, folate, manganese, and selenium. These substances are important in the body because they help defeat damage-causing free radicals. This is what makes nuts and seeds protective against cancers. They are also a healthful source of energy-producing nutrients, such as zinc, magnesium, and B vitamins.

The protein, fiber, and fat in nuts help you feel full for a long period of time, so you may end up eating less during the day, thus finding it easier to reduce unwanted weight. Nut consumers have also been shown to have a lower incidence of diabetes when compared to those who rarely ate nuts.

Eating nuts and seeds also helps ensure that your fat intake comes from healthy unsaturated fat rather than potentially harmful saturated fat found in meats and other animal products.

You can use nuts and seeds to add texture to different dishes, including pureed soups. They make convenient snacks when flavored with spices, such as cinnamon or paprika, and then baking until slightly browned. At best, nuts and seeds are a welcomed topping for casseroles, hot or cold cereals, soups, salads, and sandwich wraps.

SEEDS

Chia seed	Poppy seed	Sunflower seed
Hemp seed	Pumpkin seed	Sesame seed

SEED BUTTERS

Sesame seed	Sunflower seed	Tahini butter*

NUTS

Almond	Cashew	Walnut

NUT BUTTERS

Almond	Hazelnut	Pine nut
Brazil nut	Macadamia nut	Pistachio
Cashew	Peanut	
Chestnut	Pecan	

* Tahini is made from the inner sesame seed.

THE MOST HEALTHFUL NUTS AND SEEDS

HERE ARE THE most healthful nuts and seeds, according to the George Mateljan Foundation's list of the world's healthiest foods:

Almonds: High in vitamin E, magnesium, copper, vitamin B_2, and phosphorus, and concentrated in protein. The fat in almonds is heart-healthy monounsaturated fat.

Cashews: High in antioxidants, monounsaturated fats, and phosphorus with a lower fat content than most other nuts.

Flaxseeds (linseeds): High in omega-3 fatty acids, which is beneficial for anti-inflammatory properties, and vitamin B_6, fiber, and manganese.

Peanuts: High in monounsaturated fats, flavonoids, antioxidants, and folic acid. They are also high in vitamin B_3 and contain resveratrol, an antioxidant with antiaging effects.

Pumpkin seeds: High in essential fatty acids, potassium, magnesium, phosphorus, and vitamin K. They may benefit arthritis sufferers and help lower cholesterol.

Sesame seeds: Excellent source of Vitamin B_1, monounsaturated fats, and phytosterols, which prevent cholesterol production.

Sunflower seeds: High in linoleic acid, fiber, magnesium, and phytosterols.

Walnuts: High in omega-3 fatty acids, manganese, and copper. In addition, they contain essential amino acids that help manufacture nitric oxide, essential for keeping blood vessels flexible.

Animal Protein for Optional or Transitional Diet

The emphasis on plant-based whole foods is one that offers the optimum healing possibilities. In excessive amounts, the chemical breakdown of animal-based proteins can result in potentially harmful acids that threaten our valuable mineral status. For individuals who cannot digest bean protein, animal protein can be substituted until the intestines become better accustomed to breaking down bean starches. The real problem with animal protein consumption is one of volume and quantity; we eat too much, too often. Generally, it's best to use animal protein, if craving, in limited amounts during the transitional phases of the food plan.

FISH, CHICKEN, RED MEAT

White-meat fish: Snapper, haddock, halibut, sole, flounder, perch, cod

Salmon: Wild, *not* farmed

Turkey, chicken: Free-range, hormone-free (for Transitional Diet)

Red meat: Grass-fed, hormone-free (for Transitional Diet, according to craving)

Eggs: Free-range, naturally raised: (for Transitional and Prevention Diets)

MINIMIZE OR AVOID

Seafood high in cholesterol, such as crab, shrimp, and lobster, which also hold more ocean-floor toxins

Cured or processed meats (for Transitional Diet)

Whole eggs, once to twice weekly, at the maximum, when craving (for Transitional Diet)

Fruit: The Natural Sweet

Although fruits contain many valuable nutrients, one thing that should be remembered is that they also contain the fruit sugar, fructose. A naturally occurring sugar found in many foods, fructose is easily consumed in excess due to the high sugar content in fruits that are grown today. Through a process called hybridization, modern growers are now able to produce fruits that are higher in sugar than their wild counterparts, which grow uncultivated. If you compare the taste of a wild berry that you've just picked outdoors to a berry grown by a modern farmer, you'll immediately notice the difference in sweetness.

Another problem with high fruit consumption is that it can potentially lead to problems involving the hormones that regulate blood sugar, specifically insulin, glucagon, and growth hormone. A consistent imbalance of these hormones can lead to the development of cardiovascular disease, digestive imbalance, and diabetes. In addition, excess fruit sugar can raise serum triglyceride levels, which is another factor for cardiac risk.

The high glycemic load of some forms of fruit can also provoke insulin resistance and worsen diabetes. Individuals sensitive to fruit sugar should rely on whole fruits and limit their servings of dried fruits to a quarter cup per day.

SEASONAL (BEST TO EAT IN SEASON)

Apple	Honeydew	Prunes
Apricot	Lemon	Raisins
Blackberry	Nectarine	Raspberry
Blueberry	Orange	Strawberry
Cantaloupe	Peach	Watermelon
Cherry	Pear	
Grapes	Plum	

MINIMIZE OR AVOID

Tropical fruit tends to be more concentrated in sugar and is best if used less frequently.

Fruit juice is especially concentrated in sugar and is best minimized, diluted with water, or eliminated completely.

Fruit syrups are strong concentrates and best minimized.

Dried fruit should be eaten in moderation; a small handful might be equivalent to many portions of fresh fruit as well as being highly concentrated in sugar.

Natural Sweeteners

Natural sweeteners, while still being simple sugars, are slightly less concentrated than refined sugars. They have unique flavors and each has a different compatibility as a dessert ingredient. To keep immunity and general health sharp, minimize their use. They are considered a pleasure food, not a healing food.

On a hot summer day, nothing beats some fresh-squeezed lemon juice, water, mint leaves, and a dash of maple syrup to make a refreshingly natural lemonade. Barley malt, rice syrup, honey, maple syrup, or fruit juice, can also be unique sweeteners for making cookies or a sweetened dough.

These concentrated sweeteners have varying strengths. For example, to make 1 gallon of maple syrup requires 40 gallons of tree sap; 1 teaspoon of honey contains the same amount of sugar as four to five apples. Respect the sugar concentration of these sweeteners and use sparingly.

Amasake	Maple syrup	Stevia (natural
Barley malt	Molasses	plant
Fruit juice	Rice syrup	sweetener)

Avoid refined sugar (white, brown, turbinado, and so on), agave
syrup, high-fructose corn syrup, all chemical sweeteners (sac-
charin, NutraSweet, Splenda), fructose powder, and evaporated
cane sugar or syrup.

HONEY: NOT AN IDEAL SWEETNESS

HONEYBEES TURN NECTAR into honey by a process of regurgitation
and evaporation. It's stored as a primary food source in wax hon-
eycombs that they build within their beehives. Honey has no real
significant phytochemical or antioxidant content, and its sweetness—
identical to granulated sugar—comes from a concentrated mixture of
fructose, glucose, and sucrose. In 1 tablespoon of honey, there are
approximately 64 calories and all in the form of sugar amounting to
over 17 grams!

Honey, either in raw or cooked form, is practically all sugar and
contains no fiber. Fiber is critical because it reduces the rate of carbohydrate absorption from the small intestine. This reduction delays
the after-meal flow of glucose into the blood. Without fiber, glucose is
absorbed rapidly, elevating blood sugar, fostering inflammation, and
neutralizing valuable minerals.

In addition, the pH of honey is very acid—somewhere between 3.2
and 4.5. This acidic pH level prevents the growth of various bacteria.

Note, too, that honey often contains dormant endospores of the
bacterium *Clostridium botulinum*, which can be dangerous to infants
because the endospores change into toxin-producing bacteria within
infants' immature intestinal tracts. This leads to illness and can be
potentially fatal.

Although there are some therapies that claim certain kinds of honey
can be beneficial for treating cancer, it is important to remember that
honey, as all sweet syrups, is still a simple sugar and a source of immediate nourishment for cancer cells.

Flavorful Fermented Foods

Natural food fermentation precedes human recorded history. Since ancient times, humans have been controlling and manipulating the fermentation process of a variety of foods and beverages. In fact, the earliest

evidence of an alcoholic beverage was made from fruit, rice, and honey and dates back to 7000 to 6600 BCE.

Fermented foods and beverages are part of the human diet and have a long cultural history of being passed down from generation to generation. In some areas fermented foods might make up a small 5 percent of daily dietary intake, while in others can be as high as 40 percent.

Practically all preindustrialized cultures soaked or fermented their grains before making them into porridge, breads, cakes, and casseroles. Looking at grain recipes from around the globe will illustrate this point: In India, rice and lentils are fermented for a minimum of 2 days before they are prepared as idlis and dosas. Some traditional African peoples routinely soak coarsely ground corn overnight before adding it to soups and stews. They also ferment corn or millet for several days, producing a sour porridge called ogi; a similar dish made from oats was traditional among the Welsh. In some Asian and Latin American countries, rice is fermented for at least a day before it is prepared. Ethiopians make their delicious injera bread by fermenting a tiny grain called teff for several days. The culinary tradition of Mexico ferments corn cakes, called pozol, for several days and for some recipes, as long as two weeks in banana leaves. Before the use of commercial brewer's yeast, Europeans made thoroughly kneaded slow-rise breads from fermented starters that were used over and over; America pioneers were famous for their sourdough breads, pancakes, and biscuits. Across Europe, particularly in Scotland, grains were soaked overnight, sometimes for as long as several days, in water or soured milk, before being cooked and served as a porridge or gruel.

This valued and cherished wisdom from our ancestors used fermented foods and drink as a dietary staple, either naturally or by adding starter cultures that contain plentiful amounts of microorganisms. Microorganisms are the instigators that transform these raw materials into edible products that became an integral part of many traditional diets.

Fermented foods are unique in that they can be fried, boiled, or eaten in curries, stews, side dishes, pickles, confectionery, salads, soups, and desserts. They have been used in the form of pastes, seasonings, condiments, and even food colorants. Fermented beverages can be either alcoholic (beer and wine) or nonalcoholic, such as buttermilk, teas, and vinegars.

While most fermented foods have health-promoting benefits, their global consumption has been in decline as traditional food practices have become overwhelmed by the influence of Western diets and the popularity of fast foods. A remnant of this cultural habit today is a tiny pickle in the center of a hamburger, a long cucumber pickle when served deli meats, and artificially colored hot dog relish or a mound of sauerkraut.

Fermentation of different foods was important for three primary reasons:

Food preservation
Microorganism health benefits for intestinal bacteria
To enhance nutrition

Fermented foods improve digestion as well as the potency of the food being cultured. The probiotic bacteria that is developed as a result of fermentation is an important foundation for good intestinal and immune health. Fermentation also maximizes protein and other vitamins, allowing these nutrients to become more available to our bodies. Antioxidants, B vitamins (including B_{12}), and omega-3 fatty acids can all be created by fermenting specific foods.

Another advantage of fermented foods is that they retrain our immune systems to become more resilient in the presence of toxins and other unwelcomed invaders. In addition to preserving nutrients and preventing food spoilage, the fermentation process releases hidden nutrition from food and, in doing so, creates new compounds. Some of these compounds—digestive enzymes, lactobacilli, glutathione, beta-glucans superoxide dismutase, glucose tolerance factor (GTF) chromium, and phospholipids—have received much scientific attention in recent years, particularly for alternative cancer treatments.

Although many foods contain natural toxins, such as oxalic acid, phytic acid (found in all grains), glucosides, nitrites, and nitrosamines, they are all either completely neutralized or greatly diminished through the chemical process of fermentation.

There are a great variety of fermented foods. Generally, grains, beans, vegetables, fruit, honey, fish, diary, meat, and various teas have all been used to create fermented foods. The most popular, health-producing, and widely available fermented foods that are recommended for the Nature's Cancer-Fighting Foods program, are the following:

FERMENTED FOODS
Kimchi (Korean fermented vegetables)
Miso soybean paste
Natural soy sauce (tamari)
Sauerkraut (cabbage)
Sourdough bread
Tempeh

PICKLES
Brine or herb pickles (dill)
Miso pickles*
Umeboshi (salted plums)

Oils

Excessive body fat is considered a major risk factor for cancer, particularly colorectal cancer. Obesity is also a documented risk factor for breast cancer. Increased fat tissue has been shown to elevate circulating estrogen levels. This raises the risk factor for breast cancer. Studies have shown that vegetarian women who follow a low-fat, high-fiber diet tend to have lower blood levels of estrogen, which also means a greater excretion of estrogen in their stools (due to the whole grain fiber content of their diets) and therefore are less prone to breast cancer. It is also known that obese men have a higher rate of prostate cancer. For these reasons, it's best to keep your diet low in total fat and low in saturated fats. Studies have demonstrated two ways that dietary fat contributes to cancer development:

+ Tumor cells require low-density lipoproteins (LDLs) to grow. It would make sense, then, that a dietary plan that helps reduce LDL levels could inhibit potentially cancerous cells from growing.
+ Fat consumption stimulates the production of bile into the duodenum, where fat is primarily broken down. Bile helps digest fat. If excess amounts of bile are allowed to stagnate for a long period of time within the colon, it can be converted into apocholic acid, which is a known carcinogen.

Based on this information, it would be best to limit daily saturated fat intake to approximately 15 percent of daily total fat intake. Not including the fat content of the daily food consumed, this additional oil amount could be a maximum of 1 to 2 teaspoons, or 8 to 10 grams. This does not include your use of nuts or seeds as condiments.

The smoke point of oil can help you decide if the type you've chosen is healthful. The smoke point is the temperature at which visible gaseous vapor from the heating oil becomes noticeable. This is used as a marker for the point at which oil decomposition begins to occur. Decomposition

---

* Miso pickles can be easily made by acquiring a large amount of miso and cutting up vegetables and storing them in the miso for up to a month.

results in chemical changes that not only reduce flavor and nutritional value but also generate harmful cancer-causing compounds (oxygen radicals). Therefore, it's important to *not* heat oil past its smoke point. Inhaling smoked vapors can also prove damaging. The smoke point of a variety of oils in listed in the chart below. It's also important to make sure to choose organic and cold-pressed oil.

Essential fatty acids (EFAs) are fats that our body does not produce and so must be obtained from food sources. Of these, two EFAs are known to be health essential: omega-3 (alpha-linolenic acid) and omega-6 (linoleic acid). Although we require both of these EFAs, most of us have an imbalance of this pair.

When modern research revealed that fats such as butter and lard were a threat to our health, natural plant oils emerged as a healthier and more available choice. You can find very high levels of omega-6s in oils like sunflower, safflower, and corn oil, and very little, if any, omega-3 content. Because these oils have become commercially popular, they're now usually made from produce that has unfortunately been genetically modified.

Someone who naively consumes a standard Western diet of fried and processed foods is typically consuming far beyond the amount of omega-6 fatty acids that the body can tolerate. Research has shown that omega-6 is connected to inflammatory diseases, such as cardiovascular disease, obesity, and type 2 diabetes. Lowering omega-6 and increasing omega-3 fatty acid is connected to fewer occurrences of inflammatory disease, which influences cancer growth.

The immediate goal is to lower your omega-6 intake. Nutritional researchers agree that the omega-6 to omega-3 ratio should ideally range from 1:1 to 5:1. However, the sad reality is that it frequently ranges from 20:1 to 50:1 for most Americans, who are getting far too many omega-6 fats. This is especially dangerous as they are obtaining this EFA in the form of highly processed vegetable oils that exclude most of the original nutrients. The modern processing of oils has also introduced aberrations like trans-fats, now banned in many states and countries and tightly regulated in others.

For frying or sautéing, choose an oil with a fairly high smoke point and avoid letting it smoke because this increases the damaging free radical molecules. While smoke points are relevant, they can also give a false impression of stability and safety. Changes do occur at temperatures far below the smoke point, which can produce free radicals; therefore, be very wary about overheating oils. For a healthier salad or raw oil choice, choose oil with low omega-6 value.

OILS	SMOKE POINT (IN °F)	OMEGA-6 TO OMEGA-3 RATIO
Avocado	520	12:1
Walnut	490	12:1
Rice bran	490	21:1
Extra-virgin olive	405	13:1
Sesame	350	42:1
Coconut	350	4:1 to 4:0
Hempseed	330	3:1

LIMIT OR AVOID

Margarine, lard, shortening, palm oil, refined and chemically processed vegetable oils

Beverages

Sipping moderately hot tea after a meal is a satisfying way to finish a meal and usually will have the effect of finalizing your appetite. But, tea without caffeine is a healthier choice.

Generally, a more fragrant tea usually means a more acid tea. The teas listed below are a combination of tea, herb, and fruit infusions and are widely available. Dandelion root tea is a strong tea, with a similar bitter bite to the taste of coffee and great for heavier meals at which you had oil or sautéed dishes; dandelion is known to help bile production and detoxify the liver. It is also heart healthy and used in many herbal preparations for strengthening the heart or as a mild diuretic.

Twig tea, a traditional Asian tea that is popular in macrobiotic circles, has a very mild amount of caffeine that rarely can be felt and is a good aid to digestion. Rooibos tea (African red bush tea), like green tea, has many antioxidants and also offers a nice variety to your tea selections.

As a non-tea drink, I recommend hot water with lemon because it can help accelerate weight loss and diminish fat storages.

TEAS

Dandelion root

Green tea

Herbal (many varieties)

Rooibos

Twig (kukicha)

MINIMIZE

Mineral water (for Transitional and Prevention Diets)

Natural (sugar-free) soda (for Transitional Diet)

Nonalcoholic beer (for Transitional and Prevention Diets)

Naturally brewed beer (for Transitional and Prevention Diets; otherwise, occasional)

Sugar-free rice, almond, oat, or soy milk (for Transitional Diet)

Wine and spirits (for Transitional Diet; otherwise, occasional)

AVOID

Caffeinated beverages, sugared soft drinks, tap water, hard liquors, frozen mixed drinks, and frequent use of fruit juice

The Nature's Cancer-Fighting Foods Plan

The next step after introducing the foods and their categories is to look at how we can group them in an individualized plan format. The Nature's Cancer-Fighting Foods Plan offers three dietary plans that focus around changing the percentages of the main essential foods (primary foods), foods that support and supplement primary foods (secondary foods), and small amounts of nonessential foods for enjoyment (pleasure foods). The three dietary plans are as follows:

THE TRANSITIONAL DIET. This plan offers a gradual change for increasing cancer-fighting agents by adding new, healthful, whole foods and decreasing foods that are not health supportive. This introductory plan is best suited to someone who is not familiar with many of the recommended foods because it permits greater dietary flexibility.

THE PREVENTION DIET. This plan greatly increases cancer-suppressing foods with a higher percentage of wholesome healthful foods and further reductions of foods that are not health supportive. It can yield quicker results for general health, which can be noticed within weeks.

THE HEALING DIET. This plan focuses on cancer-fighting foods as well as cancer-fighting strategies. This program offers the highest level of anticancer protection. It minimizes or eliminates animal protein, eliminates dairy products, and raises the percentage of whole grains, vegetables, beans, bean products, sea vegetables, and fruits in the daily diet. This is a more demanding approach; however, it can be flexibly interchanged with some of the transition plan, if desired.

What Diet Plan to Choose?

If you are new to the whole foods approach, then your best bet is the gradual introduction of the Transitional Diet. If your goal is to heal and time is of the essence, begin with the Prevention Diet and work your way into the Healing Diet. There can be no real fixed plan, as our needs and cravings frequently change. Sometimes it becomes easier and sometimes it's necessary to modify your eating plan. As you become familiar with the range of foods and your physical sensitivity sharpens, you will be able to make appropriate adjustments because you'll have a better understanding of your limitations.

From personal and professional experience, I've learned that understanding more about healthful whole foods can create more value for their simplicity and uniqueness. Knowing more about the recommended foods, their origins, and how they can fit into your daily life can sustain your will to heal and your respect for their profound healing qualities. What follows are food lists and information about each of the diet plans.

THE TRANSITIONAL DIET PLATE

The Transitional Diet introduces essential whole foods, while reducing refined foods. The term *transitional* describes foods that you are still consuming from your past but are in the process of decreasing. The circle diagram below shows the approximate percentage in volume of foods consumed in the course of one day.

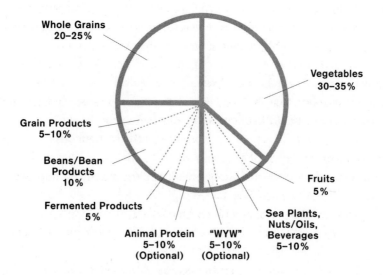

Whole Grains
20–25%

Vegetables
30–35%

Grain Products
5–10%

Beans/Bean
Products
10%

Fruits
5%

Fermented Products
5%

Sea Plants,
Nuts/Oils,
Beverages
5–10%

Animal Protein
5–10%
(Optional)

"WYW"
5–10%
(Optional)

Diet Distinctions: This diet plan reduces animal protein and limits sugar to fruit and some natural sugars, while increasing whole grains, vegetables, and beans. It allows a small percentage of whatever you want (WYW, or pleasure foods), but be sure to use the best quality. New foods such as sea vegetables are introduced, while flour products (as in grain products) are minimized.

PRIMARY FOODS

Whole grains (20 to 25 percent): Brown rice, oats, barley, millet, quinoa, buckwheat, and others

Grain products (5 to 10 percent): Unrefined whole grain bread, pasta, crackers, and so on

Vegetables (35 percent): Root, green leafy, and ground vegetables in a variety of preparations

Beans and bean products (10 percent): Dried and canned beans and bean products (tempeh, tofu, miso)

SECONDARY FOODS

Animal protein (5 to 10 percent; optional category): Fish, poultry, and wild game

Small percentages: Seed or vegetable oils, nuts, seasonal fruits, sea plants, beverages

Fermented foods: Miso soup, pickles, sauerkraut, and so on

PLEASURE FOODS

Small percentage: WYW (From time to time, we find ourselves in social situations in which we need to exercise more flexibility with food choices or when we experience random strong cravings.)

Approximate Amounts for One Day

Naturally, everyone has different appetites, but the recommended diet plan translates to the following approximate amounts:

Whole grains: ¾ to 1¼ cup, cooked

Grain products: 1 to 2 slices bread, approximately ¼ cup dry pasta,* small amount of crackers

Vegetables: 2 to 3 cups prepared in a variety of cooking styles

Animal/bean protein: 4 to 5 ounces of fish or poultry (red meat,

---

* Note: 2 servings = 1 bunch dry spaghetti measuring about 1 inch in diameter.

rarely) three times a week; ½ to ¾ cup cooked beans or bean
products (tofu, tempeh) on vegetarian days

Sea vegetables: ¼ cup dry or 2 tablespoons added to soups

Fruit: 2 to 3 servings (approximately ½ cup), if craving

Oil: 1 to 2 teaspoons

Beverages: After meals and in between meals (tea preferably)

Approximate Protein Profile

The protein profile shows quality animal and vegetable proteins and how
to gradually substitute vegetable proteins for animal proteins during this
transitional stage. You can start with 3 or 4 days of animal protein, once
daily every other day, and eat bean protein on alternate days.

MONDAY	TUESDAY	WEDNESDAY	THURSDAY	FRIDAY	SATURDAY	SUNDAY
Fish	Beans or bean product	Turkey	Beans or bean product	Fish	Beans	Beans

THE PREVENTION DIET PLATE

The Prevention Diet increases the amount of whole foods (grains, beans,
and vegetables) as more of a maintenance protocol. The circle diagram
below shows the approximate percentage in volume of foods consumed
in the course of one day.

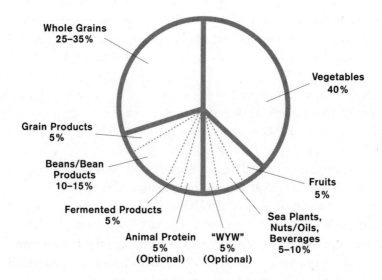

Diet Distinctions: This plan minimizes animal protein and restricts sugar to fruit. It increases whole grains, vegetables, and beans to larger percentages than the Transitional Diet, while still allowing a small percentage of WYW. New foods such as sea vegetables are encouraged in small quantities.

PRIMARY FOODS

Whole grains (25 to 35 percent): Brown rice, oats, barley, millet, quinoa, buckwheat, and others

Grain products (5 percent): Unrefined whole grain bread, pasta, or crackers

Vegetables (40 percent): Root, green leafy, and ground vegetables in a variety of preparations

Beans and bean products (10 to 15 percent): Dried and canned beans and bean products (tempeh, tofu, miso)

SECONDARY FOODS

Animal protein (5 percent; optional category): Fish, poultry, or wild game

Small percentages: Seed or vegetable oil, nuts, seasonal fruits, sea plants, and beverages

Fermented foods: Miso soup, pickles, sauerkraut, and so on

PLEASURE FOODS ("WHATEVER YOU WANT")

Small percentages: WYW (From time to time, we find ourselves in social situations in which we need to exercise more flexibility with food choices or when we experience random strong cravings.)

Approximate Amounts for One Day

Naturally, everyone has different appetites, but the recommended diet plan translates to the following amounts:

Whole grains: 1 to 1¾ cups, cooked

Grain products: 1 to 2 slices bread, approximately ¼ cup dry pasta, and/or a small amount of crackers

Vegetables: 3 to 4 cups of cooked vegetables, prepared in a variety of cooking styles

Animal/bean protein: 4 to 5 ounces fish or poultry (preferably white-meat fish) twice a week (if craving); ¾ to 1 cup cooked beans or bean products (tofu, tempeh) on vegetarian days

Sea vegetables: ¼ cup dry as a side dish, 2 tablespoons added to
  soups (as stock) or as a condiment

Fruit: 1 to 2 servings (½ cup), if craving

Oils: 1 to 1½ teaspoons

Beverages: After meals and in between meals

Approximate Protein Profile

The protein profile shows quality animal and vegetable proteins and how
to gradually substitute vegetable proteins for animal proteins during this
prevention stage. At this point, you should be consuming animal protein
a maximum of 2 days a week, once each day.

MONDAY	TUESDAY	WEDNESDAY	THURSDAY	FRIDAY	SATURDAY	SUNDAY
Beans or bean product	Fish	Beans or bean product	Beans	Fish	Beans or bean product	Beans

THE HEALING DIET PLATE

The Healing Diet offers the highest level of anticancer protection. The
circle diagram below shows the approximate percentage in volume of
foods consumed in the course of one day.

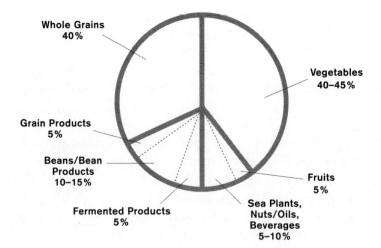

Whole Grains 40%

Vegetables 40–45%

Grain Products 5%

Beans/Bean Products 10–15%

Fermented Products 5%

Sea Plants, Nuts/Oils, Beverages 5–10%

Fruits 5%

Diet Distinctions: This plan suggests eliminating animal protein and
minimizing fruit, while increasing whole grains, vegetables, and beans. It
suggests frequent, but small amounts of sea vegetables and minimizes all
white flour products. It also includes increased fermented foods.

PRIMARY FOODS

Whole grains (40 percent): Brown rice, oats, barley, millet, quinoa, buckwheat, and others.

Grain products (5 percent): Unrefined whole grain bread, pasta, crackers, or 1 serving of pasta.

Vegetables (40 to 45 percent): Root, green leafy, and ground vegetables in a variety of preparations

Beans and bean products (10 to 15 percent): Dried and canned beans and bean products (tempeh, tofu, miso)

SECONDARY FOODS

Small percentages: Seed or vegetable oils, nuts, seasonal fruits, sea plants, and beverages

Sea vegetables: Try a variety

Fermented foods: Miso soup, pickles, and sauerkraut

Approximate Amounts for One Day

This plan is quite strict and considered a medicinal dietary approach. Naturally, everyone has different appetites, but the recommended diet plan translates to the following amounts:

Whole grains: 1½ to 2½ cups, cooked

Grain products: Minimum amount of bread, pasta, crackers, only if craving

Vegetables: 4 to 5 cups prepared in a variety of cooking styles

Bean or bean products: ⅔ to 1 cup beans and/or bean products; avoid animal protein unless experiencing a strong craving (and then minimize)

Sea vegetables: ¼ cup dry as a side dish, 2 tablespoons added to soups (as stock) or as a condiment

Fruit: Minimize, according to cravings

Oils: 1 teaspoon, maximum

Beverages: After meals and in between meals

Approximate Protein Profile

The protein profile shows quality animal and vegetable proteins and how to gradually substitute vegetable proteins for animal proteins during this medicinal stage. At this point, you should not be consuming animal protein, unless you are experiencing a strong craving.

MONDAY	TUESDAY	WEDNESDAY	THURSDAY	FRIDAY	SATURDAY	SUNDAY
Beans or bean product	Beans	Beans or bean product	Beans	Beans	Beans or bean product	Beans

Food Exchanges

It's easy to get attached to certain food habits and rituals that are simply not health supportive. The chart below offers healthier options that can replace old unhealthy habits. These new choices can make your transition to healthful, whole foods easier, more economical, and stress free.

Keep in mind that as you make dietary changes, your preferences begin to naturally change and foods that you thought would be a struggle to avoid suddenly prove easier to resist.

Fortunately, as your taste buds become accustomed to the simple flavors of whole natural foods, those less healthful choices will no longer taste as wonderful as they used to.

FOOD EXCHANGES

STANDARD FOODS	WHOLE FOOD CHOICES
Red meat	Reduce volume and frequency of red meats; move toward white meats; consume more vegetable protein sources (beans and bean products)
Dairy products	Reduce or eliminate dairy foods; increase vegetable oils, nuts, and seeds; eat more mineral-source foods (green vegetables and sea vegetables)
White breads, enriched breads, pasta, muffins, etc.	Whole grain cereals, whole grain bread, and whole grain pasta
Canned and frozen vegetables	Minimize frozen vegetables, maximize fresh vegetables (organic, when possible)
Refined sugar and sweetened desserts	Fruit, limited juices, natural jams, cookies with natural sweeteners such as barley malt, rice syrup, or maple syrup
Soda pop	Fruit spritzers (fruit juice and carbonated water)
Coffee and caffeinated beverages	Gradual caffeine reduction; black tea, green tea, herbal and grain teas
Alcohol	Occasional natural beer and spirits; nonalcoholic beer

Daily Serving Strategies

Grams, calories, and ounces. Three words synonymous with the word *diet*. Get an earful of television commercials or glance at cover titles of popular women's magazines and you'll be reminded about our national obsession with serving sizes, ounce and gram measurements, and calorie counting.

The dietary guidelines of the Nature's Cancer-Fighting Foods Plan makes daily volume measurements unnecessary. Cup suggestions are given only as an approximation. The natural fiber content of its staple foods will fill you up without filling you out—so to speak. Another way to look at amounts is by visualizing the general percentages for an entire day's consumption, as illustrated by the circle diagrams. If you've been very active, you'll naturally crave more food.

The importance of thorough chewing cannot be overemphasized. Complex carbohydrates first begin digesting in the mouth. Alkaline enzymes found in saliva initiate carbohydrate breakdown. Thorough chewing is how we expose the surface areas of food to these powerful enzymes. While you may notice an increase in your appetite and an ability to tolerate more food, be wary of stuffing yourself, because even good-quality food in excess can result in hyperacidity, poor assimilation, and subsequent fatigue, not to mention later cravings for an energy stimulant such as sugar. The key here is, *Less in Volume, More in Frequency*.

Here are the daily summary guidelines for the Nature's Cancer-Fighting Foods Plan:

+ **A regular portion of whole grain:** This will help with bowel regularity, provide valuable B vitamins, regulate blood sugar, help bond and remove toxins from the body, and naturally curb cravings for sugar and dietary fat. Sample whole grains: brown rice, oat, barley, millet, buckwheat, quinoa, and amaranth.

+ **A generous daily serving of dark leafy greens:** Dark leafy greens are natural blood cleansers, high in valuable minerals with documented anticancer qualities. Most people have no idea, aside from making salads, how to cook greens. Truth is, it's easy! You can steam them, add them to soups, include them in a vegetable sauté toward the end of cooking, or even quick-boil. Sample leafy greens: broccoli, collards, mustard greens, turnip greens, bok choy, kale, Chinese and regular cabbage, Brussels sprouts, and others.

✦ **A serving of root vegetables:** Containing concentrated vitamins, minerals, and fiber, root vegetables offer a very satisfying meal addition. Sample root vegetables: carrot, beet, celery root, red and white (daikon) radishes, parsnip, rutabaga, turnip, burdock, onion, leek, scallion.

✦ **A serving of yellow-orange vegetables:** High in the cancer-fighting antioxidant beta-carotene, many of these vegetables offer a pleasing and naturally sweet taste. Sample yellow-orange vegetables: squash (summer and winter), carrot, yam, sweet potato, rutabaga.

✦ **A protein serving:** Limit animal-source proteins according to the plan you choose (from zero to three times weekly and in 4- to 5-ounce portions at the maximum). Sample quality vegetable proteins: beans, tofu, tempeh, miso.

✦ **A fruit serving:** Tropical fruits, more concentrated in sugar, should be limited. Fruit juice is not recommended as frequent fare because it's highly concentrated in simple sugars. Fruit is best enjoyed separately, between meals but should be limited in cases of fatigue, especially if you're on the Healing Diet or if you're concerned about maintaining weight. Ideally, focus on seasonal fruits with ample fiber. Sample fruits: apple, pear, peach, apricot, melon, berries.

✦ **A small portion of oil:** Watch your oil serving. A modest amount of healthful oil can make meals more satisfying and reduce cravings for dairy and meat products. In the course of one day, the average person's combined fat intake of oils, nuts, seeds, and animal protein might be excessive, so be aware of the overall fat content in your diet. Generally, 1 to 2 teaspoons of oil per day is all that is necessary, if that. This can vary slightly either way, but as a general rule, it should suffice. Among the recommendations for healing many diseases is restricted animal protein and a drastic reduction of oils, thereby making you obtain your oils from a whole foods menu.

✦ **Liquids:** Drink as thirst permits. Our needs for liquids are exaggerated and based on diets that are either too dry or stimulate water loss. A cup of tea after meals, soup, and additional fluid when thirsty might be your best barometer. Don't feel you have to constantly hydrate or chug-a-lug fluid throughout your day. Contrary to popular opinion, your kidneys are not little toilets that flush. They are delicate, structurally complicated organs that can easily suffer from excessive fluid by swelling and causing edema in other parts of the body. Unfortunately, even physicians have bought into the myth that everyone should be drinking 8 glasses of fluid daily. A recent article in the British medical journal the *Lancet* claimed that this is not a healthy habit and traced this notion back to a 1945 recommendation from the U.S. Nutrition Council. Your liquid needs will naturally increase if you have a higher percentage of salt or flour in your diet, if you exercise consistently and for longer periods of time, frequently eat sugar or simple-sugar treats, consume more animal products, or currently take medication(s). Generally, it is best to drink *after* meals, as opposed to *during* meals—and in small quantities. By the same token, you do need fluids, so restricting is not wise, either. Allow your cravings and intuition to guide you and not static charts that generically recommend fixed amounts. For more, see page 255.

Making New Food Choices

Making new food choices is rarely easy because we become comfortable with what is familiar and convenient. However, consider your changes part of a valuable experiment: the opportunity to challenge yourself in a bigger way to take more control of your health and become more sensitized to what works and what doesn't for your body. Your reactions will be your most enduring and articulate teacher.

12

The Healing Kitchen
Healthful Ways for Preparing and Cooking Nurturing Food

When you have helped to raise the standard of cooking, you have helped to raise the only thing in the world that really matters. We only have one or two wars in a lifetime, but we have three meals a day— there's nothing in the world that we do as much as we do eating.

—Will Rogers

No Time to Cook?

The most common reaction I hear about cooking is, "I don't have time to cook." Whenever I hear this, I'm reminded of the cynical remark I once heard an 89-year-old naturopath from the Pacific Northwest say to his patients:

That's all right. Then, you should just wait . . . wait until you come out of the hospital after the bypass or any other number of diseases you're headed for and as you recuperate—hopefully— you'll have plenty of time to plan and cook.

I doubt most of his patients appreciated his sardonic humor, but the point was clear. Why wait until become too sick to care for your own health? A healthier option is to choose changing now, instead of later feeling forced to change.

When I first began counseling, I was asked to do an in-home consult with a highly successful single businesswoman in her mid-60s. She arrived in a chauffeured Bentley as I waited by her mansion's gate, then signaled me to follow her car into the compound.

Her 22-room mansion had high-tech security, perfectly manicured landscapes, thick natural-fiber carpets, antique furniture (probably belonging to Louis XIV himself), and recognizable art and sculpture throughout the main rooms. Personal assistants, dog-walkers, maids, contractors, and landscapers kept busy as she took me on a brief tour.

While her interest was in becoming healthier, she clearly had no desire to cook but was adamant that she would be doing any "necessary kitchen work" by herself. "Know this," she warned: "I don't cook . . . I *warm*. And if it's going to take me more than 10 minutes, I'm not interested in hearing about it."

She was consulting me because her friend had found immediate relief from arthritic pain with my program, and another friend's breast lumps had noticeably reduced within a very short period on my program as well. I gave her all the details of the Nature's Cancer-Fighting Foods Plan, customizing my recommendations for her specific needs and cooking requests. To keep her interested and within that 10-minute window, I suggested boxed, canned, and frozen items that required no preparation and that could be quickly cooked. It was a large compromise for me, but I rationalized that *any* positive change in her condition would probably inspire her to do more.

I explained that this was a personalized recommendation for her and that if she found improvement, she might want to accelerate her progress by doing some real cooking. With that statement, she peered at me from over the rim of her jewel-encrusted spectacles and succinctly said: "Don't bet on it."

I dropped the matter and smiled understandingly.

Two weeks later, my voice mail carried this message:

Hello, Mr. Varona. This is Ms. ———. Surprisingly, I seem to be doing quite well on this program of yours. For the first time in 9 years, I am off all pain medication and sleeping very well. Let me ask you . . . *if* I were going to actually cook, could you furnish me with some easy-to-follow recipes?

It was a definite triumph for her. A noticeable improvement in her energy levels, sleep, bowel regularity, and pain had suddenly opened her mind to the reality that she had more control over her health than she had previously realized. She now felt a new value for preparing food because of the recent changes that occurred as a result of her new diet and lifestyle.

Ultimately, this is the core of the matter: *redefining your relationship with your kitchen.* Instead of viewing cooking as a chore or a laboriously futile exercise, we change our perspective to think of the kitchen as an "Alchemical Center for Health Transformation."

Another important perspective is to think of cooking, food preparation, and planning as simply another, healthier way we can self-parent. We assume responsibility for our health to the best of our abilities by recognizing the first step as the commitment to take control in a disciplined and consistent way. This begins with the fundamentals of educating ourselves, planning meals, creating new cooking rituals, and developing a willingness to venture into self-experimentation. Eventually, through trial and error, you'll discover numerous shortcuts that will save time without compromising the integrity of your efforts.

Planning the next day's meal, having staples on hand, making sure you have leftovers for fast and easy dishes makes cooking more efficient, less stressful, and quicker.

Creating Dietary Variety

The Western diet has an enormous amount of variety, from textures and colors to consistencies and tastes. Not being conscious of how to use these elements can result in kitchen, meal, and postmeal boredom. Here are some general suggestions to create more variety before I get into specifics about cooking styles:

FOOD SELECTION. A wide array of foods allows for more creativity in the kitchen. Even with an emphasis on plant-based foods, you have almost unlimited choices: whole grains, cracked or rolled grains, grain products, vegetables, beans and bean products, sea vegetables, fruits, condiments and seasonings, herbs, and naturally fermented products. By choice, you may include limited animal proteins (meat or dairy products).

FOOD PREPARATION (CUTTING, SLICING, AND CHOPPING). Foods can also be prepared in different shapes and sizes to quicken cooking times, concentrate flavors, and be visually appealing.

METHODS OF COOKING. Foods can be prepared in a variety of ways that will support health and good flavor. Using different methods of cooking also provides a sense of texture variety, something that many diet plans overlook. (See "Four Traditional Cooking Methods" on page 267.)

COOKING TIME. Lengths of time usually vary according to the season. In warmer weather, we are more inclined to cook less for a more cooling effect, whereas in winter, long-cooked stews and porridges are appealing, particularly because they produce more internal warmth.

USE OF LIQUID. The amount or type of water or stock used in cooking can also lend variety and taste, whether preparing soups, stews, sautéing in a liquid, or cooking grains.

SEASONINGS AND CONDIMENTS. Use a range of herbal seasonings, sea salt, soy sauce, vinegar, miso, flaked sea vegetables, spices, or roasted nuts and seeds to create a variety of flavors and textures.

COMBINATIONS. The mixing of various dishes, different foods, colors, and flavors creates a greater sense of variety in taste as well as visual appeal.

THE H2O FACTOR

HAVE YOU HAD your 8 glasses of water today? Did you have to force it down, or were you genuinely thirsty? Contrary to popular thought, it's really not necessary to drink large volumes of fluid throughout the day—unless you're eating in a way that might require it—because our kidney systems are much more complex than simple flushing mechanisms.

The common factors that make drinking plenty of liquids a necessity are the following: high salt use, abundant animal proteins, high-fat consumption from dairy foods, oils, nuts, and seeds, flour products, and frequent simple sugars. In addition, the typical American diet often lacks the inclusion of soups as another liquid source as well as whole grains, vegetables, and fruits with their natural water content.

Our modern diets, laden with fat, thicken the blood, causing red blood cells to clump, a process also known as blood-cell aggregation, in the narrow capillaries of the body. Because these blood cells carry oxygen, clumping partially prevents much-needed oxygen from entering tissues and cells. Research has documented a 32 percent reduction in oxygen from the action of blood clumping, which can take up to 72 hours to normalize if fats are suddenly restricted.

(CONTINUED)

Physician Otto Warbug discovered that cancer cells have poor vascular systems and tend to be deficient in oxygen. When a normal cell was deprived of oxygen, it would become cancerous. Therefore, any diminishing of oxygen for the individual challenged by cancer increases the risk of disease progression.

Increased consumption of animal protein breaks down into harmful byproducts of sulfur, ammonia, and purine wastes, such as uric acid. Now, include meat hormones, pesticide residues, assorted bacterial strains, food industry chemicals, and a large volume of refined sugar, and you're left with a highly carcinogenic modern diet mixture.

It stands to reason that such dietary habits create a need to irrigate with fluids. It may be that this desired liquid helps dilute the effects of the carcinogenic mixture, keep the blood thin, and the kidneys in continuous eliminative mode. Therefore, the idea that we should drink more to flush toxins has a practical basis. However, an alternative strategy might be better phrased as, "Eat fewer toxins and more whole foods to reduce the need for irrigating your body."

A Chinese doctor I once interviewed told me that he thought the American diet created so much internal heat that Americans "needed to drink to put their fire out." On a whole foods diet, you'll find your thirst at a minimum and the need for fluids far less than during your previous diet. The idea is not to *restrict* your fluids, but to *reduce*. Big difference, and a difference determined by your changing needs and based on your individual condition, exercise profile, daily diet, and sensitivity.

WHEN FLUIDS BECOME DANGEROUS

There is a clear danger to taking excessive amounts of fluid. This common practice can put unnecessary stress on your body in two ways:

- Excessive fluid increases your total blood volume. Our blood volume works within the closed system of our circulation. This increase of blood volume on a regular basis can burden your heart and blood vessels.
- Our kidneys miraculously function with a filtration system necessary for helping us heal that is composed of a series of unique and incredibly small capillary beds called glomeruli. The constant flood of fluids to be filtered essentially drowns the glomeruli, potentially damaging them.

When excess fluid dilutes the circulatory system, the concentration of electrolytes in the blood decreases relative to the concentration of electrolytes in the cells. To keep an equal balance of electrolytes between the blood and the cells, water seeps into the cells from blood, causing the cells to swell. In the brain, this can sometimes cause intracranial pressure because the bones of the skull cannot flexibly expand, creating symptoms of headache, impaired breathing, and fatigue.

Our needs for liquid can also be based on a number of factors, such as excessive salt or animal proteins, sugar, stress, excessive supplement consumption, strenuous exercise, pregnancy and lactation, excessive use of spices, or taking chemotherapy, so it's difficult to issue hard-and-fast rules for liquid consumption.

Most people will find that once on the Nature's Cancer-Fighting Foods Plan, their liquid needs naturally lessen. Between the natural liquid content of whole foods, soups, a cup of tea after meals, and water as a thirst quencher in between meals, little more is necessary.

Use your intuition and craving symptoms as a guide, not mechanical rules based on generalities. Drinking with meals can sometimes dilute nutrition from your food and leave little incentive to actually chew your food. Ideally, liquids should be taken separately, preferably after your meal, and sipped slowly.

Cold liquids, frequently brought to the table before meals in most restaurants, can inhibit digestion. In studies done with ultrasound that observed the swallowing of cold liquids, stomach contractions were inhibited by liquid temperatures of less than 98.6°F (body temperature), thereby cooling the stomach down for about 20 to 30 minutes and delaying its emptying. Yet, this is an automatic practice in nearly every restaurant in the United States.

Become more sensitive to your liquid needs. If you have to attack a pitcherful of water immediately after a meal, this is an obvious sign that your meal was not balanced. Find a way to satisfy your thirst and be more conscious of balance in your food preparation for the next meal.

COMPROMISED HEALING WITH MUNICIPAL WATER TOXINS

Tap water from municipal sources is rapidly becoming a major concern in the United States. This problem is not limited to the well-documented problem of pesticides and agricultural runoffs, it's about a more serious concern: 1 out of every 4 public water system has violated

(CONTINUED)

federal standards for tap water. Municipal water can contain numerous contaminants, including potentially hazardous levels of lead, disease-causing bacteria, radioactive particles, heavy metals, gasoline solvents, industrial wastes, chemical residues, and synthetic organic chemicals, along with disinfectant byproducts.

Even groundwater may contain toxic substances. According to William L. Lappenbusch, a water toxicologist: "Radionuclides (a decay product from underground rock beds that can enter groundwater) in drinking water cause more cancer than any other stressor in that medium, challenged only by pesticides."

A survey of 100 municipal water systems and suppliers found significant levels of cancer-causing arsenic, radon, and chlorine byproducts, reported the Natural Resources Defense Council in October 1995. An estimated 19 million Americans drink water with radon levels that exceed federal safety standards, and two-thirds of the 300 major water suppliers and agencies have failed to give consumers information about their tap water.

Polluted drinking water can raise the risk of developing cancer in addition to causing metal toxicity. Lead, copper, and other heavy metals found in public drinking water can accumulate in body tissues. It is estimated that 70 percent of water toxins enter the body through the skin via baths and showers.

THE FLUORIDE DECEPTION

> **In point of act, fluoride causes more human cancer death,**
> **and causes it faster, than any other chemical.**
> **—Dean Burk, U.S. National Cancer Institute**

Since the 1950s, fluoride has routinely been added to public drinking water and toothpaste, despite the increasing evidence of its multiple health hazards. Fluoride is a poison, second in toxicity only to arsenic.

The practice of water fluoridation was first introduced by an aluminum industry lawyer who had become head of the U.S. Public Health Service. Advertised as a way to improve the public's dental health, it was also a profitable way for the aluminum industry to rid itself of its main toxic waste product, sodium fluoride.

The scientific research paints another picture: These fluoride compounds added to the drinking supply are literally unrefined toxic waste products of phosphate fertilizer production. Fluoride consumption can *produce* cancer. At minimum, concentrations of only 1 ppm (parts per million) fluoride has the power to transform normal human cells into cancerous ones. Fluoridated water has the ability to increase the cancer-producing potential of other cancer-causing chemicals. Low levels of fluoride can increase the incidence of skin cancers from 12 to 100 percent, sometimes in a matter of days. As little as 1 ppm of fluoride in water was found to increase the tumor growth rate in mice by 25 percent. A National Cancer Institute study compiling 14 years of data showed that the incidence of oral and pharyngeal cancer rises with increased exposure to fluoride by as much as 50 percent, which accounts for 8,000 new cases yearly.

Considering it too toxic for public health, fluoridated water has been outlawed in 14 European countries as well as in Egypt and India. However, in the United States, up to 4 ppm is still considered a safe level, and the American Dental Association will not endorse any dental product unless it contains fluoride.

HEALTHIER WATER CHOICES

The choices for healthy water are artesian well water, springwater, filtered water, purified water, and distilled water. Well water, natural springwater, and filtered water might be your best bet.

- **Artesian well water:** Often available in small cities as a free public water source. Check to see if it has been recently tested and cited for its purity. Its mineral content can be beneficial if it checks out as a clean water source.
- **Springwater:** Available from local distributors (look online or in the Yellow Pages), springwater is also a healthful choice. However, in many cases, bottled water is no more than tap water with a small percentage of local springwater mixed in. In addition, you have potential chemical leeching from the plastic bottle into the water and have to contend with higher bacterial counts.
- **Filtered water:** Probably the best and most practical choice for urban dwellers. Water that is filtered through an activated-charcoal filter system retains its water-soluble minerals. It usually has more flavor and is more natural in mineral content than purified water. Unfortunately, filters do not remove water-soluble toxins such as nitrates and sodium fluoride. Filtered water is a

(CONTINUED)

good choice if your city's water does not contain these toxins. Whole-house, under-the-counter, countertop, and faucet units are usually available.

- **Purified water:** Reverse osmosis (RO) water is demineralized via a two-tank process. For every 1 gallon produced, this process wastes 2 to 5 gallons of water. From an environmental point of view, this might be hard to justify. In addition, RO water has been called dead water because it is devoid of minerals and tends to be slightly acidic. If ingested for long periods of time, it can potentially leech out valuable body minerals, such as potassium, magnesium, sodium, and calcium. Sometimes, RO water is recommended to individuals with excessive mineral buildup and arterial plaques for a short-term benefit, but it could result in fatigue and mineral loss over the long term.

- **Distilled water:** Distilled water is completely devoid of minerals is and the most acidic of water choices. Many distillation units cannot remove harmful hydrocarbons. Both RO and distilled water should *not* be stored in plastic jugs or plastic bottles because the mineral-deficient water can draw polycarbons from the plastic. Be wary of purchasing purified water in plastic containers.

The Five Tastes

While most of your meals should contain a minimum of 60 percent "sweet" foods (whole grains, vegetables, beans, fruit, and so on) aim for a full range of other tastes at every meal. In traditional Chinese and Ayurvedic medicine (India's traditional medicine), each taste is correlated with a season, a type of warming or cooling energy, and a specific body organ or system. Theoretically, each taste nourishes a specific organ or organ system.

The more you include a variety of the five tastes in food preparation, the more satisfying and nutritionally enhanced your meals will be. Sometimes, just a small amount of a particular taste can contribute significantly (for example, a sprig of bitter-tasting parsley leaf on an otherwise sweet dish).

The five tastes are bitter, salty, sweet, sour, and pungent. A food will never contain one taste exclusively but each food is characterized by its dominate taste. It is said that a little of a particular taste can strengthen an organ system, whereas excess can weaken it. Each of the tastes, including associated foods, are detailed in the following list:

✦ **Bitter:** Associated with early summer and midsummer plant growth, bitter foods are thought to stimulate the heart and small intestine. These foods include dandelion, parsley leaves, mustard greens, collard greens, burdock root, sesame seeds, cereal-grain coffee substitute, and some types of corn.

✦ **Salty:** Associated with winter plant growth (and used to make food more warming and fortifying), salty food imparts strength and is thought to influence the kidneys and bladder. These foods include sea vegetables, miso, soy sauce, sea salt, and natural brine pickles.

✦ **Sweet:** Associated with late-summer plant growth, sweet food is thought to influence the pancreas, spleen, and stomach—our organs of sugar absorption and distribution. Its nourishing effect is calming. The sweet taste refers to natural whole foods, not the excessively refined sweetness we know from white sugar. This category should make up the largest percentage of our meals. These foods include whole grains, vegetables (especially cabbages, carrots, onions, squashes, parsnips, and sweet potatoes), and chestnuts.

✦ **Sour:** Associated with spring plant growth, sour-tasting food has a constrictive effect, releasing quickening energy and in classical Chinese medicine, thought to influence the liver and gallbladder. These foods include sourdough bread, vinegar, wheat, sauerkraut, lemon, and lime.

✦ **Pungent:** Associated with autumn plant growth, the pungent taste gives off a hot, dispersing energy and is said to be beneficial for the lungs and colon. However, an excess of these foods can irritate the intestines. Pungent foods have been known to stimulate blood circulation and help break down fatty accumulations in the body, commonly caused by animal protein and high-fat foods. These foods include scallions, daikon radish, ginger, peppers, wasabi, dry mustard, and horseradish.

The savory tastes can be represented in side dishes, sauces, and condiments, emphasizing a particular taste you may crave. You can achieve satisfying flavors and nutritional balance by including the five tastes in your meals.

Meals that include all the tastes will prove more satisfying in terms of reducing cravings and making your dishes more fortifying. For example, this balance factor can be seen in recipes that call for oil; pungent or sour flavors taken in combination with oil help make oils easier to digest. Dishes with this balance are mustard (pungent) and tamari (salty) with fish and salt added to water-fried (or sautéed) onions. Eventually, this will become a natural practice as you develop your cooking ability and planning habits and comfortably ease into your new way of eating.

THE FIVE SAVORY TASTES: FOODS

BITTER	SALTY	SWEET	SOUR	PUNGENT (COOKED)
Arugula	Miso	Cabbage	Fermented dishes	Fruits
Celery	Pickle	Carrot	Lemon	Garlic
Collards	Scallion	Corn	Lime	Ginger
Endive	Sea salt	Grain	Pickle	Parsnip
Grain beverages	Sea vegetables	Onion	Sauerkraut	Raw onion
Kale	Tamari	Squash	Umeboshi plum	Red and white radish
Mustard greens	Umeboshi plum	Yam		Spices
Parsley				Wasabi

AN EVOLVING SALT PERSPECTIVE

A 2006 STUDY published in the *American Journal of Medicine* reveals that sodium intake of less than 2,300 milligrams (the daily recommended allowance) was associated with a 37 percent increase in cardiovascular disease mortality and a 28 percent increase of all-cause mortality.

Blood, sweat, and tears share a common ingredient: salt. We cannot live without it. The functions of the heart, liver, kidneys, digestion, and adrenal glands all depend on some percentage of salt. Yet, we have been told repeatedly that salt will elevate blood pressure.

Opinions on the value of salt run the gamut from bad to good, unnecessary to vital. For years, physicians have pointed their fingers at salt and attributed numerous degenerative conditions to excessive intake. *Excessive* is the key word here. Some research shows that salt intake in Japan can be as high as 3 to 6 teaspoons daily, while in America conservative estimates put intake at 3 to 4 teaspoons per day. These levels are particularly common for the fast-food consumer. Considering that the American Heart Association recommends 1 to 1¼ teaspoons (2,400 milligrams) salt daily for healthy adults, this gross consumption of salt personifies excess.

Today, low-salt diets are frequently prescribed to relieve kidney problems and hypertension. In hypertension, the blood vessels are constricted by many factors, one being salt excess. This forces the heart to pump blood through strangled capillaries (an incredibly small diameter of approximately 4 microns). The sodium draws water from blood cells and blood vessels, shrinking surrounding tissues and resulting in dehydration, lower backache (kidney pain), thirst cravings, and eye or facial puffiness.

But the need for salt cannot be devalued. A lack of salt can lead to poor intestinal muscle tone and symptoms of loose bowels (diarrhea). Salt also helps keep blood vessels and cells slightly contracted, which aids in keeping the body warm. This is one of the reasons cultures native to temperate climates increase their consumption of salt in the winter. Of course an excess of salt can also restrict circulation, thus creating more vulnerability to cold.

Playing a major role in the human body is an enzyme called renin, which controls blood volume and blood pressure. Renin is produced in the kidney by our renal cells. A drop in sodium levels will cause an increase in renin levels, which stimulates a cascade of reactions in the body that ultimately causes the blood pressure to elevate. This demonstrates the body's balancing mechanism; too much salt can elevate blood pressure and, conversely, too little can do the same.

While salt is necessary in a diet, many people are unaware of the poor and harsh quality of ordinary table salt. All salt is actually sea salt, or at least, once was sea salt. Inland rock salt deposits were once dissolved in the great ocean that covered Earth over 300 million years ago, and rainfall over eons has leeched some of the non–sodium chloride minerals out of rock salt deposits and washed them into the sea. As a result, sea salt is somewhat higher in trace minerals (silicon, copper, calcium, nickel) than common rock salt. In fact, there are approximately 84 buffering elements in natural, solar-dried sea salt to protect our bodies from the harshness of pure sodium chloride.

Natural salts (those dried by a solar evaporation process) are made of larger crystals and still contain their matrix of valuable trace minerals. However, natural salts do not flow free. Because they are not

(CONTINUED)

coated with a water-repelling chemical, salt naturally attracts moisture from the air. Sun-dried sea salt cannot be evenly shaken from a salt shaker.

WHAT'S WRONG WITH COMMON TABLE SALT?

Mass-produced and refined table salt is 99.99 percent sodium chloride, regardless of its origin. This refined salt is made of uniformly fine crystals—made fine by first being heated to 1,200°F and then flash-cooled. The salt is then combined with a number of additives: potassium iodine is added to salt to iodize it, providing anti-goiter comfort. Although iodine is essential to the functioning of thyroid hormones, it is very volatile and oxidizes immediately when exposed to light. Because of this, dextrose, a simple sugar, must be added to stabilize the iodine added to table salt. This gives birth to another problem: Adding only the two ingredients of potassium iodide and dextrose would turn the salt purple. This is not considered marketable; therefore, a little sodium bicarbonate is mixed in to bleach the color. Finally, the crystals are coated with a compound such as sodium silicoaluminate (note all the extra sodium compounds in table salt) to make sure that the salt will be free flowing in humid conditions.

SEA SALT VERSUS TABLE SALT

Naturally solar-evaporated sea salt has a uniquely different taste; judge for yourself by taking a simple taste test: Put a couple table salt grains directly on your tongue. Notice that the initial taste is sharp, salty, acrid with a lingering flavor that can be harsh, metallic, and distinctly unpleasant.

Now, rinse your mouth with water and taste several grains of sea salt. Notice a difference? Its taste is slightly sweet, smooth, pleasant, and satisfying. This is when you realize the unique sensitivity of your taste buds. They have an ability to distinguish subtle differences of artificial ingredients and natural ingredients from two separate salts in an identical sodium chloride base. Good-quality sea salt has the natural advantage of being able to enhance and concentrate the flavors of other ingredients.

THE VEGETARIAN SALT-DEFICIENCY DILEMMA

People who have been on a high-fat, meat-and-potato diet and suddenly decide to change their habits find their need for salt is minimal, if not unnecessary, in the beginning. Their bodies are usually saturated with salt, and they would do well to avoid the substance for a period of time. Therefore, there is no universal rule for salt use.

However, for vegetarians, it's another story. Biochemist Jacques de Langre, offered the following observation:

> [Vegetarians] have so much ingested potassium from the green leafy vegetables that this cannot be neutralized by sodium—if potassium is excessive in relation to sodium. This can also make the body lose its ability to produce hydrochloric acid, which can produce digestive problems, quite common in vegetarians.

The blood relationship of sodium to potassium is essential. Potassium always predominates. However, if we take an excessive amount of sodium, potassium can restore the balance. Heavy meat eaters (obtaining salts via the animal muscle) who suddenly choose to eat a strict vegetarian food with no salt added tend to feel almost euphoric, at least initially. They feel lighter, more energetic, experience greater mental clarity, and so on. However, while there are some exceptions, excessive potassium can steer these positive conditions to their opposite; the new vegetarians become lethargic, mineral deprived, emotionally negative, and depressed. They begin craving meats or products containing salt.

Because they've usually been indoctrinated about the negative effects of meats and salt, they invariably end up replacing those cravings with stimulants and fats. Such new vegetarians typically use stimulants (essentially simple sugars) to maintain their declining energy and fats (oils, nut butters, avocados) to keep a sense of fullness with meals. For those who want to follow a vegan diet, reducing sugars and adding a little salt to their food during cooking (or using fermented salt products) can work wonders and reverse their complaints.

Sea salt added to the diet, either in its direct form or in fermented preparations such as miso or tamari, can be highly alkalizing to the body fluids while alleviating fatigue.

There is a sister fruit to the apricot called the ume plum in Japan. The Japanese pickle this plum in salt for a number of months and package the fruit as umeboshi salt plums. Highly salty with strong citric acid properties, umeboshi plums are excellent for neutralizing

(CONTINUED)

digestive acidity. They are handy to have when traveling for cases of indigestion or to neutralize the effects of overeating and most forms of digestive acidity.

HOW MUCH SALT IS TOO MUCH?

How can you determine when you've taken too much salt? The following seven symptoms might indicate you're taking salt beyond your needs:

- **Thirst:** Excessive salt will inspire thirst. If you drink fruit juice in an attempt to satisfy this craving, you'll notice that the sugar will also create increased thirst. Filtered water or hot noncaffeinated tea, in small quantities, will help if taken throughout the day.
- **Overeating:** Excess salt can increase your desire for greater amounts of food. This is especially true for individuals who avoid sugar. Their craving becomes transferred to one that demands volume.
- **Sweet and alcohol cravings:** Salt and sugar, a perfect union of extremes. Each creates cravings for the other. A salty meal's complement is a sweet dessert, as seen in the fast-food staples of burger, fries, and a sweetened milk shake. Alcohol is a distillation of sugar, which means concentrated sugar. Remember this fact the next time you are in a tavern or bar and notice the owner making certain the nuts, chips, popcorn, or other salty snack is well supplied to patrons. It's rarely because the owner is considerate. It's about increasing the patron's desire for alcohol.
- **Irritability:** Excessive salt may also produce irritability. This may be due to the physically constricting effects of salt (fostering a state of being uptight), its lowering of blood sugar, or its depressive effect on the nervous system.
- **Swelling:** In some people, swelling of ankles, hands, or around the eyes may be due to excess salt.
- **Coloring:** While there are many reasons for darkness beneath the eyes, one of them can be from taking an excess of salt.
- **Pain:** Excessive salt can also show as kidney pain, more commonly in one kidney, but potentially in both. How do you know your kidney pain is the result of excess salt? Immediately cease consuming *all* salt, salted products, flour, and sugar. Squeeze the juice of one lemon into a pitcher of water and drink through-

out the day. If your pain is the result of excess salt, lemon juice will usually help you desalt very quickly, eliminating all signs of pain.

The Nature's Cancer-Fighting Foods Plan suggests small amounts of salt that generally range from 500 to 1,500 milligrams (¼ to ¾ teaspoon). The salt recommended is natural, solar-dried sea salt that should be cooked into the food, as opposed to adding it raw to an already prepared dish. This allows the salt to become absorbed into the food and, therefore, easier for absorption in your body.

Four Traditional Cooking Methods

There are many methods of cooking that can be used to create a sense of variety or enhance nutrition. Some methods are considered more healthful than others, but ultimately, your developing sensitivity and intuition will be the best guide in choosing the right methods for your diet.

WOOD. Unless you're living in the country and have the time (and the wood), this might be a bit impractical. However, it is considered a very strengthening form of cooking. Many upscale restaurants and ethnic eateries (Southwestern cuisine, Indian, and so on) advertise their natural wood ovens and mesquite grills for the unique flavoring and taste they produce. On the downside, the physical and chemical properties of particulate matter from wood burning have a strong influence on how these particles may affect our health. Worsening of cardiovascular and respiratory diseases such as chronic obstructive pulmonary disease and asthma are main concerns with the use of wood-burning stoves.

NATURAL GAS. While many people claim gas cooking tastes better than food cooked on electrical ranges and that it is easier to regulate heat and gauge temperature, it still has a downside. Fire and carbon monoxide poisoning are the dangers most often associated with gas cooking stoves. In fact, Johns Hopkins research scientists reported that high levels of a noxious gas can aggravate asthma symptoms by driving up nitrogen dioxide concentrations. Good ventilation, such as a room fan and kitchen exhaust can minimize this toxin.

ELECTRIC. One of the disadvantages of electric ranges is the limitation they impose on the cook's creativity because the heat settings are limited to fixed temperatures and cannot be quickly adjusted to go from, say, a high boil to a simmer because it takes time for the element to cool down or heat up. Some alternative medicine theories suggest that electric cooking diminishes, rather than enhances, a food's energetic composition. Still, for some, particularly those with respiratory problems, which might be exacerbated by cooking with wood fire or gas, this form of cooking might be preferable.

MICROWAVE. Developed in response to our on-the-go lifestyles and now used by more than 50 percent of home cooks in the United States, microwaving is a questionable method of cooking food for health on a regular basis. The advertised convenience factor reduces the attention we give to its potential harm. Microwaving diminishes a food's energy pattern by disrupting its biomolecular structure. This form of nonionizing radiation, accelerated beyond electricity, makes a food's water molecules vibrate so rapidly that their motion is responsible for cooking the food. This might be a concern for healing purposes. Available studies on microwaving have shown the following:

- ✦ According to the *Lancet*, Britain's premier medical journal, microwaved foods, upon ingestion, can cause "structural, functional, and immunological changes in the body. It transforms the amino acid L-proline, a proven toxin to the nervous system, liver, and kidneys."
- ✦ Light and radiation researcher and author John Ott suggests that consumption of microwaved foods can reduce normal muscle strength.
- ✦ A study reported in the *Journal of the American Dietetic Association* concluded that microwave heating of human milk destroys vital immunoglobin A. Immunoglobin A is a protein necessary for a baby's essential physical development and for increasing natural immunity.
- ✦ Another study suggested that fats are denatured by microwave radiation, resulting in free radical formation, a highly carcinogenic occurrence.
- ✦ Andrew Weil, frequent media personality and author of numerous nutritional books, offers the following on microwaving:

> There may be real dangers associated with microwaving food. We don't know enough about how microwaves affect our bodies to feel entirely safe with them. This longer waveform of radiation can cook human tissues exposed to it directly, and even low doses may disrupt the delicate op-

erations of biological control systems in our bodies. Weak electrical currents and electromagnetic fields are known to affect cellular growth and development and to aid in the healing of tissue.

In some cases, particularly in restaurants, having something microwaved is practically unavoidable. While there have been a number of studies that warrant concern, it is still an area of investigation that must be more thoroughly explored before conclusive claims can be made. Despite this, discretion in choosing an established, healthful, and worry-free form of cooking might offer more mental comfort by not potentially compromising long-term good health.

Cooking Styles to Fit Your Needs

Often, I've suggested to clients that they should eat more vegetables. A common response is, "Fine! I love salad—could eat it all the time."

This response overlooks that salad is not a vegetable *category*. It is a *cooking style*—and one of many.

There are a great number of cooking techniques, which can be generally grouped into the following categories: as dry, wet, fat based, mixed medium, device based, and nonheat. The chart below shows the different cooking techniques for each of the broad categories. The most common cooking styles are easy to master.

DRY	WET	FAT BASED	MIXED MEDIUM	DEVICE BASED	NONHEAT
Dry-roasting	**Blanching***	**Stir-frying**	Barbecuing	Clay pot cooking	**Fermentation**
Baking	**Boiling**	Deep-frying	Flambéing	Earth oven cooking	Pickling
Grilling	Poaching	**Sautéing**	Braising	**Pressure cooking**	Souring
Searing	Stewing	Browning	Blackening	Microwaving	Pressing and marinating
Smoking	Pot cooking		**Steaming**	Pan-frying	Mixing

* The most popular cooking techniques are in boldface.

STEAMING. Steamed food usually has a light taste, cooks quickly, and retains little water. The key to steaming vegetables is to bring the water to a boil *before* adding the vegetables. This can be done with a double-layered pot, with stainless-steel steaming trays, or with Asian bamboo steaming baskets. Many items can be cooked or reheated with steam. Steaming works especially well for broccoli, cauliflower, cabbage, cut onions, and various root and ground vegetables.

PRESSURE COOKING. The value of cooking under pressure is in the way high pressure forces the heat through the outer covering of a grain, for instance, softening it to make it more digestible and easier to assimilate its outer-layer nutrients, which brings out a sweeter taste. Pressure cooking is especially warming for winter cooking. In many cultural folk medicines, pressure cooking is considered a strengthening form of cooking. Pressure cooking, once considered a daring way to cooking given the potential hazards of early pressure cookers, has become much simpler, safer, and faster today.

SAUTÉING (WATER OR OIL STIR-FRYING). Traditionally stir-frying, popular in Asian cuisine, is done with small amounts of oil over medium-low heat to avoid burning. Small amounts of water can be added to create steam inside a covered pan to finish off the dish. Water-frying uses a small amount of water instead of oil. It is a good way to prepare hard leafy greens, such a kale and collards. This method brings out the natural sweetness without the added calories of the oil.

BOILING. In different culinary traditions, there are many styles of boiling. With blanching, or quick-boiling, vegetables are cooked in boiling water for only 15 to 60 seconds. Although they still keep their crunch and maintain their color, blanched vegetables can be easier to digest than raw. The long-simmer method, often used in cold-weather cooking, especially for starchy and root varieties (squash, radish, turnip, carrot, onion, and so on), allows for cooking in a very small amount of water in a tightly covered pot until tender. A light sprinkle of sea salt helps the vegetables surrender additional water.

BAKING. This method is commonly used for preparing hearty root vegetables, ground varieties (such as squashes and pumpkins), onions, and in combinations (casseroles). Baking brings out the natural sugars in the vegetables, giving them a rich, syrupy sweet taste. Some vegetables can be baked in their whole state, such as squash and onions, or cut and baked in a covered or uncovered glass or ceramic dish.

BROILING. Broiling is a preferred method for cooking animal protein, but it can give vegetables a distinctive, bitter, or slightly burned flavor. Broiling allows soft vegetables (such as asparagus) to retain their natural shape.

THE GRILL AND BARBECUE MENACE TWINS: PAHS AND HCAS

WHENEVER FAT DRIPS on a flame, heating element, or hot coals, chemicals called polycyclic aromatic hydrocarbons (PAHs) form. The PAHs waft up in the smoke and land on the food. They can also form directly on food when cooked to a crisp.

As early as 1775, PAH-containing soot was linked to cancer of the scrotum in chimney sweeps. Today, grilled meat is the major source of PAHs in our food. Of more than 100 PAHs found in the environment, at least 19 have been identified in cooked food. As many as 12 of the 18 PAHs found in cooked food have been shown to cause cancer in laboratory animals. Proof that they can cause cancer in humans is still yet to be confirmed, but not far off. Preventing PAHs is simply a matter of keeping the fat from dripping on the heat, which is why broiling (using a heat source above the food), or any type of cooking in a pan, stewing, or baking, results in few if any PAHs. That's also why grilled fatty meats like pork contain more PAHs than leaner cuts.

Cooking meat, poultry, or fish at high temperatures can also present a problem. There are about six potentially cancer-causing chemicals called heterocyclic amines (HCAs), which are created when animal meats are cooked at high temperatures.

"We know these compounds can probably cause cancer in humans," says Elizabeth Snyderwine, chief of the Chemical Carcinogenesis Section at the National Cancer Institute. "What we don't know yet is how significant a problem they are in the American diet."

Until there's more evidence, "It makes sense to avoid [HCAs] when we can," says Mark Knize of the Lawrence Livermore National Laboratory in California.

"Meat and poultry produce the most HCAs because they contain the most amino acids and creatine, which are converted into HCAs," comments Lawrence Livermore's James Felton. "Seafood produces much less, and plant foods like veggie-burgers, fruits and vegetables little or none."

Cooking with liquid—as in boiling, steaming, poaching, or stewing—generates no HCAs because the temperature never tops the boiling point of water.

Creating the Healing Kitchen

As you transform your kitchen into a healing space, there are some very simply guidelines that will help you. Some may seem obvious and others less intuitive but together they will contribute to your health in innumerable ways:

- ✦ Try to clean up as you cook, to keep chaos at bay. Keeping a calm and ordered kitchen is the start of a harmonious meal.
- ✦ Live plants offer a kitchen and other parts of your home beauty, a sense of freshness, and life-sustaining oxygen.
- ✦ Your feelings and attitudes have a subtle yet energetic influence on your preparation and cooking and a positive impact on your healing strategy.
- ✦ Cooking for yourself and others can be an expression of your love and friendship. It's about energy.
- ✦ Commit to making one new recipe each week from a cookbook or other reliable source. Having a number of familiar recipes to rely on inspires confidence and creativity.
- ✦ Consider taking a natural food or ethnic cooking class to learn how you can substitute natural ingredients for ones that are not health supportive and to expand your culinary horizons.
- ✦ Plan in advance: When you devise a week's menus and shop accordingly, you will save time and reduce anxiety. Many grains, beans, soups, and desserts can often be prepared in advance, although you have to allow time to prepare fresh vegetables at meal times.
- ✦ Use the best tools available. Sharp knives and other kitchen conveniences reduce time and effort in preparation. Avoid aluminum or chemically treated, nonstick cookware because some finishes can eventually dissolve into your food. The best cookware is ceramic, glass, earthenware, stainless steel, and cast iron.

Shopping Hints

Menu planning is a good first step so that you shop wisely and efficiently. But once you head to the supermarket, your local health food store, or your local farmers' market, here are a few essentials to keep in mind:

- Buy local, seasonal, fresh, and organic products whenever possible.
- Find out if your city has farmers' markets. Visit them and get to know your growers. Often farmers' market produce is substantially lower in price than in commercial markets.
- Buy in bulk whenever possible. This requires storage room but offers substantial savings in the long run.
- Read labels! Remember, *natural* is just a marketing slogan. Sugars usually end in *-ose* (such as fructose, dextrose). And beware of corn syrup, evaporated cane juice, Sucanat, and brown sugar—these are still highly concentrated forms of sugar. Don't be content after reading the words *natural flavors*; this is often marketing lingo for, "Yeah, there's something natural about it, but you don't need to know more . . ."

THE REAL MEANING OF "NATURAL FLAVORING"

IN MANY PRODUCT labels there is a very deceptive two-word ingredient that is obviously designed to pacifiy consumer concerns about the quality of ingredients that they are purchasing. "Natural flavoring" has an innocent ring to it, but if you read the legal definition, the truth is alarming: The definition of *natural flavor* under the Code of Federal Regulations (21CFR101.22) is:

> The essential oil, oleoresin, essence or extractive, protein hydrolysate, distillate, or any product of roasting, heating or enzymolysis, which contains the flavoring constituents derived from a spice, fruit or fruit juice, vegetable or vegetable juice, edible yeast, herb, bark, bud, root, leaf or similar plant material, meat, seafood, poultry, eggs, dairy products, or fermentation products thereof, whose significant function in food is flavoring rather than nutritional.

Watch for hidden sources of oil in baked goods, crackers, cookies, tofu, veggie and soy burgers, tofu salads, and so on. (In most cases, from-scratch is the best. It's worth the investment of your time, and often simpler than you imagined.)

13

Salud!
Nutritious, Delicious,
and Easy-to-Make Recipes

salud (sah-lood) Sp. {origin f.}—A salutation of
blessing for good health. *¡Por tu salud!* ("For your
health!")

THE general guidelines for preparing and cooking foods given in this
chapter provide a good starting point for your journey to health. You will
find detailed discussions for cooking grains and vegetables, in particular
because they are such an important part of a healthful diet.

Some Notes on the Recipes

Regarding Recipe Ingredient Amounts

In contrast to Western cookbooks, which give very specific amounts,
many traditional Asian cookbooks just list approximations. They leave
it up to you to figure out your specific needs. This is considered a matter of personal intuition. Instead of a pinch of salt, you'll be advised to
add salt to taste. This can drive some people crazy if they're approaching
cooking mechanically. So, while I do try to provide specific amounts,
please keep in mind that these are suggestions, as opposed to doctrine.

Trust your intuition. If your recipe seems to flop, remember the words of inventor Thomas Edison: "I haven't failed, I've just found 10,000 ways that it did not work."

Regarding Substitutions

In some recipes, vegetables are sautéed in oil. According to current research, short-time low heating of oil is not harmful. High heating of oils, especially to the point of smoking, creates potentially harmful free radical elements, which are considered carcinogenic. In the event you are restricting oil or are not comfortable with heating oils or for whatever reason do not want to cook oil, by all means, feel free to eliminate this recipe step. Water can be substituted in place of oil to create a water-fry style of cooking.

SAVORY GRAIN-AND-VEGETABLE COMBINATIONS

IF EATING WHOLE grains is new to you or if you'd like the sensation of more tastes, consider combining whole grains with fine-cut vegetables (as in pilaf recipes), either precooked in a water-sauté style or cooked at the same time as the grain. Toasted nuts and chestnuts make a flavorful and naturally sweet addition to grains. The greater variety of tastes you can experience, the more satisfying your transition will become.

There are an infinite number of ways to prepare grains for taste, variety, and increased nutritional protection. Here are some of my favorite basic combinations:

- Brown rice with brown sweet rice, onions, and shiitake mushroom
- Brown rice with wild rice, fresh corn, and roasted pumpkin seeds
- Brown rice with millet or polenta and roasted almonds
- Brown rice with minced radish, parsley, and sunflower seeds
- Brown rice with lentils and onions
- Brown rice with chestnuts
- Brown rice with chickpeas, minced carrots, and onions
- Brown rice with millet and chickpeas

(CONTINUED)

- Brown rice with barley, leeks, and carrots
- Brown rice with quinoa, watercress, and walnuts
- Brown rice with sweet brown rice, black beans, and scallions
- Brown rice with amaranth
- Sweet brown rice with black beans, onions, and corn
- Sweet rice with millet, and almonds
- Sweet rice with millet, leeks, and black beans
- Sweet rice with sesame seeds
- Millet with onions, carrots, and cabbage
- Millet with squash (or sweet potato), onions, and carrots
- Millet with cauliflower and tahini
- Millet with squash and adzuki beans
- Rolled oats and quinoa with sesame salt
- Barley with mushrooms, carrots, celery, and onions
- Quinoa with black beans and onions
- Quinoa with Chinese greens and roasted cashews

You can also add the following to any grain:

- A second grain: Any two or three whole grains
- A seed or nut: Roasted seeds or nuts as a garnish or cooked into the dish
- A bean or legume: Cooked beans or bean product (tofu, tempeh)
- A vegetable: Preferably from the sweet category, cut into small pieces.
- Condiments: Sesame salt, sea vegetable flakes, spices, herbs, mild spices

COOKING TIMES FOR COMMON GRAINS

- **Quick-cooking grains** (up to 15 minutes): Instant or rolled oats, buckwheat, basmati rice, couscous, corn grits, quinoa, teff, amaranth
- **Medium-cooking grains** (20 to 35 minutes): Millet, sweet brown rice, white rice
- **Long-cooking grains** (45+ minutes): Brown rice, wild rice, un-hulled barley, pearl barley, oat groats, kamut, rye, spelt, wheat (soak these grains for added nutritional benefits)

Mealtime Rituals:
What You Eat and When Count

About Breakfast

According to a recent statistic, 1 in 4 Americans never eats a morning meal, while 12 percent does so only occasionally. Modern researchers report that individuals eating ample morning meals are less likely to gain weight, when compared to those who skip the morning meal or eat later. These findings also indicated that those who eat breakfast repeatedly outperform those who abstain from breakfast in both physical and mental activities.

Avoiding breakfast frequently leads to a mild low blood sugar level that resembles fatigue and instigates strong cravings for sugar or refined foods that are capable of quickly elevating the blood sugar level. Breakfast skippers usually reverse the order of eating, having little or nothing for breakfast, average lunches, and large dinners (see "Late-Night Eating" on page 279) instead of the more healthful opposite pattern. So having healthful breakfasts often sets up a positive eating cycle that will keep you from sabotaging your diet and compromising your health.

VEGETABLES FOR BREAKFAST?

Breakfast-eating habits vary widely throughout the world. Traditional fare in northern Great Britain was a whole-oat cereal, cooked all night, with a side helping of local dulse sea vegetables. Throughout Asia, standard breakfast fare is cooked vegetables with grain porridges. In some countries, mildly salted pickles are served as an alkalizing morning side dish, presumably to help counter accumulated acids from the previous evening's dinner.

In China, a common breakfast dish is congee, grains cooked to a porridge texture often containing pickled egg, small amounts of various kinds of meats, cooked vegetables, spices, raw scallions, and sometimes brine pickles. This nourishing stew fortifies one with energy throughout the morning, which makes it a stark contrast to the American machine-blown, enriched, colored, artificially flavored, and puffed cereals to which we add over 45 percent refined sugar and sometimes fruit pieces.

Many people find a bowl of fresh fruit appealing at breakfast. Although this might be initially satisfying, the simple sugar of fructose usually fails to sustain endurance energy for the work ahead. Such a breakfast, contrary to a number of fad diets that speak glowingly of fruits as cleansing foods, usually results in a late-morning energy slump.

The trick to enjoying a whole grain breakfast is relearning to chew. Thorough chewing of whole grains brings out their subtle natural sweetness—one that is not overwhelming and one that energizes. Whole grains can also be soaked for several hours (or overnight) in a small amount of water to minimize the acid content held in their vitamin-charged seven-layer covering. This makes the assimilation of fiber nutrients easier and far more nourishing. A pinch of sea salt also increases grain digestion by reducing its net acid effect and enhancing the grain's natural sweetness, in the same way a couple of salt grains can make an apple slice sweeter.

Become a willing adventurer and experience vegetables as a small part of your breakfast. They make a delicious complement to combined-grain porridges, topped with seeds or nuts and other condiments.

GENTLY BREAKING OLD BREAKFAST HABITS

Most of us eat specific foods for certain meals. We generally like something soft for breakfast, because few of us want to jump up from a deep sleep and begin the work of active chewing So, our established custom has been to eat soggy cereal with fruit, gooey sweetened oatmeal, or sweet rolls or donuts. Some prefer soft eggs accompanied by a popular breakfast addition that contrasts the soft texture with a bit of coarseness: the ubiquitous buttered toast. All is washed down with a hot beverage (coffee or tea).

I've found that most people can handle lunches and dinners creatively, but when it comes to breakfast, anything that deviates from the traditional norm can be very stressful and disorienting.

Because of breakfast traditions, you might find yourself missing what has been familiar to you. Therefore, if the morning meal becomes the struggle of the day, I'd suggest you fashion it as much as possible with what has been familiar, using better-quality ingredients. Start with a few simple substitutions:

Instead of instant flavored oatmeal with sugar, fruit, and milk
Try rolled oats flavored with some cinnamon, small amounts of raisins, apricots, or dates, and nut milk (such as almond), rice milk, or soy milk. You can also cook any whole grain with extra water for a longer period of time (usually the night before) and warm it

up for breakfast. Try topping it with roasted nuts or seeds, or cinnamon. Sometimes, I recommend diluting a level teaspoon of miso paste until creamy and then mixing it into hot cereal, along with nut toppings. Cereals such as this are naturally sweet, warming, and nourishing. It might be more satisfying to have a piece of toast with a thin spread of nut or seed butter along with the soft grain if you miss that familiar texture combination.

Instead of eggs with toast and bacon
Try scrambled tofu (see page 289), egg-white omelet with vegetables, and/or fried or baked tempeh strips.

Instead of commercial dried breakfast cereal
Try a natural version of a boxed dried cereal without sugar and use a substitute milk such as soy, rice, oat, or almond milk instead of dairy milk.

Look over the vegetable and grain recipes. Although these are unfamiliar breakfast foods to most, they are worth the effort in terms of health benefits, and you might find these foods to be surprisingly satisfying in the morning.

Late-Night Eating

Late eating or snacking causes digestion to occur during times when our bodies should be resting and distributing their daily intake of nutrients, which frequently results in fatigue the following day.

Other conditions associated with late-night eating are unwanted weight gain, morning sluggishness, depression, and a lack of mental clarity, making coffee practically a necessity. One important factor in cancer recovery is keeping the immune system in top shape. Weight gain, insulin swings, high blood acidity, or nutritional depletion can hinder immune function.

NEW RULE: DON'T SWALLOW YOUR FOOD BEFORE YOU TASTE IT

Drink your food and chew your drink.

—Mohandas K. Gandhi

OFTEN, I'VE HEARD clients complain: "Grains are soooooo bland tasting!" While it might seem that way, the real problem is twofold: It's in our eating habits and our taste buds, which have become dulled by concentrated sweet foods. We've forgotten how to really taste and chew our food. That's principally because the food we're eating today has little real taste. Rather, it's an overwhelming sensation of sweetness or flavor-trapped-in-fat quality. In addition, the more you chew poor-quality (non–health supportive) food, the worse it tastes. When a mother complains that her child never eats vegetables, I point out that because many children have high-volume sugar consumption, they cannot be expected to appreciate the subtle sweetness of vegetables.

On the other hand, real food increases in sweetness the more it is chewed because its natural complex sugars are gradually reduced to simpler forms. Gandhi's famous quote about chewing underlines the need to break everything down to practically a liquid in the mouth. The first stage of digestion is when the saliva begins to break down nutritional components, and that process occurs in the mouth. Still, many of us of us bolt and inhale our food. In fact, food inhalation (literally choking on food) was ranked as the sixth major cause of accidental death in the United States—just ahead of airplane crashes!

BREAKFAST MENUS AND RECIPES

BREAKFAST MENU I

CINNAMON RAISIN, QUICK-TIME OATMEAL

WHOLE WHEAT TOAST WITH ALMOND CREAM

ROOIBOS TEA WITH LIME

The toast provides a satisfying texture and the rooibos tea, which contains no caffeine, helps seal the appetite at the end of the meal with its natural sweet flavor and heat.

Cinnamon Raisin, Quick-Time Oatmeal

This is an easy and familiar breakfast. It's best to add the raisins about two-thirds of the way into the cooking, allowing them to absorb some of the water. You may also like to add roasted seeds or nuts as a garnish.

Serves 3 to 4

4 cups filtered water
⅛ to ¼ teaspoon sea salt
1½ to 1¾ cups rolled oats
2 tablespoons organic raisins
Pinch of ground cinnamon

In a medium pot over medium-high heat, bring the water and salt to a rapid boil. Gently stir in the oats. Reduce the heat to simmer. Partially cover the pot to allow steam to escape and cook, stirring occasionally, for 10 minutes. (Quick-cooking flaked oats cook in 3 to 5 minutes.) If the oats begin to look dry during cooking, gently stir in ⅓ to ½ cup water, as needed for a creamier texture. After 10 minutes, add the raisins and cook until slightly creamy, 5 additional minutes. Don't forget to stir in the cinnamon just before serving.

(recipe continues)

Note: If you'd like a nuttier-tasting oatmeal, try dry-roasting the uncooked oats in a medium dry skillet over low heat until slightly brown, about 5 minutes, before adding them to the boiling water.

Variation: For a sweeter version of this morning oatmeal, without added sugar, stir in a heaping tablespoon of chopped dates and 1 tablespoon of tahini.

Whole Wheat Toast with Almond Cream

If available, try non-yeast bread (usually stored in market refrigerators), which are a bit more chewy and more substantial. Making a cream from a seed or nut butter makes this more easily digestible as a spread—good for a two-toast spread.

Serves 2

> 1 tablespoon almond butter
> 2 tablespoons water, or 1 to 3 tablespoons sugar-free soy milk or almond milk
> ½ teaspoon tamari or pinch sea salt (optional)
> Dash of pure vanilla extract (optional)
> 1 to 2 slices whole wheat bread, toasted

In a small bowl or cup, mix the almond butter with the water to create a creamy consistency. Blend in the tamari and vanilla extract, spread on the bread, and refrigerate the remainder. It can last up to a week in your fridge.

Rooibos Tea with Lime

Rooibos, also known as African red bush tea, is available at most natural food stores and some gourmet specialty markets.

Steep the tea for several minutes in boiled water, and add a squeeze of fresh lime juice.

BREAKFAST MENU 2

OATMEAL-QUINOA PORRIDGE AND ROASTED SUNFLOWER SEEDS

SWEET ONION KALE

RYE TOAST BRUSHED WITH SESAME SPREAD

DANDELION ROOT TEA WITH LEMON

Oatmeal-Quinoa Porridge and Roasted Sunflower Seeds

This hearty porridge is a blend of oatmeal and a quick-cooking South American grain called quinoa. Quinoa is a uniquely delicious small grain with high protein content.

Serves 2 to 3

¾ to 1 cup any type of the different blends of colored quinoa (brown is the most popular), washed and drained (see Note)
4 cups filtered water
Pinch sea salt
¾ to 1 cup rolled oats
1 to 2 teaspoons roasted sunflower seeds (see Note)
½ to ¾ teaspoons tamari

In a medium pot, bring the water and salt to a full boil over medium-high heat. Gently stir in the quinoa and oats and lower the heat to a simmer. Partially cover the pot to allow steam to escape, and cook for 15 minutes. If the grains begin to look dry during cooking, gently stir in ⅓ to ½ cup water, as needed for a creamier texture. After 15 minutes, add the sunflower seeds, and cook with a covered lid about 5 minutes more. Add the tamari toward the end and stir into the mixture.

Note: (1) To wash the quinoa, place it in a large bowl and cover with filtered water. Stir with your hand to cleanse, and then pour the water out through a fine-mesh strainer. (2) To roast the sunflower seeds, place in a small dry skillet over medium-high heat and cook, stirring several times, until medium brown.

Sweet Onion Kale

Sometimes a sweet vegetable like onion can be a perfect complement to greens. While it might sound strange to have greens with breakfast, we seem not to mind when we order an omelet. This is just a small side dish that allows you to get more calcium and important minerals in the morning.

Serves 2

> 1 to 2 cups filtered water
> 1 large onion, peeled, cut in half, and sliced into thin crescents
> Pinch sea salt
> 1 bunch kale

In a large skillet, bring 1 cup of water to a boil over medium-high heat. Add the onion and sea salt and cook covered for 4 minutes until the onions are transparent. Add ⅓ cup of water, or less, and continue to cook, covered, for 5 to 7 minutes.

In the meantime, rinse the kale leaves, finely chop, and put aside. When chopping, chop the entire vegetable. The stems will soften quickly if the leaves are chopped more finely. After two minutes, add the chopped kale, adjust the heat to medium-low, and cook for another 3 to 4 minutes.

Then, shut off the heat and move the kale and onion mixture into a serving bowl, otherwise the retained heat in the pan will continue to cook the kale. This way you avoid overcooking and having everything appear dark and limp.

Rye Toast Brushed with Sesame Spread

Makes one large slice for each person, or two small ones for each, according to the size of your loaf.

> 1 tablespoon tahini
> ½ teaspoon tamari
> 1 to 2 slices rye bread, toasted

Mix the tahini and tamari in a small bowl to thoroughly combine. Spread on the toast.

Dandelion Root Tea with Lemon

You can purchase roasted dandelion root tea bags (*not* dandelion leaf) from a number of companies; check online or at your supermarket or natural food store. This hearty tea, considered a tonic for the liver in Native American herbal medicine and popular in Italy, is a nice finish to any meal, often naturally reducing the desire to continue eating afterward.

Steep the tea as you normally would in boiling water to release its full flavor. Add a squeeze of fresh lemon juice.

BREAKFAST MENU 3

7-MINUTE MORNING MISO-VEGETABLE SOUP

CORN TORTILLAS WITH TEMPEH, CORN, AND ONIONS IN

CILANTRO-KUZU SAUCE

LIGHT GREEN TEA

7-Minute Morning Miso-Vegetable Soup

This quick miso soup recipe is a great way to begin your day!

Serves 3 to 4

- 1 (2- to 3-inch) piece of dried dulse
- 5 cups filtered water
- 1 small onion, peeled, cut in half, and sliced into thin crescents
- 1¾ to 2 tablespoons barley miso paste, diluted with 3 to 4 tablespoons filtered water
- Minced parsley to taste (or dried organic parsley)

Add the dried dulse to the water and bring to a boil in a medium saucepan over medium heat. Add the onion and simmer until soft, 4 to 5 minutes.

(recipe continues)

Stir in the diluted miso, and turn off the heat. Add the parsley and allow to sit for 1 minute. Divide into serving bowls.

Corn Tortillas with Tempeh, Corn, and Onions in Cilantro-Kuzu Sauce

Tempeh combined with corn and onions in a kuzu sauce makes for a delicious, high-protein meal. Because the tempeh is fermented, the protein is easily broken down for maximum nutrition.

Serves 4

- 1 tablespoon sesame oil
- 8 ounces tempeh, cut into 1-inch cubes
- 2 onions, sliced wedge-style
- 2 cups fresh or frozen corn kernels (no need to thaw)
- 3 cups filtered spring water
- ½ teaspoon tamari
- ¾ teaspoon ground ginger
- ⅓ cup finely chopped cilantro
- 1 teaspoon umeboshi vinegar
- 1½ tablespoons kuzu diluted in 2 tablespoons cold water (see Note)
- 4 (6-inch round) corn tortillas, lightly toasted to make them warm and bendable (if overtoasted, they will become hard)

Heat the sesame oil in a heavy skillet over medium-low heat until hot (do not let it burn or smoke!). Add the tempeh cubes and sauté until crisp, about 4 minutes on each side. Remove the tempeh from the pan and let it drain on a paper towel. In a medium soup pot, layer the onions, corn, and sautéed tempeh. Add the water, cover the pot, and bring to a boil over medium-high heat. Lower the heat and cook until the onions are fairly soft, 5 to 7 minutes.

Stir in the tamari and ginger. Simmer for another 5 minutes. Stir in the cilantro and vinegar and cook for 1 to 2 minutes. Add the diluted kuzu in cold water, stirring continuously, until the sauce begins to thicken, about 4 minutes.

Divide the mixture into 4 bowls and serve with the tortillas on the side or use them to make a breakfast wrap.

Note: Kuzu is a natural thickener, and as you add this milky liquid, it signals its readiness when it becomes clear or translucent.

BREAKFAST MENU 4

NATURAL COLD CEREAL WITH SEASONAL FRUIT

SOURDOUGH TOAST WITH PEANUT CREAM

TWIG (KUKICHA) TEA

This breakfast is a familiar one to millions across the country, only it has more healthful ingredients. It is not particularly nourishing, but sometimes we need foods that are familiar. Commercial boxed breakfast cereals typically get anywhere from 22 to 58 percent of their calories from refined sugar and a host of other unnecessary artificial ingredients. Choose more healthful quality cereals from your natural food stores that are fruit sweetened, if at all. Milk can be substituted with better-quality and more healthful soy, oat, almond, or rice milks (be sure to pick sugar-free brands). This is strictly a Transitional Diet breakfast.

Natural Cold Cereal with Seasonal Fruit

Your supermarket and natural food store will offer many types of commercial cereals. Make sure that you pick one with no added sugar.

Serves 1

2 cups sugar-free natural dry cereal
Small amount of soy, almond, oat, or rice milk, to taste
Fresh fruit, preferably organic and in season

Mix the dry cereal with the milk. Add the fruit.

Sourdough Toast with Peanut Cream

Serves 1

1 round tablespoon organic peanut butter (diluted with 2 teaspoons water for a creamy texture)
1 to 2 slices sourdough bread, toasted, if desired

Spread the peanut cream on the toast.

Twig (Kukicha) Tea

This popular tea from the famous tea bush contains about 5 to 7 percent caffeine and provides a full-bodied taste to end a meal. Tea from the twigs are called kukicha and tea from the leaves (higher in caffeine) are called bancha.

Serves 1

Add 1 teabag into a cup with boiling hot water. Steep for 2 to 3 minutes.

BREAKFAST MENU 5

SCRAMBLED TOFU AND VEGETABLES ON WHOLE WHEAT TOAST

TEMPEH BACON

BARLEY BREW

■

Scrambled Tofu and Vegetables on Whole Wheat Toast

This scrambled tofu recipe has been adapted from New Zealand cookbook author Cheryl Beere. It's a great substitution dish in place of eggs and has a similar consistency.

Serves 4

2 tablespoons sesame oil

1 medium carrot, diced

1 rib celery, diced

1 medium onion, diced

¼ teaspoon finely grated fresh gingerroot

2 blocks (approximately 4 ounces each) firm or medium-firm tofu, crumbled

¼ cup finely chopped coriander

¼ teaspoon ground turmeric

¼ teaspoon freshly ground black pepper

2 teaspoons tamari

4 slices sourdough toast

Toasted sesame seeds, for garnish

Heat a large cast-iron skillet or frying pan over low-medium heat. Add the sesame oil. When the oil is hot (*not* burning), add the carrot, celery, and onion and sauté, covered, until soft, approximately 5 minutes. Occasionally, stir the vegetables back and forth to evenly cook. Add the ginger and tofu. Stir gently to combine, and add the coriander, turmeric, pepper, and tamari. Cover and cook, 4 to 5 minutes.

Place a piece of toast on each of 4 plates. Divide the tofu mixture evenly over the toast. Allow to spill over the sides of the toast. Sprinkle each portion lightly with toasted sesame seeds and serve immediately.

Tempeh Bacon

This delicious tempeh bacon recipe was adapted from cookbook authors Mary Estella and Lenore Baum. It calls for cooking the tempeh in a marinade before broiling.

Serves 2

MARINADE

2 tablespoons sweet white miso

½ cup boiling filtered water

1 teaspoon prepared natural mustard

2 bay leaves

2 garlic cloves, minced

¼ teaspoon ground white pepper

8 ounces tempeh cut into small strips

In a large saucepan, use a spoon to mash and dilute the miso with the boiling water. Add the mustard, bay leaves, garlic, and pepper. Stir gently until all ingredients are thoroughly blended. Over medium heat, carefully add the tempeh strips. Turn down to a simmer, cover the pan, and cook for 20 minutes.

Remove the tempeh strips from the marinade and drain on a paper towel. Preheat the broiler.

Place the tempeh strips in single layer on a lightly oiled baking pan. Discard the marinade. Broil the tempeh 6 to 8 minutes, until brown and crisp. Flip the tempeh pieces and broil for an additional 5 minutes, until brown and crisp on the second side.

Note: Tempeh bacon can also be added to stews, sandwiches, stir-fries, and salads.

Variation: For juicier bacon, add 1 teaspoon toasted sesame oil to the marinade before adding the tempeh.

Barley Brew

There are several companies that make a delicious barley coffee, usually called something like barley brew. It's made from barley that has been lightly roasted and ground. You make it in a drip coffeemaker or with a coffee filter. It has a familiar coffee-like taste and its slightly bitter flavor adds a nice finish to a meal. You might want to add a couple of drops of lemon juice for an added zing.

LUNCH MENUS AND RECIPES

LUNCH MENU I

PATRICIA'S LEMON RED LENTIL SOUP

BRUSSELS SPROUTS AND GINGER-PLUM GLAZE

LEAFY GREEN SALAD WITH PARSLEY-LEMON DRESSING

CHILLED MANDARIN ORANGE WEDGES

KUKICHA TEA

Patricia's Lemon Red Lentil Soup

This delicious soup comes from the inspiring kitchen of Patricia Wemhoff.

Serves 4

1 tablespoon sesame oil
2 medium onions, peeled, cut in half, and sliced into thin crescents
2 garlic cloves, minced
½ teaspoon sea salt
1 teaspoon ground cumin
1 cup dried red lentils
4 cups filtered water
1 bay leaf
Small portion lemon zest
1 tablespoon freshly squeezed lemon juice

Heat the sesame oil in a 4-quart pot over medium-high heat. Add onions and sauté until translucent, 5 to 7 minutes. Mash the garlic cloves and mix with the sea salt. Add the garlic mixture and cumin to the onions. Cook about 4 minutes. Add the lentils and water to the onion mixture and bring to a boil, skimming off any foam.

As soon as the soup has reached a boil, reduce the heat to a simmer, add the bay leaf and lemon zest and cook, covered, 25 to 30 minutes. The lentils should be broken and soup mix creamy. Remove from the heat, stir in the lemon juice, remove the bay leaf and whatever lemon zest is visible, and serve hot.

Brussels Sprouts and Ginger-Plum Glaze

This elegant side dish stew from the kitchens of television personality Christina Pirello offers a nice complement to the lentil soup.

Serves 4

> 1 to 2 medium sweet onions, cut into wedges
> 4 to 5 cups whole Brussels sprouts, trimmed and scored on the base
> 1½ teaspoons tamari, or to taste
> 1 cup filtered water
> 2 to 3 teaspoons fresh ginger juice (see Note, page 317)
> 1½ tablespoons kuzu, diluted in 2 tablespoons cold water
> 2 teaspoons umeboshi vinegar, or brown rice vinegar

In a medium pot, layer the onions and then the Brussels sprouts. Sprinkle 1 teaspoon of the tamari over the vegetables. Add the water, cover the pot, and turn the heat to medium. Bring the vegetables to a simmer and cook until the Brussels sprouts are tender, 25 to 40 minutes, testing to make sure the sprouts do not get mushy.

Season with ½ teaspoon tamari, or to taste. Add the ginger juice and simmer for an additional 5 minutes. Gently stir in the kuzu and cook, stirring gently to avoid breaking the vegetables, until a thin glaze forms, 2 to 3 minutes.

Remove from the heat and sprinkle with the vinegar. Serve warm.

■   ■   ■

Leafy Green Salad with Lemon-Parsley Dressing

Serves 4

DRESSING

1 cup organic vegetable stock

1 tablespoon freshly squeezed lemon juice

1 tablespoon balsamic vinegar

1⅓ cups finely chopped fresh parsley

¼ teaspoon sea salt

4 handfuls of mixed wild greens

To make the dressing: In a 1-quart saucepan over high heat, bring the vegetable stock to a boil and let it reduce to 5 to 6 tablespoons, 7 to 12 minutes. Remove from the heat.

Place the still-warm reduced stock, lemon juice, vinegar, parsley, and salt in a blender and blend thoroughly.

Place the greens into a large bowl. Add the dressing, and toss well.

Chilled Mandarin Orange Wedges

Chill a mandarin orange and serve peeled.

Kukicha Tea

Kukicha, or twig tea, is a Japanese blend that is made of stems, stalks, and twigs from the traditional tea bush. It is roasted in a gas-fired cauldron and aged for 2 to 3 years. It has a unique flavor and aroma among teas, due to its being composed of parts of the tea plant that are excluded from most other teas. The health benefits of kukicha tea lie in its alkalizing properties, which help neutralize acidity. It's also an excellent source of catechins, which are polyphenols also found in green tea and known for having cancer-fighting abilities. These are antioxidants with enough power to minimize the effects of free radicals. One of them in particular, called epigallocatechin, contains as much as 100 times the antioxidants of vitamin C and is found in both brown and green tea varieties! Studies have indicated that not only is this catechin capable of preventing cancers but it may also minimize tumors and the spread of cancerous cells. Brew kukicha twig tea in loose form by boiling for 7 to 10 minutes, or from a tea bag.

LUNCH MENU 2

TOFU AND VEGETABLE SESAME STIR-FRY

WALNUT RICE

ASSORTED GREENS WITH CITRUS SPARKLE DRESSING

HERBAL TEA

Tofu and Vegetable Sesame Stir-Fry

Serves 4

1 tablespoon safflower oil
1 medium yellow onion, cut into wedges
2 carrots, sliced on an angle
1 cup corn kernels (fresh or frozen)
2 pounds extra-firm tofu, cut into ½-inch cubes
5 bok choy leaves and stalks, thinly sliced
1½ cups snow peas
½-inch piece gingerroot, peeled and minced
1 garlic clove, minced
1 tablespoon tamari or Bragg Liquid Aminos

Heat the oil in a large skillet over medium-high heat. Add the onion and cook for 2 minutes. Stir in the carrots and corn and cook for 2 minutes more. Add the tofu, cover, and continue to cook, stirring frequently, for 4 minutes. Add the bok choy, snow peas, ginger, and garlic. Cook, stirring, until the bok choy is tender, 3 to 4 minutes more. Mix in the tamari and serve hot.

Walnut Rice

Serves 4

- ¾ cup chopped walnuts
- 2 cups long-grain brown rice, rinsed and drained
- 4 cups filtered water
- ½ teaspoon sea salt
- ⅓ cup minced parsley

Place the walnuts in a small skillet over medium-high heat and roast until fragrant and golden, 15 to 20 minutes.

In a medium pot, add the rice, water, salt, and walnuts. Cover and bring to a boil over medium-high heat. Lower the heat to low and let simmer until the rice is tender, about 45 minutes. Remove from the heat and fluff gently while mixing in the parsley.

Note: If the top of the rice appears dry, gently mix the rice and continue cooking over a low heat for another 2 minutes.

Assorted Greens with Citrus Sparkle Dressing

A similar version of this dressing appears in Christina Pirello's *Cooking the Whole Foods Way.*

Serves 4

DRESSING

- 2 tablespoons olive oil
- 1 teaspoon tamari
- Juice of one lemon
- Juice of 1 orange
- Peel of 1 orange, grated
- 1 scallion, finely chopped
- ¼ roasted red or green bell pepper, finely minced
- Pinch sea salt
- ½ teaspoon powdered ginger
- 3 tablespoons balsamic vinegar

4 handfuls of assorted greens

Warm the oil and tamari in a small saucepan over medium heat for 2 minutes. Add the lemon and orange juices, grated orange peel, scallion, bell pepper, salt, ginger, and vinegar. Whisk together until blended on a low heat. Allow to cool.

Place the greens in a large bowl and toss with the dressing.

LUNCH MENU 3

REBECCA'S GRILLED MILLET AND BUTTERNUT SQUASH CAKES

MISO-GLAZED CARROTS

PRONTO BLANCHED WATERCRESS

GREEN TEA

Rebecca's Grilled Millet and Butternut Squash Cakes

This delicious grilled millet recipe comes from old friend and award-winning author Rebecca Wood.

Serves 4 (3 cakes each)

- 1 cup millet
- 1 teaspoon mustard seeds
- ½ teaspoon curry powder
- 2½ cups filtered water
- 2 cups peeled and diced butternut squash
- 1 teaspoon ground ginger, or minced gingerroot
- ½ teaspoon sea salt
- ½ cup chopped cilantro

Heat a heavy-bottomed skillet (preferably cast iron) over medium-high heat. Add the millet and roast, stirring constantly, until the first seeds pop, about 4 minutes. Rinse the roasted millet with cold water, drain, and set aside.

(recipe continues)

Reheat the skillet over medium-high heat. Add the mustard seeds and curry powder, and roast until the aroma is released, about 1 minute.

In a medium to large saucepan, over high heat, mix the millet, mustard mixture, water, squash, ginger, and salt. Bring to a boil, lower the heat to medium, and simmer, covered, until the millet has absorbed all the water, about 25 minutes. Remove from the heat and allow to cool.

Preheat the broiler to 350°F.

Add the cilantro to the millet mixture and combine well. Wet your hands and form the millet mixture into 12 uniform cakes. Place the cakes on a lightly oiled baking sheet and broil for approximately 3 minutes on each side, or until golden. Serve hot.

Miso-Glazed Carrots

This dish is a simple favorite of mine from Patricia Wemhoff's kitchen.

Serves 4

> 1 tablespoon sesame oil
> ½ cup finely chopped onion
> 3 cups (½-inch slices) carrots
> 1 tablespoon light miso paste
> ¾ cup vegetable broth or filtered water
> 2 teaspoons grated orange zest
> 1 teaspoon grated gingerroot
> ¼ teaspoon toasted sesame oil
> Sea salt to taste

In a heavy, deep skillet, heat the 1 tablespoon sesame oil over medium-high heat. Add the onion and carrots and sauté until the onions are softened and translucent, 5 to 7 minutes.

Cream the miso with ¼ cup of the broth and stir it into the vegetable mixture. Add the remaining vegetable broth, the orange zest, and ginger. Reduce the heat to medium and simmer uncovered until the liquid is reduced to a glaze and the carrots are tender and crisp, 7 to 9 minutes. Remove from the heat, stir in the ¼ teaspoon toasted sesame oil and season with salt.

Pronto Blanched Watercress

Blanching greens is a speedy way to heat a vegetable for better assimilation while retaining its rich green color and without cooking it limp. Blanched greens can be added to salads, tossed in sandwiches, or simmered in the last 3 minutes of soup making. Alternate greens for blanching are kale, collards, mustard greens, bok choy, dandelion, broccoli rabe, turnip greens, and daikon greens.

Serves 4

DRESSING

Pinch sea salt

1 tablespoon freshly squeezed lemon juice

2 teaspoons umeboshi vinegar

1½ teaspoons flaxseed oil

¼ cup filtered water

3 bunches watercress, soaked and drained (see Note)

1 quart filtered water

⅛ teaspoon sea salt

To make the dressing: Place the salt, lemon juice, vinegar, oil, and water in a small jar with a tight-fitting lid. Shake to mix well.

Roughly chop the watercress. In a medium pot over high heat, bring the water to a hearty boil. Add the salt. Drop the watercress into the boiling water and remove after 20 to 30 seconds with a slotted spoon. Transfer the greens to a large bowl, rinse in cool water to stop the cooking process, and toss with the dressing just before serving.

Note: Wash the watercress well and soak it for at least 15 seconds in a bowl of water, scanning for bugs. Raw watercress is known to harbor bugs. Drain before using in the recipe.

LUNCH MENU 4

CREAM OF CELERY-LEEK SOUP

TEMPEH REUBEN

PLAIN AND EASY STEAMED BROCCOLI

CHEF ST. JACQUES'S SPICE COOKIES

DANDELION ROOT TEA

■

Cream of Celery-Leek Soup

This nondairy soup gets its creamy consistency from rolled oats!

Serves 4

2 small leeks, sliced lengthwise, rinsed, and diced
4 to 5 cups filtered water
¾ cup sliced celery
⅔ cup old-fashioned rolled oats
2 tablespoons white miso
Finely chopped parsley, for garnish
Thinly sliced scallion, for garnish
Flaked dulse, for garnish (optional)

In a soup pot over medium heat, add the leeks, add enough of the water to cover, and bring to a boil. Add the celery, and reduce the heat to medium. Simmer for 3 to 4 minutes. Add the remaining water, increase the heat to medium-high, and return to a boil. Add the oats, lower the heat to low, and simmer about 15 minutes.

In a small bowl, combine the miso and ¼ cup of the broth; stir until dissolved. Add the miso to the soup and simmer 1 to 2 minutes. Divide the soup among 4 bowls and garnish each serving with the parsley, scallion, and dulse, if using.

Tempeh Reuben

Of the many tempeh Reuben recipes I've tried, this one from Lenore Baum's *Lenore's Natural Cuisine* is one of my favorites.

Serves 4

- ½ teaspoon toasted sesame oil
- ½ pound tempeh, cut into 1-inch strips
- 1 teaspoon prepared natural mustard
- 1 teaspoon barley miso
- ½ cup filtered water
- 2 garlic cloves, minced
- 1 tablespoon mirin
- 4 cups finely shredded green cabbage
- 1 cup low-salt sauerkraut with juice
- 4 to 5 tablespoon grated uncooked plain mochi, to taste

In a large cast-iron skillet, heat the oil over medium-high heat. Add the tempeh and sauté until golden brown, about 5 minutes on each side.

In a small bowl combine the mustard, miso, and water. Pour the mixture over the tempeh. Add the garlic, mirin, cabbage, and sauerkraut (and its juice) to the tempeh and mix together gently. Simmer, covered, for 20 minutes until the tempeh is tender. Add additional water, if no liquid remains.

Preheat the broiler.

Transfer the mixture to a 2-quart casserole. Sprinkle the mochi over top. Place the casserole under the broiler until the mochi melts and is golden brown, 2 to 3 minutes. Or bake at 350°F, covered, approximately 20 minutes, until melted and golden brown.

Plain and Easy Steamed Broccoli

Sometimes it's important to simply enjoy the natural taste of vegetables without feeling like you have to improve on nature with a sauce, glaze, or dip. This makes an excellent complement to a very flavorful dish such as the Tempeh Reuben.

Serves 4

(recipe continues)

4 stalks of organic broccoli (see Note)

2 to 3 cups filtered water

Chop the broccoli stems and florets. Place a steamer in a medium pot, add the water, and bring to a boil over medium-high heat. Place the broccoli in the steamer, cover, and steam until crisp tender, 4 to 6 minutes. Do not overcook.

Note: Rinse and soak the broccoli for about 1 minute in a large bowl of cold water. Look for little critters, which organic broccoli often contains. Rinse again before using.

Chef St. Jacques's Spice Cookies

For this menu, I've included a recipe for North Carolina chef Benoit St. Jacques's spice cookies, which I adapted from cook and publisher Merle Davis. Merle informs me that, to her knowledge, there is no known cure for spice cookie addiction—you've been warned!

Makes 7 to 10 cookies

1 cup old-fashioned rolled oats

1 cup walnuts

1½ cups pastry flour

½ teaspoon ground cardamom

½ teaspoon ground nutmeg

½ teaspoon ground allspice

½ teaspoon ground cinnamon

1 teaspoon baking soda

½ cup dried currants

Pinch sea salt

2 tablespoons freshly squeezed lemon juice

⅓ to ½ cup safflower oil

½ cup maple syrup

Preheat the oven to 350°F.

Combine the oats and nuts in the bowl of a food processor or blender and process until coarsely chopped. Transfer to a large mixing bowl and add the flour, cardamom, nutmeg, allspice, cinnamon, baking soda, currants, and salt. Mix to combine. In a large bowl, mix the lemon juice, oil, and maple syrup. Add the dry ingredients to the wet and mix well. For each cookie, scoop out about 2 tablespoons of dough, form into a round cookie shape, and place on a lightly oiled baking sheet, about 1 inch apart. Bake 15 to 20 minutes, until browned and fragrant.

LUNCH MENU 5

SWEET RICE AND CHESTNUTS

REFRIED BEANS

CHOPPED MIXED GREENS WITH AVOCADO VINAIGRETTE

HERBAL TEA

Sweet Rice and Chestnuts

This simple rice dish comes from Aveline Kushi's *Complete Guide to Macrobiotic Cooking*. It is a special dish reserved for the Japanese New Year's Day. Unlike other nuts, chestnuts have a very low fat content, 3 to 5 percent. The best part is the unique sweetness they add to the rice. Brown sweet rice is a unique variety containing a slightly higher protein and water percentage than ordinary brown rice. Once cooked, it comes out slightly sticky. I've never grown tired of this dish.

Serves 4

   ½ cup dried chestnuts, soaked overnight (see Note), or 1 cup fresh
   2 cups brown sweet rice
   2 cups filtered water
   ⅓ teaspoon sea salt

Chop the chestnuts in half, set aside. Using cool water, wash the rice free of impurities.

In a medium heavy-bottomed pot, add the chestnuts, rice, water, and salt. Cover and bring to boil over high heat. Lower the heat, and

(recipe continues)

allow the rice to simmer undisturbed, until tender, 50 to 60 minutes. Mix thoroughly and transfer to a serving bowl.

Note: Place the dried chestnuts in a large bowl and cover with 1½ cups of filtered water. The chestnuts will swell as they absorb the water. Canned chestnuts can be used in a pinch but fresh or dried are better.

Refried Beans

The classic Mexican staple of refried beans (*refrito*) doesn't mean fried twice but fried well. You can cook the beans from scratch or more conveniently purchase organic cooked beans in enamel-lined, lead-free cans.

Serves 4

½ to ¾ cup water
⅔ teaspoon sea salt
2 cups canned pinto beans, drained
1 carrot, diced
1 bay leaf
1½ tablespoons olive oil
1 to 1½ cups diced onion
1 teaspoon dried oregano
½ teaspoon dried basil
2 teaspoons ground cumin

Bring the water and salt to a boil in a medium pot over high heat. Add the beans to the pot and stir thoroughly. Add the carrot and bay leaf. Cook until carrots are soft but still firm, approximately 8 minutes.

Meanwhile, in a large, deep-sided skillet, heat the oil over medium heat. Add the onion and sauté until soft, 6 to 8 minutes. Stir in the oregano, basil, and cumin. Continue to sauté until the onions are soft, 5 minutes more, adding some of the bean liquid to prevent the onions from burning.

Lower the heat to low, add the beans, and mash to a thick paste. Cook, stirring and adding water to prevent burning, until heated through, 5 to 8 minutes. Serve hot.

Chopped Mixed Greens with Avocado Vinaigrette

This vinaigrette comes courtesy of Cheryl Beere from *The Atomic Café Cookbook.* Use any kind of greens for this dish, such as spinach, romaine lettuce, arugula, or kale.

Serves 4

VINAIGRETTE

1 garlic clove

1 medium onion, minced

¼ cup rice vinegar

1 tablespoon mirin

½ teaspoon sea salt

1 tablespoon freshly squeezed lemon juice

1 teaspoon black pepper

1 ripe avocado, peeled and roughly chopped

⅓ cup olive oil

4 handfuls of chopped mixed greens

In a blender, combine the garlic and onion and purée until smooth. Add the vinegar, mirin, salt, lemon juice, pepper, and avocado, and blend again until smooth. Add the olive oil and blend fully.

Place the greens in a large bowl and toss with the dressing.

DINNER MENUS AND RECIPES

DINNER MENU I

CREAMY CAULIFLOWER SOUP

LINGUINI WITH ORANGE ROUGHY, PORTOBELLO MUSHROOMS,

AND SUN-DRIED TOMATOES

MIXED BABY GREEN SALAD WITH TAHINI-TART DRESSING

STRAWBERRY KANTEN

MINT TEA

■

Creamy Cauliflower Soup

This recipe comes thanks to Anna MacKenzie, courtesy of the Kushi Summer Conference.

Serves 4

1 large cauliflower, separated into florets
Filtered water
Pinch sea salt
¼ cup white miso
¼ cup umeboshi vinegar
1 teaspoon toasted sesame oil
½ teaspoon freshly grated nutmeg
4 large sprigs parsley, for garnish

Place the cauliflower in a heavy pot. Add enough water to cover it by about three-quarters. Cook the cauliflower over medium-low heat, covered, until tender, about 6 to 8 minutes.

Add the miso, vinegar, and oil, mix to combine and cook until heated through, about 5 minutes. Place the vegetable mixture in a blender and process until smooth.

Divide the soup into 4 bowls, sprinkle each with nutmeg and garnish with a sprig of parsley.

Linguini with Orange Roughy, Portobello Mushrooms, and Sun-Dried Tomatoes

Vegetarians can substitute tempeh or fried tofu in place of fish as a protein component.

Serves 4

1 tablespoon olive oil

2 green onions, finely chopped

1 cup thinly sliced Portobello mushrooms

Sea salt, to taste

1 tablespoon tamari

1 cup sliced sun-dried tomatoes

2 garlic cloves, minced

10 thinly sliced basil leaves, plus additional whole leaves for garnish

¼ cup filtered water

¾ cup sugar-free rice or soy milk

4 (5-ounce) orange roughy fillets (optional)

1 pound dry linguini or spaghetti

Fill a large pot with water and bring to a boil while you prep the rest of the recipe. Add ½ teaspoon sea salt.

In a large skillet, heat the oil over medium-low heat. Add the green onions and sauté until transparent, 4 to 6 minutes. Add the mushrooms and a pinch of salt. Sauté 5 minutes. Add tamari, sun-dried tomatoes, and garlic. Cook, stirring, 2 to 3 minutes. Add the basil leaves, water, milk, and another pinch of sea salt.

Cut the fish into bite-size pieces. Place the fish on the vegetable mixture, lower the heat to low, cover, and continue cooking until tender, 4 to 6 minutes.

Add the linguini to the boiling water and cook according to package instructions, or until the pasta is al dente (tender but firm), usually 5 to 7 minutes. Drain the linguini, but do not rinse. Return the linguini to the cooking pot, add the fish and vegetable mixture. Mix thoroughly, but gently. Divide onto four plates, garnish with basil leaves, and serve hot.

(recipe continues)

Note: If you have oil-packed sun-dried tomatoes, pat dry with a
paper towel before slicing.

Mixed Baby Green Salad with Tahini-Tart Dressing

This salad may be served before, with, or after the main course, according to
your preference.

Serves 4

DRESSING

2 tablespoons umeboshi paste

2 tablespoons toasted tahini (see Note)

2 tablespoons grated onion with the juice

Filtered water, as needed

3 springs fresh parsley, diced

Choice of mixed salad greens and assorted raw vegetables (carrot, white,
radish, tomato, cucumber)

Mix the umeboshi paste, tahini, and grated onion with juice in a small
bowl. Add water to thin to the consistency of standard salad dressing.

Tear any large greens and chop the vegetables into bite-size pieces.
Place the greens and vegetables in a large bowl and toss with the dressing to coat evenly.

Note: Tahini, one of the main ingredients used in the popular
sandwich spread known as hummus, is made into a creamy
spread from shelled sesame seeds and then roasted. It can be purchased in natural food stores and most standard markets.

Strawberry Kanten

Light and refreshing, this is the nearest thing to a natural version of chilled
fruit gelatin, but it is 100 percent vegan. Softer fruits such as cherries, berries,
peaches, and melons do not require cooking before combing with the kanten.
However, firmer-textured fruit such as apples and pears need to be cooked in a
juice and agar-agar mixture to soften.

Serves 4

2½ cups apple juice, or other unsweetened fruit juice of your choice
Pinch of sea salt
3 tablespoons agar-agar flakes (see Note)
1½ to 2 cups chopped strawberries
Mint leaves and orange slices for garnish

Combine the juice, salt, and agar-agar in a large saucepan. Bring to a *slow* boil over low heat. (If you are using firm fruit, add it now.) Simmer, stirring frequently, until the agar-agar is dissolved, 10 to 15 minutes.

Place the strawberries in a serving dish and carefully pour the agar mixture over top. Allow to stand 30 minutes, then refrigerate until firm, at least 30 minutes more. Cut into servable sections, and garnish each serving with mint leaves and an orange slice.

Note: Be sure to bring the mixture to a slow boil. The most common mistake is boiling the agar too quickly, making it sink to the bottom of the pot still intact.

DINNER MENU 2

10-MINUTE SAVORY BROCCOLI-CAULIFLOWER MISO SOUP

NATIVE WILD RICE WITH PECANS AND SHIITAKE-ONION TOPPING

ROASTED ROOT VEGETABLES

PEACH MOUSSE

BARLEY BREW

10-Minute Savory Broccoli-Cauliflower Miso Soup

Serves 4

4 cups filtered water

1 stick dry kombu or 2-by-2-inch piece of dried dulse

1 large cauliflower, chopped, with 3 or 4 small florets reserved

1 bunch broccoli, chopped, with 3 or 4 small florets reserved

2 cups vegetable stock

2 tablespoons kuzu

¼ cup cold filtered water

1½ to 2 tablespoons barley miso paste

3 tablespoons grated mochi, for garnish

1 scallion, finely chopped, for garnish

In a soup pot, bring the 4 cups of water and kombu to a rapid boil. Add all the cauliflower and broccoli. Bring to a boil, cover, lower the heat to simmer, and cook until soft but still firm, 6 to 8 minutes. Gently stir in the vegetable stock, and continue to cook for 1 minute more. Remove from the heat.

Set aside the cauliflower and broccoli florets and transfer the rest of the mixture to a blender. Blend to a puree. Return the puree to the pot and bring to a near boil over medium-high heat. Return the reserved florets to the pot.

Mix the kuzu into the ¼ cup cold water and stir into the soup. Continue to cook until thick, 1 or 2 minutes.

In a small bowl, mix the barley miso paste with ¼ cup of the hot soup, and then stir the paste back into soup. Stir to combine. Divide soup into 4 bowls and garnish with the mochi and scallion.

Native Wild Rice with Pecans and Shiitake-Onion Topping

While I recommend hand-harvested varieties of wild rice (as opposed to the darker colored mainstream varieties), they are harder to come by and usually more expensive. Hand-harvested rice has a distinct nutty and woodsy taste and also requires less water to cook.

Serves 4

TOPPING

2 teaspoons sesame or olive oil

1½ cups filtered water

1 cup minced onion

1 cup shiitake mushroom, diced

2 tablespoons tamari

RICE

2 to 2½ cups springwater

¼ to ⅓ teaspoon sea salt

1 cup wild rice, rinsed under cold running water and drained

½ cup roughly chopped pecans, roasted (see Note)

Finely chopped parsley, garnish

Make the topping: In a saucepan over medium-low heat, add the oil and cook the onion until it becomes clear, 5 to 7 minutes. Add the mushroom and cook, stirring, until soft but not crumbly. After 3 to 5 minutes, stir in the tamari, then remove from heat and set aside.

To make the rice: In a large heavy saucepan, bring the water and salt to a vigorous boil over high heat. Add the rice, cover, and lower the heat to a simmer. Cook until tender (about 45 minutes). Stir in the pecans, cover, and allow the dish to steam for another 10 minutes.

Divide onto 4 plates, top with shiitake mixture, garnish with parsley, and serve hot.

(recipe continues)

Note: To roast the nuts, cook in a heavy-bottomed dry skillet over low heat until brown and fragrant—4 to 6 minutes. They can also be roasted in a 375°F oven for 6 minutes, or until brown and fragrant.

Variation: A popular addition to this dish is ½ cup corn kernels (cooked fresh or frozen and thawed). Stir the corn into the rice mixture before the topping is added.

Roasted Root Vegetables

Thanks to Patricia Wemhoff for this recipe.

Serves 4

> 2 beets, peeled
> 2 parsnips, scrubbed or peeled
> 2 medium rutabagas, peeled
> 1 to 2 tablespoons safflower oil
> Sprinkle sea salt

Preheat oven to 375°F.

Cut the beets and parsnips into ¼-inch slices. Cut the rutabagas into ½-inch cubes. In a baking dish or pan large enough to hold the vegetables in a single layer, toss the vegetables with the safflower oil to coat lightly and dust with sea salt. For best results make sure that each piece touches the pan surface. Bake 30 to 45 minutes, turning once or twice, until thoroughly tender but still firm.

Peach Mousse

Thanks to cook and author Melanie Waxman for this delicious treat.

Serves 4

> 4 cups unsweetened peach juice
> 2 cups filtered water
> Pinch sea salt
> 2 bars agar-agar, rinsed and shredded, or 3 tablespoons agar-agar flakes
> 2 tablespoons almond butter

1 teaspoon pure vanilla extract

2 peaches finely chopped

3 to 4 tablespoons chopped, roasted almonds (see Note, page 312)

In a medium pot over low-medium heat, cook the juice, water, salt, and agar-agar until the agar-agar dissolves, as you continually stir. Pour into a serving dish and refrigerate until it sets, about 60 minutes.

After the mixture has set, transfer it to a blender. Add the almond butter and vanilla and process into a smooth cream. Transfer the cream to a bowl and fold in the peaches. Divide into individual serving dishes and garnish with the almonds.

DINNER MENU 3

DILLED CORN CHOWDER

MILLET MASHED POTATOES WITH CARAWAY

MESCLUN SALAD AND CREAMY LEMON DRESSING

ALMOND DROP COOKIES

TWIG TEA

Dilled Corn Chowder

Serves 4

6 cups springwater

Corn kernels from 4 to 5 ears (reserve cobs, roughly chopped)

Pinch sea salt

3 tablespoons fine-ground cornmeal

2 ribs celery, minced

2 small carrots, minced

1½ tablespoons mellow miso

1 tablespoon chopped fresh dill

(recipe continues)

In a large pot, bring the water to a boil over high heat. Reduce the heat and add the chopped corn cobs, sea salt, and cornmeal, stirring constantly to prevent lumps. Simmer for about 10 minutes. Remove the corn cobs and add the vegetables.

Simmer over medium heat for 15 minutes more. In a cup, dilute the miso with ¼ cup of the soup broth and mix to combine. Add the miso to the pot. Stir and simmer, without letting the soup come to a boil—1 to 2 minutes. Stir in the dill and immediately remove the pot from the heat. Divide into 4 bowls and serve hot.

Millet Mashed Potatoes with Caraway

This delicious millet recipe can be made to have the taste and texture of mashed potatoes. Originally, this dish was created for people who wanted to avoid potatoes but missed that familiar taste and texture. Some research has shown that nightshade family vegetables might cause inflammation for people diagnosed with arthritis. Whether this may apply to you, it's a unique way to enjoy millet as a whole grain entrée.

Serves 4

　　3½ cups filtered water
　　1 cup millet, rinsed and drained
　　1 small onion, diced
　　½ head cauliflower, cut into chunks
　　1 tablespoon caraway seeds
　　⅛ teaspoon sea salt
　　1 tablespoon tamari
　　1 tablespoon finely chopped fresh parsley

In a heavy-bottomed pot with a lid, bring the water to a boil over medium-high heat. Add the millet, onion, cauliflower, caraway seeds, and salt. Cover and cook until the millet is soft and fluffy, about 30 minutes. Check and stir occasionally to prevent sticking or add more water if the mixture becomes too dry.

Remove from heat, add the tamari, and mash the millet. Divide onto individual plates, garnish with parsley, and serve warm.

Mesclun Salad and Creamy Lemon Dressing

Serves 2

DRESSING

2 tablespoons avocado oil

1 tablespoon umeboshi paste

1 tablespoon freshly squeezed lemon juice

¼ cup soft tofu

6 tablespoons filtered water

4 handfuls of mesclun salad greens

To make the dressing: In a small bowl, whisk the oil, umeboshi paste, lemon juice, tofu, and water until well blended.

Place the greens in a large bowl and toss with the dressing until lightly coated.

Almond Drop Cookies

These flourless, oil-free almond cookies are full of delicate flavor with the subtle sweetness of barley malt.

Makes 18 cookies

3 cups sliced almonds

⅓ cup unsweetened apple juice, or as needed

Juice of 1 orange

1 cup rice syrup or barley malt

1 teaspoon pure vanilla extract

½ teaspoon ground cinnamon

⅓ teaspoon sea salt

Preheat the oven to 325°F.

In a blender, grind the almonds to a meal-like consistency. Add enough apple juice to make a smooth paste. In a bowl, mix the almond paste with the remaining ingredients.

Drop the mixture by tablespoons onto a well-oiled baking sheet, 1 to 2 inches apart, and press each cookie lightly with a fork. Bake on a high oven rack for 10 minutes, or until the cookies look golden. They are easy to burn and require careful attention. Cool and store in an airtight container.

DINNER MENU 4

AZTEC BUTTERNUT SQUASH SOUP

GINGER SALMON BAKE

NATIVE AMERICAN HOLIDAY RICE

WATER-FRIED BOK CHOY, SWISS CHARD, AND NAPA CABBAGE

GLAZED APPLES

ROOIBOS TEA

Aztec Butternut Squash Soup

This version of Aztec soup, inspired by Jody Main, makes for a festive table when served in a carved-out pumpkin.

Serves 4

- 1 medium butternut squash
- 2 onions, chopped
- 1 red or green chili, seeded and chopped
- 3 garlic cloves, crushed
- 1 teaspoon sunflower oil
- ⅔ cup raw pumpkin seeds
- 5 to 6 cups filtered water
- ⅓ to ½ teaspoon sea salt

Preheat the oven to 350°F.

Poke several holes in the squash with a fork and set on a baking sheet. Bake for 30 to 40 minutes, until tender.

While the squash is baking, place a medium frying pan over low-heat and sauté the onions, chili, and garlic in the sunflower oil, stirring regularly to avoid scorching, until softened, 8 to 10 minutes.

Toast pumpkin seeds in a heavy skillet over medium heat while the squash is roasting, stirring constantly until they are puffed, popping, and deliciously fragrant, 3 or 4 minutes. Set aside half the seeds for garnish, and blend remaining half in a blender until finely ground, while the seeds are still warm.

Remove the squash from the oven, cut it in half, scoop out seeds and fibers, and cut the flesh into cubes with a sharp knife.

In a large pot, bring the water to a boil over medium-high heat. Add the squash and vegetables from the frying pan. Lower the heat, cover, and simmer gently until the vegetables are tender, 15 minutes. Stir in the ground pumpkin seeds and sea salt. Simmer, coveed, 15 minutes more.

Serve in a tureen (or hollowed-out pumpkin), garnished with the reserved pumpkin seeds.

Ginger Salmon Bake

This is a simple, no-frills recipe anyone can master in minutes.

Serves 4

MARINADE

2 teaspoons fresh ginger juice (see Note)

2 tablespoons tamari

4 tablespoons filtered water

2 scallions, finely chopped

4 (5-ounce) wild salmon fillets

Preheat oven to 400°F.

In a small bowl, whisk together the ginger juice, tamari, water, and scallions. Set aside.

Rinse the salmon fillets in cold water and place in glass baking dish. Cover with the marinade and bake 15 to 20 minutes, or until done to your taste.

Note: To make ginger juice, grate a 1-inch piece of peeled gingerroot to extract about 2 teaspoons fresh ginger juice.

■ ■ ■

Native American Holiday Rice

This rice dish is a holiday staple, and a very popular dish with my clients. It is suitable for any occasion, but especially appropriate for Thanksgiving.

Serves 4

> 1 cup brown rice
> ½ cup wild rice
> 3 cups filtered water
> Pinch sea salt
> ½ cup corn kernels, fresh or frozen
> ½ bunch watercress, minced
> 2 tablespoons roasted tahini butter, thinned in 5 tablespoons water (optional)
> 2 teaspoons tamari (optional)

In a large heavy-bottomed pot, add the brown rice, wild rice, water, and salt. Bring to a boil, then simmer covered for at least 1 hour, or until the water is fully absorbed. (For this dish, pressure-cooking works well, and if this is an available choice, add 1⅓ cup water to 1 cup grain, add sea salt, cover, bring up to pressure, and then cook on a simmer for 55 minutes. This is the most common way to cook short-grain brown rice, but it is optional.)

In a separate pot, break up the corn kernals and add to boiling water for 1 minute. Add the watercress and boil 1 minute more. Drain. Combine the corn and watercress with the brown and wild rice.

Mix in the tahini butter and tamari, if using, and serve warm.

Water-Fried Bok Choy, Swiss Chard, and Napa Cabbage

This green vegetable combination is nutritious and subtly sweet.

Serves 4

> 1 bunch bok choy
> 1 bunch Swiss chard
> ½ napa cabbage
> 1 to 1½ cups filtered water
> 1 tablespoon toasted sesame seeds (see Note)

Wash all the greens and pat thoroughly dry, then chop into small, uniform pieces. In a large pot, bring the water to a boil over medium-high heat. Add the greens. Cover by about one-third, lower the heat to medium, and cook 4 to 6 minutes. Greens should be tender and easy to chew. Drain and serve warm with a garnish of toasted sesame seeds.

> *Note:* To toast the sesame seeds, heat them in a dry skillet over medium heat, stirring frequently to prevent burning, until lightly brown, about 10 minutes. Make extra to have handy as garnish for other dishes. They keep well in a sealed container.

Glazed Apples

Thanks to Christina Pirello for this recipe from *Cooking the Whole Foods Way.*

Serves 4

4 ripe medium apples

Pinch sea salt

1 cup unfiltered, unsweetened, organic (if available) apple juice

1 tablespoon kuzu or arrowroot, dissolved in 3 tablespoons cold filtered water

½ teaspoon fresh ginger juice (see Note, page 317)

Preheat the oven to 350°F.

Cut the apples in half and remove cores. Lay apple halves in a shallow baking dish, cut sides facing up, and dust with sea salt. Cover and bake for 15 minutes, or until tender.

While the apples are baking, heat the apple juice in a small saucepan over low heat until hot. Stir in the dissolved kuzu, stirring until the mixture thickens and clears, 3 to 4 minutes. Add the ginger juice.

Pour the mixture over the cooked apples.

Increase oven heat to 400°F and return the apples to the oven. Bake uncovered, for 15 minutes, or until the glaze sets. Serve warm.

DINNER MENU 5

BROILED HALIBUT WITH LEMON AND CAPERS

SIMPLY BAKED ONIONS

MIXED GREEN SALAD WITH ROMA TOMATOES IN

BASIL-GARLIC VINAIGRETTE

APRICOT SLICES

HERBAL TEA

Broiled Halibut with Lemon and Capers

This recipe has been adapted courtesy of author Christina Pirello.

Serves 4

1 tablespoon olive oil

2 leeks, washed well, and cut thinly lengthwise

1 to 2 teaspoons tamari

2 tablespoons capers, thoroughly drained

1 carrot, cut into 1½-inch matchsticks

4 (4- to 5-ounce) halibut fillets

Filtered water

Juice of 2 lemons

In a large heavy-bottomed skillet, heat the olive oil over medium heat. Add the leeks and tamari and sauté for 2 to 3 minutes. Add the capers and sauté for 1 minute. Add the carrot and continue sautéing for 1 minute more.

Evenly layer the vegetables across the bottom of the skillet and place the halibut on the vegetables. Add a small amount of water to cover the skillet bottom. Cover and cook, until the halibut is tender, 10 to 12 minutes. Transfer the fish and vegetables to a serving dish and pour lemon juice over the fish.

Simply Baked Onions

This is a very simple recipe that requires advance planning because it has to bake for 2 hours. It has an appealing texture and very satisfying sweetness.

Serves 4

    4 medium yellow onions

Preheat oven to 350°F.

    Place the whole, unpeeled onions on a cookie sheet. Bake for 2 hours. Allow the onions to cool until you can handle them. Peel the skins off, slice into quarters, and serve as a side dish.

Mixed Green Salad with Roma Tomatoes in Basil-Garlic Vinaigrette

Serves 4

VINAIGRETTE
2 tablespoons brown rice vinegar
5 tablespoons olive oil
½ cup whole basil leaves
½ teaspoon sea salt
1 garlic clove, coarsely chopped
2 to 3 small Roma tomatoes
4 handfuls mixed greens

To make the vinaigrette: In a blender, combine the vinegar, olive oil, basil, salt, and garlic. Blend until smooth.

    Dice the tomatoes and toss with the mixed greens in a large bowl. Toss well with the vinaigrette to coat evenly.

Apricot Slices

Serves 4

20 slices fresh apricot
Mint leaves, for garnish

Divide the apricot slices among 4 plates. Garnish with the mint leaves.

Agar, agar-agar (ah-gahr): Also known as kanten, agar has a complex carbohydrate quality that acts as a gelling agent. It is the vegetarian alternative to gelatin, which is made up from animal skin, tendons, ligaments, and/or bones.

Barley brew: Barley brew is essentially ground up and roasted barley. When steeped and made into a dripped tea, it has a bold and coffee-like flavor. A nice finish to a dinner meal.

Barley malt syrup: Similar in appearance and taste to molasses, barley malt is composed chiefly of maltose sugar and is made by cooking sprouted barley until it's concentrated into a sweet syrup.

Brown rice vinegar: This unique vinegar has a sharp, tangy flavor. Most superior brands have been fermented for 1 year.

Chestnuts: As well as being extremely low in fat (4 to 8 percent), chestnuts offer a unique texture and unusual sweetness. Their season is the fall. Dried chestnuts can be found in many natural food markets as well as in Asian groceries.

Daikon (dye-kon): This long, white radish is popular in Asian cooking. According to the dietary traditions of Asian medicine, daikon has strong healing properties. It aids in the breakdown and digestion of fat and protein and, for this reason, is often served with fish dishes. It has a subtle diuretic effect.

Gingerroot: A pungent tropical vegetable typically used in stir-fries, animal-protein dishes, and many Asian medicinal preparations. Ginger juice can be easily extracted by grating the root on a porcelain or stainless steel grater, gathering the small ginger fragments, and squeezing them to liberate the juice.

Kanten: See agar.

Kombu (kom-boo): I like to refer to this dried sea vegetable, also known as sea kelp, as Asian bay leaf because it is used much like a bay leaf in soup stocks, medicinal preparations, and bean dishes. Known as the original and natural form of monosodium glutamate, but without the side effects or danger of the excito-toxin concentrate commonly called MSG, kombu is a natural flavor enhancer. Its mineral content is helpful for reducing the gas-producing starches in beans.

Kukicha twig tea (ku-key-cha): A mild, very low-caffeine tea, high in minerals and made from both the stems and twigs of the tea bushes. The stems and twigs are generally roasted, which reduces its caffeine content further. (Most of the caffeine from the tea bush is concentrated in the leaves.) The best brands will be labeled "twig only," to indicate the omission of leaves.

Kuzu (coo-zoo): Also know in the American south as kudzu, this valuable, chalky white root starch is usually used as a thickening agent in sauces and icings. It dissolves only in cold water and must be gradually stirred into a warm liquid so it will thicken and not separate. According to Asian folk medicine, kuzu makes the blood alkaline, is beneficial to the intestines and stomach, and helps relieve muscle pain. It has far more medicinal properties than arrowroot starch powder. Use 1 tablespoon of kuzu to thicken 1 cup of liquid.

Mirin (mihr-ihn): A unique cooking wine from Japan, mirin is made from sweet brown rice, koji rice, and water. It has a light and sweet taste and is often used to complement stronger flavors such as miso, tamari, or vinegar. Purchase only naturally brewed versions that can be found in natural food stores.

Miso (mee-so): An aged, fermented soybean paste that is typically made from grain, soybean, and sea salt, miso is found in a wide array of products. The two common types are dark and light. The darker the miso, the longer it has been fermented, which is considered more strength building and medicinal. Light miso tends to be sweeter, contains less salt, and is fermented for a shorter period of time.

Mochi (moh-chee): Mochi is made from cooked sweet brown rice that has been pounded, formed into square cakes, and dried. Used in Asian folk medicine for its energy-producing effects, mochi was traditionally added to miso soup to help nursing mothers produce more milk. Mochi is very versatile: It can be grated and added to dishes to produce a cheese-like effect; it can be used to produce a flourless and sweet waffle, used in soups or served as a side dish with other foods.

Rice milk: A mildly sweetened (usually with barley malt) grain beverage that can be substituted for milk.

Sea salt: The differences between mine (land) salt and sea salt are a matter of mineral content and bioavailability. The best sea salt is slightly damp, indicating that it has been solar, and not oven, dried. Sea salt is best added during the cooking process, which allows it to chelate to the food. This bonding "vegetablizes" the salt, making it easier to digest. The vegetable, vitamin, and mineral factors help sodium absorption.

Sea vegetable flakes: Many of the more common sea vegetables used worldwide can be purchased in dry, flaked form to be used as a mineral supplement or to neutralize excessive acids in the diet. These include nori, dulse, wakame, and kombu. Flakes are handy to use when you cannot use the whole seaweed (as in dry dulse flakes versus dried whole dulse), otherwise using the actual seaweed is best. These are usually sold on the same rack in natural food stores.

Sesame oil: Sesame oil is a light and nutty-flavored oil that can be used in many dishes. The toasted version is generally used as a flavoring accent and is usually not cooked for any length of time.

Sesame salt (also known as gomashio, goh-mah-shee-o): This condiment is a delicious blend of toasted sesame seeds and sea salt, usually made in a large proportion of 20:1 or 24:1—that is, 20 teaspoons of toasted sesame seeds to 1 teaspoon of sea salt. The seeds are roasted, mixed in a *suribachi* (Asian mortar and pestle with serrated edges) and ground until the sesame seeds are crushed and their oil covers the salt. If made properly, it should not inspire thirst. It is commonly used to enhance the flavor and digestion of whole grains.

Shiitake mushrooms (shee-tah-kay): Shiitake mushrooms, which have a more delicate flavor than other mushrooms, are prized for their medicinal qualities, especially because they help neutralize animal proteins by reducing cholesterol. It is always best to buy loose mushrooms as opposed to those packaged in plastic-wrapped cartons. The dried mushrooms, which are suitable for many cooked dishes and tend to be more concentrated in flavor, are a favorite in many traditional Asian culinary dishes. They can be soaked in water for 10 to 60 minutes before cooking. Their nutritional value is similar in both dried and fresh. Shiitakes have been shown to reduce cholesterol levels and stimulate immune function.

Shoyu: Shoyu is the Japanese term for soy sauce that is naturally fermented and made from soybeans, roasted wheat, and salt. It is fermented in wooden kegs for 18 months to 3 years. See **tamari** to understand the differences between these natural soy sauces.

Soy milk: Soy milk is more of a milk-transitional food. Soy that is not fermented (as are miso, tamari, and tempeh) contains phytoestrogens called isoflavones that may mimic the activity of the estrogen hormone in your body. The effects of soy isoflavones on human estrogen levels are very complex and not identical for all. For many people, soy is generally safe to consume in moderation and can have a modest effect on estrogen levels. When used in many traditional dishes in Japan, the amount is minuscule compared to what is being suggested in current Western natural food cookbooks. So, it comes down to a matter of volume and frequency. Soy milk has lower fat and chemical residue than cow's milk, a small molecular structure (which prevents allergy reactions), fewer calories, and virtually no cholesterol. However, it should still be used, if at all, in moderation, and *not* as a replacement for dairy milk.

Soy sauce: This is a standard term for the dark and very salty liquid on every Asian restaurant table. Unfortunately, commercial soy sauces are not brewed with traditional methods, which take many months or even years. Many commercial brands use chemicals and/or yeast to speed the fermentation process. Also, many contain sugar, corn syrup, artificial colors and flavors, and MSG.

Tahini (tah-hee-nee): Made from unhulled sesame seeds, tahini has a nutty flavor that lends well to such dishes as hummus. However, tahini is high in oil content, which means fat, and is something that should be minimized in daily foods. Canned tahini is often bitter, grainy, and rarely organic. Arrowhead Mills, Westbrae, MaraNatha, Brad's, and

Tohum all distribute organic, quality tahini butters. Roasted tahini has a fuller flavor and is used more frequently in recipes. Ideally, since toxins are usually stored more easily in fats, insist on organic when buying nut butters or seed oil.

Tempeh (temp-pay): This fermented soybean product, originally from Indonesia, contains more than 50 percent more protein per volume than hamburger, yet it is cholesterol free. Frequently flavored with strong seasonings such as ginger, vinegar, soy sauce, mustard, and garlic, it can be grilled, steamed, sautéed, or baked. Tempeh can be found in the refrigerator section of natural food stores and in many well-stocked supermarkets.

Tofu (toe-fu): Made from soybeans, tofu is a healthy source of calcium and vegan protein. Traditionally, tofu was eaten in small quantities in soups and side dishes. Its blandness makes it a good candidate for mixing with other foods due to its unique ability to absorb flavors. It comes in soft and firm white blocks. Soft tofu is more frequently used in soups and for creamy sauces. Firm, especially extra-firm, tofu is best for frying, baking, and grilling. You can enhance the degree that tofu can absorb flavors by draining off the excess water. Place the tofu between two small wooden cutting boards in a shallow pan or dish, add a weight to the top board, and let sit for 20 to 25 minutes to drain the excess water.

Umeboshi paste (uhm-ee-bou-she): The bright pink umeboshi plum is similar to the apricot, but with a salty and sour taste. The plums are picked unripened and fermented in a wooden keg for nearly 1 year. High in iron, they have an exceptional natural antibiotic quality and are used in many Asian folk remedies. The paste is made from the pureed meat of the plum. Umeboshi paste is most frequently used in salad dressings, sushi, and sauces. Used 1 level teaspoon of umeboshi paste in 1 cup of twig-only tea to remedy an upset stomach fairly quickly. It's a standard part of my first-aid travel kit!

Umeboshi vinegar: This vinegar is a byproduct of the umeboshi process and is actually more of a salt brine liquid than a vinegar. It is most frequently used in salad dressings, pasta sauces, and with cooked greens.

Zest: This is another word for the colored part of citrus fruit skin, prepared by scraping or cutting the rind of unwaxed fruits. It is most commonly used from lemon, orange, citron, and lime. Too often, the white part (the underskin), which gives a bitter aftertaste, comes away with the zest when a knife is used.

RESOURCES

ALTERNATIVE PHYSICIAN ORGANIZATIONS

Physicians Committee for Responsible Medicine: Promotes preventive medicine, whole foods nutrition, ethical research practices, and compassionate medical policy. It publishes *Good Medicine*, a quarterly journal. (pcrm.org)

ALTERNATIVE APPROACHES TO CANCER: ORGANIZATIONS AND PATIENT SERVICES

National Center for Complementary and Alternative Medicine: Evaluates and provides information about complementary and alternative medicine to health providers and the public. (nccam.nih.gov)

Ralph Moss, PhD: Leading author and cancer treatment consultant. (cancerdecisions .com)

Prostate Cancer Research Institute: It hosts an annual conference in Los Angeles and has an impressive faculty of leading physicians and researchers who share cutting-edge therapies, new research, and support services. (prostate-cancer.org)

Cancer Control Society: Maintains an online list of alternative physicians and therapies and sponsors an annual exposition. (cancercontrolsociety.com)

Annie Appleseed Project: Provides information, education, advocacy, and awareness for people with cancer, their family, and their friends. It sponsors an annual conference. (annieappleseedproject.org)

RECOMMENDED BOOKS ON ALTERNATIVE APPROACHES TO CANCER

Blum, Ralph and Mark Scholz. *Invasions of the Prostate Snatchers*. New York: Random House, 2010.

Hirshberg, Caryle and Marc Ian Barasch. *Remarkable Recovery: What Extraordinary Healings Tell Us about Getting Well and Staying Well*. New York: Riverhead Books, 1995.

Lerner, Michael. *Choices in Healing: Integrating the Best of Conventional and Complementary Approaches to Cancer*. Cambridge: MIT Press, 1994.

LeShan, Lawrence. *Cancer as a Turning Point*. New York: Plume, 1994.

Moss, Ralph. *Antioxidants against Cancer*. New York: Equinox, 2000.

Moss, Ralph. *The Cancer Industry: The Classic Exposé of the Cancer Establishment*. New York: Paragon House, 1989.

Quillin, Partick with Noreen Quillin. *Beating Cancer with Nutrition*. Rev. ed. Tulsa, OK: Nutrition Time Press, 1998.

RECOMMENDED BOOKS ON GENERAL NUTRITION

Appleton, Nancy. *Lick the Sugar Habit*. New York: Warner Books, 1986.

Dufty William. *Sugar Blues*. New York: Warner Books, 1975.

Northrup, Christiane. *Woman's Bodies, Woman's Wisdom*. New York: Bantam Books, 1994.

Shurtleff, William and Akiko Aoyagi. *The Book of Miso*. New York: Ballantine, 1981.

Varona, Verne. *Macrobiotics for Dummies*. New York: Wiley Publications, 2009.

RECOMMENDED BOOKS ON HERBAL NUTRITION

Moss, Ralph. *Herbs against Cancer: History and Controversy.* New York: Equinox Books, 1998.

Yance, Donald R. Jr. with Arlene Valentine. *Herbal Medicine, Healing and Cancer.* Chicago: Keats Publishing, 1999.

RECOMMENDED BOOKS ON SPECIFIC NUTRITIONAL TOPICS

Campbell, T. Colin. *The China Study.* Dallas, TX: BenBella Books, 2006.

Cohen, Robert. *Milk: The Deadly Poison.* Englewood Cliffs, NJ: Argus Publishing, 1998.

Lyman, Howard F. *Mad Cowboy: Plain Truth from the Cattle Rancher Who Won't Eat Meat.* New York: Scribner, 1998.

Oski, Frank. *Don't Drink Your Milk.* New York: Health Services, 1983.

COOKBOOKS

Baum, Lenore. *Lenore's Natural Cuisine.* Farmington Hills, MI: Culinary Publications, 2000.

Kushi, Aveline with Alex Jack. *Aveline Kushi's Complete Guide to Macrobiotic Cooking.* New York: Warner Books, 1985.

Legg, Roanne. *For the Love of Eating.* Ashland, OR: Laughing Rain, 2013.

McCarty, Meredith. *Fresh from a Vegetarian Kitchen.* New York: St. Martin's Press, 1995.

McCarty, Meredith. *Sweet and Natural.* New York: St. Martin's Press, 1999.

Nishimura, Mayumi. *Mayumi's Kitchen.* Tokyo: Kodansha International, 2010.

Pirello, Christina. *Christina Cooks.* New York: Perigee Books, 2004.

Pirello, Christina. *Cooking the Whole Foods Way.* Rev. New York: Perigee Books, 2007.

Sroufe, Del. *Forks Over Knives: The Cookbook.* New York: The Experiment, 2012.

Watson-Tara, Marlene. *Macrobiotics for All Seasons.* Berkeley, CA: North Atlantic Books, 2013.

Wolff, Meg. *Becoming Whole.* Camden, ME: Lulu.com, 2006.

Wolff, Meg. *A Life in Balance: Delicious Plant-Based Recipes for Optimal Health.* Camden, ME: Down East Books, 2010.

Wood, Rebecca. *The Splendid Grain.* New York: William Morrow & Co, 1997.

RELATED HEALING BOOKS: STRESS MANAGEMENT, PSYCHOLOGY, SPIRITUALITY

Frankl, Viktor. *Man's Search for Meaning.* Rev. ed. New York: Touchstone Books, 1984.

Siegel, Bernie. *How to Live Between Office Visits.* New York: HarperCollins, 1993.

Siegel, Bernie. *Love Medicine and Miracles.* New York: Harper & Row, 1986.

Wolpe, David. *Making Loss Matter.* New York: Riverhead Books, 1999.

RECOMMENDED BOOKS ON THE HAZARDS OF MEDICAL RADIATION

Committee on the Biological Effects of Ionizing Radiation. *Health Exposure to Low Levels of Ionizing Radiation.* Washington, DC: National Academy Press, 1990.

Gofman, John. *Radiation-Induced Cancer.* San Francisco: CNR Books, 1990.

Moss, Ralph. *Questioning Chemotherapy.* New York: Equinox Books, 1995.

RECOMMENDED BOOKS ON VISUALIZATION AND GUIDED IMAGERY

Naparstek, Belleruth. *Staying Well with Guided Imagery: How to Harness the Power of Your Imagination for Health and Healing.* New York: Warner Books, 1994.

Simonton, O. Carl, Stephanie Matthews-Simonton, and James L. Creighton. *Getting Well Again.* Rev. ed. New York: Bantam, 1992.

MAIL-ORDER (AND ONLINE) NATURAL FOODS

Eden Foods: edenfoods.com

GoldMine Natural Foods: goldminenaturalfoods.com

South River Miso Company: southrivermiso.com

Westbrae Natural Foods: westbrae.com

Hand-Foraged Natural Organic Wild Rice

Leech Lake Band of Ojibwe: www.llojibwe.org/drm/fisheries/wildrice.html

Wild Rice Direct: wildricedirect.com

Sea Salt

Recommended: Fleur de Sel (Flower of the Ocean), a hand-harvested top layer of highly
mineralized sea salt available at natural food stores or directly online. (selinanaturally
.com/flower-of-the-ocean)

Specific Nutrients Mentioned in *Nature's Cancer-Fighting Foods*

Maitake D-fraction: Mushroom extract and capsules. Available at natural food markets
and online retailers. (allstarhealth.com)

Maitake dried whole mushroom. (goldminenaturalfoods.com)

Milk thistle: Recommended brands include Jarrow Formulas, Source Naturals, and
Mariposa Botanicals.

Miso: Recommended brands include South River Miso Company. (southrivermiso.com)

Sun chlorella: Available at natural food markets.

MISCELLANEOUS INTERNET RESOURCES AND INFORMATION

Cancer Guide: Steve Dunn's cancer information page, cancerguide.org

Christina Pirello: TV cooking show personality, christinacooks.com

Commonweal: commonweal.org

Holistic Holiday at Sea Cruise: Yearly Caribbean cruise with quality natural foods and
on-board educational programs, atasteofhealth.org

Meredith McCarty: Cookbook author, healingcuisine.com

National Center for Complementary and Alternative Medicine: nccam.nih.gov

Ralph Moss, PhD: cancerdecisions.com

REFERENCES

INTRODUCTION

Doctors interrupting patients: Shannon Brownlee, "The Doctor Will See You—If You're Quick." *Newsweek*, April 16, 2012.

Courses in nutrition: John Robbins, *Reclaiming Our Health* (Novato, CA: Kramer, 1996).

Barnard quotation: Neal Barnard, *Foods That Fight Pain* (New York: Three Rivers Press, 1998), pp. xvi–xvii.

Medical schools: Kelly M. Adams, Karen C. Lindell, and Steven H. Zeisel, "Status of Nutrition Education in Medical Schools," *American Journal of Clinical Nutrition* 83, no. 4 (2006): 941S–944S.

Research on smoking: Sophie Egan, "Why Smoking Rates Are at New Lows," *New York Times*, June 25, 2013, well.blogs.nytimes.com/2013/06/25/why-smoking-rates-are-at-new-lows/?_r=0.

Signed statement (1992): Supriya Lahiri et al., "Employment Conditions as Social Determinants of Health, Part I: The External Domain," *New Solutions: A Journal of Environmental and Occupational Health Policy* 16, no. 3 (2006): 267–288.

Research on cancer: S. Epstein, "Winning the War Against Cancer? . . . Are They Even Fighting It?," *The Ecologist* 28, no. 2 (1998): 69–80.

Cancer and nutrition:

American Cancer Society, "Cancer Facts and Figures 2013," cancer.org/research/cancer factsstatistics/cancerfactsfigures2013/index.

R. R. Butrum et al., "NCI Dietary Guidelines: Rationale," *American Journal of Clinical Nutrition* 48 (1988): 888–895.

Department of Health and Human Services, *The Surgeon General's Report on Nutrition and Health*, DDHS Publication 88-50210 (Washington, DC: U.S. Government Printing Office, 1988).

National Academy of Sciences, National Research Council, and Food and Nutrition Board, *Diet and Health: Implications for Reducing Chronic Disease Risk* (Washington, DC: National Academy Press, 1989).

Charles Simone, *Cancer and Nutrition: A Ten-Point Plan to Reduce Your Risk of Getting Cancer* (New York: Avery, 1994).

World Cancer Research Fund: Cancer Society of New Zealand, "Reducing Your Risk of Bowel Cancer," 2013. cancernz.org.nz/assets/files/info/Information%20Sheets/Info%20Sheets%202013/BowelCancer_Risk2013FINAL.pdf.

Cancer and the rise of technology: R. Waller, "The Diseases of Civilization," *The Ecologist* 1, no. 2 (1970).

Cancer and blood sugar: Par Stattin et al., "Prospective Study of Hyperglycemia and Cancer Risk," *Diabetes Care* 30, no. 30 (2007): 561–567.

Scientific support:

"Harvard Heart Letter," Havard Health Publications, October 2009. health.harvard.edu/newsletters/Harvard_Heart Letter/2009/October/11-foods-that-lower-cholesterol.

J. S. de Munter, F. B. Hu, D. Spiegelman, et al., "Whole Grain, Bran, and Germ Intake and Risk of Type 2 Diabetes: A Prospective Cohort Study and Systematic Review," *PLoS Med* 4 (2007): e261.

A. Schatzkin, T. Mouw, Y. Park, et al., "Dietary Fiber and Whole-Grain Consumption in Relation to Colorectal Cancer in the NIH-AARP Diet and Health Study," *American Journal of Clinical Nutrition* 85 (2007): 1353–1360.

Frank Speizer, "The Nurses' Health Study," 1976. channing.harvard.edu/nhs/?page_id=70.

L. Strayer, D. R. Jacobs Jr., C. Schairer, et al., "Dietary Carbohydrate, Glycemic Index, and Glycemic Load and the Risk of Colorectal Cancer in the BCDDP Cohort," *Cancer Causes and Control* 18 (2007): 853–863.

CHAPTER 1: TEN ESSENTIAL KEYS FOR TAKING CONTROL OF YOUR TOTAL WELL-BEING

A call to meaning: Viktor Frankl, *Man's Search for Meaning* (New York: Touchstone Books, 1984).

Positive attitude: Paul Pearsall, *Super Immunity* (New York: Fawcett Books, 1988).

Taking responsibility: Sheldon Greenfield, Sherrie Kaplan, and John Ware Jr., "Expanding Patient Involvement in Care: Effects on Patient Outcomes," *Annals of Internal Medicine* 102, no. 4 (1985): 520–528.

Experiment: Bernie Siegel, *How to Live Between Office Visits* (New York: HarperCollins, 1993).

Active, healthful lifestyle:

D. Albanes et al., "Physical Activity and Risk of Cancer in the HANES I Population," *American Journal of Public Health* 79 (1989): 744–750.

L. Berstein et al. "Physical Exercise and Reduced Risk of Breast Cancer in Young Women," *Journal of the National Cancer Institute* 86 (1994): 1403–1408.

C. M. Freidenreich et al., "Physical Activity and the Risk of Breast Cancer," *European Journal of Cancer Prevention* 4 (1995): 145–151.

R. E. Frisch et al., "Lower Prevalence of Breast Cancer and Cancers of the Reproductive System among Former College Athletes Compared to Non-Athletes," *British Journal of Cancer* 52 (1985): 885–891. Cited in Joseph Keon, *The Truth About Breast Cancer* (Mill Valley, CA: Parissound, 1999), p. 142.

Maryce M. Jacobs, ed., *Exercise, Calories, Fat and Cancer* (New York: Plenum Press, 1992).

R. S. Paffenbarger and I. M. Lee, "Physical Activity and Fitness for Health and Longevity," *Research Quarterly for Exercise and Sport* 67, suppl. 3 (1996): S11–S28.

A. P. Simopoulous et al., "Energy Imbalance and Cancer of the Breast, Colon, and Prostate," *Medical Oncology and Tumor Pharmacotherapy* 7 (1990): 109–120.

P. Suadicani, H. Ole Hein, and F. Gyntelberg, "Lifestyle, Social Class, and Obesity: The Copenhagen Male Study," *European Journal of Cardiovascular Prevention and Rehabilitation* 12, no. 3 (2005): 236–242.

I. Thune et al., "Physical Activity and the Risk of Breast Cancer," *New England Journal of Medicine* 336 (1997): 1269–1275. Cited in Joseph Keon, *The Truth About Breast Cancer* (Mill Valley, CA: Parissound, 1999).

Stress reduction: Interview with Hans Selye in Robert Oates, *Celebrating the Dawn* (New York: Putnam, 1976).

Humor as medicine:

L. S. Berk et al., "Eustress of Mirthful Laughter Modifies Natural Killer Cell Activity," *Clinical Research* 37 (1989): 115.

L. S. Berk et al., "Humor Associated Laughter Decreases Cortisol and Increases Spontaneous Lymphocyte Blastogenesis," *Clinical Research* 36 (1988): 435.

L. S. Berk, "Neuroendocrine and Stress Hormone Changes During Mirthful Laughter," *American Journal of Medicine* (1989): 298–396.

Larry Dossey, *Healing Words: The Power of Prayer and the Practice of Medicine* (New York: HarperCollins, 1994).

Larry Dossey, "'Now You Are Fit to Live': Humor and Health," *Alternative Therapies* 2, no. 5 (1996): 8–13, 98–100.

W. Fry and W. Salameh, eds., *Handbook of Humor and Psychotherapy* (Sarasota, FL: Professional Resource Exchange, 1986).

Love:

David McClelland et al., "The Effect of Motivational Arousal Through Films on Salivary Immunoglobulin," *Psychology and Health* 2 (1988): 31–52.

H. Medalie and U. Goldbourt, "Angina Pectoris Among 10,000 Men II: Psychosocial and Other Risk Factors as Evidenced by a Multivariate Analysis of Five-Year Incidence Study," *American Journal of Medicine* 60 (1976): 910–921. Cited in Larry Dossey, *Healing Words* (New York: HarperCollins, 1994).

Strong sense of faith:

Gerald Bonner, *St. Augustine of Hippo: Life and Controversies*, 3rd ed. (Norwich, UK: Canterbury Press, 2009).

Theodore M. Brown, "The Growth of George Engel's Biopsychosocial Model," Corner Society Presentation, May 24, 2000. human-nature.com/free-associations/engel1.html.

Larry Dossey, *Prayer Is Good Medicine: How to Reap the Healing Benefits of Prayer* (New York: HarperCollins, 1996).

A. Scott Dowling. "George Engel, MD (1913–1999)," *American Journal of Psychiatry* 162, no. 11 (2005): 2039.

Bruno Klopfer, "Psychological Variables in Human Cancer," *Journal of Projective Techniques* 21, no. 4 (1957): 331–340.

Gratitude: Robert Emmons and Michael McCollough, "Counting Blessings Versus Burdens: An Experimental Investigation of Gratitude and Subjective Well-Being in Daily Life," *Journal of Personality and Social Psychology* 84, no. 2 (2003): 377–389.

CHAPTER 2: EATING HABITS, FOOD QUALITY, AND CANCER PREVENTION

Increased meat consumption: Earth Policy Institute, "Rising Meat Consumption Takes Big Bite Out of Grain Harvest," November 22, 2011. earth-policy.org/data_high lights/2011/highlights22.

Staple foods:

G. Griffiths, L. Trueman, T. Crowther, et al., "Onions: A Global Benefit to Health." *Phytotherapy Research* 16, no. 7 (200): 603–615.

"Meat Production Wastes Natural Resources," People for the Ethical Treatment of Animals. peta.org/issues/animals-used-for-food/meat-wastes-natural-resources/#ixzz2oqOxj6Z7.

Andrew Muhammad et al., "International Evidence on Food Consumption Patterns: An Update Using 2005 International Comparison Program Data," U.S. Department of Agriculture, March 2011. ers.usda.gov/publications/tb-technical-bulletin/tb1929.aspx#.UtVRoKW5jDc.

Diet and cancer:

Neal Barnard, *Foods That Fight Pain* (New York: Three Rivers Press, 1998).

Keith I. Block and Charlotte Gyllenhaal, *Nutrition: An Essential Tool in Cancer Therapy* (Washington, DC: Office of Technology Assessment, U.S. Congress, 1990).

Colin T. Campbell, *The China Study* (Dallas: Benbella Books, 2004).

J. J. Decosse, H. H. Miller, and M. L. Lesser, "Effect of Wheat Fiber and Vitamins C and E on Rectal Polyps in Patients with Familial Adenomatous Polyposis," *Journal of the National Cancer Institute* 81 (1989): 1290–1297. Cited in Neal D. Barnard, *Foods That Fight Pain.*

Robert J. Hatherill, *Eat to Beat Cancer* (Los Angeles: Renaissance Books, 1998).

M. A. Malfatti and J. S. Felton, "Susceptibility to Exposure to Heterocyclic Amines from Cooked Food: Role of UDP Glucuronosyltransferases," in *Nutritional Genomics: Discovering the Path to Personalized Nutrition*, eds. Jim Kaput and Raymond L. Rodriguez (Hoboken, NJ: Wiley: 2006): 331–352.

The Million Woman Study, Oxford University, 1996–2001. millionwomenstudy.org/introduction.

David E. Nelson, Dwayne W. Jarman, and Timothy S. Naimi, "Alcohol-Attributable Cancer Deaths and Years of Potential Life Lost in the United States," *American Journal of Public Health* 103, no. 4 (2013): 641–648.

Madlen Schütze et al., "Alcohol Attributable Burden of Incidence of Cancer in Eight European Countries Based on Results from Prospective Cohort Study," *BMJ (British Medical Journal)* 342 (2011): d1584.

R. Sinha et al., "High Concentrations of the Carcinogen 2-Amino-1-Methyl-6-Phenylimidazo-[4,5] Pyridine (PhIP) Occur in Chicken but Are Dependent on Cooking Method," *Cancer Research* 55 (1995): 4516–4519.

P. Toniolo et al., "Calorie-Providing Nutrients and Risk of Breast Cancer," *Journal of the National Cancer Institute* 81 (1989): 278. Cited in Neal D. Barnard, *Foods That Fight Pain* (New York: Three Rivers Press, 1998).

CHAPTER 3: NUTRITION'S TOP TRIO: CARBOHYDRATES, FATS, AND PROTEINS

Jean Anthelme Brillat-Savarin, *Physiologie du goût* [The Physiology of Taste] (Gloucestershire, UK: Echo Library, 2008). Originally published 1825.

Carbohydrates:

N. F. Boyd et al., "Effects at Two Years of a Low-Fat, High-Carbohydrate Diet on Radiologic Features of the Breast: Results from a Randomized Trial," *Journal of National Cancer Institute* 89, no. 7 (1977): 488–498.

M. Digirolamo, *Diet and Cancer: Markers, Prevention and Treatment* (New York: Plenum Press, 1994).

Will Durant and Ariel Durant, *The Story of Civilization* (MJF Books, 1993).

D. B. Leeper et al., "Effect of IV Glucose Versus Combined IV. Plus Oral Glucose on Human Tumor Extracellular pH for Potential Sensitization to Thermoradiotherapy," *International Journal of Hyperthermia* 14, no. 3 (1998): 257–269.

F. Rossi-Fanelli et al., "Abnormal Substrate Metabolism and Nutritional Strategies in Cancer Management," *Journal of Parenteral and Enteral Nutrition* 15, no. 6 (1991): 680–683.

P. Smith-Barbaro et al. "Carcinogen Binding to Various Types of Dietary Fiber," *Journal of the National Cancer Institute* 67, no. 2 (1981): 495–497.

N. E. Spingarn, L. A. Solcum, and H. G. Weisburger, "Formation of Mutagens in Cooked Foods. II. Foods with High Starch Content," *Cancer Letters* 9, no. 1 (1980): 7–12.

D. Steinhausen et al., "Evaluation of Systemic Tolerance of 42.0 Degrees C Infrared-A Whole-Body Hyperthermia in Combination with Hyperglycemia and Hyperoxemia. A Phase-I Study," *Strahlentherapie und Onkologie* [*Journal of Radiation and Oncology*] 170, no. 6 (1994): 322–334.

T. Volk et al., "pH in Human Tumor Xenografts: Effect of Intravenous Administration of Glucose," *British Journal of Cancer* 68, no. 3 (1993): 492–500.

M. Von Ardenne, "Principles and Concept 1993 of the Systemic Cancer Multistep Therapy (SCMT). Extreme Whole-Body Hyperthermia Using the Infrared-A Technique IRATHERM 2000—Selective Thermosensitisation by Hyperglycemia—Circulatory Back-Up by Adapted Hyperoxemia," *Strahlentherapie und Onkologie* [*Journal of Radiation and Oncology*] 170, no. 10 (1994): 581–589.

O. Warburg, "On the Origin of Cancer Cells," *Science* 123 (1956): 309–314.

World Health Organization report. Cited in V. Melina, B. Davis, and V. Harrison, *Becoming Vegetarian* (Macmillan Canada, 1994).

Fats:

Bob Arnot, *The Breast Cancer Prevention Diet* (Boston: Little, Brown, 1998).

Neal D. Barnard, "Cancer and Your Immune System," *Nutrition Advocate* 1, no. 4 (1995): 4-5.

BreastCancer.org, "U.S. Breast Cancer Statistics," breastcancer.org/symptoms/under stand_bc/statistics.

D. M. Demke et al., "Effects of a Fish Oil Concentrate on Patients with Hypercholesterolemia," *Atherosclerosis* 70 (1988): 73–80.

Mary G. Enig, "A New Look at Coconut Oil," 2000, westonaprice.org/know-your-fats/ new-look-at-coconut-oil.

Caldwell B. Essenstyn Jr., *Prevent and Reverse Heart Disease: The Revolutionary, Scientifically Proven, Nutrition-Based Cure* (New York: Avery, 2008).

W. S. Harris et al., "Effects of a Low-Saturated-Fat, Low-Cholesterol Fish Oil Supplement in Hypertriglyceride Patients," *Annals of International Medicine* 109 (1988): 465–470.

Donald Hensrud, "Olive Oil: What Are the Health Benefits?," mayoclinic.com/health/ food-and-nutrition/AN01037.

C. Paddock, "Omega-3 Fish Oil Supplements May Not Offer Heart Benefits After All," *Medical News Today*, 2012, medicalnewstoday.com/articles/250142

Timothy Regan, "Myocardial Blood Flow and Oxygen Consumption During Postprandial Lipemia and Heparin-Induced Lipolyses" *Circulation* 23 (1961): 55–63. Cited in Julian M. Whitaker, *Reversing Heart Disease* (New York: Warner Books, 1985).

R. Talamini, "Special Medical Conditions and Risk of Breast Cancer," *British Journal of Cancer* 75, no. 11 (1997): 1699–1703.

Paolo Toniolo et al., "Calorie-Providing Nutrients and Risk of Breast Cancer," *Journal of the National Cancer Institute* 81 (1989): 278.

J. J. Vitale and S. A. Broitman. "Lipids and Immune Function," *Cancer Research* 41 (1981): 3706–3710.

Robert Vogel et al., "The Postprandial Effect of Components of the Mediterranean Diet on Endothelial Function," *Journal of the American College of Cardiology* 36, no. 5 (2000): 1455–1460.

Fiber: Denis Burkitt, *Don't Forget Fibre in Your Diet: To Help Avoid Many of Our Commonest Diseases* (London: Martin Dunitz, 1979).

Glycemic load: Bill Campbell, "Glycemic Load (GL) vs. Glycemic Index (GI)," Age Management Optimal Wellness Centers, July 18, 2011. http://agemanagement optimalwellnesscenters.com/weight-loss/cat-weight-loss-female/glyemic-loadgl-vs -glyemic-index-gi.html.

Proteins:

"Diet, Nutrition and the Prevention of Chronic Diseases," scientific background papers of the joint World Health Organization and the Food and Agricultural Organization of the United Nations (WHO/FAO) expert consultation, Geneva, January 28–February 1, 2002. *Public Health Nutrition* 7, no. 1A (2004): Supplement 1001.

R. B. Mazess and W. Mather, "Bone Mineral Content of North Alaskan Eskimos," *American Journal of Clinical Nutrition* 27, no. 9 (1974): 916–924.

National Kidney and Urologic Diseases Information Clearinghouse (NKUDIC), "Diet for Kidney Stone Prevention," February 2013. kidney.niddk.nih.gov/Kudiseases/pubs/kidneystonediet/index.aspx#protein.

National Research Council, Committee on Diet, Nurtition, and Cancer, *Diet, Nutrition, and Cancer* (Washington, DC: National Academies Press, 1982). nap.edu/openbook.php?isbn=0309032806.

"Protein and Amino Acid Requirements in Human Nutrition," Report of a joint World Health Organization and the Food and Agricultural Organization of the United Nations (WHO/FAO) expert consultation, 2007. who.int/nutrition/publications/nutrientrequirements/WHO_TRS_935/en.

William J. Visek, "Intestinal Cancer May Be Increased by Meat Ammonia," *Medical Tribune* (1972). Cited in A. Thrash and C. Thrash, *Nutrition for Vegetarians* (Seale, AL: New Life Style Books, 1996).

CHAPTER 4: PHYTOCHEMICAL SUPERHEROES AND AMAZING ANTIOXIDANTS

Lawrence J. Appel, Edgar R. Miller, et al., "Effect of Dietary Patterns on Serum Homocysteine: Results of a Randomized, Controlled Feeding Study," *Circulation* 102 (2000): 852–857.

"Calming the GI Tract," *Science* 284, no. 5423 (1999): 2053.

E. Cameron and L. Pauling, "Supplemental Ascorbate in the Supportive Treatment of Cancer: Reevaluation of Prolongation of Survival Times in Terminal Human Cancer," *Proceedings of the National Academy of Sciences* 7 (1976): 4538–4542.

A. B. Caragay, "Cancer-Preventative Foods and Ingredients," *Food Tech* 46, no. 4 (1992): 65–68. Cited in Winston J. Craig, "Phytochemicals: Guardians of Our Health," Andrews University Nutrition Department Paper (Berrien Springs, MI: Andrews University, 1997).

J. H. Cohen, A. R. Kristal, and J. L. Stanford, "Fruit and Vegetable Intakes and Prostate Cancer Risk," *Journal of the National Cancer Institute* 92 (2000): 61-68.

Winston J. Craig, "Phytochemicals: Guardians of Our Health," *Journal of the American Dietetic Association* 97, no. 10 (1997): S199–S204.

E. A. Decker, "The Role of Phenolics, Conjugated Linoleic Acid, Carnosine, and Pyrroloquinoline Quinone as Nonessential Dietary Antioxidants," *Nutrition Review* 53 (1995): 49–58.

Mark Fuhrman, "Healthy Times," March 2004.

T. Hirano et al., "Antiproliferative Activity of Mammalian Lignan Derivatives Against the Human Breast Carcinoma Cell Line, ZR-75-1," *Cancer Investigation* (1990): 8595–8601.

Kathi J. Kemper, "Burdock (*Arctium lappa*)," Longwood Herbal Task Force, 1996. longwoodherbal.org/burdock/burdock.pdf.

A. R. Kennedy, "The Evidence for Soybean Products as Cancer Preventive Agents," *Journal of Nutrition* 125 (1995): 733S–743S.

Alan Kristal, M. J. Messina et al., "Soy Intake and Cancer Risk: A Review of the In Vitro and In Vivo Data," *Nutrition and Cancer* 21, no. 2 (1994): 113–131.

Thomas Moore, Laura Svetkey et al. *The DASH Diet for Hypertension* (New York: Simon & Schuster, 2001).

K. Morita et al. "A Desmutagenic Factor Isolated from Burdock (*Arctium lappa* Linne)," *Mutation Research* 129, no. 1 (1984): 25–31.

"Move Over Tomatoes! All Vegetables—Especially the Cruciferous Kind—May Prevent Prostate Cancer," Fred Hutchinson Cancer Research Center, January 4, 2000. fhcrc.org/en/news/releases/2000/01/Veggiesprostat.html.

Y. Ohsake et al., "Combination Effects of Caffeine and Cisplatin on a Cisplatin Resistant Human Lung Cancer Cell Line," *Gan To Kagaku Ryoho* 17, no. 7 (1990): 1339–1343.

B. Patterson et al., "Fruits and Vegetables in the American Diet: Data from the NHANES II—Survey," *American Journal of Public Health* 80 (1990): 1443–1449.

D. Schardt, "Phytochemicals: Plants Against Cancer," *Nutrition Action Health Letter* 21, no. 3 (1994): 9–11.

M. Serraino and L. U. Thompson, "The Effect of Flaxseed Supplementation on Early Risk Markers for Mammary Carcinogenesis." *Cancer Letters* 60 (1991), 135–142.

M. Serraino, L. U. Thompson, and K. Oka, "The Effect of Flaxseed Supplementation on the Initiation and Promotional Stages of Mammary Tumorigenesis," *Nutrition and Cancer* 17 (1992): 153–159.

H. Sies and N. I. Krinsky, "The Present Status of Antioxidant Vitamins and Beta-Carotene," *American Journal of Clinical Nutrition* 62 (1995): 1299S–1300S.

Margaret Smith, *Phytochemicals* (Baltimore, MD: Johns Hopkins Hospital, Department of Nutrition, 1997).

K. A. Steinmetz and J. D. Potter, "Vegetables, Fruit and Cancer, II. Mechanisms," *Cancer Causes Control* 2 (1991): 427–442.

L. U. Thompson, "Antioxidants and Hormone-Mediated Health Benefits of Whole Grains," *Critical Reviews in Food Science and Nutrition* 34 (1994): 473–497.

L. U. Thompson, "Potential Health Benefits of Whole Grains and Their Components," *Contemporary Nutrition* 17, no. 6 (1992): 1–2.

Andrew Weil, "Better Boost from Broccoli Sprouts?" Dr. Weil Q & A, April 10, 2012. drweil.com/drw/u/QAA401093/Better-Boost-From-Broccoli-Sprouts.html.

G. Q. Zheng, J. Zhang, P. M. Kenney, and L. K. T. Lam, "Stimulation of Glutathione *S*-Transferase and Inhibition of Carcinogenesis in Mice by Celery Seed Oil Constituents," in *Food Phytochemicals for Cancer Prevention I: Fruits and Vegetables*, eds. M. J. Hang, T. Osawa, C. T. Ho, and R. T. Rosen (Washington, DC: American Chemical Society, 1994), 144–153.

CHAPTER 5: MEAT, DAIRY, AND THE VEGETARIAN OPTION

Epigraph: Cited in F. Sussman, *The Vegetarian Alternative* (Emmaus, PA: Rodale Press, 1978).

Asian vs. American diet:

Michael Klaper, *Vegan Nutrition: Just What the Doctor Ordered*, Ahimsa videotape 12 (Malaga, NJ: American Vegetarian Society, 1993).

Robert M. Kradjian, *Save Yourself from Breast Cancer* (New York: Berkley, 1994).

Jean A. T. Pennington and Judith Spungen, *Bowes and Church's Food Values of Portions Commonly Used*, 19th edition (Philadelphia: Lippincott Publisher, 2010).

Jeremy Rifkin, *Beyond Beef* (New York: Dutton, 1992).

Nutrient content of beef and chicken: USDA National Nutrient Database for Standard Reference, ndb.nal.usda.gov.

Wartime nutrition: M. Hindhede, "The Effect of Food Restriction During War on Mortality in Copenhagen," *Journal of the American Medical Association* 74, no. 6 (1920): 381–382.

Historical references: Robert M. Kradjian, *Save Yourself from Breast Cancer* (New York: Berkley, 1994).

Unsafe beef and dairy:

Keith Block and Charlotte Gyllenhaal,"Nutrition: An Essential Tool in Cancer Therapy," Report for the Office of Technology Assessment, Washington, DC: U.S. Congress, 1990.

Robert M. Kradjian, *Save Yourself from Breast Cancer* (New York: Berkley, 1994).

J. W. Wilesmith, J. B. Ryan, and W. D. Hueston, "Case Control Studies of Calf Feeding Practices and Meat and Bonemeal Inclusion in Proprietary Concentrates," *Research in Veterinary Science* 52, no. 3 (1992): 325–331.

Fats, meat, and breast cancer:

P. Mills et al., "Dietary Habits and Breast Cancer Incidence among Seventh-Day Adventists," *Cancer* 79 (1989): 465–471.

F. de Waard, "Breast Cancer Incidence and Nutritional Status with Particular Reference to Body Weight and Height," *Cancer Research* 35 (1975): 3351.

E. White et al., "Maintenance of a Low-Fat Diet: Follow-Up of the Women's Health Trial," *Cancer Epidemiology, Biomarkers and Prevention* 1, no. 4 (1992): 315–322.

Plant fat and breast cancer:

T. Hirayama, "Epidemiology of Breast Cancer with Special Reference to the Role of Diet," *Journal of Preventative Medicine* 7 (1978):173–174.

Robert M. Kradjian, *Save Yourself from Breast Cancer* (New York: Berkley, 1994).

Meat and acid production: G. Hepner, "Altered Bile Acid Metabolism in Vegetarians," *American Journal of Digestive Diseases* 20 (1975): 935.

Diet and endometrial cancer: M. Goodman et al., "Association of Soy and Fiber Consumption with the Risk of Endometrial Cancer," *American Journal of Epidemiology* 146, no. 4 (1997): 292–306.

Meat and general nutrition:

J. R. Mead, "The Essential Fatty Acids: Past, Present and Future," *Progress in Lipid Research* 20 (1981): 1–6.

S. D. Phinney, R. S. Odin, S. B. Johnson, and R. T. Holman, "Reduced Arachidonate in Serum Phospholipids and Cholesteryl Esters Associated with Vegetarian Diets in Humans," *American Journal of Clinical Nutrition* 51 (1990): 385–392.

T. A. B. Sanders, F. R. Ellis, and J. W. T. Dickerson, "Studies of Vegans: The Fatty Acid Composition of Plasma Choline Phosphoglycerides, Erythrocytes, Adipose Tissue, Breast Milk and Some Indicators of Susceptibility to Ischemic Heart Disease in Vegans and Omnivore Controls," *American Journal of Clinical Nutrition* 31 (1978): 805–813.

D. Schmahl et al., "Experimental Investigations on the Influence upon the Chemical Carcinogenesis. Third Communication: Studies with 1,2-Dimethylhydrazine," *Z. Krebsforch* 86 (1976): 89–94. Cited in Keith Block and Charlotte Gyllenhaal, "Nutrition: An Essential Tool in Cancer Therapy," Report for the Office of Technology Assessment, Washington, DC: U.S. Congress, 1990.

Klaper and milk: Nutrition for Optimum Health, "Dr. Klaper Presents Important Facts about Heart Disease, Fat, Nutritional Needs, Calories, Milk, Osteoporosis and Vitamin B-12," vegsource.com/klaper/optimum.htm. Cited in John Robbins, *Diet for a New America* (Walpole, NH: Stillpoint, 1987).

The Hawaii diet: Terry Shintani, *Hawaii Diet* (New York: Pocket Books, 1997).

Milk and general health:

John McDougall, *The McDougall Plan* (Clinton: New Win, 1983). Cited in Nathaniel Mead, "Don't Drink Your Milk!," *Natural Health Magazine* (July–August 1994).

Physicians Committee for Responsible Medicine, "What's Wrong with Dairy Products?" scienzavegetariana.it/nutrizione/pcrm/pcrm_dairy.html.

Dairy products and ovarian cancer:

D. W. Cramer et al., "Galactose Consumption and Metabolism in Relation to the Risk of Ovarian Cancer," *Lancet* 2 (1989): 66–71.

Lawrence H. Kushi, Pamela J. Mink, et al., "Prospective Study of Diet and Ovarian Cancer," *American Journal of Epidemiology* 149, no. 1 (1999).

P. MacDonald, "Effect of Obesity on Conversion of Plasma Androstenedione to Estrone in Postmenopausal Women with and Without Endometrial Cancer," *American Journal of Obstetrics and Gynecology* 130 (1978): 448.

John Robbins, *Diet for a New America: How Your Food Choices Affect Your Health, Happiness, and the Future of Life on Earth* (Walpole, NH: Stillpoint, 1987).

John Snowden, *Journal of the American Medical Association* (1985). Cited in John Robbins, *Diet for a New America* (Walpole, NH: Stillpoint, 1987).

Dairy products and prostate cancer:

J. M. Chan et al., "Plasma Insulin-Like Growth Factor-1 and Prostate Cancer Risk: A Prospective Study," *Science* 279 (1998): 563-5.

P. Cohen, "Serum Insulin-Like Growth Factor-I Levels and Prostate Cancer Risk: Interpreting the Evidence." *Journal of the National Cancer Institute* 90 (1998): 876–879.

Physicians Committee for Responsible Medicine, "Milk Consumption and Prostate Cancer," pcrm.org/health/health-topics/milk-consumption-and-prostate-cancer.

D. J. Pusateri, W. T. Roth, J. K. Ross, and T. D. Shultz, "Dietary and Hormonal Evaluation of Men at Different Risks for Prostate Cancer: Plasma and Fecal Hormone-Nutrient Interrelationships," *American Journal of Clinical Nutrition* 51 (1990): 371–377. Cited in Keith Block and Charlotte Gyllenhaal, "Nutrition: An Essential Tool in Cancer Therapy," Report for the Office of Technology Assessment, Washington, DC: U.S. Congress, 1990.

World Cancer Research Fund/American Institute for Cancer Research, "Food, Nutrition, Physical Activity, and the Prevention of Cancer: A Global Perspective," (Washington, DC: AICR, 2007). aicr.org/assets/docs/pdf/reports/Second_Expert_Report.pdf.

Dairy products and breast cancer:

J. L. Outwater, A. Nicolson, and N. D. Barnard, "Dairy Products and Breast Cancer: The IFG-1, Estrogen, and bGH Hypothesis," *Medical Hypothesis* 48 (1997): 453–461.

Ronald Phillips, "Nutrition in the Causation of Cancer," *Cancer Research* 35 (1975): 3231.

Dairy and Non-Hodgkin's lymphoma and lung cancer:

A. Cunningham, "Lymphomas and Animal Protein Consumption," *Lancet* 2 (1976): 1184.

S. Franceschi, D. Serraino, A. Carbone, et al., "Dietary Factors and Non-Hodgkin's Lymphoma: A Case-Control Study in the Northeastern Part of Italy," *Nutrition and Cancer* 12 (1989): 333–341.

Nathaniel Mead, "Don't Drink Your Milk!," *Natural Health Magazine* (July–August 1994).

Dairy and bone mineralization: J. Cadogan, R. Eastell, N. Jones, and M. E. Barker, "Milk Intake and Bone Mineral Acquisition in Adolescent Girls: Randomised, Controlled Intervention Trial," *British Medical Journal* 315 (1997): 1255–1269.

Humans as meat eaters:

Barbara Parham, *What's Wrong with Eating Meat?* (Denver: Ananda Marga, 1977).

C. Prosser, *Comparative Animal Physiology*, 2nd ed. (Philadelphia: Saunders, 1961).

Vegetarianism and vitamin B12:

"Harmful B12 Breakdown Products in Multivitamins?" *Medical World News* (1981): 12–13.

V. Herbert, "Multivitamin Mineral Food Supplements Containing Vitamin B12 May Also Contain Dangerous Analogues of Vitamin B12," *New England Journal of Medicine* 307 (1982): 255.

A. Immerman, "Vitamin B12 Status of a Vegetarian Diet—A Critical Review," *World Review of Nutrition and Dietetics* 37 (1981): 38.

John McDougall, *The McDougall Plan* (Clinton, NJ: New Win, 1983).

M. Murphy, "Vitamin B12 Deficiency Due to a Low-Cholesterol Diet in a Vegetarian," *Annals of Internal Medicine* 94 (1981): 57–58.

J. Stewart, "Response of Dietary Vitamin B12 Deficiency to Physiological Oral Doses of Cyanocobalamin," *Lancet* 2 (1970): 542.

S. Winawer, "Gastric and Hematological Abnormalities in a Vegan with Nutritional B12 Deficiency: Effects of Oral Vitamin B12," *Gastroenterology* 53 (1967): 130.

Vegetarianism and sugar:

J. Berstein et al., "Depression of Lymphocyte Transformation Following Oral Glucose Ingestion," *American Journal of Clinical Nutrition* 30 (1977): 613.

E. Nasset, "Movements of the Small Intestine," in *Medical Physiology,* 11th ed., ed. P. Bard (St. Louis: Mosby, 1961).

A. Sanchez et al., "Role of Sugars in Human Neutrophilic Phagocytosis," *American Journal of Clinical Nutrition* 26, no. 11 (1973): 1180–1184.

D. Yam, "Insulin-Cancer Relationships: Possible Dietary Implication," *Medical Hypothesis* 38, no. 2 (1992): 111–117.

Vegetarianism and cancer: R. Phillips, "Role of Lifestyle and Dietary Habits in Risk of Cancer," *Cancer Research* 35 (1975): 3513.

Flaxseed oil and prostate cancer:

E. Giovannucci et al. "A Prospective Study of Dietary Fat and Risk of Prostate Cancer," *Journal of the National Cancer Institute* 85 (1993): 1571–1579.

Charles Myers, *Prostate Forum* (February 2000).

P. K. Pandalai et al. "The Effects of Omega-3 and Omega-6 Fatty Acids on In Vitro Prostate Cancer Growth," *Anticancer Research* 16 (1996): 815–820.

Vegetarianism and circulatory health:

W. Collens, "Phylogenetic Aspects of the Cause of Human Atherosclerotic Disease," *Circulation* 2, no. 7 (1965): 31–32.

J. Dietschy, "Regulation of Cholesterol Metabolism (Third of Three Parts)," *New England Journal of Medicine* 282 (1970): 1241.

CHAPTER 6: BALANCING OUR ACID–ALKALINE CHEMISTRY

Acids and bases: Michael Worlitschek, "Deacidification: A Basic Theory—Acids and Bases Require Equilibrium in the Organism," *Semmelweis Institut Verlag für Naturheilkunde* (1995).

Lymphocyte research:

G. Frentz et al., "Increased Number of Suppressor T-Lymphocytes in Sun-Induced Multiple Skin Cancers," *Cancer* 61 (1988): 294–297.

"Neoplasia: Six Years Later," *New England Journal of Medicine* 308 (1983): 1595–1597. Cited in James J. Sparandeo, "Scientific Relationships Between Diet and Cancer Survival," *Comprehensive Nutritional News* 308 (1983–1991): 1595–1597.

D. S. Robbins and H. H. Fudenberg, "Human Lymphocyte Subpopulations in Metastatic," *New England Journal of Medicine* 308 (1983): 1595–1597.

A. W. Ritchie et al., "Lymphocyte Subsets in Renal Carcinoma—A Sequential Study Using Monoclonal Antibodies," *British Journal of Urology* 56 (1984): 140–148.

T. Watanabe et al., "T-Cell Subsets in Patients with Gastric Cancer," *Oncology* 42 (1985): 89–91.

L. J. Wesselius et al., "Lymphocyte Subsets in Lung Cancer," *Chest* 91 (1987): 725–729.

Elevating blood glucose in cancer patients: Fanelli F. Rossi et al., "Abnormal Substrate Metabolism and Nutritional Strategies in Cancer Management," *Journal of Parenteral Enteral Nutrition* 15, no. 6 (1991): 680–683. Cited in Patrick Quillin and Noreen Quillin, *Beating Cancer with Nutrition* (Tulsa, OK: Nutrition Times Press, 1994).

Therapies:

James Ewing, *Neoplastic Diseases,* 4th ed. (Philadelphia: Saunders, 1942): 3.

Ralph W. Moss, "Simoncini's Bicarbonate Treatment for Cancer," August 22, 2009, whale.to/cancer/simoncini.html.

Kevin Passero, "Four Scary Side Effects of Heartburn Medicines," *Live in the Now,* liveinthenow.com/article/4-scary-side-effects-of-heartburn-medications.

Y. Yang, J. D. Lewis, S. Epstein, and D. Metz, "Long-Term Proton Pump Inhibitor Therapy and Risk of Hip Fracture," *Journal of the American Medical Association* 296, no. 24 (2006): 2947–2953.

Acid–alkaline research:

L. A. Frassetto and A. Sebastian, "How Metabolic Acidosis and Oxidative Stress Alone and Interacting May Increase the Risk of Fracture in Diabetic Subjects," *Medical Hypotheses* 79, no. 2 (2012): 189–192.

Gabe Mirkin, "Acid/Alkaline Theory of Disease Is Nonsense," *Quackwatch*, January 11, 2009, quackwatch.org/01QuackeryRelatedTopics/DSH/coral2.html.

Fermentation and cancer cell growth: Otto Heinrich Warburg, "The Prime Cause and Prevention of Cancer," lecture delivered to Nobel laureates, Lindau, Lake Constance, Germany, June 30, 1966.

Caffeine and breast cancer:

H. W. Borger, A. Schafmayer, R. Arnold, et al., "The Influence of Coffee and Caffeine on Gastrin and Acid Secretion in Man," *Deutsche Medizinische Wochenschrift* [*German Medical Weekly*] 101, no. 12 (1976): 455–457.

Kate Devlin, "Caffeine 'Can Increase Breast Cancer Risk,'" *The Telegraph*, October 13, 2008, telegraph.co.uk/health/3189530/Caffeine-can-increase-breast-cancer-risk.html.

Ken Ishitani et al., "Caffeine Consumption and Risk of Breast Cancer in a Large Prospective Cohort of Women," *Archives of Internal Medicine* 168, no. 18 (2008): 2022–2031.

David M. Mrazik, "Reconsidering Caffeine: An Awake and Alert New Look at America's Most Commonly Consumed Drug" (2004). dash.harvard.edu/bitstream/handle/1/8846793/Mrazik.html?sequence=2.

M. R. Olthof, P. C. Hollman, M. N. Buijsman, et al., "Chlorogenic Acid, Quercetin-3-Rutinoside and Black Tea Phenols Are Extensively Metabolized in Humans," *Journal of Nutrition* 133, no. 6 (2003): 1806–1814.

CHAPTER 7: INCREASING AND STRENGTHENING IMMUNE FUNCTION

Epigraph: Robert Good, "Toward Cancer Control," *Time* (March 19, 1973).

Natural immunity: Michio Kushi, *A Natural Approach to Allergies* (Tokyo: Japan Publications, 1985).

Lymph system:

R. Pinner et al., "Trends in Infectious Diseases Mortality in the United States," *Journal of the American Medical Association* 275, no. 3 (1996): 189–193. Cited in Patrick Holford, *Say No to Cancer* (London: Judy Piatkus, 1999).

Robert Roundtree and Carol Colman, *Immunotics* (New York: Putnam, 2000).

Development of the lymph system:

R. K. Chandra and A. Hamed, "Cumulative Incidence of Atopic Disorders in High Risk Infants Fed Whey Hydrolysate, Soy, and Conventional Cow Milk Formulas," *Annals of Allergy, Asthma, and Immunology* 67 (1991): 129–132.

Robert Roundtree and Carol Colman, *Immunotics* (New York: Putnam, 2000).

Stress:

L. R. Derogatis et al., "Psychological Coping Mechanisms and Survival Time in Metastatic Breast Cancer," *Journal of the American Medical Association* 242 (1979): 1504–1508.

Robert Roundtree and Carol Colman, *Immunotics* (New York: Putnam, 2000).

Martin Seligman, *Learned Optimism* (New York: Pocket Books, 1998).

Emotions and cancer:

Breast Cancer Research 10, no. 2 (2008). breast-cancer-research.com/content/pdf/bcr1881.pdf.

S. O. Dalton et al., "Depression and Cancer Risk," *American Journal of Epidemiology* 155, no. 12 (2002): 1088–1095.

E. Dedert, E. Lush, A. Chagpar, et al., "Stress, Coping, and Circadian Disruption Among Women Awaiting Breast Cancer Surgery," *Annals of Behavioral Medicine* 44, no. 1 (2012): 10–20.

M. Irwin et al., "Impaired NK Cell Activity During Bereavement," *Brain, Behavior, and Immunity* 1, no. 98 (1987). Cited in Paul Martin, *The Healing Mind*.

Lawrence LeShan, *Cancer as a Turning Point* (New York: Plume, 1994). cancerasaturning point.org.

Paul Martin, *The Healing Mind: The Vital Links Between Brain and Behavior, Immunity and Disease* (New York: St. Martin's, 1997): 220–221.

Ross Pelton and Lee Overholser, *Alternatives in Cancer Therapy* (New York: Fireside Books, 1994).

D. Spiegel, "Social Support: How Friends, Family, and Groups Can Help," in *Mind Body Medicine*, D. Golrman and J. Gurin (Yonkers, NY: Consumer Reports Books, 1993).

D. Spiegel, J. R. Bloom, and E. Gottheil, "Effects of Psychosocial Treatment on Survival of Patients with Metastatic Breast Cancer," *Lancet* 2 (1989): 888–891.

Nutrition and immunity:

R. K. Chandra, *Nutrition and Immunology* (New York: Liss Press, 1989).

Maureen Keane and Daniella Chace, *What to Eat If You Have Cancer* (Chicago: Contemporary Books, 1996).

Charles B. Simone, *Cancer and Nutrition* (New York: Avery Publishing, 1994).

Vitamins and immunity:

W. R. Beisel et al., "Single-Nutrient Effects on Immunological Functions," *Journal of the American Medical Association* 245 (1981): 53–58. Cited in: Joseph Pizzorno, *Total Wellness* (Rocklin, CA: Prima, 1998).

R. K. Chandra, "Nutrition and Immunity: Basic Considerations, Part 1," *Contemporary Nutrition* 11, no. 11 (1986). Cited in Joseph Pizzorno, *Total Wellness* (Rocklin, CA: Prima, 1998).

R. Suskind, "Immunological Mechanism and the Role of Nutrients," in *Principles and Practice of Environmental Medicine*, ed. A.B. Tarcher (New York: Plenum Medical, 1992).

Sugar and immunity:

J. Bernstein, S. Alpert, K. Nauss, and R. Suskind, "Depression of Lymphocyte Transformation Following Glucose Ingestion," *American Journal of Clinical Nutrition* 30 (1977): 613.

W. Ringsdorf, E. Cheraskin, and R. Ramsay, "Sucrose, Neutrophilic Phagocytosis and Resistance to Disease," *Dental Survey* 52 (1976): 46–48. Cited in Joseph Pizzorno, *Total Wellness* (Rocklin, CA: Prima, 1998).

A. Sanchez et al., "Role of Sugars in Human Neutrophilic Phagocytosis," *American Journal of Clinical Nutrition* 26 (1973): 1180–1184. Cited in Joseph Pizzorno, *Total Wellness* (Rocklin, CA: Prima, 1998).

C. J. Van Oss, "Influence of Glucose Levels on the In Vitro Phagocytosis of Bacteria by Human Neutrophils," *Infection and Immunity* 4, no. 54 (1971). Cited in Charles B. Simone, *Cancer and Nutrition* (New York: Avery, 1994).

Animal protein and autoimmune diseases:

R Cheung et al., "T Cells from Children with IDDM Are Sensitized to Bovine Serum Albumin," *Scandinavian Journal of Immunology* 40, no. 6 (1994): 623–628.

John McDougall, "Boosting Immunity," *McDougall Newsletter* 9, no. 3, May–June 1995.

Dietary fat and immunity:

J. Barone, J. R. Hebert, and M. M. Reddy, "Dietary Fat and Natural-Killer-Cell Activity," *American Journal of Clinical Nutrition* 50 (1989): 861–867. Cited in Neal Barnard, *Foods That Fight Pain* (New York: Three Rivers Press, 1998).

J. Clausen and J. Moller, "Allergic Encephalomyelitis Induced by Brain Antigen after Deficiency in Polyunsaturated during Myelination," *International Archives of Allergy and Applied Immunology* 36, no. 224 (1969).

H. P. Hawley and G. B. Gordon, "The Effects of Long Chain Free Fatty Acids on Human Neutrophil Function and Structure," *Laboratory Investigation* 34 (1976): 216–222. Cited in Neal Barnard, *Foods That Fight Pain* (New York: Three Rivers Press, 1998).

J. Nordenstrom, C. Jarstrand, and A. Wiernik, "Decreased Chemotactic and Random Migration of Leukocytes during Intralipid Infusion," *American Journal of Clinical Nutrition* 32 (1979): 2416–2422. Cited in Neal Barnard, *Foods That Fight Pain* (New York: Three Rivers Press, 1998).

Obesity and immunity: G. M. Halpern and C. L. Trapp, "Nutrition and Immunity: Where Are We Standing?" *Allergologia et Immunopathologia* 21 (1993): 122–126.

Allergies and immunity: Joseph Pizzorno, *Total Wellness* (Rocklin, CA: Prima, 1998).

Metals, immunity, and cancer:

Robert J. Hatherill, *Eat to Beat Cancer* (Los Angeles: Renaissance Books, 1998).

David Steinman, *Diet for a Poisoned Planet* (New York: Ballantine Books, 1990).

J. Stejskal, "Beware of Metals: A Possible Cause of Immunological Disorders," paper presented at the Center for Functional Nanostructures (CFN) Symposium: Immunotoxicity and In Vitro Possibilities, Stockholm, September 19–21, 1993. Cited in Joseph Pizzorno, *Total Wellness* (Rocklin CA: Prima, 1998).

The importance of quality sleep:

Carol Everson, "Sustained Sleep Deprivation Impairs Host Defense" (1993). gwern.net/docs/algernon/1993-everson.pdf.

Michael Irwin, "Fail to Snooze, Immune Cells Lose." *Science News* 147 (1995): 11.

D. Uthgenannt, D. Schoolmann, R. Pietrowsky, et al., "Effects of Sleep on the Production of Cytokines in Humans," *Psychosomatic Medicine* 57 (1995): 97–104.

Moods and illness: Blair Justice, *Who Gets Sick? How Beliefs, Moods and Thoughts Affect Your Health* (Houston Peak Press, 2000).

Effects of exercise:

H. W. Baenkler, "Exercise and the Immune System: The Impact on Diseases," *Rheumatic Diseases and Sport Rheumatology* 16 (1992): 5–21. Cited in Joseph Pizzorno, *Total Wellness* (Rocklin, CA: Prima, 1998).

D. C. Nieman, "Exercise, Upper Respiratory Tract Infection, and the Immune System," *Medicine and Science in Sports and Exercise* 26, no. 2 (1994): 128–139. Cited in John McDougall, *McDougall Newsletter* 9, no. 3, May–June 1995.

Optimum diet to maximize immunity: Darshan S. Kelley et al., "Concentration of Dietary n-6 Polyunsaturated Fatty Acids and the Human Immune Status," *Clinical Immunology and Immunopathology* 62 (1992): 240–244. Cited in John McDougall, *McDougall Newsletter* 9, no. 3, May–June 1995.

CHAPTER 8: PRACTICAL STRATEGIES TO ELIMINATE SUGAR, FAT, AND OVEREATING

B. Cortés et al., "Acute Efects of High-Fat Meals Enriched with Walnuts or Olive Oil on Postprandial Endothelial Function," *Journal of the American College of Cardiology* 48, no. 8 (2006): 1666–1671.

J. Le Magnen, "A Role for Opiates in Food Reward and Food Addiction." In P. T. Capaldi (ed.), *Taste, Experience, and Feeding* (Washington, DC: American Psychological Association, 1990): 241–252.

C. S. Mott, "National Poll on Children's Health" (January 8, 2009). Children's Hospital, the University of Michigan Department of Pediatrics and Communicable Diseases, and the University of Michigan Child Health Evaluation and Research (CHEAR) Unit.

Lawrence L. Rudel, John S. Parks, and Janet K. Sawyer, "Compared with Dietary Monounsaturated and Saturated Fat, Polyunsaturated Fat Protects African Green Monkeys from Coronary Artery Atherosclerosis," *Arteriosclerosis, Thrombosis, and Vascular Biology* 15 (1995): 2101–2110.

Michael G. Tordoff, Rebecca L. Hughes, and Diane M. Pilchak, "Calcium Intake by Rats: Influence of Parathyroid Hormone, Calcitonin, and 1,25-Dihydroxyvitamin D," *American Journal of Physiology: Regulatory, Integrative, and Comparative Physiology* 274 (January 1998): R214–R231.

A. Wakui et al., "Randomized Study of Lentinan on Patients with Advanced Gastric and Colorectal Cancer (Tohoku Lentinan Study Group)," *Gan To Kagaku Ryohosha* 13, no. 4, part 1 (1986): 1050–1059 [in Japanese].

CHAPTER 9: DETOXIFYING YOUR BODY, NATURALLY

Pesticides and breast cancer:

Robert J. Hatherill, *Eat to Beat Cancer* (Los Angeles: Renaissance Books, 1998).

Joseph Keon, *The Truth About Breast Cancer* (Mill Valley, CA: Parissound, 1999).

Y. Zhang, P. Tallalay, C.G. Cho, and G. H. Posner, "A Major Inducer of Anticarcinogenic Protective Enzymes from Broccoli: Isolation and Elucidation of Structure," *Proceeding of the National Academy of Sciences* 89 (1992): 2399–2403. Cited in Jeffery Bland, Jeffery, *The 20-Day Rejuvenation Diet Program* (New Canaan, CT: Keats, 1997).

Liver detox: C. W. Sies and J. Brooker, "Could These Be Gallstones?" *Lancet* 365, no. 9468 (2005): 1388.

Fasting detox:

Paul C. Bragg, *The Miracle of Fasting:* Paul C. Bragg, *The Miracle of Fasting* (Santa Barbara, CA: Health Science, 2004).

Norman Walker, *Become Younger* (Prescott, AZ: Norwalk Press, 1995).

Heat detox: David Steinman, *Diet for a Poisoned Planet* (New York: Ballantine Books, 1990).

Exercise and detox: David Shier, Jackie Butler, and Ricki Lewis, *Hole's Essentials of Human Anatomy and Physiology*, 10th ed. (Burr Ridge, IL: McGraw-Hill Higher Education, 2008).

P. Anand, C. Sundaram, et al., "Curcumin and Cancer: An 'Old-Age' Disease with an 'Age-Old' Solution," *Cancer Letters* 267, no. 1 (2008): 133–164.

Milk thistle: H. Wilhelm, "The Effect of Silymarin Treatment on the Course of Acute and Chronic Liver Disease," *Zeitschrift fur Therapie* 10, no. 8 (1972): 482–495. Cited in Jeffery Bland, Jeffery, *The 20-Day Rejuvenation Diet Program* (New Canaan, CT: Keats, 1997).

CHAPTER 10: CANCER-FIGHTING SUPPLEMENT STRATEGIES

Vitamins and supplements:

G. Dennert et al. "Retinoic Acid Stimulation of the Induction of Mouse Killer T-Cell in Allogeneic and Syngeneic Systems," *Journal of the National Cancer Institute* 62 (1979): 89.

G. Dennert et al. "Retinoic Acid Stimulation of Killer-T Cell Induction," *European Journal of Immunology* 8 (1978): 23.

Anette Dickinson, "Who Uses Vitamin and Mineral Supplements? People Seeking a

Healthier Lifestyle," in *The Benefits of Nutritional Supplements*, ed. Council for Responsible Nutrition, 2002, crnusa.org/benpdfs/CRN011benefits_whovms.pdf.

R. H. Goldfarb and R. B. Herberman, "Natural Killer Cell Reactivity: Regulatory Interactions among Phorbol Ester, Interferon, Cholera Toxin, and Retinoic Acid," *Journal of Immunology* 126 (1981): 2129.

E. R. Greenberg et al., "A Clinical Trial of Antioxidant Vitamins to Prevent Colorectal Adenoma (Polyp Prevention Study Group)," *New England Journal of Medicine* 331, no. 3 (1994): 141–147.

Joanne Larsen, "Vitamin Supplements," Ask the Dietitian, dietitian.com/vitamins .html#.Uidqx9K3_To.

Arlene Weintraub, "Dietary Supplements: Latest Government Uproar No Match for Industry Lobbying Money," CBS News, May 28, 2010, cbsnews.com/8301 -505123_162-40042284/dietary-supplements-latest-government-uproar-no-match -for-industry-lobbying-money.

Beta-carotene:

C. La Vecchia et al. "Dietary Vitamin A and the Risk of Invasive Cervical Cancer," *International Journal of Cervical Cancer* 34, no. 3 (1984): 319–322.

M. S. Menkes et al., "Serum Beta-Carotene, Vitamins A and Selenium and the Risk of Lung Cancer," *New England Journal of Medicine* 315 (1986): 1250.

Vitamin E:

C. E. Myers et al., "Effect of Tocopherol and Selenium on Defenses against Reactive Oxygen Species and Their Effect on Radiation Sensitivity," *Annals of the New York Academy of Sciences* 393 (1982): 429–425.

Sharon Palmer, "Therapeutic Controversy: Is Supplementing Cancer Treatment with Antioxidants Helpful or Harmful?" *Today's Dietitian* 12, no. 4 (April 2010): 26.

K. N. Prasad et al., "Vitamin E Increases the Growth Inhibitory and Differentiating Effects of Tumor Therapeutic Agents on Neuroblastoma and Glioma Cells in Culture," *Proceedings of the Society for Experimental Biology and Medicine* 164, no. 2 (1980): 158–163.

Janet Roper, "The Effect of Vitamin E on Immune Responses," *Nutrition Reviews* 45, no. 1 (1987): 27.

Coenzyme Q10: Emile Bliznakov and Gerald Hunt, *The Miracle Nutrient Coenzyme Q10* (New York: Bantam, 1987).

Modified citrus protein: P. Nangia-Makker, V. Hogan, Y. Honjo, et al., "Inhibition of Human Cancer Cell Growth and Metastasis in Nude Mice by Oral Intake of Modified Citrus Pectin," *Journal of the National Cancer Institute* 94 (2002): 1854–1862.

B vitamins:

T. K. Basu, "Significance of Vitamins in Cancer," *Oncology* 33 (1976): 183.

W. R. Beisel et al., "Single Nutrients and Immunity," *American Journal of Clinical Nutrition* 35 (1982): 417–468.

J. Diamond, Lee W. Cowden, and Burton Goldburg, *Alternative Medicine: Definitive Guide to Cancer* (Tiburon, CA: Future Medicine, 1997).

H. A. Ladner et al., *Nutrition, Growth and Cancer* (New York: Alan Liss, 1988). Cited in Patrick Quillan, *Beating Cancer with Nutrition* (Tulsa, OK: Nutrition Times Press, 1994).

R. S. Panush and J. C. Delafuente, "Vitamins and Immunocompetence: Group B Vitamins—World Review," *Nutrition Digest* 45 (1985): 97–132.

B. M. Posner et al., "Nutrition in Neoplastic Disease," *Advances in Modern Human Nutrition and Dietetics* 29 (1980): 130–169.

Vitamin C:

E. T. Cameron et al. "Ascorbic Acid and Cancer: A Review," *Cancer Research* 39 (1979): 663–681.

R. A. Good et al., "Nutrition, Immunity and Cancer: A Review," *Clinical Bulletin* 9 (1979): 3–12, 63–75.

R. A. Jacob and G. Sotoudeh, "Vitamin C Function and Status in Chronic Disease," *Nutrition in Clinical Care* 5 (2002): 66–74.

S. J. Padayatty, H. Sun, Y. Wang, et al., "Vitamin C Pharmacokinetics: Implications for Oral and Intravenous Use," *Annals of Internal Medicine* 140 (2004): 533–537.

C. H. Park, "Vitamin C in Leukemia and Preleukemia Cell Growth," in N*utrition, Growth and Cancer*, ed. G. P. Tryfiates and K. N. Prasad (New York: Alan R. Liss, 1988).

R. H. Yonemoto, "Vitamin C and Immunological Response in Normal Controls and Cancer Patients," *Medico Dialogo* 5 (1979): 23–30.

Vitamin D:

J. Boik, *Cancer and Natural Medicine* (Princeton, MN: Oregon Medical Press, 1995).

"Dietary Reference Intakes for Calcium and Vitamin D," Institute of Medicine, Food and Nutrition Board (Washington, DC: National Academy Press, 2010).

C. D. Davis, "Vitamin D and Cancer: Current Dilemmas and Future Research Needs," *American Journal of Clinical Nutrition* 88 (2008): 565S–9S.

C. D. Davis, V. Hartmuller, M. Freedman, et al., "Vitamin D and Cancer: Current Dilemmas and Future Needs," *Nutrition Reviews* 65 (2007): S71–S74.

Wayne Martin, "Anti-Cancer Effect of Vitamin D," *Townsend Newsletter for Doctors and Patients*, October 1966, p. 111.

Selenium:

"Dietary Fact Sheet on Selenium," Office of Dietary Supplements, National Institutes of Health (November 22, 2013). ods.od.nih.gov/factsheets/Selenium-QuickFacts.

C. Ip, "Prophylaxis of Mammary Neoplasia by Selenium Supplementation in the Initiation and Promotion Phases of Carcinogenesis," *Cancer Research* 41 (1981): 4386–4393.

J. T. Rotruck et al., "Selenium: Biochemical Role as a Component of Glutathione Peroxidase," *Science* 179, no. 4073 (1973): 588–590. Cited in J. Diamond, Lee W. Cowden, and Burton Goldburg, *Alternative Medicine: Definitive Guide to Cancer* (Tiburon, CA: Future Medicine Publishing, 1997).

G. N. Schrauzer, "Selenium for the Cancer Patient," paper presented at the Adjuvant Nutrition in Cancer Treatment Symposium, Tampa, FL, September 29, 1995.

Calcium:

H. Schroeder, *The Poisons Around Us* (Bloomington: Indiana University Press, 1974).

M. L. Slattery, A. W. Sorenon, and M. H. Ford, "Dietary Calcium Intake as a Mitigating Factor in Colon Cancer," *American Journal of Epidemiology* 128, no. 3 (1988): 504–514.

"Vitamin and Mineral Requirements in Human Nutrition." Report of the Joint FAO/ WHO Expert Consultation, World Health Organization. who.int/dietphysicalactiv ity/publications/trs916/en/gsfao_osteo.pdf.

Magnesium:

J. M. Blondell, "The Anticarcinogenic Effect of Magnesium," *Medical Hypothesis* 6, no. 8 (1980): 863–871.

V. V. Ranade and J. C. Somberg, "Bioavailability and Pharmacokinetics of Magnesium After Administration of Magnesium Salts to Humans," *American Journal of Therapeutics* 8 (2001): 345–57.

R. K. Rude, "Magnesium." In P. M. Coates, J. M. Betz, M. R. Blackman, et al., eds. *Encyclopedia of Dietary Supplements.* 2nd ed. (New York: Informa Healthcare, 2010): 527–537.

Iodine:

"Dietary Reference Intakes for Vitamin A, Vitamin K, Arsenic, Boron, Chromium, Copper, Iodine, Iron, Manganese, Molybdenum, Nickel, Silicon, Vanadium, and

Zinc," Institute of Medicine, Food and Nutrition Board (Washington, DC: National Academy Press, 2001).

V. W. Standel, "Dietary Iodine and the Risk of Breast, Endometrial and Ovarian Cancer," *Lancet* 1, no. 7965 (1976): 890–891.

Zinc: "Dietary Reference Intakes for Vitamin A, Vitamin K, Arsenic, Boron, Chromium, Copper, Iodine, Iron, Manganese, Molybdenum, Nickel, Silicon, Vanadium, and Zinc," Institute of Medicine, Food and Nutrition Board (Washington, DC: National Academy Press, 2001).

Omega-3 fatty acids:

K. L. Fritsche and P. V. Johnston, "Effect of Dietary Alpha-Linolenic Acid on Growth, Metastasis, Fatty Acid Profile, and Prostaglandin Production of Two Murine Mammary Adenocarcinomas," *Journal of Nutrition* 120 (1990): 1601–1609. Cited in J. Diamond, Lee W. Cowden, and Burton Goldburg, *Alternative Medicine: Definitive Guide to Cancer* (Tiburon, CA: Future Medicine Publishing, 1997).

J. Prudden, "Use of Cartilage in Cancer Treatment," paper presented at the Adjuvant Nutrition for Cancer Treatment Symposium, Tampa, FL, September 30, 1995. Cited in J. Diamond, Lee W. Cowden, and Burton Goldburg, *Alternative Medicine: Definitive Guide to Cancer* (Tiburon, CA: Future Medicine Publishing, 1997).

E. I. Wynder et al., "Diet and Breast Cancer in Causation and Therapy," *Cancer* 58, no. 8 (1986): 1804–1831.

Curcumin: Jane Higdon et al., "Curcumin," Linus Pauling Institute, Oregon State University, reviewed January 2009, lpi.oregonstate.edu/infocenter/phytochemicals/curcumin.

Chlorella: Ralph Moss, *Cancer Therapy* (Equinox Press, 1996).

Garlic: J. M. Chan, F. Wang, and E. A. Holly, "Vegetable and Fruit Intake and Pancreatic Cancer in a Population-Based Case-Control Study in the San Francisco Bay Area," *Cancer Epidemiology Biomarkers and Prevention* 14, no. 9 (2005): 2093–2097.

Supplement toxicity:

A. Bendich and L. J. Machlin, "Safety of Oral Intake of Vitamin E," *American Journal of Clinical Nutrition* 48 (1988): 612–619.

Food and Nutrition Board, *Recommended Dietary Allowances*, 10th ed. (Washington, DC: National Academy Press, 1989).

K. J. Rothman et al., "Teratogenicity of High Vitamin A Intake," *New England Journal of Medicine* 333 (1995): 1369–1373.

U.S. Preventive Services Task Force, "Routine Iron Supplementation during Pregnancy; Policy Statement and Review Article," *Journal of the American Medical Association* 270 (1993): 2846–2848.

"Vitamin and Nutritional Supplements," Medical Essay, *Supplement to Mayo Clinic Health Letter,* June 1997. Cited in Janet R. Hunt, "Position of the American Dietetic Association: Vitamin and Mineral Supplementation," *Journal of the American Dietetic Association* 96, no. 1 (1996): 73–77.

Limitations of chemotherapy:

Lily Giambarba Casura, "Twenty Questions with Ralph Moss, PhD," *Townsend Letter for Doctors and Patients*, January 1998.

Ralph Moss, *Questioning Chemotherapy* (New York: Equinox Press, 1995).

New England Journal of Medicine (1986). Cited in Peter Barry Chowka, "Alternative Medicine and the War on Cancer: Is There Light at the End of the Tunnel?" *Better Nutrition* (August 1999).

"Why Is Chemotherapy Not Very Effective?" CYTImmune Sciences Inc. cytimmune.com/go.cfm?do=Page.View&pid=75.

Alternatives to chemotherapy:

S. Bhatia et al. "Breast Cancer and Other Second Neoplasms After Childhood Hodgskin's Disease," *New England Journal of Medicine* 334 (1996): 745–751. Cited in Peter Barry Chowka, "Alternative Medicine and the War on Cancer: Is There Light at the End of the Tunnel?" *Better Nutrition* (August 1999).

Peter Barry Chowka, "Alternative Medicine and the War on Cancer: Is There Light at the End of the Tunnel?" *Better Nutrition* (August 1999).

Robert J. Hatherill, *Eat to Beat Cancer* (Los Angeles: Renaissance Books, 1998).

Prevention of nausea: F. de Blasio et al., "N-acetyl cysteine (NAC) in Preventing Nausea and Vomiting Induced by Chemotherapy in Patients Suffering from Inoperable No Small Cell Lung Cancer (NSCLC)," *Chest* 110 (1996): 103S.

Vitamins and treatment:

M. Nakagawa et al. "Potentiation by Vitamin A of the Action of Anticancer Agents against Murine Tumors," *Japanese Journal of Cancer Research* 76 (1985): 887–894.

K. N. Prasad et al. "Vitamin E Increases the Growth Inhibitory and Differentiating Effects of Tumor Therapeutic Agents in Neuroblastoma and Glioma Cells in Culture," *Proceedings of the Society for Experimental Biology and Medicine* 164 (1980): 158–163.

H. S. Taper et al. "Non-Toxic Potentiation of cancer Chemotherapy by Combined C and K3 Vitamin Pre-Treatment," *International Journal of Cancer* 40 (1987): 575–579.

R. G. Wadleigh et al., "Vitamin E in the Treatment of Chemotherapy-Induced Mucositis," *American Journal of Medicine* 92 (1992): 481–484.

Coenzyme Q10 and treatment: K. Folkers and A. Wolanjuk, "Research on Coenzyme Q10 in Clinical Medicine and in Immunomodulation," *Drugs Experimental Clinical Research Journal* 11 (1985): 539–545.

Adriamycin toxicity:

K. Fujita et al., "Reduction of Adriamycin Toxicity by Ascorbate in Mice and Guinea Pigs," *Cancer Research* 42 (1982): 309–316.

E. J. Ladas et al., "A Randomized, Controlled, Double-Blind, Pilot Study of Milk Thistle for the Treatment of Hepatotoxicity in Childhood Acute Lymphoblastic Leukemia (ALL)," *Cancer* 116, no. 2 (2009): 506–51.

R. Ogura, Y. Humon, and R. Young, "Adriamycin Amelioration of Toxicity by Alpha-Tocopherol," *Cancer Treatment Reports* 60 (1976): 961–92.

L. A. Wood, "Possible Prevention of Adriamycin-Induced Alopecia by Tocopherol," *New England Journal of Medicine* 312 (1985): 1060.

Magnesium and treatment: J. E. Buckley, V. L. Clark, T. J. Meyer, and N. W. Pearlman, "Hypomagnesemia after Cisplatin Combination Chemotherapy," *Archives of Internal Medicine* 144 (1984): 2347–2348.

Glutathione and treatment:

S. Cascinus et al. "Neuroprotective Effect of Reduced Glutathione on cisplatin Based Chemotherapy in Advanced Gastric Cancer: A Randomized Double-Bind Placebo-Controlled Trial," *Journal of Clinical Oncology* 13 (1995): 26–32.

R. Molina, C. Gabian, M. Slavik, and S. Dahlberg, "Reversal of Palmar-Plantar Erythrodysesthesia (PPE) by B6 without Loss of Response in Colon Cancer Patients Receiving 200 mg/m²/day Continuous 5FU," *Proceedings of the American Society of Clinical Oncology* 6 (1987): 90.

J. F. Smythe et al., "Glutathione Reduces the Toxicity and Improves Quality of Life of Women Diagnosed with Ovarian Cancer Treated with Cisplatin: Results of a Double-Bind, Randomized Trial," *Annals of Oncology* 8 (1997): 569–573.

S. J. Vukelja, F. Lombardo, W. D. James, and R. B. Weiss, "Pyroxidine [sic] for the Palmar-Plantar Erythrodysesthesia Syndrome," *Annals of Internal Medicine* 111 (1989): 688–689.

Recommended supplement plan: Ralph Moss, *Questioning Chemotherapy* (New York: Equinox Books, 1995).

Sugar and immunity: A. Sanchez et al., "High Sugar Content and Weakened Immune Function," *American Journal of Clinical Nutrition* 26 (1973): 180.

CHAPTER 11: FOOD FOR HEALING

Sea vegetables and cancer:

D. O. Thompson and J. Teas, "Seaweed Blocks the Mammary Tumor Promoting Effects of High Fat Diets," paper presented at the International Breast Cancer Research Conference, Denver, March 1983.

Eiichi Furusawa et al., "Anticancer Activity of a Natural Product, Viva-Natural, Extracted from *Undaria pinnatifida* on Intraperitoneally Implanted Lewis Lung Carcinoma," *Oncology* 42 (1985): 364–369.

James J. Sparandeo, *Foods and Tumor Growth Inhibition* (Easton, PA: Comprehensive Nutritional News, 1991). Cited in Rachel Albert Matesz and Don Matesz, *The Nourishment for Life Cookbook* (Seattle: Nourishment for Life Press, 1994).

Jan Teas et al., "Dietary Seaweed and Mammary Carcinogenesis in Rats," *Cancer Research* 44, no. 27 (1984): 58–61.

I. Yamamoto et al., "Antitumor Activity of Edible Marine Algae: Effect of Crude Fucoidan Fractions Prepared from Edible Brown Seaweeds Against L-12100 Leukemia," *Hydrobiologia* 116–117 (1984): 145-148.

Tanaka Yukio et al., "Studies on Inhibition of Intestinal Absorption of Radioactive Strontium," *Canadian Medical Association Journal* 99 (1964): 169–175.

Norman Childers, *Nightshades and Heath* (Emmaus, PA: Rodale Press, 1977).

CHAPTER 12: THE HEALING KITCHEN: HEELTHFUL WAYS FOR PREPARING AND COOKING NURTURING FOOD

Food and medicine: Burton Goldberg, in *Alternative Medicine: The Definitive Guide*, ed. John W. Anderson and Larry Trivieri (Tiburon, CA: Future Medicine Publishing, 1995).

Water toxicity and choices:

Gabriel Cousens, "Health Today," *New Frontier* (1994).

George Glasser, "Dental Fluorosis: A Legal Time Bomb," *Health Freedom News* (1995): 40–46.

B. Goldberg et al., .*Definitive Guide to Cancer* (Tiburon, CA: Future Medicine Publishing, 1997).

A. D. Keet, *The Pyloric Sphincteric Cylinder in Health and Disease* (London: PLiG, 1998).

William L. Lappenbusch, *Contaminated Drinking Water and Your Health* (Alexandria, VA: Lappenbusch Environmental Health, 1986).

John Cary Stewart, *Drinking Water Hazards* (Hiram, Ohio: Envirographics, 1990). Cited in B. Goldberg et al., *Definitive Guide to Cancer.* (Tiburon, CA: Future Medicine Publishing, 1997).

U.S. Environmental Protection Agency, "Basic Information About Fluoride in Drinking Water," July 2013. water.epa.gov/drink/contaminants/basicinformation/fluoride.cfm.

Val Valerian, "On the Toxic Nature of Fluorides—Part 2: Fluorides and Cancer," *Perceptions* (1995): 30–37.

John Yiamouyiannis, *Fluoride: The Aging Factor* (Delaware, OH: Health Action Press, 1993).

Salt:

American Heart Association, "Shaking the Salt Habit," April 23, 2013. heart.org/ HEARTORG/Conditions/HighBloodPressure/PreventionTreatmentofHighBlood

Pressure/Shaking-the-Salt-Habit_UCM_303241_Article.jsp.

H. W. Cohen, S. M. Hailpern, J. Fang, and M. H. Alderman, "Sodium Intake and Mortality in the NHANES II Follow-Up Study," *American Journal of Medicine* 119, no. 3 (2006): 275.e7–14.

Jacques de Langre, *Sea Salt's Hidden Powers* (Happiness Press, 1987). seventhwaveuk.com/content/31-sam-biser-interviews-jacques-de-langre-.

Cooking styles:

Eleese Cunningham, "What Is a Raw Foods Diet and Are There Any Risks or Benefits Associated with It?" *Journal of the American Dietetic Association* 104, no. 10 (October 2004): 1623.

James Felton, quoted in "Beat the Heat" by David Schardt and Leila Corcoran, Center for Science in the Public Interest (June 1998). cspinet.org/nah/6_98heat.htm.

Mark Knize, quoted in "Beat the Heat" by David Schardt and Leila Corcoran, Center for Science in the Public Interest (June 1998). cspinet.org/nah/6_98heat.htm.

Lisa Lefferts, "Great Grilling," *Nutrition Action Health Letter*, 1998. cspinet.org/nah/grilling.html.

G. Lubec et al., "Amino Acid Isomerisation and Microwave Exposure" (letter), *Lancet* 2, no. 8676 (December 9, 1989): 1392–93.

John Ott, *Health and Light: The Effects of Natural and Artificial Light on Man and Other Living Things* (Ariel Press, 1976).

R. Quan et al., "Effects of Microwave Radiation on Anti-Infective Factors in Human Milk," *Pediatrics* 89 (4 Pt 1): 667–69.

"Research Confirms It: Noxious Gas Stove Emissions Worsen Asthma Symptoms in Young Children," John Hopkins Children's Center (October 13, 2008). hopkinschildrens.org/noxious-gas-stove-emissions-worsen-asthma-symptoms-in-young-children.aspx.

Elizabeth Snyderwine, quoted in "Beat the Heat" by David Schardt and Leila Corcoran, Center for Science in the Public Interest (June 1998). cspinet.org/nah/6_98heat.htm.

Anthony Wayne and Lawrence Newell, "The Hidden Hazards of Microwave Cooking," *Health-Science.* health-science.com/microwave_hazards.html.

Andrew Weil, "Nuking Your Nutrients?" DrWeil.com, December 26, 2006. drweil.com/drw/u/QAA400107/microwaving-nutrients.

Rebecca Wood, *Be Nourished: The Complete Guide and Cookbook Celebrating Whole Foods Naturally* (Grant Junction, CO: Grand Cooking School, 1995).

Natural flavoring: U.S. Food and Drug Administration, "Code of Federal Regulations Title 21," vol. 2, April 2013. www.accessdata.fda.gov/scripts/cdrh/cfdocs/cfcfr/cfrsearch.cfm?fr=101.22.

CHAPTER 13: SALUD! NUTRITIOUS, DELICIOUS, AND EASY-TO-MAKE RECIPES

Lenore Yalisove Baum, "Lenore's Natural Cuisine: Your Essential Guide to Wholesome, Vegetarian Cooking," Culinary Publications (2000). lenoresnatural.com/cookbooks/aboutbook.php.

Cheryl Beere, *The Atomic Café Cookbook* (New Zealand: Godwit Publishing, 1995).

C. Cabrera, R. Artacho, and R. Giménez, "Beneficial Effects of Green Tea: A Review," *Journal of the American College of Nutrition* 25, no 2 (2006).

"Choking Is a Leading Cause of Injury and Death Among Children," *ScienceDaily.* February 28, 2010. sciencedaily.com /releases/2010/02/100226212559.htm.

Christina Pirello, *Cooking the Whole Foods Way* (New York: HP Books, 2007).

ACKNOWLEDGMENTS

The only end of writing is to enable the readers better
to enjoy life or better to endure it.
—Dr. Samuel Johnson (1709–1784)

At the end of the play, the audience applauds the actors. The actor's bow and point to other cast members, including them as recipients of the applause. However, behind the scenes, so many others have a hidden and equally important part of realizing this production.

In writing this book, I have been advantaged by the loving and supportive influence of family members, teachers, friends, colleagues, and clients. The reader will kindly indulge me while I offer a public thanks to those who have made a difference in my life and have helped me realize this book. I am rich in friendships and fortunate to have this way of expressing my gratitude:

To my loving daughters, Sara, Desire, and Haley: May you have long, healthy, happy, loving, and creative lives. Thank you, Sara, for your culinary support and for late-night-awakening shoulder massages that kept me from banging my head against the keyboard.

To Robert Davis: whose faith, brotherly counsel, and constant support in 2000 allowed me to devote full-time efforts to researching and writing the first edition of this book. To my teachers: Michio and Aveline Kushi, Herman and Cornelia Aihara, Jacques and Yvette de Langre, Duncan Sim, and Nomboro Muramoto. My deep gratitude for your hard-earned wisdom and generosity in sharing it.

To my past clients: I have had the benefit of thousands of clients who over the years motivated (and in some cases, *forced*) me to broaden my perspective in the face of rigid ideology. Your have all been teachers of the most noble and enduring kind. Thank you for your continued feedback and patience. This book and its revision is the result of your collective efforts.

Thanks to Margaret Hollander; Peter and Brenda Gignac; my high school buddy, Jack Bone, who initially encouraged me, over 40 years ago in a Culver City health food store to investigate alternative medicine. See what you started, Jack! To my brother-in-spirit, Eduardo Longoria, for his continued friendship and for optimistically holding a vision of possibility when it was needed most; Martin Fallick for your caring of my mother; Barbara DeAngelis for your inspiring support; Glenda Twining for your relentless promotion of my work throughout Texas; Jack and Dora Ledbetter for thoughtful support and encouragement; Olivia Cerco for your encouragement and research assistance; Amanda Fieldhouse for being the loving and exceptional mother that you are to Haley and for your caring encouragement and support of my writing; my Omaha sister-in-spirit, Sandy Aquila, of Omaha Healing Arts for your friendship and support; Tom DeSilva of Erewhon Inc. for your efforts to popularize whole foods and your personal support; Diane Bradshaw for supportive friendship and seminar organizing; dear Ruska Porter for her faith and support (we all miss you!); Phil ("Bass-Man") Chen for your friendship and being a one-man support team; Monique Guild for intuitive insight and timely suggestions; Jimmy Israel for your friendship and positive encouragement.

The following friends have acted as seminar organizers in numerous cities throughout the country. Thank you Patricia Becker; Terry Rex Cady, Seattle; David and Anita Catron; Carol and Jim Gordon; Judy Grill; Will Hoglund; Joel Huckins; Patrick McDermott; Vesna Vuksa; Victoria Barayev; the Monday Night Palo Alto Alto Group, empowered by Gerard Lum, Ilona Pollack, and Gary Alinder; Mary Tataryn; Arturo Rodriguez, president of the United Farm Workers; and professor Jeffery Rockwell, DC, of Parker Chiropractic in Dallas, Texas, for the opportunity to guest-teach classes and for the special assembly student-body presentation. Gratitude to Lorraine Rosenthal, cofounder of the Cancer Control Society, who put me in front of 5,000 convention participants and said, "They need your help!"

I want to thank the following organizations for their seminar sponsorship: Larry Cooper's Annual Health Classic; Carl Ferre, director of the French Meadow's Annual Summer Camp, in Lake Tahoe; The Kushi Summer Conference staff of Olaf Fischer and John and Cathy Russo. Thank you all so much for such consistent support.

For their culinary contributions, I am grateful to Aveline Kushi, Cheryl Beere, Rachel Albert-Matesz, Patricia Wemhoff, Ann Sherman, Merle Davis, Christina Pirello, Lenore Baum, Meredith McCarty, Julia Ferre, and Debra Singletary.

A heartfelt and loving thank-you to Heather Wlodek, whose faith, love, and eagle-eyed grammar corrections sustain me.

I am indebted to a number of medical practitioners for their support and encouragement:

Michael Brown, MD, for taking the bold initial step and including me in your practice at Calabasas Medical Group. That was a working demonstration of faith.

Joshua Leichtberg, MD, for the opportunity of working together, your faith, and the Summa Medical Group experience—an inspiring and profoundly educational experience for me.

Theresa Dale, ND, of the International College of Naturopathy, for featuring me in your programs and supporting my work with your student body.

Keith Block, MD, of Block Medical in Evanston, Illinois, for suggestions, dedication, and inspiration.

Mark Scholz, MD, of Prostate Cancer Research Institute, for outstanding and consistent support of my work, for allowing me to be a keynote speaker at PCRI's annual medical conferences, and for the much appreciated introduction to this book.

I am indebted to the kindness and keen editorial eye of Doris Kanter, who for the original edition of this book graciously cheered me through each chapter with savvy commentary and interminable optimism. Thank you to my original senior editor, Ed Claflin, from Prentice Hall, for his editorial work, his patience, and flexibility beyond the call of duty.

A special thank-you goes to my literary agent, Doug Corcoran, who initially, as a former editor of Prentice Hall green-lighted this book publication.

To John Duff, publisher of Perigee Books, for his editorial guidance and support in encouraging this update. And a much appreciated thank-you to Morgan Vines and Amanda Shih for their infinite patience, diligence, and editorial savvy in making this revision a reality.

My deepest gratitude to my former literary agent, Bob Silverstein of Quicksilver Books, for a 21-year working friendship. Bob passed away during this current rewrite. He was the inspiration for me to do this revision. Thank you, Bob. Your presence can be felt in these pages, and you are so dearly missed.

. . . and finally, I wish to thank you, dear reader. It is my hope that this work will help you positively transform your health and be able to reach out to others to do the same.

Good health,
Verne Varona,
New York City

INDEX

Page numbers in *italics* indicate tables.

Acid-alkaline balance, 127, 129, 155. *See also* pH factor
  of blood, 111–12
  body fluids and, 112, 124
  buffers for, 123–24
  cancer and, 112–13
  fruits and, 120
  medicine and, 121–22
  misunderstandings about, 124, 128
  sugars in, 119–20
Alcohol, 50, 142, 145, 235–36, *248*
  craving for, 168–69, 266
Alkalinity, 71. *See also* Acid-alkaline balance
Alliums, 84
Almonds, 232
Amaranth, 223
Ammonia, 79–80
Anderson, Greg, 7
Anger, 29–31, 137
Animal proteins, 41–42, 50–51, 167, 169
  advice on, 102, 145–46
  as cancer healing food, 232–33
  consumption of, 96
  human bodies compared to, 46, 105–6
  immune system and, 141
  natural resources and, 45–46
  plant protein compared to, 46
  in transitional diet, *242*, 243–44
Antioxidants, 82–90, 204
Arame, 230
Arthritis, 117–18, 225–26
Artificial additives, 42
Atomic Café Cookbook, The (Beere), 289, 305
Avocados, 45, 305
Awareness, 32

Bathing, 194
Baum, Lenore, 290, 301
Beans, 44, 81, 87, 289, 295, 304
  gas from, 197, 226–27

Become Younger (Walker), 181
Beef, 97–100
Beere, Cheryl, 289, 305
Behavioral toxicology, 142
Beta-carotene, 205
Beta-glucans, 162
Beverages, 188, 198, 240–41, 250–51. *See also* Water
  Barley Brew, 291
  coffee, 125–27
  Dandelion Root Tea with Lemon, 240, 285
  Kukicha Tea, 294–95
  Rooibos Tea with Lime, 282
  Twig (Kukicha) Tea, 288
Beyond Beef (Rifkin), 96
BGH. *See* Bovine growth hormone
Blood chemistry, 53, *123*
Blood pressure, 118–19
Blood sugar, 67–69, 175
  hormonal, in cravings, *156*, 156–58
Bone density, 80–81, 96–97
Book of Changes (I Ching), 5
Bovine growth hormone (BGH), 99
Bovine spongiform encephalopathy (BSE), 99–100
Bragg, Paul, 181
Bread, 168, 171–72
  toast, 60–61, 282, 284, 288–89
Breakfast, 277–79. *See also* Beverages
  Cinnamon Raisin, Quick-Time Oatmeal, 281–82
  Corn Tortillas with Tempeh, Corn, and Onions in Cilantro-Kuzu Sauce, 286–87
  Natural Cold Cereal with Seasonal Fruit, 287
  Oatmeal-Quinoa Porridge with Roasted Sunflower Seeds, 283
  Rye Toast Brushed with Sesame Spread, 284

Breakfast (*cont.*)
    Scrambled Tofu and Vegetables on
        Whole Wheat Toast, 289
    7-Minute Morning Miso-Vegetable
        Soup, 285–86
    Sourdough Toast with Peanut Cream, 288
    Sweet Onion Kale, 284
    Tempeh Bacon, 290
    Whole Wheat Toast with Almond
        Cream, 282
Breast cancer, 76–77, 100–101, 105
    obesity and, 238
    stress and, 137–39
Breast milk, 134, 174
Breathing, deep, 193, 195
Brillat-Savarin, Jean, 52
Broccoli, 91–92, 301–2, 310–11
BSE. *See* Bovine spongiform encephalopathy
Bunai, Russell, 103
Burdock, 91
Burk, Dean, 258
Burkitt, Denis, 63–64
Bush, George H. W., 91–92

Caffeine, 125–27, 168, *248*
Cairns, John, 213, 215
Calcium, 126, 152, 208, 212
Cancer, 50, 58, 71–72, 137. *See also specific types*
    acid-alkaline balance and, 112–13
    caffeine and, 125–27
    CP and, 48–49
    detection versus prevention, 47–51
    exercise and, 20–21
    fats and, 76–77
    fiber and, 65
    immune system and, 112–13, 131
    meat and, 96, 98, 100–102
    metastasis of, 47
    oxygen related to, 75–76
    phytates and, 59
    prevention research on phytochemicals
        and, 85–87
    protein and, 79–81
    sex hormones and, 48
    stress related to, 137–39
    toast related to, 60–61
    tumor growth in, 214
    vegetarianism and, 49
Cancer healing food
    animal protein as, 232–33
    beans as, 226–27

beverages as, 240–41
daily serving strategies and, 249–51
fermented foods as, 235–38
fruit as, 233–34
grains as, 220–24
natural sweeteners as, 234–35
nuts and seeds as, 230–32
oils as, 238–40, *240*
seaweed as, 227–30
vegetables as, 224–26
Carbohydrates, 92, 106, 170–71, 198
    cancer and, 71–72
    energy from, 53–54, 81
    GI of, 68–69
    sugars from, 54, 65–66
    whole grains and, 54–55
Carcinogens, 50, 60–61, 101
Cardiovascular disease, 26, 74
Carotenoid absorption, 87–88
Carrots, 44–45, 298
Cauliflower, 306–7, 310–11
Celery, 45, 300
Cereal, 57, 287
    oatmeal, 58, 69, 281–83
Chemicals, 42, 99, 185
    against immune system, 142–43
    phytochemicals, 84–87
Chemotherapy
    choice of, 218–19
    enhancement of, 216
    heart damage from, 216
    limitations of, 213–15
    minimization of, 215–17
    nausea from, 215–16
    prevention and, 215
    questions about, 214–15
Chewing, 188, 197–98, 280
    overeating and, 175–76
    of vegetables, 92–93, 108
    of whole grains, 55, 59, 106, 108, 278
Chicken, 97–98
Childers, Norman, 226
Children, 27, 133–34, 235
China, 56, 277
China Project (CP), 48–49
Chinese medicine, 30–31
Chlorella, 211
Chocolate, 157–58, 164–65
Choice, 5–7, 14, 218–19
Chronic obstructive pulmonary disease
    (COPD), 191

Cicero, 40
Citrus, 200–201
Coconut oil, 73–74
Coenzyme Q10, 205–6, 216
Colon cancer, 22, 51, 101
Comfort food, 174
Commitment, 3–5, 7, 10, 28
Complete Guide to Macrobiotic Cooking
        (Kushi), 303–4
Confidence, 23
Constipation, 183
Control, 31–32, 135–36
Convolvulaceous vegetable, 85
Cooking, 86, 88–90, 93
    baking in, *269*, 270
    boiling in, *269*, 270
    broiling in, *269*, 270
    electricity for, 267–68
    grilling in, *269*, 271
    kitchen and, 272
    microwave for, 268–69
    natural gas for, 267
    no time for, 252–54
    pressure cooking in, *269*, 270
    sautéing in, *269*, 270
    shopping for, 272–73
    steaming in, *269*, 269–70
    tools for, 272
    variety in, 254–60
    wood for, 267
Cooking the Whole Foods Way (Pirello),
        296–97, 319
COPD. *See* Chronic obstructive pulmonary
        disease
Copper, 140
Cortisol, 22–23
CP. *See* China Project
Cramer, Daniel, 104
Cravings, 110, 148–50. *See also* Fats
        cravings; Sugar cravings
    acid-alkaline balance in, 155
    for alcohol, 168–69, 266
    for animal protein, 167
    for caffeine, 168
    categories of, 153–64
    for chocolate, 157–58
    elimination-detoxification in, 163
    emotions related to, 158–60
    equilibrium compared to, 151–52
    expansion-contraction of, 163–64
    for familiar foods, 164–69, *166*

    food allergies and, *161*, 161–62
    food group imbalance in, 153–54, *154*
    genetics and, 160–61
    hormonal blood sugar in, *156*, 156–58
    hormones and, 159–60
    nutrient imbalances in, 153–55, *154*
    opposite attractions in, 165
    substitutes for, 167–69
    taste in, 166, *166*
    texture in, 166–67
Creativity, 23–24
Cruciferous, 84–86, 185, 225, 306–7,
        310–11
Cucurbitaceous vegetables, 85
Cultures, 11, 236–37
Curcumin, 210–11

Dairy, 77, 102, 168, *248*
    cancer and, 103–5
Davis, Merle, 302–3
Death, 5–6, 10, 37
    humor and, 24–25
Defensiveness, 1–3
Depression, 137
Detoxification, 163, 177, 228
    blame about, 182–83
    breathing for, 193, 195
    constipation and, 183
    digestive system in, 187–88
    exercise for, 195
    fasting for, 181
    fatigue as, 183
    fruit sugar and, 181–82
    herbs for, 195
    kidneys in, 186–87
    liver in, 180–81, 184–86
    lymphatic system in, 192–94
    marketing of, 179
    massage for, 193, 195–96
    Master Cleanse for, 181
    natural process of, 178, 183–98
    nutrient concentration and, 181–82
    respiratory system in, 191–92
    sauna for, 196
    through skin, 183, 189–90, 192, 195
    sleep for, 194
    variety for, 179–81
Diet, 48, 50, 76–77, 99
    animal protein in, 41–42, 45–46
    artificial additives in, 42
    blood chemistry related to, 53

Diet (*cont.*)
    for cardiovascular disease, 74
    colon and, 51
    for detoxification, 194
    of early humans, 53
    excesses in, 18
    fiber in, 42, 49
    healing diet, 241, *246*, 246–48, *248*
    health foods for, 42–43
    for immune system, 145–46
    lifestyle and, 42
    macrobiotic, 79, 107
    pH factor of, *115–16*
    pleasure foods for, 47
    prevention diet, 241, *244*, 244–46,
        246
    quantities for, 90, 181–82, 187
    refined sugar in, 41
    saturated fats in, 42
    supportive foods for, 46
    teeth related to, 46
    transitional diet, 241–44, *242*, *244*
    unsaturated fats in, 42
    vegetable protein in, 42, 82
    whole grains in, 41
Diet, Nutrition, and Cancer, 79
Dietary change. *See also* Cravings
    gender in, 150–51
    willpower related to, 148–51
Dietary Supplement Health and Education
        Act (DSHEA), 199
Diet for a Poisoned Planet (Steinman), 190
Digestion, 19, 52–53, 73, *122*
    enzymes for, 88–90
    time and, 63–64, 146, 279
Digestive system, 187–88
Dinner. *See also* Beverages; Sweets
    Aztec Butternut Squash Soup,
        316–17
    Broiled Halibut with Lemon and
        Capers, 320
    Creamy Cauliflower Soup, 306–7
    Ginger Salmon Bake, 317
    Linguini with Orange Roughy,
        Portobello Mushrooms, and Sun-
        Dried Tomatoes, 307–8
    Mesclun Salad and Creamy Lemon
        Dressing, 315
    Millet-Mashed Potatoes with Caraway, 314
    Mixed Baby Green Salad with Tahini-
        Tart Dressing, 308

    Mixed Green Salad with Roma
        Tomatoes in Basil-Garlic
        Vinaigrette, 321
    Native American Holiday Rice, 318
    Native Wild Rice with Pecans and
        Shiitake-Onion Topping, 311–12
    Peach Dilled Corn Chowder, 313–14
    Roasted Root Vegetables, 312
    Simply Baked Onions, 321
    10-Minute Savory Broccoli-Cauliflower
        Miso Soup, 310–11
    Water-Fried Bok Choy, Swiss Chard,
        and Napa Cabbage, 318–19
Disease, 7–8, 14. *See also specific diseases*
DNA, 22, 202
Dominy, Nathaniel, 53
Don't Forget the Fiber in Your Diet (Burkitt), 63–64
Dossey, Larry, 37
Drugs, 161–63
DSHEA. *See* Dietary Supplement Health
        and Education Act
Dulse, 230
Durant, Will, 56–57

Earth Policy Institute, 41–42
Edison, Thomas, 275
Education, 16–17, 93, 199, 272–73
EFAs. *See* Essential fatty acids
Elimination system, *123*
Emmons, Robert, 39
Emotional eating, 158–60
Emotions, 174, 196, 198. *See also specific emotions*
    cravings related to, 158–60
    expression of, 28–34, 137
    hormones and, 159–60
    network support for, 144
    resonance and, 32–33
    six-step feeling process for, 32–34
    sugar cravings and, 170–71
Empowerment, 7, 15
Endometrial cancer, 101–2
Engel, George, 37
Enthousiasmos (having the God within), 9
Environment, 21, 190
Enzymes, 88–90, 205–6, 216
Epictetus, 38
Eskimos, 97
Esselstyn, Caldwell B., Jr., 74
Essential fatty acids (EFAs), 239
Estella, Mary, 290
Estrogen, 238

Ethnicity, 80–81, 98, 152
Even in Summer the Ice Doesn't Melt (Reynolds), 28
Everson, Carol, 144
Ewing, James, 113
Exercise, 20–21, 34, 145
    for detoxification, 195
    food and, 188
    for lymphatic system, 192–93
    sugar cravings and, 170
    swimming, 190
Eyes, 44–45

Faith, 34, 37–38
    willpower and, 35–36
Fat-emulsifying foods, 172–73, *173*
Fatigue, 183
Fats, 42, 110, 155, 157
    cancer and, 76–77
    digestion of, 73
    intolerance of, 72
    in nuts and seeds, 231–32
    oils and, 77, 238
    oxygen and, 75–76
    reduction of, 145
    for taste, 72–73
    vegetable oil, 77
Fats cravings
    bread and flour products and, 171–72
    carbohydrate imbalance and, 171
    comfort food and, 174
    fermented foods and, 172
    food combinations and, 173–74
    protein and, 172
Fat-stimulating foods, 173, *173*
Fatty acids, 209–10, 239
    coconut oil and, 73–74
    immune system and, 141–42
    sugars and, 66–67
    types of, 73
Fear, 29
Felton, James, 271
Fermented foods, 235
    in cultures, 236–37
    fats cravings and, 172
    recommendations of, 237–38
    toxins and, 237
Fiber, 42, 49, 188
    in beans, 226
    cancer and, 65
    honey and, 235
    phytates and, 64–65

Fish, 46, 143, 307–8, 317, 320
Fish oils, 74–75
Flax, 87
Flaxseed oil, 108, 209–10
Flour, 61, 171–72
Fluoride, 258–59
Folic acid, 200, 207, 212, 216
Folk medicine, 163–64, 201
    doctrine of signatures from, 44–45
Food, 42. *See also* Cancer healing food
    combinations of, 173–74
    exercise and, 188
    fluids and, 256–57
    raw food movement, 88–90
    before sleep, 187–88
    staple, 43–45
Food allergies, 142
    cravings and, *161*, 161–62
Frankl, Viktor E., 5, 9
Frassetto, Lynda, 122
Free radicals
    antioxidants versus, 82–90
    nuts and seeds against, 231
    oxidation from, 83
    from oxygen, 82
    toxins for, 83
Freud, Sigmund, 9
Friendship, 10, 144
Fromm, Eric, 13
Fruits, 85–86, 90, 250, 265–66, 287
    acid-alkaline balance and, 120
    as cancer healing food, 233–34
    consumption of, 92
Fruit sugar
    detoxification and, 181–82
    hormones and, 233
Fuhrman, Mark, 88–89
Funk, Casimir, 201–2

Gandhi, Mohandas K., 10, 280
Garlic, 211–12, 321
Gas, 196
    from beans, 197, 226–27
    chewing and, 197–98
    for cooking, 267
Gastroesophageal reflux disease (GERD), 121
Gender, 150–51
Genesis 1.29, 56
GERD. *See* Gastroesophageal reflux disease
GI. *See* Glycemic index
Gilles, Robert J., 113

Ginseng root, 45
GL. *See* Glycemic load
Glutathione *S*-transferase (GST), 86–87
Gluten. *See also* Nongluten grains
    whole grains and, 59
Glycemic index (GI), 68–70
Glycemic load (GL), 69–70
Good, Robert, 130
Gordon, James, 9
Gori, Gio B., 95
Grains. *See also* Nongluten grains; Whole
        grains
    for animals, 46
    bread as, 60–61
    as cancer healing food, 220–24
    categories of, 220–21
    consumption of, 96
    refined, 109–10
Gratitude, 38–40
Great Britain, 277
Greece, 56–57
Green, Alyce, 13–14
Green, Elmer, 13–14
Greenfield, Sheldon, 14
Greenland Inuit, 74
Greens, dark leafy, 249
Greens, leafy, 84, 294, 296–97, 305, 308, 321
GST. *See* Glutathione *S*-transferase

Hair loss, 217
HCAs. *See* Heterocyclic amines
Healing, 15. *See also* Cancer healing food
    choice in, 5–7, 14, 218–19
    in vitamin-disease connection, 203–4
Healing food plan
    healing diet in, 241, *246*, 246–48, *248*
    prevention diet in, 241, *244*, 244–46,
        246
    transitional diet in, 241–44, *242*, *244*
Healing Wisdom (Anderson), 7
Healing Words (Dossey), 37
Health foods, 42–43
Helping
    love and, 28
    purpose related to, 27–28
Herbal Medicine, Healing and Cancer (Yance
        and Valentine), 147
Herbs, 91, 217. *See also specific herbs*
    for detoxification, 195
    for immune system, 147
Heterocyclic amines (HCAs), 271

Hill, Benny, 24–25
Hirayama, Takeshi, 100–101
Hiziki, 230
*Hole's Essentials of Human Anatomy and
        Physiology* (Shier), 193
Honey, 66, 120, 234–35
Hopkins, Frederick, 201–2
Hormones, 48, *156*, 156–58
    BGH, 99
    cravings and, 159–60
    fruit sugar and, 233
    stress hormones, 22–23
Hospitals, 135–36
    emotions in, 31–32
Human bodies, 105–6
Hyperuricemia, 80
Hypoglycemia, 157

IBS. *See* Irritable bowel syndrome
I Ching (Book of Changes), 5
IgA. *See* Immunoglobin A
Ikigai ("a reason to get up in the morning"),
        11
Imagination, 37
Immune system, 117
    alcohol and, 142
    animal proteins and, 141
    beta-glucans for, 162
    brain and, 137
    burdock for, 91
    cancer and, 112–13, 131
    chemicals against, 142–43
    of children, 133–34
    cortisol and, 23
    defense of, 130–32
    diet for, 145–46
    fatty acids and, 141–42
    food allergies and, 142, 162
    herbs for, 147
    laughter and, 25
    lymphatic system with, 132
    maximization of, 143–47
    nourishment balance and, 18–19
    nutrition and, 139–41
    psychoneuroimmunology and, 26–27
    stress related to, 134–35
    sugars related to, 140–41
    supplements for, 146
Immunoglobin A (IgA), 25, 27
India, 10, 56
Internet, 16–17

Intestines, 132
Intuition, 16
Inuit, 74, 80–81
Iron, 64, 140, 213
Irritable bowel syndrome (IBS), 88, 121
Ishitani, Ken, 125

Japan, 10–11, 211, 265–66
Jefferson, Thomas, 77
Jungle, The (Sinclair), 99
Justice, Blair, 144

Kaplan, Sherrie, 14
Karma, 35
Keller, Helen, 12
Kidney beans, 44
Kidneys, 118, 266–67
    in detoxification, 186–87
    sleep and, 187
    water and, 186
Kidney stones, 80
Klaper, Michael, 97, 102
Klopfer, Bruno, 35–36
Kombu, 230
Kristal, Alan, 86
Kuninaka, Kancho, 118
Kushi, Aveline, 303–4

Lambe, William, 98
Langre, Jacques de, 265
Lappenbusch, William L., 258
Laughter, 24–26
LDL. *See* Low-density lipoprotein
Lead, 143
Learned Optimism: How to Change Your Mind and Your Life (Seligman), 136
Legumes, 84. *See also* Beans
Lenore's Natural Cuisine (Baum), 301
LeShan, Lawrence, 137
Lifestyle, 19–21, 42, 143–45, 175
Lignans, 228
Lind, James, 200
Liver, 66, 71, 91, 118, 132, 157
    chemicals and, 185
    chemotherapy and, 217
    tasks of, 184
    toxins and, 184–86
Liver flush, 180–81
Logotherapy, 9
Love, 26–28
Low-density lipoprotein (LDL), 74

Lunch. *See also* Beverages; Sweets
    Assorted Greens with Citrus Sparkle Dressing, 296–97
    Brussels Sprouts and Ginger-Plum Glaze, 293
    Chopped Mixed Greens with Avocado Vinaigrette, 305
    Cream of Celery-Leek Soup, 300
    Leafy Green Salad and Lemon-Parsley Dressing, 294
    Miso-Glazed Carrots, 298
    Patricia's Lemon Red Lentil Soup, 292–93
    Plain and Easy Steamed Broccoli, 301–2
    Pronto Blanched Watercress, 299
    Rebecca's Grilled Millet and Butternut Squash Cakes, 297–98
    Refried Beans, 304
    Sweet Rice and Chestnuts, 303–4
    Tempeh Reuben, 301
    Tofu and Vegetable Sesame Stir-Fry, 295
    Walnut Rice, 296
Lung cancer, 105
Lungs, 45, 191–92
Lymphatic system, 119, 132
    breathing and, 193
    in detoxification, 192–94
    exercise for, 192–93
    massage for, 193, 195–96
    rebounders for, 193
    skin brushing for, 192
    temperature and, 194

MacKenzie, Anna, 306–7
Macrobiotic diets, 79, 107
Mad cow disease, 99–100
Magnesium, 208, 217
Main, Jody, 316–17
Man's Search for Meaning (Frankl), 9
Maple syrup, 66, 120, 234
Marcus Aurelius, 6
Marijuana, 163
Mazess, Richard B., 81–82
McClelland, David, 27
McCollough, Michael, 39
McDougall, John, 53, 141
MCP. *See* Modified citrus pectin
Meaning, 9–11
Meat, 77–78
    cancer and, 96, 98, 100–102
    in history, 98
    love of, 95–98

Meat (*cont.*)
    mad cow disease, 99–100
    osteoporosis and, 96–97
    quality of, 98–100
    substitutes for, *248*
Medicine, 16, 30–31
    acid-alkaline balance and, 121–22
    folk medicine, 44–45, 163–64, 201
    humor as, 24–26
    Krebiozen, 35–36
Mencken, H. L., 111
Mercury, 143
Mexico, 57
Micronutrients, 202
Microwave, 268–69
Milk, 50, 99
    breast milk, 134, 174
Miller, Edgar R., 83
Millet, 222, 297–98, 314
Million Women Study, 50
Minerals, 65, 152, 202–3
Miracle of Fasting, The (Bragg), 181
Modified citrus pectin (MCP), 206
Monounsaturated fatty acids (MUFAs), 74
Montagu, Ashley, 27
Moreau, Jeanne, 199
Moss, Ralph, 113, 211, 214
Mother Teresa effect, 27
Motivation, 1–3, 12
Mrazik, David M., 125
MUFAs. *See* Monounsaturated fatty acids
Muscle, 119
Mushrooms, 225, 307–8
Myers, Charles, 108

Natural flavoring, 273
Natural foods, 42–43
Natural gas, 267
Natural immunity, 130
Natural killer (NK) cells, 144
Natural sweeteners, 234–35
Natural toxins, 89
Nature's Cancer-Fighting Foods program,
    70–71
Nestle, Marion, 52
Neurotransmitters, 25
New Age, 35
Nightshade vegetables, 225–26
NK. *See* Natural killer (NK) cells
Nongluten grains, 221
    amaranth, 223

    buckwheat groats, 223
    millet, 222, 297–98, 314
    oats, 58, 223–24, 278–79
    quinoa, 222, 283
    rice, 222, 296, 303–4, 318
    teff, 223
    wild rice, 222, 311–12
Non-Hodgkin's lymphoma, 105
Nori, 229
Nourishment balance
    digestion in, 19
    education for, 16–17
    immune system and, 18–19
Nutrients, 89, 175, 181–82
    absorption of, 215
    imbalances in, 153–55, *154*
    micronutrients, 202
Nutrition, 116–17
    immune system and, 139–41
Nuts and seeds, 230–32. *See also specific nuts and seeds*

Oatmeal, 58, 69, 281–83
Oats, 58, 223–24, 278–79
Obesity, 238
Oils, 73–75, 107–8, 209–10, 250, 275
    EFAs from, 239
    fats and, 77, 238
    omega fatty acids and, 239
    smoke point of, 239–40, *240*
    tumors related to, 238
Omega-3 fatty acids, 209–10, 239
Omega-3 supplements, 74–75
Omega-6 fatty acids, 239
Onions, 45, 284, 286–87, 311–12, 321
Opportunity, 3, 6–8
Optimism, 136
Organs, 118
Ott, John, 268
Ovarian cancer, 104
Overeating, 146, 158–59
    blood sugar fluctuation in, 175
    chewing and, 175–76
    emotions for, 174
    gas from, 197–98
    lifestyle and, 175
    nutrients and, 175
    salt in, 174–75
Oxygen, 75–76, 82, 191

PAHs. *See* Polycyclic aromatic hydrocarbons
Pancreas, 118

Pancreatic cancer, 211–12
Paracelsus, 44
Pasta, 61, 307–8
Peanuts, 232, 288
Pearsall, Paul, 13–14
Personal philosophy, 13–15
Perspective, 5, 11, 35–36
    of gratitude, 38–40
    humor for, 26
    imagination in, 37
    positive attitude in, 6–7, 12–15
    present in, 6–7
Phenolic compounds, 86
pH factor, *115–16*
    in body, *122–23*
    of body fluids, 114–15
    imbalance of, 116–19
    measurement of, 128
Phillips, Ronald, 105
Phosphate, 152
Physical activity. *See* Exercise
Phytates
    advice about, 64
    fiber and, 64–65
    whole grains and, 59
Phytochemicals
    cancer prevention research on, 85–87
    cooking of, 86
    defense from, 84–85
    sources of, 84–85
    in soybeans, 87
    in whole grains, 87
Pirello, Christina, 293, 296–97, 319–20
Pizzorno, Joseph, 147
Placebo response, 35–36
Pollan, Michael, 82
Polycyclic aromatic hydrocarbons (PAHs),
    271
Positive attitude, 16
    in perspective, 6–7, 12–15
Prayer, 37–38
Pregnancy, 117, 152
Prevention diet, 241, *244*, 244–46, *246*
Process, 32
Prostate cancer, 49, 76, 104–5, 211
    vegetables and, 86–87
Protein. *See also* Animal proteins
    cancer and, 79–81
    fats cravings and, 172
    gas from, 198
    LDL, 74

meat for, 77–78
    need for, 78, 81
    recommendations for, 78–79, 81
    sources of, 78–79
    vegetable, 42, 82
Psychology, 117
    sugar cravings and, 171
Psychoneuroimmunology, 26–27
Publilius Syrus, 19
Pumpkin seeds, 232
Purpose
    goal compared to, 12
    helping related to, 27–28
    motivation and, 12
    survival related to, 9

Questioning Chemotherapy (Moss), 214
Quinoa, 222, 283

Radiation toxicity, 215–17
Raw food movement, 88–90
RDA. *See* Recommended daily allowance
Recipes. *See also* Breakfast; Dinner; Lunch;
    Sweets
    quantities in, 274–75
    substitutions in, 275–76
Recommended daily allowance (RDA), 67
Regan, Timothy, 75–76
Relaxation therapies, 145
Resilience, 5
Respiratory system, 191–92
Reynolds, David K., 28
Rice, 222, 296, 303–4, 318. *See also* Wild
    rice
Rifkin, Jeremy, 96
Rogers, Will, 252
Rolled oats, 58
Russell, Bertrand, 22, 134
Russell, Rollo, 98

Sachs, Frank, 177
SAD. *See* Standard American diet
St. Augustine, 28
St. Jacques, Benoit, 302–3
Salads, 225, 249, 294, 308, 315, 321
Salt, 164, 198
    detoxification with, 190
    excess of, 266–67
    in overeating, 174–75
    as savory taste, 261–62, *262*
    sea salt, 263–64

Salt (*cont.*)
    sugar cravings and, 155, 169, 266
    for vegetarianism, 264–65
Saunas, 163, 189–90
SCMT. *See* Systemic Cancer Multistep
    Therapy
Scurvy, 200–201
Seaweed
    beans and, 227
    lignans in, 228
    research on, 228–29
    types of, 229–30
Secretory immunoglobulin A (SIgA), 22
Seeds, 230–32, 283. *See also specific nuts and seeds*
Selenium, 140, 208
Self-empowerment, 7
Self-love, 26
Seligman, Martin, 136
Selye, Hans, 23, 134
Seventh-Day Adventists, 49, 100
Shakes, Ronnie, 24, 135
Shaw, George Bernard, 34
Shintani, Terry, 103
Siegel, Bernie, 17
SIgA. *See* Secretory immunoglobulin A
Simoncini, Tullio, 113
Sinclair, Upton, 99
Skin, 119, 131
    breakouts, 183
    brushing of, 192, 195
    detoxification through, 183, 189–90,
        192, 195
    heat for, 189–90
Sleep, 119, 144
    for detoxification, 194
    food before, 187–88
Snacking, 92
Snowden, John, 104
Snyderwine, Elizabeth, 271
Sodium, 107
Solanaceous foods, 85–86
Sophocles, 26
Soup, 90, 285–86, 292–93, 300, 306–7,
    310–11, 316–17
Soybeans, 87
    tofu, 289, 295
Spiegel, David, 138–39
Spiritual perspective, 11, 37–38
Spontaneous remission, 13–14
Squash, 297–98, 316–17
Standard American diet (SAD), 49

Staple foods
    doctrine of signatures in, 44–45
    whole grains as, 43–44
Steinman, David, 190
Stomach, 132
Stress, 20
    biochemistry of, 134–39
    cancer related to, 137–39
    of detoxification, 182
    DNA and, 22
    general adaptation response to, 134
    hormones and, 22–23
    immune system related to, 134–35
    learned helplessness as, 135–36
    love and, 27
    management of, 144–45
    Type C individuals and, 138–39
Stress of Life, The (Seyle), 134
Sugar cravings
    animal protein and, 169
    emotions and, 170–71
    exercise and, 170
    food volume and, 169
    salt and, 155, 169, 266
    strategies for, 169–71
    substitutes for, 167
    time and, 170
Sugars
    in acid-alkaline balance, 119–20
    avoidance of, 145
    beans and, 227
    blood sugar, 67–69, *156*, 156–58, 175
    cancer and, 71–72
    from carbohydrates, 54, 65–66
    consumption of, 65–66
    dangers of, 67, 107–9
    fatty acids and, 66–67
    fruit, 66, 181–82, 233
    gas from, 197
    immune system related to, 140–41
    liver related to, 66, 71
    marketing of, 120, 273
    natural sweeteners or, 234–35
    refined, 41
    substitutes for, *248*
    whole grains and, 54, 63
Super Immunity (Pearsall), 13–14
Supplement cancer protection, 204, 218
    beta-carotene in, 205
    calcium in, 208
    chlorella in, 211

coenzyme Q10 in, 205–6, 216
curcumin in, 210–11
garlic in, 211–12
iodine in, 209
magnesium in, 208, 217
MCP in, 206
omega-3 fatty acids in, 209–10
selenium in, 140, 208
vitamin B6 in, 217
vitamin B complex in, 206–7
vitamin C in, 207
vitamin D in, 207
vitamin E in, 205, 217
vitamin excesses or, 212–13
zinc in, 209
Supplements, 199, 203–4. *See also specific supplements*
    for immune system, 146
    popularity of, 199
    vegetables or, 93
Survival, 18, 136. *See also* Death
    characteristics of, 8–9
    complexity of, 8
    ikigai for, 11
    making moments count in, 15–16
    purpose related to, 9
    spontaneous remission in, 13–14
Sweets, 234–35, 261, *262*, 294. *See also* Sugars
    Almond Drop Cookies, 315
    Apricot Slices, 322
    Chef St. Jacques's Spice Cookies, 302–3
    Glazed Apples, 319
    Peach Mousse, 312–13
    Strawberry Kanten, 308
Sweet vegetables, 225
Swimming, 190
Systemic Cancer Multistep Therapy (SCMT), 72

Tannock, Ian, 113
Tastes, 72–73, 165, 260. *See also* Salt
    in cravings, 166, *166*
    natural flavoring and, 273
    savory, 261–62, *262*
Teeth, 46
Teff, 223
Tempeh, 286–87, 290
Tobacco, 143–44, 164
Tofu, 289, 295
Tongue, 127

Toniolo, Paolo, 76–77
Total parenteral (TPN) solution, 72
Total Wellness (Pizzorno), 147
Toxins, 21, 63, 196, 215–17, 257–58. *See also* Detoxification
    fermented foods and, 237
    for free radicals, 83
    honey and, 235
    laughter and, 25
    liver and, 184–86
    natural, 89
TPN. *See* Total parenteral (TPN) solution
Transitional diet, 241–44, *242*, *244*
Twain, Mark, 176
Type C individuals, 138–39

Umbelliferous vegetables, 85–86
Uric acid, 80

Valentine, Arlene, 147
Vegetable oil, 77
Vegetables, 42, 44, 48, 82, 85, 173, *173*
    as cancer healing food, 224–26
    carbohydrate consumption or, 92
    chewing of, 92–93, 108
    classifications of, 45, 224–26
    consumption of, 92
    cooking education about, 93
    nightshade, 225–26
    pigments of, 93
    prostate cancer and, 86–87
    raw versus cooked, 87–89
    supplements or, 93
    sweet, 225
Vegetarianism, 101, 105, 107–10
    cancer and, 49
    dairy and, 77
    salt for, 264–65
Visek, Willard J., 79–80
Vitamin A, 139, 212
Vitamin B, 108, 140
Vitamin B6, 217
Vitamin B complex, 206–7
Vitamin C, 139, 207, 213
Vitamin D, 207
Vitamin-disease connection
    healing in, 203–4
    history of, 201–3
Vitamin E, 63, 139–40, 212
    in supplement cancer protection, 205, 217

Wakame, 230
Walker, Norman, 181
Walnuts, 44, 232, 296
War, 98
Warburg, Otto, 71, 124, 256
Water, 46, 186, 318–19
    contaminants in, 257–59
    excess of, 256–57
    fluoride in, 258–59
    in food preparation, 257–60
    health from, 259–60
    need for, 255–56
    purification of, 259–60
Waxman, Melanie, 312–13
Weil, Andrew, 89, 268–69
Wemhoff, Patricia, 292–93, 298, 312
WHO. *See* World Health Organization
Whole grains, 41, 60, 62–63, 84, 87, 109.
    See also specific whole grains
    additions for, 276
    cancer and, 58
    carbohydrates and, 54–55
    cereal as, 57–58

chewing of, 55, 59, 106, 108, 278
combinations with, 275–76
cooking times for, 276
determination of, 55
gluten and, 59
history of, 56–57
phytates and, 59
as staple foods, 43–44
sugars and, 54, 63
Wild rice, 222, 311–12
Willpower, 35–36, 148–51
Women, 50, 76, 160, 238
    breast milk of, 134, 174
    language and, 150–51
    pregnancy in, 117, 152, 200
Wood, Rebecca, 297–98
World Health Organization (WHO),
    64–65
Writing, 33

Yance, Donald R., Jr., 147
Yeast, 172

Zinc, 140, 209, 212–13

 **VERNE VARONA** studied oriental medicine and cultural folk medicine at the East West Foundation of Boston (1970–1974) and is the 2012 recipient of the Aveline Kushi Lifetime Achievement Award. For more than 40 years, he has been a highly sought-after speaker and consultant on health, fitness, and motivation.

For 5 years, he was the nutritional consultant and cofounder of a popular Los Angeles medical group with clientele that featured well-known entertainment and sports professionals. With his physician associate, Verne cocreated the ODDS Program (Off Dangerous Drugs Safely); a dietary program designed to reverse pharmaceutical drug dependency using dietary and lifestyle guidelines featured in his books.

He has been a part of educational programs for West Coast chapters of the Multiple Sclerosis Foundation and the Prostate Cancer Research Institute in Los Angeles. He is founding director of the Exceptional Health Foundation, a nonprofit organization developed for promoting principles of holistic health.

Varona is also the author of *Macrobiotics for Dummies*, a comprehensive work that embraces a flexible, multicultural perspective on body, mind, and spiritual health.

A native New Yorker currently residing in New York, Verne is also a professional fine-art photographer whose work is featured by several U.S. galleries. He is presently involved in creating media projects that document natural disease reversal with physician monitoring.

Visit his website at vernevarona.com.